THE
NEW
QUEEN'S
CROWN

LINDSEY SANFORD

Printed in the United States of America

First Printing, 2018

ISBN 9781724112439

Amazon Kindle Direct Publishing

Cover design by Lindsey Sanford

Cover image credit goes to **Duong Tran Quoc** on Unsplash.com

THE
NEW
QUEEN'S
CROWN

THE HAVAAN CHRONICLES BOOK I

For anyone who's ever been told they don't have what it takes to rule — make your own crown and rock it!

BEFORE.

It is the year 2160 and the world is very different than that in the history books.

Earth was ill, dying. Country after country, continent after continent, was being destroyed by war and poisoned by famine. Natural resources were disappearing daily. The population was fading by the hundreds; in some places by the thousands. There was chaos and panic. Law was long gone. It was every man and woman for themselves.

The world would not have survived another fifty years.

Toward the end of the old days, it was discovered that the sleight-of-hand magicians were not frauds as was always assumed, but instead people with real powers. Magic, for many years following, was celebrated and worshipped; and those with said abilities banded together and rose to the top. They studied what had worked in civilization and what hadn't. They pushed and pulled the continents into one landmass and shrank it down until it was 800 miles wide and 800 miles tall. Then they sealed the seams together and dropped those who remained into this new place, thus healing and uniting a broken and damaged world.

They called it Havaan.

Resources abounded. Health returned to the sick. The population replenished.

For nearly a hundred years, things were good. Things were peaceful.

But the second generation of magicians became egotistical and greedy, wanting power more than peace, love or compassion. They selfishly hoarded their magic, using it to benefit only themselves, and soon an inevitable rebellion began. However, before the citizens of Havaan could destroy themselves further, from the shadows came a new ruler, one with an army that quickly defeated the magicians and their allies.

As the story goes, after the Great War, this new leader forced every magician—those who had fought against him as well as those who had fought beside him—to drain their powers into decanters. He tossed the glowing bottles into the ocean, where they were carried far away and no one could ever get to them. This commander, warmly received by the people of Havaan, established a new dynasty, one that mimicked a monarchy of the time before. He called himself King Orion and it is he who currently presides over Havaan.

With the new ruling system came a new tradition: The Queen's Gala. On this night, the eligible young ladies of Havaan are invited to spend a glamorous evening at the king's home, all with hopes of being chosen to rule beside the eldest prince, making her not only a princess but the future queen.

It is on the eve of the second official Queen's Gala that we begin our story.

I.

The bed bowed and Avaleigh let out a low "oof" as her best friend landed on top of her.

"How are you still sleeping?" Delilah whined in her ear.

Ava hadn't been asleep since she'd heard the front door slam and Delilah clomp up the stairs. For such a petite thing, Delilah made a *lot* of noise.

"Because it's not time to get up," Ava mumbled into her pillow. She rolled, trying to free herself from the body lying on her. Delilah held tight, like a baby koala, and ended up on Ava's back, shaking her.

"It *is* time to get up. You promised you'd go to the market with me. Avie, please—" Delilah was the only person who ever called her Avie, mainly because she knew how much Ava hated it. But as Delilah would say, nicknames were a best friend perk. "If we don't get there early all the good dresses will be taken."

A low growl escaped from Ava's throat. Part of it was out of frustration. A bigger part was because she knew she had no choice but to get out of bed. When she wanted something, Delilah was relentless.

"I can't get up if you don't get off of me."

"If I get off do you promise to get up?"

Ava huffed. "Sure."

"Doesn't count."

"I promise!" Ava said, louder than intended. She was not a morning person, which was something Delilah was privy to more than anyone. Ava knew she wouldn't get offended by her grumpiness, just like she knew there would be a strawberry and mango smoothie sitting on the stand next to her bed, as well as a lemon scone with sweet butter from her favorite bakery.

Before unsticking herself, Delilah ruffled Ava's already messy hair. Ava sat up, reaching for the drink without looking. She tossed the thick curtain of sleep-tousled curls from her face with her forearm then took a giant bite of her breakfast. While she ate in silence—it never really prepared her for the things she'd have to deal with each day—she watched Delilah flutter around the jewelry box, like a moth drawn to sparkly things. The hand-carved box, a birthday present from the moth herself, was always filled with cast-away bracelets or practice necklaces.

Ava's mother, Cordellia, was one of Havaan's best and most sought-after jewelry designers. The pieces she made were beautiful and elegant—opposite of the woman who designed them—and often times incredibly expensive. Expensive meant perfect, and a chip in a stone or an off-center diamond wouldn't cut it. So, they ended up in Ava's box, became costume jewelry for all the fancy events she'd never attend.

"Are you almost done?" Delilah asked as she slipped a thick golden bracelet over her thin wrist. It was a gorgeous piece, studded with a thin row of tiny diamonds, but there was a chink in the metal, rendering it imperfect. "The last thing I want is to have to purchase a dress from Erock. He gives me the creeps."

"Erock isn't creepy," Ava replied. "He's just awkward. And you make him nervous."

Delilah scrunched her nose. "Yeah, well. He's got to get over me. It's been six years." Ava shook her head, a slight smile on her lips. "Besides," Delilah added, "I'm saving myself."

Ava snorted. "For the prince."

"Of course." Delilah held up a chunky silver necklace. The layered chains were embedded with rubies of varying shades. The stones painted Ava's bedroom in lava when the sun filtered through them. "Have you thought about what *you're* wearing to the gala?"

"Probably the blue dress."

Delilah's face pinched as if she'd suddenly tasted something sour. It was a look she had acquired in the years since she'd moved from Meridian to Typhony. Ava hated it. It spoke volumes; words of judgment which all translated into "I'm better than you." Though Delilah would never say them, Ava knew there were times when she wanted to.

"I—"

"You hate the blue dress," Ava interrupted as she hoisted herself out of bed. "I know." She pulled her hair into a thick bun at the base of her neck then shuffled down the hall to the bathroom. She could hear Delilah padding after her on her small, dainty feet. Ava left the door cracked a sliver, like she had during sleep-overs when they were younger.

"You could buy something new at the market, you know. I'm sure we could find something cheapish."

Ava inhaled deeply and glared at the door. Delilah often reminded her of the gap in their wealth, although since Orion had mounted the throne, the difference between the social classes was not nearly as drastic as it had once been. In fact, the division between them was so minute it didn't even leave room for a lower class. Just a middle and upper. Still, those in the latter never failed to ensure that those in the former remembered a difference *did* exist.

Ava and her mother lived comfortably, but comfortably wasn't what the people in the upper class liked. It was fine with Ava that she was destined for a life in Meridian. Fancy dinners with dishes that looked like pieces of art, expensive dresses that tangled around her feet, and having to hold her tongue simply weren't things she wanted in her life.

Besides, the spotlight was where all your secrets came through.

She doesn't mean it the way you're taking it, Ava reminded her reflection. Big doe eyes stared back at her, irises the same teal as the indicolite tourmaline stones her mother kept in jars in the basement. Ava was often described as stunning, with her cascading waterfall of light brown curls and perfectly shaped nose—the hoop through her right nostril (a small act of defiance at eighteen) had altered that just a fraction. Her lips were full in a nude-blush color that made women constantly ask her what shade of lipstick she was wearing. Her tall frame curved and bent, creating the perfect hourglass figure.

Once upon a time, all of that would have mattered.

But none of it made her special now, because *everyone* in Havaan was beautiful.

When the magicians created the new land, they used their powers to breed mythical features into the coming generations: slight points to ears, unnatural hair colors, eyes in hues that hadn't existed before. Part of it was to redefine who and what the world was to become, but they'd also learned from the history of the old world that appearances had been a deciding factor in countless things, and those who were deemed physically attractive were offered greater advantages.

The first generation wanted every citizen of Havaan to be on equal playing ground, to be able to succeed and thrive the same as their neighbor. And citizens had no qualms about working hard to achieve such things.

With the second generation, all of that had been for naught. Then it became about who had magic in their veins and who was willing to pay the bounty to get it. With magic now eradicated in Havaan, beauty once again reigned supreme.

Yet to Ava it didn't matter. When she looked at herself she saw a simple girl: a plain woman, twenty years old who was just sort of there. Maybe it was because that's what she wanted to be—not someone who stood out in a crowd but faded into one.

The less people looked at her, the less she had to try to hide everything.

She was more than happy to let the other women in Havaan fight for the spotlight; to let it shine on the darkest, deepest parts of *their* closets and reveal the skeletons hanging alongside extravagant dresses.

Ava didn't have a lot of dresses, but she had plenty of skeletons.

After taking a few calming breaths, Ava stepped out of the bathroom and went back to her bedroom. Delilah prattled on about the upcoming gala while Ava dressed in a pair of faded jeans and a striped shirt with green sleeves that went to her elbows. Then she let her curls loose, the spirals falling over her shoulders and halfway down her spine.

"Did you happen to see my mom?" Ava asked as she shoved her feet into laceless shoes. She had a feeling she knew what Delilah was going to say, but there was still an embarrassing lilt of hope attached to her words.

As they stepped out of the hallway, Delilah shook her head. Her brows creased sympathetically and the corners of her lips turned down.

Her pin-straight hair looked a darker pink in the dim hallway light, making her light brown eyes fairer than normal.

Sighing, Ava paused in front of her mother's bedroom door. "I'll meet you downstairs in a minute then." Delilah nodded once, knowingly, and retreated without another word as Ava's knuckles rapped against the wood. She waited a breath, two at the most, then turned the handle and slipped inside. She closed the door behind her before the light from the hallway could leak in too much and permeate the darkness.

She did not want to see what it would reveal.

With death comes a specific smell. Not death like the decaying of a body, but the loss of a person. It lingers like smoke after a fire.

Depending on the room in the Toliver house, that smell varied. In the basement it was metallic, particularly silver and gold, with a slightly burnt aftertaste. It was the aroma of working as a distraction from the absent voices that should fill the home.

In the living room, it was old. Antique. The distinct smell of dust and abandonment. Occasionally—rarely—in the kitchen it was sugar and lemon. Home cooked meals that vibrated with laughter; memories that clung to the corners like cobwebs.

In her mother's bedroom, it was stale. Old vanilla seeped into carpets and blankets. It was the sickly-sweet smell of spoiled milk that had coagulated in bowls of uneaten cereal. It was day-old coffee, the grounds making fortune predictions in the bottom of cracked mugs.

Ava wrinkled her nose. Faint remnants of the incense burned to try and mask the smell of mourning hung in the air. It mingled with nightmare sweat and unwashed skin.

"Mom," Ava whispered as she crossed the overly vacuumed carpet. It had long ago lost its plushness. The fibers were now bristled and frayed. The lump on the bed stirred slightly and like a snake shedding its skin, the blankets shifted from her mother's face to her neck.

"'Morning." Ava's voice was soft as she approached the bed. Her mother only slept on one side of the mattress. The other was always undisturbed, the blankets wrinkled only at the center of the linen. The pillows there were full and unnaturally clean, untouched by any head, even the ghost of the man who had stopped warming the spot years ago.

Cordellia groaned, stretched, and then glanced at the clock. "What time is it?"

Ava replied, "Somewhere around nine."

Her mother sat up, bunching her flat pillows against the headboard as she did. The braid Ava had pleated two days ago was a mess, chunks of it having escaped the elastic band. The back of her hair was pressed to her head, flattened from laying on it, and the contours of her face were deeper than normal.

"Do you want me to make you breakfast?" Cordellia asked, tossing the blankets aside as if she were going to get out of bed. It was a good act, almost convincing even, but they both knew that's all it was.

"It's okay," Ava replied, saving her mother the effort of having to put on more of a show. "Delilah and I are going to go to the market to try and find her a dress for tomorrow."

"Is the gala here already?" Cordellia asked as she covered herself back up. Ava nodded gently. "What are you going to wear?"

Ava shrugged. "The blue dress."

A soft smile of fondness touched her mother's dry lips, and in that brief second the woman she was on a good day pressed through. "I love the blue dress," she said.

"Me, too." Silence settled between them, but before Ava could choke on it, she cleared her throat. "Alright, well, I'll be home later." She moved to her mother and kissed her forehead. As she turned away, she retrieved the bowl of soggy cereal she'd brought up last night and asked, "Do you need anything before I go?"

Waving her away with a callused hand, Cordellia replied, "Go. Have fun. There's some money in the jug if you need it."

"Thanks," Ava said as she opened the door. Before she stepped out she added, "Don't forget that Mrs. Jacobi's order is due today. It *has* to take priority over the others. Her daughter needs that necklace for the gala and she's already given you a week grace period. I'll be home in time to deliver it, just make sure it's done. Please."

Without having to look behind her, Ava knew that her mother's eyes had narrowed to slits. Ava had spent many years being not only a child then a teen then a young adult, but also her mother's deliverer, secretary, secret keeper, and parent when the time called. They never acknowledged it though, the messed-up relationship they had. Ava hated what their life had become almost as much as Cordellia hated being reminded of her failure as a parent.

Her voice was flat, lacking any sort of emotion behind the lie when she scolded, "I don't need you to remind me of how to do my job, Avaleigh."

We both know that's not true, Ava thought. Instead of the words dancing on her tongue, she replied with, "I'll see you when I get home." Then, using the toe of her shoe, she pulled the door shut.

From the top of the stairs she had a perfect view into the living room, and from this position she watched as Delilah, propped against the back of the couch, twisted a piece of her rose-gold hair around her finger. Ava tried to find a fragment of the girl D had once been.

Before she worried what people thought about her.

Before her father left and her mother married a man from Typhony, and residential status mattered.

Seemingly overnight, Delilah had developed the same air of pretentiousness they had always despised in their schoolmates. It made Ava sad to think about the girl Delilah had once been versus who she was now. She was the only best friend Ava had though, so she tolerated the person Delilah had become. Part of it, Ava hoped, was an act—as if Delilah was playing a part so people would forget she had once been a simpleton from Meridian.

In the kitchen, Ava dumped the remaining gunk from the bowl down the disposal.

"Ready?" she asked Delilah, her voice too high-pitched and eager, as she made her way around the island.

"How is she?" D asked. She pushed herself off the couch and met Ava at the money jug. Really, it was more of a jar with a lid, the knobby handle broken and re-glued more times than seemed possible. At one time it had held freshly baked cookies—peanut butter and sugar, chocolate chip and macadamia nut. But now it was the place where the extra money went—when there was extra money. Ava had warned her mother multiple times that it was the least safe spot for something like this to be kept, but crime wasn't a thing in Havaan, not since the end of the second generation. There had been a time when they would have worried, but now everyone had what they needed and no one needed to pillage or steal to make a living.

Or to buy potions and spells.

Things had gotten rough at one point—before King Orion—when the second generation became too powerful, too egotistical, and used their abilities to manipulate those without. The war and the only decree that followed—the prohibition of all use of magic—rectified that.

Now everyone was happy again.

Outwardly, at least.

The walls of the houses in Havaan were thick, and many secrets could be hidden behind closed curtains. Ava knew all about that—the walls of *her* house were practically pregnant with them.

"She's Cordellia," Ava replied as she grabbed a wad of cash from the bottom of the money jar. She counted out fifty Havaanian dollars, then put thirty of it back and stuffed the rest into her pocket. She had no intentions of buying anything besides food at the market.

The two women stepped out of the house and immediately Delilah took off, making up for the minute or two she believed they'd lost.

"What's the rush?" Ava asked.

"A minute could be hours in market time," Delilah said in one struggling breath. She was shorter than Ava by a couple of inches, her legs not nearly as long. "I could have missed out on the perfect dress already."

"Whatever shall you do?" Ava replied sarcastically, her breathing even and steady.

The market was set up just past the invisible border between Meridian and Typhony, across the bridge which divided Brene in two. Every day, sellers trundled their carts downtown and spread out in a two-mile radius. They sold exotic spices, tapestries woven from freshly spun wool, flower crowns and small, handcrafted trinkets. The most popular items, especially during the weeks leading up to the Queen's Gala, were dresses made of the finest fabrics, encrusted with beads and jewels that would sparkle like the heavens under the lights of High House. The closer to the event one shopped, the higher the prices, but the more sophisticated and elegant the garment. That was the *only* reason Delilah had waited so long to find a dress. She needed something that would wow the king the moment she passed through the gates.

As they got farther from the neighborhood, Delilah took the time to catch her breath. It was as though she'd been trying to get away from Meridian as fast as possible. To outrun the memories of her life before.

"I wish you were more excited about the gala," she said, not for the first time.

Ava let out an exasperated sigh. "It's not my fault girls from Meridian can't audition to be queen."

"I also hate when you call it an audition."

"What would you have me call it then?" She waited for Delilah to reply, but when D failed to provide a better word, Ava continued. "That's exactly what the Queen's Gala is and you know it. You primp and preen, then prance around like a peacock hoping your plumage is big enough to attract Orion. You're being chosen based purely on who's the prettiest. But beauty doesn't mean you have any sort of intellectual qualities, let alone the capacity to be queen. It's a shallow and ridiculous tradition, and I'm sorry if I can't fake excitement over something I have no desire to be a part of."

Delilah rolled her eyes. "I realize you're perfectly content being the daughter of a jewelry maker, but you can't fault those of us who have higher aspirations," she said.

It wasn't *what* Delilah said, but the *way* she said it, that made Ava stop in her tracks.

Ava had never heard anyone speak about her mother's profession with such disgust, especially Delilah. It was as if the words had taken on a tangible form—something mucky like tar—that rooted Ava in place. She was tempted to turn around and head back home, but her anger had locked her legs.

Home was not her favorite place.

Home was a continuous funeral with a few days of happiness.

At that moment, though, she would have much rather been there.

Her mother's job wasn't glamorous, and they were destined to live in Meridian forever, but Cordellia was good at what she did. Hell, her mother had been selected to design the crown for the queen-elect. That in and of itself made her more than just a simple jewelry maker.

Ava would have reminded Delilah of this, but all she could muster was, "That was really mean, D."

The two women stared at each other. Ava's nails dug into her palms as she curled her slender fingers into fists. So often she let Delilah's words slide to avoid an argument, but not today. Not now.

Ava could handle anyone else in Havaan judging her family...

Finally, Delilah sighed and moseyed to her, dragging her feet slightly. "I'm sorry," she mumbled as she offered Ava a sad, apologetic look. She took her hands, uncurling them at the same time. "I just...I *need* this to matter to you as much as it matters to me. I want you to be excited, if not with me, at least *for* me." Delilah let out a slow breath before continuing. "You're all I have, Avie. My mother thinks it's a stupid, dumb dream, and maybe it is, but it's *my* stupid, dumb dream. I don't want to settle for marrying some guy from Typhony and being his precious little wifey. I've dreamed of attending the Queen's Gala since Orion announced it. You know this."

Ava did know.

When they'd both been citizens of Meridian, Delilah had talked fervently about the Queen's Gala. She'd made lists and sketched dresses for an event in which, at that time, she could not participate. She'd fawned over a younger Sebastian as if he were just a boy in their astrology class; as if she had any sort of chance with him. She had sobbed uncontrollably for two days when one of the girls at school snidely informed her that only women from the upper classes were eligible candidates for Havaan's future queen. When Delilah's mother remarried, her excitement was for nothing other than her ability to attend the Queen's Gala as more than just a spectator.

It wasn't that Ava couldn't understand the excitement about being queen. As someone who had grown up on fairytales and Prince Charming, she got the appeal. It was that she refused to rally behind the one factor that would make the king's choice. To Ava, a queen should be more than just the most beautiful face in the crowd. She didn't believe it was so farfetched to think the sovereign should possess brains, compassion; the ability to think beyond the crown.

To see beyond the gates of High House.

But no.

Who would sit on the throne simply came down to the one who would catch the king's eye.

It was why having the most attention-grabbing dress was of the utmost importance. There would be thousands of women in attendance, all hoping their genetics would deem them worthy of carrying on the royal bloodline. They had a fleeting breath to gain King Orion's approval or be forced to return home with nothing more than a fancy dress, sore feet, and crushed dreams.

"Do you think you can find it in your uncaring heart to conjure up even a grain of excitement for me this weekend?" Delilah squeezed Ava's hands. "Because if you're not happy too, there's no reason for me to go. And I will never forgive you if you make me miss my chance at being queen. I need you there, in my corner, rooting for me."

When Delilah looked at her this way, when she was genuine, she was the person with whom Ava had once had dance parties. She was the same girl she'd jumped into leaf piles with in the fall and built snowmen with in the winter. Ava would sacrifice her life for this Delilah.

And for this Delilah, she would attend some stupid gala.

Which was why, with a resigned sigh, Avaleigh forced a weak smile to her lips. "Just make sure you don't forget about me when you become queen." She was good at faking excitement for Delilah, especially over something as foolish as the Queen's Gala.

She'd been doing it for the last ten years.

But the probability of Delilah getting crowned wasn't pretend. She had just as good a chance as anyone, if not more. She was gorgeous, with mid-length hair that was a mixture of light pink and deep gold. Where Ava was tall and curvy, Delilah was petite, with a slender frame that made her easy to dress. Her light brown eyes always danced with the same mischief perpetually smirked on her lips. The king would notice her, and Ava would help.

Delilah squealed and tossed her arms around her friend's neck. It required her standing on the tip of her toes, but she squeezed with a force that surprised Ava.

"Forget you? You're going to be my assistant, silly girl." Delilah tapped the end of Ava's nose then linked their arms together.

As long as the focus was back on Delilah, all was right in their world. It was a small price to pay to have her as a friend. Delilah was an honest and kindhearted person when she let her real self shine through the dirt of Typhony.

Because of this she would make the perfect queen. That was if they could ever make it to the damn market.

II.

On the morning of the Queen's Gala, the city was alight with a harmonic blend of sounds beginning at the crack of dawn. From the center of town, the pre-celebration celebrations carried on the wind and filtered through Ava's bedroom window, waking her with the jingling of bells, flirty giggles of women and the boisterous shouts of men. Even her neighborhood, which was typically quiet and peaceful, was in high spirits.

While most of Havaan was up early and prepping for the coming evening, it was just another day in the Toliver household. Ava laid in bed, trying to find some sort of commonality with the merriments taking place. As her fingers worked through the knots in her hair, she mentally prepared herself for what her day could hold. Would she have to deal with angry citizens screaming at her about their necklaces and earrings not being ready? Would she have the strength to drag Cordellia out of bed and into the shower? Would she——

The scent of cinnamon invaded her thoughts and beckoned her downstairs.

She was surprised, and slightly suspicious, to see her mother sitting at the kitchen table with her hair freshly washed and pulled back in the antique clip Ava had gotten her for her 45th birthday. Especially after the way she'd been yesterday. When Ava had returned home from the market, Cordellia was still burrowed under her blankets, having vacated her bed only to use the restroom and make a cup of tea. Ava had begged her, in the least demanding way possible, to go downstairs and finish at least *one* project.

One out of the twelve she'd half started.

One out of the four that were needed for the gala.

Especially that damn Jacobi piece.

Cordellia had just laid there though, her back to her child, ignoring her pleas.

Ava was relieved to see her up and about this morning, wearing her mask of normalcy.

Seeing her relaxing, a cup of coffee in one hand and a cracked-spine paperback in the other, was a rare but welcomed sight.

As Ava entered the kitchen, Cordellia looked up and smiled at her daughter. It was hard to miss the deep grooves around her mouth and the valley of wrinkles that had started to form between her eyebrows. Despite the markings of age, her mother was still sophisticatedly beautiful, which was somewhat rare. Beauty withstanding the test of time was not something the first generation had been concerned about. Thus the visual effects of the passing years still etched itself into flesh as it aged.

Cordellia wasn't yet an elder, but Ava had a feeling that even when she was, her good looks would remain.

Delilah always said she hoped to age as well as Cordellia.

Ava didn't really care.

Mother and daughter shared the same milk-and-honey skin tone— softly tanned—and full, round lips. Cordellia was narrow from her shoulders to her toes and a few inches shorter than her child. Ava's height, her eyes, and her hair had all come from her father's side. She had no memories of the man and knew very little of him. Once, when she was twelve and her mother had been mentally present for a handful of days, she had asked Cordellia to tell her *anything* about the man with who she shared genetics, but just the mention of him had sent her into a dissociative state.

Ava never asked again.

A couple of years later, she came home from school to find one of only four photos she would ever see of her dad sitting on her bed. It was a faded image in shadowed sepia tones, parts of it obscured by tears shed long ago. The man in the picture was square-shouldered with short, curly locks and a smile almost too big for his face. Holding the picture, Ava could almost hear his voice telling her nursery rhymes and feel his strong hands tossing her in the air; all things she had never gotten to experience.

When she awoke the next morning, the photo had vanished from her bedside table. She never asked Cordellia about it. It was rare that her mother ever spoke of her father aside from mentioning him in passing, though Ava had gathered some information through the years. She knew his name: Dante Noriega, and that he had been a great fisherman. She never gave up hope that one day the pain of his death would alleviate enough for her and Cordellia to have an actual conversation about him.

For now, Cordellia spent endless hours either holed up in her bedroom or working in the basement; both as a distraction from her loneliness. On better days, she would work well into the night melding pieces of metal together until her fingertips blistered while the meals Ava left on the stairs grew cold. It wasn't uncommon for her to be slumped over her workstation or curled up on the old couch downstairs, only to wake a few hours later as if her fingers had never stopped setting stones.

Ava rarely saw her mother not in the basement when she was having a good day.

Taking advantage of this rare moment, she slid into the chair across from her with a large, homemade cinnamon roll and a tall glass of milk.

"Big day today," her mother said as she folded the corner of her book and set it down in front of her.

Ava shrugged and shoved a piece of roll into her mouth. "Not for me," she mumbled around her chewing. Cordellia gave her a chiding look and Ava swallowed before apologizing.

"It could be a big day for you as well. You never know if you'll meet your own prince at the gala."

Sticking her finger in her mouth, Ava mimed a gag. "I'm not going tonight to hook a husband. I'm going because Delilah needs the support and I need to be there whether she wins or she loses."

"I'm just saying. It wouldn't hurt anyone for you to lady-up a bit."

Ava lowered her thick but shapely brows and scowled at her mother. "I'm lady-upping it enough. I'm going to wear a dress. More than that is asking a lot."

For a moment, Cordellia looked at Ava and something passed behind her eyes. Sadness maybe, combined with a smidge of guilt.

"What?" Ava asked once the discomfort became too much.

The slight smile her mother gave was forced. "I just wish I could give you more opportunities, is all. That we could live in a place like Typhony so you could have a chance at being queen. You would make such a wonderful one."

Ava sighed. This was not a new conversation. Ava was aware her mother thought a life in Typhony, or one of the other region-equivalents, would open more doors, provide a better life. While it was true, Ava had seen how the other half lived, and it wasn't something she desired.

There was nothing Ava would change about her life except for one thing, and that was the way Cordellia had handled—was handling—Dante's death. If a move to an upper class could rescue her mother from the never-ending trek through the badlands, Ava would sell her soul in a heartbeat. She would happily attend daily galas and don as many jewels and dresses as required. She would even sneer down at those in the middle class. But no amount of taffeta or wishful thinking was going to chase away Dante's memory, so they would stay planted in their moderate-sized house with the unused pillows and continue to grow in the sadness plowed by his death.

Reaching across the table, Ava took her mother's scarred, scuffed and calloused hand and said, "I don't need more than what I have, Mom. I'm happy with the life we have. Besides, no one cares about living in a place like Typhony except for the people who live in a place like Typhony."

Cordellia squeezed her daughter's fingers, then asked, "How do you think Delilah is holding up this morning?" before taking a slow sip from her mug.

"She's probably an absolute mess," Ava answered, grinning. The idea of Delilah being a wreck brought a sort of warped satisfaction to Ava. Seeing her best friend frazzled, on the rare occasions when it happened, returned the normalness the move to Typhony seemed to have syphoned from her small body.

Cordellia stood and crossed the kitchen to the sink. "There are a few things I've got to finish up and deliver before tonight. Including the Jacobi piece." She gave Ava a sharp look then kissed her on the top of the head, smoothing the wild curls at the back of her hair at the same time. "I love you, sweet girl. I'll try and wait up so I can hear all about your evening." Ava looked up and smiled at her. "Don't work too hard."

Her mother laughed—a sound Ava didn't realize she missed until it was absent for days at a time—as she made her way toward the basement stairs. "Perhaps when Delilah becomes queen she can make a decree banning all work for jewelry makers."

"Unlikely," Ava replied as she scraped frosting from the edge of her plate with her fork. "Who would dress her in diamonds and pearls?" With a wink and a tinny laugh, Cordellia vanished into her workroom. It wasn't long until a steady bass slithered up the stairs and permeated the rest of the house.

Avaleigh showered, dressed, grabbed the garment bag with the blue dress and her shoes in it, and then headed to Typhony. If hell had ever existed, like the prophets and religious zealots of the old world had claimed, places like Typhony had no doubt been their inspiration.

In the time between the elder magicians and King Orion was the second generation. Learning nothing—or perhaps just the wrong things from those who'd come before—they allowed greed and power to corrupt them. They had almost destroyed Havaan in their need for dominance. It was during this time that they separated Havaan into four regions, and from there another division happened: four areas quickly became eight as two social classes emerged in each; an upper class and a middle class. Many believed the divisions were another way for the magicians to gain control, that by giving those in the now-formed upper class a reason to think they mattered more, they would have allies. As long as there was someone on the bottom, power could be had.

The citizens of Havaan knew nothing of rebellion or protest, so they settled into their districts without question. But there was a group who refused to be oppressed and ruled under the avaricious thumb of the magicians. Thus, the war began.

To keep as much peace as possible, King Orion refused to make a decree that would merge the social classes. Since becoming king, he'd made only one declaration, and that was the eradication of magic.

Under no condition was magic allowed. Seeking information on or even attempting to gain access to it would result in immediate exile to the lowest level of Havaan.

Noples.

Nopels was the boogeyman to children; a terrifying place where its residents were hollow and emaciated shells of the people they'd once been. It was the place where those who'd fought against Orion resided; their hands trapped in metal cages to prevent conjuring and their tongues cut blunt to keep them from speaking. While no one knew the location of Nopels—aside from the king—it was not a place people willingly tried to find.

Typhony was Ava's version of Nopels. She hadn't been lying when she'd said that the only people who cared about being in the upper class were those who were there. The difference between the two classes was marginal and ultimately came down to one thing: a citizen's occupation.

Those who chose jobs that required a more hands-on approach such as sculpting, baking, record keeping or jewelry making lived in the middle class. Those who held positions that kept the cogs and gears of Havaan turning—bankers, teachers and the king's guards—had homes in places like Typhony. Though the houses were only slightly bigger and the yards only moderately better kept in the upper, by the way they were scowled at, one would assume the people of the middle lived in boxes and ate garbage for dinner.

Judgments ran especially high in Typhony.

Luckily for citizens like Ava, noses were so upturned into the air she could slip through the city without a second, or even a first, glance her way.

Without knocking on the door of the Witicker-Finn compound, Ava bypassed the maid and took the carpeted staircase to the second-floor landing. She hurried past the wall of family photos and snagged a wrapped peppermint from the glass bowl sitting below the eight-foot high painting of Doctor Finn, his acquired wife and daughter, and their youngest child, Ashton.

Delilah didn't have any feelings toward her brother one way or another. She tolerated him, but there wasn't much they could do to forge a fourteen-year age gap. Ava, who'd always thought it would be nice to have a sibling, adored the brown haired, blue eyed six-year-old. He was too smart for his age and his grown-up sarcasm amused her. He was a breath of fresh air and she was a bit disappointed she hadn't gotten to see him this day before having to deal with his sister.

"Oh, thank the stars you're here!" Delilah said as she pulled Ava into the bedroom seconds after she'd knocked.

Delilah was definitely anxious.

Ava had assumed she'd be at least half-way finished getting ready, but Delilah's hair was in rollers and her face was bare of makeup. There were puffy bags under her brown eyes and she paced in nothing more than a black slip and pink silk robe. High heels of varying heights were scattered around the large bedroom. The bedsheets were tossed aside aimlessly and there were three half-full mugs of coffee sitting on the vanity.

"Did someone rob you this morning?" Ava joked as she looked around the normally organized room. "Don't tell me they took your dress!"

Delilah stopped making circles in her carpet long enough to give Ava a look that could freeze fire, and then she started up again, mumbling to herself. Before she could start an inferno with her feet, Ava stepped into her path. "What's wrong with you?" she asked gently, holding her friend's arms so she couldn't move.

"What if this is a mistake? There are going to be so many other women there…the chance of me making an impression on the king is like, one in a million."

"One in a couple thousand, really."

"You're not helping!" Delilah pouted, crossing her arms over her chest to emphasize her point.

"You're right. I'm sorry." Ava offered her an apologetic smile. "What do you need from me?"

Taking a deep breath, Delilah answered, "I need you to tell me that tonight isn't a waste of time. That everything is going to be okay…Tell me something—*anything*—to keep me from staying home."

Ava rested her hands on the sides of her best friend's face. "This is not a mistake," she started, as convincingly as possible. "All it takes is a glance. One second, a second and a half if the king lingers, for his choice to be made. One blink of an eye for your entire life to change. But you have to be there for it to happen. If you don't go tonight, if you sit this out, you forfeit that chance and you will spend the rest of your life regretting it." As she spoke, Ava steered Delilah to the cushioned seat of her lit vanity. She turned her toward the mirror then leaned down and rested her chin on Delilah's shoulder. Looking at her through the mirror, like some weird two-headed creature, she added as casually as possible, "And if you don't go tonight I will murder you."

Delilah turned to her quickly, her eyes large with confusion. "Excuse me?"

"If you make all those hours I spent listening to you rant and rave about this damn gala mean nothing, I will end you. And then I will befriend the new queen and become *her* assistant." Ava smiled and finally Delilah laughed. Ava could feel the physical change in her; the loosening of her shoulders and the softening of her face.

"I adore you. You know that, yeah?"

Shrugging a shoulder slightly, Ava nodded. "What's not to adore? Now, let's get you glammed up. We can't have you looking a mess for the king."

"You don't think I would get his attention with rollers in my hair?"

Laughing dryly, Ava replied, "Not the kind you want."

The friends fell into a fit of giggles as the rest of the tension left the room.

Ava had discovered she was surprisingly good at cosmetology at a young age. Delilah had always insisted she become a beautician, but if she was going to have any career it was going to be in a kitchen. She would never own her own restaurant while living in Meridian, but she was more than okay with just working in the back of one. She'd had an internship lined up after graduation, but first Zarah died and subsequently her mother's already splintered mental state cracked even more, so she'd given that up. If the whole queen's assistant thing didn't pan out, she would look into employment at a bistro or something similar. She needed to start contributing to the household income, especially since Cordellia's dark days were becoming more frequent.

She worked for an hour on Delilah's makeup, starting over twice when the color combinations didn't feel right. Eventually she found satisfaction in a look that accentuated Delilah's beautiful eyes and delicate face. It paired well with not only D's pink-gold hair, but also the dress she'd purchased. Most of her hair was pinned to one side, soft waves caressing her neck. A few wispy pieces were pulled from the pins to frame her face.

When Delilah emerged from the closet fully dressed, Ava's eyes welled with unexpected tears. "You look stunning," she whispered, completely awed by the transformation. The top of Delilah's dress was gilded—with actual gold rubbed into the fabric—and a neckline that plunged almost to her bellybutton. The flakes glittered in the light of the bedroom and would no doubt absorb the ones at the ball. The bottom half of the dress was made from sheer black chiffon that swooshed gently with each step. There was a slit cut on the left side that reached the middle of Delilah's thigh, showing off her smooth porcelain skin.

She looked sexy but elegant.

Enchanting and a little dangerous.

Everything expected from a queen.

There was a fleeting second, as Delilah primped in the mirror, when Ava felt a sting of jealousy. She wasn't sure where it came from, because she had never cared about the Queen's Gala or even slightly wanted to be queen—and she still didn't—but the idea of getting glammed up for a night of attention suddenly seemed appealing. Swallowing the bitter taste, she forced the thought from her head.

When Delilah pulled herself from the mirror, Ava handed her a small green box. "What's this?" Delilah asked as she untied the silk ribbon and removed the lid. "Wow," she gawked, pulling a chain from the box. Set in a black iron frame, the edges curving and twisting in on one another like scorched ivy branches, was a perfectly round sapphire. It was surrounded by twenty small diamonds that cast mini prisms around the room. Delilah looked up at Ava, rainbows from the stones glinting off her face.

"When did your mother find time to make this?"

Smiling sheepishly, Ava replied, "I made it. There are a couple diamonds that probably aren't set correctly, but—"

Delilah launched herself at her best friend and wrapped her arms tightly around her neck. "It's beautiful. You're the most wonderful best friend a girl could ask for."

"Don't you mean a future queen could ask for?" she mumbled, returning the hug.

"You're damn right!" Delilah laughed and turned around so that Ava could fasten the piece around her neck.

Just as her fingers were closing the clasp, the bedroom door was thrown wide by the tornado known as Celeste Witicker-Finn; also known as Delilah's mother.

"Avaleigh," she greeted as she breezed by, giving her the sneer she reserved only for Ava. It was a look that said, "I tolerate you because you're my daughter's friend, even though you've given me no reason to actually dislike you." If she weren't one of Ava's least favorite people she would care, but as it was, she simply gave the matriarch her biggest and brightest smile.

Celeste had been born and raised in what was now Ramenell, the middle class of Paranick. When she'd turned eighteen, she moved to Meridian, met the man who would become Delilah's father, and at twenty she gave birth. After three years, Delilah's father decided parenthood was not in his wheelhouse and split, leaving Celeste to take care of a toddler on her own. Orion had been in power a few short months when he'd announced he was looking for a wife. Celeste jumped at the chance to become queen. At that time, every woman in Havaan was eligible to do so. But she left the first Queen's Gala with mascara-stained cheeks and returned to her job as a florist. Nine long years later, she met Doctor Barrett Finn, baby-birther extraordinaire. They married within six months and she took to her new life in Typhony quite well. It wasn't High House but it wasn't Meridian.

It especially wasn't Ramenell.

Celeste circled Delilah like a hungry shark. She cocked her head this way and that, a motion that reminded Ava of a curious bird. Celeste tugged on the shoulder straps of Delilah's dress, trying to raise the neckline. She frowned when it dropped back into place as soon as she let go. With an exaggerated sigh, she crossed her arms and said, "I really wish you hadn't waited so long to buy a dress. We could have had it altered."

Glancing down, Delilah shrugged. "I don't want it altered," she challenged. "I bought it this way on purpose. I need the king to notice me."

"And you would willingly reduce yourself to your breasts and a high slit?"

For once, Ava and Celeste were on the same page.

Delilah rolled her eyes and mimicked her mom, her crossed arms hiding her cleavage slightly. "What would you have me do? It's not like he's going to interview us. I've got one shot and if it takes a little thigh to get his attention, so be it."

Tsking, Celeste let out a deep huff. "Delilah," she started, trying to soften her annoyance. "If for whatever reason tonight doesn't work out in your favor, this fantasy of yours has to end." She paused long enough to tuck an intentionally loose piece of hair behind Delilah's ear. Perhaps it was her own disappointment at being passed over at the first gala that made her so reluctant to let her daughter participate in the second.

"You have the potential to be extraordinary," Celeste continued, "but you can't achieve those things with your head in the clouds. So, if you aren't chosen tonight, promise me you'll move on and let it go. That you'll find yourself a suitable husband and begin your life."

"I won't exactly have much of a choice, will I?" Delilah's sarcasm was as smooth as her dress and as sharp as her eyeliner. Though Ava was not a fan of Celeste, she disliked this version of Delilah even more—the snarky, somewhat disrespectful monster Typhony had created. However, a large part of her transformation came from Celeste pushing D to be great and wonderful, to defy expectations, while in the same breath berating her for making her own plans to achieve such things.

Luckily for all three women, the moment was interrupted by the man of the house. Doctor Finn was, like his son, an inhalation of clean, unpolluted air. With his short-cropped salt-and-pepper hair and pale green eyes, he carried himself with a level of confidence that wasn't at all off-putting. His smile was contagious and his laugh infectious. He was good to Celeste and especially Delilah, whom he doted on and adored as if he'd had a part in creating her.

Delilah had been a bit hesitant of the man at first, worried that he, too, would abandon her. But it didn't take long for her to take to the good doctor. Eight years later, they were inseparable. At times, their interactions seemed so personal Ava had to look away.

Of all the things Delilah had, a father was the one thing Ava envied.

"Your ride for tonight's festivities is here, ladies," he said, sticking his head into the bedroom. Upon seeing Delilah, he stepped into the room carefully, as if approaching too quickly would startle her. "Oh, Delilah, you look absolutely beautiful."

She made a low, dramatic curtsy and grinned.

"You don't think the neckline is a little low?" Celeste piped, hoping to corral an ally.

"Possibly," he started, "but there isn't much we can do about it now, my dear." He turned to Ava, who was leaning casually against the wall in her modest blue dress, and tipped his head to her. "Avaleigh," he greeted kindly, smiling. She bowed, eliciting a sweet chuckle from Delilah. "You look as radiant as always."

"Thank you, Doctor Finn."

"Shall we get you two beauties off for the evening? I wouldn't want you to miss a second of tonight."

With arms linked, Ava and Delilah led the other two down the stairs, through the foyer, and out the front door where a horse-drawn carriage waited. Both girls gasped at the unexpected chariot. The buggy was a large half-circle, flat on top and matte black with painted purple filigree around its edges. The ornate top looked very similar to the current queen's crown, with jewels strung between the delicate spikes. The two white horses hitched to the front had braided manes with bright bellflowers tucked into the pleats.

"This is for us?" Delilah asked her stepfather. He nodded and ushered them forward, a hand on each of their shoulders. They greeted the rider before mounting the steps into the carriage. The seats were plush and satin, upholstered in the same purple as the flowers in the horses' manes. It was more elegance Ava had ever experienced and she couldn't help but feel almost as excited as Delilah, who was practically bouncing out of her skin.

Doctor Finn reached inside and grabbed D's hand. "No matter what happens tonight, I want you to know that I am incredibly proud of you. You are the daughter I always wanted, but never thought I would have, and I love you very much."

Smiling against the tears that were filling her eyes, Delilah squeezed his hand in return. "Thank you, Dad."

It was one of those moments when Ava had to look away.

"You two have a great time tonight. Take care of our girl," he added, patting Ava's knee as he disembarked and closed the door.

The two friends stuck their heads out of the window and waved ferociously, as if the bones in their wrists didn't exist, until the carriage rounded the corner and the Witicker-Finn house vanished from sight.

Then they settled into their seats for the twelve-mile trek to High House.

III.

The seats of the carriage welcomed the two as they sank into them. The hooves of the horses marked a steady rhythm against the road; a clip-clop that echoed Delilah's excited heart.

Trotting through Havaan was like moving through a living piece of art. When the first generation pulled the world together and created Havaan, they joined the people under one singular sky. Before, there had been locations where winter affected some and not others; where the summer months had existed longer in particular regions. Nixing that, they stirred the seasons together and spread them evenly amongst the land.

The Queen's Gala could not have taken place at a more perfect time. The spring mornings were warm and stuffy with the coming heat of summer. The sun bore down on exposed shoulders and drew forth smatterings of freckles. The evenings, by comparison, were cool and comfortable. The wind blew steadily and carried with it a faint hint of grass and potting soil. The leaves were at their greenest and the flowers fully bloomed. Patches of wildflowers sprouted along the sides of the roads, little blips of yellows and whites, pinks and blues.

The sun was barely beginning to set and it blanketed everything in melted copper. Soon, houses faded and the land opened into countryside that resembled some of the paintings the first generation had allowed to remain.

Looking away from the breathtaking scenery, Ava glanced at Delilah, whose long fingers stroked the jewel of her necklace. Her gaze was far away as she stared out the window, and Ava could almost read her thoughts as they swirled. The casting sun played with the browns of Delilah's eyes and highlighted the gold of her hair. It danced on the planes of her face and hid in the shadows of her cheekbones. Ava had always been a bit envious of the mystical features Delilah had gotten. Nothing about her seemed natural, from her slender frame to her wicked smile and earthly beauty—as if she'd been birthed from Mother Nature herself.

As if she could feel Ava's eyes on her, Delilah turned with a cocked brow. "What?"

"Are you nervous?"

Dropping her hands to her lap, Delilah shook her head no, and then nodded. "Yes," she laughed. "This is the biggest night of my life. I've been waiting for this for ten years."

"Oh, I'm aware," Ava teased, grinning.

Delilah offered her a soft smile back. "Everything is going to change tonight," she said as she rubbed the sapphire with the pad of her thumb and looked back out the window. Ava followed her line of sight. To the southwest, sitting atop the hill from which it got its name, the silhouette of High House was barely visible above the tree lines. White clouds, perfectly round and full, hung in the background as if suspended from invisible strings.

"Have you thought about what you'll do if tonight doesn't go your way?" Ava questioned as she tore her eyes away from the mansion. They would be there soon enough; she had no desire to track their approach.

"I think about it every time I imagine what I'll do if this *does* go my way. They're always there, together, playing off one another."

"Care to share that plan with your best friend?"

Delilah looked her in the eyes and said simply, "I'm leaving."

"What do you mean you're leaving?"

"That's my plan. If I'm not chosen as queen, I'm leaving Typhony. Leaving Brene entirely."

For a moment Ava wondered if Delilah was joking, but when she didn't start laughing, the truth settled on her skin in goosebumps. It had never crossed her mind that Delilah wouldn't remain in Typhony. She assumed she would spend a few days—maybe weeks—wallowing in both her sorrow and her pajamas, but that she'd eventually pull herself together and carry on with life. At no point had Ava imagined the latter happening away from Brene.

Away from *her*.

"Where will you go?" Ava asked, trying to keep her voice from shaking.

Delilah shrugged a shoulder as she played with the fabric of her skirt. "West. Until something tells me to stop and settle there. That may be somewhere in Zyprah or closer, like Lyyard. I don't have the logistics worked out because I'm not planning on having to actually leave. But if it comes down to it…" She let the rest hang in the air between them.

"It's as good a plan as any, I suppose," Ava said, looking away. The horses were slowing gradually as they neared the gates. A line of carriages and cars at least a mile long could be seen up ahead, vanishing around a curve. They were all full of women with the same dream as Delilah.

Suddenly, the possibility of Delilah leaving seemed more and more likely.

Delilah's words brought Ava back to the buggy, with its ceiling of miniature lights that glinted and glittered. The diamonds in Delilah's necklace bounced tiny rainbows off the taupe colored walls.

"What?" Ava asked when she realized Delilah had spoken.

"I said you could come with me," Delilah repeated. "If I leave."

"Yeah," Ava agreed, chewing the inside of her lip. It was not lost on her that just as she had never considered Delilah's leaving, she had never thought of her own, either. Delilah and Cordellia, living in Brene—none of it had ever stopped being a part of her future; even if she did decide to let love in and become a simple-man's missus. In her mind, Delilah was there for everything that would follow tonight. She was in her wedding and holding her hand as she gave birth. Her mother was in a rocking chair, sending those children into Slumberland with the same lullabies she'd sung to Ava. None of this was ever meant to happen elsewhere in Havaan, but instead of telling D this, she merely replied, "Maybe."

Noticing her friend's discomfort, Delilah reached across the small distance and squeezed her knee. "Nothing we need to worry about right now though, yeah? The night is young."

Ava nodded and smiled. "We don't even need a night. Just one second," she reminded.

Sitting back in her seat with a wide grin on her face, Delilah nudged Ava's foot gently. "You look really pretty, by the way."

While Delilah had been changing, Ava had slipped into her simple dress. She'd woven a small braid across the top of her head and let the rest of her hair do whatever it pleased. Adding a tinge of gold shadow to her lids, a coat of mascara to her feathery lashes and a layer of coral lipstick satisfied her enough. She looked fine, better than she had before, and passable enough that they wouldn't turn her away at the gates of High House.

"I meant to tell you at the house, but Celeste didn't leave much room to do so."

"That's because she was barely able to contain her excitement," Ava said sarcastically.

"She's the greatest."

As their carriage came to an almost complete stop, both women leaned out the window to look ahead. The horses had made quick work of their journey. They were less than a half mile away at this point. It was only a matter of the other buggies and cars, some stretched to accommodate larger parties, dropping off their passengers then retreating down the opposite side of the hill. At this pace, they would be at High House within the next few minutes. In that mere span of time, the culmination of ten years would come together and by the end of the night everything *would* change, just as Delilah had said.

How it would change, though, they were still hours from knowing.

Nearing their destination, gaieties of laughter and shouts of greetings filled the carriage. The noise grew thicker as they arrived at the massive wrought-iron gates. They were normally closed, but tonight they were wide-open as citizens of Havaan filed in. Delilah disembarked, followed by Ava, with the help of the carriage driver.

"I will meet you here at the end of the evening for your return home," he said as he locked the door.

They thanked him before stepping into the surge of mostly women. There were many men in attendance, but tonight, ladies from all regions of Havaan dominated. They wore dresses of fiery reds and lush greens. There were fabrics of royal purple and crisp white. It was easy to tell the upper class from the middle by the amount of stones on their fingers and gold around their necks. Ava even spotted a few pieces Cordellia had crafted.

It was a sea of beautiful, strong, elegant, ravenous women, all with one thing on their mind: catching the attention of their king.

"Promise me you'll try to have fun tonight," Delilah said, her tone slightly pleading as she hooked her arm with that of her friend.

Avaleigh rolled her eyes. She wasn't out to make this night anything but wonderful for Delilah. "Of course I'm going to have fun. Just because I think this whole thing is stupid doesn't mean I'm against dancing the night away."

"I heard there's going to be seventeen different kinds of desserts." Delilah wiggled her eyebrows.

Mouth wide, Ava looked at her. Slowly, her shock morphed into genuine excitement, her grin all but splitting her face. Ava loved sweets—desserts especially—and more than anything cake was at the very top. Hearing this news made being here worthwhile. She wouldn't go home with a potential husband, or even the crown, but her stomach would undoubtedly be happier than either of those things could ever make her.

"You just made my night," she said, throwing an arm around Delilah's shoulders.

"Let's see if we can make mine, too," the pink-haired beauty replied as she pulled her friend into the courtyard.

In fairytales of the old days, kings and queens resided in grand castles with massive towers and moats protected by dragons. High House wasn't a castle by any stretch, and since dragons didn't exist there was no need for a drawbridge. The home of the royal family *was* large and extravagant however, the biggest in Havaan, with a courtyard that wrapped around the entire house. There was a smooth cobblestone walkway that bisected two large patches of lush grass, making up the front and back yards. The property stretched at least a mile in all directions and was encased by a black metal fence no less than ten feet high. All of it sat upon a hill overlooking Brene. The royal family had homes in each of the regions, but High House was their main headquarters.

The quad was full of people milling about, as well as performers on stilts and servers dressed in neatly pressed suits. The tuning of a band could be heard as it set up in a corner of the yard. The air was tainted with spun sugar and roasted pig. It was sweet and savory, and made the taste buds of the citizens tap-dance hungrily.

At the horizon, the sun was finally beginning to set. It brushed everything around them with warm lilac, tangerine orange and vibrant blue. Soon the sky would be dark and the strings of lights looped between the tall trees would look like thousands of makeshift stars.

Ava whistled as she took it all in. It really was beautiful and impossible not to get swept up in the grandeur of the night. Regardless of her feelings toward the Queen's Gala, tonight would be one for the memory books. She would have the magic of the evening to look back on; and one day she would tell her children all about it—how she had shared the same air and space with whomever would become queen.

"Come on." Delilah pulled her to a table filled with glasses. Delilah settled on a flute of champagne and Ava a sweet wine. Side-by-side, drinks in hand, the two friends wove through the crowd. They waved hello to classmates they'd not seen since their last day of school and engaged in light conversation with strangers. When the music picked up, the notes floating above their heads, they made their way to the designated dance area. There were no lyrics to the songs, just steady rhythms that forced them to twirl and spin, jump and shuffle. They flowed from partner to partner in a quick dosey-doe and ducked under the arms of handsome men.

There was a hum of electricity in the air that looped its way over Ava's skin like silk.

It was easy to forget why they were there until the music faded and a hush fell over the crowd. It made its way through them like a wave until Ava could hear nothing but her own heartbeat. As one, the crowd turned toward High House and one of the balconies that loomed over them.

King Orion, Queen Bernadette, and Prince Levi stood as still as statues, smiles plastered on their faces. Ava wondered where Prince Sebastian was, seeing as this whole fanfare was for his benefit. After a few breaths, the king raised his hand and everyone around Ava burst into applause. There were even a few whistles tossed in for good measure. Ava looked around and then clapped quietly until the silence returned.

"Citizens of Havaan, greetings on this celebratory night!" King Orion's voice boomed. Ava didn't see a microphone, but she assumed it was hidden in his gold trimmed jacket.

From the corner of her eye, she spotted someone moving through the crowd. It wasn't the decent looking waiter who caught her attention, but the tower of cupcakes he was balancing on a tray. She followed him with her eyes, craning her neck as much as possible, until he disappeared.

Next to her, Delilah elbowed her side, and when Ava turned toward her, she mouthed "Pay attention." D's face was stern, so Ava gave her the most apologetic smile she could muster before refocusing on the king's speech.

"—thank you for your journey. Many of you have traveled a great distance to be here and your dedication does not go unappreciated. Tonight, we have gathered to celebrate the birth of my eldest son—your prince and future king—Sebastian. For it shall be his time to reign soon and as we all know, behind a great king is an even better queen." King Orion turned to the queen and tipped his head to her. Her smile was short, tight, but convincing enough to earn a round of applause. "This evening we will find our next queen amongst you. Until then, enjoy the festivities. Eat, drink and be merry!" Orion lifted a goblet to the crowd. "Long live Havaan!"

"In our king we give thanks!" the crowd shouted as one. It was the official motto of Havaan, a reminder as to who was responsible for their current unity and peace.

The horde remained in place, some whispering to one another, as the royal family disappeared back inside. Once the balcony doors were closed, conversation picked up again, much of it centered on the deciding of a future crowned head.

"How do you think he'll decide?"

"Will we know tonight?"

"Do you think I still have a chance?"

When the plucking of strings and tapping of drums began again, the citizens of Havaan dispersed. Some hurried to the dance area while others hung back, sipping from their glasses and making eyes at one another. Delilah held up her first finger to a group of girls then took

Ava by the elbow, pulling her the opposite direction in which she was trying to go.

"A few of us are going to explore the grounds. Come with us."

Ava shook her off. "I'll pass. You go though. I'm going to see how many types of cake I can get through before I throw up."

In a moment of hesitation Delilah asked, "Are you sure?"

"Absolutely," Ava assured. "This is your night. Go get acquainted with your future home."

Delilah smiled before hugging her quickly. "I'll meet you at the cake table within the hour, okay?" Ava barely got off a nod before Delilah was gone. She joined the group, most of them old school peers, and then turned back to Ava. She wiggled her fingers in a girly wave before she was swallowed by chiffon dresses and black tuxedos.

Not nearly as disappointed as she should have been at being left alone, Ava made a casual beeline toward the desserts. On her way, she snagged another glass of wine and tried to appear as inconspicuous as possible.

It took only a few minutes to find the spaced designated for dining. Circular tables with gold and black cloths dotted the lawn. Longer buffet tables held an array of food. Juicy pork freshly sliced from the pig glistened next to bowls of creamy mashed potatoes. The earthy pallet of vegetable displays contrasted with the bright ones of colorful fruit arrangements designated for the chocolate fountain. It all smelled and looked delicious, but there was a very specific section of tables in which Ava was interested, and she finally made her way to them after rejecting four different invitations to dance and one request to meet behind the greenhouse.

A little disheartened there were only fifteen different sweets—ranging from cupcakes to spongy lemon bars—she set to work, collecting only a few to begin with. It was still early and she would have to pace herself; but if the rest of the desserts were anywhere as close to mouthwatering as the red velvet cupcake had been, she was in trouble. *The sugar will keep me awake for the ride home,* she theorized as she sank her teeth into a small piece of chocolate sachertorte cake. Its smooth mirror icing melted in her mouth. Ava sighed contently while she finished the slice and looked around.

The sheer number of people in attendance was overwhelming, especially considering how many women were there solely with hopes of becoming queen. While they seemed to be taking the night in stride, enjoying the evening as if it were just a random gathering at the king's home, Ava couldn't begin to fathom how nervous they were. When they swiveled their heads, were they simply taking in their surroundings or was there something more to it; were they hoping to catch a glimpse of King Orion, make eye contact with him and send a silent plea of *pick me, pick me?*

She did not envy them.

Lost in her thoughts, Ava turned to refill her plate and bumped into the side of someone. "Oh," she gasped, taking a step back. A tanned arm shot out to steady her, but she was already planted firmly on her feet. "Sorry. I didn't see you there."

"Are you enjoying yourself?" he asked. His voice was deep and smooth, graveled. It stirred something in her soul, dragged like a wooden spoon along the edges of her stomach. She let her gaze travel up his torso and over his muscular arm. She inhaled when she reached his face. His eyes drew her in the most. They were nearly black, the pupil taking up the entire iris, except for a small ring that blazed like fire.

"I am," she replied once she blinked and forced herself to look away.

"And the cakes, as well?"

"The cakes are the *reason* I'm enjoying myself." She picked a piece of cheesecake from her plate and popped it into her mouth.

The stranger turned his attention to the crowd and Ava risked another glance at him. His jaw was squared and his nose a perfect triangle with a high bridge. His lips fit his face well and her fingers twitched with desire to feel the strands of his earlobe-length black hair between them.

Even his profile was attractive and she had to bite the inside of her cheek to keep from sighing dramatically.

The man exhaled, the sound almost regretful. "If you can pull yourself away from your sampling for a moment, the king would like to speak with you."

It was the k-word that finally broke the spell and for the first time she took note of what he was wearing: black pants and pristine white dress shirt under a black vest, into which a thin red tie disappeared. It was on the front of his vest where she noticed King Orion's crest—two crossed swords with a row of three stars between the points. It was designed as a reminder that Orion was their third ruler, and that his rise to power was forged from steel and sacrifice, not magic and privilege.

She looked up at him slowly. "Excuse me?"

He met her eyes and once again she found it impossible to think. He was the most handsome man she'd ever seen. And his smell…it was mint and clean clothes and all things comforting and safe. But her immodest feelings could not distract from what he had said. Words he repeated for her sake. "The king would like a word with you."

"Just one?" she asked. She tried to sound playful, but it came out awkward, forced. "I guess in that case it'll be a quick conversation and I can get back to my cakes. I have ten more to get through." The man—*a guard*, she reminded herself—quirked a thick brow at her but said nothing else. She set down her plate, ran her tongue over her teeth and then smiled fully. "Do I have anything in my choppers?"

He frowned at her, eyed her almost curiously, and then shook his head. Without another word, he waved her ahead of him. He placed a hand on the small of her back, steering her through the crowd. People hardly glanced their way as they moved amongst them. Not that Ava would have noticed anyway; she was too focused on trying not to trip. The pressure of this stranger's hand was melting her uncaring heart, which was currently trying to escape by way of her throat. His scent filled her nostrils and made it impossible to breathe anything but him.

She wanted to lose herself in all the things of which he was made.

"Do you want to give me some sort of idea what I'm in for?" she asked as soon as they crossed the threshold into High House. Her voice echoed off the marbled floors of the foyer. The black, grey and deep red swirls complimented the burgundy walls. There were two carpeted staircases, mirrors of each other, that curved outwards from their middle and met at one landing.

The ceilings were high, with large skylights. Etched white vines with hundreds of leaves stretched across the glass in intricate twists and curlicues. Right now, the windows offered a magnificent view of the star-spattered sky, but in the daytime they no doubt let in a copious amount of warm sunlight.

Across from the front door was a set of double doors that led to the backyard. Ava could see an array of people socializing beyond them, and she couldn't help but wonder where Delilah was, if she was okay, if she was looking for her…

In the center of the room was a round table with onyx legs supporting a glass top. An expensive looking vase, which held a lavished bouquet of lilies, was the only decoration in the otherwise empty room. Its bareness wasn't uninviting but it certainly didn't calm Ava's nerves. Neither did the vow of silence Mr. Elusive Guard had suddenly decided to take as he led her up the staircase to the left, its ornate banister of overlapping swirls cold in her hand.

Maybe I ate too many cakes, she thought as they neared a large door. It was brushed gold, with the same looping pattern as the stair railing engraved so deeply the shadows made it look black. When her escort reached for the handle, Ava grabbed his arm.

"Wait." She could not mask the slight tremor of her voice. His attention snapped to her hand, which she cautiously removed. Only then did he raise his eyes to her face. "I'm sorry. I'm just…I don't know what's going on and I feel like I might throw up on your shoes. Can you break your silence long enough to tell me if I'm in trouble for something? Please."

With a sigh he answered, "You're not in trouble." His voice melted over her, though his reassurance did not help. They stood in the hall, stillness around them, looking at one another for the passing of six heartbeats before he reached for the door again. "Are you ready?"

"No." She took a deep, steadying breath as she ran her hands down the skirt of her dress, trying to press out any wrinkles.

"Do you need a minute to gather yourself?"

"No," she said again, more certain this time, and squared her shoulders. She nodded firmly to the guard, who opened the door and ushered her inside.

As she crossed in front of him, she gave him a look that said *wish me luck*. The corner of his mouth twitched a fraction of a centimeter before his solemnity was back. Once she was inside, he closed the door behind them. The echo bounced through the massive room, which seemed to stretch for miles. Countless windows, all nearly reaching the tall vaulted ceiling, had thick red curtains pulled across them. Slivers of light leaked around the edges and cast moonbeams on the grey wood floors.

Pillar after ivory pillar, each carved with intricate images, filled the room like trees in a forest. Ava and the guard were passing by too fast for her to catch what the scenes were, but she could make out rolling hills and very small people. It was beautiful, and she wanted to stop to look at each one, but the presence behind her pushed her forward until they reached the opposite end of the room.

Seated in thrones on a raised platform were King Orion and his wife, Queen Bernadette. Ava had never seen either one in person, though she would know them anywhere. Posters of the king plastered the outside of buildings in the town square and his face was printed on all of their currency.

As for the queen, years ago there had been a statue of her erected in the very center of Havaan, four hundred miles from all the edges of their world. Havaan was not a very big land mass, having been molded and shrunk by the elder magicians. It was equally eight hundred miles north to south as it was east to west, and the stone monument marked the exact middle.

Ava had attended the revealing when she was nine.

She and Zarah had traveled two-hundred and sixty-two miles just to watch a sheet be pulled from the sculpted image of Queen Bernadette. It had been impressive, if for nothing more than its sheer size, but Ava had been far too young to appreciate it for anything more than a statue.

Standing in front of the inspiration, she couldn't help but feel awed; even if Bernadette's face was not as smooth as that of the carving. She really was as majestic as everyone said, especially with her shock of silver hair and penetrating, seafoam green eyes. Sitting next to her, King Orion's typical good looks seemed average. The only off-putting thing about the queen was the invisible coldness that seemed to roll off her.

Ava wasn't sure why, but she didn't feel quite safe in her presence.

Orion and Bernadette sat tall in their chairs, looking down at her—wordlessly—for seconds that felt like an eternity.

"Thank you, Nixon," the king finally said, addressing the guard. Nixon tipped his head, a casual bow, but said nothing. She was surprised the king's voice was gentler than it had been during his speech, less demanding and authoritative. It was the sort of voice that should be telling stories to children, not one that belonged to a ruler. And for a moment Ava felt her shoulders relax; at least, until he stood.

He was a monster of a man, with a wide berth and the shoulders of an ox. His voice, nor his size, made much sense with the gentle angles of his face. As he meandered down the short flight of stairs to where she was standing, his large hand stroked his neatly trimmed brown beard, as if he were considering her. Up close, Ava could see shallow cracks forming in his peach skin and radiating from his bright emerald eyes.

In her peripheral, she saw Nixon step away. He ascended the stairs and stood behind the king's now empty throne, disappearing into the shadows.

"What is your name, my dear?" the king asked.

"Ava," she said quietly, her nerves choking her words. She cleared her throat and spoke louder. "Avaleigh Toliver." She bowed slightly to him, something she realized she should have done as soon as she'd approached, then stood as tall as her 5'8" frame would allow. Most people would shrink away from the king, humbled to be in his presence, but not Ava. She met his eyes. Yes, she was nervous, but she refused to let any of them see that.

She took pride in one thing above all, and that was her strength.

Her entire life she had watched her mother crumble little by little, afraid to pull herself from the rubble. Ava knew firsthand what weakness could do to a person and she would be damned before succumbing to it.

"Did Nixon tell you why you've been summoned?" the king questioned.

"No," she replied, suddenly angry. She couldn't help looking toward the darkness at the mention of his name, searching for the soldier. The golden disks of his eyes glowed in the black like two flickering candles. "He's a fortress."

The king gave her a wide smile. It crinkled the skin around his eyes, making him look jolly. For whatever reason, Ava wanted to like him.

"It's because he knew I wanted to give you the good news myself."

Ava looked at him curiously, her large eyes narrowing a fraction. "And what good news would that be?"

King Orion threw his arms open excitedly. "Avaleigh Toliver," he started, his voice booming once again. The words ricocheted off the floors and clung to the rafters as if they, too, were awaiting his announcement.

"Congratulations. You have been selected as the future queen of Havaan!"

IV.

The king's words hit her like a bullet from a gun.

Then everything besides her racing heart slowed.

She scanned the faces in the room.

The king's mouth was stretched wide, pure excitement tugging on the corners of his eyes and lips. The queen sat in her throne, one of her perfectly defined, thinly plucked eyebrows arching in silent anticipation. Nixon stepped from the shadows just enough to differentiate himself from the darkness; his face an emotionless mask aside from the slight flare of his nostrils. It looked as if he, too, were taken by surprise at the king's proclamation.

Where is the prince? she wondered, noticing his absence for the second time.

Ava's gaze continued past them and to the door at the back of the room.

She realized she was still waiting.

Waiting for Delilah to pop out and tell her it had all been a joke; that it was *D* who had been chosen for the prince and that Ava was just there to be knighted as her assistant.

Assistant I can handle, Ava thought as she counted the seconds. *Queen I cannot.* She refused to blink, to miss the moment the door opened and her best friend's smiling face poked through. But as time began to move forward again and Delilah failed to appear, the truth settled on her like a blanket of wet wool.

Then she began to laugh. At first they were short chuckles, like hiccups, but before long they were rolling out in waves.

"No, no, no, no, no," she said in the breaks between breaths.

The queen's voice cut through the room. "What is the meaning of this?" she demanded as she floated from the platform to Ava in a matter of seconds.

"She's just excited, my love," the king assumed. He stepped closer to his wife and put a stilling hand on her shoulder. "Isn't that right?" His attention focused on Ava once again.

Ava's honest answer came quick. "No," she said as her laughter died down.

"What do you mean *no*?" Queen Bernadette's eyebrows lowered and her eyes flashed a pale blue so light it almost looked silver. It flared in a ring around the queen's pupils and combined with something Ava couldn't quite identify. It was in the sneer of her red lips that she understood it was disgust.

Not that it wasn't a warranted response.

Ava had no doubt this was the opposite reaction they'd been expecting.

"I'm…" She paused, searching for the right word. "Flattered. Really. But you're making a huge mistake. I—"

"Are you a murderer?" the queen questioned snidely.

"No," Ava replied, dragging the word out.

"Are you married already? Do you perform magic despite your king's decree?"

"Well no, but—"

"Then your king has not made a mistake."

"I'm from Meridian," she offered. It was her last lifeline. She was certain that, if anything, her status would instantly default her.

That assurance was crushed when, at the same time, the other three in the room said, "That isn't a real rule."

It was the king's turn to speak. "This is great news!" he exclaimed.

Maybe it's a dream, Ava rationalized as she pinched her wrist and then flinched as the pain rocketed up her forearm and drew her attention back to Orion's words. "The people of Havaan will not be able to claim favoritism." Orion looked at Ava hopefully, as if he wanted her to feel the same way he did. The belief of his words erased the years from his face. For a moment he was the king who had taken power twenty-five years ago, full of great expectancy and dreams of an impeccable life for his citizens.

Orion fully believed in what he was saying, in his decision, and Ava wanted nothing more than to reciprocate his enthusiasm. If it were *any* other woman from the middle classes, Ava would rally behind her without hesitation, so she could understand the potential Orion saw in this decision.

But it was upon *her* head they wanted to place the crown. Her life— everything she knew, everything she was—was going to be stripped from her, and in that she could not find happiness. She could not find the strength to support the king's dreams when her own were at stake.

"I appreciate your vote of confidence, King Orion, but I can't accept. I'm sorry. There are thousands of women out there who want this *so* much. Give it to one of them. They would make excellent queens, I'm sure of it. But I am not the right person for this."

Before the last word passed Ava's lips, Bernadette put her face close enough to Ava's that she could count the queen's lashes. Their shadow cast angry veins down her cheeks. This close, she looked a little ill; the corners of her eyes had a slight droop and the undertone of her skin was grey, not unlike the stone from which her statue was built.

Bernadette lowered her voice to a near whisper. As she gripped the top of Ava's arm, her nails bit into the flesh the sleeveless dress left exposed. Ava had to grind her teeth to keep from flinching, but she refused to let the pain register. When people talked about the queen they spoke of her beauty, of her sereneness and quiet nature. They said nothing of her cruelty or how her silence was really just icy judgment. *Perhaps because no one knows of those things.* Maybe they never got close enough to see the flickering of hate that flashed in her eyes like lightning or to feel the shiver run down their spine as her threat-tainted lips brushed their earlobes.

But Ava was getting a first-hand experience, and if she *had* ever wanted to be queen, all desire would have ceased the moment Bernadette took hold of her.

For as much as she wanted to like the king, she already hated the queen.

"You would be stupid to refuse this," Bernadette said, the words simple but laced with frightening malice. She held her attention for a few tense seconds and then kissed Ava's cheek before pulling away. Her face was once again calm, her smile sweet but tight. Her voice was back to normal when she spoke loud enough for the other two to hear.

"There is no reason that you won't make a fine queen, Avaleigh. This is a rare and special gift you are being offered. Do not let uncertainty in yourself make you question your king's decision. It was not made lightly, I assure you." She ran her hand down the area her fingers had just been, as if she could smooth away the dull thrumming her grip had left, then she turned to her husband. "An excellent choice, my king. Her fierce fire will benefit Havaan in ways not yet seen. Sebastian, as well as the citizens of our country, will love her."

"I've no doubt you will reign over your people will an honest heart," King Orion added, patting her shoulder. "I am sorry our son is not here to celebrate with us, but you two shall meet in seven nights at the Welcome Dinner. Now, before we get you home so you can share the news with your family, I must ask you one thing." He took her hands gently in his, the fists she was making enveloped by his massive paws.

The touch was gentle, almost tender, and she could understand why people liked him. He seemed sweet, too nice for someone like Bernadette. Ava wondered if even *he* was privy to his wife's true nature, or if she had him just as fooled as the rest of Havaan. It made Ava's stomach churn knowing she had been lied to, manipulated into believing the queen was a woman of great and wonderful things. These were the footsteps so many young women had been hoping to follow.

Shoes Ava was being forced to wear.

More than anything, she wanted to kick them off—preferably at the queen—and run as far from High House as she could. She knew, though, in the deepest part of her heart that none of that was possible.

Ava could only hope Sebastian took after his father more than his mother. A nice husband she could tolerate. One with Bernadette's temperament would be a different story.

The king's words brought her back to the moment. "Avaleigh Toliver, do you accept this honor being given to you? Do you agree to marry our eldest son and take up the throne by year end?" She blanched. So soon...*too soon*. "To stand proudly by his side as our future queen?"

She wanted to say, "As if I have a choice," but instead settled on a dry, emotionless "Sure."

Suddenly, everything around her was closing in, as if her words had sealed her inside a crypt far too small. Her dress, which had always felt safe, like a second skin, was now a boa snaking up her body, squeezing and compressing her bones. The walls were rolling toward her, boxing her in to a life she had never desired. She took deep breaths and tried to swallow the stale air of the room. She just hoped she could keep the nausea away, at least until she could get outside.

Thankfully, no one seemed to notice the panic because the king exclaimed, "Such wonderful news!" as he wrapped Ava up in his tree-branch arms. Part of her wanted to burrow into his trunk-like body and stay there forever. Safe. Hidden. Protected. But too soon were his arms gone and quickly replaced by the willowy ones of the queen.

Bracing herself for another onslaught of harsh words, Ava was taken aback when the queen kissed both of her cheeks this time and said, "I look forward to knowing you better."

"And I you," Ava lied, her response automatic. She would say whatever she needed if it meant she could escape this damn room, with its curtains blocking out the better options for queen—women who had dreamed of this moment for years, who would willingly lay their heads upon the guillotine for a chance to wear the crown. Women who had practiced writing their names with *Queen of Havaan* tacked on the end.

Women like Delilah.

Ava cringed inwardly at the mere thought of having to break the news to her best friend. It would, without a doubt, go over equally as well as the king's declaration had. Worse even, if that were at all possible…

"We shall announce you to all of Havaan one week from tonight at the Welcome Dinner. Share this great opportunity with those closest to you." With a subtle tip of his head, the king acknowledged the guard for only the second time that night. "Nixon will ensure you get home safely."

"It's okay," Ava started. Her voice, her mere existence, sounded far away. She struggled to speak. She was tired; physically and mentally drained. "I have a ride home."

"Nonsense. Nixon will take you."

Shrugging, she laughed once without mirth. "Sure. Whatever."

Having said all that needed to be said, the king and queen took their seats once again. Nixon was by her side in four long strides and leading her back toward the door through which they'd come.

"Thank them," he mumbled from the side of his mouth.

Ava looked up at him with heavy eyes. "What?"

He gave her a look and motioned behind them with a jerk of his head.

She stopped and faced the king and queen. "Thank you," she said with as much strength as she could gather. Then she turned back to the door and hurried ahead of her escort. She let him steer her down the staircase and through a hallway to the right of it, away from the veranda doors and the unsuspecting party guests. More than once, her body swayed into him, the reality of the coming days settling on her shoulders. After the third or fourth time, he stopped trying to prop her up and instead gave her his strength. He maneuvered her away from her impending future, making little protest when he had to practically carry her out. She should have been running, but she could barely stand. It was as though she were walking under water, the currents continuously pushing against her.

They approached another door, concealed by the darkness, and when Nixon pushed it open they were greeted by the chill of fresh air. Ava, grateful to feel its embrace, drank it in. She filled her lungs until they felt cleansed. Only then did she let the gathering tears flow freely. Nixon waited against the house, veiled by the shadows, while she had her silent cry.

"Can you please take me home?" Her voice came out barely above a whisper. It was all she had left. Thankfully Nixon heard her and approached with caution.

Once he was by her side, he held something out to her. She glanced down at it then up at him. "Why do I need this?" she asked, reaching for the matte black helmet.

"I don't think the king would be very happy if something happened to you." He took her elbow, the contact sending a slight zing through her blood, and coaxed her over to a two-wheeled vehicle. It was sleek, all black and chrome, with two seats and a neon green zigzagging pattern along the side. She had never seen something so dangerously gorgeous before. Most people in Havaan who owned vehicles had simple cars. Airplanes no longer existed, since traveling between the regions was simpler. Most transportation was provided by the two trains that made the voyage across Havaan daily. One went east to west while the other went north and south. Each region had a handful of docking stations, making travel easily accessible for all.

Ava had been on the train twice: once with Zarah and once when she and Delilah had, without permission, traveled to Ramenell to visit

D's cousin. They were sent back home the very next morning and grounded from one another for a week.

Cordellia owned a car—a gift from her parents before their passing—and though she knew how, Ava never drove. She never ventured beyond Typhony, so her legs and her bicycle sufficed. She had never ridden a motorized bike though, and expressed her concern as she mounted the seat behind Nixon.

"Just hold on and lean with the bike," he instructed as she wrapped her arms around him loosely. He took her wrists and pulled her arms tighter, securing her against him. His touch lingered a fraction longer than necessary, but not long enough. His fingertips grazed the tops of her hands before he reached for the handles. Clearing his throat he asked, "Where to?"

"Holland Avenue, Number Six."

With a nod of his head, the visor of his helmet fell into place.

With a flick of his wrist, the engine roared to life.

The machine vibrated between her thighs and shook her from the inside out. If the night had not panned out the way it had, she would've enjoyed this moment a bit more; her arms encircling the insanely attractive guard, with his eyes of burnished gold and hair of inked secrets. She would delight in feeling his strong back tucked against her front and the way the wind carried to her his clean scent of cool mint. It should have awoken her spirit and delighted her senses, but all she felt was fatigue.

After a while, the gentle bends of the road and the low hum of the engine as it took her further and further away from High House lulled her closer and closer to sleep until she was lying, not *against* Nixon's back, but on her own, floating lazily down a river. Schools of minnows kissed her calves. In that moment, everything was perfect; life was right again and she was still just Ava Toliver, daughter of a jewelry maker, and nothing more.

But dreams, like the first taste of love or the innocence of childhood, never last as long as they should. Before she knew it, the rumble of the bike was replaced by Nixon's deep voice calling her back to the shore.

She sat up and looked around as he dismounted. Her neighborhood was silent, the lights in almost all the houses switched off for the evening. Even her own home was dark aside from the porch light her mother always kept on. Ava had never found such peace in it as she did this very moment.

The sky was a solid sheet of navy, with tiny pinpricks of scattered light. She felt as though she hadn't slept for days. Her blood had become cement in her veins and her usual grace gone as she slinked, rather than climbed, off Nixon's bike. He was by her side in seconds, his arms at the ready in case she collapsed under the burden of her future. She moved slowly toward the front door, literally dragging her feet, each step more difficult than the one before. As she placed her hand on the knob, the metal chilled from the early spring temperature, she spoke over her shoulder.

"Thank you for the ride," she said, offering him a small smile. "The king and queen will be glad to know you got their investment home safely."

"Get some sleep, Ms. Toliver. Tomorrow will hopefully be better for you."

"Call me Ava, please."

Nixon nodded once then climbed back onto his bike. Before she could turn the handle fully, his voice cut through the night like a heated knife through melting butter. He spoke lowly and she shouldn't have been able to hear him, yet somehow did as if he were standing right behind her. Part of her wished he was, so she could fall into his firm chest and sleep the rest of this horrible night away in his warmth and earthiness.

"I am sorry tonight went the way it did for you. But if it's any consolation, I think the king made the right choice. I will gladly follow you anywhere."

She closed her eyes as his words wrapped themselves around her heart and a fresh batch of tears tickled her lashes. People who didn't know her had such faith in her ability to rule. She was filled with pre-guilt at the disappointment they would inevitably experience, especially when they realized how wrong a choice she would be.

The roar of his bike sounded as she flicked her tears away before turning toward him fully. She felt compelled to not only see him once more, but to respond. What she would say though, she hadn't a clue. But, it was too late. He was already retreating the way they had come.

Ava watched until he and his bike meshed flawlessly with the night sky and the darkness of the unlit road. As soon as he was out of sight, the exhaustion hit hard. Her eyes were heavy, as if tiny weights hung from her lids. She forced herself into the house, its silence saddening and almost as dense as her heart. The basement was dark and still; the living room empty of all life, filled only by the steady ticking of the clock.

She dragged herself step…by…step…by……step…up the stairs.

Leaning against the wall for balance, her shoulder bumped the family photos, skewing them on their nails. She went straight for her mother's bedroom door.

It was slightly ajar and Cordellia's deep breathing called her forth like a beacon, promising safety and comfort. Familiarity. It was a reminder of all the things she needed at that very moment and of all the things that were to be ripped away from her in seven short days.

Lumbering into the bedroom, she was met by the scent of her mother's lotions. She crawled into the large bed and curled up on the side that was always empty. The moment her body hit the feather-filled mattress, her eyes closed and she was pulled immediately under, greeted by a welcomed nothingness.

"Are you okay?" a voice sounded. It hooked her feet and dragged her back to the surface. It was a nauseating emergence, like spinning around too fast and then suddenly stopping.

"No," she answered. How many times had she said that word tonight?

"Do you want to talk about it?" Cordellia asked as she combed her fingers through her daughter's twisted hair.

"Tomorrow," Ava replied, her tongue heavy in her mouth. "I'm just...I'm tired."

"Tomorrow, then."

Ava nodded and pulled into herself more, as if she could become so small no one could take her away. "I love you," she muttered, the words barely making it past her lips.

It had been a long time since Cordellia had held Ava, and even longer since Ava had wanted her to do so, but when her arms came around Ava and her callused hands gripped her daughter's firmly, her only child sank into the embrace. "*Mikor orada es tidak svar , enged dashuri fi itu clave,*" Cordellia whispered.

The words had always brought Ava comfort, though she hadn't a clue what they meant. She had asked her mother once while Cordellia was pleating Ava's thick hair. Back then, Cordellia's good days had trumped the bad.

"I don't know," Cordellia had admitted. "It was something your father used to say."

"And you just assumed it was a good thing? What if he was telling you that you have the breath of an onion farm?"

Cordellia had laughed, the sound low, coming from a peaceful crevice in her soul. "*Do* I have the breath of an onion farm?"

"No," Ava replied, grinning, "but how do you know they're meaningful? That they're something worth repeating?"

When her response didn't come immediately, Ava looked back at her mother. Cordellia had gotten a far-off, almost dreamy look in her eyes. "I asked him once what they meant," she finally said. Her fingers continued their deft braiding. "He told me that the words held great power and because of such, there was no way to adequately define them. The translation would get lost. But the *way* he said them, Ava, the authority of his voice when they passed his lips, there was no way to doubt they were significant. Important.

"After a while, they became our thing. When I love you didn't suffice, when the intensity of our feelings for one another became too much, *mikor orada es tidak svar, enged dashuri fi itu clave* became our way of saying more."

Ava cleared her throat before speaking. "I can't believe you never questioned him more about it," she said. She didn't want her mother to see how hurt Ava was that she would never hear her father speak them.

Would never get to witness the power behind his voice when they tumbled from his mouth.

"I am not like you," Cordellia had said affectionately. She'd tugged on the two braids and tilted Ava's head back. "I don't demand answers for everything." She had paused long enough to kiss Ava's forehead. "Sometimes I am okay with letting things be."

Though Ava had long ago stopped wondering about the saying's origin, after all these years, she was still that girl. Still the one who wanted answers for things: like how it was so easy for her mother to vanish inside herself. And why, after it had mattered all her life, the social divide held no weight when she needed it to the most.

The familiar mantra barely registered as Ava gave in to the enervation. In her dreams, she jumped headfirst into the smooth, blue ocean below her, and once she broke the surface, swam lower and lower until there was nothing but quiet and peace and blackness.

Which is where she stayed until dawn.

V.

Cordellia shook her daughter by the shoulder gently. "Ava, darling," she coaxed. "Honey, you have to get up. It's almost noon."

Turning into the pillow more, Ava grumbled but refused to rouse. Cordellia combed her fingers through her daughter's soft curls and hummed quietly until two blue eyes—slightly bloodshot and red-rimmed—looked up.

"I'm awake," Ava said, her voice as dry as sandpaper.

There were countless questions running through her mind, but instead of voicing them, Cordellia set the steaming cup of raspberry and lemon tea on the side table then kissed her forehead. "Drink up and shower. Then meet me downstairs for lunch. I'll make your favorite."

Ava nodded but said nothing more as Cordellia stood from the bed and left the room. At the doorway, she turned and looked over her shoulder at her beautiful daughter, her heart full of motherly concern.

Ava only slept in *this* late when she was ill. Her skin hadn't felt warm under her lips, though. Perhaps she'd drunk too much wine or nibbled too many sweets. Maybe she'd met someone last night, only to have her heart broken at midnight. There were endless possibilities, but they all led back to one thing: something was wrong. Ava was so strong—sometimes *too* strong for her own good—and Cordellia had sensed her daughter's weakening resolve like a crumbling wall.

Even as a child Ava had rarely cried. It had happened only three times in Cordellia's presence: when Zarah had passed away, at Ava's first taste of true heartbreak, and when Delilah moved from Meridian to Typhony. Though she hadn't heard any indication of tears last night, the evidence was obvious. Ava's normally vibrant eyes were inflamed and puffy. Her cheeks were lined with black rivers. The end of her nose was red.

Call it a mother's instinct, or her own mastered dance with demons, but something had happened last night; something which had put her daughter in a state of despondency.

Something that had—for now, at least—cleared away the cobwebs in Cordellia's mind.

She had always idolized Ava's resilience and self-awareness, especially during the times—of which there had been many—when Cordellia needed to draw from it just to get through the day.

Things had not been easy for them since the beginning.

Cordellia had been born when magic still flourished in all the best ways. People were happy and always found reasons to celebrate. From country-wide dances during the first rainfall to meditative afternoons greeting spring blooms. It was at one of these celebrations, the welcoming of the summer months, where she had met Dante. He was charming and handsome, with eyes so intense they cut through the smoke of the bonfire and homed in on her like she was the only girl in the world. He complimented her flower crown, compared her hair to the glow of the embers, and then asked her to dance. He spun her around the flames until her heart and her skin heated; whether from the blaze or his touch, she would never know.

That was all it took—one night under the incoming summer sky and she was his.

And he, hers.

If any two people had been made for each other, Cordellia and Dante were the epitome of such design.

When the war began, their life shifted. Dante, like most men in Havaan, played his part—a part he refused to discuss. It kept him away for days, sometimes a full week, and during the nights when Cordellia was forced to sleep alone, the grey returned.

That's what she called it—the darkness living inside of her.

It had been there ever since she was a child.

For as long as she could remember, Cordellia sometimes saw people in color. Happiness was yellow; sadness was collisions of red and orange. When she looked in the mirror, more often than not, she was buttery and soft.

But there were also times when she was grey. It was a hazy layer that rippled around her like a drizzle. Her parents had always considered her reserved, quiet. They never questioned when she'd spend two or three days holed up in her bedroom or ask about the greyish tear-tracks staining her cheeks.

It was one reason why Cordellia had been hesitant about having children. She was scared she would pass it on; that as she was giving life, she would also be burdening them with this lingering shadow. But those doubts, that fear, had burned away in the blazing bonfire the night she met Dante. He erased her gray, pushed it away with his calm ocean blue. Whenever the grey threatened to make an appearance, Dante filled the space with the promise of a new and better tomorrow.

When Ava was born, she arrived in a swirl of peaceful teal and lemony serenity. She pulsed with the vibrant life of lilac. She hummed with the gentleness of green. The red of life flowed through her like a current. In Ava there was not a pinprick of grey. She had inherited all the good of her father and none of the bad from her mother.

Dante's death had come so unexpectedly they'd had no time to prepare for the onslaught of darkness that would come to mourn with them. Ava was only eight months old when Dante died, and even though Cordellia loved her, she was a reminder of what had been lost.

They had gotten through their life together because of Ava's colors. It was the purple, the mint green, the chartreuse, that Cordellia had selfishly drawn from, all in an effort to try and keep the grey at bay as best as possible.

Ava had always been the light to Cordellia's dark.

But that morning, the grey had settled on Ava like a layer of ash and stifled the bright with which she so often beamed. If her strained voice and red-rimmed eyes had not been an indication something was wrong, then her wavering hue would have been.

Cordellia was not often attuned to the world, but she was always aware of Ava's colors.

To know her only child was suffering made Cordellia uneasy. It was enough to force her out of bed for something more than work. It gave her the will—the desire—to be a mother. She so rarely got the opportunity to be such because Ava rarely needed her to be.

I hope it is something I can fix. She flipped the grilled cheese sandwiches. *I owe her that much.*

As she was ladling warm chicken soup with veggies—soup Ava had made and frozen for days like this—into bowls, Ava stepped into the kitchen. Her wet hair was gathered atop her head and dark circles surrounded her eyes. She smiled weakly and slid into a chair. She watched her mother flutter around, filling glasses with iced water before setting two of her favorite comfort foods in front of her. Yet the succulence of the hearty soup and the oozing of melted cheese did nothing to chase away her hebetude. Her stomach churned at the idea of putting anything into it.

The lulling of her mother's voice that morning had almost convinced her the last twelve hours had been a dream. Waking in Cordellia's bed with the silk of the blue dress wrapped around her legs assured her that it had not.

Her sleep had been restless, punctuated with scenes from the gala. It was during the times when Nixon's face appeared that she was able to get a solid bout of sleep. But those times were quickly shattered by a continuous looping of the king's words and the penetrating glare of the queen.

She had been conscious when the sunlight filtered through the curtains pulled across the window. It was then, once the night was officially over, when she fell into a deep sleep void of High House or crowns or a forced future.

Now that she was awake, she was living a nightmare.

All the reminders of the night before eddied like a mist in her memories.

She swirled her spoon around the bowl, the metal scraping the sides in a melodic, hypnotizing tune. She pushed the diced chicken, chunks of veggies, and spirals of noodles to one side of the bowl then the other, watching the broth flood away. That was what she was soon to become: separated from her home, her life—her mother...

Glancing up at the thought, she caught Cordellia staring at her, her eyebrows pulled together with concern. She hadn't touched much of her food either, Ava noted.

"Growing up," Ava started, forcing the words past the tightness of her vocal chords, "I would watch you fall apart and I didn't get it. I didn't understand how you could be so sad that not getting out of bed seemed a reasonable thing to do." She sniffled and ran her fingers under her eyes, wiping away gathering tears. "But it makes sense now. I'm getting my own dose of it." A forced smile was all she could give before her eyes were encased with fresh tears.

Cordellia was by her side in seconds. She gathered her daughter in her arms and held her while she cried. Ava had tried to keep it together, but the dam broke and all her emotions came pouring out. Deep sobs quaked her body. She clung to her mother as if the fear and desperation inside of her had grown arms. She released muffled screams into her shirt and wept until every part of her ached.

"Tell me what happened," her mother pleaded as she took her child's face in her hands. "Were you hurt? Did someone..." She made herself say the words. "Were you taken advantage of?"

Ava snorted and took a shaky breath. "Not in the way you're thinking."

She pulled away from Cordellia's touch and took a long drink of water as her mom moved to the seat next to her. The two women looked at one another for a solid minute as Ava tossed the words around on her tongue, tried to manipulate them into something tangible, something less sour. It was as if her body was rejecting the word-vomit. Her mouth opened then closed immediately whenever she tried to speak. It would be the first time she would say them aloud, and once they were expelled there was no taking them back.

It would be real.

Her future would come to be.

"Avaleigh, just spit it out," Cordellia said, gripping her hand tightly. All of the questions, the concern she felt, had pushed her patience to the brink. "Tell me so I can fix it."

"You can't fix this, Mother. Unless you have some magical ability to change the king's mind."

"Change his mind about what…?"

With a final breath, Ava replied, "About me being queen."

She watched as her mother's face twisted with the full range of emotions. First confusion, her head tilted slightly, her lowered eyebrows casting shadows over her eyes. Then, understanding, those same brows wrinkling. Her hands, calloused and nicked from shaping metal and setting stones, covered her gaped mouth.

"Oh, Ava," she finally whispered. Ava shrugged a shoulder, feigning nonchalance, and slumped back against her chair. Her confession had left a bitter taste in her mouth, one she couldn't get rid of, even with water and lukewarm soup. "But you're not even from an upper class."

"Yeah, apparently that's not a real rule," Ava responded sarcastically.

"I'm…I'm sorry, honey. How…how do you feel?"

Ava glowered at the absurdity of her question. *It should be pretty obvious how I feel.* "How do you *think* I feel? Disappointed. Upset. Angry. Hateful. Annoyed. Shocked. Appalled. Take your pick." She pushed her chair back angrily and stood. The front legs lifted from the ground before rocking back. "This whole thing is so fucking stupid!" she shouted as she stomped through the house toward the back door.

"Avaleigh Toliver, stop." Ava barely heard her mother's words as she stepped into their yard. She had invested hundreds, if not thousands, of hours here while growing up. She had taken her first barefooted steps through the grass. When she'd gotten her first boyfriend, they'd painted their names in a heart on one of the fence posts; it was later covered with a flower mural when they broke up. Tents had been erected in the summers for backyard campouts with Delilah and snowmen built in the same spot during blustery winters. The tire-swing that had been suspended from the thickest branch of the oak tree was still there. Even though the ropes were slightly frayed and a bit uneven, the black wheel spun lazily in the spring breeze of the morning.

How long had it been since she'd spent time out here for longer than it took to rake fallen leaves or mow the lawn in the nicer months? *Where has all the time gone?* she asked herself as she let the warm rays kiss her skin and the soft wind wrap around her like a comforting hug. In this moment, she could forget everything that was happening and pretend she was little again. She waited with childish anticipation for her mother to come up behind her and sweep her into her arms, spin her around and around until they fell to the ground laughing.

Cordellia *did* fill the space at her back, but instead of wrapping her in her arms, she circled Ava's wrist with her fingers and squeezed, a small gesture that said *I'm here, but you have to let me be.*

Right now, even that was more difficult than rationalizing what had happened last night.

Ava's throat constricted as a new wave of emotions threatened to take over. She pushed them down though, refusing to let the king have any more of her tears. She turned to her mother and shrugged again, shaking her head at the same time. She didn't have any words, but she also had too many.

Not knowing where to start, but knowing she needed to, she began at the gates. She told Cordellia about the dancing and losing herself in the excitement of the night. She spoke about the air of celebration and how she got swept up in it; raved about the piles of delicious treats and cakes and how her entire goal was to eat them all. She talked about Nixon—not about his beauty or the effect he had on her—but about him leading her through the crowd and to the king.

"I tried to tell him no," Ava said, exasperated. "That I was the wrong choice, the *worst* choice, but he wouldn't listen. He just went on and on about how great of a decision I am." She paused and growled her frustration through clenched teeth.

"The king is very insistent," Cordellia said, almost to herself.

"I hate him. I hate all of them."

"You don't know them, Ava…"

"Know them? I don't need to *know* them. They're robbing me of my entire life. They're taking me away from *you.*" She emphasized the last word, angry that her mother hadn't made the realization before. "They're forcing me into something I have no desire to do. I don't even have a choice in the matter. I can hate them all I want and don't you dare try and tell me otherwise. Whose side are you even on?"

"I'm on your side, always. But Ava—"

"But *what?*" she snapped, venom dripping from her words. She had a feeling she knew what her mother was going to say, and she began bracing herself for the words. *Don't say it* she mentally begged her. *Do not let me down again. Not right now.* She had only two people in her life who mattered beyond words and measure, and one of them was sure to hate her by day's end.

If her mother abandoned her too…

"This doesn't have to be the horrible thing you're making it out to be. Ava—" Cordellia took a step forward and reached for her hands.

Ava recoiled as if physically repelled by the words coming out of her mother. "You just said there isn't anything you can do about it. If you leave Brene he'll find you. If you hole up at home, he'll send someone for you. One way or another, it's going to happen. But there are positives that can come from this. You can get out of Meridian and have—"

"I don't want to leave Meridian. *You* want me to leave Meridian."

Ava pushed by her mother and went back inside. Cordellia followed her up the stairs.

"It's my job to want better things for you." Cordellia was at her heels. Her voice was clear, rational. It was a voice Ava hadn't heard in what felt like years. For some reason, that fueled her choler like gasoline to a flame. "You can't fault me for that," Cordellia continued. "Sometimes, my love, life makes our choices for us and we have to face them, we have to deal with them head on." Cordellia chased Ava down the hall, past photos of their life together: Ava's birth, her first "big girl" bicycle, the start of her schooling all the way to graduation. The years had blurred together, images rolled into each other until each day and every event became one solid picture.

There had been good days—sometimes it was hard to recall them, but they did exist. But there had always been something missing, something keeping Cordellia's smiles from fully meeting her eyes.

When Ava reached her bedroom door, she turned on her heels and glared at her mother. "Like you did when Dante died?" she challenged.

Cordellia stopped short, the harsh words yet another barrier keeping her and her child separated. It was a name that had done the exact thing for the past nineteen years. When she didn't reply, Ava laughed once, humorlessly, and then slammed her bedroom door. Silence pressed on both sides of it, pulsating and thrumming as Ava hastily dressed in a pair of tight running pants and an old t-shirt. She laced her shoes angrily, tugging on the strings harder than necessary. As she sat on the floor, stretching her tense muscles, her mother's resigned voice filtered into her room.

"I didn't handle your father's death the way I should have, I know that. But Ava, you're better than me. You always have been." A deep sigh. "I know that none of this is the life you wanted, but if you don't deal with what's in front of you, you will be just like me. And I know you don't want that, probably more than *I* don't want it for you. Probably more than you don't want to be queen."

She couldn't hear Cordellia retreat from her door but there was a physical shift when she left. With her elbows pressed into the floor between widely spread legs, Ava inhaled the words along with warm air. Her feelings toward the way her mother had dealt with Dante's passing had always been unspoken. Though Ava had never been in love—she'd thought she was at one point—she couldn't imagine disappearing from the world for days, sometimes even weeks.

Let alone abandoning your only child...

Cordellia had never quite gotten the hang of what it meant to be a mother. She'd tried, but there was always some level of it she couldn't reach.

What she'd said was true. Ava *didn't* have any other options besides conceding to the king's wishes, and even though she'd toyed with the idea of fleeing Meridian, leaving Brene just like Delilah had planned, that's all it had been. She just didn't want to *hear* it. She wanted Cordellia to be as upset as she was, but that was the part of mothering she'd always lacked: the ability to know what Ava needed and when she needed it. Ava didn't want a better life or more from it, she just wanted…well, that didn't matter much now.

She padded back down the stairs and headed for the front door, walking by her mother without a glance, even when she asked, "Where are you going?"

"To tell Delilah the great news," she answered acrimoniously, her reply swollen with lingering resentment. "She's going to hate me by the time I'm finished, but at least someone will agree that the king has made a horrible choice."

Giving Cordellia zero time to reply, she took off toward Typhony at a measured jog.

Normally she would walk or ride her bike the four miles to D's house—or occasionally drive when the colder months forced her to do so—but today required more. She needed to clear her head, and the rhythm of her feet hitting the pavement would do that.

The swish of her feet leaving the ground interspersed with the quiet thump of them returning to the earth lulled her thoughts until there was nothing of the Queen's Gala's or her ill fate.

Most days she would take the bridge that connected Meridian to Typhony, but today she veered away from it and followed the road as it snaked along the River Caine, a path of water that ran from the west coast to the east coast of Havaan. Ava wasn't entirely sure what part it played in the division of social classes in the other regions, but in Brene it was the only physical thing separating the two. It was a one-and-a-half-mile wide stretch of roiling water sandwiched between banks of soft black sand.

Twenty-five years ago, the battle between the magicians and King Orion's army took place at the river's edge. Eight hundred miles of dirt that had once been ivory and pure was soaked by magic and blood. Seared into each grain was a reminder of the war, of a rebellion coaxed forth by greed and mystical elements too great for anyone to possess. Some doubted the validity of the story, but much of Havaan's overall history was comprised of stories passed from mouth to mouth until the final version was simply accepted.

Acceptance was a part of Havaanian life.

It was easier for the people to take things at face value than to ask questions.

Maybe they just didn't want to be let down by the lack of answers they would receive.

But questions fueled Ava daily.

She wasn't content with things being the way they were just because that's how they were. Perhaps that's why the premise behind the Queen's Gala had never made sense to her. The royal family based their entire legacy and rule in Havaan on a beauty contest, choosing a future queen on nothing more than cheekbones and body shape. There was no substance expected, just a willingness to accept the choice without challenge. Well, if the king thought she was going to bury her head in the sand and give up her freedom readily, he had another thing coming. She would fight until there was nothing left in her; and if they had to drag her kicking and screaming down the aisle, then so be it.

Her mother was right about one thing.

She would face them all head on until one of them surrendered.

And it sure as hell wasn't going to be her.

At some point in her mental pep-talk she'd circled back to the bridge and this time she crossed it, her steps echoing against the wooden planks. The rushing of the river below mimicked the shallowness of her breathing. The sun beat on her and sweat trickled down her face, salty rivulets on her lips. The fabric of her already fitted shirt clung to her as perspiration dripped down her back. The baby hairs around her forehead stuck to her skin while the humidity in the spring air made her curls an unruly mass at the base of her neck. The thick ponytail bounced against her spine with each step. Her lungs begged her to stop, to breathe deeply, but she pushed herself the one and a half miles until her feet hit pavement again.

Welcoming her into Typhony was her favorite deli.

Though a resident of Meridian, Mr. Fillion had opened his place of business at the edge of Typhony. It was a welcome pit-stop to travelers looking for on-the-spot sandwiches, fresh veggies, a small assortment of groceries, or his famous, homemade fruit-infused water. Which is what Ava snagged from the cooler.

Instead of heading straight to Delilah's—intentionally putting off the inevitable for a bit longer—she hoisted herself onto a low wall, the stones within the cement faded and cracking lightly. She positioned herself so she was facing High House. It loomed over them, a speck in the far distance, but a constant presence.

In less than a week it would be her home, with its columns of finely detailed etchings and courtyard large enough to fit roughly twelve of her current home. She would be sleeping in a bed that didn't conform to her body and sharing meals with complete strangers. Thinking about relocating no longer filled her with a sense of dread; she was too numb for that at this point. It just made her sad.

When she tired of looking at the house, she hopped down and walked leisurely through the streets toward her destination. Typhonies ignored her, as they so often did, oblivious to the fact that they were brushing shoulders with and breathing the same air as the future Queen of Havaan. She spent the journey rehearsing what she would say to Delilah, debating whether to spring it on her or build up to it. She mentally prepared herself for the onslaught of harsh words that might come her way and braced herself for the likely ending of their friendship. She hoped for the best but planned for the worst.

Because what else can I do, Ava thought, when I'm about to tell my very best friend her dreams aren't going to come true...all because of me?

VI.

The thought of knocking on the front door crossed her mind, but Ava decided against taking away the one remaining normalcy in her life. The brass knob turned easily in her hand—no one ever worried about break-ins in Havaan, especially in a place like Typhony—and she pushed her way inside. A wave of sage incense mixed with the astringency of lemon polish greeted her. The Witicker-Finn household was always eerily quiet, as if only ghosts lived there, and today was no different; though it was a bit bewildering. She'd expected screaming and shouting from Delilah's room. The silence made her wonder if anyone was even here. She had no idea if Delilah had made it home safely from the gala. There was no way she was still at High House, but what if—

"I was wondering if you were ever going to show up," Delilah's mother said as she blew into the foyer, clearly exasperated. Ava stopped her ascent up the stairs, one foot on the second step. "She is in a frightful mood. As I'm sure you know, last night did not go as she planned. I tried to tell her, you were there, but she never listens to me. See if you can calm her down, won't you?" Taking Ava's hand in hers, Celeste pressed something into her palm. "Try and get her to take these," she added before fluttering back from where she'd come.

As Ava arrived at the top of the stairs, a small version of Dr. Finn stepped out of a room at the end of the hall. "Hey dude," Ava said, holding her hand out for a high-five as Ashton passed by.

"Hey dudette," he replied, slapping her hand and smiling at her. His two bottom teeth were missing. She knelt to the ground so they were eyelevel and motioned with her head at his sister's door.

"How is she?" Ashton shook his head by way of answer. "That good, huh?" Sighing, Ava stood and tousled his already messy hair, sending him on his way. When she turned back to Delilah's bedroom door, fist ready to knock, she was startled by her best friend's warzone of a face. It was clear she had slept—and sobbed—in her makeup. Rivers of black ran down her pale face, turning her into a human-zebra hybrid. There was a fury in her eyes that Ava had only seen a handful of times, but never directed at her.

Until now.

Just wait.

"Hey…" Ava dragged the word out as she approached the door with measured caution.

"Where the hell were you?" Delilah asked, her voice husky and raw. Ava skirted past her and stepped into the bedroom. Looking around, she whistled at the destruction. Scraps of D's black and gold dress were haphazardly thrown around; only the top half remained whole, though it had taken a few hard hits from the scissors sticking out of it. The carpet had been replaced with sheets of paper—page after page of diary entries—ripped from their binding. Ava didn't need to read them to know what was written in cute, feminine handwriting. Delilah had started journaling the day after the king announced the Queen's Gala, writing every scenario she could think of when it came to Orion presenting her the news of her future queenship.

Never once, Ava guessed, did the scenario at hand make it onto those lines.

"Rough night?" Ava asked casually, trying to speak past the rock that lodged in her throat. She was having a difficult time breathing, as if the state of disarray around her was sitting on her chest—a ball of lost hope, disappointment, and crushed dreams.

"You would have known this if you'd ridden home with me," Delilah responded as she slammed her door. The panes of her window rattled with the force.

Ava turned to her. "About that," she started before she was cut off by D's rant.

"Guess what. I wasn't chosen."

"Yeah, I know. D—"

Delilah raised a curious brow. "You know? How?" She waved the question off with a tick of her wrist. "Celeste must have intercepted you. Did she give you drugs to make me calm down? She's been trying to peddle them on me all morning." Ava opened her hand and revealed the two green capsules sitting in her palm. Delilah smacked them away, sending them flying into opposite corners of her room to be lost amongst her dreams for the crown.

"She doesn't even care that I'm upset, ya know?" Delilah sniffled. "She's just waiting until I'm 'over it' to rub it in my face that she was right all along." She sat on the edge of her bed in a huff and flicked a finger over her cheek, brushing away a new trickle of tears. "*You* were right," Delilah said, looking up at Ava with her sad eyes. "It was just a stupid beauty pageant. I bet the person they picked is some ditzy, dumb blonde from Oxyphyn with big boobs and a box of rocks for brains."

Ava quietly said, "It was me." She hadn't intended for Delilah to hear it, not with her ranting and raving; she'd just wanted to test them out, see if they felt any less horrible than before.

They didn't.

"They won't even tell us who she is until the Welcome Dinner. Probably to keep people from trying to kill her or something. Ugh…" Delilah fell onto her back and pulled a pillow to her chest, hugging it tightly. "I just want to know who they picked so I can better understand why it wasn't me."

"It was me," Ava said a bit louder.

Delilah sprang up, and Ava wondered if she'd heard her that time, but then she lowered her head into the pillow and screamed, the cotton muffling it. "I just don't get it," she said after her short fit. "I wanted this so freaking bad. I just…who is she? What does she have that caught his eye over me?"

"Delilah," Ava said, cutting through her words.

Her best friend looked at her. Glared more like it. "What?" she growled.

"I have something to tell you."

Delilah rolled her eyes. "I'm having an existential crisis right now but you have something to tell me? Please. By all means, Avie. The floor is yours."

For a second, Ava considered keeping the news to herself and letting Delilah find out on the night of the dinner, but even when D was at her cruelest, Ava refused to sink that low. If she was going to hurt her, she wanted to do so when she had a chance to at least explain herself. To possibly smooth over the pain just a little.

"It was me," she said for a third time, ensuring her voice was loud enough.

Clearly exasperated that the spotlight had shifted, Delilah sighed. "*What* was you?"

Ava licked her dry lips then swallowed the words. "The king's choice." They came out softer than she would have liked, but she knew they'd been heard by the look on Delilah's face. At first there was confusion, but only for a fleeting moment before anger replaced it.

Anger she had expected, but not the way in which it was delivered.

"What a horrible thing for you to say to me!" Delilah exclaimed as she tossed her pillow at her. "This isn't a joke, Ava. I am genuinely upset and you think it's funny to play some stupid trick on me? How could—are you *crying?*"

Ava covered her eyes with the palms of her hands and pressed against them. She didn't want to cry, let alone in front of Delilah. She was tired of being a weepy mess—it felt so foreign to her. How women did this on a constant basis she would never understand. It hadn't even been 24 hours and she was already over the tears.

Her hands were lowered and replaced by a now concerned face. "You're not kidding, are you?" Delilah whispered as she dropped Ava's hands. Ava shook her head. "But how? Why? You're not—"

"Yeah, I know. Not a real rule."

Delilah lowered to the edge of her bed again, this time as if in slow motion, and looked around the bedroom like she'd never seen it before. Her gaze settled on Ava last. "I don't understand…"

Ava threw her hands up, a silent 'that makes two of us.' "I was just eating cake, and then this guard was there telling me the king wanted to talk to me. When I was told the news, I asked them to reconsider, to pick someone else—*anyone* else—but they refused. I wasn't left with much of a choice but to agree." She squatted next to Delilah and gripped her hands, desperate for her to understand how remorseful she truly was. "I don't want this, D. I'm sorry that—"

"Did you ask him or did you beg?" Delilah questioned, almost robotically. Her face was calm but her gentle brown eyes blazed with something more than anger. Her eyebrows were pulled high, a look that said 'well?'

"Did I ask or beg what?"

"For the king to make a different decision. Did you ask him or did you beg him? Because if you just asked nicely—"

"I pleaded with him, Delilah." Ava stood indignantly and stepped away from her friend, as if she could physically feel the heat of her irascible stare. "How could you think anything else? I did *everything* I could, short of falling down and throwing a tantrum, to get him to change his mind. But he wouldn't budge."

The two women looked at each other, tension building between them like smoke. Delilah's face remained still until she rolled her head into her shoulders, as if working a kink from her neck. She pushed herself off the bed and shuffled through the layer of black chiffon and worded pages. She opened the door to her bedroom then turned to Ava.

"I need you to leave."

"D, please…" Fear bubbled up inside of her. First the king took away her freedom, her family, and now his choice was going to take away her best friend. Though Ava had prepped for this possibility, it was still devastating in its actuality. She could get through whatever Orion and his nefarious wife tossed at her; she could wear the crown and be a queen, but only if Delilah was there beside her.

Sure, Delilah could be selfish and mean, but she was also passionate and steadfast.

She was all the things Ava was not.

When Ava was sixteen, she fell in love with a boy named Connor. They were the center of the other's world for two years, until one day he told her it was over, breaking her heart into a million little pieces. He gave her countless excuses except for the truth: that he had started seeing one of their schoolmates, Juliet Graham. After Ava's three-day mourn over the death of their relationship, she and Delilah headed to the market for a little retail shopping, only to spot Connor and his new lady. Ava, wrought with emotion, had stood in the shadows while Delilah, brave as could be, stomped over to the couple, said a gamut of very harsh and colorful words, then proceeded to dump her blueberry smoothie on the lovebirds.

That was how their friendship had always been. In the moments where Ava wasn't courageous or strong, Delilah was her backbone. When Delilah's emotions got the best of her and her mouth was destined to get them into trouble, Ava calmed her. It had always seemed that they needed one another to survive, and at least for Ava that was true. Now it appeared as though that was going to be forgotten, tossed aside, all because of some stupid ball and some stupid, very wrong decision.

"I'm mad," Delilah said, her voice shaking a little. "But not at you. I need to process what you just told me and I can't do it with you here. I can't work through my thoughts while looking at you, okay?"

Nodding numbly, because she didn't know what else to do, Ava walked to the door and stopped at the threshold. "I'm sorry," she said again, biting her bottom lip to quell her feelings.

"I know," Delilah replied, smiling sadly. Then she closed the door, the faint click of the lock saying more than any words could.

The descent down the stairs seemed to take forever, each step slow and sluggish. The thought of having to make the walk back home was taxing. Now that the hard part was over, all the adrenaline building up to it was gone, left in a puddle on Delilah's floor, seeping into her diary pages and making them soggy.

"How is she?" Dr. Finn asked as Ava neared the front door. She hadn't even seen the three of them standing there, all in a stacked row like a Babushka doll.

She looked to the archway of the dining room and replied, "As well as can be expected." "Did you at least fix her?" Celeste asked.

With an exasperated sigh, Ava replied. "She isn't broken,"

As if Ava hadn't spoken, Celeste's tired voice probed, "Well, do you think it'll take her long to get over this? She really needs to get a move on with her life."

Ava, fueled by every possible emotion a person could experience, spun on her toes and marched over to her. Their faces half a yard apart, she spoke sternly but evenly, her words controlled. "Your daughter's dreams were crushed last night," she started. "Pulverized, even. You of all people should understand how she feels. The gala may have seemed silly to you, but it mattered to her. And you are treating it like it's nothing more than a hangnail. Some burden on *you*. You are her mother." Each word was delivered with measured emphasis. "It is your job to want better for her, but more than that, it is your job to support her dreams, no matter how childish or ludicrous they may seem. You aren't supposed to make her feel like shit, especially as often as you do. You are lucky to have a daughter who aspires to great things the way Delilah does. If you could pull your head out of your own pompous ass longer than to just take a breath, you would realize that."

Celeste's mouth, as well as those of her husband and young child, formed perfect O's. "How *dare* you," she hissed through wine-stained red lips. "Who do you think you are to speak to me that way?"

"Your future queen," Ava replied, her spine straightening instinctively. She took great pride in the startled look that came over Celeste's face. She had never seen the woman so taken aback, so unhinged. Leaving no time for anyone to say anything more, she pivoted away from them and walked back to the door. From the corner of her eye she caught a blur of movement, and when she looked up toward the staircase she saw Delilah sitting at the top, knees pulled to her chest.

Ava's smile was soft, sad. Delilah returned the gesture and mouthed *thank you.*

The realization this might be the last time she saw her best friend hit her hard. What if, in her processing, Delilah made Ava a target for her resentment? What if she decided it would be too hard to remain friends, after all?

With a hundred more 'what if's' playing jump rope with her fears, she stepped out of the suffocating Witicker-Finn compound and was greeted by a high sun, the vast sky of Havaan streaked with clouds as white as snow.

By the time she made it home, the sun was hanging low in a sky the color of a wildflower field. A few glittering stars kept it company.

It was the end of day one post Queen's Gala.

Six more remained.

VII.

For the two days following the big reveal, Ava heard nothing from Delilah. It was the longest they'd gone without speaking and the void was tangible. Ava spent those lonely days sorting through twenty years of memories.

When she'd returned home from crushing Delilah's dreams, there'd been a small red box adorned with a rolled piece of paper waiting on her dresser. Inside the box was an empty key ring with a tag attached. The king's emblem was engraved into the metal, along with her first name. She'd slipped the black ribbon off the note then unrolled it carefully. Written in beautiful, elegant script were words expressing the royal family's great appreciation in her decision to take on the role of queen and how they were looking forward to welcoming her into their fold. There was also a formal invitation to the Welcome Dinner, which would take place on Saturday evening—exactly one week after the Queen's Gala—following her move-in that same day. A caravan would arrive at two that afternoon to escort her and her luggage to High House.

She was being given a total of seven days to decide which items were important enough to make the trek to her new home and which ones were to remain behind, locked in her bedroom like a museum display of her old life. Citizens of Havaan could tour her home while her mother said things like, "This is where Queen Avaleigh slept" and "Oh, this is the closet where the dress she wore to the Queen's Gala hung for so many years." They could *ooh* and *ahh* over a pair of ratty slippers or hair-stuffed brush.

Her mother had been staying out of Ava's way the last couple of days, as well. They had apologized to each other over bowls of ice cream that same night, Ava for her attitude and the harsh words she'd said, and they'd forgiven one another like they always did. But things were still tense. They acted as though the impending days could cease to exist if they pretended that it wasn't going to happen. Ava didn't have the luxury of ignoring it, though, as she sorted through stacks of loose photos, putting them into two piles: ones to take and ones to tuck away in the corner of her dresser, along with the tattered t-shirts and old jeans she figured wouldn't be welcomed in High House.

They hadn't given her a list of things she could and couldn't bring, and it wasn't like she had *that* many possessions to start with, but going through it piece by piece was grueling and never-ending. This was one of the hundreds of moments she'd had in the last couple of days where Delilah's absence was heavily noticed. D would have no qualm telling her to ditch the photo of them dressed as belly dancers when they were thirteen, or encouraging her to keep the one from when Ava had turned a year old and smashed cake on, not only her own face, but that of her mother and Zarah, as well.

As she was re-shuffling through the one-hundred and six photos in the 'take' pile, trying to whittle it down even more, the floor outside her room creaked before the door opened a smidge. Glancing up, she expected to see her mother's face peeking through, but was overcome with a wave of relief when blue eyes met light brown ones.

"Hey," Delilah said, a bit apprehensively. "Can I come in?"

"Of course you can," Ava replied as she hopped up from the bed, moving quickly across her small room. "What a stupid question."

"Yeah, well, I've done a few stupid things lately," Delilah answered as she stepped over the threshold. She took in the bare walls and empty bookshelves before settling on Ava. She sighed and then pursed her lips. "I was an ass the other day. I treated you like shit and you didn't deserve that. I was shocked, as you can imagine. Like, how does the one person who wants to be queen the least end up getting chosen?"

"Your guess is as good as mine," Ava mumbled.

"But what happened wasn't your fault and I can't imagine it's been easy for you."

"It hasn't been," she agreed, shrugging. "But you reacted exactly how I figured you would." Delilah's face contorted as if she was offended, and Ava couldn't help but laugh. "Not like an asshole," she explained when she regained herself. "Just the anger. Honestly, as much as I hate the king's decision, I was more worried about you and how hurt you were going to be. You've wanted this for years…"

Cupping her face, Delilah smiled her radiant grin, and it was in that moment that Ava knew they were fine, that she was forgiven and their friendship would remain as it had always been.

"And that is one of the million reasons why you're going to make such an amazing queen."

Ava smiled—really smiled—for the first time since midway through the gala. "I adore you," she said as she wrapped Delilah in her arms. Despite all that was going on, everything was right in her world for now. And in retrospect, that was all that mattered.

"Do you wanna take a break for a bit?" D asked once Ava let go.

Looking around her room, Ava laughed. "Please."

"Though I'm sure you've already packed it away, the blue dress isn't going to cut it at the Welcome Dinner—"

"So, shopping we shall go?"

Delilah winked and gave her a playful smirk. "You need a garment that is going to wow your citizens. But more importantly, one that will make Sebastian drag his jaw on the ground. We'll find you a piece worthy of the crown. My treat. Consider it my congratulations gift. And a thank you for saying what you did to Celeste."

Ava had completely forgotten about her tiff with D's mother. At the reminder, she cringed while she laced up leather boots. "What a great start to my ruling," she said sarcastically.

Shrugging a shoulder, Delilah twisted a piece of light pink hair around her finger. "It needed to be done."

"Maybe, but not in front of everyone. Including Ashton."

Ava hadn't been outside the last couple of days. She'd watched her curtains dance with the occasional breeze, but she hadn't felt the wind twist in her curls or the sun welcome her like a heated blanket. Stepping into a white-clouded sky to the symphony of twittering birds was like breathing after holding her breath for too long. Most of her neighbors were at work or school, but a young couple sat on the rickety porch swing of the house across from hers, kissing with such zeal Ava wondered if they had enough oxygen between them.

She was seeing her neighborhood with fresh eyes: the cracks in the sidewalks, the chipped paint on houses she'd walked by thousands of times. She had taken it for granted over the years, the simplicity and normalcy of everything. She had complained to her mother on multiple occasions about the early, excited shouts of the neighborhood kids in the summer. She wouldn't have those tiny voices or elaborate sidewalk chalk doodles much longer. She would no longer walk the snow-covered sidewalks with Delilah and comment on the beautiful—but mostly gaudy—winter decorations that adorned houses and yards. *What will the seasons be like at High House?* she wondered.

Did they, too, have weird traditions like using the first big snowfall to build a snowman?

"He did ask what a 'pompous ass' was," Delilah said as they walked leisurely toward the market. The air was already filtered with scents of fried dough and roasted meats, invisible tendrils of mouthwatering temptations beckoning them forth.

"Who?" Ava asked, her brows crinkling.

"Ashton."

Ava felt her cheeks redden with embarrassment as she groaned. "Well, at least your mother has a reason to hate me now. I can just hear Celeste telling all her garden club buddies what a rude, foul-mouthed hoodlum their new queen is." Ava cleared her throat before pitching her voice an octave higher, adding a pretentious accent for dramatic effect. "Can you *believe* what she said to me?" she mocked, fanning herself.

"The audacity of such a lowly person," Delilah chimed in with a Celeste-cadence all her own. She giggled and bumped her shoulder against that of her best friend. "You should definitely talk like that when you're queen."

Ava smirked at her before they settled into a comfortable quiet. She had always found an ease in Delilah's presence, whether they were having a full-force gabfest or doing homework with a bowl of popcorn between them. In high school, a few of the more popular girls had started a rumor about the two of them being lovers. But Ava felt for Delilah didn't bloom from romantic feelings. Rather, it came from the faith Delilah had in her; from the fullness of their friendship, regardless of the quarrels or negative beats. She was one of the only people Ava had ever cared about letting down.

"What are they like?" D asked suddenly, interrupting the steady tap-tap-tap of their shoes down the sidewalk.

Ava kicked a rock with the toe of her boot and asked for the second time, "Who?"

"The royals. The king. Queen. Your future husband." She wiggled her eyebrows at the mention of the prince.

"Well, Sebastian wasn't there—"

"Where was he?"

Ava gave her a look that said *as if I would know*. "I didn't really ask. Much of my vocabulary that night consisted of why me and please no."

"Fair enough. But the other two?"

"King Orion is...*huge*. Delilah, that man is a giant," she exclaimed, lifting her hand above her head as high as her arms would allow. "He seems nice enough though. Sure of himself and his decisions, even if it's the wrong one."

Delilah squeezed her hand gently. "It's not the wrong one," she reassured with more certainty than Ava felt.

Giving her a skeptical look, Ava returned the friendly gesture before saying, "The queen is..." She paused as she racked her brain for the right word to describe Bernadette. Finally she settled on vile. Her mouth agape, Delilah listened with wide eyes as Ava told of her exchange with the queen. She rubbed her arm unintentionally when she described the pinch of her nails as they dug into her skin.

After digesting the information, Delilah cautiously asked, "Do you think it's possible that your opinion of her is tainted by your shock?

Like, you hated what they were telling you, so you just automatically hated *her*?"

"Maybe," Ava agreed, though she didn't think so.

"Then again, you *are* her replacement. Maybe she really does hate you."

"Also a possibility."

"I'll see for myself when I move in. Make sure to watch how she is around you."

Ava looked at her curiously. "What do you mean when you move in?"

"I assumed the queen's assistant lives at High House, as well. Does she not?"

"D, about that," Ava started, her voice hesitant. "I was sure you were going to end our friendship once I told you what happened, so I asked Juliet Graham to be my assistant." Delilah glared at her so intensely her eyes became thin slits. "I can't have the ashes of burned bridges following me around when I'm queen," she added, apologetically. She was doing her best to hoodwink her friend and was proud at how well she was keeping a straight face.

"I would assassinate you," her minx of a friend replied nonchalantly. "You don't get to keep me from High House twice and live to tell about it."

Grinning, Ava wrapped her arms around Delilah's shoulders and squeezed her tightly. "Do you think you'll be able to handle waiting on me day in and day out?"

"As long as there are attractive men around for me to get into trouble with once in a while, I think I'll survive." She smiled sweetly, batting her long lashes at the same time.

There's at least one.

Ava's brain flooded with memories of the handsome guard. Of his golden eyes and the way his touch had lingered on her skin. Suddenly, the intoxicating combination of mint and clean laundry filled her nose, so real it was if he had passed. The whole thing had taken only seconds, but she was so lost in thoughts of Nixon she had to intentionally refocus her attention on Delilah's words to get away from him.

"I never really thought I'd be queen, ya know?" D said as they neared the market. Other citizens flowed around them, heading to the same destination. "Sometimes I could almost convince myself it was a possibility, but that night, seeing all of those other women there hoping for the same thing…" She shook her head as an end to the sentence.

"You had just as much a chance as anyone else."

Delilah ran her hand through a bowl of beads at one of the seller's carts, letting the small red globules slip through her fingers. "It doesn't matter now," she answered, giving Ava a smile that didn't fully light her eyes the way it normally did. She had no doubt that D was still upset about the king's verdict. Ava didn't, and couldn't, hold it against her. Honestly, she was surprised Delilah was keeping it together as well as she was and that they could speak of Ava's future title without either one of them having an emotional breakdown. She still wasn't happy about the way things had progressed, but she *was* happy Delilah would be a part of the insane adventure that was to come.

Just that made the future a little easier to stomach.

They traversed the busier than normal market for most of the day, sampling finger sandwiches and sipping on frozen lemonade. They slipped golden bangles onto their wrists and admired the beautiful artwork in several pop-up carts. Delilah pointed out hundreds of dresses, some exquisite and others downright garish, but deemed none worthy of a queen. They talked and joked, made eyes at good-looking men and swayed out of the path of running children. It felt like any other day—two girlfriends hanging out—even though there was an obvious cloud following them around.

Suddenly Delilah, who had stayed behind to chat with an old classmate while Ava searched for more food—ran up to her, nearly knocking over a display of elaborately frosted cookies. Ava, with a sample piece of cinnamon bread halted on its journey to her lips, looked at her out-of-breath friend with startled concern.

"Avie," Delilah started, hopping from foot to foot, "he's coming!"

Popping the square of bread into her mouth, Ava asked, "Who's coming?" around bites.

"Sebastian. He's heading this way."

A chunk of chewy cinnamon deliciousness lodged itself in her throat as Ava inhaled a surprised breath. She coughed, clearing it before sputtering, "Why?"

"Does it matter?" Delilah replied as she grabbed her hand and pulled her away from the sweets cart.

Why is everyone always doing that? she pondered as they meshed with a small cluster of sixty or so people. The news of the prince's presence was starting to spread and citizens lined the streets to make a clear path, as if there were a parade rolling through and not just the eldest son of the king.

It didn't take long for their whispers to settle as two figures made their way down the now empty street. Even the vendors had quieted, and seemingly the birds in both cages and the sky, as if they too were paying respect. As the duo, still silhouettes from where the friends were standing, made their way past the streams of people, their progress was tracked by the bowing of bodies. Once the prince and his escort passed, the folded citizens straightened, hoping to catch a glance at the man who would soon become their king.

My future husband, Ava thought without any sort of emotion on either end of the spectrum. Delilah, who was standing on her tiptoes, vibrated with the excitement and anticipation Ava couldn't seem to find. What she did feel, as the prince neared them—only three hands worth of people away—was the change in the atmosphere; a building of electricity in the air that made the hairs on her arms stand. She still couldn't see their features clearly—except for the chock of sterling hair on one and the glowing, fiery eyes of the other.

When they were close enough, Ava made brief eye contact with Nixon, long enough for him to nod at her almost unnoticeably, then Delilah tugged on her arm, pulling her down into a jerky bow. The women made furrow-browed faces at one another before Ava watched the feet of the two men pass. Certain the coast was clear, she stood enough that she could see over the person next to her. Nixon leaned into the prince and whispered something to him; and in the second it took her to blink, they both turned toward her.

"Crap," she muttered, bending back down slightly. She hoped the curtain of her hair would hide her face as she looked at her best friend, cringing.

"What?" Delilah asked so only Ava could hear.

Opening her mouth to answer, someone cleared their throat above them. Ava gave Delilah a look that could only be interpreted as *oops*, then took a deep breath and stood, coming face-to-face with none other than the Prince of Havaan.

VIII.

They eyed one another, took in the other's features. She could understand why women—and probably some men—drooled over him. He was gorgeous, with mature definition to his cheeks, jaw, and nose. His looks were beyond those typical for Havaan, exceptionally so that he pushed past handsome and into the territory of beautiful. His dark eyebrows and the silver hair he shared with his mother made him look like some gallant mystical creature.

Sebastian's emerald green eyes, the same as his father, were intense and never ventured past her neck before connecting with Ava's blue ones. As she mimicked him, scanning all the parts of his face, Ava couldn't quite figure out if she liked the way he looked or if she was a bit intimidated by it. But when he smiled—the same boyish grin as King Orion—his features softened and he looked his twenty-one years.

He was the first to speak, his voice calm, deep but not as gravely or cavernous as that of his cohort. "Why do you bow to me?" he asked her.

She shrugged. "Seemed like the thing to do," she replied as she motioned to the people around them. Some were still half bent, while others, like Delilah, rose slowly to take in the scene before them.

"You're my intended, though, are you not?"

"That's what they tell me." She smirked, her lips twisting to the side, and he returned the look. Anyone watching would assume they shared a joke only the two of them knew.

"As such, you should never put yourself below me. We are meant to be equals." He regarded her again, as if waiting for her to argue. Unable to do so, for once in her life, she simply nodded. "I have looked forward to meeting you since I was informed my parents had found a suitable match."

"Well, isn't it lucky you don't have to wait any longer?" She stuck her hand out and after staring at her for a second more, Sebastian gripped it. He wasn't bulky like the king, nor was he svelte like the queen. He was somewhere in between, a happy medium, with the same overly-creamed-coffee skin tone and strong grip as his father.

"Avaleigh Toliver," she introduced.

"Sebastian Calder, first Prince of Havaan."

"That's a fancy title," Ava jested as he dropped her hand.

"Tiresomely fancy, at times," he agreed. His finger traced the curve of his bottom lip as he considered something. "Have dinner with me tonight," he blurted.

From beside Ava came a small squeak. She had almost forgotten her best friend but glanced over with the sound. Delilah was grinning like a fool, her eyes moving between Ava and Sebastian as if she were watching two cheetahs play tennis. Ava wasn't sure if D was more excited about witnessing the first exchange between the future king and queen, or of Sebastian himself.

"We're having dinner together in four days," Ava reminded as she pulled her gaze from her friend.

"You and I and a mass of Havaan are having dinner together in four days. Consider this an apology for my absence the night of the gala. It'll be small, simple. Just the two of us. A chance for me to get to know you, and for you to know myself." He looked at her expectantly, with something more masculine than puppy-eyes but with a similar effect.

"I have a feeling I don't have much of a choice. Seems to happen a lot with you people." She raised a brow at him quickly, challengingly.

"You and I have that in common."

"Do we?" she said, doubt evident.

Sebastian leaned closer to her, as his mother had done, and her spine tightened. *If he tells me I'm stupid…*she thought, pre-anger bubbling inside of her. Instead, his voice was gentle and almost a little sad when he replied, "Just because it's my life doesn't mean I have much control over it."

He pulled back and looked into her eyes through a long piece of hair. Something shifted inside of Ava. She realized, for the first time since everything had happened, that she and Sebastian were, if not in the same boat, at least similar ones. He had been raised knowing a wife would be chosen for him and they would rule Havaan together the same way his parents had. At no point, though, had Ava even considered the possibility that he would have his own qualms about the process; that he, too, would feel shoved into a future that had been decided for him.

It wasn't necessarily acceptance of the king's choice, but she felt a bit of relief knowing she and Sebastian shared at least one thing, and that in him—in that regard, at least—she had an ally.

Because of that, she found herself saying, "Dinner sounds doable."

She was thanked with Sebastian's luminescent grin as he pushed the silver tresses from his forehead. His hair wasn't as long as Nixon's, but it was somewhat shaggy. The sides were buzzed short, but the longer strands brushed the tops of his ears. It was surprisingly unkempt for someone of his title.

"Great," he said. "Tell your guard to have you to High House at…shall we say, 6:30 this evening?"

Both Ava and Delilah cocked their heads curiously at the silver-haired prince, a look of smug confusion on Ava's face. "Yeah, I'll just tell…my guard…"

"I'm missing something here," Sebastian said after a glance between the two women. "Do you not have one?" She gave him a look that said *you got it*. With a sly smile, Sebastian nodded his head once. "I assumed my father had assigned one to you."

"It must have slipped his mind during all the excitement of the night."

Sebastian reached up and slapped Nixon, who hadn't spoken a word this entire time, on the back. "Take Nixon with you, then. He is my most trusted friend and protector."

"No——" Ava said while Delilah happily sighed, "Okay."

Six eyes turned toward the shorter woman, though she was oblivious to it all. Her attention was sliding over Nixon with an intensity Ava reserved for five-layered cakes with thick frosting and sprinkles.

"I don't need an escort. Especially one who's a guard, as well," Ava replied, ignoring her friend once again. She crossed her arms over her chest and planted her feet defiantly. Her face was set, her shoulders squared. She had four days of normalcy left. She wasn't going to have *that* taken away by another royal family member. Even if it was the prince—*especially* if it was the prince. With the other two, she hadn't had much of a chance against their wishes. But Sebastian wasn't in control of Havaan yet, let alone her.

Not that she would ever let him *be* in control of her…

"Avaleigh." He said her name as though the argument was exhausting already. Resting a hand lightly on her forearm, he looked at her seriously. "If you haven't yet noticed, there are a couple hundred eyes on us." He paused long enough for her to look around, and with a heavy heart she realized he was right. They were all standing like mannequins, watching the two with intense curiosity. They were committing every look, smile and touch to memory for future retelling. When she found Sebastian's gaze again, hers had softened marginally.

"Whether they know who you are or have even a slight suspicion, people are going to ask questions now. It will make things a lot easier if you have someone to help deter their attention. I know it's not ideal, but I would hate for something to happen all because I needed to stop and speak with you. I should have waited, and for my impatience I apologize, but the moment I saw you I *couldn't* wait. So please, for me, take this protection."

Ava glanced at the guard, who seemed equally as excited about escorting them around. She had a tickling suspicion they would end up with his company whether she wanted it or not. So instead of arguing, she conceded. "Fine, but under one condition."

Amused, Sebastian mumbled, "My mother did say you were a bit—"

"Difficult?" Ava interrupted, though she was certain the queen had used something much more unpleasant.

He chuckled and confirmed her suspicions when he retorted, "Something along those lines."

"I'm sure she found me incredibly endearing."

"Not quite," he answered honestly, his voice playfully sweet. "But I do." She couldn't help the blush that warmed her cheeks. "What are your terms?" Sebastian asked, clearly pleased with her decision as well as the pink coloring creeping into her face.

"He has to change," she demanded.

"What?" Nixon's deep voice was clipped with a controlled anger. Next to her, Delilah shivered. Ava understood entirely the effect his voice had, especially the first time it was heard. She'd felt the same tremor rack her body and was doing everything in her power to keep it under wraps even now.

Ava held his gaze, as difficult as it was. Looking at Nixon felt like flying; like her feet were hovering off the ground and at any moment the string keeping her tethered to the earth would snap and she would float away.

"I don't want to draw anymore unwanted attention to myself," Ava began, "and having you decked out in the king's emblem will do just that. So, you either change or you don't get to hang out with us." Ava raised a cocky brow at him. She had to steel her face when his eyelids dropped into a look she was sure he meant to be intimidating, but her brain processed as something else.

Something dangerous.

Something tempting.

Regardless of what was going on internally, externally she was a stone.

It was a standoff, one from which she refused to back down. Part of her hoped Nixon wouldn't concede either, giving Sebastian no choice but to take his guard with him and leave the girls to do their shopping alone. But after a minute of silence and staring, Nixon grumbled, "I get to keep my weapons."

Sebastian turned to Ava with a look that said *well?* She shrugged, content that she had held her ground as well and as long as she had. She was starting to realize that control of her life was going to become more and more finite the closer and closer she got to the crown. It was imperative she establish herself now; that she force Sebastian and the rest of the Calder clan to take her seriously as the strong, independent woman she was.

"Fine," she said nonchalantly.

They passed the next couple of minutes making arrangements for the evening and ridding Nixon of all things King Orion. Luckily for everyone—or not so much for Delilah, who was hoping they'd have to strip him fully—the red t-shirt he wore underneath his fitted jacket was plain; as were the black slacks that hid his weapons, whatever they were.

Nixon handed his discarded clothing to Sebastian before the prince addressed Ava once more. "I'll send a car by your place around six this evening to pick you two up. Is that okay?"

Ava nodded once. "Works for me." And then she added, "Will you be okay getting home without your bodyguard?"

She wasn't sure where her concern came from—genuine concern at that—but it granted her another flawless Sebastian smile. She liked the way it crinkled his eyes and softened his face while still retaining his grown-up features.

"I'll be fine, I promise," the prince assured. He took her hand and kissed the top of it. Next to her, she was certain Delilah melted into a sticky, gooey mess of whatever it was that romantic gestures turned people into. And it would be a lie if Ava herself hadn't felt some sort of warmth in the pit of her stomach.

They had migrated to an uncongested area of the market but there were still prying eyes glued in their direction. At that moment, she was very thankful for Sebastian's insistence about adding Nixon to their twosome. Not nearly as thankful as Delilah, however, who was having a hard time keeping her eyes off the soldier. It was slightly amusing, but Ava still felt sorry for him. Delilah was a viper, especially when she set her sights on someone. If she were a betting woman, Ava would have started a pool to see how long Nixon could avoid Delilah's snare.

With a few parting words, the threesome headed towards a small dress shop Delilah had scouted while Sebastian went the other way, continuing his journey back to High House.

"Are you sure he'll be okay?" Ava asked, looking up at Nixon.

"I'm sure," he replied.

"But *how* can you be sure?"

With a sigh Ava was coming to recognize as something a bit less than annoyance, he cocked his head backwards. She turned in the direction Sebastian had gone. No longer alone, he was joined by a much taller, thicker built man—in the same jacket with the same kingly insignia sewn into the back—that Nixon had worn only a handful of minutes ago.

"There's never just one of us around when the royal family is concerned," he explained simply.

Ava didn't find that very comforting, but she was glad Sebastian would have protection as he made his trek home. She wasn't worried about him being attacked violently—no one worried about that in Havaan—she was more concerned about the hordes of fanatics waiting to swarm him. His new escort looked more than capable of swatting them away if need be, and that helped ease her worry enough that she was suddenly aware of the eyes following her around carts and through the once-again bustling streets.

They made their way to a less crowded corner of the market, where whispers of the excitement had yet to reach the shoppers. She had no doubt the news would spread like a virus though. Sooner rather than later everyone around them would be infected. She wasn't one to bask in attention. She preferred to blend in to her surroundings, but because of a weird twist of fate and timing of coincidence she wouldn't be able to do so much longer. *I suppose I should get used to it,* her inner voice reminded as she and Delilah neared the dress shop.

Delilah turned, and walking backwards asked, "You know Prince Sebastian pretty well, yeah?" Nixon, who remained a few steps behind them, nodded firmly. "Good. Then it'll be your job to help us decide on a dress he'll like. Something that'll make it impossible for him to take his eyes off his future wifey." Delilah winked at Ava before she spun back around and linked their arms together.

"I don't think that will be difficult," Nixon said, his comment sliding over Ava like melted chocolate. *Is he flirting with me?* she wondered. The thought vanished quickly when he amended, "He could barely keep them off of you just now."

She and Delilah exchanged a look as they stepped into the small dress shop, the bell above the door jingling an excited welcome. A woman with chaotic blonde hair and glasses perched on the end of her nose popped up from behind the desk with an armful of fabrics.

"Can I help you with anything?" she asked, clearly frazzled.

"We're just looking," Ava replied as Delilah made a beeline for the display across the store. The saleswoman gave her the smallest glance, shrugged, then vanished back from where she'd come.

Sighing, Ava plopped down onto the cushioned bench in the corner. Nixon took his time wandering over, where he leaned against the wall beside her. "Are you not going to help?" he asked, motioning to Delilah, who already had three or four garments tossed over her shoulder.

"I'm pretty sure she has it handled," she answered, smiling fondly at her best friend. She was overjoyed that Delilah was here. It had been a scary couple of days thinking their friendship had ended.

Ava gathered her hair and tucked it behind the back of her head as a makeshift pillow. Closing her eyes, her head cradled in the thickness of her curls, she let the warmth of the shop settle over her. Each deep inhale brought with it the intoxicating smell of the man next to her. Before she knew it, her head had lolled to the side, as if her nose were drawn to it like a magnet.

When she opened her eyes and looked up, his eyes weren't the only thing on fire. It was still a breathtaking experience looking at him, and in that moment, he was all she could see. All she *wanted* to see. It was both fortunate and unfortunate she was destined to marry Sebastian, because she had a feeling Nixon could be her undoing.

"Long day?" he asked gently, quietly, somewhat compassionately.

"Long three and a half days."

"I'm—"

"Here," Delilah interrupted. She dropped a stack of dresses onto Ava's lap, the weight of the garments eliciting from her a throaty grunt. "I know a few of them are going to be no's but I figured I'd give you a few options. Now where…is that woman?" Delilah asked, the last part mumbled as she headed to the counter.

While D tracked down the saleswoman, Ava sauntered over to one of three dressing rooms.

"If we need adjustments, how long will that take?" Delilah questioned as she and the squat female made their way toward the other two.

"Two weeks," the shop owner replied as she puffed a piece of frizzy hair from her eyes.

"Well, what if she's——" Ava, certain of where the question was going, elbowed her friend as covertly as possible and scowled at her. After Delilah recovered from the jab to her ribs, she finished with a revised, "In a hurry?"

"Oh, in that case," the associate said as she unlocked the fitting room with one of at least seventy-five keys, "two weeks."

"That's absurd," Delilah protested.

"I'm sorry, but it's just me and…"

Ava closed the door on their bickering and hung up each garment. Delilah had, as promised, chosen a few definite no's, which she set aside immediately. After sorting them out she was left with five choices in five different colors, all elegantly as beautiful as the next.

The taupe-grey one she shimmied into was covered in rhinestone swirls and filigree. It was pretty but it didn't feel…right. It didn't feel enough. No, that wasn't it. *She* didn't feel enough in it.

The next one she stepped into was carnation pink with a full ball gown bottom. Around the middle was a faux-diamond decorative belt. Another good choice but it reminded her of the princess cake Cordellia had made her one year, with its frosted-loaf dress.

As she slid the third dress up, the fabric wrapped around her like skin. It draped over all her curves as if it were melted glass. The top was a fitted corset and the slit of the skirt played peek-a-boo with her thigh. The curtain-like fabric pooled at her feet like a puddle of blood. *Like all the women I slayed in order to reach the throne.* She chuckled at the delirious thought.

"I'm so tired," she muttered as she admired herself in the mirror. It was a neutral red that rivaled not only the macabre, but also roses and ripe cherries. It brought out the amber undertones of her hair which intensified the blue of her eyes. If she squinted hard enough, she could almost see the crown; could feel its weight sitting heavy on a cushion of curls.

This is the one, her conscience assured as she stepped into the lobby, hiking the skirt up so she could walk. Nixon's low chatter and Delilah's giggling ceased when she emerged. They both gawked at her, wide-eyed with mouths unhinged. She looked between the two of them a few times before shrugging and saying, "Well?"

"Holy shit," Delilah exhaled in one breath.

Ava laughed and then turned to Nixon. "Is it good enough for High House?"

He met her eyes, the golden irises blazing more than normal, and nodded once. "It's better than good enough."

Before the blush could make it to her cheeks, Ava turned on her tiptoes and went back into the room to change. She made slow, chary movements as she peeled the fabric off and hung it carefully back on the hanger. She ran her fingers over the draped cloth of the skirt; let it slip through her fingers like warm sand. This would be the dress in which all of Havaan would meet her, the dress that would say "I am your future queen. It's a pleasure to make your acquaintance." The thought wasn't as overwhelming as it had been a few days ago, and a slight tinge of unexpected acceptance settled in her stomach.

"What are you turning me into?" she chided the dress.

When she handed it over, she was careful not to wrinkle it as she laid it on the counter. "I'm going to step outside while you pay," she told Delilah as they hugged. They'd argued for ten minutes about splitting the bill, but Delilah had finally won when she pulled a stack of cash from her back pocket.

Nixon fell into step behind her as she pushed the door to the shop open, the little bell jingling a sweet goodbye. Ava sat against the wall of the small shop and Nixon settled into a corner, the shadows welcoming him as if he were one of them. It was eerie how easily he could melt into the darkness, which she supposed was a good trait for a guard.

Ava hadn't realized how suffocating the shop had been until she stepped outside. It was at least ten degrees hotter now than it had been when they'd gone in, but the air felt cool. Refreshing. Perhaps it was the wide-open space that gave it that feel, as if her world were still full of countless possibilities and not just the singular one blurring in her peripheral.

She inhaled a long pull through her nose and closed her eyes. She tilted her face to the sun and tried to count the white specs dancing across her lids. The familiar hum of the market carried on the wind and wrapped her in a safe, protective bubble.

It was shattered when Nixon questioned, "Are you okay?"

Her eyes opened slowly before she turned to where he was standing. "A bit overwhelmed," she admitted, "but it's okay. *I'm* okay."

He seemed to consider something for a second. "Ava, I—"

"I'm sorry today has been so weird for you," Ava spoke over him. She lowered her eyes apologetically and waited for him to continue. When it was obvious he was doing the same, she added, "That you got saddled with babysitting us."

"Protecting," he amended. There was a nip of playfulness to the word, but it drew a different feeling from Ava.

"Of course," she snipped. "Wouldn't want anything to happen to the king's precious investment." She hated the way she sounded, the childish tone riding her words, and she turned from him, hiding behind her hair.

Nixon's voice was low when he replied, "No, I would not." Her gaze snapped to him and they let the statement swell between them. Gather like cotton candy, thin and airy, but full of flavor that could melt on their tongues if they just risked a taste. Nixon cleared his throat, and at the same time the sugar vanished. "Besides," he started, "today has been different, yes, but not weird."

"Are you telling me you and Sebastian don't go dress shopping often?" Ava teased, trying to sweep away the tension.

"You would be surprised how little that happens," Nixon said. Though he didn't smile, Ava could feel it on the lightness of the words. They locked eyes once more and the intensity of Nixon's gaze sent a shiver down Ava's spine. She watched his lips part, saw his chest rise as he gathered breath to speak, and then took note of the way his brows dipped when Delilah exited the shop with a pink garment bag folded over her arm.

"Thank the stars this dress fit you perfectly," she said, "because that woman is a nightmare." She swept past them without a second glance at either. Ava gave Nixon an annoyed smile, then turned and followed her best friend. "I don't know why you wouldn't just let me tell her you were the next queen. She probably would have given us a great discount."

"D, if the dress was too expensive—"

"It wasn't, but that's not the point."

"Then what is?" Ava asked as she pulled her hair into a messy bun. The midday sun was at its highest point and a cloudless sky let loose its full intensity. If the spring days were any indication of how the summer months were going to be, they were in for a hot one. She couldn't help but wonder if High House had a pool. If it didn't, she would request one be built. If the king and queen were adamant on making her part of the royal family, she would use her position to get as many frivolous amenities as possible. First a pool and then an entertainment room, stocked with fresh desserts every day! Maybe she'd skip the pool entirely and go straight for a waterpark. *The world is my oyster*, she thought.

Delilah gave Ava a confused look. "It's the principal of it," she said flatly.

Ava, not wanting to continue the pointless conversation, changed the topic as she steered them toward a display of gaudy necklaces. Nixon remained an ever-present shadow at their backs while they aimlessly wandered the market. Ava tried to ignore the pointed stares and obvious whispers, but after a while it became a physical heaviness, as if the air were depleting of oxygen. She could almost feel each look, a tiny jolt of blistering pain to her back. The unsaid words of the people around her trickled into her ears and rolled around in her brain, a constant popcorn sound like rain on a roof.

It wasn't Delilah who noticed how Ava all but curled in on herself, but Nixon. "Are you alright?" he asked for the second time that day. This time, Ava shook her head and looked at him, a silent plea that spoke volumes. It took very little to convince Delilah it was time to leave once she was made aware of her friend's discomfort. Never one to miss an opportunity to shoot dagger-like glares, Delilah made certain to spare as few citizens as possible from the look as they wove their way through carts of jewels, food and framed artwork.

Once they cleared the fog of curious stares, Ava unfurled, and the threesome fell into step with one another. They talked casually as they made their way to Delilah's house before continuing onward to Meridian. There were only a few hours left before Ava's first official date with Sebastian and, much to her chagrin, it would require those hours plus some for her to be even close to presentable for dinner at High House.

Maybe the king will change his mind if I wear my pajamas, she joked mentally, smiling to herself at the absurdity of such a thing before focusing back on the conversation at hand.

Although that didn't stop her from contemplating just *how* far she could test her limits…

IX.

After depositing Delilah at home, Ava and Nixon strolled casually toward Meridian. Ava learned it was the first time the guard had spent this much time away from High House, and she took a weird sort of pride in pointing out important landmarks; places of which she had distinct memories but had always taken for granted. She did that a lot, she was starting to realize.

There was a time during their walk home when there was nothing to see besides tree after tree, and the two settled into a comfortable silence. Ava's life was rarely quiet between her mother's work music or the sobbing that leaked through the walls like mold or Delilah's constant presence or just the lives that existed outside her window. Because silence was rare, she was never the type that felt a *need* to fill the stillness with words.

It was still bright out and the canopy of trees above shaded them from the heat. She had no idea what time it was, but she knew there were at least a couple of hours until the car would arrive. She still needed to figure out what to wear, how to do her hair, what shoes—

"You two are very close." Nixon's deep bravado cut through the air, startling her and seemingly a flock of birds as they sprung from their branch and took to the sky.

"Delilah and me?" she asked, looking at him. He nodded. "We are. She's my number one."

"Your number one...what?" he asked as he switched the garment bag from one hand to the other then tossed it over his shoulder. She'd insisted on carrying it, but he had insisted harder, leaving her no choice when he'd hoisted it above his head. She'd given him her best death-glare, but it had done very little to deter him.

"My number one friend. My *best* friend, at that. Though honestly, I was a little worried that would cease once I told her about the king's decision."

"Why is that?"

Ava sighed. "I wasn't at the gala for myself. I was there for her. Delilah had dreamt about being queen for ten years. What happened that night was worst case scenario for both of us, and I was so scared that when I told her what happened, she would hate me, that she would think I had taken it from her."

"But you didn't," Nixon reminded, his voice gentle. She smiled softly at him.

"I didn't, no, but I wasn't entirely sure she would see it that way. And for a moment she didn't. We're okay now. I think. I'm sure she's still a little sour about the whole ordeal, but who wouldn't be? She gets to move to High House, though, like she always wanted, and be a part of the whole fanciful lifestyle. It might not be in the way either of us had planned but—" Ava paused for a shrug. "I'm sure she'll get over it much quicker now that she knows you're part of the package." She winked at Nixon then laughed as he lowered his eyebrows and cocked his head curiously.

"What do I have to do with anything?" he asked, his confusion genuine.

"She was practically drooling over you," Ava replied. "You're probably so used to women throwing themselves at you, you don't even notice it anymore."

After a handful of wordless steps, Nixon said, "There's no shortage of attention."

Ava looked up at him then shook her head and tossed in a Delilah-sized eye-roll for good measure. She said sarcastically, "Sounds awesome." She wasn't surprised by his admittance, but hearing it stirred something inside of her, a sleeping green monster she'd never had to worry about waking. Now it shifted, flexed a foot and looked around before curling back up and drifting off to sleep, less deep than before.

"Not so much," he answered. Sincerity coated his voice. "As I'm sure you're aware, it can be taxing."

"Ya know…" Ava kicked a rock with her toe and watched it skitter down the road. "Women don't hit on me as often as you would think." Her eyes turned to him just in time to see Nixon's mouth twitch, but he remained his stoic, serious self. "Man," she sighed. "Do you *ever* smile?" He raised a brow at her. "I'm hilarious and you haven't laughed once."

"Maybe you're just not that funny."

As she considered what he'd said, she kicked the stone again. It rolled a few feet before changing directions and ending up in a boulevard with a piece of wet newspaper and an empty cardboard box. Finally, she shook her head in disagreement. "No, that's not it. It's definitely you."

He exhaled through his nose, a sound that could have almost been a laugh laced within the breath. "I smile," he said. Ava gave him a skeptical look. "But only in the mirror. To ensure the muscles don't rust."

She couldn't help but laugh as she imagined him practicing different grinning styles, as if he were some high-tech robot or being from another planet trying to mimic human emotions.

"Good looking *and* funny. Who knew?" she joked, gently shoving him with her shoulder.

"Don't tell anyone. I've got a reputation to uphold."

She tapped the space above her heart with two fingers. "I will keep it close to my chest always."

Nixon considered her, his lips pursed to the side as he did. "I imagine you do that a lot," he finally said as they rounded the corner to Holland Avenue. Her street was calm once again. Bicycles leaned against the spring grass, discarded for plates of spaghetti before bed. Working citizens crossed their yards with patches of flour in their hair or ink-stained fingertips.

"Do what?" she asked.

"Keep secrets."

"A girl can't show all of her cards at once. And if I'm not as funny as I thought, I've got nothing else going for me except my air of mystery."

She'd said it playfully, but there really *was* a reason she had a hard time letting people in. She lived with the ideals that the less someone knew about you, the less ammunition they had when they decided to hurt you. She wasn't so jaded as to believe everyone in the world had an ulterior motive, but it was a lesson Cordellia had drilled into her from a young age. Everyone you love, everyone you care about, at some point will leave; but if you give less of yourself, it doesn't hurt as much when they do.

"You have much going for you," Nixon said, more to himself, like he hadn't wanted her to hear his words. She pretended she didn't as she turned away from him to hide the heat warming her cheeks.

Uncomfortable with the weird silence this time, she cleared her throat and asked, "So you and Sebastian…are you two close? Is he your number one?"

"He is my brother," he said simply.

Ava stumbled over her feet. "Excuse me?"

The corner of his mouth twitched in amusement. "Not by blood. The king and the queen are not my parents." He debated saying more, considered how many of his own cards he wanted to lay down on the table so soon, but before he could make a final decision, he heard himself add, "I've been with them since I was young."

"How young?" Ava asked without missing a beat. They were nearing her house, only half a block away, but their steps had slowed considerably, as if unconsciously trying to prolong their conversation. The ease with which it came was unfamiliar to both. Ava had a difficult time opening up to even Delilah sometimes, and Nixon didn't speak much in general. He'd been training as a guard since he was twelve, and in those lessons had learned the importance of listening over speaking. Both tended to observe more than engage.

"Since I was ten," Nixon answered.

Ava's deep blue eyes widened in surprise. She was prepared to ask a follow up question, mulling it between her teeth, but when she looked at the guard, *really* looked at him—beyond his unnaturally good looks— the gold ring in his eyes blazed dully under a layer of still-fresh sadness. His squared jaw was set and she almost missed the slight flare of his nose. She understood better than most the signs of mourning and was good at reading the cues that said *I don't want to talk about it*. She had developed many of her own over the years.

So, instead she said, "Sounds like tragedy has visited us both."

"It's difficult to avoid when war is involved."

Ava nodded absently. "Maybe one day we can share our stories. You show me yours, I'll show you mine." She smiled at his amused grunt. "See," she added as they approached her house, "I'm hilarious."

Nixon followed her up the small flight of stairs to where she leaned against the door, her hand resting on the handle. "Listen, I don't know what state of mind my mother is going to be in. She isn't crazy," she defended as his brows furrowed with question. "She just…sometimes she's really sad and other times she gets really focused on her work and in doing so gets a bit um…frazzled? Just…if she seems a little off…" Ava looked at him, her teeth worrying her bottom lip. She looked tragically vulnerable, the way abandoned homes do when the sun sets behind them. A million words flooded his mind, things to say that could comfort her, but all he said was, "I had a sad mother once, too."

Whether he knew it or not, those words were more than she needed to push the door open.

A sonic boom of music flew at them, as if the closed door had been a dam, and opening it let loose a flood of wordless melodies and vibrating bass. Ava looked at Nixon and sighed, relieved, then repeatedly flicked a light switch at the top of the staircase. Within seconds the music quieted and then ceased.

"Can I get you something to drink?" she asked as Nixon laid her dress bag atop the kitchen table.

"No, I'm fine. Thank you though." He stepped into the small, cozy living room that opened directly off the kitchen, and made a beeline toward the framed photographs lined across the fireplace mantel. Cordellia kept no photos of Dante out in the open aside from the one front and center in the arrangement. That, along with the one Ava had briefly possessed as a teenager, were the only two pictures she'd seen of her father. In the one over the fireplace, Ava was no more than three months old and sound asleep on her dad's chest. His arms were wrapped around her tiny body and a small smile tugged the corner of her lips.

Nixon picked up the photograph carefully and brushed a fingertip over the glass, leaving a clean streak in the fine layer of dust that had gathered. "Your father?" She smiled tightly and nodded. "Is he still around?" he asked. There was a small tremor in his question and his hand shook ever so slightly as he set the photo back in its place. Standing beside him, Ava shook her head and adjusted the photo. A deep sigh escaped her as she turned away from it. Nixon tapped his fingertips against his chest and looked at her in a silent question. Her smile was more natural this time and she mimicked his motion, creating between the two of them their own little signal. It was sort of like the secret codes she and Delilah had developed as pre-teens.

It forged between Ava and the guard—as it had done many years ago between she and D—a special bond, one that would be impenetrable to outsiders. Little did either of them know, this new bond would play a larger role than anyone could predict. Many days from now, one of their lives would hinge upon it.

For now, it might have been a simple, insignificant thing to anyone else, but she felt a peacefulness bloom in her sternum, and as Nixon's plush lips contorted into his own satisfied smirk, she knew he felt the same. They both opened their mouths to speak, to say something that would shatter the heavy silence between them, but Cordellia's voice did it for them instead.

"Avaleigh, honey," she called as she rounded the corner. "I didn't know you and Delilah—"

Cordellia stopped. She inhaled a startled breath. One hand went to her mouth while the other braced against the doorframe.

Faintly, she heard Ava call out to her before she was at her side. "Are you okay?"

"Yes," Cordellia replied breathlessly. She blinked a few times, trying to focus on Ava. "I think I just...um...I got a little lightheaded." Uncertain grey eyes traveled back to Nixon.

"Have you eaten?" Ava questioned. She helped steady Cordellia. Her mother shook her head, her eyes still trained on the guard. "I'll make you a sandwich. Are you sure you're alright?"

"I'm fine."

Ava pulled her hands away slowly, keeping them close enough in case Cordellia passed out. She stayed upright, though, which Ava took as a good sign. From the corner of her eye, she caught a flash of red and followed Cordellia's curious gaze.

"This is Nixon," Ava started, reading the question in her mother's eyes. "One of the king's guards. This is my mother, Cordellia."

Nixon extended his hand and waited for Cordellia to shake it. "It's a pleasure to meet you, Mrs. Toliver."

Her voice wavered, as if caught in her throat, as she replied, "Please, call me Cordellia. Mrs. Toliver was my mother."

"You and Ava's father never married, then?" he asked as he dropped her hand.

"No," Cordellia replied quickly. Whatever had hit her seemed to have passed, so Ava made her way into the kitchen. "We never had the chance," Cordellia added. She tugged on the front of her black apron.

Microscopic shards of silver and gold coated it as if she had fallen into a pile of stars.

"I'm sorry to hear that." With a sad, curious pull to his eyebrows, Nixon looked over Cordellia's head at Ava, who was leaning against the wall of the archway, a plate in hand. She tapped the space over her heart and he nodded once in understanding. "You have a very lovely home," he said, changing the subject, for which both Toliver women were thankful.

"I'm sure it's nothing compared to High House," Cordellia said, waving off his compliment. "What are you doing so far from there?"

"Sebas—the prince—was insistent that I have an extra level of protection, and Nixon got forced into the role." Ava handed her mother the chipped sage-colored plate. She'd cut the ham and cheese sandwich across, not diagonally, which struck Nixon has a bit strange.

Cordellia turned toward her daughter quickly, her eyebrows raised. "You saw the prince? Today?"

"At the market," Ava replied. "It would have been fine if he hadn't stopped and talked to me, but apparently I'm irresistible." The last bit dripped with sarcasm and was accompanied by a slight roll of her eyes.

"That was nice of him to look out for you. I'm sure his presence there drew some unexpected attention." Cordellia directed her focus back to Nixon, who was encased in shadows and orange embers from the sun. "Thank you for getting her home safely. I hope she didn't give you too much of a hard time."

Nixon looked at Ava, the intensity of his eyes even more vibrant as the setting sun poured in through the large window of their living room. It left streaks of tangerine across the hardwood floor, spotlights for the dust particles dancing in the beams.

The film that had settled in the unused space had been disturbed by the new presence.

Very little time was spent in the living room. Cordellia and Ava often looked past it on their way from the front door to the basement or kitchen to bedroom. It was the only place in the house where photos of a stolen life resided, and they treated it almost like a mausoleum, a shrine to what should have been but never would be.

It seemed no part of Ava's life would go untouched by the guard.

"She gave me just enough of it to keep me busy," Nixon joked, winking at Cordellia. "You've raised a wonderful daughter. She will make an excellent queen."

Looking at her child, Cordellia smiled fondly. "I have, haven't I?" Ava scrunched her nose and offered her own cheeky grin. There was a beat of silence, Cordellia clicked into hostess mode. "Will you be staying for dinner, then? I didn't know what time you'd be home and haven't thought much of it, obviously." She raised the plate. Only one bite had been taken from a half of the sandwich. "But I assume—" She looked at her watch. "—it's very close to that time."

"I'm actually having dinner with Sebastian tonight. I just came home to change."

"Oh," Cordellia replied, almost sadly, but then she forced a smile that could fool anyone but Ava and waved a hand in the air. "That should be fun. I've got a few pieces I need to get finished anyway." She turned back to Nixon. "It was…" She shook her head, as if silently scolding herself. "It was a pleasure meeting you. Again, thank you for taking such good care of her."

Nixon tipped his head and bowed slightly, a gesture that created a lump Ava had to swallow. Most people, especially those in the upper class, never paid extra respect to her mother, even as she was handing them a necklace or headdress she'd spent days shaping to perfection. To them, she was a jewelry maker—that was her trade—and she was there only to provide them such a service. They weren't rude, they just weren't kind. To see someone, a near stranger, pay even a slight reverence...

"I'm going to raid your closet for something to wear. Do you mind?" Ava asked as Cordellia kissed her forehead.

"Of course not," she replied, touching her cheek lightly with the palm of her hand. "I am very proud of you," she whispered. Ava blinked away the wetness forming in her eyes. Cordellia tossed Nixon a final goodbye smile before she headed back downstairs, setting her uneaten food on the kitchen island as she passed. A steady thumping seeped up from the floor almost immediately.

Ava looked at Nixon, held his blazing gaze for a few beats of the music, and then gestured to the stairs with a flick of her head. "You can wait down here or you can hang out in my bedroom. Whatever you prefer."

He shrugged a shoulder, his movement flexing the muscles below his fitted shirt. Ava tore her eyes away from his chest and let her bottom lip slip through her teeth. "I can do whichever makes you the most comfortable," he replied.

She wasn't sure if it was the sudden rush of blood to her ears, or if his voice had actually dropped an octave, but whatever it was pressed in through her bellybutton and squeezed her heart. It didn't seem fair that he was not only good looking, but also possessed a voice that could tempt the wings off angels.

"I guess you can just wait in my bedroom. You can't get into as much trouble up there," she said, hoping her lie sounded truthful enough. *We could get into a lot of trouble,* she thought as they started up the faux wood stairs.

"Your mother is very nice," Nixon said from behind her. "I can see where you get your beauty."

"Really?" Ava asked with genuine surprise. "I've always heard I look like my dad."

"Then he must have been beautiful, as well."

Ava turned over her shoulder. "You charmer," she teased as she opened her bedroom door. "Welcome to my humble mess of a bedroom. Forgive the chaos. I'm not sure if you've heard, but I'm the next queen." Nixon flicked an eyebrow at the joke. "I'm sorting through stuff and having a difficult time determining what to take with me."

Boxes were stacked in all the available corners of the bedroom, as well as on the bench below her reading window. Piles of clothing lined the foot of her bed, the covers arranged haphazardly.

"Purple must be your favorite color," he stated, taking in the deep violet curtains, soft lavender walls, lilac chevron comforter, and accent pillows with white silhouettes of nature scenes printed on the fronts.

"You're observant. I can see why you're a guard." She winked at him. "Make yourself comfortable. I'm going to go snag something presentable from my mom's wardrobe." She stepped into the hallway then flung herself back in, her arms holding her in suspension. "I don't suppose the queen prances around in oversized t-shirts and holey jeans very often, does she?"

"Not as often as you would expect," Nixon replied.

She nodded once and clicked her tongue in disappointment. "Bummer."

"I suppose Delilah will have to go shopping and fill your new closet."

"How will she ever survive?" she feigned dramatically. With that, she was gone, leaving the raven-locked serviceman to wander. He shifted through stacks of photographs and ran his finger down the spine of books that had yet to be packed away.

A string was stretched across the head of the bed, draped between the posts of it, with quotes hanging by clothes pins. Some were cut from books while most were written in rounded handwriting—a chirography that no doubt belonged to Ava. Some spoke of hope, like one from Oscar Wilde: *"We are all in the gutter, but some of us are looking at the stars."* Many of friendship: *"Friendships are fragile things, and require as much handling as any other fragile and precious thing."* And even some of love, ranging from the requiem of it to the need to open oneself up despite the pain that it may cause.

"Do you want to know what my favorite quote is?" Ava's voice pulled his attention from the mantras and he turned toward the doorway from which it had come. She had a dress slung over her folded arms, and she leaned her shoulder against the frame.

"I do," Nixon answered honestly. He suddenly wanted to know everything about her, from her favorite meal to whether someone had hurt her so much she reserved little room for love.

"It's particularly the last stanza, but it's '…for it says that no matter how hard the world pushes against me, within me there's something stronger, something better, pushing right back.'"

Nixon's fiery gaze settled on her, heating her from the inside out. "Makes sense," he finally said.

She waited for him to explain, but when he continued to stare at her, she held up the dress in her arms. "Is this okay for tonight?" There had been a weight to his words, a passion she didn't have the time or energy to delve into right now. The car would arrive in less than an hour.

Nixon nodded curtly at her clothing choice.

Ava mimicked him and turned out of the room, only to return less than thirty minutes later. The black dress hit her just below the knee and the thin white and green houndstooth-printed belt cinched her waist classily. It was sleeveless, with a thick white stitching along the seam. She'd paired it with strappy white shoes with a low heel. Her hair was done in a tight French twist, a few shorter strands framing her face, onto which she'd lightly dusted makeup. She looked elegant but not overly done, and it took conscious effort for Nixon to pry his eyes away.

"Do I look respectable?" she asked, swishing the skirt around her legs.

He cleared his throat. "You look great."

"I guess great will have to do for the night then," she replied as a horn beeped from outside. "That must be our ride. Are you ready to go?"

"Are *you* ready to go?" Nixon echoed, waving her out the door in front of him.

"As ready as I'll ever be." She shrugged as she headed down the stairs. "I hope we're having pizza."

Behind her, Nixon snorted. "Very unlikely."

"You can be such a downer sometimes," she replied playfully, poking him in the side. Her finger hit a solid block of muscle, and she cradled it gently as it pulsed with pain. She yelled down to Cordellia, though it was a wasted effort, and then stepped outside into a warm but breezy evening.

The vehicle that waited for them was simple but sleek. It had been polished recently, probably that very day, and the blue and silver streaks in the sky reflected off the hood. Standing next to the back passenger door was a wall of a man, with broad shoulders and biceps the size of grapefruit. As his travelers approached, he tipped his head slightly.

"Evening Ramiro," Nixon said, slapping the big man on the shoulder. "This is Sebastian's intended, Miss Avaleigh Toliver."

"Nice to meet you, Miss Toliver," the driver replied.

Ava flashed him a toothy greeting. "And you, as well."

"Shall we go?" Ramiro asked as he opened the door. "We should arrive close to six-thirty."

"Let's get a move on," Ava said as she slid into the car, tucking her skirt under her as she did. "Wouldn't want to keep the prince waiting."

Ramiro, unlike Nixon, gave her a slight smile before closing the door. As he rounded the front of the car, Nixon circled the back. They said a few words to one another before their doors opened simultaneously and they entered the vehicle at the same time. Their synchronicity fascinated Ava, and when Nixon looked over at her, he questioned what she was grinning about.

"Nothing," she replied. "I just enjoy smiling. You should give it a go sometime."

He frowned at her, but the light reflecting in his eyes reassured her that his ire was for naught. As the car pulled away from her house, Ava had her first glimpse of how things would be at the end of the week. While nervous excitement bubbled in her stomach at this moment, the next time she watched her home fade away through the back of a windshield would be with a sadness she never knew possible.

X.

As the sleek black car maneuvered the winding road to High House, Ava rolled the tinted window down so she could see the blur outside. Everything was so different on this journey up the hill, even the way the world passed. It blended and streaked together, like paints smeared on a giant canvas. The occasional car would pass by them, interrupting the scenery for nothing more than a second. Ava had never considered how significant a second could be, how quickly things could change in a blink or the beat of a heart. But she had been forced to see things with new sight during the last four days.

Sometimes it felt as if she were an outsider, watching a life she barely recognized.

Now more than ever.

She sighed and rested her head against the plush seat. She tapped her feet in sync with the gentle jazz tune coming through the car speakers and hummed quietly, harmonizing with the undercurrents of the instruments, all the while trying to be as relaxed as the music. When the song ended, she opened her eyes and instinctively glanced over at Nixon.

What she saw stopped her breath in her throat. Amusement danced in the embers of his eyes and set them alight even more than normal. There was even a slight tilt to the corners of his mouth, a soft curve that teased the start of a smile.

"What?" she asked, suddenly self-conscious under the heat of his gaze. He looked ready to say something, then he shook his head and looked away. "No way, mister. You can't look at someone like that and then act like it was for no reason." She crossed her arms over her chest and set her face.

Nixon adjusted his body until he was facing her, his strong back pressed against the door, one knee resting on the suede seat. She'd never seen anyone so comfortable just existing, and she envied him. She had never experienced that. Ava had always been conscious of the space she took up and was constantly doing whatever she could to minimize it.

"I was thinking about why you like that poem so much," he said.

A frustration she couldn't quite pinpoint rose in her, but she swallowed it down. "Oh yeah?" she challenged as she mimicked his casual pose. She crossed her legs at the ankles and stretched them across the seat bench. The girth of the car was wide enough that even extended fully there was still five inches between the two of them. "Tell me."

Nixon rubbed his stubbly jaw. A thin layer of shadow had emerged through the day, and it escalated his devilishly good looks. Ava had a difficult time looking at him as was, but now it took everything to stay in her seat and not slide closer to him.

"It is your motto. Your life anthem. It is the rhythm that beats in your veins." Ava cocked her head slightly but said nothing. "I saw it the night of the gala, as well as today in the market."

"Saw what?"

"Your tenacity," he replied calmly. His eyes blazed as if they were a sun on fire. "The writer encourages the reader to never back down, especially against things they have no control over. It may be futile, but refusing to bend and concede makes everything worth it in the end.

Someway. If you can remain true to yourself, if you face even the preordained parts of life with courage and strength, you'll survive. It is a poem about surviving because of resistance. It's about you."

"I highly doubt he had me in mind when he wrote the words," Ava refuted.

Nixon shook his head and looked at her, his frustration weighing down his features. Aside from Sebastian, no one ever really asked him his opinion, and never to this extent. He'd never had to try and explain the meaning behind a poem before, and he hadn't intended doing so when Ava had said the few lines to him. But sitting in the car, watching her absorb the jazzy notes, she had looked peaceful. Though he was sure she was anything but, certain there was a storm of dissonance brewing under her skin, in those quiet moments she'd looked ready.

Ready for whatever the throne threw at her. It looked, to anyone who hadn't seen her break down at the gala, like she'd accepted her fate. He knew that wasn't the case, just as he knew she wouldn't settle into it without making a ruckus. Others may frown at her obstinacy, but he admired her defiant spirit, even envied it a bit. He couldn't very well tell her that, though—speaking ill toward the king was not an infraction he was looking to pin to his name, but as he sat there watching her, the two simple lines ran through his mind. An endless loop, like a battle cry, and he understood not only the meaning behind them, but also *why* Ava liked them.

"I do not mean you were his muse," Nixon started, trying to choose the right words to say what he needed to without saying it outright. "But your will to avoid surrendering is impenetrable. You will fight until you can't fight any more if it's something you truly believe in. You are strong, especially in moments that would buckle the knees of others."

Ava gave him a sad smile and disagreed with a slight shake of her head. "I'm not strong, though. I thought I was. *Everyone* has always believed I am, but I'm not." She licked her lips, letting her top teeth drag along her lip as she tried to quell her emotions. "I couldn't even convince the king to change his mind. I told him I would marry his son without a fight. I did exactly the opposite of what you're saying. I conceded. I gave in. I backed down. I didn't push back. That isn't strength, Nixon, that's cowardice."

"How can you not see that none of that is true?" he asked, almost sternly. When she opened her mouth to argue, he held up a hand. She looked at him incredulously, surprised by his audacity, but she sat back against the door and scowled. "You could have fled," he continued. "You could have gone to any other area of Havaan and vanished, yet you didn't. You're here still. It didn't matter how loud you got, how much you screamed at the king, nothing was going to change his mind. But you still tried, you spoke bravely and you didn't make an effort to hide your anger of the situation. Anyone else would have bowed immediately and taken whatever he handed them without argument, without question. But not you, because Ava, you *are* strong. You rage, even when it seems pointless, because there could be that one crack that shatters the whole thing. You remain constant in yourself. And that's what matters in the long run."

In one swift motion—barely giving her time to move her legs—

Nixon slid next to her, their faces mere inches apart. *Holy shit.* Ava glanced at the driver, but his eyes were on the road. She didn't care if he could hear them. She worried he would get the wrong impression and say something to Sebastian, though. But when Nixon said her name, demanded her attention with the gravelly growl of his voice, she didn't care about any of that. Instead, she swallowed the nervous lump in her throat and pulled her eyes slowly from his lips.

When he spoke again, the words were nothing more than a breath between them. "When you move to High House, do not lose sight of who you are. You have the potential to be the best queen Havaan has ever had, but to succeed you have to stay Ava. The Ava you are *right now*. Fight, whenever it is called for. Push back. The king has *not* made the wrong choice."

Nixon held her gaze, forcing the belief of his words into the car. The air between them sparked, and Ava was afraid to breathe in fear of starting a fire no one could put out.

"Promise me," he whispered, almost begged. His words, his faith in her, stirred the deepest desire to never let him down; to not only become an amazing queen, but more importantly, the best version of herself.

"I promise," she mouthed.

In the following moment, he did something she never thought he would do.

He smiled.

Not a half grin or the sly smirk he'd trademarked.

This was a heart-stopping, world ending grin full of straight white teeth and a magic all its own. Ava swore she could hear the loud thud of angel wings being tossed aside. He was...perfect...as if the elder magicians had created him from all things beautiful, and pure, and good.

"Oh my god," she exhaled in a rush.

"What?" he asked, his eyes ablaze. "I told you I smiled."

Ava laughed.

She felt light—free—as if every care in her world ceased to exist. All because of this dark-haired, copper-eyed guard whose smile could calm the raging rapids. The moment was interrupted all too soon as their driver—Ramiro—cleared his throat and pressed a button on the console of his car.

"We're here," he informed as the large metal gates of High House began to slowly swing open. Nixon and Ava looked at one another for a beat longer, then, just as quickly as before, he was back on his side of the car, looking out the window with a demeanor so calm Ava wondered if she'd imagined the whole thing. But when she looked ahead and caught the dark brown eyes of Ramiro, he winked at her. She wasn't entirely sure where the certainty came from, but she knew that what had transpired between she and Nixon would remain in the backseat.

The certainty, however, did very little to calm the feeling settling in her stomach. She shifted her focus to the world outside her window and tried to banish everything Nixon made her feel.

As she attempted to justify a guilt that had no reason for existing, her door suddenly opened, jerking her back to reality. She looked beside her but Nixon had moved out of the car and was on the wide porch, waiting. She cleared her head then slipped out of the car.

She thanked Ramiro, for more than just their safe arrival, and then smiled up at Nixon as she stepped into the foyer of High House.

Sebastian was sitting on the last step of the staircase, leaning against the one above him. When he saw them, he grinned. Where Nixon's smile—Ava was still having a difficult time believing she'd actually seen his—strengthened the slants and shadows of his face, making him seem even older and more mysterious, Sebastian's did the opposite. It softened his features and took away years.

They were light and dark in every way possible, these two.

"You're here!" the prince greeted as he pushed his lithe body up and sauntered toward them. His movements were fluid, as if he were gliding over ice.

Sebastian held her forearms then kissed both of her cheeks. He smelled like cinnamon and apple, and woods, like the handmade cedar chest where Cordellia kept all the winter blankets. It wasn't as intoxicating as Nixon's scent, but it wasn't off-putting. In fact, it was quite pleasant.

"You look beautiful," Sebastian praised as he held her an arm's length away.

"You look very nice yourself," she replied. He was dressed in slate-grey trousers, the shape emphasizing the length of his legs, and a crisp butter-yellow dress shirt. It was more casual than Ava would have imagined and she made a mental note to ask about the expected attire.

Sebastian gave her one of his glowing smiles then gripped Nixon's shoulder. "My friend," he said fondly, "thank you for keeping my lady safe today." He turned to Ava and said, "I hope he wasn't too much of a bother."

"Nothing I couldn't handle," she replied, echoing Nixon's earlier sentiment.

"You two got along well, then?"

Nixon nodded. "She's a pleasure to be around. You're a very lucky man."

Sebastian's eyes twinkled. She didn't quite understand the look, but still it brought warmth to her cheeks. "I've had no doubt about that," he answered simply. Then he switched gears and placed his hand on the small of her back. "Shall we head to dinner?" He steered her toward a sliding door to their left. It was made of solid oak and gleamed even in the low light of the wall sconces.

"Enjoy your meal," Nixon called half-way up the stairs.

"You're not joining us?" Ava asked. She sensed his separation already, having spent most of the day with him by her side.

He gave her a soft, tight smile. Though it wasn't the fullness of the one she'd seen in the car, it stilled her heart regardless. "I think you can manage dinner without my protection." With a slight nod of his head, he continued his journey with quick ease up the left staircase.

Ava turned back to Sebastian and smiled her thanks as he pulled the heavy door open, revealing a beautiful dining room with a long table, as well as—

"Mother. Father." The prince's words were short and hooked with a question. "What are you doing here?" There was a clear annoyance to his voice as Sebastian stepped into the room to find his parents seated side-by-side at the table. The polished wood reflected the lights of the low-hanging chandeliers.

"It's dinner time. We always eat together," Bernadette said. Her tone was sickly-sweet. She grinned at Ava, though her eyes remained emotionless. She did, however, look better than she had at the gala. Gone were the lines that had etched her face and the ill paleness of her skin. She looked renewed, younger by at least ten years. "Avaleigh, it's so great to see you again."

"Thank you. It's nice to see you two, as well," Ava lied through a forced smile.

"I was unaware I wasn't allowed one dinner to myself," Sebastian replied flatly while he pulled Ava's chair out. She mouthed a *thank you* before sitting in the seat closest to the king.

Bernadette waved her son's comment away with a flick of her wrist. "You'll have hundreds of dinners together. Your father and I wanted to take the evening to learn a bit more about Avaleigh."

"So did I," the prince mumbled. He dropped into the seat next to his mother.

Bernadette reached out and cupped the side of his face, forcing him to look at her. Neither said anything as they stared the other down, a silent argument building in the space between them. In the next instant, an array of servants flooded into the room with trays and pitchers. One pair—two young women in all-black attire—filled the glasses in front of each diner. The smell of grapes wafted from one decanter before the first drop of liquid hit Ava's glass.

"I'm sure she won't mind us joining you, will you, dear?" The queen acknowledged Ava, her eyes dancing with calculated mischief.

Ava had two options: she could cower under the queen's intense look and the razor-sharp smile that stretched her already taught skin; or she could meet her directly, head-on in the middle of a game that two could play.

Fight, she heard Nixon whisper. *Push back.*

Those words gave her the answer she needed, and when she replied, "Of course not," it was with the same pretentious saccharinity. She then reached across the short distance of the table and touched

Sebastian's arm with her fingertips. "We'll have plenty of dinners together," she said.

Sebastian's tense face softened slightly, and he squeezed her fingers before she pulled her hand away.

"Then it's settled. We shall stay," King Orion chimed in as he lifted his goblet to his lips.

"It doesn't seem like it's up for debate anyway." Sebastian sat up in his chair, defiance and irritation still obvious in the carriage of his shoulders.

"It isn't," Queen Bernadette snapped. The sharp finality of her words could not be ignored.

Ava followed the king's movements as she sipped the semi-sweet dinner wine from her glass. Another wave of servants bustled around, serving all four a plate of stuffed Cornish hen, halved and seasoned redskin potatoes and a hot buttered biscuit. She was a bit disappointed the meal was not pizza, but she could not ignore the way her mouth salivated at the steaming meal before her. The bird glistened in a way that promised juicy, flavorful meat. The scented curlicues of garlic and herbs coming off the potatoes were direct targets to her stomach, which grumbled as if on cue. She wanted to delve into it like a starving banshee, but instead she tucked her hands in her lap as the king gave a heartfelt speech, most of it focused on the mutual excitement of him and his wife being able to share in this meal with their future daughter-in-law.

The foreign pairing of words sent a new wave of resentment down her spine. She was trying to accept her up-and-coming title of queen. And if she didn't overanalyze it, she could almost get through a whole thought of being Sebastian's wife without wanting to cry. But there was something about the realization of forever being married to the king—and more unfortunate, the queen—that angered her once again.

Everyone in Havaan got to pick their spouses, and if they ended up hating their in-laws they could call off the whole relationship. But Ava wouldn't have that choice—or many others, it was starting to seem—and it was just another reminder of the things King Orion was taking from her. She was angry at herself for forgetting what he was not *asking* of her but *demanding* of her.

She wanted nothing more than to throw her plate across the room, along with her glass of wine, and storm out. But she would not let them get the best of her; she would *not* let them see her vulnerable.

Never again.

Instead, after running her thumb along the serrated edge of her knife, she picked it up, along with her fork, and cut into the delicate meat. Conversation ceased for a few minutes as they let the tension from the earlier exchange dissipate, pushed aside by the scraping of cutlery against china and the muffled noises from the hidden kitchen.

"So Avaleigh," the king began as he gathered bits of stuffing onto his fork, "how did your family react when you shared with them the good news of your future queenhood?"

"After the shock wears off, everyone I've told has been quite excited."

"At least someone in your life is," Queen Bernadette said.

"Bernadette…" the king warned the same time Sebastian cried, "Mother!"

Ava glowered at the queen over the brim of her water glass before setting it down with slow, difficult control. "What was that?" she asked as if she hadn't heard anything.

"It doesn't matter," Sebastian answered sternly. He pulled his gaze away from his mother and relaxed the furrow of his brows before looking at Ava. "She was told not to say anything."

"I wish you would though," Ava said. She smiled coldly at the queen. "We're going to be family soon, right? We should be able to speak honestly with one another, don't you agree?"

Queen Bernadette replied with a slight sneer to the corner of her lips, "Oh, I very much agree."

Ava sat back in her chair and folded her hands in her lap comfortably. She refused to lose herself under the queen's hateful stare. She had always been the girl who didn't quite fit in. Having people silently judge her wasn't anything new. She had long ago learned that cowering would give them power, so she did everything she could to hold on to what little she had.

Her whole life she had refused to break herself to fit into a mold, and she would not surrender any part of who she was to the Calder family. She would marry into it because she had no choice, but she would give them hell however many days required it. She would not be their puppet, their little lap dog that followed them blindly like so many others. Her mother, Delilah, and now Nixon all saw in her the passion and fervor she'd worked so hard to establish. Though three was not the biggest number, it was enough to keep that fire burning. As long as she held on to their faith, it would never be extinguished, no matter how hard anyone huffed and puffed.

Including the queen.

Especially the queen.

Next to her, the king shot his wife a look of warning. She caught it from the corner of her eye and exhaled in frustration before closing her mouth.

Sebastian either didn't see the same look or chose to ignore it because he said, "My mother was a bit put-off by your reaction the night of the gala, by your…lack of enthusiasm. She feels as though your dejection was disrespectful and that you don't fully grasp the magnitude of their decision." Each word was glazed with a layer of disgust, but not toward her. He snagged the chunk of potato off the prong of his fork with his teeth. Leaning back enough to look at his parents, Sebastian chewed his food with a smug look on his face.

It took all of Ava's self-control to not smile at the obvious declaration of sides. Knowing he was choosing hers helped to solidify the bond they'd made in the market earlier that day. *Was that just a few hours ago?* she asked herself. So much had happened in that short timeframe, and especially in the couple of days since the gala.

Ava not only appreciated Sebastian's support but also that he had told the truth. She had worried how her response had come across, and though she wasn't entirely thrilled that the king and queen would be her marital family one day, she also didn't want to provide the queen with any extra ammunition in her obvious dislike toward her future daughter-in-law.

After a passing second of tense silence, Ava calmly replied, "I can understand how my reaction could have been misinterpreted as disrespect. And I'm sorry that there was even a possibility for it to be seen as such, but you have to understand that hearing I had been chosen was the last thing I expected." She addressed all three, but shifted her gaze between the king and queen more often. "I didn't have time to think about how I was *supposed* to respond. What you saw was genuine confusion, and surprise, and yes—even frustration and disagreement. None of that means I'm at all oblivious to the honor being given to me. I'm well aware how important this tradition is for Havaan."

Now she turned her full attention to the queen and said with mock sincerity, "I hope you can accept my apology, and allow me the chance to prove to you how very wrong your first impression of me was." She didn't *really* care what they thought of her, but the queen already hated her without preamble. She could only imagine what would happen if she had a genuine reason to do so.

With six eyes upon her, all varying shapes and hues, the queen had no choice but to plaster on her fake smile, though it wasn't as spiteful as normal. There was even a bit of resigned sadness in it that Ava could take no pride in. "Of course I accept your apology, Avaleigh," she said. "It is a huge undertaking we are asking of you. It is understandable that you responded the way you did. I am sorry there was a misinterpretation of your actions."

"Thank you," Ava said as she picked up her wine glass and took a hearty swig. While she remained impressively calm and collected on the outside, inside she was a raging sea. She hated that this was a game she was going to have to play, a tête-à-tête between she and the queen that would undoubtedly come full-force at some point.

When that time came, she would be ready for it.

"Now that we've cleared the air on that matter, Avaleigh, have you considered who you'd like for your assistant? Your move to High House is only a few days away." King Orion pushed his chair back so the staff could clear away their near-empty plates. They kept their eyes down the entire time and spoke to no one.

Ava watched them with fascination. They reminded her of the worker ants they'd studied in one of the science classes she'd taken during school. Ants, like the small women who stacked plates and refilled empty glasses, worked quickly but efficiently. Their all-black uniforms made the resemblance even more uncanny.

"Um, yes," Ava replied as her dishware was whisked away and in equally as quick a motion replaced with a beautiful slice of cheesecake drizzled with strawberry puree. Though the main course had been beyond delicious, Ava knew without even tasting the dessert that this was going to be here favorite part of the meal. She forced herself to focus on the king's question instead. "My best friend. Delilah Witicker."

"And if she declines? Assistant to the queen is not an easy feat."

"She won't," Ava assured, her tone leaving no room for argument. "Delilah has wanted a place in High House since you announced the gala. Of course, she had always hoped that would come by way of being queen, but…" She shrugged and left the rest of it hanging. None of it mattered—it wasn't the king's business—and it certainly wasn't going to change anything. There was zero chance of her explaining the situation and Orion suddenly going, "Oh, well in that case, she can marry Sebastian. You are free to go."

"Perhaps we should have offered the crown to Ms. Witicker," Bernadette said. "She would have at least accepted humbly and willingly." Ava could taste the sourness of her words, despite how casual she tried to make them.

"I told you that from the start," Ava replied without missing a beat. Her fork clinked against her plate as she cut into the dessert.

King Orion set his glass down a little too hard, a drop of his drink splattering onto the table. "Are you so openly questioning my choice?" he asked his wife.

Bernadette stared down the king for a few seconds before she dropped her eyes. "Of course not," she said. "I look forward to fostering Ava into her crown. That is, if she'll let me."

Ava had thought they were done with this, but she did not miss the challenge brewing between them. Nixon's words echoed in her ears once more: *push back*. But pushing back was exactly what Bernadette expected her to do. They already had one idea of who she was; that she was a spoiled brat who didn't appreciate this "gift" she was being given. If she responded in the way the queen was hoping, she would only give merit to that belief. What she needed to do was prove to them that their perception of her was wrong, because while their opinion of her didn't *really* matter, it would affect the kind of life she had at High House.

She did not want to make it harder than it was already going to be.

"Make no mistake," she began, her eyes jumping between the king and the queen, "I will do whatever is necessary to become the queen Havaan deserves."

"There you have it," Orion said. His words shattered the silence before it could begin. "There shall be no more talk of secondary choices."

"Of course," Bernadette agreed.

"And Mother," Sebastian chimed, "I really hope you will stop trying to pick a fight with Ava."

Bernadette said nothing in reply but the look she gave her oldest son spoke volumes. The queen was not a woman who took kindly to being challenged, especially by her sons. Never had they so boldly done so. There was something about Ava, she realized as her gaze languorously traveled to her, which brazened up her son.

It was yet another thing she'd have to fix, and quick.

Bringing the conversation back to its starting point, Orion said, "We will have an invitation for Ms. Witicker delivered tomorrow. I look forward to meeting her."

"Thank you," Ava replied, sincerely. "And she, all of you. Especially you, Queen Bernadette."

There was no way for Ava to know the effect those words would have and the things they would set into motion. Things from which there would be no turning back. Things she would regret just as much as she regretted attending the gala.

But that was later.

For now, Sebastian's words echoed through the dining room.

"A toast then," he said, his earlier anger seemingly gone. He held up his wine glass and the other three followed. "To our future queen and all the fun that is to come."

"To Avaleigh," the king echoed.

Ava motioned to them all with her flute, her smile soft, forced, and then she took a swig of wine before diving back into her cheesecake.

She'd been right—it *was* her favorite part of the meal.

XI.

While King Orion asked surface-level questions of Ava throughout the meal, Bernadette stayed quiet. Sebastian chirped in occasionally, but the tension remained palpable and Ava could not have been happier when the king and queen took their leave. When Sebastian offered to show her the grounds, she agreed.

"I'm sorry dinner didn't go as planned," he said as they strolled across the spacious backyard. There was a dense forest bordering the hill and clumps of mini gardens dotted the lush grass, their pinpricks of colors like splatters of paint on a green canvas. Ava was beyond giddy when she noticed the large swimming pool, its edge so thin it gave the impression of continuing into the horizon. The stillness of the water looked like a mirror and reflected the evening sky. A million stars coated the surface with such clarity they looked tangible. She was tempted to reach her hand in and scoop them out.

"That's okay," she answered. "I think we all needed an opportunity to clear the air before I move in. Hopefully it'll make the transition smoother for everyone."

"I didn't miss the fact that while you were defending your actions, you failed to mention a change in your lack of excitement." Scrunching her nose, she looked at him sheepishly. She'd done it on purpose, avoided having to outright lie to the three of them, but leave it to Sebastian to catch such a minor thing. "Is it safe to assume it's because you're *not* excited?"

"Yes," she answered after a few contemplative steps. A chunk of her heart broke at the look of disappointment that passed over his face.

"It's not because of you, though," she added quickly. She gathered her thoughts. "I spent ten years being told girls like me weren't eligible for the crown. So I never got excited about it. I didn't dot my I's with little hearts as I tacked your last name onto my first. I just…didn't care. But I want to be excited about this," she insisted, because she really did. "I don't want to feel bummed every time I think about the future. If I could flip a switch, I would, but unfortunately I can't."

She looked at him then, pointedly stared into his eyes and tried to convey the truth of her words. She wanted him to understand, because as much as she disliked his parents, she felt connected to Sebastian. They were both being tossed into the same crazy situation. They would become a steadfast point for one another, and she looked forward to that.

Nodding his head repeatedly, like a fishing bobber in the water, Sebastian replied, "I can respect that. It's a good thing my excitement is based purely on the fact that you're gorgeous." He gave her a playful half smile when she gasped, her mouth agape. Then his face and tone changed, both serious once more. "I will give you however much time you need, if you can promise me one thing."

"And what would that be?"

Sebastian stopped walking and Ava had to back-track a step to stand in front of him. He reached for her hands and she let him hold them tightly in his own. As he ran his thumbs across her knuckles, there was a soft tickle in the back of her knees, as if someone had brushed a feather there. "Promise me you won't take ten years to find joy in being my wife. That seems like a large chunk of time to be married to someone who isn't all that fond of you." He gave her a slow grin. Ava couldn't help but return it, along with a few amused chuckles.

"I promise you I will do my very best."

"That is all anyone can ask of another," Sebastian replied as he brought her hands to his lips. He kissed the top of each before dropping only one. He intertwined their fingers, and she would be lying if she said it wasn't a nice, somewhat missed feeling.

"Do you have much to do before the big move?" he asked as they passed the all-glass greenhouse tucked securely in the corner of the garden.

"So much," she sighed. "Mostly just sorting all of my stuff and deciding what's appropriate to bring and what should be left behind. Speaking of, this may be a dumb question, but what sort of attire is expected?" She hadn't failed to miss the queen's sleek jumper or the king's dress-pants with simple red polo. She'd even felt a bit overdressed, which *never* happened.

"That's not a stupid question," the prince reassured. "Anytime there's an event where we're expected to be front and center, like the gala, the Welcome Dinner, our wedding, formal wear is required. Any other time, the dress code is what mother calls 'always ready casual.' Meaning if we unexpectedly need to meet with someone or make an appearance, we're ready to go."

"I take it old jeans and overly worn t-shirts don't fall into either of those categories?"

Sebastian laughed. "I'm afraid not."

"Bummer," she grumbled at her confirmed suspicions. "Looks like I'll have to add 'update wardrobe' to my list of things to do."

"You should have someone with you when you go," Sebastian replied without missing a beat.

"I will," Ava assured just as quickly. "Delilah would kill me if I didn't bring her along."

With amused green eyes, her silver-haired prince smirked at her. "While I'm sure Miss Witicker is capable of taking care of herself, as well as you, she isn't necessarily who I had in mind."

"Yeah, I know," she affirmed with a clearly annoyed huff.

"Did you and Nixon really get along well?" he asked.

"I guess," Ava said, thankful that her voice didn't shake. Just thinking about him painted a new coat of guilt on her conscience. "I forgot he was even there sometimes, which I'm pretty sure says a lot more about me than it does him," she joked.

"And do you have a spare room at your house?" he asked.

She looked at him with a raised eyebrow, perplexed by the new direction of their conversation. "Yes..." she answered, dragging the single word out and tossing a question-mark at the end.

"Then Nixon shall stay with you until the Welcome Dinner."

She pulled her hand away, the gesture an emphasis on her words. "I don't need a babysitter." Especially one who distracted her as much as the guard did. She would get nothing done if constantly worried if he was comfortable, if he was enjoying himself. It wasn't only unwarranted, but an interruption to the last few days of normalcy she would have. How many more of those days was the royal family going to take from her, without her permission, without even giving her a choice?

"Ava," Sebastian said in the tone that told her he was already over the argument he knew was coming. "People are going to begin piecing together who and what you are. This isn't a question of whether or not you can protect yourself, but an extra precaution in case there's a moment when you can't."

By all the stars in Havaan, she wanted to argue. She was already tired of being forced into things by the damn Calder family. "Why do I have a feeling he's going to end up at my house whether I agree or not?"

Sebastian's lips twitched, testing a smile. "I'm sure he would prefer a bed to the hard ground."

Ava glared at him for a moment, and then an idea formed. "I'll accept without complaint if I can ask something of *you*."

"You are going to be my wife," Sebastian said. "You are free to ask anything of me, and I promise to do my best to deliver."

The narrow of her eyes decreased ever so slightly. "My mother…she has a difficult time managing her emotions. She's a rollercoaster most days, and it's just the two of us. I'm worried what will happen when it's just her." Ava took a deep breath and let it out slowly, her cheeks puffing at the same time. Telling Sebastian about Cordellia was scary. But to get what she wanted, doing so was essential. She just hoped it didn't create a gateway for more secrets to spill out.

"I've heard rumors about medications," she said, "remedies that she can take to make sure she's okay. To stabilize her. But they're incredibly difficult to gain access to."

"Say nothing more," the prince said. "I will see to it that your mother gets what she needs."

Ava thought she was going to cry. Relief sat heavy in her chest. Honestly, she hadn't expected Sebastian to confirm the existence of said tinctures. The crown would have its citizens believe such mental instabilities weren't feasible in a place like Havaan. Acknowledging the existence of these stabilizers admitted the opposite. It proved there were flaws in Havaan's veneer, and one little crack could shatter the whole thing.

"Is she one of the reasons you're so against becoming queen?" Sebastian asked once she'd peppered him with appreciative thank yous.

Nodding, Ava replied, "She's never been on her own. I've always been there to hold her up when she can't do it."

"I can understand your reluctance even more now."

Offering him a soft smile, Ava squeezed his fingers before he linked their hands together again. "Let me walk you to the car, and then I'll go tell Nixon. It won't take him much time to gather clothing for the next few days. When you plan to do your shopping, send word, and I'll make sure to have the market cleared out for you."

"That seems unnecessary."

"You're already limited on time. Having to weave through a crowd would only be a hindrance. You will come to find that being a member of the royal family has many perks. Having the marketplace to yourself is just one of them. It will, with time, become easier to accept the others."

"Having no choice in things isn't one of them as well, I hope," she said, the words mixed with a playful seriousness. The point was driven home by the look she gave Sebastian.

"It'll be better once you're here. I promise."

She chose not to express her doubt as they approached the sleek car. Ramiro was already waiting with the back door hanging open.

"I appreciate you coming tonight. And for amusing my need to keep you safe. Even though the latter is with great reluctance."

"Wouldn't want to change things up too much," Ava answered.

The prince grinned at her, pure delight twinkling in his candy-apple eyes. "I so look forward to having you here." He leaned into her, invading her personal space, and kissed her on the corner of her mouth. When he pulled away, he held her attention for a moment then turned to Ramiro. "Nixon will be joining you momentarily."

Ramiro tipped his head to the prince, who gave Ava one last wave before he vanished into High House. Giving the dark-haired, muscular chauffeur a quick glance and light smile, Ava slid into the car and waited for Nixon.

She wondered if Nixon would risk arguing with Sebastian, even though he—like Ava—knew it would be for nothing; or if he would pack a bag, quietly resigned to doing whatever the prince ordered. What if he was angry? What if he blamed *her* for this needless provision? If that were indeed the case, the next few days would prove to be even less enjoyable than she already imagined.

As she was worrying these thoughts over and over, the front door opened. A flood of yellow spilled onto the porch before being eclipsed by Nixon's frame. He stopped inside the doorway and said a few words to someone. Then, with a large duffle bag slung over his shoulder, he walked to the car. He handed the bag to Ramiro, and as he was placing it in the trunk, Nixon slid in beside her. The shift in the air was obvious.

"I'm sorry," Ava whispered, almost immediately.

He turned to her and raised an eyebrow in question. "For what?" he asked. He didn't sound mad. In fact, he sounded...happy?

Ava shrugged. "That you still have to babysit me."

"As long as I don't have to change any diapers, I'm fine." He winked before giving her a quick glimpse of his sanity-ending grin. She wondered if it would ever stop having the effect on her that it did. She knew she should want it to, but not yet.

"Mom and I have been working pretty hard at the whole potty training thing. You should be off the hook for that one." Ava caught Ramiro's laughing brown eyes in the mirror before she and Nixon settled into casual conversation. Occasionally she would lean through the divide in the seats and pull Ramiro into it, as well. She learned that not only was he a driver for the royal family—of which there were two others—he was also a guard and one of the trainers for the fleet. He had a wife, two sons, and an infant daughter, all whom he loved dearly.

It was obvious he and Nixon had a bond from the way they joked and teased one another. Now that the seal had been broken, and Nixon had revealed human emotions, he laughed freely, his chuckles vibrating in his chest like thunder. Ava couldn't remember the last time she'd been so content or when she'd laughed until her sides hurt. There hadn't been much of it in the last few days, but she was glad the tears forming in her eyes now were not from anger or frustration or any other emotion on that side of the scale.

When the car stopped in front of her house, her disappointment hummed like the porch light. She and Nixon unloaded and bid farewell to Ramiro, who expressed his great joy in the king's choice.

"I look forward to many more nights like this with you," he said out of the window before shifting into drive and gliding away from them.

Ava mused, "I like him." Her words dripped with sincerity.

"He seems taken with you, as well."

When the two-some pushed their way into the house, Cordellia was standing at the counter, bent over a piece of paper while a cup of tea steeped next to her. It filled the air with raspberries, hibiscus flowers, lemon and orange zest.

Cordellia, her hair a frazzled, messy braid, did a double-take when her daughter and Nixon entered the house. "You're back," she stated, adding, "Both of you."

Ava exhaled through her nose and nodded. "Long story, but Nixon is staying with us until the Welcome Dinner."

"He is?" Cordellia replied, leaning her hip against the counter. "I can't wait to hear the long story, but I am happy to have you, Nixon."

"Thank you, Ms. Toliver."

"Cordellia," she reminded as she pulled her teabag from the mug and set it on a plate. "The guest room is all set with fresh linens. The closet and dresser are both empty, so please make yourself at home. Would either of you like a cup of tea before I retire for the evening?" Ava smiled at the question. It was a rare sight to see her mother so cohesive, effortlessly existing in the world. She longed for days like these, but they were becoming fewer and further between. She crossed her fingers that Sebastian would be able to get his hands on whatever medication Cordellia needed, because if the past proved anything, these types of days would be coming to an end soon. Ava could not stomach the idea of her mother sinking into the pit of despair in which she so often lived without having someone—or something—to coax her out.

Ava and Nixon both shook their heads at the offer of tea. "I'm still pretty stuffed from dinner," Ava said, poking at her stomach. Behind her, Nixon laughed from the back of his throat. She glared at him over her shoulder, but the tilt of her lips assured him that it was all in jest.

"Well, then I am going to head to bed. I've got another busy day tomorrow, but I look forward to hearing all about your evening."

Cordellia smoothed the back of Ava's hair with her hand then pulled her near and kissed her forehead. "Help him get settled."

"I'll think about it."

Cordellia looked at her daughter, her eyes soft and full of love. Then she turned her attention to Nixon. "Let us know if you need anything, okay?" He nodded once, firmly, his dark strands flicking with the movement. He ran both hands through his hair then, pushing it back. The ends fell a little below his earlobes, but not in a feminine way. There was nothing feminine about him, from the square cut of his jaw to his strong, defined physique...

"Avaleigh." Her mother's stern voice interrupted her thoughts.

She blinked a few times. "Mmhm?"

"Did you hear what I said?" Ava, afraid to speak for fear of drooling, simply shook her head. "I said that maybe we could find some time tomorrow to go over the design for your crown."

"Oh. Sure."

With a final, unreadable look at her child and a shared, amused one with the guard, Cordellia bid the two of them goodnight then took the stairs to her bedroom, cup of tea in hand. Ava would be surprised if she made it halfway through the brew before she zonked out.

Ava turned on her toes and straightened her spine, her arms hanging rigidly at her side. Then she put on a charming accent and asked, "Would you like to head up to your suite, sir?" Nixon did his best to keep a straight face but his lips contorted with the effort. "Shut up," Ava said, punching him in the arm. Her knuckles stung immediately. *I really need to stop doing that,* she scolded as pain lanced through her cradled hand.

Unable to control himself any longer, Nixon let out a full-belly laugh. Before he could see the blush on her cheeks, Ava started up the stairs. Nixon followed behind.

"You're cute," he said between dying chuckles.

"Careful," Ava warned as she leaned her back against the closed door of the guestroom. She dropped her voice a level. "People might think you're flirting with me."

"We wouldn't want that now, would we?" he replied, bringing his voice down even lower. The vibrato clenched her stomach and her brain sent a quick SOS to the rest of her body.

"We definitely wouldn't want that," she whispered. "Seeing how I'm technically engaged to the prince. You know. Your not-by-blood brother."

"It's super creepy when you say it like that." Nixon's eyes were bright, even in the darkness of the doorway.

She smiled but said nothing more as the door fell open behind her. Nixon entered the room and flipped the light switch.

Seeing the room hurt in a way Ava had not been expecting. It hadn't been used in the two years since Zarah's passing, and yet Ava had half expected Zarah to be pacing around.

She had been Cordellia's best friend since they were teenagers. When she'd seen how hard a time Cordellia was having with life after Dante, she'd moved in and never left. Zarah had no children of her own, but she'd loved Ava as if she'd carried her in her womb.

The bedroom welcomed them with the lingering hint of Zarah's lavender lotion, almost as though a few drops had bled into the carpet fibers. It made Ava's eyes well instantly. She couldn't help but wish her other mother was here, especially during this monumental part of her life. Would she be happy for her? Or would she, like Ava, find the whole thing ludicrous?

"You are meant for great things," Zarah had once told her. "So be great at them."

Was this one of those great things of which she'd spoken?

"Are you alright?" she heard Nixon ask. It was quickly becoming a very common question.

The look she gave him was sad and made the nod of her head unconvincing. "I'm good." She swallowed the lie, not wanting to share Zarah with him quite yet. *One day, maybe, but not tonight.* She was giving so much to the royal family and had already revealed a bigger part of herself to Nixon than she had ever intended. She wasn't ready to give him this.

Thankfully, Nixon didn't press her, though he did look at her skeptically before dropping his duffle bag on the bed. Then he put his hands on his hips and surveyed the small room, taking in the storm grey wallpaper, with its faint pattern of ivy, and the freshly made bed with white bedding. Ava had a fleeting image of the bed being too small for him, of his feet sticking out of the blankets and dangling over the edge. She covered her giggle with a cough then gave Nixon the rest of the upstairs tour, which consisted of the bathroom and linen closet.

"Help yourself to whatever you need," Ava said as she walked the few steps to her bedroom door. "I'll check on you before I head to bed."

Though he looked like he wanted to say more than, "It has been a long day for the both of us," he settled for that, then tipped his head to her before vanishing into the bedroom. The latch of the door clicked softly.

Ava stood in the hallway for a handful of breaths wondering what he was doing, if he was changing into his pajamas or doing the thousand pushups she assumed he did daily. But that pesky pang of guilt snaked around her conscience, stopping her thoughts before they got too out of control.

Nixon was dangerous and his close proximity was equally so. It would be different if she was just a citizen and he was just a guard and they'd caught each other's eye at the gala, or the market, or any place in Havaan. In another world, in another reality, her attraction to him would be acceptable. There would come a time, very soon, when even looking at him the way she did would be inappropriate.

"I just have to get through the next couple of days and then my time with him will be limited." She cleared from the bed the piles of clothing that, just this morning, she'd thought would be acceptable to take with her. She couldn't wait to tell Delilah the news about her required wardrobe facelift.

She changed into a pair of baggy black workout pants and pink t-shirt while she listened for the bathroom sink to turn off. She tracked Nixon's footsteps from the washroom to the bedroom as she pulled her hair loose from all the pins and clips it had taken to secure her mane into the tight French twist. She tousled her curls with quick fingers and they settled into a messy mass of spirals. Delilah had said for years how Ava's hair looked difficult, that the twists and turns of it seemed cumbersome and exhausting to deal with. Sometimes it *was* frustrating, especially when pieces wouldn't lay the way she wanted, but Ava had always loved her hair. The fullness of it; the plush softness that was like lying on a woolly sheep past shearing. Most importantly, it was one of the few features she shared with her father. Though she remembered nothing of him or the few months they'd spent together, her hair was one of those biological traits that would always remind her of him and keep them connected.

After washing her face and brushing her teeth, she did as promised and stopped by Nixon's temporary room. She didn't knock right away, but instead listened to the old squeaks and exhausted sighs from the bed. There was an ache in her chest at the ghostly reminders of Zarah's existence. Once she was sure she wasn't going to cry, Ava rapped the door with her knuckles. When his hearty voice welcomed her in, she nudged the door open with her toe. Nixon glanced up from the large book perched on his tented knees.

"Do you have enough pillows and blankets?" she asked, resting against the doorframe.

"I have plenty. Thank you for asking, though."

"That's all you're getting from me in terms of hospitality," she joked. "This isn't a hotel."

"Does that mean I shouldn't expect breakfast in bed?"

Ava laughed. "Absolutely not. But you can expect breakfast downstairs at the table with the rest of us common folk."

He smiled, all his teeth on display and Ava had to steel herself for the effect it had. *He's so damn hot,* her inner voice reminded, as if she'd ever be able to forget.

"That'll be just as fine."

They looked at one another for a few breaths then Ava inhaled slowly. "I'll let you get back to your reading. I just wanted to say goodnight. And while I'm still sorry you got stuck watching over me, I'm glad you're here."

"Me, too," he replied. "You're pretty easy to guard."

"It's unfortunate we're not putting those fine protecting skills to use. Maybe I'll cause some trouble tomorrow," she teased, although a part of her really did want to see just how well he handled his weapons.

"I'll make sure to get plenty of sleep so I can keep up with whatever you throw at me."

"Good," she said. "You're gonna need it." She tossed him a wink and a sly smile before going into her room.

As soon as her body hit the mattress and her head the pillows, she had barely enough time to get the blankets tucked around her before Mr. Sandman pulled her under. She welcomed his lover's embrace, as well as the scent of minty cotton that carried her deep into her slumber.

XII.

Nixon ran his hand down the side of Ava's face, his palm cupping her jaw as her lips grazed the coarse prickles of his stubble. Lost in his embrace, focused on only him, she almost didn't hear the creak from the side of the bed. But she did, and when she looked, she found Sebastian, his face contorted in both rage and pain at finding his best friend and his *wife*—she looked at the gold band—

Ava gasped as she sat up in her bed, the glint of the ring forcing her awake. She brought her hands to her chest, her heart thudding relentlessly under her ribcage, and glanced down. There was no vow of promise wrapped around her finger like a vice. Though she finally managed to get the arrhythmia in her chest under control, she failed to keep the images of her dream from replaying like a choppy, sloppily spliced movie.

As she flopped back down against her pillow and stared at the crosshatching on her ceiling, she rationalized her dream—why it was she'd ended up in Nixon's arms—with the fact that she'd been around him more than she had Sebastian. In her dream, she had been where she'd belonged, like the water and the shore. But Nixon wasn't the man she was to marry.

Sebastian isn't the worst choice for a husband, she'd had to remind herself multiple times since the Welcome Dinner. He would be a good husband and she could be a good wife, and with time she was certain she could come to love him as was expected.

"Maybe I'll even be able to love him with the same intensity my mother loved my father," she tried to convince the shadows. She rolled over to face the window. A blanket of soft grey settled on the horizon, waiting to welcome the day. Ava lay awake for a while, listening to the sounds of her house and the shifting groans of the bed the next room over.

Each one brought with it a flash of skin, of hands, of lips on lips...

After an hour, the images became too overwhelming. Instead of waiting for morning to greet her, she tugged a hooded sweatshirt over her pajama top, pushed her feet into a pair of old slippers, made a cup of blackberry tea with far too much sugar, and shuffled into the backyard to meet the sun.

The world was tranquil, the faint chirping of bird song the only sound, the beginning soundtrack to a new day. As she sat sipping her tea, her body warming from the inside out, it was the first time in a long while—even beyond the last few days—that Ava's mind was completely still.

The next thing she knew, someone was shaking her gently, a deep hum of a voice repeating her name. Her eyes opened slowly and when they did, she was peering into honey.

"Morning," Nixon said, smirking down at her.

"Hey," Ava answered, her voice thick with sleep. She cleared her throat and sat up, looking around. Gone was the taupe haze of predawn and the silence it possessed. It had been replaced with the vibrant sun sitting high in the sky and the symphony of a Thursday morning. Her muscles protested as she stood. She gathered her tea cup from the ground, where she'd apparently placed it before crashing out, and looked at Nixon. His hair was tied away from his face and a shadow of stubble coated his jaw. Seeing it made her lips tingle and she looked away quickly.

"How'd you sleep?" she asked him as they moved into the house.

"Mostly on my stomach," he replied from behind her. She looked at him over her shoulder and rolled her eyes. "In terms of quality of sleep, though, it was fine. More comfortable than a chair, I'm sure."

"That was only for a few minutes," she said, assumed, as she placed her cup in the sink. Then she faced him and hoisted her body onto the countertop at the same time. "Where are you off to?" she questioned as she took in his black athletic pants, plain mint-green t-shirt and white sneakers.

Nixon leaned casually against the wall across from her, his muscular forearms crossed over his chest. "For a quick run. We train every morning at High House, but I don't imagine you have a full facility for such tucked away here, so a jog will have to suffice. Would you care to join me?"

Ava shook her head, loose pieces of hair whipping around her face. "Pass. But I *will* make sure breakfast is ready by the time you get home." Nixon raised a brow at her. "Back here, I mean. To my home." She hoped her awkward smile would distract from the color creeping into her cheeks.

"Breakfast sounds great," he answered, returning her grin, but with a genuine one.

"Okay cool, awesome." Ava hopped off the counter and moved to the fridge. She needed something—anything—to distract herself. Every time she looked at Nixon, every word he spoke and each flash of a smile rolled the images of her dream on a loop. They were starting to feel like memories instead of a fantasy and filling her with a false belief that she could have him…

"Have a nice run," she said to the food.

She could feel the heat of his gaze on her back, heard his footsteps as he came closer. She held her breath at their halt and exhaled at the opening of the door as he left.

"Good morning," he said, causing her to glance up.

"And to you," Delilah replied, her voice rising curiously as she stepped into the house. Her neck craned as she watched him.

Nixon's "See you for breakfast," filtered in a second before Delilah closed the door. She turned her head slowly, cocking it as she looked at Ava, her eyebrows raised as if to say *you better explain.*

Ava held up her hands, proclaiming her innocence. "Sebastian's idea. Apparently, he was worried about the fallout from our meeting at the market."

"So he gave you protection in the form of the hottest guy in all of Havaan?" Delilah practically swooned. "He's so considerate."

As she began gathering food and dishes for breakfast, Ava made a valid effort to change the subject. "You're up early," she said. Delilah had a habit of sleeping in until almost lunchtime except for one thing: shopping. Then she was unable to sleep past the cracking of dawn. But shopping was not on the agenda today, though this was the point at which Ava explained the need to get an entire new arsenal of clothing. Delilah was, as expected, beyond excited and Ava made a note to 'send word' that the mission would begin tomorrow afternoon.

"How was dinner last night?" Delilah asked over the cracking of eggs.

"Ugh," Ava groaned, whisking them more violently than necessary, an observation Delilah did not fail to mention before Ava told her everything from start to finish—at least the events of her time at High House. She kept the car ride out of the story. Nothing about *that* needed to be reiterated. Ramiro had witnessed the close proximity the two had shared, and while Avaleigh doubted he would ever say anything to anyone, that was already one too many opportunities for the prince to find out and think something conspiratorial of it.

"It was…okay though, I guess," she finished while flipping the strips of sizzling bacon.

"And you got a new roomie for a few days," Delilah said, wiggling her eyebrows. Ava laughed dryly and shook her head. "Did he sleep with you?"

Ava blanched, of this she was sure, and swallowed the lump in her throat. "Of course not," she answered. "He slept in Zarah's room. The guestroom," she amended.

Her best friend looked at her with sorrowful eyes. "That must have been weird for you." Ava smiled sadly. She loved this version of Delilah. The gentle soul who had written a gym-excuse note, signed in an almost perfect replica of Cordellia's elegant flourish, when Ava started her period in sixth grade.

"You know what we haven't done in a long time," Delilah started. She snagged a piece of bacon from the plate, narrowly missing Ava's swat, and popped it into her mouth. Ava flashed angry eyes at her as she pushed the lever on the toaster down. She then pressed the START button on the coffee maker, the water gurgling and releasing the aroma of freshly ground beans into the air.

"We haven't done a lot of things in a long time," Ava said.

"True," Delilah agreed, "but I'm talking specifically about having a sleepover."

Ava raised a brow higher than normal. "That's because we're not children anymore."

"I know that," D replied. She rolled her eyes at her best friend as she took the stack of plates from her and began setting them around the table. "This is the last time we'll be able to do it here, though."

Nearly convinced by the tease of sadness in her voice, Ava almost believed her friend. "This wouldn't have anything to do with Nixon staying here as well, would it?" she asked.

Delilah feigned surprise. "How dare you!" she joked. "It has *everything* to do with him."

Before she could help it, Ava found herself not only in a fit of giggles but also agreeing to the sleepover. Delilah's reminder, although done entirely for selfish reasons, really had touched Ava. There were a lot of things that would be her last in the house where she'd grown up. The next two nights would be the last ones spent in her bed, in her nursery turned big-girl room. There were only a handful more meals she would prepare in this kitchen, in a space that held endless memories; some good and some bad. She had fallen to the linoleum floor like a house made of feathers in a storm when Connor had broken up with her, but she had also spent hours with Delilah at the kitchen table, painting their nails and playing Checkers™ while ranking the hotness of guys at their school.

It was in these memories which she was trapped when Nixon returned. The closing of the door pushed her back to reality, to the almost-burnt bacon still in the pan and the getting-cold toast that had popped in the toaster.

"Shit!" Ava grabbed for the pan and lifted it from the heat as quickly as possible.

"Shit is right," Delilah sighed next to her.

Following D's line of sight, all the air in Ava's lungs stopped moving. The pounding of her heart echoed like voices in a cave. Nixon stood in the kitchen, sweat soaking his shirt. Pieces of his hair had come loose from the hair-tie and framed his face. She was pretty sure his shallow, quick breaths matched hers. Next to her, Delilah's mouth hung open as if her jaw had disconnected from her skull. Ava reached over, pushing it closed.

"Hey," she finally said as the heat from the skillet's handle began to burn her palm. She set it into the sink then acknowledged the spread on the island with a wave of her hands. "Breakfast is ready."

Nixon nodded once. "I can see that," he said between deep breaths. "I'll grab a shower then join you."

"Do you need help?" Delilah blurted. Then she slowly turned to Ava. Her brown eyes were large and round, screaming *help me!*

"With getting everything else out?" Ava asked, not entirely convincing. Delilah, afraid of speaking, just nodded repeatedly. "Sure." Pinching her best friend on the hip, where Nixon couldn't see below the island, Ava addressed the guard. "Towels are in the linen closet in the hallway. Take your time. We'll keep it warm."

Nixon looked between the two women, with their forced smiles, and chuckled. Then he winked at Delilah—who all but melted into a gooey mess—before he ascended the stairs.

Ava shook her head at her best friend, laughing to herself at first then breaking into another fit. After scowling at her for a few seconds, and once her embarrassment passed, Delilah joined her. Cordellia entered the kitchen minutes later, wrapped in a light blue cotton robe, her thick hair braided down her back. She got her coffee and settled at the table while the other two filled her in on Delilah's Freudian slip.

"I get it, Delilah," Cordellia said, grinning.

"Mother!" Ava's outcry set the three women into another bout of giggles that lasted until they heard the water shut off. By the time Nixon emerged, his hair wet but non-dripping, they'd regained their composure. The conversation flowed as easily as the orange juice and coffee creamer. They passed the serving dishes around and loaded their plates, then dived into the warm meal while enjoying the company of one another.

It had been a very long time since they'd had more than just Cordellia and Ava—more often than not, just Ava—at the table, partaking in a large, hearty meal together. As she sat back and took it all in, Ava's heart crumbled a little over the realization that in a few short days the faces of the people she would enjoy meals with would change. As sobering as it was, those days were still a bit off. She would, she vowed, enjoy the moments while she could and worry about High House later.

Zarah had a nephew named Ryder. He was only a year older than Ava and had spent every summer with his Aunt Z starting at age nine. It was weird at first, having a boy around, but by the time they were teenagers, both Ava and Delilah found themselves looking forward to the week when Ryder was around.

They spent nights camped out in the backyard or under elaborate blanket forts in the living room. They would ride their bikes to the market and spend an entire day at the carnival when it was erected in

Brene. Ryder was perhaps the one boy Delilah had never been crazy over, though the same could not be said for Ava.

One summer night, when Ryder was fourteen and Ava thirteen, he kissed her on the bridge connecting Meridian and Typhony. They kissed many more times that summer and the ones following. Their weird summer-love never got in the way of the trio, however, or the adventures they had for seven days every year.

Having Nixon around reminded Ava of those summers. Though there was no kissing with Nixon, there *were* many hours spent joking and laughing while he and Delilah kept Ava company during her sorting and packing. The three of them meshed as if they'd known one another their entire lives. Delilah also provided a buffer from the occasional flirting of Ava and Nixon. There was very little time when Nixon wasn't with the women. Not because Ava needed to be guarded while at home, but because he genuinely enjoyed their company as much as they enjoyed his.

The only time the two left Ava's side was when Nixon borrowed Cordellia's rarely driven convertible to take Delilah home so she could get sleepover necessities and to give word to Sebastian that they would venture to the market the following day at noon.

As Ava watched the two speed off down the road, Delilah's hands thrown in the air as the wind blew her pink-gold hair behind her, she felt the gut-punch of jealousy.

This is good, she had to remind herself as she rubbed the pain from her chest. Maybe the two of them would fall in love and get married, raise their children alongside those of Sebastian and Ava. It was a nice enough thought, if nothing more.

Taking advantage of the alone time, Ava wandered downstairs. For as long as she could remember, the basement had never been anything other than Cordellia's workspace. There had only been a few jars of jewels when she was little—perhaps that was all she could see at her small height—but now the built-in shelving unit was stuffed with glasses, boxes and other sorts of containers full of gemstones in varying sizes, colors, shapes and density. There was also yard after yard of chain—gold, silver, platinum, even black—and all the accoutrements that went with creating the elaborate and regal pieces from which Cordellia made her living.

It was at least ten degrees warmer downstairs than in the rest of the house, and there was a continuous haze of silver and gold in the air; infinitesimal particles that danced like fireflies in the beams of the bright lights hanging from the ceiling. Growing up, Ava had loved spending time here. She would tuck herself in the corner of the couch with a book and listen to her mother hum while she worked.

When she worked.

Cordellia was a master at what she did, and it seemed at times that the hours she spent slaving away were the only minutes of peace she allowed herself; a few hours reprieve from her mourning and feelings of failure as a mother. She could never forgive herself for not meeting the standards of parenting and livelihood that she herself had set.

When Dante died, so too did all her dreams.

"I don't know how fancy you want to get with your crown," Cordellia said as she laid out ten or so roughly sketched ideas, "but having the future queen living in my house means I don't have to try and guess."

Ava smiled at the pieces of paper in front of her. They were all so different, some with many embellishments and others with very few. Ava, being the simple girl she was, was instantly drawn to the latter, but there was also a subtle flair of excitement when her eyes scanned over the ones that were a bit....more.

There was one, above all, which stood out the most. The band (also known as a circlet) was solid. Instead of the traditional spikes, they were twisted and bent to look like flowers. The one in the middle was largest, a jagged rose, surrounded by squared-looking daisies, carnations and metal dahlias. The flowers did not go fully around the circlet, but stopped three-quarters of the way back. It was the most elegant flower crown Ava had ever seen and perfect in every sense of the word.

"This one," Ava said, jabbing it with her finger.

Cordellia smiled. "That one's my favorite. I tried to envision what sort of crown would look best on you and this one felt the most honest."

As Cordellia wrapped a measuring tape around Ava's head and jotted down all sorts of notes that meant nothing to Ava, she said, as nonchalantly as if she were discussing the dinner plans for the evening, "It would be best to not mention anything about your father to the king and queen."

Ava looked at her mother. It took her a few seconds to even be sure the topic had actually veered that way. "That should be pretty easy," she said. "I don't *know* anything about him." Her voice shook with uncontained anger.

Sighing, Cordellia sat on the arm of the couch, looking up at her daughter. Ava hadn't realized it until just that moment, but the years had, at some point, attached themselves to her mother. Her face was etched with worry lines and her eyes had lost some of their luster. Ava was immediately filled with worry about leaving her. *Will she be okay when I'm gone?* she wondered, too afraid of the answer to ask the question aloud.

As a child, Cordellia had had two wonderful parents. When Dante came along, he filled her days with love and wonder. Within a year her parents died, then Dante was gone but Zarah was there, until she passed away. But still she wasn't alone because Ava existed.

Someone had always been around, but in a couple of days there would be no one.

"Avaleigh," she started, her voice sounding older as well, "I haven't kept information about your father from you because it isn't important. I've done it to protect you, so that no one can ever use him against you. I would have loved—I *would* love to—tell you everything about him, about the wonderful man who helped create you." She flicked away a fallen tear. "But it's safer the less you know."

"That doesn't make any sense though, Mom," Ava contended. "It's not as if you were holding out all of these years because you expected me to become queen. What if I hadn't gone to that gala? What if none of this had happened? Would you *ever* tell me anything?"

"When the time was right," was all Cordellia said back. Ava was so tired of hearing that—it was the same excuse her mother gave her every single time she asked about Dante. As she opened her mouth to argue, her mother took her hands in her own calloused ones and looked at her child with desperate eyes. "One day though, when you're officially queen, I will tell you anything you want to know, okay?"

She had never been more confused about her father in all her life. That confusion brought a whole new list of questions, like why was he such a secret? And just who was Cordellia so insistent on keeping him a secret *from*? She knew she would get no answers at this time, which left her with no other option but to agree.

"I'm going to hold you to that," she half-joked.

"I expect nothing less from you." Her mother smiled and kissed her forehead. Then she rested the palm of her hand on the soft jawline of her child and looked at her the way only a mother could: with extreme pride and deep love and a resigned sadness at having to let her go. "I love you," she said, the creases at the corner of her eyes crinkling.

"I know," Ava teased before giving her mother a tight squeeze.

From above came a stomping of feet and a trill of laughter as Nixon and Delilah burst into the house. "They're heeere," Ava said in an ominous voice. Cordellia giggled into her hand and swatted at her daughter with a piece of paper.

"Go be with your friends."

"You'll join us for dinner, yeah?" Ava insisted when she was half-way up the stairs. Getting her mother to eat daily was sometimes a struggle, especially when she was overwhelmed with orders. Which, judging by the chaos on her desk, was her current state. Cordellia nodded though. Ava smiled tightly then hurried up the stairs, where she was instantly swept up in the barrage of merriment.

One summer, Ryder and Ava built an uneven but useable bonfire pit off-center in the backyard. When Ryder stayed with Zarah and the weather was nice it was often put to good use. They—along with Delilah and sometimes the adults—would watch logs burn and listen to the popping of the flames while licking melted marshmallow from their fingertips. It had been years since the pit had been used, since the charring of wood filled the air, but sitting around it again flooded Ava with fond memories and gave her a warm, calming sense of resolution.

It was hard to believe that this would be her last night at Holland Avenue Number Six.

They had utilized the rarely used grill Thursday night to cook seared steaks and corn on the cob. While Nixon manned the barbeque, Delilah had whipped up a decadent chocolate cake. Everything between the four of them felt natural. Not for the first time, Ava couldn't help but wonder what her life would have been like if Dante hadn't been on that boat nineteen years ago. Would her parents have had another child who liked to bake things like cookies and cakes? Would Ava have brought home the guys she dated—guys like Nixon—who would hang out with her father around the grill as they discussed guy stuff?

Regardless of those answers, and the ones to the thousand other questions that ran through her mind daily, she was certain of two things: one, her life would have been incredibly different; and two, this Friday night would have been just like any other, instead of the bitter one it was becoming.

Things had happened so quickly over the last week, from the start of the gala to this very moment. Her entire life had begun around a campfire, when the blue eyes of her father had met the grey ones of her mother. The irony that *that* life was ending around one, too, was not lost on her.

When she looked across the curling flames and her eyes locked with Nixon's, the gold of his irises heated her almost as much as the fire. She allowed herself time to appreciate his beauty. The lines of his face were hidden in the shadows, while the light from the fire painted the highpoints in an ember's glow. *Is this how my parents felt?* she wondered. *Was their attraction to one another as palpable as ours?*

She'd noticed his covert glances through the last few days, the way he sometimes seemed lost while looking at her. While she wanted to deny there was an attraction between them, it was impossible. She'd had yet another dream about him, this one interrupted not by Sebastian's presence but by Nixon's name caught in her throat. She'd avoided waking Delilah, thankfully, but had spent the rest of the night curled up in Cordellia's bed.

Now it was just the two of them, separated by a small fire and a hint of melted chocolate in the air.

Nixon's deep voice cut through the violin sounds of crickets and the hooted laughter of owls. "Are you worried about tomorrow?" he asked with knowingness in his voice. She contemplated lying but instead nodded her head. "Is it because of what is being asked of you?"

Sighing, Ava gathered her hair over her shoulder and pulled her knees into her chest. "I don't worry about being queen," she started. "I get the importance of it and I understand the honor. There's even a tiny part of me that is kind of excited about the whole thing. I'm not indifferent to being queen. It's the fact that nothing is being *asked* of me. I'm being told I have to do all of this, and no one asked if I was okay with it." She hated how weak her voice sounded, and that even after six days she was still emotional about the whole ordeal. She wanted, so desperately, to be the strong, brave woman everyone kept insisting she was. But she was still just a twenty-year-old being forced into a life—a future, a marriage—over which she had no say.

"I imagine you do not do well with being told what to do," the guard replied, his lips twitching in amusement.

She shrugged and gave him a look that said *what can I tell ya?* It was followed by a small smile when he chuckled. It was quickly becoming one of her favorite sounds.

Having Nixon around had surprisingly been fun—something that didn't happen much at High House from what he'd told her. Keeping Havaan operating sounded mechanical: training, meetings, dinners, traveling, speeches, functions, soirees. "There isn't room for fun," Nixon had said. "Even the galas and parties are done for political reasons."

If she hadn't already been unimpressed by everything, that would have been enough to convince her to hightail it out of town.

But she didn't—couldn't—so instead they sat wordlessly for a few minutes and watched the dying flames creep along the last bits of untouched wood, charring every spot it licked. "I don't want to lose myself in the madness of the crown," she admitted. She looked up at him slowly, the fear and sadness in her deep blue eyes made his heart break.

He wanted to reach through the fire and comfort her, but instead he simply replied, "Then don't." In a glance, she confessed all her self-doubt, as well as her ability to remain the person she was in a place that was already trying to mold her to fit their desires. "The king didn't know it when he selected you, but you've got a fire in your soul that is going to set that whole place alight. Just because you have no say in what is happening doesn't mean you can't still give them hell."

"You're encouraging mutiny?" she chided, only half joking because this wasn't the first time he'd told her to fight against the tide of power, to kick against the undercurrent of a mandatory destiny.

He gave her the smallest smile, one that barely tickled the fullness of his lips. "I'm encouraging *you*. Don't let them put your light out," he said as he tossed a bucket of water on the pit, dousing what was left of the flames.

XIII.

Soggy cereal swirled around in its bowl, the spoon circling a pool of mushy, colorful rings.

Morning had come sooner than Ava wanted. Instead of lying in bed unable to sleep, she'd sneaked into the kitchen and devoured half a pint of cookie dough ice cream. Then she'd snagged the photo of herself and Dante from the mantel and packed it into a box. She got in a catnap before the other two woke, and then they'd spent forty-five minutes moving boxes from her bedroom to the living room. To say she was dragging would be an understatement. She was barely moving, as if there were shackles of quicksand around her ankles, hindering her every step. Her eyes were dry, that same sand rubbed into them, and her head was a balloon threatening to detach from her neck. She knew she looked as messy as she felt, but thankfully no one had mentioned it.

No one had really said much that morning.

She and Cordellia sat in silence, neither touching their breakfast. Nixon was out for a longer than normal run; because while he hadn't said so, he'd known the two Toliver women needed all the time together that they could get. Even if that meant giving one another sad glances across the table.

No longer able to take the questions—one in particular—rolling through her mind, Ava blurted, "Are you going to be okay once I'm gone?"

Cordellia furrowed her brows and looked at her daughter like she'd spoken a different language. "Of course I will," she replied as if the question was the most absurd thing she'd ever heard. But Ava had every right to ask. There had been countless times over the years when Ava had been forced to step into the role of parent, ensuring Cordellia ate, slept, bathed…remained a sane member of society. Nearly 228 moons had passed since Dante's death and Cordellia relived the loss every single day. Ava would never discredit her misery, even if she didn't feel it the same way, but she had never really understood it. She *could*, however, doubt Cordellia's "I can take care of myself" attitude.

It was just the two of them, and in a few hours, it would be one.

One who sometimes forgot how to live.

Ava worried, more than anything, that her mother would lose sight of life, of herself, and that the shroud of darkness in which she kept herself wrapped would swallow her whole.

There was one glimmer of hope, however. Just a day after her dinner with Sebastian, a package had arrived. In the box was a large bottle of small green pills, along with a note in heavy handwriting: **I hope these are what you wanted, and that they help to ease the transition for both you and your mother. –Sebastian.**

Her mother had been taking the pills consistently through the last couple of days, and already Ava had noticed a change. Yet Ava could not ignore the worry overshadowing that glimmer. Because this was the woman who would lose track of days, who would forget her own name sometimes. What was to stop her mother from forgetting to take a pill, and then two, and then three? Before a week's end, she would be right back where she'd started.

This time, Ava would not be there to pull her out.

That was what scared her the most.

She wanted to argue with Cordellia.

She wanted an outlet for all she was feeling about this day and everything it would bring unto their family. She wanted to argue about everything she'd felt leading *up* to this day. Scream about all the times Cordellia had ignored life and made Ava suffer right along with her. But while her mother was the right target for all her anger, none of it would make a difference. She had failed to see anything from Ava's point-of-view—ever—but especially regarding her becoming queen. She believed Ava deserved it more than anything.

Nothing Ava could say was going to convince her mother otherwise. She'd always wanted better for her child, which Ava loved her for, but *this*? All the arguments and reasoning Ava could give had fallen on deaf ears since the night of the gala, and there was no reason to believe it would be any different now.

Especially not today.

So instead, she swallowed the words she wanted to say and dropped the spoonful of mush back into the bowl.

"Will you be able to visit often?" Cordellia asked nonchalantly, her tone changed within seconds, as if Ava were simply moving the next town over.

Ava shrugged, exhaling her frustrations at the same time. "I don't know what my routine will be like," she replied. Her words were angrier than she'd intended. Softer, kinder, she added, "But I hope so." After a few seconds, she continued, "You can always come and visit, too." Ava knew it would be like pulling alligator teeth trying to get Cordellia to High House, which led her to ask another question that had been brewing. "You *are* coming to the Welcome Dinner, right?"

Cordellia was part of the Havaan Woman's Choir: a group of twenty-five women who performed mostly at banquets and weddings throughout their country. She had a powerful, beautiful voice. It was sweet like nectar and her vibrato shook like an earthquake. This year, the choir would be featured at the Welcome Dinner. For most of the women, it would be the first time they'd ever go to High House.

Cordellia, however, had been invited to the king and queen's home once.

It hadn't gone well.

When news of the boating accident had spread, King Orion held a vigil for the lost fisherman. While no bodies had been recovered, assumingly washed far beyond the reaches of Havaan, there was still a continent-wide funeral at High House for friends and families of the lost. Cordellia had made it to the gates before falling into a fit of despair, her wailing heard for miles in all directions. Zarah had physically carried her back to the car. She'd wrapped her in a blanket, but it could not compete with the one of mourning in which Cordellia cocooned herself daily.

Even after all these years she still turned her eyes away from the looming mansion when she passed by, as if the ghost of Dante might linger in the windows.

Cordellia smiled tightly, a forced assurance that Ava wanted to believe but just couldn't. "Of course," she answered again, as if those two words would wipe away all uncertainty. "The choir will be there."

"I know, but—"

There was a bit of hostility—at whom, Ava wasn't sure—when her mother interrupted. "It's been twenty years since your father died. I think that's enough time to stop avoiding the place, don't you?"

Yes! Ava wanted to scream. I think it's been enough time for many things!

Her mother spoke of time as though it were sutures, but it had not healed the gaping, bleeding wounds Dante's death had left.

With her frustration bubbling, threatening to spill onto the floor, Ava pushed her chair back and stood. "I hope so, Mother," was all she said. She placed her bowl in the sink then turned to the mountain of boxes stacked neatly by the front door. Two racks of new clothing had already been delivered to High House after their day of empty-market shopping. Her bedroom closet was packed from wall to door with boxes of mementos, clothing, books, photographs and other knick-knacks that would stay behind.

Maybe she would come back for them one day.

What would that be like, she wondered, returning after living at High House? Would Holland Avenue Number Six still feel like home?

With a glance at the grandfather clock Ava mumbled, "I'm going to go and shower before they get here." As she passed her, Cordellia's rough hand reached out and grazed Ava's arm.

"I'm sorry I have not always been the mother you deserved," she whispered.

Ava looked down at her with a sad smile. "You were the best mother you could be," she said sincerely before making her way through the kitchen and up the stairs.

Nixon pushed the partially jarred door open, making as little noise as possible. He stood in the doorway and just watched her. She wasn't doing anything besides sitting on her bed, looking out the window, but those moments of stillness were when he found her the most beautiful.

When she was unguarded, when she put away the protective armor and simply existed in the world, she was…perfect. Havaan, and especially Sebastian, were lucky they would soon get to call her theirs.

"Avaleigh," he said quietly, a hushed word that fluttered to her ears.

She turned her head quickly, her curls, full of volume, moving with her like a mane. She wasn't sure how long she'd been sitting there—long enough for her mass of hair to dry—staring out the window she'd counted stars from and watched the sun rise through. The same window she'd marked the passing of each year, the flipping of seasons framed in the panes. The world outside had changed, the world *inside* had changed countless times over, but the window had not. It always looked down into her backyard, the view of the sky uninterrupted.

I wonder what my view will look like tonight, she was thinking when she heard her name, as quiet as if carried on the wind. When she turned, she met Nixon's bright gaze, his eyes so on fire it was as though he were burning from the inside out. They didn't say anything for a few seconds, and she reveled in the peace that came with his presence. Even standing on the other side of the room he brought with him a sense of calm she'd come to appreciate the last couple of days. It would be weird not having him around all the time, though she was sure they would pass one another in the many halls of High House.

"Things are never going to be the same after today," she had said to herself in the shower. It was an echoed sentiment, words Delilah had said in the carriage. She had been right then, and it was equally as true now.

How much of her life, up until this very moment, would remain once she was no longer here, once she became someone else?

Someone new.

"They're here," Nixon said once he'd cleared his throat. His voice was lower than normal, reverent, his words the final nail in the coffin of her fate. The arrival of the movers meant no escape, no running in the other direction. They were there to take her, and her belongings, away from this life and into her next. Like Charon, the ferryman on the River Styx, except death was not her final destination.

Ava stood and looked around her room one last time. When she faced Nixon again, her blue eyes shone like diamonds in a clear pool. Her bottom lip trembled and she bit down to calm it, but it moved through her body in small tremors until she was a shaking, blubbering mess.

Nixon was across the room before she even registered him moving. His strong arms wrapped around her, holding her tightly, and she clung to him, her fingertips digging into the muscles of his back as she sobbed into his chest. He rested his chin atop her soft curls but said nothing, just traced her spine with the palm of his hand, a steady rhythm that calmed her and anchored her to his serenity. It took a while for the tears to end and her breathing to return to normal, for her body to stop shaking.

Until, that is, she was doing so for an entirely different reason.

His nearness was too much to handle, her senses on an emotional overload. She wiped at her eyes with the palms of her hands then stepped back as far as his caged arms would allow. Her eyes roved from the dark spot on his black shirt to his face, his full lips parted just enough that she could smell the cool mint of his breath. The embers in his eyes had calmed slightly, and concern creased his brows. But when she looked at him, her hands resting on his stomach, they blazed to their full inferno again and it took her breath away.

"Your eyes are super blue when you're sad," he said quietly.

"My own orbital mood rings," she answered, laughing through sniffles.

He loosened his arms, but she stayed where she was, frozen in place by the intensity of his gaze. "You're going to be okay," he assured, and the certainty in his voice was almost enough to convince her.

"How can you know that?" she asked, barely above a whisper.

This time he smiled, the brilliance of it on full display, as he ran his thumbs along her cheeks, removing any remaining traces of her breakdown. "Because I know your greatness."

"Yeah?"

He nodded once. "Yeah."

From the way he wet his lips and cocked his head, she thought he was going to kiss her. Instinctively, she tilted her head the opposite direction, ready for it, while the part of her that knew better tugged at her hair, trying to pull her away from him. She wanted to feel his lips, to share a single breath with him. Damned be the crown, and Sebastian, and her pending commitment to him. He didn't have claim to her yet, and if Nixon wanted that right, she would give it to him willingly.

Because the things she wanted she couldn't have, and the things she was being given she would gladly hand to someone else.

This realization lit a spark inside of her, one she had felt the first time her eyes had scanned the lines of the Albert Camus poem. It had felt like a battle cry then, a steady beating in the deepest part of her soul she had wanted to answer. Now, it was starting again, the pounding of drums and sharpening of blades, soldiers at the ready to rebel, to fight against whatever barriers were in their way.

To push back.

Right now, it was against the king and his rules. Rules which were forcing her into a life she had never desired. If Nixon's lips were one of the sacrifices her warrior-self had to make, she would make it without question.

But instead of pressing his lips to hers, he did the one thing she couldn't find within herself to do, and stepped away. Not a moment too soon, either, because within two breaths her mother was at her bedroom door.

She looked between the two of them, her eyebrows lowering a fraction. "The truck is loaded. Ramiro sent me to get you."

With a sad, tight smile Ava squared her shoulders and took a deep breath. "I'm ready," she said, looking at Nixon when she said it.

"I know you are," he replied. "Take whatever time you need," he added before heading out of the room. He tipped his head to Cordellia as he crossed her and then was gone, his shadow bouncing off the wall as he went downstairs.

Ava and her mother looked at one another, saying nothing because there was too much to be said. Finally, Cordellia spoke first through a tight throat. "I'm going to miss you."

"Me, too." Ava traversed the room quickly and hugged her. She didn't cry though, because she knew that if she started again she would never stop.

When they parted, Cordellia reached a small hand to her face and cupped Ava's cheek lovingly. "Your father would be so proud of you."

Ava scoffed before she had a chance to stop it. "I haven't done anything to earn this."

"Maybe not," her mother replied, her words kind, "but you will do great things to prove you deserve it. Even though this may not be what you want, I know that you are too good to let everyone down."

"I'll do my best," she promised, and she meant it, even though a part of her was screaming *why does it matter if I let everyone down? Who are they to me that I would care so much?*

They walked down the stairs and through the kitchen together, past the fridge with drawings Ava had done as a young child and by the living room with its mantel of photos. If Cordellia had noticed the missing picture, she didn't mention it. Without a look back, they made their way outside. A caravan three vehicles long was parked in front of the house: two of them were large black trucks, the cabs loaded with her stuff; the other was a familiar car with Ramiro standing next to the passenger side.

Most of the neighbors had come out of their homes and stood in their lawns, watching the commotion. Assuredly, a handful of them would bum-rush the Toliver house the moment the cars pulled away, harassing Cordellia with an onslaught of questions of what was going on? Where was Ava going? Who were those men? What did it all mean?! And Cordellia would no doubt barricade herself in the house until Naomi, or another member of the choir, came by to take her to the Welcome Dinner.

On the porch, Ava turned to her mother. "I'll see you tonight, right?"

Cordellia nodded. "Yes, my love. We will get through this together, I promise."

That one word, *promise,* put Ava at ease. It was not a word Cordellia used lightly. She was aware of how quickly you could break it, most of the time unintentionally. Dante had promised to return home to her until old age took him, but he hadn't. And that shattered vow had set in motion a life no one could have seen coming. So she and Ava made it a point to avoid the p-word.

Unless they meant it.

Unless it was something they could deliver on.

They hugged again, this time the grip much tighter. Ava didn't want to let her go, because it was just another certainty that things were about to change and that everything she'd grown up knowing was going to be gone. She refused to be the first to let go, and thankfully she didn't have to be.

"I love you, sweet girl," Cordellia whispered before pulling apart. She wiped her tears away with the sleeve of her shirt but not before Ava could see them.

"I love you, too," her only child replied as her own tears fell gently down her cheeks. Ava exhaled slowly. Then, with shoulders as squared as before—if for nothing more than a performance for the neighbors—she walked, with more confidence than she felt, to the lead car.

"Are you ready to go?" Ramiro asked, his deep voice full of kindness.

She nodded once, firmly, like her favorite guard so often did, and then slid into the vehicle.

"Where's Nixon?" she asked as soon as Ramiro was inside. She had expected him to be in the car already. An overwhelming panic gripped her chest when she realized she was alone.

"He's in one of the trucks. He thought you would want some time to yourself," Ramiro answered as he shifted the car into gear and began to pull away from her house. She turned on her knees and looked out the back window, her hand pressed to it as Cordellia held hers up in a motionless wave.

"Stop the car," Ava whispered as tears welled in her eyes and fear filled her lungs like tar. "Stop the car!" she demanded, this time while reaching for the handle. As the door flung open, Ramiro swore and slammed on the breaks a second before she was out. She heard Nixon yell her name but ignored it as she sprinted the short distance back to her house. She threw herself at her mother, who pulled her into her arms, crushing her to her chest.

"I can't do this," she repeated through her sobs. She held onto Cordellia with a ferocity she had never experienced before. She had never needed her mother more than she did in this very moment. She was the anchor to everything Ava was, and she knew the moment she let go, she would be swept far, far away. She had no idea how she was supposed to handle anything that was about to happen without Cordellia a room or two away. Yes, their relationship had always been rocky, but they had also been that light for one another, a beacon welcoming the other home.

"You are not alone in this," her mother replied. Ava wanted to believe her, she really did, but she *felt* alone, like she was the last remaining person in this crazy, messed up world. When she finally calmed down—minutes, though it could have been hours—later, Cordellia, like she had countless times before, took her child's face in her hands, held it like it was the most beautiful thing she had ever seen, and repeated words that only three people in the world knew.

"*Mikor orada es tidak svar, enged dashuri fi itu clave.*"

Sometimes Ava swore she'd heard the words while in the womb, said proudly by her father in his calming voice. She had, unbeknownst to her mother, read them on letters Dante had written to Cordellia. Pieces of paper held so many times they were thinning, the words worn in some places. It was their own mantra, a secret shared between only three pairs of lips.

They had the effect Ava had been looking for. They seeped into her pores and flowed through her veins like ice, giving her the courage and willpower to make it back to the car.

"I love you," she said one last time before heading there. "I will do my best to make you and dad proud of me."

"Oh, sweet girl," Cordellia replied, tucking a chunk of curly hair behind Ava's ear. "I could not possibly be more proud of you."

They embraced again, one final hug before Ava became an official resident of the High House Institution, and then she marched back to the car, her spine straight. giving, for the first time in a week, the appearance of a queen. There was no way of knowing what was going to happen in the following days, hours, months. Even years. But as they pulled away from her house again, and this time she stayed rooted to her seat, Ava knew whatever situations were to come her way, she could handle them.

As long as she kept that fire burning inside of her and pushed back when she was shoved.

There would be times where her arms would go weak from doing so, of this she was certain.

But I am ready.

She spent the car ride to High House trying to believe it.

XIV.

One moment they were pulling *away* from Holland Avenue Number Six and the next they were pulling *up* to High House, so soon it was almost as though they'd teleported.

It felt that way to Ava, at least. Sleep had overtaken her almost immediately. Perhaps it was the lack of it from the night before or a need to avoid, for as long as possible, what awaited her at the end of the curved and twisted road. Maybe it was a combination of the two, along with the heavy dose of all the doom and gloom with which she was filled. Whatever it was, it held her captive even as the car eased to a stop.

It was the gentle closing of doors, one after another, that startled her awake. She stretched and took in her surroundings, familiarizing herself with where she was and why. Her mood immediately turned sour as tired eyes settled on the multi-story house, its grandiosity looming over her like a giant, ready to crush her under its boot.

Delilah and Sebastian waited on the porch wearing matching smiles. Ava returned their waves with more excitement than she felt. Her best friend was practically bouncing out of her skin, her grin so wide it should have split her face in half.

From the corner of her eye, Ava watched two long legs emerge from the truck behind her. Nixon unfolded from within it, his single duffle bag hoisted over his shoulder. He walked past the car and to the porch without a glance her way. The dismissal pained Ava, sent a tiny shock to her heart. It filled her eyes with salty tears, but she blinked them away. Sebastian and Nixon exchanged a few words, along with a friendly slap on the back, while Delilah eyed Nixon with an intensity that made even Ava blush.

Then he was gone, gulped up by the doorway.

In the next moment, the prince had her door open. After gathering a deep breath and pushing away all the emotions crawling under her skin like spiders, she placed her hand in his outstretched one and exited the car. Around them, a crew of at least a dozen soldiers, dressed in simple king-crested t-shirts, unpacked the moving trucks with the efficiency of a well-oiled machine. It was all very impressive, if not just a little bit off-putting. Ava was already terrified of losing her sense of self and independence within the walls of High House, and watching these men work like robots did nothing to subdue that fear.

"Welcome home," Sebastian said. His words drew her attention from the guards to his elegantly handsome face. His green eyes sparkled with unmatched excitement as they met hers.

Ava gave what she hoped was a convincing smile. "It's good to see you," she added, and it was. She liked Sebastian—not as much as she liked Nixon—but she *wanted* to feel for him what she did for Nixon. More even. It would help the whole being married to him thing if she more than tolerated the guy, if she felt *their* attraction like an incoming storm.

"Thank you for getting those pills for my mother," she whispered. Her appreciation was evident on her face. Cordellia had been offended initially that Ava thought she needed such a thing, but within taking the first pill she seemed more balanced than she'd been in twenty years. Where a bad day or two would have normally followed such a high, her mood remained steady. She was emotional at times, but that was expected with all that was going on. Both women were shocked by the transformation, by the life just a couple of pills had breathed back into her. Ava didn't know what sort of sorcery was behind them, nor was she going to ask. As long as they continued to help her mother, that was all that mattered.

Sebastian's grin spread across his face and crinkled the corner of his green eyes. "I was wondering if the package made it to your home. I hope they help."

"They seem to be," she replied. "I really do appreciate it."

Sebastian ran a finger down the back of her arm. "We're in this together, Avaleigh," he said, his voice kind. Warm.

She knew he wasn't 100% on board with the whole shebang either, and it was sort of nice knowing they would conquer this journey together. Knowing she wasn't going to have to figure it all out on her own was comforting.

Speaking of…

Glancing over Sebastian's shoulder, Ava smiled at her best friend. "Hi, D," she said. The pink-haired beauty ran over to her and flung herself at her taller friend.

"Can you believe this is happening?" she exclaimed.

"Not even a little," Ava replied, squeezing Delilah. *How could I have ever believed I'd be alone in this?* Having Delilah living at High House with her was one of the few things Ava could get excited about. Her number one would be under the same roof; she would be the biggest anchor to her old life, one she would cling to until she was able to float on her own.

"How long have you been here?"

Delilah flicked a piece of hair from her eyes and shrugged. "Not long. Less than an hour. I can't wait for you to see my room. It's gorgeous." She drew the last word out and sighed dramatically.

"On that note," Sebastian said as he placed his hand on the small of Ava's back, steering her up the walkway toward the house. "Allow me to show you to yours."

They were trailed by Delilah, who filled her in on her exciting morning with barely a breath between words. They followed the silver-haired prince up the right staircase, away from the door to the Throne Room and down a short hallway. Rounding the corner led to an even longer passageway with doors scattered on both sides, like that of a hotel. Sconces dotted the baby blue walls, illuminating their path. She wasn't sure how many people lived at High House, but Ava imagined it was a large number based on how many doors had nameplates next to them. Four doors down was one with Delilah's name etched in beautiful cursive, and on one across the hall but a few feet away, was Ava's.

"You guys put me this close to her?" she joked, hip-checking her best friend.

"I figured she would have my head if I didn't," Sebastian replied playfully.

Delilah giggled. "Right you were! Now open the door so she can see it."

Chuckling, Sebastian turned the handle, revealing one of the most beautiful rooms Ava had ever seen. It was modern and sleek, with a bed big enough to fit at least ten of her. Three of the walls were off-white. The fourth, the one against which her bed rested, was true sapphire blue. Directly across from the door were two large French doors that opened onto a balcony. It overlooked the backyard and gave her an uninterrupted view of the horizon. Her boxes were all piled by the wall, stacked neatly, waiting to be unpacked. The mountain had been so large in her kitchen, but now seemed tiny compared to the grandness of the bedroom.

The dresser was black, as were the end tables on either side of the bed. There was also a chaise lounge in the corner and a small bookcase. A thick faux-fur rug rested in the middle of the room, and Ava couldn't wait to step onto it with bare feet or lay across it while the circular fireplace warmed her. The bedroom also had its own full bathroom with a claw-foot tub, large glass shower, and lighted vanity.

"Check out the closet," Delilah gushed as she slid the panel. The space was huge, easily big enough to be another bedroom, and filled with all the clothing they'd gotten the day at the market. Once the few articles she'd brought from home were added, in total everything would take up maybe a third of the storage. There was also a rack underneath for shoes, on which a few pairs already nestled comfortably.

"It's awesome, right?" Delilah's eyes were large and she was filled to the brim with an exhilaration Ava found impossible to mirror. How was it possible that Delilah, who was settling for her second option, could be this thrilled, but Ava couldn't find it in herself to feel the same?

"It is," Ava agreed as she exhaled a warm breath. It was lovely, but more than she was used to. While she couldn't wait to test out the comfort level of the bed or take a relaxing soak in the tub, nothing about it was even remotely similar to her bedroom at home.

Maybe once I'm unpacked…she rationalized, trying to stay positive. She really didn't want to be a sourpuss for the next however many years of her reign.

It wasn't until after she took it all in, did a complete 360° spin, that she really noticed how unbroken in the room was. Everything was too clean, too fresh, too new…

"Are we not sharing a room?" she blurted, her gaze cutting to Sebastian.

Sebastian cocked his head slightly and his brows lowered in confusion. "Do you want us to?" he questioned cautiously.

"No," she replied immediately, but then added quietly, "I just assumed…" Sebastian stepped closer and took her hands. They were only slightly larger than hers and warm, but not sticky. He wasn't nervous, she realized. He may not be sold on the idea either, but he wasn't worried about any of it. She envied that.

"I'm a mess," she said by way of apology.

"It's a messy time," Sebastian replied, his tone kind. He lowered his voice and leaned closer to her, as if he were going to tell her a secret. "You are going to be my wife one day, and I am very much looking forward to all the things that will entail. But you and I are strangers, and I know how uncomfortable and overwhelming all of this is for you. The last thing we need is to share a private space so soon. I want you to have your *own* space, where you can decompress at the end of the day, or in the middle of it, without me being around."

Ava sighed, a bit of tension leaving her body with the exhale and squeezed his hands.

"That's super considerate of you," she whispered. Her mouth curved slightly at the corners, all on their own. "Thanks."

Sebastian brushed her cheek with his thumb, and she turned her eyes down at the intimacy of the small gesture. "My bedroom is down the opposite hall." Then he added, as if he needed a justification for giving her this information, "In case you ever need to find it." He lifted her face with his finger and looked her in the eyes. He grinned, a cute, flirtatious gesture that knotted her stomach, but not necessarily in a bad way. Sebastian seemed to have that effect on her, an ability to smooth over even the roughest of moments. It was just another thing she liked about him—another thing to add to a small but growing list. He was like Nixon in that way.

Nixon.

At just the thought of his name, her heart swelled and warmth crept up her neck to her cheeks. Noticing it, Sebastian's eyes glinted with a hint of mischief. She didn't have the heart to tell him she hadn't misread his implication, as the look implied.

Behind them, Delilah cleared her throat. They turned to her and found another woman standing in the doorway. She was dressed in a tight red pencil skirt and striped blouse. Her very blond hair was twisted and pinned on the top of her head. She was all legs and in her slender fingers was a clipboard.

"I don't mean to bother you two," she said. There was a bit of a drawl to her words, saccharine and thick like strawberry jam. All the regions of Havaan had them, little tonal lilts that varied person to person. They were fragments of the old world, pieces of it that could not be erased.

"You're not bothering us, Claudia," Sebastian replied. He turned his smile up to high, and Ava was almost certain she saw a slight buckle to

Claudia's knees. "Avaleigh, this is Claudia MacIntire. She is the events coordinator for High House."

Claudia crossed the room in an impressively high pair of black heels, her arm extended the whole time. Ava was ready for it, and when the woman was close enough, they shook hands firmly. It was one of the things Ava's mother had drilled into her as a teenager: "A strong handshake can make you seem more confident than you actually are."

"It is an absolute pleasure to meet you. It's nice to put a face with the name I've been hearing tossed around all day."

"Hopefully it's been tossed around positively," Ava said. She could only imagine the things Queen Bernadette had been saying.

Claudia laughed a pure, sweet sound like wind-chimes. "It's been all good, I promise. I came by to let you know we'll be gathering in the Throne Room in twenty minutes. We've got quite an evening ahead of us and need to go over the itinerary."

"Twenty minutes?" Ava blanched. She'd just stepped into High House and she was already—

"Hey," Sebastian said gently as he ran a hand down her arm. She looked at him, worry tugging at the corner of her blue eyes. "It won't take long. We just need to make sure everyone, especially you, knows how the night is going to go. You'll have many hours to rest, relax. Wander around and learn the layout of the house. I know it's a lot, but you're going to be fine."

"I wish I had as much faith as you do," Ava mumbled.

"I've got enough for the both of us until you find your own." The prince smiled at her as he reached up and twisted a curl around his finger. She wanted to pull away from him—the little touches were too intimate too soon—but she resisted. *He is going to be your husband,* she repeated to herself. "Take the remainder of the time to catch your breath. I'll see you in a few." He held her eyes for a couple of seconds before turning from her. He squeezed Delilah's shoulder as he passed her and then was gone.

"You might want to change," D said once they were alone.

Ava glanced down at her outfit. Her fitted shirt was solid green and her jeans were without tatters. She'd even worn a newish pair of calf-high black boots. She glared up at her friend through slits. "Already taking your job as assistant to heart, I see."

Delilah rolled her eyes. "Please," she started with that undercut of passive-aggressive abhorrence Ava had never heard in anyone other than D. "That piece of advice was because I'm your friend. You're not on Holland Avenue anymore. You've got to dress for the life you have now, not the one you left behind."

"I appreciate your honest candor," Ava replied with her own bite of sarcasm.

The pink-haired sprite did a slight raise with her brow. "Don't be mean. I'm just looking out for you," she retorted. "But by all means, wear whatever you want. Give the queen yet another reason to dislike you." Then she left the room without another word.

As soon as she was gone, Ava pushed the door closed with a little more force than she'd wanted and leaned her back against it. Slowly, she slid down it and brought her knees to her chest. As her gaze moved around the room, her eyes settled on the glass doors across from her.

She suddenly had a deep desire to throw herself off the balcony.

"With my luck, I'd survive," she muttered. She dropped her head against the door, the thud of it muffled by her hair.

After a few minutes, she tired of being the only guest at her pity party. She hoisted herself off the very soft carpet and went to the too-large closet to reluctantly find something more presentable to wear.

XV.

The Throne Room was an undulating wave of voices. Words ricocheted off the tall ceilings. Pieces of conversations crumbled down like plaster and collected in a thin layer on the floor. Most of High House's residents and staff were gathered, filling rows of the same cushioned chairs from the gala. The king and queen sat perched on their thrones, lost in their own conversation, although Bernadette's eyes constantly scanned the crowd.

There were forty or so people in attendance. Aside from all four members of the Calder clan were Ava and Delilah, roughly twenty guards in their familiar black pants and crested shirt uniform; lastly, there was nine women and one man who looked like common folk, all dressed in regular clothing that gave no indication of their jobs or designated titles. As Ava tugged on the hem of her skirt, she envied those wearing casual trousers and what looked like very comfortable shoes. She took her seat in the front row, sandwiched between Delilah and Sebastian, and crossed her legs.

"Ava, I'd like for you to meet my brother, Levi." Sebastian motioned to the younger, simpler version of himself, seated in the next chair over.

The same green eyes that seemed to run on the male side of the royal family twinkled behind a pair of black-framed glasses. No one in Havaan needed glasses, but many people wore them for the aesthetic. Bad eyesight was one of the old world flaws the first magicians had eliminated—along with acne and crooked teeth.

Anything to keep the citizens as close to perfect as possible.

Levi was no exception. His hair was brown and cropped short, though there was a slight wave to the texture. His features were overall softer than Sebastian's, from the shape of his eyes to the curve of his nose. He was thinner, less muscular, but still attractive in that 'coming into one's features' kind of way.

"It's great to meet you, Ava," Levi said. His voice was not as deep as his brother's, either. If her lackluster knowledge of the royal family served her right—*probably should have studied up*—Levi was only seventeen. Still a young buck, by all standards.

"And you," Ava replied as she shook his hand. "I can't wait for you to tell me embarrassing stories about this one." She glanced up at Sebastian and grinned.

The three of them shared a smile then sat back in their seats as Claudia tapped into the room. The heels of her shoes echoed off the large space, like a steady drip in a metal sink. She looked a bit disheveled, her tight bun slightly looser than it had been less than thirty minutes ago. She fanned herself with her clipboard as she hurried down the aisle.

Ava, as inconspicuously as possible, scanned the faces in the room, looking for one in particular. He slipped in through a crack in the large door, all muscles and long limbs, like a detached shadow. His hair was pulled away from his face, but pieces of it clung to his damp forehead and his sleeveless shirt was a bit wrinkled. Ava looked from Claudia, who was whispering to the king and queen, then back to Nixon, who was whispering to a tall, baldheaded man next to him. A thousand scenarios raced through her mind, images of her—*not my*—fire-eyed kingsman and the bubbly events coordinator. She swallowed the bile in her throat as she willed Nixon to look at her. To simply acknowledge her.

And he did.

Finally.

His gaze swept the crowd and settled on Ava for a second, maybe even half of one, before he directed his attention to the woman up front. She did not fail to miss the pulse of his jaw or the bob of his Adam's apple. It was the second time he'd dismissed her today. This was not the same guy she'd spent the last three days with, who'd slept in the bedroom next to hers and laughed freely at her corny jokes. This was a Nixon she did not recognize and was not too fond of, either. She sat back with a huff, her arms crossed over her chest as she tried to focus on Claudia's words.

"...such an exciting evening," the blonde said, her sweet voice now grating on Ava's eardrums. "This meeting is just to make sure we're all on the same page. Guards." Claudia paused and ran her eyes along the group of large, fit men. "We are expecting a ton of people tonight, so make sure you're being vigilant and making yourselves known amongst them. Not that there will be any sort of trouble, of course," she said, laughing to herself.

Ava raised her hand slowly and waited until she was called upon. "Exactly *how* many people are we expecting?" she asked, hoping no one else noticed the slight tremor in her voice. She wasn't sure if it was coincidence or just a perfectly timed gesture, but Sebastian rested a hand on her knee and squeezed gently.

"We've got about 20,000 citizens coming." Ava blanched. Her lungs closed off and her heart raced as if it were trying to make up for the lack of air. "But you'll only be doing a face-to-face meeting with about a quarter of them," Claudia added, as if that would make any difference.

Delilah leaned over and from the corner of her mouth mumbled, "Breathe," as she slapped her near panicked friend on the back. It was the jumpstart her body needed. Ava inhaled the stale air of the room.

She reminded herself to steer as clear as possible from the Throne Room from now on——nothing but bad news was ever delivered here.

"It really isn't as bad as it sounds," Claudia assured. "They will file in and shake your hand, along with those of the royal family, then move along. It'll all be very quick and very simple. You just have to stand there, really. These 5,000 or so citizens made a very generous donation to Havaan for the opportunity to meet you. They're eager to welcome their new queen." Ava, afraid to speak, just nodded and offered Claudia a tight smile. Instinctively, as though she were being controlled by a force unseen, her hand covered Sebastian's.

"Now," Claudia continued, her attention still on Ava, "after the meet-and-greet, the king will say a few words to introduce you and then it'll be time for your speech. Once——"

Ava leaned forward in her chair and blurted, "Speech? What speech?"

Claudia looked at Ava as if she'd lost her mind before glancing down at her clipboard. She flipped a few pages and said, mostly to herself, "I wasn't told we wouldn't be doing the speech." She glanced up at Ava. "I assumed you knew about it?" Claudia looked first at Ava then Queen Bernadette, as did everyone else in the room.

The queen simply shrugged, her thin lips cocked to one side. She was clearly amused by the unraveling of her future daughter-in-law, but by the dagger-sharp glare her eldest son was shooting her, *he* was not.

"It must have slipped my mind in all the chaos at the gala. I do apologize, Avaleigh, for the mistake."

"It wouldn't do any harm if we nixed the speech," Orion interceded, his features, as well as his thunderous voice, as lax as he could make them.

Aware of the mounting tension, and with a desire to keep the room as light and airy as her personality, Claudia removed a pen from behind her ear. "We can *totally* skip the speech, it's not——"

"No," Ava interrupted. Her eyes locked on those of the queen. It was obvious Bernadette was playing at something. Maybe she was trying to prove a point or punish Ava for the way she'd behaved at the gala. Whatever the reason, it didn't faze Ava. What the queen didn't know was that these little games only added fuel to an already burning fire. The current sovereign had seen her falter once; she would not do so again.

"When you move to High House, do not lose sight of who you are," Nixon had said, and those words played like a record stuck on repeat. "Fight, whenever it is called for. Push back. Do not go gentle into anything." And fight she would. She would push back harder than anyone suspected possible of her. The king and queen had already taken so much from her. She would not let them take her sense of self, as well.

"I'll do the speech," Ava said, sitting higher in her seat.

"There isn't much time to prepare," Claudia warned, her pen suspended above her clipboard.

Ava shrugged, mimicking the queen's cold gesture. "Then I'll wing it."

"Ava, are you certain?" Sebastian questioned. She turned to him and nodded once. Firmly. Surely. She glanced at the queen from the corner of her eye and took pleasure in the missing smirk that had been there only moments ago.

Claudia cleared her throat and tucked the pen back behind her ear. "Excellent," she chirped before moving on. "Following the meet-and-greet, Ava will do her speech. Then dinner will be served. Once that's all done and over with, there will be an opportunity for everyone to mingle with the guests. Before you know it, the night is over and everyone gets to go to bed. Any questions?"

In the silent moment, Ava looked at Delilah for the first time since the meeting had begun. Delilah was staring at her, her eyes big and alight with…not necessarily *amusement* but something else. Pride, maybe?

"Great, then," Claudia continued when no one spoke up. "I will be around all evening, so if you need me, I'll be somewhere. Dressers." Claudia focused on the group of plain-clothed citizens. "You are expected in the rooms of your charges at four o'clock sharp. Meet-and-greet begins at six this evening and we need everyone dressed and primped by quarter 'til. Understood?" The dozen people nodded and Claudia let out a deep breath. "Thank you, all, for taking the time to meet with me. It was… interesting, to say the least." Then she tucked her precious clipboard under her armpit and clapped her hands. "Dismissed!" she announced, laughing to herself yet again.

There was an immediate scuffle of chairs and conversations restarted. As Ava stood, her body wound tight with frustration, she risked a glance across the vast room at Nixon. Even from a distance she could see the gilt of his eyes, two glowing disks that reminded her of melted gold. He tipped his head to her, a barely noticeable tick, and then exited the room as quickly and quietly as he'd arrived.

Sebastian was in front of her before she could blink. "Ava, I am so sorry my mother didn't tell you about the speech," he said quickly. His apology read across his face.

She shook her head, a section of loose hair falling over her eye. She tucked it behind her ear with more aggression than necessary. "It's okay. Really. It's obvious she hates me, though, so that's fun."

"She doesn't know you," he replied, his voice full of compassion. "You're coming in to take her place. She isn't adjusting well, either."

Ava was pretty sure there was more to it than that, but what it was, she couldn't begin to fathom. Still, she agreed with a short, "Maybe."

"Avaleigh." The queen's voice slid over her like curdled milk. "Don't forget dear, that all of Havaan will be tuning in for your speech. You might consider taking a bit of time to prepare instead of simply *winging it*." There was a warning to her advice, one Ava chose to ignore, because if she acknowledged it she would be welcoming another wave of panic. She could not afford to be a weakling tonight—not with all the eyes of Havaan watching—and especially under the scrutiny of the queen.

If she had to be here, if she had to be a part of all this, then she would do so with her head held high, every bit of courage she possessed front and center.

"I look forward to hearing what you have to say," the king said as he and the queen made their way to the door in the back of the room. Ava watched them through narrowed eyes until they were gone, though the chill of Bernadette still lingered in the air like the first breath of winter.

Sebastian, Levi, and Delilah were lost in conversation, which made Ava's exit easy. She slipped away like a ghost and avoided most of the curious eyes as she made her way through the giant room with its floor-to-ceiling windows and carved pillars, up the bulbous staircase and back to her room. She assumed the staff knew who she was, who she was going to become, but only one person attempted to stop her for small talk. She obliged the man, who, she learned, was one of the floral arrangers, and told him that she preferred lilacs over roses. She made it to her bedroom without any other interference and locked the door as soon as she was inside.

She looked around the empty space, took in the bare bookshelves and flawlessly made bed.

The starkness, the lack of life it held, was making her anxious.

She kicked off her shoes, pulled off her socks and then hurried across the room to the stack of boxes, making sure to take a moment to appreciate the softness of the rug between her toes. It took a few minutes to find the box she wanted, but once she did, she ripped the tape off the flaps and removed her framed photos one by one. She'd purchased a hodge-podge set of ten varnished black frames—each a different style and size—at the market. The photos inside were a pretty accurate telling of her life: her as a newborn, screaming on Cordellia's chest; the first time she and Delilah had broken into Zarah's extensive makeup collection when they were six; "wacky outfit day" at school and her eighteenth birthday. There were others, smaller moments when the person in the snapshot had been caught simply existing.

They were her favorites.

Ava arranged the pictures across the top of her dresser and bookshelf. She placed the one of her and her father on the nightstand.

The one Delilah had taken for her photography class of Ava and Cordellia went next to it. They were laughing at something Ava had long forgotten, but the pure, honest happiness on their faces and love in their eyes was what she would always hold dear. The times when Cordellia's mind was clear was when Ava loved and admired her mother the most.

School was one of the biggest carry-overs from the old world. Education was important, and because citizens were only required to go until they turned eighteen, the classes were vigorous: five days a week for core classes, with the extracurricular ones taking place on Saturday.

When the second generation of magicians was of school-age, the "arts" hadn't been painting and sculpting, but sorcery and manipulation. They would later grow up to bring war to Havaan, using their teachings to destroy the peace and unity their ancestors had worked so hard to establish. When Orion came into power and banished magic, he also expatriated the teaching of such. Little by little the idea of magic, of its once reign, ceased to exist.

At the beginning of the king's rule, even the *mention* of sorcery was justification for banishment to Nopels. Once the horror stories of the place reached the ears of Havaan's citizens, not speaking of it seemed like the smarter idea.

Not speaking of it left no room for questions.

Ignorance was just another of the cogs keeping Havaan operating.

When Ava sat at the foot of her bed and surveyed her very small decorating effort, she realized none of the photos were in her direct line of sight. After some grunting and a lot of pushing and pulling—which was easy seeing how both the dresser and bookcase were currently empty—the faces of her loved ones would be the last thing Ava saw before she fell asleep.

Delilah had come to her door to make sure she wasn't breaking anything, and Sebastian had stopped to ask if she was hungry, which she declined. Other than those two, she was able to rearrange in peace.

Not only was she happy with the new placement of the pieces, but she was also a sweaty mess. She'd discarded her blouse for a tank top a solid hour ago, and opened the doors of the veranda, but even the cool breeze of April did little to keep her hair from frizzing and clothes from sticking.

While the conditioner soaked into her hair, she paced the length of the large shower and mentally organized words and sentences into a somewhat cohesive speech. At one point, she considered turning the whole thing into a roast, calling out the queen for her hatred and the king's reluctance to speak up against his wife.

"I could start with 'I know I can't be the only one who doesn't want to be here tonight…'" She laughed as she imagined the horrified look on everyone's faces. *That would teach them to set me up.*

As she was lying on her bed in nothing but a towel, her stomach growled. She glanced at her watch. It was a little past two in the afternoon. She hadn't had anything to eat since that morning, and even then she'd only taken a handful of bites before her cereal turned into milky rainbow vomit.

How had it only been that morning when everything had changed? Already it felt like she'd been living at High House for at least a month.

"Fine, we'll go find the kitchen," she said to her gut as she dressed in a pair of striped leggings and a long black shirt. The hem brushed her knees and its small sleeves barely covered her shoulders. She didn't really care if it was dressy enough for High House, and cared even less what the queen would think about it. She had two hours until she had to be in her evening wear, and it seemed pointless to trade one swanky outfit for another.

She hurried down the carpeted stairs in a pair of black flats. She knew where the dining room was, and from what she remembered, it had sounded as though the kitchen was directly off of that. Before she could even begin her search, she heard from behind her the purest, holiest of notes.

It halted her in her tracks.

"Mom," she whispered, her heart contracting with excitement. It had only been a few hours since she'd seen her mother, but just the idea of Cordellia being at High House filled Ava with happiness so intense it was almost overwhelming.

Two things could entice Cordellia from the darkness: work and the choir. Cordellia seemed to be better when she had something to do. Sometimes she was functional but still refused to go outside, so the choir would practice at their house. Ava was twelve when her mother had joined the acapella group. Many times, she had sat at the top of the basement stairs while the women practiced, their voices taking her far away from Holland Avenue Number Six.

Away from the never-ending funeral of Dante.

Hearing it echoing down the hall of High House filled Ava with that same expectation. If she could listen to their voices blend seamlessly into one another, maybe it could take her away from here, too.

Just for a little bit.

As the women progressed from their starting note into a song with which Ava was all too familiar, she changed course and followed the melody. It wrapped around her feet like a silk scarf and wove under her like waves, carrying her toward the back of the mansion. She stood outside the door, listening to their warm-up song and as she did, the excitement she'd had just seconds ago started to dissipate. Cordellia had a unique voice, one Ava could easily distinguish from all the rest. Without having to open the door, she already knew what she would find. The part of her that had grown up always being let down by her mother begged her to walk away, but the childlike side of her that was always holding on to some sort of hope was in control of her hand as she reached for the door and pushed it open.

A sea of familiar faces met her sweeping eyes, but the one she wanted to see was not present. She turned her attention to the second-best option. Naomi Biddwater was a no-nonsense woman. Ava had never seen her smile, and her low brow bone gave the impression she was always scowling. She was also the only member of the choir who Cordellia spent time with outside of rehearsals.

Which is why she sought her out.

"Where's my mom?" Ava asked, her voice steady. She already knew the answer but that damn part of her kept gripping at optimism like it was a kite string. She wanted to believe that perhaps Cordellia was simply in the bathroom or maybe just running behind.

Lonnie, one of her least favorite chorus members, leaned around the person in front of her. "Avaleigh? What are you doing here?" Her whiney, nails on a chalkboard voice was laced with confusion.

Ignoring the whispers of "is she the new queen?" and "...not eligible" Ava again asked, "Where is my mother?" Her tone was firmer and demanded an immediate answer.

"She's ill," Naomi replied. The way she said *ill*, with a sardonic tilt to the word, told Ava she didn't believe it for a second. Naomi wasn't privy to all of Cordellia's demons, but she had more of an idea than most.

Anger flared inside of Ava.

Anger at her mother, yes, but also at herself for even believing she would show.

She had been let down by Cordellia countless times, but she'd always let it slide because you can't control ones sadness. She had never doubted the authenticity behind the depression, had never yelled at her for missing important school functions because she didn't—couldn't—*wouldn't* get out of bed for three days. Maybe she'd never addressed her disappointment with Cordellia because she'd been too busy hiding her mother's mental state. It fell on her to deliver finished orders, maintain the house, and balance her schoolwork, all while trying to coax Cordellia back to the land of the living. There had never been time to face how genuinely thwarted she felt. Maybe Ava's haste to take on the extra responsibilities had somehow discouraged Cordellia from getting better.

Ultimately, she hadn't needed to.

Ava had always been there to clean up the mess. To make sure she was okay, that she held onto even the smallest shred of sanity.

But now...

Suddenly, the anger she felt was replaced with unease. Worry.

Ava could feel her mask slipping. Her voice trembled as she asked, "Did you see her?"

Naomi shook her head. "There was just a note on the door."

That concern settled in her stomach like a boulder as it morphed into something even bigger. Something that twisted her heart like children's clay.

It wasn't fear anymore.

It was dread.

XVI.

Ava ran from the room and back down the hall. She needed to find Sebastian *now*. She'd had no time to explore the house and had no idea where he could possibly be. Luckily, she didn't have to look too far, since he was coming down the stairs as she came around the corner.

His bright, cheerful face dropped as soon as he saw her. He hurried down the last half and met her at the bottom. "What's wrong?" he asked, his dark brows creased with concern.

"I have to go home," she said quickly.

"Why? What's going on?"

There wasn't time to explain, but she was going to have to if she had any chance of getting out of here. She took a deep breath and rambled. He already knew a little about Cordellia's disorder, but she elaborated enough to give him a true sense of its depth. She told him of the choir and how her mother was supposed to be at High House practicing, but wasn't.

"I'm all she has left," she said lastly. She tapped her foot anxiously and tried to keep the pressure behind her eyes from spilling over. "I just...I just need to go home and make sure nothing's happened. That she hasn't...done something."

"Ava," Sebastian started, reaching out for her. She crossed her arms over her chest, unintentionally closing herself off from him. She registered the hurt in his face but didn't care. She *couldn't* care, not right now. "The Welcome Dinner is in three hours. With—"

"I'll be back in time," she cut in.

Around them, people went about their jobs, though a few glances slid their direction. Ava could only imagine what was going through their minds. *"Lover's quarrel already? She sure is a handful."* But neither Sebastian nor Ava's attention was on them. They focused only on one another. There was a war raging in his eyes as he weighed the choices.

"The traffic is going to be insane," he finally said. "I just don't see how you can make it there and back, and have enough time——"

The answer was immediate. "Nixon." Sebastian raised a questioning brow. Her head was clear, for a moment at least, and again, hope filled her. "He can take me on his bike. We could maneuver through the traffic and make it back with plenty of time to spare." This time, Ava reached out for the prince and brushed her fingertips against his. "Please," she whispered.

They regarded one another for a few seconds more, though it felt like hours to Ava. She would get to her mother one way or another, a resolve Sebastian must have read on her face.

Finally, almost reluctantly, he nodded. "If Nixon will take you then I will cover for you. For as long as I can, at least."

Ava released a shaky breath. "Thank you," she said. Then, without thinking it over, she hugged him. It was quick, but strong and honest and it felt nice when he returned the gesture.

"Come with me." He took her hand—this time she let him—and followed him up the left staircase. They veered left at the top this time and went down a hallway identical to the one that contained her bedroom. Sebastian's room was four doors down, sandwiched between someone named Raymon and Nixon's.

Sebastian pounded on the appropriate door with his fist, the sound reverberating like a thunder clap. "Nix!" he shouted, pounding harder.

There was a shuffle behind the door and then it opened. The doorframe bordered the guard like the most forbidden piece of art. There was no question the first generation would have burned him, frame and all.

A towel was wrapped around his waist and a t-shirt clung to his wet skin. His black locks were pushed away from his rugged, handsome face and his eyes flickered between the two.

"What's wrong?" he asked as his eyes scanned Ava's pained face.

"My mom isn't here," she replied through a tight throat.

Nixon's brows pulled in as he tightened his hold on the towel. "Is she okay?" he asked.

Ava shrugged as Sebastian explained, "Ava needs you to take her home so that she can find out. Your bike will be the quickest and easiest way to avoid the traffic. But you have to hurry. There isn't much time until we have to start getting ready."

Nixon looked between Ava and Sebastian again, but his gaze finally settled on Ava. He massaged the back of his neck and chewed the inside of his cheek. Ava was growing more worried—about her mother and that Nixon would refuse—but also annoyed that he could even consider doing so. This was the guy who had spent time under the same roof as her, laughing and joking and hell, even flirting a bit. She had pricked a part of herself open and bled her secrets and fears into his hands. She had even introduced him to a few of the skeletons in the graveyard that was her life. She thought they were, if anything, at least friends; but since they'd gotten back to High House, he had built a fortress around himself and ignored the bloody handprints on the wall.

Her disbelief was mounting. Was he *really* considering saying no?

"Please," Ava begged. This one was even more urgent than the one she'd given Sebastian. She sent Nixon a telepathic message, begged him with her eyes. *If you won't do this for me, at least do it for my mom.* Through clenched teeth she said his name. She hated how small her voice sounded, how scared, as if she were a little kid afraid of the monsters under her bed.

She wouldn't ask anything from him again, she vowed. She just needed him to—

"Fine," he answered. His diffidence was evident in the one word.

She bit the inside of her lip and blinked away the tears of relief that welled in her eyes. *Thank you*, she mouthed, unable to speak.

"I'll meet you at the garage." Without another word, he closed the door.

Ava faced Sebastian, who offered her a kind smile. "Go take care of your mother. But get back as soon as you can, okay?"

She nodded eagerly, pecked the prince on his cheek, then turned from him and rushed back down the hall.

It felt like it took an eternity for Nixon to appear. She'd already rolled the speedster out of the garage and was straddling the seat, helmet on, when he did. His eyes roved her body, and with a sigh he shrugged off his jacket and handed it to her. "You're going to get cold," he explained before taking his place in front of her.

She hadn't even thought to change out of her flimsy shirt and was immediately thankful for the offering as they took off. The wind was chilly against even the clothed parts of her.

They rode in silence, which didn't bother Ava. It gave her time to think, to prepare.

Throughout the city, crews of people were erecting what looked like giant white sheets positioned between two very tall metal poles. They were the size and width of billboards, except they weren't billboards.

They were projection screens.

"All of Havaan will be watching," Bernadette had said, and she hadn't been lying. Claudia said they were expecting 20,000 or so citizens. That was only a fifth of the population of Havaan. Those who owned a television—used only when the royal family had an announcement to make—would watch from the comfort of their home. The rest would line the streets, maybe pull out lounge chairs and pop some popcorn, to enjoy the show. That was how Ava had started to think of the whole fanfare: as a show. A spectacle.

She couldn't worry about any of that right now. Images of her mother flashed and fizzled in her mind each time she started to. Cordellia had never seemed suicidal, but then again, she'd never been truly alone. There had always been someone there to hold her up when the weight of reality became too much. But with Ava out of the house now, she had all that space for dark thoughts to flourish from the seeds of her melancholy.

As Ava swayed this way and that with the curves of the road, she felt unsteady. Both mentally and physically. Her grip on Nixon was not as tight as it should have been, and when she got too lost in her thoughts she'd forget to lean with him, tossing the bike off balance. It wasn't like she didn't want to tighten her hold. By all the blood and magic soaked in the black sand of Havaan, she wanted to press herself firmly to him. But it was like the wall he'd put up was tangible, creating an invisible shield meant to keep her from getting too close.

Besides, holding onto him like she once had felt too personal after what had almost happened in her bedroom.

And too invasive considering he was hardly speaking to her.

She would deal with the root of his taciturnity after she dealt with whatever was waiting for her at Holland Avenue Number Six.

Even if…

She couldn't stomach the idea of being too late. Would not allow her mind to go there. She took her thoughts the opposite direction: perhaps Cordellia had just gotten so caught up in her work that she'd lost track of time. That was a possibility. Or maybe she'd fallen asleep and hadn't set an alarm, which was also probable. Neither of those, nor the other scenarios in which Cordellia was fine, explained the note she'd left on the door.

Ava refused to let logic get in the way of believing her mother was okay.

That she was alive.

Sebastian had been right; traffic was a cluster. But as expected, Nixon had snaked through it and made surprisingly quick work of the drive. Ava was off the bike and across the yard before it came to a complete stop. She tugged the helmet off—snagging her ear in the process—and threw it in the grass as she ran across it.

The street was surprisingly empty. No neighbors were milling around, waiting for a chance to bombard Cordellia with questions. No vultures from any of the newspapers were camped in the yard, hoping to get an exclusive with the mother of their future queen. Nothing big ever happened in Havaan unless the royal family was involved, and by now people in her neighborhood must have put two-and-two together.

It didn't matter if they had.

Ava was just glad she didn't have to fight anyone to get inside.

The note was still stuck on the door, the bottom half flapping softly in the wind, waving like a white flag of surrender.

Ava placed her hand on the knob and closed her eyes as she took a deep breath, preparing herself for the worst. Then she turned the handle. She'd done it a thousand times before, but for whatever reason it felt heavier, as if something were leaning against it.

After a bit of shoving, Ava forced herself through the space and kicked her mother's shoe out of the way. The door opened freely then, and Ava stopped dead in the kitchen, her entire body shaking at what she saw.

Cordellia was fine.

She was more than fine.

She was wrapped in a soft, cashmere robe with a glass of wine in one hand and a novel in the other.

Ava had never understood the term "seeing red" until that very moment. She had also never hated her mother before, but it seemed today was a day full of firsts.

Clearly as startled at seeing her child as her child was at seeing her, Cordellia fumbled with her glass, barely setting it upright on the table before standing. "Avaleigh. What are you doing here? You're supposed to be getting ready for the dinner."

Ava balled her hands into fists and focused on the sharp bite of her nails digging into her palms. "I could say the same for you," she said through clenched teeth. "What happened to we'll get through this night together? What happened to I promise?"

"Ava, there are things you don't understand. Things that I can't explain to you, but please, I need you to know I tried, I just—"

"You didn't, though," Ava interrupted with certainty. She wasn't sure how she knew her mother hadn't made any effort to make it to High House, but she knew. "What's even worse than that," Ava continued, "is that you lied to me." She shook her head and rolled her eyes, laughing dryly. "I was so stupid to believe that you would actually be there for me for *once*. I don't even know why I'm surprised. You have *never* been there. Ever."

Cordellia took a step around the table but stopped at the rage in Ava's eyes. If looks could kill, Cordellia would be a corpse on the floor. She sighed, a lifeless sound of its own, and her shoulders dropping as she said, "That isn't fair," with little conviction.

"No," Ava snapped, her voice rising with every word. "What isn't fair is how easy it is for you to let me down all the time. I *need* you. I need you by my side. I need you to, for once in your life, act like a parent and you can't even do that. With all your talk about facing our fears and being strong, one would think you'd be capable of taking your own advice."

"You know how hard it's been for me," Cordellia replied, her tone matching that of her daughter. Tears streamed down in rivulets. They cut into the lines and creases of her face before dripping down her chin. "If your father were still here, things would be different. I could do all the things you need me to do. We could do it together and it would be easier."

Ava felt no sympathy, though the regret of her words would come later. For now, however, her mouth was a rifle and her anger the deadly bullets shot from her lips. "Well Mother, news flash. Dad is dead." Cordellia bit down on a knuckle. "But you're not. You still have a choice and you're choosing to make the wrong one because what?

You're scared?" Ava gripped the fabric above her chest tightly, her knuckles turning white with the force. "*I'm* scared." A few seconds passed between them. Air cycled from her nose to her lungs then back out. "You still have time to get to High House, to prove to me you're better than you've been my entire life. But if you stay here, holed up like a coward, there will be no making this up. Don't try and fix this after tonight, because you will not exist to me."

Cordellia stood there, her face buried in her weathered hands, her body shaking with each heartfelt sob. Damn the childish part of Ava that wanted to run to her, to give mommy a Band-Aid for her owies; as if a piece of tape and a square of gauze could fix the gushing wound that was their relationship. This moment had always been there, a festering infected scab they kept picking at and bandaging, but never allowing to fully heal. Until one day it became toxic, and no amount of sterilization or patches could make it better.

It was clear that her mother had retreated inside of herself, gone to the place she often ventured when the notion of life became too much to handle. Ava knew, with a heavy heart, that Cordellia wasn't going to be at the Welcome Dinner. She wasn't even going to make the effort to try. Perhaps that was the saddest part in the whole mess: that Ava, her own flesh and blood and living breath, mattered less to her than a memory.

As she went to leave, her entire body shaking, Ava said, "Dad would not be proud of *you*."

"Ava!" Nixon scolded. She had forgotten he was there, watching the entire thing. She felt small, embarrassed he had witnessed the unleashing of her fury, but she also didn't care. If he wanted to be an asshole to her, now he had a reason.

She pushed past him and grabbed the helmet from his hands. Her hair whipped around her face as she stomped across the yard back to the bike. He called her name again, and she considered ignoring him, but instead she spun on her toes and glared.

"*Now* you want to talk to me?" she yelled. She was gripping the visor of the helmet so tightly she wasn't sure it wouldn't crack in her hand. He opened his mouth to reply, to argue, to chastise her again, but she held up her hand before a single letter could pass his lips. "Don't. Just…" She exhaled through her nose, a harsh sound like a bull getting ready to charge. "Just get me back."

The traffic was even more backed up on the way *to* High House, the roads congested with people traveling from all areas of Havaan. It was still surreal to think this many people wanted to have dinner in the presence of the royal family. Some had donated money, large chunks from the way Claudia had made it seem, to simply shake their hands. They had no idea who her hand even belonged to, yet they'd paid to touch it, anyway. The priorities of some people would never cease to amaze Ava, and not necessarily in a good way.

Today was not shaping up to be anything like she'd expected, and she had planned for the worst. Between Bernadette's blatant dislike, Nixon's vow of silence, and Cordellia, Ava had already had all she could handle. The grip she had on her emotions was even weaker than the one she had on Nixon. If there'd been a barrier between them on the ride into Meridian, the ride out of it was twofold. Now Ava was as distant and withdrawn as he'd been. Her arms barely encased him and there were multiple times where she considered, for just a fleeting second, letting go entirely. Being tossed from the bike would be the cherry on top of a very shitty pie, but Ava had always liked cherries.

But for a reason she didn't quite understand, she kept herself on the bike as they zipped and zagged between a line of cars. They made it back to High House without incident *and* with two minutes to spare before her 'dresser' was to arrive.

Ava was thankful for neither.

When they docked, she took off her helmet, glad to drink in some fresh air, and walked away from Nixon without a word. He called her name once and even asked her to wait, but she ignored him and went straight up the staircase, then down the hall where she ran—literally—into Delilah.

"Is everything okay?" she asked as they recovered from their collision. "Seb told me you went home to check on your mom."

Ava raised a brow and curled her top lip in disgust. "Seb?"

Her best friend shrugged sheepishly. "I would never call him that to his face. It just saves time not having to say Sebastian. But that isn't important. How's Cordellia?"

She wanted to tell Delilah everything. She needed an hour, even half of one, to have a vent fest and pile it all on her friend. Delilah was rationally emotional and that made her a great person upon which to unload one's burdens. She would take them, sort it all out, and then hand them back in a nicer package with a pretty bow. Ava, however, compartmentalized everything. She put her emotions in their own boxes, battered ones that had holes so sometimes her feelings escaped and ran wild in her brain. Sometimes they even made it all the way to her lips. But she didn't have time—there was never enough time—to do anything besides stuff her thoughts and feelings into a box too small to adequately contain them all.

It would have to do for now.

"I will tell you everything later," Ava promised as she backed away from Delilah. "But I just…" She sighed, exhaled a quick breath. "Right now I need to get ready. And you need to get ready. I *will* tell you though, okay?"

Delilah, who was not used to being dismissed, especially by Ava, just nodded. Her tight smile could do nothing to mask her true feelings. Ava hated seeing Delilah upset, even more so when she was the cause of it, but she pushed her guilt aside and opened the door to her room. Before she stepped inside, she looked over her shoulder at her pink-haired friend. "I'm really glad you're here with me," she said, her voice choked with one of those pesky emotions trying to escape its container.

When she crossed the threshold, she was greeted by not only her barely decorated, full of its own boxes bedroom, but also a short, heavy-set woman who was eyeing her family photos. Ava was happy to see she wasn't touching them, her hands behind her back, but the fact that she was simply looking at them set Ava on edge. It shouldn't have, she knew this, but she couldn't keep herself from asking, "Can I help you?" with controlled anger.

The woman looked at her, an emotion on her face that Ava didn't understand, and then she smiled, as if she'd filtered out the aggression in Ava's question. The woman had been at the meeting. Claudia had addressed her as a 'dresser.'

"Sebastian wasn't sure when you would be here and so—"

"So you thought you'd just take a look around?" Ava crossed her arms and stared at the woman, her big eyes even larger.

"The photos are the only interesting thing in here right now," the woman replied—not argued—as she took a pointed look around the room.

"They're also the most personal."

The woman bowed her head slightly. "I didn't mean any disrespect. I apologize." She had a low voice, husky, as though she were speaking from the very hollows of her throat. She sounded wise, like the years that had turned her hair grey had also imparted wisdom into her speaking.

Ava sighed and rolled her eyes. "It's fine. Where do we start?" she asked, making no effort to hide her agitation.

"We start over," the woman said as she waddled over to Ava. "I'm Helen Yabritza." She extended her hand. Ava eyed the woman's round face. She had kind, stormy grey eyes and a nose that hooked at the tip. When she smiled, her cheeks became perfect cherubic circles, as if she were smuggling two Ping-Pong balls in them. She stared at Ava, her lips curved expectantly.

Finally, despite her desire to be left alone, Ava took Helen's hand in hers. "Avaleigh Toliver. Call me Ava, though."

"It's a pleasure to meet you," Helen replied. Ava's attention shifted to the foot of the bed, where two dresses hung off the edge: the fiery, feisty red one Delilah had purchased for the evening, and the blue one. Helen looked behind her then back at Ava, her smile small but gentle. "I wasn't sure which one you were wearing tonight."

Ava eyed her curiously. "The nice one."

"They both seem very nice to me."

Ava scoffed and walked around Helen. She ran her fingertips along the soft, worn fabric of her favorite dress. "Only one of them is worthy of High House, though," she contended as she grabbed the newer, more expensive of the two and stomped into the bathroom.

"Says who?" the short woman asked.

"Says everyone," Ava replied through the closed door. She was still shaking, riled up from the confrontation with her mother and overfilled with rage she couldn't release. All she wanted to do was curl up in bed and sleep the night, maybe even the week, away. Helen's game of devil's advocate wasn't helping the matter much, either.

"You should wear what you want, not what you think everyone wants you to wear."

Ava yanked the bathroom door open harder than intended. It hit the wall with a loud bang. "Yeah, well, what I want hasn't mattered in a week." Her reply was short, clipped, dripping with resentment.

Helen gave her a once over. "It's a very beautiful dress, and you look beautiful in it." She walked over to the blue dress and cradled it like it was a child, like it was precious. She handed it to a misty-eyed Ava and smiled at her, her cheeks at their fullest. "Now this one."

"Why?" Ava asked. It came out as a whisper as she cuddled the fabric to her chest. "It isn't good enough," she added. What she had really meant was *I'm* not good enough, with my cheap, handmade dress and mess of a life.

Helen pushed the dress into her more. "Just appease an old woman."

Exhaling a deep, quick breath Ava did as she was asked. As she let the fabric hug her body, it felt like coming home. Not the home where all Ava's stuff was gone and her mother was holed up, refusing to face her responsibilities; but home where her father left muddy footprints in the carpet and Zarah's laughter filtered from room to room. Home where life was perfect and Ava could drift to sleep every night in its comfort and safety.

She had never known perfect, had never known peace. The blue dress though…the blue dress was as close to either of those things as she had ever gotten. It had been made for her not as an obligation, but out of love, and from the first time she'd put it on, it had become a pinnacle part of her.

Of her growing, both in the world and into herself.

Maybe it wasn't red hot and regal, but it was hers—it was the one thing she would never let anyone take from her. Her life had changed in the blue dress, just seven days ago, and she would introduce herself as the future queen in it. All the eyes of Havaan would see it, see her homage to one of the women who had played a part in the person Ava was this very day. And maybe—wherever Zarah was, with Dante even—the two of them would see it, too.

When Ava walked out of the bathroom this time, she opened the door like a normal person. Helen looked up from her arsenal of makeup and nodded. "Perfect," she said, beaming.

Ava bit the inside of her lip and then smiled. She felt…better. Not great. She wasn't sure she would ever feel great about everything that was going on, but as long as she was wearing the blue dress, it was almost as if Zarah was giving her the longest never-ending hug.

And a Zarah hug had always made everything…better.

"Shall we get you ready?"

Ava shrugged nonchalantly. "If you don't want to lose your job, then yeah, probably."

Helen had dragged a chair in and Ava planted herself in it. Next to them was a large rolling cart with combs, brushes, tonics, a curling iron, clips, and the biggest collection of makeup Ava had ever seen.

As she set to work on Ava's hair, separating the loose curls into sections, Helen hummed. Ava wasn't sure of the melody, but that, combined with the gentle tugging of hair was calming, and Ava found herself sinking into it. She followed the thread of relaxation down a bright hole that smelled vaguely of mint and cotton.

Helen's voice cut through, but not intrusively. It was soft, another layer of serenity. "I imagine all of these changes are wearing on you." Ava nodded repeatedly. "If it's any consolation, I will say that you seem to be holding yourself together quite well."

Ava scoffed. "I'm a wreck."

"I didn't see a wreck today, when you stood up for yourself against the queen."

"That woman hates me," Ava stated, without emotion one way or another.

Helen's voice held a bit of amusement when she replied, "The queen hates most people."

Ava snapped her fingers sarcastically. "Then I'm not as special as I thought."

"I have a feeling you're very special."

The corners of Ava's mouth flickered slightly at the compliment. Helen reminded her of Zarah—not physically, as Zarah had been as exotic as a gypsy—but with their sweet, friendly dispositions. Ava didn't know much of Helen, but she could tell she was a kind, caring person. And Ava needed kind and caring right now.

"I'm sorry I was rude to you when I came in," she apologized. "It's just been a really rough day."

"It's okay," Helen reassured. A blast of heat brushed against Ava's neck as she twisted a strand of hair around the barrel of a curling iron. "Now, tell me why the queen has such a vendetta against you."

Ava growled and slumped in her chair, but like one continuous stream of conscious thought, she recapped all the interactions she'd had with Bernadette, starting from the night of the gala. She embarrassingly told her about the tantrum she'd thrown and how that had been the catalyst for the queen's dislike. She kept out the part about Bernadette's vice-like grip on her arm, though, because while she liked Helen, she wasn't entirely sure she could trust her motives. She was, after all, the queen's assistant.

There was, of course, the fact that Ava wasn't entirely sure she could trust *anyone* in High House, except for Delilah. She had thought at one point she could do the same with Nixon. Her gut had told her that he was good and honest and worthy of that trust, but being blatantly ignored by him felt a little like betrayal.

She would worry about Nixon later. She had too much on her plate for the night; and not enough time to fret over anything else. If he wanted to distance himself from her, if he wanted to withdraw back into himself, be the stoic guy she had met a week ago who only spoke when he was delivering orders, so be it.

"You remind me of my niece," Helen said as she gathered three chunks of hair and began to pleat them into a loose French-braid down the side of Ava's head.

"Is she moody and rude, too?"

Next to her, Helen chuckled. "Not always. But she is defiant." Her voice was warm when she said it, full of admiration.

Ava looked up at the woman, her eyebrows drawing towards her hairline cynically. "That isn't a good thing."

Giving her a half smile, the elder woman repositioned Ava's head. "It isn't always, no," she agreed as she began pinning the rest of Ava's hair into place with a purpose. "But it isn't always bad. And in this case, it's the latter. She never quite understood why the women in the middle classes weren't eligible to be queen. For a country that prides itself on togetherness, that stipulation always seemed ironic to her."

"I can understand that," Ava agreed quietly.

"She never settled into the idea that she didn't have a shot, though. Of course, she went through her life not expecting to ever be queen. She got a job and dated, but she refused to believe that the king would be able to tell she wasn't from an upper class just by looking at her."

"She couldn't have known that wasn't a real rule, so why would she want to risk it? What if it had been, and what if he did select her only to find out she wasn't as well-to-do as expected?"

Though she couldn't see it, Helen shrugged. "Because she's defiant. She has always believed that having a queen from a middle class would better for the country. It would finally give those citizens some representation. Why the division between citizens is so necessary doesn't make any sense. There isn't a need for one, and Madeline has always been passionate about that. She wanted to make a difference as queen, wanted to be the face of 'the people'. We're not an unhappy nation overall, but there *are* complaints. I think that was the biggest reason she refused to not participate in the Queen's Gala. She just wanted the opportunity, even if it was small, to make Havaan more united."

"Was she at the gala?" Ava asked. Helen maneuvered to the front and leveled herself with Ava as she adjusted her bangs, framing her face with them. Her pudgy, semi-wrinkled face was focused but her concrete colored eyes shone as the corners of her mouth turned up.

"She was."

Ava sighed and frowned slightly. "Orion should have given it to her, then. She sounds like she'd be a much better queen."

Helen's eyes met Ava's. "But he gave it to you. You have a right to be angry, to feel unsettled by all the changes you've been forced to make, and anyone who tells you otherwise isn't worth listening to unless they've been in your place. But eventually…" She paused and covered Ava's face with her hand before unleashing a copious amount of hairspray into the air. Then, as she began painting Ava's face, continued. "Eventually that anger will lessen, be it that you come to accept your new role or because time heals everything, but all the energy you've spent focusing on how much you don't want this will need to be routed somewhere else. Hopefully into something good. That's up to you, however. Personally, I would like to see you do something like Madi wanted to do. You can make a difference. *You* can be the face of the people, bring Havaan together."

Ava looked up at the ceiling as Helen coated her lashes with mascara. *Would it really be that simple?* she wondered. "There are going to be a lot of really jealous people," Ava said, not maliciously or even arrogantly, but as a general statement.

A reminder.

Because there *were* going to be a lot of jealous, and confused, citizens when they found out that she—a person from a middle class—was selected to be queen. How many of those women would be like Delilah and Madi? How many would have spent years prepping and planning, reaching for the crown? How many more had been denied their shot, all because of some stupid rule which hadn't existed?

"Yes," Helen agreed as she pushed a loose piece of grey hair out of her eyes with the back of her hand. Then she made an open-mouthed O face, which Ava mimicked and held. "But there would be a lot of jealous women even if it wasn't you," she said as she ran a lipstick brush over Ava's pouty lips. "Did you know that the population of the middle class is higher than that of the upper?"

Ava smudged her lips together a few times. "I wouldn't have thought that." She took the tissue being offered and blotted her lipstick.

Helen gave her a look she couldn't decipher and then continued. "That jealousy will pass, too, and when it does, eyes will turn toward you. They will rally behind you, but you have to be worth rallying behind, or you will waste many opportunities. Orion and Bernadette rule from a mountain, where only the voices of the upper class can reach. You don't have to do that." Helen took Ava's chin in her fingers and turned her face this way and that, admiring her handiwork.

"Make them want to follow you," she added before tapping the end of the future queen's nose with a fluffy brush.

"Be my best self," Ava answered, smiling the first real, genuine one in…how long had it been since she'd been truly happy?

Helen returned her grin as she adjusted a piece of hair. "I believe you're ready, my dear."

Ava was both excited and nervous to see herself, afraid that even with a fancy up-do and expertly applied makeup she would still look like a girl from Meridian; that she would feel as though she were simply playing dress-up, pretending she actually had a shot at becoming queen.

She fought through that fear and made her way to the mirror. She closed her eyes, took a calming breath, and then looked at herself.

"Wow," she breathed, tears instantly springing to her eyes. She blinked them away before they could fall, clearing her vision at the same time. She looked…gorgeous. Her makeup was elegant, her lipstick a rich plummy stain. Her thick curls were looped and folded into an intricate bun at the base of her neck with a large, beautiful hairpiece tucked into it. It looked like baby's breath and white roses made of metal and wires, a much smaller version of what her crown would be.

Ava almost didn't recognize herself—couldn't see the distraught girl who had practically thrown herself at the mercy of the king's feet just a week ago.

"I almost look like a queen," she said. It was the first time she had acknowledged that side of herself. Honestly, she hadn't believed she could ever feel like she was good enough for the crown, for the throne. For the title. And it wasn't that she entirely felt it at this moment, either; but looking the part was a good first step.

It was also the first time the voice in her head whispered, "you can do this. You belong here," and she agreed with it.

"You clean up pretty well," Helen teased as she stepped next to Ava. The comment cleared away the overwhelming emotions that were building in the room like a dense fog.

"Not too bad, huh?" she replied, looking at Helen through the reflective surface. "Thank you."

"It's my pleasure." Helen glanced at her watch. "I've done my part, now you have to do yours."

Ava nodded and adjusted her posture. She tightened her spine and dropped her shoulders, taking on a battle stance. All she needed was a few stripes on her cheeks and she'd be ready for war.

As Helen began to clean up her tools and Ava slipped on a pair of open-toed sandals that crisscrossed up her ankles, she asked, "What does your niece do?"

The older woman looked up from wrapping the cord of the curling iron around her hand. "Pardon?"

"Madi. You said she worked. What does she do?"

"She's a pastry chef," Helen answered with that prideful lilt to her voice again.

Ava's ears, eyebrows, and interest perked up. "Like desserts?" Helen nodded. Ava decided right then that, "If she wants it, she has a job here."

Cocking her head slightly, Helen eyed Ava. "What do you mean?"

The younger of the two shrugged a shoulder. "I know it isn't the crown, but she sounds like someone I would like to have around. So, if she wants it, there'll be a position for her in the kitchen. I'll talk to Sebastian and we'll make it happen," she promised.

It didn't seem possible, but Helen's face softened and her cheeks rounded even more. "I'll let her know," she said, her voice even lower as she tried to keep the tremor of emotion from her words.

"Just leave me her information and I'll get in touch with her," Ava said. She placed her hand on the knob of her bedroom door and prepared to step into the hall, readied herself for the clash of citizens, and greetings, introductions and speeches. Before exiting, however, she made her way back to Helen and hugged her, squeezing the small, portly woman. She whispered her thanks again—for the makeover, for the words of advice—but more importantly for the courage she'd given Ava without knowing she was even doing so.

Helen's name was now on the very short list of people that Ava couldn't—*wouldn't*—let down.

Then, without another word, she crossed the soft carpet of her uninspired boudoir and made her way down the hall. Toward the battle front she marched, waving her banner of house Toliver and wearing her armor of blue.

XVII.

The only room Ava had seen that was big enough to hold thousands of people was the Throne Room, so she made her way there. She had to weave through a conveyer belt of staff; men and women hurrying this way and that with chairs or platters or fabric, table settings and place cards…a podium. The air was perfumed with rosemary and sage, tinges of garlic mingled with a singed odor of chargrilled meat that would make anyone's mouth water. As Ava made her way through the foyer, she glanced up at the large clock on the wall. It had no frame or faceplate, just metal numbers in a perfect circle and two hands in the middle. There was still at least fifteen minutes until everyone was expected to gather, but she continued to the meeting room anyway.

She could do with a few minutes of alone time.

Ava closed the heavy door behind her, the sound of it shutting echoing through the cavernous room, and *really* looked around. During her first visit here, she'd been so focused on the king she hadn't had time to take in its sheer grandeur. The red curtains hanging over the floor to ceiling windows were heavy velvet and swept the marbled floor.

The view outside of the windows was almost more extraordinary than the actual space. The room sat slightly above ground-level and looked out over the vastness of the backyard. It was at least the size of two football fields, if not three, with plush green grass in varying shades. A woodsy area, miles deep, encompassed the yard like a fern and evergreen fence. To the far left was an old greenhouse. Ivy vines covered it like a wall, clinging to its glass windows and slanted roof. Hundreds of citizens had heard from a friend of a friend of a friend about the rare and sometimes dangerous plants housed there. Ava planned to be one of the people who *actually* went inside. Not because she cared all that much about the florae, but simply because she wanted to be able to say, "I've been there."

Set slightly behind the greenhouse was a large barn shaped from corrugated steel. She hadn't a clue what the building was used for, though her familiarity of the layout of High House was null.

All around the yard, tables were being erected and golden cloths tossed across them. They weren't the only things going up. A large platform, at least four feet off the ground, was being built, its pieces snapped into one another like an oversized child's puzzle. It looked like a performance stage, or the makings of a hangman's gallows.

Ava could barely differentiate between the two.

She turned away from the construction and shuffled over to the main focus of the room, the one thing that had drawn her attention each time she stepped into the extravagant but overwhelming space. From the corner of her eye, the two large chairs loomed, and while she was tempted to see if they were as uncomfortable as they looked, she resisted as she neared one of the many carved pillars instead. They were the entire height of the room and it would take at least two of her to get her arms around them completely. It wasn't the mass of them that impressed her, but rather the delicate carvings in each.

The scenes were nearly at eye-level and took up only ten inches or so, but they wrapped fully around the circumference of the column. From a distance they looked like random lines and shapes haphazardly etched into the smooth white surface, but up-close they were…magnificent. As Ava moved to each one, starting closest to the door, they told the story of the history of Havaan. The first showed the mass of the world being stitched together by a giant needle, the thread controlled by the minds of the first magicians. One pillar wordlessly described the selfishness of the second generation: the characters played tug-of-war with something, kicked each other while they were down. This was followed by a grisly recreation of the war on the banks. In the background, coming from both the sky and the ground was the silhouette of a man who would inevitably claim victory over the magi.

Below him, two sides blasted one another with magic and weapons. Magicians lay dead on the ground, arrows and swords through them, tendrils of smoke evaporating from their chests. Everyday citizens, those without magic at their control, had limbs blown off by a simple will of fingertips. One image confused Ava, but also stirred in her a feeling she couldn't quite explain. In it, a man stood in the middle of the battlefield with his hands raised toward the sky. From graves surrounding him, emaciated bodies emerged, weapons of steel already gripped in their dead fingers.

The rest of the stories Ava had heard. They'd been recited to her over the years and she'd been taught a watered-down version of them in school. All except for the man raising the dead.

"They're beautiful, aren't they?" She heard footsteps approach from behind her and she ran her finger over the sculpted, faceless man.

"I don't know this story," she said to Sebastian. She gave him a quick up-and-down, taking in his dark grey suit and baby blue tie. His silver locks were slicked away from his face and he looked at least four years older.

He looked at her curiously, and replied, as if the answer were obvious, "It's the history of Havaan."

"I know that much. I meant *this*." She tapped the carving. "This scene."

"Ah. The Necromancer." Sebastian walked around the pillar, his hands behind his back, studying the image as if it were the first time he was seeing it, as well. Ava watched him as patiently as possible and gave him time to speak. "As the story goes, during the war there were mixed allegiances on both sides. Citizens fought citizens and magicians battled magicians. Father's side happened to have a man with a rare and extraordinary ability."

"He could raise the dead," Ava finished. Her voice was full of wonderment. There was never any mention of such power in the history books and she would wager most people didn't know this tidbit, either.

"When the war was over, Father gave those with power the option to relinquish it or suffer the same fate as everyone else. Those who willingly sacrificed their abilities were given immunity and allowed to live normal lives. Those who refused were banished to Nopels. Regular citizens who'd decided to fight against him were automatically banished. Those who had fought *with* him were given the same two options. As I'm sure you can imagine, most took the better of the deal."

Ava didn't know the part about Orion giving the magicians a choice. In her head he had always forced them to give up their powers, and then they were banished regardless. Now she couldn't help but wonder how many people were walking around Havaan with old, dried veins that had once throbbed with magic.

"How have I never heard any of this?"

Sebastian shrugged casually. "Every world has their own myths. The old days had tales of a man who broke into homes and left gifts. The Necromancer is ours. No one before him and no one since has ever had that ability. You haven't heard about it because it's just a fable, a fun element to add to an otherwise harrowing war story."

She rounded the opposite side of the column and came face-to-face with him. "But he's included in the pillars."

"The winners always get to write the history books, and in it they can embellish what they want. This is one of those times. No one talks about the war. There are no record books of it, only retellings of an edited story. But Father loves to tell the story of The Necromancer, because who wouldn't want a dead-raising magician on their side? So, he became a part of the unauthorized history, immortalized forever in ivory stone."

Ava's eyes drifted to the spot once more. The inkling in the base of her skull returned, as if something—a memory, maybe?—had grown claws and was trying to dig its way to the surface. But it never emerged and finally settled back into the cave in which it'd been hiding.

"You look beautiful, by the way," Sebastian said, his words diverting her attention.

She gave him a full grin and curtsied cheekily. "And you look quite dashing."

The prince glanced down at his wardrobe and shrugged before lifting his eyes to meet hers. "This old thing?" he joked, waving off her compliment.

Their laughter was cut short as Delilah entered the room, continuing a conversation with Ava that Ava hadn't even been a part of. "—and I went to your room, but you were already gone. I wanted to be the first to——" She halted mid-step, the toe of one shoe hovering off the ground as her eyebrow slowly rose into a comma. "What are you wearing?"

Mimicking Sebastian, Ava looked down her tall body. "The blue dress."

"Right," Delilah replied, drawing the word out. "The *blue* dress. Not the red one."

Rolling her eyes slightly at Sebastian, Ava excused herself and hurried to her best friend. By the elbow, she tugged D into a corner. As soon as Ava let go, Delilah crossed her arms and glared, but said nothing. Taking a deep breath, Ava explained, "The red dress is…perfect, but it's perfect for something else. D——" She held up a finger to mute her friend. "I know that you think this dress is simple and nothing special. But so am I. All of Havaan is going to meet me tonight, and I don't want their first impression to be of me in an expensive, saucy dress that alludes to someone I'm not. I will wear the red dress, but I have to wear it when the occasion is right. Tonight just isn't that night. Can you understand that?"

Delilah pursed her lips and cocked them to one side, then she dropped her arms as she let out an exasperated breath. "I guess," she finally agreed, though Ava could tell she wasn't entirely happy about the whole thing. "At least you pulled it together with your hair and makeup."

"Pulled it together." Ava shook her head, laughing. "I'm pretty sure you look hot enough for the both of us."

Delilah's emerald green dress was fitted so perfectly to her body it looked like paint. It hit just above her knee and showed off her legs. Peek-toe black heels made her eyelevel with Ava. The neckline was a bit more modest than Delilah preferred, but it didn't take away from the palpable sensuality D omitted no matter what she wore.

"I'm hoping it'll tempt Nixon into ravishing me tonight," Delilah said, wiggling her eyebrows.

"It's as good a dress as any to tempt such a man," Ava replied with hopeful nonchalance.

Their conversation ended abruptly as the door swung wide and the rest of the royal family trailed in. "Speak of the devil," Delilah mumble-whispered from the side of her mouth as Nixon brought up the rear. Even if she'd been blindfolded and encased in a tomb ten feet under, Ava would have known he'd entered the room. The air changed, charged with the static that always crackled when he was around.

Ava's mouth was suddenly dry as she drank him in. He was dressed in the traditional guard attire: a fitted black jacket—military cut that hit at the hips— with the king's emblem in white on the back and three golden buttons down the front. The sleeves were three-quarter length and cuffed, held in place by polished onyx links. The lapels of a crisp red dress shirt lined up perfectly with those on the jacket. Straight-leg black pants finished the sleekness of the attire. He looked as dark and dangerous as he always did, but also intimidatingly in control. There was power rolling off him that wrapped around Ava's feet like an invisible lasso, tugging at her ankles. She wanted to go to him. It wasn't the outfit that was doing it, she realized. It didn't matter what he wore—she'd probably still be drawn to him if he donned a burlap potato sack.

He just had that effect on her.

She recognized it for what it was: unadulterated attraction.

Tight throat, racing pulse, constricting pupils, pounding heart, ribcage full of monarchs.

His eyes swept the room before settling on the two women. They jumped from Ava to Delilah very quickly, as though he'd realized he was looking at her, but then they were back to Ava almost as fast. Even from a distance she noticed the flare of his nostrils and the spark in his eyes. She wanted him to say something, anything—she would even settle for a smile—but he blinked and cleared his head with a slight shake as Claudia entered.

"You all look exquisite," she praised as she looked at each person. Ava had to agree. Everyone looked elegant and regal, but not overly done or too extravagant. No one was dripping in jewels or finely spun gold. Even the crowns on Orion and Bernadette's heads were modest, as far as crowns went. Ava didn't even feel all that underdressed in her simple gown. Was it in the same league as Bernadette's, with its collar of green gems? Not even close, but it did pair well with Sebastian's tie and Levi's aqua dress-shirt. It was even in the same spectrum as the other two dresses in the room. Standing in a row together, as they were now that Claudia had arranged them in front of the throne platform, they looked coordinated but not tackily so. It was as if they had chosen their outfits on purpose but also intentionally picked garments that weren't too similar. It would be a nice family photo for the wall.

The order was a little odd, and not at all what Ava had expected it to be. Orion was first and next to him was not Bernadette but Ava herself. The king would make introductions as the lucky 5,000 filed in one by one. Sebastian was on Ava's other side, followed by his mother and finally Levi, who looked about as over the whole thing as Ava felt. Although, she couldn't deny the fanfare was a *little* exciting.

On the first step of the platform was Delilah—allowed in the mix because she was the assistant—and Nixon, the stoic, most trusted of all the guards, who still refused to speak to or even look at Ava.

She'd said hi to him once Claudia had her positioned, but all she'd gotten was a heated look and quick twitch from the corner of his lips. With an eye-roll that would have impressed Delilah and a scoffed, "Whatever," she'd turned away from him and resigned to stop trying. She was making herself look like a fool, thirsty for even the smallest acknowledgement as if she were parched—minutes from death—and in his hands he held the living water.

No more, she thought as she felt Sebastian's attention on her. When she turned to look at him, his smile was radiant and his eyes full of pure, genuine joy. Why was she wasting time being upset over Nixon, who felt a million miles away, when she had a wonderful and beautiful man right beside her?

Claudia began to prattle off the order of operations for the meeting, cutting through her thoughts. "It's all going to be very quick," she promised. "Everyone will file in in an orderly fashion, King Orion will introduce Ava to them, and then they will make their way down the line. Once they reach Levi, a guard will escort them into the backyard where they'll enjoy some lite hors d'oeuvres until everyone has made it through. Then the rest of you will join them, speeches will take place and finally dinner will be served. Any questions?" She looked down the line, her plastic smile unwavering. Elated that there were none, she looked over her handiwork one last time then instructed a young guard to open the doors.

With a glance back at Delilah, who gave her an ecstatic pair of thumbs-up, and a gentle hand-squeeze from the prince, Ava let out a slow breath, forced her lips into something that hopefully mimicked enthusiasm, and steeled herself for the 5,000 hands she was about to shake.

XVIII.

The first thousand and a half people went smoothly, and surprisingly fast, just as Claudia had promised. Even so, at citizen number one-hundred and fifty-three, Ava's hand was sore from being gripped, her wrist limp from all the shaking, and her face tense from the plastered-on smile.

Even Before that, the faces and names of the bankers and architects, lawyers and artists, and the men who Orion had named "governors" over the different regions of Havaan, had all begun to look and sound the same. The king did a pretty decent job remembering to introduce his future daughter-in-law, though the boom of his voice only required him to say, "I'd like for you to meet Avaleigh Toliver, future queen of our great land" every twenty people or so.

Occasionally the king would get caught up in conversation, halting the line. People seemed to handle the hold-up surprisingly well, and if they didn't, at least had the forethought to not complain within earshot of Orion. The reprieve allowed Ava a moment to shake out her hands or granted Sebastian an opportunity to regale her with anecdotes about citizens who would be coming up to them soon. Some of the tales made it difficult for her to keep a giggle under wraps when they approached, but it also helped to ease some of the tension and nervousness she was feeling.

She tried to avoid looking at Nixon, but sporadically there was a shock to the back of her neck, like someone had touched her with a live wire. When she turned her head to see if it was because *he* was looking at *her*, his eyes were either facing forward or he was whispering nothings to Delilah sweet enough to make her cheeks match the ruddiness of her hair. Ava had to swallow the building lump in her throat each time she caught sight of it, but she also had to remind herself how good this was, that maybe something positive could come from Nixon acting like a complete asshole.

Having a crush on the golden-eyed sentry was not beneficial, especially when she was expected to marry the jade-eyed mensch next to her. And she couldn't do that if Nixon was always around like he'd been at her house. She rationalized, as she smiled without validation at another portly man with thinning hair, that the less time she spent with Nixon and the more unavailable he became, the better chance she had at falling in love with Sebastian.

Love.

It seemed like such an easy thing to tumble into. People did it all the time. Some even loved multiple people at the same time. People like Connor, who she'd thought she had loved, but had merely mistaken hormonal infatuation with the word. By all the stars in the sky, though, she *had* been infatuated…by his nimble fingers and the way they'd peeled apart her innocence. By the way his lips moved when he told her she was beautiful. She had believed him, every lie he had spoken. Each promise he had made against her flesh had imprinted into her naivety like a cattle prod. When he left, scars had formed where his name had once resided, and the new tissue hardened her against feeling anything for anyone again.

She hadn't been surprised when he'd left her for Juliet.

Just sad.

So much sadness. So deep and dark she was certain it was going to drown her.

But it hadn't.

Connor and Juliet were the kind of people who were meant to end up together. They both came from upper class families. She was one of the popular girls and though Ava had teetered somewhere between popular and non-popular, she and Juliet hadn't really been friends. They didn't *not* get along, but not getting along and getting along are two very different things when you're a teenager.

Ava hadn't realized how hurt she was by the breakup until she'd seen them together, only a few short days after he'd kicked her to the curb, sitting in the market as though *she* hadn't spent the last couple of days being a mirror of her mother. That hurt had turned into anger in a matter of seconds, and there had been a wicked delight in seeing them covered in blueberry smoothie. She hadn't seen Connor or Juliet since that day, at least not until—

"Hi." The familiar voice pulled her from her memories and brought her face-to-face with the one person she hadn't thought she'd ever see again. Let alone here.

The forced smile she'd been wearing all night slipped when she replied, "Hey."

From behind her came a growl, quiet but there, like a warning from a dog. Ava didn't need to look to know it had come from Delilah, her small but scrappy, never afraid of confrontation, best friend.

If Juliet heard it, she didn't give any indication. Instead she just said, "It's been a while." Her voice sounded different, dejected almost. It was not the same sharp-edged one she'd had throughout their school days.

"It has," Ava confirmed.

"You look really good though."

"So do you." It wasn't a lie or said out of courtesy. Juliet looked almost as polished as she had while growing up. Her syrup-colored hair was still long and thick and hung down her back in loose waves. Her violet eyes were still tilted and tapered, surrounded by the longest lashes Ava had ever seen. Juliet had always been a pretty girl, but was now a beautiful woman. The only thing different about her, aside from the bags under her eyes, was her weight. She'd always been fit, slender but toned with definition in all the right places. Now she was willowy, like a tree that had been stripped of all its foliage and left with droopy, thin limbs.

Juliet smiled, though it was sad and changed her face none. "I never thought, in a million years, that you would be queen one day."

Ava laughed. "That makes two of us.

"It also makes sense. You were destined for wonderful things. I'm glad to see that you are finally getting them."

Against her control, Ava angled her head and made her doe-eyes thin as she tried to figure out Juliet's angle—because she had always had one—because there was no way she was being nice without some sort of hidden agenda. Instead, she replied with an insincere, "Thanks." There was a breath of a pause before Ava asked, "So, are you and Connor still together?" while her eyes acknowledged the large ring on Juliet's finger. Juliet held her hand up and looked at the diamond. It was impressive, especially on her skinny fingers, but there was no joy behind her eyes. "We have a son," she answered, almost robotically.

"Oh. That's great."

Glancing over at Orion, who was again lost in conversation with a man whose nose was so sharp he reminded Ava of a human-penguin hybrid, Ava was left with no choice but to converse with Juliet, who clearly had no intention of moving on until she was forced. But then Ava realized it was because she had something to say. She mushed her lips together, almost anxiously, then blurted, "I'm sorry," the same time that Ava asked, "What else have you been up to?"

"You're sorry?" It was the last thing she had expected Juliet to say, and it showed in the way her eyes widened and her brows reached toward her forehead. "For what?"

Juliet looked around nervously before her purple eyes found Ava's blue ones. "I didn't know," she started, leaning closer to Ava. Her voice dropped to a near whisper and Ava had to strain to hear her. "I didn't know you two were still dating when he asked me out. He told me he had broken things off months before we got together. Ava, if I *had* known I never would have agreed to go out with him. I know it doesn't matter now, but I just thought you should know that I never meant anything ill toward you."

It was the explanation she had wanted two years ago, when it felt like Connor had ripped her heart out and tap-danced on it with spiked shoes. She had felt stupid for believing she had mattered to him, that she had been more than a conquest; and she had felt replaced when he'd moved on to the other woman so quickly. Ava had always assumed there'd been an overlap in the two relationships, that she had been splitting his attention with another, but she had never had confirmation. At that time, she had wanted validation so she could stop feeling like a paranoid ex-girlfriend, but getting it now felt like…nothing. There was no peace, no resolution, because she had stopped caring a long time ago.

About Connor.

About Juliet.

About any of the pettiness that came with being young.

What she did feel, however, was guilt and sadness…so much sadness…when Juliet added with tears on the rim of her eyes, "Between the two of us, you got the better deal." The movement that followed was subtle, a natural flick of hair off her shoulder before she moved it back into place, but Ava didn't fail to miss the dark bruises on her neck——angry red on top of healing green that looked very much like fingermarks.

"Juliet," she whispered, because that's all her brain could come up with. There was nothing she could say that would adequately express how truly sorry she was that Juliet was in the position she was. She may not be that fond of her, but Ava would never, in a million lifetimes, wish such treatment upon anyone——even Bernadette.

Without thought she looked at Sebastian, who was joking around with his younger brother across his mother. In that second, Ava felt the first of many moments of thankfulness. Maybe this wasn't the life she had planned, but it wasn't the worst one she could have been dealt. It would have been so easy for her and Juliet to be in each other's shoes, on the opposite side of the line between them. Though Ava could never imagine letting someone put their hands on her in a violent manner, she could have imagined Juliet doing so even less. She'd been strong, intimidating, the kind of girl you didn't want to piss off. Standing here was the first time that Ava had ever been glad Connor had ended their relationship. Sure, she'd gotten a broken heart out of it and was incredibly jaded toward love—but Juliet had gotten far worse. Ava had no doubt that there were other bruises, ones hidden by the long-sleeved canary colored dress the other woman wore.

Next to her, the conversation between Penguin-Man and the king was finishing up. Ava had heard him use the lines "we'll get together soon" and "we'll have to make plans" enough that evening to know it was coming to an end, but she wasn't ready for her own conversation to do so. There were so many questions she had for Juliet, ones that would no doubt pry into her darkest moments, but she wanted to know how someone so high up could fall so quickly.

Instead, she quelled her curious mind and asked, "Is he here?" Her voice was more controlled than she felt.

Juliet nodded. "He got pulled out of line so he's a few people behind me." As nonchalantly as possible, Ava scrutinized the thirty-five or so people inside the room. It didn't take long to find her target. He looked exactly the same. Connor was tall and solidly built, with buzzed hair and a goatee. Everything about him was oversized—from his giant head to the wide berth of his shoulders. Even his ears and nose were larger than average, but none of it looked weird or misplaced. He was just a big guy and the extra-large features made sense.

But Connor had a secret—an ugly secret—and ugly secrets can snatch away beauty in the blink of an eye. Juliet was a prime example of that.

As if he could sense eyes on him, Connor began to turn from the conversation in which he was engaged. Ava diverted her attention back to Juliet before their eyes could meet. She could only imagine what sort of punishment his wife would endure at his hands if he thought for even a second that Juliet had made anyone privy to the violence their marriage had borne; and Ava was awful at hiding her thoughts and feelings from her face.

"What about your son?" she asked, her stomach a bundle of nerves at all the possibilities a monster like Connor could wreck on his own flesh and blood.

"He's a great father," Juliet defended, her voice shaky. "Ava, you can't let him know—"

At the first sight of tears, at the first crack in Juliet's veneer, Ava wrapped the woman in a tight hug. She was pretty sure the shocked inhale of breath from behind her depleted the room by at least half its oxygen, but she didn't care. At first Juliet just stood there, her scrawny arms limp at her too thin sides, but after a few seconds she returned the embrace, tighter than Ava would have thought possible. It said so much, words that Juliet's fear would never let her say, but Ava got it. She understood.

"I will get you out of there," she whispered with as much promise and conviction as she could. She didn't know why she said it, but as soon as the words passed her lips she knew she meant them.

When the two women parted, Mr. Penguin ready to move the line along again, Ava saw for the first time that night a flicker of optimism in Juliet's sad, lost eyes. It was only there for the single tick of a second, and Ava couldn't help but wonder how many times she'd heard that already, only to awake in the same nightmare over and over and over.

The man behind Juliet cleared his throat. "Congratulations," she said. Her voice was steady again. "I can't wait to see what you do as queen."

Ava nodded once and offered her a friendly smile, which she returned. As she went to walk away, Ava reached out and touched her arm lightly. "Hey Jules?" The dark-haired woman looked at her with expectancy. "We're good."

It was back—for longer than a second this time—that same hope Ava had so desperately clung to all her life; hope that burned bridges could be mended and lives put back together, even after they'd been demolished, obliterated into nothing but microscopic shards. She wanted to believe that as long as something remained, even the tiniest sliver, that reconstruction could begin; that regrowth could happen.

It had to start somewhere.

She and Juliet would never be best friends; that title was already reserved for the pink-haired pixie who leaned over Ava's shoulder and whispered, "You have some serious explaining to do," into her ear. But it wouldn't hurt to have another person on her side.

You never knew when you'd have to traverse that bridge again, use it to get to safety.

Ava shook the hand of the beak-nosed man and smiled sweetly at him as Sebastian bumped his shoulder with hers. "Was she a friend of yours?" She followed his line of sight to Juliet, who was being escorted out of the room.

"They shared a boyfriend," Delilah piped, doing very little to hide her disdain for the whole situation.

Sebastian's eyebrows rose quickly and a flicker of mischief sparked in his eyes. "Is that so?"

"Not like that," Ava replied almost immediately, the corner of her lips lifting in amusement. "I did not agree nor was I made aware of the sharing," she explained just as her fingers were gripped by a feeble old woman.

"Sounds like an interesting story either way," the prince replied.

Ava shook her head. "It's not," she disputed, but quickly added, "I will tell it to you one day." The promise smoothed away the small wave of disappointment that had creased Sebastian's forehead. He really was a good looking guy, especially when he smiled, and she hoped one day his nearness would elicit a frenzy of butterflies in her stomach.

At the thought of such winged creatures, she risked a glance at Nixon. His glowing eyes were facing forward and his face was still, but she did not miss the bob of his Adam's apple as he swallowed or the slow exhale through his nostrils. What it meant, Ava couldn't be sure, but there was no question that he had heard the exchange between herself and Sebastian. She had been so quick to promise entrance into her past just then, an almost eager willingness to offer a peek into what was a very hard and depressive memory. But with Nixon she had been hesitant. She had given him multiple glimpses at many memories, but some she had been reluctant to hand over to him. There was no reason for the guilt she was feeling, and the simple fact that she was feeling *any*, especially about her alacrity to share herself—important pieces that made up the whole of her—with her future husband, was outlandish.

Lost so deeply in thought and focused so intently on the sudden resentment she was feeling toward the guard, Ava didn't realize whose hand had been placed in hers until a rush of memories came flooding back. She trailed her eyes up the long fingers that had traced the tender parts of her body, up an arm that had branded around her waist as, sticky with sweat, they'd tried to count the stars in the sky. She skipped his torso and went immediately to his face, familiar but also not—a stranger you've passed so repeatedly in a store that you begin to feel maybe you knew them in a past life.

She watched as his lips, two thin lines that had once pressed against hers and told her he loved her, formed her name in the same way they had when he'd told her it was over. "Avaleigh." His voice was like an ice cube down her spine and she clenched her teeth to keep from shivering—not in the way she once had when her name would cross his lips.

"Connor," she replied, dry and flat.

Behind her, Delilah made a sound like a feral cat. Ava didn't need to see her friend to know there was a sneer to her lips and a look so vindictive it could convince the devil to hand over his pitchfork.

It didn't bother Connor, though, who had always taken a sort of sick delight in agitating the small but vicious woman. Knowing what she did now, it made sense. "Delilah. Always a pleasure to see you."

A helpless look at Sebastian told her that he was eating this up, and since his posture was relaxed, she knew he had no intentions of jumping in to save her. Not because he wouldn't, but because he knew she didn't need him. At least, not yet.

Connor returned his vibrant, kiwi-green eyes to Ava and grinned viper-like. Deadly. Poisonous. Full of everything bad in the world hidden behind two rows of teeth as white as a dove's wing. "This is the last place I ever thought I'd see you."

She pulled her hand out of his grasp, and as conspicuously as possible wiped it on her dress. "I've always been full of surprises," she replied emotionlessly.

Rubbing his chin with his thumb and first finger, his index one patting his well-groomed facial hair, her ex-boyfriend's eyes roved her body. His spacey, "That you have been," was laced with innuendos and Ava could almost feel the detestation rolling off of Delilah. D had never liked Connor, had never trusted his intentions of being with Ava—mainly because boys from the upper class didn't date girls from the middle. After he'd shattered Ava's purity, and later her heart, Delilah's dislike for him had only intensified in an almost *I told you so* sort of way.

Nixon cleared his throat, pulling Connor's attention off Ava. Whatever look the kingsman was giving the other man forced a wicked, un-intimidated smirk to Connor's lips. Then he held out his hand to Sebastian, who shook it firmly but cautiously. "Connor Avery. This one—" He motioned to Ava with a thumb. "—and I dated."

"Sebastian Calder. That one and I are going to be married." He winked at Ava.

"I guess you could say I did you a favor breaking things off, huh?"

Ava's nose scrunched, as if she'd suddenly smelled something foul. "I'd say that even if I wasn't going to be queen."

Behind her, Delilah chuckled. On her left, the king's eyes darted to the scene taking place. On her right, Sebastian's chest puffed with pride. Above her, Nixon remained statuesque, aside for the small flicker at the corner of his mouth.

Connor's true colors flashed for a heartbeat. The cracking of his knuckles as his hands clenched into fists was as audible as the conversation around her. One thing Connor had always hated was being challenged.

Especially by a woman.

Especially in front of others.

Ava should have been afraid, and maybe she was a little—but she was less scared for herself and more so for the woman who had, for whatever reason, agreed to marry him. Ava had protection. Juliet didn't.

And she wondered if standing up to Connor meant Juliet was going to have to pay the price.

She couldn't think about it too long, because suddenly Claudia was there, her ruby red lips pulled tight across her jaw as if they'd been surgically placed that way by a madman. She turned her back to the king and in a hushed voice asked, "Everything okay here?" Her eyes darted between the small group. "I know how exciting it is to meet the queen, but we have a lot of people looking to do so as well, so we need to keep the line moving, please," she chirped, though her bravado faltered a bit at the tension she'd walked into.

Ava's eyes continued to bore into Connor's. Eyes she had looked into almost as deeply once before, but this time hers held not passion but a dare: do something.

But then he laughed. A condescending guffaw that, with just a sound, was repetitive of the words he'd said to Delilah the day she'd confronted him in the market. "Why Ava?" she had asked. *Why hurt kind, sweet, naïve Ava?* His reply was as cold as winter. "I got tired of pretending she was worth something."

It wasn't fair to say he had been the catalyst for her walls, for her difficulty in letting people in, but he had played a major part.

Between Connor and Cordellia, they'd really fucked Ava up.

And poor Sebastian, who had stepped even closer and placed a protective hand on her back, had to be the one to deal with all of it.

With a final rest on all the faces, his eyes lingering on Ava's a few seconds longer than everyone else, Connor gave her his disgustingly charming grin before moving down the line. As soon as he was to Bernadette, Ava exhaled the breath she hadn't known she was holding. It came out of her in one gasp, a collapsing of lungs and hunching of shoulders. She turned away from everyone, her back to the line, and ran a finger under her eye, wiping away the teardrop that had fallen from her lashes. Then she rolled her neck, cracking the tightness from her spine and put her mask back on. Around her, her posse, her support system, settled as well, though there were still cautious, apprehensive glances shared between them.

They got through the rest of the line without incident. A few of Ava's neighbors had made it into the line, no doubt using a large chunk of their savings to do so. They promised to look after Cordellia, to check in on her frequently, because that's "just what neighbors do." And as much as Ava wanted to believe that they would—or at least were agreeing to do so—purely from the kindness of their hearts, she just couldn't. After tonight, the speck of faith she'd had in people was stretched even thinner. She was going to be queen in a very short amount of time. There would undoubtedly be a cost to that; people coming out of the woodwork hoping their good deeds would somehow be rewarded.

Seeing Connor had reminded her how easy it was for someone to manipulate another, to use their kindness and compassion against them. Though she thanked her neighbors, told them that she would appreciate it, she couldn't help but question the sincerity behind their words.

And when they exchanged low-fives and expectant looks between one another, she couldn't help but doubt it even more.

XIX.

As soon as the last citizen exited the room, there was a collective sigh from the remaining eight.

"You all did so well," Claudia praised, though her tone didn't hold its normal enthusiasm. It seemed the entire event had drained even the perkiest of them. "Take a few minutes and breathe, gather yourselves again, and then head into the yard, okay?"

Numbly, they all nodded. It had never occurred to Ava that shaking hands for three hours could be so exhausting, but she was spent in all possible ways. The instep of her feet ached from her shoes. Her cheeks were sore to the touch from smiling. Her emotions were frayed and mentally…well, mentally she was barely checked in.

Her weariness, however, did not keep her from thanking Claudia. The blonde stopped mid-tap and the look she gave Ava told her that those were not words the coordinator was used to hearing. Especially from members of the royal family, Ava would bet. Then Claudia smiled. It was not over-stretched and eager to please, but soft—the curve of her mouth showing her appreciation more than her, "you're very welcome, Ava," ever could. Then she was gone, slipped through the space in the door. The gentle closing of it still caused an echo through the room.

"I think that went quite well. Great job, everyone!" The king shared a bit of his wide grin with each of them. He rubbed his massive hand against Levi's short hair before patting him on the shoulder. It was the most interaction Ava had seen between Orion and his sons, and it warmed her heart.

Of course, it was extinguished in a matter of seconds.

"Except for that little snafu with Ava's people, I think so as well, my love." Coldness dripped off the queen's jab, turning her words into sharp icicles.

Fourteen eyes turned toward her at once, but only one set glared so intensely it was as though she were trying to bring the roof down with her eyes. "My *people*?" Ava replied through clenched teeth. "What part of that exchange looked like I wanted either of them here? Especially Connor?" Sebastian, who was on the step above her, placed a hand on her back, but she shook him off with a roll of her shoulder. "I don't know what you think you saw, but Connor Avery is one of the last people I wanted to see, let alone talk to tonight. Ever, at that."

The queen adjusted her crown then continued, lazily, "He didn't seem all that surprised to see you here, dear."

"So, *what*? You think that I invited him?" Ava asked sarcastically, and then, like a light bulb, she realized the truth in her words. The queen's smug eyebrow flick only confirmed it. "That's exactly what you think."

"I'm sure that's not what she's implying," Orion interceded, but stopped with the look Ava flashed him before she refocused her attention on the queen.

Ava pushed herself off the stair, a burst of angry energy rushing through her veins like charged blood. Each step was deliberate and controlled as she walked over to the queen. "What purpose could I possibly have for asking him to come and make a scene like he did?"

"You've made it very clear that you don't want to be here—"

"And if I showed you the sordid, ugly parts of my past I could convince you to change your mind about me?"

The queen gave a noncommittal shrug. "I wouldn't put it past you."

Bernadette was on a mission. Its main purpose was to burrow under Ava's skin like a nest of wood ticks. But Ava knew that the only way to remove the bug was to pull off its head. She had no intentions of beheading the queen, of course, but she could easily match poison with fire.

With hands gripping the fabric of her dress so tightly she could feel the sting of her nails digging into her palms through the cloth, Ava spoke clearly but with conviction, making zero effort to hide her vexation. "The night of the gala I was scared and confused and yes, incredibly angry. But I have done everything that's been required. My entire life is upstairs in boxes right now. I got dolled up and stood here with all of you, and I've never once—past that first night—complained about any of it." *At least not around any of you.* "I apologized to you, and the king, and Sebastian, for what *you* deemed unacceptable and disrespectful behavior. But I will not apologize for the behavior and actions of others."

She was aware of the wobble of her words, which came not from fear but frustration. "I don't know what else I have to do to convince you that I'm trying. But frankly, I don't care if you believe me, because I'm not marrying you." She shrugged. "You can choose to hate me, to try and belittle me every chance you get, but I was *your* choice. You're stuck with me. And it would make things a lot easier for everybody if you could get over whatever it is you have against me." Her eyes remained fixed on Bernadette's for a few seconds longer, daring the woman to argue, to say another word.

The queen straightened her spine and looked around the room before meeting Ava's eyes again. A rose blush crept up her neck and to her cheeks, and then to Ava's surprise, she dropped her eyes. Not much, but enough that Ava knew she'd won this moment. She also knew more confrontations were on the horizon. Queen Bernadette wouldn't fold forever.

Instead of letting her lips bear the triumph, Ava lifted her eyebrows just enough, a slight gesture that said *this is done*. Then she turned away from her, before the wave of saltwater crashing behind her eyes had a chance to overflow. She aimed for the darkest corner. She needed a few minutes to herself, and while she would rather leave the room altogether, she knew how doing so would look.

She watched from her shady area as Sebastian and Orion hurried to the queen. The haste with which the prince's arms flapped and flailed reassured Ava he was still on her side. The king, however, was harder to read. His face remained impassive as he rubbed his wife's back, his massive hands moving up and down her rigid spine. Ava was so focused on the scene that she didn't notice the shadowy figure until he was next to her, blending into the darkness like always.

"When I told you to fight, I didn't think you would take it literally." Nixon's voice wrapped around her like silk, but she was wound too tight to enjoy it. Its normal calming effect was absent and his closeness only added to her choler.

"Do you remember when I said Connor was one of the last people I wanted to see or talk to tonight?" she asked, looking up at him through mascaraed lashes. His head cocked a fraction in acknowledgement. "You're on that list, too." She gave him a pointed look as his eyes constricted, and through the smaller space, his pupils flared, eclipsing the sun in them.

She said nothing more as she walked away from him and met Sebastian half-way across the room. "We should probably head to the yard," she said as his hands came to hers.

He lowered his head to meet her eyes. "Are you okay?"

Nodding once, she replied, "Why wouldn't I be?" She came off more confident than she felt, but she had learned from her mother to fake it until you make it; and fake it she would. All she had to do was make it through the rest of the night and then she could sleep away the day's events. It had been a doozy and it was hard to believe it wasn't over yet. If she thought about it though, if she took even a nanosecond to reflect on the move, on her fight with Cordellia, on her fight with the queen, on Juliet's situation, even—she would lose it.

Lose her gusto, despite how small.

Lose her sanity, despite how little.

She needed both to survive the rest of the night.

She avoided the eyes of the king and queen, even Nixon, as they made their way into the backyard. As they strolled through the crowd and to the platform that had been erected, a gentle roar of applause followed them. Inwardly, none of them were in the mood for such a fanfare, but outwardly they looked like a united front, ready to take on the world. They smiled and waved to familiar faces. Sebastian said ridiculous things in Ava's ear that caused her to giggle, and Delilah glowed from all the excitement, her grin radiant and possibly the only genuine one on the stage.

Ava wished she could transfuse some of it into herself.

As it was, she held her face in a mask that almost matched Delilah's and took her place next to the king. The order of seating was as it had been during the meet-and-greet, except for Nixon, who had vanished into the crowd to make himself scarce but aware, and Delilah who was wedged between Sebastian and Levi. Ava was thankful for Nixon's distance, and as she downed the swig of ice water in her mouth, she washed down with it her remorse for the words she'd spoken to him. Hope, like guilt, seemed to be two words becoming synonymous with her life.

The royal party spoke amongst themselves while citizens made their way to name-plated tables. Delilah's parents were seated a couple of tables to the right of the stage. On the same table was a plate without a name card. Ava swallowed when she realized it was Cordellia's seat. She turned away and tried to focus on what Sebastian was saying.

The queen said a few words here and there to her sons, but for the most part remained content to stew in her malevolence toward Ava. The girl had said something during their spat, something that wasn't sitting too kindly with her—something Bernadette questioned the validity of and would for quite some time. Then she would form a plan, but that was awhile away. It didn't matter, though. Time was one of the few things of which they had a plethora.

Time and anger.

One which would allow the other to fester, to wreak havoc until it was so gross and harmful to the rest of the body, it would have to be extracted. Removed. Amputated.

Killed…?

The mere thought tugged the corner of the queen's lips.

As the crowd began to settle, Claudia mounted the stairs, looking ravishing and refreshed. Ava loved her soft pink dress and coiffed hair, and envied the confidence she exuded, especially with so many eyes focused on her. Looking out across the lawn of people, a bout of nervousness roiled in Ava's stomach. Her mouth was dry, like an arid desert, and each inhale brought with it particles of sand until her throat was like an hourglass. She took short, quick sips of water as Claudia's voice filled the backyard. Ava hadn't noticed before, but there were speakers mounted to poles, hanging high above the crowd to provide a surround-sound experience.

"Citizens of Havaan," Claudia's voice echoed. "Welcome to this monumental evening. One we have all been awaiting a very long time. Tonight, things that will set the future of Havaan on course will take place. And you, the lucky few, are here to witness it. On behalf of the royal family, we thank you for coming." She paused and waited for the clapping to subside. "Now, without further ado I present to you, your king and mine, King Orion Calder."

"In our king we give thanks!" the crowd erupted as one.

Orion stood to a rush of applause and whistles, hoots and whoops. He waved his mammoth hand and like a symphony conductor, quieted them with a lowering of his arms. An eerie hush fell over the yard. Ava's heartbeat was too loud in her ears, as if it had escaped her chest and was sitting on her shoulder. Next to her, Delilah squeezed her hand, a reminder that she had one of the toughest chicks in her corner. If Ava could conjure a bit of D into herself, she'd be okay.

"Citizens. Friends. *Family*. We welcome you to our house for this exciting celebration. In a short amount of time my son—" He turned to Sebastian, who beamed up at his father with that same lopsided smile. "—will become your king. As I have for the last twenty-five years, he will reign with a brilliant woman by his side. Something about this young lady spoke to me with just a look, and as I have gotten to know her and see her tenacity, I know I have made the right choice in selecting your future queen." He paused for dramatic effect and then turned his kind eyes to Ava. His smile was infectious and in it she forgot her nerves. It was just a few seconds, but long enough to clear her mind.

Orion finished. "Allow me to introduce to you the newest member of our family, and soon your queen…Miss Avaleigh Toliver."

Ava cleared the sand from her throat with a deep drink of wine.

"You're going to do great," Delilah whispered across Sebastian.

Ava stood and wrapped her arms tightly around the tree-trunk waist of the king, returning his surprise hug. Around them, the cheering started again, but it was gentler, like waves crashing on a far-off shore. That was, except for Delilah and Sebastian, who were making up for the audience tenfold. She grinned down at them and then slid her gaze over the people below. Their ovation died down on its own until it was just the occasional clinking of a glass, the pulsing of her heart and the sounds of nature in her ears.

She licked her lips and let out a warm breath before speaking. Her hands were shaking and she clasped them together in front of her. "Hi," she started, chuckling nervously. From the crowd, a bit of laughter was returned. "As a resident of Meridian, I never thought this was in my future. And as I say that, I'm sure many of you are just as surprised as I am that it's me who's standing here. It's safe to say I didn't handle the announcement of my queenhood very well. If you ask anyone who was in the room, they'll agree." She looked over at the queen, who nodded casually, her plastic smile playful. Again, giggles swirled up the stairs. "There was a lot of fear and confusion when the king told me I was his choice. Confusion over how someone who had been told her entire life she wasn't qualified for such a task was ever expected to rule, and fear over having to do so. Even after seven days a lot of that fear still lingers." She scanned the faces of those watching her and settled on one unintentionally.

One who was hidden by the night with halcyon in his eyes.

In the golden flames she found solace.

"At first it was fear that I may not do as great a job as King Orion and Queen Bernadette have. Now it's fear that I may not succeed in ruling how *I* want. Someone recently said something to me that hit home on so many levels. They said, 'the king and queen rule on a mountain where only the voices of the upper class can reach.' As a citizen of a middle class I can understand that." Whispers broke the otherwise stillness of the crowd, but Ava continued, her voice echoing through the massive yard. "I don't want to rule the same as the king and queen, because while they've done an amazing job, there are things that need to change. We are not an unhappy nation by any means. There are few reasons *for* us to be, but there are still complaints and those complaints cannot be heard from a house on a hill, away from you."

Ava's eyes found Helen's, who winked at her from one of the tables closer to the stage. "I, with Sebastian by my side, hope to put our eyes, and ears, and feet on the ground of Havaan. I grew up with a separation between classes—between people—an unnecessary divide that does nothing but ostracize other citizens. One that tells little girls they don't have what it takes to be queen. The old world had segregation and look what it did to them. It destroyed them. They destroyed one another. And later it destroyed the second generation. I don't want it to destroy Havaan as well. So while there is still fear, and there will probably always be a little, there is also excitement."

She turned her attention to Sebastian for a second and touched his shoulder softly. "I know it will take time for you to trust me, as it will take time for me to trust myself," Ava said as she turned back to the crowd. She wasn't sure where the camera was, but she looked ahead of her just in case. She wanted those outside the wrought iron gates to feel the weight of her words.

"I'm not going to promise you I will have a flawless reign, because I don't want to lie to you. Am I going to do everything perfectly? No. Am I going to make mistakes? Yes. Probably millions. But the one thing I can, and will promise, is that I will do everything possible to be the best version of myself that I can be, and in that the best queen. In this, I ask not only for your support, but for *your* honesty, too. I ask for time and patience as we all grow into the crown together. I ask for you to hold me accountable. If I start to sink too deeply into my title, tell me. Remind me of the woman I am tonight—right now—with humble beginnings and a dream for a better Havaan." She reached for her wine glass and held it high. Below and next to her everyone did the same, a mass cheers that was their first symbol of unity.

"To us. To Havaan," she said.

"To Havaan," came the echo of thousands of voices. It sent a shiver down her spine, one she chased away with a mouthful of alcohol. As she began to sit, there was a moment of stillness, as if all of Havaan had ended. Then the crowd exploded. Louder than they had been for the king, they also stood. Cheers and shouts of support resounded. The stage below her feet vibrated with the thunderous sound. Next to her, Orion whispered, "Well done." Delilah swooped in from behind and wrapped her slender arms around her best friend's neck.

Ava couldn't help but laugh as she was swept up in the praise. Full belly laughter that was real, and genuine, and felt...by all the stars...it felt great. It was as though she'd removed the noose from around her neck; and for the first time since she'd entered High House a week ago—on the fretful night of the Queen's Gala—she could breathe.

In that breath, she could feel a new excitement come over her.

Becoming queen had never seemed so right, so *welcomed*, until that very moment.

XX.

After dinner, which was delicious and mouthwatering and succulent and spiced and amazing—all things one would expect a royal dinner to be—the true festivities began. The Havaan's Women Choir had been spectacular as they'd regaled guests with beautifully harmonized songs during the meal. The sounds they'd produced were haunting, but it wasn't the music that sprinkled Ava's waterline with tears. There was a massive Cordellia sized hole in her heart, one even her disappointment could not lessen. She wanted her mother here more than she'd wanted anything before. Yet she painted on the mask expected of her and ignored the longing thrum in her soul.

Once the plates had been cleared away, people were free to roam the grounds. Wait-staff looped the yard with trays of varying desserts and goblets of the finest wine in Havaan. The courtyard, with its smooth cobblestone driveway, had been turned into a makeshift dance area. Strings of lights, like the ones from the gala, wove between posts above the dancers, shining through the night like hundreds of miniature spotlights. Many citizens funneled that direction, pulled forward by the jazzy music of the band, while others lazed around the bar with never an empty glass. The royal family spread like dandelion seeds in the wind and mixed themselves within the crowd.

People approached them, some with confidence and others with a charming shyness, but the number of citizens who sought them out was a much smaller crowd than Ava had imagined it would be. She enjoyed getting to talk with them on a personal level. They engaged her as if they'd known her all their lives and spoke of mundane things like the weather or their children. Perhaps it was the wine that made her feel so comfortable, but the atmosphere was almost as relaxed and easy as it had been at the gala, at least before everything had come crashing to a screeching halt.

It was during these conversations when a plan formed and took root in not only Ava's mind but her heart as well. She was eager to tell it to Sebastian, who she hoped would feel the same.

As she finished talking with a married couple from Zyprah—the region farthest west of Brene—and turned in search of both her prince and another glass of wine, a woman stepped into her path. She was stunning, with long, razor-straight black hair that glittered under the lights. Her icy blue eyes regarded Ava from under blunt bangs.

"It's Avaleigh, right?" she questioned as she thrust her hand forward. Ava nodded and gripped the slender fingers. "Brisbane McAufferman." Her skin was smooth as porcelain and as white as cooking flour. She was Ava's height with none of her curves, and her apple-red dress was a thin piece of fabric hanging off her shoulders and covering only her most intimate parts.

Her pale eyes looked around then back at Ava. "So, Meridian, huh? This must be super exciting for you."

"It's a lot of things, but exciting is definitely one of them," Ava replied as she snagged a bite-sized piece of cheesecake from the passing waiter.

"How exactly did you manage to get chosen?" Brisbane asked. The end of her question was frayed with forced nonchalance.

"The same way anyone would have," Ava started, her eyebrow cocked and her voice uncertain. "I went to the gala. Honestly, I'm just as clueless as anyone as to why me and not someone else."

"Especially when you weren't eligible." There was a hit of accusation in the statement, and Ava didn't necessarily like it. It sent up a flag as red as Brisbane's dress.

"That was never an official rule." Ava's reply came flatly, almost mechanically. How many more times was she going to have to inform people of this?

"And yet the king and queen never made an effort to dispute it."

Ava looked at her from the corner of her eye. "You would have to ask the king and queen about that. And about why they selected me, since it seems to matter so much to you."

The other woman returned her look, her brows tucked into her bangs. Her eyes were so light they looked almost white, like tinted glass marbles. "I'm not the only one it matters to. A lot of people are having a difficult time believing there wasn't *something*…" She paused, letting the implication hang in the air. "Family connection, maybe…" Ava shook her head. "It's just odd that—"

"Brisbane." Sebastian's stern voice interrupted what was surely becoming a trial of one, and Ava hadn't been looking forward to playing defense attorney on her own behalf. As difficult as it might be for some to believe, she really *didn't* have the answers to what most, if not all of Havaan, was asking themselves: how did someone from the middle class get picked to be queen? What can she possibly know about ruling a nation?

It was a never-ending list of why's and how's and who's and what's for which there would never be an adequate answer.

"Hey there Prince Charming," Brisbane replied with a cold disinterest as she flicked her bangs out of her eyes.

The tension between the two was obvious almost immediately, and was reaffirmed by Sebastian's, "Shouldn't you be off ruining someone's life?"

Brisbane scoffed, coyness playing on the corners of her lips. "Bitterness isn't a good look on you," she replied. "You should really leave that to your mother."

With a disgusted scowl on his face, Sebastian ignored her jab. "What are you doing here? We had a very clear no press rule with our security." He slid a possessive arm around the back of Ava. His fingers rested comfortably on the curve of her waist.

"You're a reporter?" Ava asked, incredulously. She was a little angry at herself for not realizing the line of questions had been asked with such an obvious agenda. *I should have known better,* she scolded.

It would become her first lesson in royal life: everyone wants something from you.

"I'm not on the job. But people are curious about some things." The coal-haired woman shrugged a bony shoulder. "I figured while she was standing here I would try to get some answers straight from Ava. Besides, I knew your family would be a little less...willing...to speak with me."

Brisbane's attention was tugged away from Ava and Sebastian as she looked over their heads and wiggled her fingers in a wave. Sebastian, who refused to do anything other than try and set Brisbane on fire with his eyes, did not look over his shoulder. Ava did. Queen Bernadette smiled fully at the reporter. It was a look Ava had never seen on the queen's face. Pure, honest, genuine joy. Something bitter like jealousy mixed with anger swished in Ava's stomach. There hadn't been *much* of a reason for her to dislike Brisbane, but now she had all the ammunition she needed to hate her as much as Sebastian seemingly did.

"Well, everyone except for one," Brisbane said as she lowered her eyes back to the duo in front of her. "Though if either of *you* are interested in doing a formal interview…" She looked at them expectantly.

Sebastian squared his shoulders and hardened his face even more. In that moment, he looked more like his mother than ever before, and Ava had to make a valid effort to not pull away.

"I'm going to say this once to you," he started, his voice coming out in a low grumble from the back of his throat. "We will never give The Report or any other newspaper an interview. We are not a story to boost your numbers."

"What would it hurt, though?" she challenged as she turned her ghostly eyes to Ava. "Don't you care what people think? *Your* people. The same ones you plan to rule one day."

Sebastian's clipped "No," mirrored his mood, but it did not reflect the response Ava would have given. Because she *did* care. She did worry. It was one of the biggest reasons she needed to speak to Sebastian. Alone. Without prying ears around.

"Can I use that as a direct quote?" Brisbane tested, clearly feeding off Sebastian's aggression.

"If you try to harass anything out of any member of my family you will regret it," he threatened. "Particularly regarding Ava or any doubt cast about my father's decision. I will end your career. You can pass that along to all your other reporter buddies, as well. You should know by now that I protect those I care about."

"Oh, Sebastian. I also know by now that your threats are nothing more than just hot air. I'm not worried though. There are other resources—friends, family, enemies—that I'm sure would be beyond giddy to sit down with me. It won't be nearly as exciting as if it were coming from you and it may not even be the truth but—"

"But you're brilliant at spinning a pretty lie," Sebastian finished.

Brisbane flashed her flawless but ravenous smile. It spread across her mouth like warm molasses. "It was great seeing you," she said as she winked at him. "But the queen is beckoning me. I'm sure she has plenty to say that won't require any sort of harassment." With a wave of her fingers she sashayed past them, making a beeline for Bernadette. The train of her dress was too vibrant against the wall of black trousers and tuxedos into which she vanished.

Ava was glad she hadn't worn the red dress tonight.

Sebastian's face was hard angles and his forehead creased with frown lines. Ava thought there was a swirl of light green right along the edge of his irises, but when he blinked it was gone. Nothing more than a trick of the lights.

"Well, she seems great," Ava joked. She smirked at him as his features relaxed, though the tension in his body and stance remained. He was tense, his anger coiled like a cobra ready to attack.

"That woman is a leech," he finally said, each word clipped.

Ava slid her hand into his and entwined their fingers loosely. "What'd she do to hurt you so much?"

Sebastian squeezed her hand. "Not me," he replied as his eyes focused ahead of him. Ava followed his line of sight to the last person she would have assumed.

"Really?" She was unable to keep the skepticism from her tone.

"Are you surprised he has a heart?" Sebastian teased as he led her into the crowd of dancers. He spun her under his arm before drawing her body close to his. One of his hands rested firm on the small of her back while the other held hers comfortably. She laid their joined grip on his shoulder and swayed with him to the smooth, moderate pace of the band.

"Not at all," she answered, glancing over at Nixon once more. "Just surprised that he gave someone the opportunity to break it."

"We were young…ish," Sebastian started, his voice quiet. "Nix was eighteen, maybe nineteen. He wanted…normalcy, and Brisbane was normal. She had no ties to High House. She was just a girl he met at a café in town. While he was falling in love, she was stringing him along, hoping to get in good with my parents. She wanted the crown and hoped she could make them like her enough that they would bypass the gala and just give it to her. She came on to me, tried to recruit me into her scheme…" He shook his head, as if he were trying to erase the memories.

"Did you tell him what happened?" Ava asked, looking into his emerald eyes.

"He's my best friend," Sebastian said by way of admittance. "Part of me wished I hadn't though, that I'd let him find out what kind of person she was on his own, but he was blinded by her. I'd never seen him so devastated as he was when he found out. She tried to deny it at first—it almost ripped our friendship apart. But she showed her true colors eventually. Unfortunately, Nixon got burned in the process. He's never let himself trust anyone after that."

"That's sad," Ava said. "He deserves to be happy."

She caught Nixon's eyes briefly across the courtyard as he flung Delilah away from him in a swift dance move. She tossed her head back in laughter, her pink-gold hair glistening under the lights, and Ava's heart contracted. There always seemed to be some sort of wall between him and everyone else, and if he caught himself coming too far around it he would retreat back into the safety of the shadows. Now she had a better understanding from where that separation came. Delilah had a battle of epic proportions ahead of her if she was going to win him over.

But if she can, Ava thought with a sad smile as she watched them move together, *she'll have herself one hell of a great guy.*

She returned her attention to the handsome man in front of her, with his intense green eyes and hair of messy steel. "I was coming to find you when Brisbane intercepted me."

"Were you? Am I in trouble?"

"Not yet." Her response was light, playful, but then she looked at him seriously as they swayed together, the tempo of the music slowing down slightly. "I meant what I said tonight."

"Which part? A lot of words have been said this evening."

She gave him an amused look. "Okay yes, that's true," she laughed, "but specifically the ones about us being down there." Ava looked through the bars of the gate, toward the miniature houses in the bowl at the bottom of the hill. "One of my biggest qualms about being chosen is that I've done absolutely nothing to earn the crown. And I'm never going to feel comfortable calling myself a queen if I can't remedy that. I need to make a difference."

"You want to rule where all the voices can reach you."

She nodded. "Exactly. Thousands of citizens have lived a majority, if not all of their lives, supporting your parents. If we ask them to now trust and support *us*, one of whom has zero experience or idea what they're doing, without giving them a reason to…I can't imagine it'll be a smooth transition for anyone. *And* it isn't fair." They moved and surged with the crash of couples, and Ava lifted the skirt of her dress to keep it from being stepped on. "I know what it's like to feel ostracized by those who sit on the throne. I don't want that for anyone anymore. I want the citizens to know us, as if we're their neighbors. I want them to feel comfortable coming to us with their issues. Big. Small. It doesn't matter. I want our rule to happen under a truly united front."

As she explained her plan, Sebastian looked down at her, the green of his irises sparkling. The way he was eyeing her said so much without any necessary words. The words he did say, however, did not match the look. "This is the most excited you've been about becoming queen."

"Yeah, well…" She shrugged. "If I'm stuck with the title I might as well do something with it," she replied, winking at him.

His laughter vibrated against her stomach. From their cocoons, the butterflies in the darkest pit of it shook a little too, as if they were stretching out their wings, giving them a test shake before curling them back around their bodies.

"I feel like you're the only woman in all of Havaan who would want to do something like this."

She blushed. "Does that make me naïve?"

He shook his head, almost unnoticeably. "No," he said quietly. "It makes you undeniably the right choice."

"Does that mean you think it's a good idea?" she asked, her voice buoyant but not overly excited, still not entirely sure he would agree with her.

She was relieved, however, when he answered, "I think it's a brilliant idea." And when he added, "I think *you're* brilliant" she lowered her eyes as a heated blush threatened to bleed through the rouge on her cheeks. No one had ever told her she was brilliant before, especially not with as much conviction as Sebastian had. It was almost as if he were awed by her, which was also not a feeling she had ever experienced. It was uncomfortable but surprisingly not off-putting.

"So how do we execute it?" he asked.

This was the part of her idea she had been most excited to tell him, but also the most nervous. It would require a lot of finagling, and a lot of convincing of other people. She was also sure it was a solid idea and that it would be highly effective in achieving what she wanted. "We go on a tour," she said.

Sebastian looked at her uncertainly. "A tour?"

"We visit all the regions of Havaan, make ourselves available via a more personal but larger scale meet-and-greet. We force the two classes to come together, to breathe the same air for one common cause. They'll listen to one another and they'll realize they're not that different, because I have no doubt that while some things will matter more to one class than the other, there will also be issues both share."

Pensively, Sebastian scratched his chin. "It could work," he said slowly. "Of course, it would take some time—"

"A week."

He stopped moving and looked down at her with wide eyes. She could see herself in the reflection of his pupils. "Why so soon?"

They were standing motionless in the middle of a spinning crowd, but he was the only one on which she focused. There was a need in her voice, one she couldn't control. "We have to show them I was serious. That I wasn't saying what I did as a 'one day when I'm queen' sort of thing. We need to set the wheels in motion *now*. We need to be preemptive so that the citizens know we stand by our words, long before we take over."

Sebastian considered this for at least a minute, which was long enough for the doubt to start. Was she being too eager, too pushy? Was she demanding too much too soon? Was she completely out of her wits in even thinking this was a good idea; that any of this was going to make a difference in the long run? Or would her status as a middle-class resident forever matter to Havaan, no matter what she did?

Nothing *would* matter until Sebastian said yes, because if he didn't agree, if he wasn't going to be next to her on this, it was going to wilt before it even had a chance to bloom.

"It'll take a few days to secure meeting locations," Sebastian finally said and she gave an audible and visible sigh of relief. Maybe it *was* a crazy idea, but now she would have the chance to find out. Now there would be two hands planting and harvesting their future instead of just hers, clumsy and uncertain and scared and with the green-thumb of a cold frost. "Our family has homes spread throughout Havaan, so lodging won't be an issue. We'll also need time to get the word out, give Nixon time to prepare—"

"Not Nixon," Ava said quickly, and then scolded herself for how hasty she had been when Sebastian questioned her.

"Did something happen between the two of you?"

"Of course not," she replied. "He's just spent a lot of time with me. He deserves a break." She gave him a quick smile that she hoped was convincing enough before she added, "Besides, Delilah has a thing for him. They could use the time to get to know one another, too."

"I'm not sure how Nix would feel knowing you're playing matchmaker," Sebastian chided though his tone was spirited.

"Then don't tell him."

His lips quirked a little before he returned to the business at hand. "Thursday is the earliest we can head out."

"Thursday is perfect," she approved.

"I'll let Mother and Father know tonight."

She grinned ear-to-ear as she flung herself at him, wrapping her arms around his neck tightly. He laughed, and she couldn't help but laugh as well. Words of "they're adorable" and "what a nice pairing" and "they'll make a great team" carried to them, and when Sebastian's eyes locked on Ava's, she knew he'd heard them too. Then he tapped her nose before sweeping her back into his arms, twirling her around the courtyard to the beat of the music. What had started out as a rough, miserable day ended with jovial merriment. Something Ava had never expected to feel in her new life.

The crown was going to be hers—she had no control over it—but she could control the sort of queen she would become. And if everything went well, if it all went according to how she expected it to, she would be the best one possible.

She would be the queen Havaan deserved.

XXI.

At night, when everyone was snuggled into comfy beds and lost to their dreams, the house was still. So much so, it was louder outside than in, with sounds of nighttime creatures carried by gusts of wind. Inside there was no creaking of stairs or rattling of windowpanes. The footsteps of the day were vacuumed up by the last remaining maids and the clock in the foyer was soundless. It was as if the house itself fell asleep, too.

When morning came, the building awoke as well. Blinds were raised like heavy eyelids and curtains yawned open to let in the sun. Voices filled the hallways and every room was alive. Though carpeted, the staircases still vibrated as the staff raced up and down them. Orders were barked from the kitchen, whisks clinking against metal bowls as dozens of eggs were scrambled. Meat sizzled on the grill. Lightly browned bread popped excitedly from the toaster before being stacked on a plate and carried to the dining room. The pipes groaned behind walls as they stretched, readying themselves to carry water to showers and toilets, garden hoses and sinks.

If the house was awake, everyone was awake. Including Ava, who was not used to being up before eight in the morning. Now she was conscious by dawn every day.

It was Monday, the first day back at High House since the tour ended. A tour which had gone surprisingly well.

Ava's expectations about the changes their trip would elicit had also given way to growing fears. What if no one showed up, or those who did only came to question how a nobody from the middle class had been chosen to rule over them? If the tour ultimately became a waste of time, it would be yet another tarnish on her already flawed crown. Ava could sow and fertilize fields with the passion she had, but if the citizens refused to grow—to yield a harvest as one united country—all her efforts would be for nothing.

Who are you that they would listen to what you want? that lingering voice of doubt would snarl as they pulled up to each venue. As they made their way to each gathering crowd. As she introduced herself and laid out her plans to each citizen. In was there, before, during, and after each meeting.

"Be honest," she asked them repeatedly. "Nothing can change if you don't let us know *what* needs to change."

Though people were hesitant at first, wary at speaking out against Orion and Bernadette, it only took one voice to encourage the others. People were not unhappy overall, which Ava had expected. Havaan had, for the most part, given its citizens everything they needed.

There were, of course, minor complaints. Ava was surprised to hear how many people agreed with her desire to unify the classes. The division created a lack of community, which few could justify. The thing Ava loved the most about the tour was not when citizens spoke to her and Sebastian, but when they spoke to one another. There was very little to discern an upper class citizen from those in the middle class, and the more they talked to each other, they realized how much they had in common.

A man named Clyde owned a dry-cleaning business in Conley, the middle class of Zyprah. Despite providing services for those in the upper class—the same family tree for twenty years in some cases—they regarded him as nothing more than a necessity in their lives. A thing that had existed for so long, like a crack in the wall, they had come to simply ignore it.

"This afternoon," he'd said to Ava, his eyes glistening in the bright midday sun, "was the first time anyone from Usealie asked me about my life and told me about theirs. Not about a wine stain on their suit shirt, but about their children and hobbies. Hobbies we shared!"

This was what Ava had wanted to achieve with the tour. A tour the queen had deemed pointless. "No one will show," she'd said to Sebastian in secret. Ava hadn't meant to overhear the conversation, but she hadn't continued walking once she had. "You will spend a week achieving nothing."

Hearing these words, though not surprised they were said, added yet another concern to Ava's lengthening list. This one about Sebastian. He had been raised in the thick of the division. If a class existed above the upper, he lived in it. There was a chance his preconceived notions would keep him on the outside of things, hovering but not participating. Listening but not hearing. Waiting for it to inevitably fail.

He had surprised her, though.

They had both agreed, before the first meeting of the tour took place, to mix themselves amongst the crowds. They would not treat the gatherings as a place to give speeches or make promises, where people would come to them one by one while they floated above them on picnic tables and stages.

"If that's the plan, we might as well stay at High House," Ava explained. Instead, they—as well as their assigned guards—melded into the crowds, inviting themselves into conversations. They asked citizens about their families, got to know them on as personal a basis as the event allowed. When the sky set itself on fire, Sebastian gave a couple of men money to buy steaks and burgers. At one of the parks between Oxphyn and Ramenell, the prince exchanged his crown for a spatula and grilled up enough food to feed the remaining citizens. He was charming in the way one would expect, but genuine in a way Ava had not. People flocked to him in drones, and he took it all in stride, laughing at their jokes, celebrating their successes—no matter how small—and sharing in the pain of their losses.

One citizen, however, played coy to Sebastian's dazzling personality.

Raphael the baby would cry uncontrollably every time Sebastian glanced his way. As soon as he looked elsewhere, Raphie, with his two tiny teeth and tear-streaked cheeks, would smile at Ava to let her know it was all a game that he was having a blast playing.

When Sebastian and Ava finally returned to High House, there was an obvious shift between the two, because she had come to see Sebastian in a new light. While on the road, they spent the evenings at the charming, quaint homes the Calder's owned throughout Havaan. The houses were rather small and simple in comparison to High House, and Ava loved each one the moment she stepped inside. Each house had at least two bedrooms, and at the first two, Ava and Sebastian had their own rooms. By their third night on the road, Ava found herself missing the prince at day's end. Even though they spent the day together, they were so tied up with citizens they rarely said more than thirty words to one another. Ava had started to cherish the couple of hours granted to them before heading to bed. Sebastian made her laugh until her sides ached and had the ability to make her forget all the things she disliked about what was happening.

He was slowly unbecoming someone she was being forced to marry and more the kind of husband she'd be happy to have. She no longer recoiled from his touch, and at times even initiated it. They were simple things, like holding his hand or setting her palm against his knee, but in the grand scheme of things, made all the difference.

Ava had tiptoed into the prince's room at their third house and curled up in the bed with him, careful not to disturb his sleep. The following morning, neither of them spoke of it, though they woke face-to-face, and from then on it was understood the extra bedrooms weren't needed.

They shared one bed.

And sometimes they snuggled.

One morning, they'd even kissed. As far as first kisses went, it hadn't been anything to write home about, but it did bring to the surface feelings and thoughts Ava later scrawled into her journal.

Feelings she hadn't experienced since Connor.

No.

Since Nixon. Since he'd crawled across the seat and smiled at her.

But the feelings I have for Nixon are feelings I cannot act upon, she transcribed on the pages of her diary. Sebastian has done everything I have asked of him. He has given me time to come around and I owe it to him—to us—to me, to make every effort I can to see him as he is; past the crown and the gala, the rules of his parents. I can love him…I just need to let myself do so. And I cannot do that while feeling something for another.

Returning to High House had been strange, because none of it was turning out as Ava had expected. She hadn't wanted to believe everyone when they told her, "just give it time, it'll get better." She hadn't wanted to like Sebastian. Her plan had been to be ruthless, to be so unlikeable that both the prince and Bernadette would demand the king dismiss her; and he would have no choice but to agree and ship her back home. At no point had she *ever* thought, no matter what she had said to anyone, that she would enjoy herself or look forward to seeing Sebastian and spending time with him.

She would have never believed there would be a part of her excited about becoming queen.

As she lay in a bed far too empty without another body in it, listening to the hubbub of her new home while cracking bones and lengthening joints, there was a knock. She rolled over and looked at the clock, then with furrowed brows shoved her feet into her favorite pair of tattered slippers and shuffled to the door.

"Good morning," Sebastian said when she emerged.

She yawned, "You're early," by way of greeting. Every morning, since her first one here, he'd come to her room at nine o'clock to escort her to breakfast. Typically, they dined in comfy clothes, the elastic of their pants allowing them to stuff more delicious food into their stomachs, but today he was dressed in a pair of khaki pants and a fitted shirt the same green as his eyes. At his feet, which were laced inside brown loafers, was a drooping bag. Her eyes locked with his.

"Where are you going?" she asked.

"I've got an errand to run," he answered casually. "I wanted to see you before I left though, so you'd know why I wasn't around the next couple of days."

"A Havaan errand?" she probed, ignoring the rest.

"A Queen Bernadette errand."

Ava looked at him curiously. She didn't like that he was being so elusive. So she tried for a more direct approach, and again asked,

"Where are you going?" This time, each word was shorter, leaving little room for him to misinterpret her question.

All he did was smile, one side of his mouth higher than the other, and shake his head. "It doesn't matter."

Annoyance crept up her body, starting at her ankles. She leaned against the doorframe and nudged his bag with her toe. "It matters to me," she challenged, looking into his eyes.

His deep sigh, like always, let her know he was already over the argument dancing in their peripheral. He reached a hand out to caress her cheek, but she pulled away from his touch and instead he got a piece of hair. He let the loose curl slip through his fingers, his foliage-green eyes transfixed on it. For a moment, he looked like he was going to say something other than, "Let me walk you to breakfast."

"I'm not ready," she said flatly.

Suddenly the air shifted.

Of course, she was the only one who could sense it. The increase in static, the goosebumps that prickled her arms, the change of her heart's cadence. She felt him before she saw him emerge from the shadows, as if he lived amongst them, as though he were a part of them. Her eyes flickered his direction as he appeared over Sebastian's shoulder.

"Hey," she said.

She felt very self-conscious in her frayed, thigh-length shorts and ratty tank-top. Sebastian had seen her in the getup more than once during their trip, but she had kept herself covered around everyone else. She crossed her arms over her chest as Nixon's eyes traveled the full length of her body before settling on her own.

"Hey," he finally replied, the word almost strangled.

"Are you going on this secret errand-run, too? A little male bonding time, perhaps?" she asked, making no effort to hide her irritation.

"I'm afraid not," Nixon replied. "I'm just here to let Sebastian know his mother would like to speak with him before he leaves for said secret errand-run."

Ava glared at both of them before righting herself again, using her shoulder to push off from the doorway. "Well," she started, still incredibly peeved, "have a safe trip. Be careful. Enjoy yourself. Don't drink too much. Don't do anything I wouldn't do. Behave." Sebastian's eyes sparkled with amusement. "I don't know which one is appropriate." She smiled, but it was not pleasant. It was sarcastic and humorless and without teeth. The queen would be proud.

"They're all appropriate," the prince informed. "I'll make it up to you, okay?"

"Presents are always nice," Delilah's cheerful voice chimed from behind the two men.

Ava nodded once. "Yeah. What she said."

"Presents I can do," Sebastian said. "I need to go check in with my parents before I leave. Don't hold this against me, love. Please."

Something tangy, like bile, rose up inside of her with the pet name. He never called her anything other than Ava or Avaleigh, and for some reason him trying one out in the current moment felt wrong. Especially one that involved the l-word, because though her feelings toward him had changed and developed into something more than just surface-level tolerance, love was a very long way off. Now he was leaving on some surreptitious mission, about which he refused to tell her nothing. Did he really think that was going to help their situation; that she was going to shrug her shoulders and bat her lashes and coo, "Anything you say Sebastian"? She scoffed internally.

Did he just meet me?

"I'll see you when you get back," was her only response.

With a resigned exhale, the prince bent and picked up his bag, tossing the strap of it over his shoulder. Then, before he turned to leave, he leaned in and pressed his lips to hers. It was quick, only a couple of seconds, but this time it felt too stiff. Too habitual. Maybe it was the unspoken words between them, or the extra sets of eyes watching, but Ava took no pleasure in it. Sebastian must have sensed it because he walked away from her as soon as they parted.

"'Morning," Delilah chirped as the friends passed her, her attention focused pointedly on Nixon.

His gruff reply of, "Hey," seemed enough to satiate D, as she did everything she could to keep from buckling at the knees. The women watched as the men rounded the corner, and then Ava looked across the hall at her best friend. She'd seen her last night at dinner, but they'd had very little time together since the big move. Even when they'd been planning the tour, there had constantly been other people around. She missed Delilah in a way she'd never had to before, and it was obvious in the sad way she said, "Hey."

"Hi," D replied in the same tone.

"You look nice," Ava said in acknowledgement of the red trousers and polka-dotted peplum top she wore.

Delilah smiled gently. "Thanks. You look…Well, you've looked worse."

Laughter escaped Ava in a giant whoosh. "Do you want to keep me company while I get ready?" she asked through her grin.

"Only if I can pick your outfit," Delilah said, though she was crossing the hall before Ava could reply. As she made a beeline for the closet, Ava dropped onto the edge of the bed and looked around her bedroom. It was homier now. She'd done some setting up before she'd left, but while she'd been away, Delilah had taken it upon herself to fully unpack. Books filled shelves. Photos were taped across an empty wall in a haphazard but chaotically organized array, much like they had been at home. Somehow D had gotten a couple hundred tiny glow-in-the-dark stars on the ceiling. Ava's first night back at High House, she'd fallen asleep trying to count them. Delilah had even strung the quote-rope from the mantel of the fireplace, though some pieces were missing—ones that spoke of change and rebellion, pictures and words the first generation had banned.

Once the old world ceased to exist, the elder magicians made the decision to remove music, literature, art, and traditions they deemed harmful or degrading to their new society. Art that depicted war and violence was burned in the city square. Music that degraded women or promoted aggression were shattered and made into a reflective mural. Words and passages, poems included, which could cause an uprising were erased from the books. Simply displaying them could have been considered an act of rebellion, but Ava had never had to worry about them being seen back home.

At High House however...

Delilah stepped out of the closet with a top and bottom and held them against herself as she asked Ava, "Where's your dude going?"

"No idea," Ava replied as she stretched out on the bed, her head at the foot.

Delilah glanced over at her with a skeptical look before disappearing back into the closet. "Secrets already?" Her voice carried over the shifting of hangers.

"It won't be a secret once he gets back," Ava threatened half-heartedly. The look her best friend gave her let her know that she didn't believe it, either.

Delilah dropped a few garments next to Ava and said, "What are you going to do, sex the answers out of him?" as she sashayed back to the closet. Ava knew she was joking. There was no way she would ever stoop to using her feminine ways to get answers. Before year's end, however, she would change her tune on this.

She would do what she needed to get what she wanted.

By that point, everything would be different, including her.

For now, she kept her morals, though for a brief second, considered going against them. As brief as it was, it was long enough for Delilah's brown eyes to widen and her jaw to go slack. She was, possibly for the first time since she and Ava had become friends, speechless. Then her eyes narrowed and her typical smugness reappeared. "You wouldn't," she confirmed as she tossed a pair of iridescent taupe flats at the bed.

Ava gathered her outfit in her arms and shrugged. "You underestimate my need to know things," she replied casually as she sauntered into the bathroom.

She left the door cracked enough so that Delilah's, "Does he know?" was unfiltered.

"Does who know what?" came her breathless reply as she tugged on the straight-legged brown trousers and jumped a few times to get them over her hips. Thankfully she didn't have to suck anything in to get them buttoned. Otherwise, she might have to consider cutting down on all the delicious desserts the kitchen kept on hand.

"Does Sebastian know that you've been deflowered?"

Ava wrinkled her nose. She'd always hated the phrase, as if she were part of some soft, holy garden and men could simply conquer her by picking a bulb. Besides, it sounded so childish, too innocent. Nothing had been childish or innocent about that night.

"No," she said when her head emerged from the flowy, sleeveless blouse Delilah had chosen. "He doesn't know I'm not a virgin." She emphasized the last word to drive her point home.

"That wasn't something that came up on your great cross-country trip?" Delilah looked up from the nails she was buffing and gave Ava an approving grin when she stepped out of the bathroom. The mint green blazer was opened at the front, allowing the looping of chains around her neck to be seen. The pop of color was nice against Ava's skin as well as the neutrals of the rest of the ensemble. Delilah was good at many things, and putting together outfits definitely ranked at the top of her skillset. Ava felt comfortable, which was something that rarely happened outside of jeans and t-shirts, but also sophisticated and well-assembled. She looked both of those things, too, which was even more important.

It was strange how well she was adjusting to her new-found self.

And at times a little unsettling.

"There wasn't really a great opportunity to regale him with the story of my drunken night in the bed of Connor's truck," Ava answered as she slipped her feet into the shoes. "As far as first-time stories go, it isn't exactly the classiest."

Delilah's first time had at least been inside and with a sober mind. Ava's not so much. The irony was never lost on her that she'd surrendered her body to someone at the same summer celebration her mother and father had met all those years ago. Except her night under the stars did not end with romance, but in the back of Connor's truck atop a pile of blankets and pillows he'd conveniently had. It started not with a bonfire and sultry looks through a flame but with too many cups of spiked punch and promised lies whispered against her skin. She had waited longer than most of her friends, including Delilah, to take the plunge into "womanhood", and at the time was glad it was with someone she was in love with—someone she thought loved her back.

Maybe he had loved her—he'd said it countless times that night—but it was difficult to believe when just a few weeks later he'd left her sobbing in her front yard. Sebastian had already gotten an up-close view of one of the worst mistakes of her life. She wasn't quite ready to let him see more of it.

"Don't you think you should tell him at some point? What if he's expecting a virginal wife? He's going to be a little disappointed when he goes to—"

"I got it, D," Ava interjected as she turned away from her best friend. She used some rouge to cover the blush settling under her skin. Delilah gave a little shrug as she ran her fingers through her shiny, pin-straight hair while Ava attempted to wrestle her thick, unruly curls into a somewhat neat bun. "I can't really tell him anything if he isn't around though, can I?"

"It's super weird that he wouldn't tell you where he's going."

This time it was Ava's shoulders that gravitated toward her ears. "Maybe you can ask Nixon, see if he'll tell *you* anything, since he and I aren't speaking."

Delilah laughed dryly, sarcastically. "That would mean that he would need to speak to *me*."

Glancing away from her reflection, three half braided pieces of hair in her fingers, Ava looked at her best friend sympathetically. "Not going so well, huh?"

Delilah tapped the end of her nose a few times. It was something they'd done since they were kids, letting the other know they were on the right track. Though she lounged back on her elbows and tried to look as if her lack of progress with the fortress that was Nixon didn't bother her, Ava knew better. Delilah was the one who turned guys down, refused offers when they went out dancing or marriage proposals—which had happened more than once—when they were at the market. She stood out no matter what group of people surrounded her, with her infectious laugh and brash but amiable personality. She was reckless, always the first into the ocean despite the remaining winter chill. She was daring, willing to crawl through the windows of their school afterhours for a dip in the pool. Delilah was used to batting her lashes and popping her gum and having men fall at her feet like dominoes. The fact that Nixon was still standing and seemed impervious to her charms was a little upsetting and a lot frustrating, despite how much she tried to pretend otherwise.

"Some days it seems like he's into me and other days it's as though he forgets I even exist." She puffed a piece of hair from her face.

"Men," Ava mumbled.

"It's okay, though. There are sixteen guards alone who meet all my potential boyfriend qualifications. I haven't even taken stock of the rest of the staff. Then there are the nephews of the governors, of course. Needless to say, options are not limited and if it comes down to it, I will devote my time elsewhere."

Ava made no effort to hide the smirk that tickled the corners of her mouth. "It'll be his loss if that happens."

"Oh, I know," Delilah said with a confidence that was all her own. It surpassed any that Ava had ever seen. No one else she knew believed the world revolved around her, and that it *should*, quite like Delilah. It was one of the things Ava envied about her—maybe not the egotism that came with such self-assurance, but the fact she was able to exude it so easily.

Pushing herself off the bed she walked toward the bedroom door. "I don't even know who you're getting fancy for. Your beau isn't even here," Delilah joked.

"Haven't you heard, D," Ava started while opening the door, "the rest of the world cares what I look like."

"Good thing you're a hottie," her best friend replied, hip-checking her as they made their way down the hall.

The two girls grinned at one another as they hurried down the staircase. When they rounded the bend leading to the dining room, Ava's name was called from the back of the house. Together, they turned. Helen and another woman, small and petite, were approaching them.

"Good morning, Helen," Ava said. It was impossible for her to contain her excitement at seeing the woman who was quickly becoming one of her favorite staff members. During the days before the tour started, Ava had spent much of it with Helen, who was not only the official dresser for both she and Bernadette, but also the current queen's assistant. It was a job she had been promoted to when Bernadette's original assistant—her Delilah—left ten years ago to start a family of her own. It wasn't until hearing this did Ava even consider that one day Delilah may not be around; that she, too, might leave to get married and have her own children. Thinking about it again, she glanced at Delilah as if to confirm she was still there.

"What?" Delilah mouthed, her face scrunched under her best friend's uncomfortably sad look.

Shaking her head, Ava's lips formed a tight smile. "Why don't you go get started with breakfast. I'll be there in a minute."

Her brown eyes moved between Helen, the other woman, and Ava before she nodded. "Sure," Delilah said. "It's nice to see you, Helen."

"And you, Delilah," Helen replied, her voice kind.

All three watched Delilah make her way into the dining room before Ava turned her attention to the two ladies in front of her. "Ava, my dear," Helen started as she placed a hand on the other woman's shoulder. She wasn't much taller than the older, who barely reached 5'5" on a good day. "I'd like for you to meet my niece."

"Madeline. Of course." Ava shook her hand and returned her excited smile. "It is a pleasure to finally meet you."

"Madi. Please. And no," Madi argued, waving off the compliment. "The pleasure is all mine, your…" She paused. "I'm afraid I'm unsure what to call you," she said, laughing.

"Ava works just fine for now. I love your hair, by the way." Madi touched her locks instinctively. It was black, shiny like dew on satin, but with highlights of different colors: green and blue, pink, purple, yellow, brassy orange. It looked like car oil had dripped onto concrete, especially when the sunshine pouring in through the backdoor bounced off. It was beautiful, and unquestionably one of those mystical, fairy-like features the first generation had bred into the next. When she was around people like Delilah or Madeline, even Sebastian with his silver hair, Ava never felt plainer. She was just one of many people in Havaan with normal hair and normal eyes. She looked like anyone else from the old world. Sometimes her mother teased her that her agility and grace was her gift from the first generation, but by comparison, it was kind of a shitty one.

Madi blushed at Ava's compliment, this time casting her eyes downward. "I can't believe I am standing here talking to you right now. You're everything I want to be."

This time it was Ava's turn to redden in her cheeks. "I'm sorry I can't give you the crown. From what your aunt tells me, you would have done extraordinary things with it." Ava's words were genuine and matched her kind smile. "But hopefully getting you into the kitchen will suffice for a while."

"Are you kidding me? This opportunity is beyond amazing, and more than you ever needed to do for someone like me."

Ava turned to Helen. "From the way your aunt spoke about you, I knew I couldn't allow someone else to snag you up. Especially if you're as talented with desserts as I've been led to believe." At the mention of Ava's favorite type of food, her stomach grumbled. All three women chuckled.

"We intercepted you on your way to breakfast, no doubt," Helen said.

"You did, but it's okay. The delay is well worth it." She took one of Madi's small hands in her own. "I am so excited to have you here. Let me introduce you to the kitchen staff and see that you get settled in okay."

"That isn't necessary," Madi refused quickly. "Go enjoy your breakfast."

Ava gave her a mockingly stern look. "As your future queen, I demand you allow me to walk you to the kitchen. I'm headed there, anyway."

"Well, if you insist…"

"I do," Ava said.

"Then I will leave you in Ava's very capable hands and go check in with Queen Bernadette." Helen kissed Madi's temple. "I'll see you in a bit. Behave yourself."

Madi's face hardened as her eyelids lowered slightly. It was an expression that said *how could you ever think I'd get into trouble?* and it made Ava snicker.

Helen shot a pointed look at Ava and poked her finger at her, wagging it. "You behave yourself too, young lady."

Ava saluted her. With a gentle shake of her head, Helen tottered up the staircase while Ava and Madi made their way into the kitchen. High House had many beautiful, elaborate, quiet rooms. There were enough bedrooms to house most of the staff, though no one besides a handful of guards and the royal family, Ava and Delilah included, lived there. From what Ava had gathered, there were two libraries as well as a sitting room with lush, fancy pieces of furniture; the Throne Room, which was empty most of the time; the greenhouse, the pavilion next to it and the training barn. But one of the most exciting rooms in the house was the kitchen, and not because of the decadent meals that emerged from within. Ava loved the electric energy buzzing throughout, from the clanking of pots and pans to the rapid-fire directions called from the two head chefs: Chef Aurdart (*ar-dough*) and Chef Neiman. Then there was Mrs. Markum, the lead pastry chef, and the eight sous chefs between them.

They all spared a moment from their work to greet Ava when she walked in, the kitchen door swinging behind her. Ava made sure to ask Chef Aurdart how his son was healing after he'd fallen from his bicycle and broken his wrist, and to stop by the dishwashing station for her daily joke from Willy, an older man of fifty-five who had been with Orion since day one. She spent a lot of time in the kitchen, and not just because they would occasionally let her taste-test. She loved watching meals go from empty plates and mixed concoctions to edible pieces of art. It was magic, seeing how it all came together.

As she teased Mrs. Markum to take it easy on Madi, then settled onto an open stool, Bernadette passed the circular window of the kitchen door. Amongst the normal sounds of cooking was something else; something new: laughing and joking. For a moment, she couldn't figure out the cause of the change, couldn't quite grasp what was so different that it would allot for the joviality. Then she saw it—not a what, but a who—with her innocent as a newborn laugh and her mass of curls tied away from her face. She was whisking something in a bowl and looked genuinely thrilled to be doing such a menial task.

Rage filled the queen. It was an ominous presence, a dark force that took on a tangible form, with talons that dug so deep into the back of her skull all she could see were pools of blood. It whispered things to her; nefarious things that lifted her higher and higher off the ground until she was hovering above it. Until she was another being altogether.

Those whisperings filtered under the door and snaked along the floor until they pushed strands of hair away from Ava's ear. She felt a tingle at her back—not the same spark she felt when Nixon was around, but something else, something evil. When she turned to the door, there was nothing and no one there. Just a shadow slithering away both too fast and too slow to belong to a human. Turning her attention back to Mrs. Markum, she gladly accepted the spoonful of chocolate ganache she was being handed. While the flavors exploded in her mouth, she couldn't shake the feeling of having been watched, of having been touched by something not quite of this realm.

XXII.

Time moved differently in High House depending on the room. It was long and lazy in the library, words stretching like shadows across the floor. In the training barn, time stood still. Suspended in sweat drops that clung to the skin. The kitchen moved at lightspeed, minutes flipping into hours like pancakes on the griddle.

Before she realized it, Ava had missed breakfast—though her stomach was full of duck sauce for dinner's meal and a perfectly folded three-cheese omelet—inadvertently leaving Delilah to eat by herself.

Yet again.

With a guilt-laden heart, she excused herself and went on a mission to find Delilah. She would be annoyed, and Ava would apologize, and Delilah would tell her to forget about it, both knowing full well it was a conversation they'd have again. Ava hated that her time had to be spread so thin now that she was here. It was not like it had been back home, where all she'd had to focus on was Cordellia and Delilah. Now, she had staff with which to acquaint herself and lessons of queenliness to learn.

The dining room was empty, aside from the two maids who were busy cleaning the table and dusting the dustless furniture. As Ava came around the corner, she spotted Levi and called his name.

"Have you seen Delilah?" she asked, hurrying to catch up with him at the back door.

"She was at breakfast but I'm not sure where she went afterwards. Is everything okay?"

Ava gave him a small, reassuring smile. "If it isn't, it will be once I find her and apologize. Where are you headed?"

With a thumb, Levi gestured out the door. "Over to the training barn. I go and watch sometimes, act as another pair of eyes for the guards." He shrugged and dropped his gaze. "It's stupid, but—"

"It doesn't sound stupid at all," Ava said. "I'm sure the senior guards can't see everyone at all times. Having an additional set of eyes is useful, I'd bet." Levi gave her a cheeky, lopsided grin that made him look a lot younger than his seventeen years. "You know," Ava started slyly, "the training area is one of the few places I haven't seen yet."

Catching her not-so-subtle hint, Levi asked, "You wouldn't want to come with me, would you?"

"How kind of you to ask," she laughed. Ava hooked her arm with Levi's and together they trekked across the vibrant, freshly mowed yard. The air was warm, but a slight breeze stirred the humidity enough to keep it from settling on the skin. It was one of those days that chased away any doubt spring had officially arrived. Summer would be upon them before they knew it, with its unbearable heat. Ava planned to avoid it via the massive pool. Before then, however, was the budding of flowers—of which there were hundreds in the garden plots surrounding High House—and arrival of baby animals.

On Holland Avenue, every year a family of finches built their nest in the big oak tree in the backyard. Ava could see the circle of twigs and leaves, fabric and other bits of found trash, from Cordellia's bedroom window. Many spring days were spent there, the panes lifted so the twittering and chirping of the winged creatures could filter in. It had been the only way to bring life into Cordellia's room.

Ava had a front row view of cracking eggs and featherless infants emerging from their shelled incubators, and later their lessons of flight. She'd given her undivided attention to them as they found their voices. When they fled the nest, took to the air with the wind in their wings and a plan she could not understand, she was struck with a bit of sadness. It was as though in their beaks they carried a part of her.

Took her into the bright sky that spanned the expanse of Havaan.

She had believed they were the only way she was going to get out of Meridian.

This would be the first spring she'd be unable to watch their birth, their growth, their leaving. The thought created a river of longing in her soul, and she found herself glancing into the trees, scanning the branches for any sign of nests. Levi, without question, slowed his pace to match hers; and though he had no idea what she was looking for, he let his green eyes scan the horizon until their view was interrupted.

"How do I get in there?" Ava asked as they passed the greenhouse. Vines of ivy hugged the glass walls and were starting to creep toward the roof. She had wandered over to the conservatory once before, intending to look inside, only to find a thick chain with an even thicker padlock barring her entrance.

"You have to have one of two keys," Levi explained. "That place is my mother's pride and joy. She doesn't even trust the gardeners to tend to whatever plants she has growing in there."

"Who has the second key?"

"Sebastian," he replied as they neared the barn door.

The sounds coming from inside the metal box did not match the peace and serenity outside. The grunts and groans, thumps and bangs, shouts and cries of bantering aggression were a dark contrast to the quiet rustling of leaves and buzzing of hedge trimmers. When Levi slid the door open, a wave of heat hit them. When the door was closed behind them, they were locked inside the catacomb of sweat and musk that was explicitly male. There were also other smells: leather and cedar wood, dirt and metal. It was heavy, seeping into her pores like a thick lotion, but it only took a few seconds to adjust to the change.

The barn was bigger than she had imagined, with a second level that was more an overhanging catwalk than anything. On the main floor were bleachers stacked nine levels high and built into the farthest wall. As Ava and Levi made their way to them, she did her best to hide her amused smile at the catcalls and hoots coming from the guards. She'd spent less time with them than anyone else, although she'd been introduced to most—if not all—at this point. She couldn't remember most their names quite yet, but they all knew who she was, so she took no offense to their flirtatious calls. It was all in jest, she understood, but it didn't seem Raymon, one of the lead training guards, had gotten the memo. He launched—one handed—a medicine ball at one of the rambunctious guards. The smaller man caught it, but not before it smacked into his torso. The sound of weight meeting muscle echoed through the large space, along with the grunt that followed. Ava tipped her chin in thanks at the bald but full red-bearded guard.

Levi and Ava settled near the top of the bleachers, high enough that they had a view of the entire training area. The floor was mostly dirt, clouds of it kicked up under shuffling feet and tumbling bodies. Some of the guards boxed portable punching bags, while others settled for a one-on-one scrimmage. A cluster of guards did condition training and more focused on curling and pressing weights heavy enough to snap Ava's arms. Nixon, Raymon and Ramiro circled the men, whose ages ranged from seventeen to fifty-five, giving them pointers or demonstrating the proper fighting technique. It was fascinating, and Ava got lost in the blur of their quick jabs and calculated though aggressive lunges.

"What do you look for?" she asked Levi. He was leaning forward, his elbows resting on his knees and his hands supporting his face. His eyes darted from one spot to another, absorbing it all. Occasionally, Nixon would glance up at him and Levi would give him a number followed by a signal—mostly thumbs up, down, or a so-so rock of the hand.

His eyes never stopped moving as he answered. "Inconsistencies. Poor posture. Dropping of hands from the face. Or if someone does something impressive, something we haven't seen before and need a demonstration of." He tipped his head to a guard in the corner. "Watch the guy with the tire." The tire in question was taller than the man and weighed no less than two-hundred pounds. The guard lifted one side of it then pushed it over, moving it across the expanse of the barn one flip at a time.

"That's impressive," Ava said, her voice full of awe.

Levi nodded. "But watch when he squats."

This time she paid closer attention to the way he was bending then standing, lifting and shoving. She didn't realize it at first, too wowed by his strength, but then she saw it. "He's lifting with his back," she said, a little too excited.

Levi smiled his response. "If he keeps doing it that way, he's going to mess up his back and render himself useless to Father. There isn't a shortage of volunteers, but we don't want to waste time training someone only to lose them for a stupid reason. Unfortunately, this isn't the first time Dalton will be spoken to about his technique." With his first two fingers in the shape of a V, Levi pointed to his own eyes and then at Dalton. Nixon understood. The return look he gave—the drop of his shoulders and the roll of his copper eyes—expressed his frustration. But when he approached the guy, who couldn't have been older than nineteen, even from a distance Ava could tell his words were kind, though firm.

Then, unexpectedly, Nixon demonstrated.

Ava couldn't help but lean forward as well, her eyes locked on him as he flipped the tire as though it were made of air. Without realizing it, she gnawed her bottom lip as vibrating warmth danced across her flesh. Even in the overwhelming heat of the barn, she felt on fire. She clearly wasn't the only one who was impressed, as a round of applause broke out. Nixon ignored it, instead focusing on Dalton as he mirrored his posture and motions almost as effortlessly. Nixon smacked praise onto the younger guard's shoulder before moving to a different part of the gym.

This time, when he looked back to the stands, his gaze met Ava's, igniting the burn in her veins even more. Their connection, which felt like it lasted days, was interrupted by Levi, who cleared his throat loudly.

She blinked a few times then leaned back on the bench, avoiding Levi's eyes. She looked anywhere besides at him or Nixon. "So, uh…do you…" She waved her hand at the guards. "Can you do any of that?"

"Some," he answered, a hint of amusement in his voice as he reclined as well, their backs supported by the bleacher behind them. "Nixon has taught me a few things throughout the years, mostly for self-defense. Mother and Father don't think I need to know anything about…" He mimicked her, gesturing below to the training center. "They do allow me to fence, though."

Ava looked over at him, surprised. "Fencing, like with the swords and masks?"

Levi sat a little straighter as, perfectly timed, the door to the barn opened and a tall, svelte gentleman entered. He was wearing a pair of white breeches that came to just below his knee and was met by a pair of calf-high white socks. On his upper-half he wore a long-sleeved black shirt. Over it was something that looked like a thin life jacket, only it was cut in half and with one short-sleeve. It was flush against his body by straps on the sides.

"It's a plastron," Levi explained when she asked about it. "It's a pad that provides protection for the sword arm." He waved to his fencing partner, a subtle but slightly eager motion, then stood and cleared his throat again. "I'm going down to practice. Do you want me to walk you back out before I begin?"

Ava shook her head, looking up at him. "I think I'll stick around and watch for a bit longer, if you don't mind. I've always wanted to see a fencing match."

Levi laughed. "I can't promise it'll be all that interesting, but stay as long as you'd like."

She grinned up at him then tracked the young prince as he made his way down the bleachers. When Levi reached the other man, they exchanged a few words before Levi vanished behind a wall, only to emerge a few minutes later in full fencing gear. He carried his mask in his hand.

With curious interest, Ava watched as the taller of the two assisted Levi with his mask, tucking the end of it into the fencing jacket. He tugged on different areas of the clothing, ensuring their protection, then discretely—to anyone not paying attention—he squeezed Levi's fingers. Ava couldn't see Levi's lips through the mesh of the mask, but he must have said something to him, because they both turned her direction. She flicked her eyes away quickly and unintentionally found Nixon's once again.

Maybe I should have left, she grumbled to herself as he made his way up the bleachers, taking every other step with the wide stride of his legs. Within seconds he was seated beside her, close enough she could feel the heat radiating off his skin. He smelled like sweat, a sweet odor that mixed with his cotton and mint. It was oddly intoxicating.

"Have you been enjoying the show?" His deep voice, laced with an unfamiliar lightness, vibrated in her sternum.

"I haven't really been paying attention," she lied.

Nixon's lips twitched. They both knew she'd been eyeball deep in the whole charade. "If you aren't here to ogle them, what *are* you doing here?"

You're the only one I want to ogle. The king's men were all big muscled, brawny and attractive. Some of them off the charts beautiful. Many would consider it unfair that Ava was surrounded by so many good-looking guys, but for her, none could hold a candle to Nixon. Every time she looked at him, a bit of her soul wilted; a reminder that no matter how on fire he set her body, how often he invaded her dreams, or how deep her attraction and desire for him ran, it would never matter.

Reluctantly, she scooted just a finger's length away, but it was enough that the entire side of her body went cold. Nixon didn't say anything, but the look he gave her let her know he noticed the distance, too.

As casually as possible, she leaned against the bleacher at her back once more. Nixon copied her. He stretched his broad torso and long legs out full length. He looked comfortable and cool while she failed at simply looking relaxed.

"I was just spending some q.t. with my future bro-in-law," she said in answer to his question.

They were silent for a moment and then Nixon said, "Ew." A small laugh escaped from his throat and she followed it with one of her own.

"That was pretty gross," she agreed, giggling. She kicked her feet in the air, her posture suspending them off the floor. "I really did come here to hang out with him, though. I don't know much about him."

"Did you learn anything good?"

She looked over at Nixon and smiled gently. It felt natural being around him, at least when he was civil and not ignoring her. "I learned that he looks up to you." There was something in the way Levi spoke about Nixon—an admiration he didn't need to explain. It was like Nixon gave Levi a purpose, held him to a standard other than just *prince*. Maybe acting as another pair of eyes wasn't that big a deal, but Nixon included Levi in things. Sometimes that was enough.

"He's a good kid," Nixon said, his words tender. They watched, like proud parents, as Levi and his fencing partner lunged and parried, blocking the swish of thin blades. The clashing of the weapons made pebble-like tings as they tapped against one another. It was an elegant, contrasting dance from the aggressive grabs and flips the guards were performing. Although those, too, had their own sort of grace.

Ava took the time to inquire about something of which she'd been curious.

"Why does the king need guards?" she asked Nixon.

"He doesn't," Nixon replied immediately.

"Okay…" She tried again. "Then why does he have them?"

He thought a moment as his fierce eyes roved the men below, cataloguing every movement. "Just in case, I suppose."

"In case another war breaks out?" Ava challenged. Nixon raised his eyebrows quickly, as if he knew something but refused to say. It was like he was waiting for her to ask the right question, one that would open the floodgates. She leaned in closer and locked her eyes with his. "Is that even a possibility?" she whispered.

"It's happened before. There's no failsafe to keep it from happening again." She considered this for a moment before returning to her spot. "There isn't a reason that it *would* happen again, of course," he added.

"Of course." Her voice took a faraway tone as she waded through her thoughts. She had never been afraid of another war, never even considered the likelihood of one; and if one did break out...it would hopefully be dealt with quickly and quietly. But now that she was close to the crown, the mere possibility of one scared her. Because if it happened once Orion was gone, it wouldn't be his war. It would be hers, and she was in no way, shape or form equipped to deal with such a thing.

Nixon must have sensed her unease because he reached over and grazed her knee with his fingertips. The simple touch sent a spark through the sinews connecting all pieces of her to one another. It was the nervous feeling that came before a major risk.

Will it always be this way between us? she wondered, momentarily distracted from the conversation they'd been having.

"Nothing like that is going to happen," he said, this time assurance backing his words. He made it easy to believe. "Havaan is better than it has ever been, and once you're in power, it will be even greater."

Ava nodded a few times then looked back at the training area. She knew there were sixty-five guards in total, though they were rarely at High House at the same time. *Is that enough?* She chewed on her thumbnail absently. It was a horrible habit, one that only happened when she was truly worried about something.

Life had demonstrated more than once that there were only so many things she could control, so she made a valid effort to stress herself out as little as possible. Life had also shown her there was nothing she couldn't handle, despite how often it may seem otherwise. She did not, however, think she would handle a war very well; and while sixty-five seemed a good, strong number—especially when one considered the size and skill of the guards—it would ultimately depend on the size and number of the people fighting against them.

If the entirety of Havaan banded together in protest, sixty-five would be just as useless as five. Things would crumble and she would—

"It's nice to have you speaking to me again." Nixon's comment cut through her thoughts, distracting her from the onslaught that was taking place in her imagination. That had been his intent, and when she responded with, "*Me*, talking to *you*?" he smirked a bit.

"You're the one who's made it a point to ignore me since I got here," Ava snapped, the last couple of words short with agitation.

"You did say I was on the list of people you didn't want to speak with," he replied calmly, almost sarcastically.

Ava faced him, her face twisted with incredulity. "AFTER you spent the entire day ignoring me!" She didn't realize she was shouting until a few of the guards looked their way. She ignored them and focused all of her attention on nailing Nixon to his seat with the heated daggers of her eyes.

"Still," he shrugged, "it wasn't very nice of you."

A dry laugh escaped her lips. "What, did I hurt your feelings?"

"Some say I don't have any," he said flatly.

She almost agreed out of spite, but she refused to lie to him. To let him perpetuate this cold, emotionless façade he'd created for himself. He had allowed someone to love him once, and he'd loved her in return. Yes, he had been burned by her, scorched by her ulterior motives, but Ava had also seen him smile. Heard him laugh. Felt the passion behind his words when he'd practically begged her to stay true to herself, no matter what.

It was almost as though he was afraid to let people see that side of him. As if having feelings would somehow make him less.

Ava wondered how much of the real Nixon even Sebastian knew.

"I'm sorry if I hurt whatever feelings you *do* have," she said, less angry.

He looked over at her, his ember pupils an animated blaze. "You're forgiven."

"Now you," she encouraged.

He raised a thick brow at her. "Now me…what?"

"Apologize."

A loud thunderclap of a laugh burst from him, but it held no actual joy. "For *what?*" he asked as if it were the most absurd thing he'd heard all year.

Her mouth hung open on its hinges as she returned his look, her face a mixture of *are you serious?* and genuine bafflement. "Oh, I don't know," she stared, every word dripping with sarcasm as thick as fresh honey. "Maybe for being a huge asshole these last couple of weeks. Or for pretending I don't exist. Or ignoring me as if I'm a plague. Pick one and start there. I at least had a reason for being mean to you."

"As did I," he said quietly, barely above a whisper.

"Care to share what that reason *was,* because I've been at a complete loss."

Nixon studied her for five beats of her heart, one and a half breaths. From the furrow of his brow and the slow lick of his lips, it appeared he was preparing to spill his guts, to cut himself open at the abdomen and share every secret he kept locked up in his depth. Instead he forced out a disappointing, "No," through clenched teeth.

Heated, and not for the reasons typically involving Nixon, Ava let loose a snarl of frustration as she stood. She needed to get away from him before she socked him in his perfectly chiseled jaw.

"Whatever," she huffed as she pushed to her feet. She hurried down the bleachers as quickly as possible, not for the first time thankful for her agility, and headed toward the exit. Around her, the gym continued. The *whap* of fists meeting bag and the *clang* of sword meeting sword echoed her angry heart, but all she could hear was the rushing of blood in her ears. She didn't even hear her name being called until Nixon was right behind her, his hand gripping her arm.

"Get off me," she demanded, twisting out of his grip.

"Ava, stop!" His tone was so full of authority it took everything in her not to obey. Under her feet, dirt clouds rose, little puffs of earth that settled on the top of her shoes and in the pleats of her trousers. "Damn it," Nixon growled. Suddenly, she was yanked from her path and set in a dark corner. Her breath was coming quick, making her head floaty. She didn't know why she was so mad, but anger burned in her veins like acid. She didn't give a second, let alone a first thought, as she shoved Nixon. He was stone. No part of him faltered when her hands met his chest, but it made her feel a little better, anyway.

"Leave me alone."

Nixon spoke over her fury. "I was ignoring you because I hoped it would stop my feelings for you." The words were heavy with a conviction all their own.

This corner of the barn was blanketed in shadows, but the smallest amount of light slinked around the wall and illuminated the deep cuts of his face. His eyes radiated brighter than normal and Ava wanted nothing more than to wade into the flames, to burn in his inferno.

His words…it took too many frozen seconds for her to understand what he'd said, but when she did, her heart dropped to her stomach and startled the butterflies from their slumber. They sprang to life, their wings carrying them up her throat where they lodged, blocking anything from coming out.

Nixon ran his fingers through his lobe-length black locks and took her stunned silence as space to say more. "In your bedroom, I wanted nothing more than to kiss you, and if I hadn't heard your mother coming up the stairs I would have. I didn't want to leave you with that, though, with the guilt of having to look Sebastian in his eyes minutes later. The fact that I was willing to was too much. I thought if I could distance myself from you, if I could keep you as far away from me as possible that I would stop…" He swallowed. "…*craving* you. That I would no longer consider betraying my best friend." His hands hung rigid at his sides, his long fingers flexing into fists repeatedly as if it were the only way he could keep from reaching for Ava.

Maybe it was.

When he said, "I'm sorry if I hurt you," and took a step forward, the world tilted. It lifted on her side, pushing Ava toward him, and she did nothing to resist the force. Her deep cerulean eyes were locked so intently on his it was like she was trying to put out the fire of his pupils with the ocean of her own.

Without warning, the butterflies in her throat broke free and brought with the flapping of wings a question asked on a shaky breath. "Did it work?" She was afraid of his answer in more ways than one.

His hands moved in slow motion to her face. His gaze traveled down her nose and to her lips as they parted, her breaths coming too fast to keep stifled behind her teeth. His fingertips were mere inches from her cheek and she shifted just a fraction into their path.

In the next second, a shrill buzzing shattered the space around them.

"What is that?" Ava asked breathlessly.

Nixon dropped his hand quickly, too fast almost, like everything was speeding up again. "Lunch. It's the lunch bell. It lets us know it's lunchtime." He stumbled over his words as if he'd forgotten how to speak. Maybe he had, because Ava had forgotten how to breathe, how to exist in anything other than Nixon's confession.

He wanted her like she wanted him.

There had never been a crueler or more unfair synchronicity in all of existence.

"You should go before they wonder where you are," he said with obvious reluctance.

It was a feeling Ava understood all too well. Her voice quaked when she asked, "Aren't you coming, too?"

He shook his head. "I'm going to go a few rounds on the bag and then maybe take a run, but I'll be at dinner."

Nodding her head mechanically, as though she could do nothing else, she pivoted away from him and floated back toward the exit. Before she rounded the corner, however, words crashed into her from behind; ones that sounded an awful lot like Nixon.

"And no," they said, "it didn't work."

It took everything within her to keep moving, to not acknowledge what he had said, though she faltered a step—enough to let him know she had heard them. She smiled at the guard who paused to let her pass, and though she wanted to turn back, to run back into the barn and launch herself into Nixon's arms—beg him to take her far away from High House—she continued across the yard, her lips twitching as her secret made every effort to spew into the wind. The world could use some good news, and this was the best she could imagine.

But this bit was all hers, even if Nixon never would be.

XXIII.

Lunch at High House was served buffet style, with a row of chafing dishes lined against the wall and filled with meats like pulled pork for sandwiches or seasoned ground beef for a nacho bar. Perfectly triangular pieces of cheesecake or moist chocolate brownies were stacked three levels high on beautiful serving trays. The meal was far less formal than dinner.

Some chose to eat in the dining room while others found their own special place to dine. There was a collection of guards who always gathered along the fence and another set who lounged at the edge of the pool, plates of food balanced on their stomachs. Ava's favorite spot was the rustic gazebo next to the greenhouse. The structure was old, but still managed to maintain its original elegance. Ornate swirls were carved into the posts like metal ivy. There was a line of forest behind the gazebo and the dotting of colors from the many gardens in front could almost convince her she was someplace enchanted and magical where only she knew. It was also quiet, peaceful; a small haven in the grandeur of the mansion in whose shadows it was encased.

Which is why Ava was always surprised no one ever made their way there.

She typically used the time alone to collect her thoughts for the day. Sometimes she'd journal, her hand and pen one entity as they flew across the page and tried to keep up with her racing thoughts. More often than not, she just ate and daydreamed.

It was quite a shock when she cut across the lush grass this day—her brain a cataclysm of Nixon and his words, of fantasies that ended with happily ever after's she knew would never happen—and found Delilah seated at the small, rusting metal table with a plate full of salad.

"Stealing food from the rabbits again?" Ava joked as she set her plate down and took the seat across from her best friend.

Delilah shoved a forkful of greens into her mouth and shrugged. "I had a big breakfast," she said between chews. "Which you'd know if you'd shown up."

She had known where D was going with her comment as soon as the words crossed her lips, but Ava still flinched. "I got held up," she said as she adjusted the cold turkey falling from her bread. "I came to find you, but you'd already left."

"A girl can only sit by herself for so long before she realizes she's been stood up," Delilah replied dryly as she violently stabbed a piece of ham with her fork.

Ava exhaled a small sigh and rested her face in her hands. Cordellia had always scolded her about putting her elbows on the table, but Cordellia wasn't here; and Ava was the future queen—she could put whatever she wanted to on the table.

"Nothing is turning out how we thought it would," she mumbled, looking at Delilah sadly.

D shook her head and pushed a few pieces of lettuce around her plate. "No, it's not," she agreed.

Ava said her name softly, and her brown eyes rotated upward. "I'm sorry."

"I know," Delilah said. What she didn't say, though it lingered on the edge of her words, was *you're always sorry*. And as much offense as

Ava wanted to take, she couldn't. She'd been unintentionally disregarding Delilah since they'd arrived and her feelings were hurt. That was one of the few things in life Ava made a valid effort to never do.

"Can I make it up to you somehow?" Ava asked as she took a massive bite of her food. "Anything you want."

Delilah drummed her fingers on her chin pensively, and then her eyes widened until they marveled saucers. "That," she said breathlessly. "I want *that.*"

Ava turned in her chair and followed her friend's line of sight. She should have known by the way Delilah had sung the simple word that *that* was really a *who*.

Nixon was crossing the yard. The towel hanging around his neck did little to catch the drops of sweat coming from the ends of his hair. As though he could feel their staring, his eyes found them. They met Delilah's brown ones first. When they flicked to Ava's blue ones, he held her attention for a second longer. His lips twitched, a quick upturn at the corners before someone called his name, severing their connection.

Swallowing a swig of water, Ava cleared away the sediment of the secret scratching at her throat. Delilah was the first person she would gush to about something like this; about how the prettiest boy thought she was the prettiest girl, but these were not normal circumstances.

It was too sensitive to even put on the lines of her journal.

It had the power to destroy the world if it didn't destroy her first.

"I don't think my title as future queen allows me to give you a person," Ava teased as she tried to contain the warble in her voice.

The look of sad desperation, of defeat, that painted itself on Delilah's face made Ava want to fold the world into an origami star and give it to her best friend.

"I just want him to see me," D whispered. The way she said *see* meant more than the obvious. It was something Ava understood more than she wanted to admit. The thing was, Nixon *had* seen her. She wasn't sure which was worse.

"It's so hard to crack him," Delilah continued, "when I can't get him to talk to me for more than two minutes at a time. We need to get away from everything that's going on and have actual time to get to know one another, ya know? I've seen him with Sebastian and he's…he's different. He's almost like he was at your house."

Ava's eyebrow raised a fraction as she popped a chip into her mouth. "So how do I come into all of this?" she questioned, because she knew somehow, she did. The sly smile that stretched Delilah's lips reaffirmed it.

"I was thinking if you orchestrated something like a double-date…" She put up a hand as Ava opened her mouth to protest. "It doesn't have to anything fancy, Avie. Just something that will allow us to be Sebastian and Ava, Nixon and Delilah instead of the prince and the future queen, the guard and the queen's assistant. An hour where we can just be ourselves, separate from all of that." She waved her hand in the direction of High House. "Please," Delilah added. The beseeching plea matched the intensity of her puppy-eyes.

As Ava's best friend, she knew Ava couldn't resist them, and felt no shame in the squeal that escaped her when she sighed a resigned, "Fine."

This was the last thing Ava wanted to do.

She didn't want to play matchmaker between her best friend and the guy who spun her world on its axis. Knowing how Nixon felt about her meant he would never feel that way about Delilah. All this build-up would lead to a massive let-down.

But things like this needed to happen, because things like falling in love with Nixon and making the sort of future with him that Delilah wanted was impossible for Ava. When Sebastian wasn't around it was easy to forget he existed, to forget that her fate was tied with his, sealed together at all the seams and edges. Sebastian *would* be around though. In a few short days he would return and their courtship would continue. The days until their nuptials would press closer together until there was no space for Nixon.

Perhaps he'd had the right idea.

Perhaps space and time apart was the best plan. It was not a plan Ava wanted to put into effect, but hopefully…maybe…it would make whatever feelings they had for one another null and void.

"When Sebastian returns, I'll figure something out," Ava promised. She dusted crumbs off of her shirt so Delilah wouldn't catch the disappointment in her eyes.

Delilah grinned. "If it doesn't work, if after that things don't change between us, I will find a new target."

Ava laughed. "There are sixteen guards alone who meet all your boyfriend qualifications," she reminded with a wink.

"I hope you don't think for a second I would ever forget that," Delilah said, giggling.

Later that night, as she sat on the chaise in her room, listening to the nighttime lullaby of High House, Ava sorted her thoughts between the covers of her journal. It was a tattered thing—two pieces of leather held together by frayed string, the 1000 pages of lined paper holed manually. It was also a gift from Zarah, given on Ava's sixteenth birthday. She'd replaced the strings at least ten times over the years and was nearing the last of the paper. It was bursting with Ava's most personal thoughts and feelings, and even when the final page was finished she would keep it.

She had spent chunks of her day mentally planning Delilah's favor— which is what she was calling it—because there was no way she would do such a thing otherwise. She had spent a larger part of her day thinking about Nixon, specifically how she could erase not just her feelings for him but his feelings toward her, as well. While he had been ignoring her, she'd hated his vacant stares and stone back; had found nothing pleasant in the way he looked beyond her when all she was doing was silently screaming for his attention.

Now she considered how he might have been on to something.

Time really was an interesting thing, and it was possible that if she spent enough of it away from him…far, *far* away from him…maybe she could stop feeling what she felt. She couldn't ban him from High House though, from his home. He was Sebastian's Delilah, and would be around for at least the next couple of years.

She could try and make him hate her, she supposed. Do something so vile he couldn't stand the sight of her, and then he would leave, and then it would just be she and Sebastian and she wouldn't have to look at Nixon's perfect face or hear the boom of his voice or absorb all the static in the world when he walked near.

What if, she wrote in handwriting that had always been described as not feminine enough, I have the same ailment as Cordellia, whatever it is that keeps her chained to Dante's ghost? What if it followed me here, shackles at the ready?

The probability she would forever miss Nixon no matter how far away he went was higher than her ever being able to fully let him go.

Ultimately, she decided she really didn't *want* to stay away from him. She liked him beyond his good looks and angsty personality. He was a shade of vibrancy she'd never had in her life. He made her laugh despite his dry humor—*especially* because of his dry humor. His wit was sharp enough to duel hers. He was passionate, and in that passion, he believed in her. When she looked at Nixon she could see within herself all her hidden potential; potential she *wanted* to live up to.

Being a sous chef and the daughter of a half-crazed woman was no longer good enough.

There would never be anything besides friendship allowed between herself and Nixon, a fact she, unfortunately, needed to accept. But friendship, she decided in the end, was better than not having him around. She needed him in her life. Needed him to keep her sane and to, more than anything, remind her how strong she could be. Without him, she feared she would forget to push back and everything would steamroll her until she fluttered into the wind.

She would become nothing but a memory, if even that.

She would need to talk to him about everything, hash out their feelings for one another and then draw a line in the sand that they could not cross. She would tell him how she felt, too, so he would know he wasn't the only one silently suffering; and then they would come up with a plan that would work for both of them.

If it didn't, well, then she would worry about scaring him off.

As hard as it will be to have him near me, knowing I will never see him is worse. I can handle feeling what I feel and not being able to act on it. I cannot handle feeling what I feel and knowing my heart will try to break through my chest every day that he's gone in an effort to get to him. I will deny myself as much of him as I can handle, but I will not put myself through more than I can take.

The second the tiny dot of ink appeared at the end of her disorganized thoughts, finalizing them, she tore the pages from their binding. She shredded the paper, her words staining her fingers, and flushed the confetti down the toilet. Then she crawled into bed, snuggled under the blanket, and wrapped her arms around her pillow as tightly as possible. Before long, the darkness behind her lids was illuminated by two blazing circles so intense they could set the world on fire.

She, without hesitation, walked through those flames.

XXIV.

A storm had ripped through the night. It announced itself somewhere in the middle of their dreams and stuck around until the dawning of morning. There was applause of thunder and paparazzi flashes of lightning before it put on a show that rattled windowpanes as it begged to come inside. Some of the flowers had been so impressed they'd thrown themselves at the rain like crazed groupies, sacrificing their petals to the Earth before collapsing from sheer exhaustion. Ava had slept through most of it, only waking when it was giving its grand finale. Delilah had dragged her out of bed that morning and forced her into the backyard, still in their pajamas, to stare at the multi-colored arch it left behind in the sky.

Ava had never seen a rainbow before, but she had heard stories about them. The old world had viewed them as a symbol of hope, a promise of all the good that would follow the storm. She didn't know if that was true, but for what she had planned today, she could use a positive omen. She decided to take a little bit of old world belief and tuck it into her pocket.

Summer's heat had been creeping in, making the air thick and skin tacky. But the squall had cooled it down, and the morning following was beautiful in both temperature and in destruction. Petals and leaves covered the grass like sprinkles, as if Mother Nature and the night had thrown themselves a party and used the rainbow to decorate cupcakes.

While she waited on the porch, Ava gathered carnation pinks, rosy reds, and iris purples into a pile next to her. She poked strands of stems through their centers. She was halfway finished with her droopy flower crown when the door to High House finally opened.

She didn't need to turn around to know who it was. The skin on the back of her neck tingled and her heart pumped as though it had been jumpstarted.

"What are you doing?" Nixon asked as he hurdled effortlessly over the four steps.

She held her ring of flowers toward him and shielded her eyes from the sun as she looked up. "Since mom and I aren't speaking right now, I figured I should get a start on my crown," she said. His lips vanished into his mouth in an effort to hide his amusement. Ava stood, dusting debris off the back of her pants. "I'm coming with you today."

Nixon raised a brow as his eyes scanned her outfit. It was similar to his: black jogging pants, except Ava's were capri-length; black tank top and worn but comfortable running shoes. Even their hair was styled similarly, the locks gathered away from their faces at the base of their heads.

"How'd you know I was going running?" he asked.

"It's almost eleven. You go running every other day around eleven."

"I must be getting predictable."

"You're going to lose your air of mystery if you're not careful," she joked.

The balance he exhibited as he pulled his left leg up and bent it behind him, stretching the muscles like a flamingo, was impressive. "I'm not going to slow down for you."

With a refusal to be outdone already, Ava pantomimed her lack of worry then bent at her waist in a wide-stance downward dog. She could feel the pull up the back of her legs all the way down her spine, and it felt…amazing. She loved yoga, had done it every day until the one following the gala. If ever there had been a time for it, it had been then, but she couldn't seem to find her center.

The world felt like it was constantly unbalanced.

This was the first time she'd done anything of the sort since that night, and the relief in tension was almost immediate. *Perhaps the old world was onto something with that whole rainbow omen thing,* she thought as she and Nixon started off.

As soon as they were past the wrought iron gates of High House, they settled into a steady jog. Nixon stayed a stride ahead of her, which she allowed. The last thing she wanted was to get too cocky and tumble over a downed log or rut in the pine-covered ground. He leaped over large rocks half buried in the dirt and ducked under low-hanging branches.

While they ran they didn't speak.

Occasionally, he would glance back to make sure Ava hadn't collapsed from exhaustion, but she was keeping up with him as though she ran this trail every day. It was a four-mile trek uphill and her body figured it out long before Nixon told her. Her calves burned and her lungs begged her for air, but she felt good.

When they reached the top of the incline, she felt alive.

The end of the trail was immediate. If Nixon hadn't stopped, Ava would have run into oblivion. The peak of the cliff hovered above a gully of knee-high grass and a pond so smooth and clear it looked like blue tinted glass. Six fully grown swans swam in circles, strings of off-white fluff-balls chasing them and each other. It was so quiet she could hear the flutter of wings at least half a mile below when one of the bigger swans took flight. Not only was it eerily silent, void of chirping birds or the clattering of dishes or the thuds of bodies hitting packed dirt, but the air was cleaner. As she filled her lungs with it, she felt like she was taking the purest breath ever.

"It's beautiful up here," she whispered, though it sounded as if she'd said it at a normal decibel. She was surprised Nixon couldn't hear the horses clopping up and down her ribs as her heart slowly returned to its normal cadence.

"It's one of my favorite places," he replied, stepping next to her. Though his chest moved up and down with each deep, quick breath, he didn't look worn or tired. *Of course,* Ava had to remind herself, *he does this daily.*

Ava looked at him from the corner of her eye and traced his profile against the backdrop of green: the sharp beak-like shape of his nose and the dip under it that led to two almost symmetrical lips, the bottom one just a fraction larger than the top. She always thought of Sebastian as beautiful, but Nixon was, too. It was just in a more masculine way, with deep angles and grooves that could cut diamonds. Nixon was also broody and intense, withdrawn and closed off, and that made him a challenge. It was the mysterious element he was so intent on keeping that made her want to know him, to learn everything about him in case the world ended one day. She would write it all down, smear it into the pages of her journal for future generations to find, and when they rebuilt civilization they would be envious men like Nixon had existed.

He cleared his throat and she blinked a few times, her eyes suddenly dry. She had been staring, but more embarrassing, she'd been *caught* staring. She coughed and then looked at her feet. "Can we sit and talk for a few?" she asked before glancing back up at him. She met his eyes unexpectedly and if she hadn't already been warm from their run, the intensity of his gaze would have reduced her to nothing more than ash. The edge of her bottom lip slipped from her teeth and his pupils dilated, dousing the fires in his eyes into a black almost as dark as his hair. He looked like a man possessed by desire. It rolled off him in a hundred-degree waves and it was too much.

Using the little bit of strength she had, Ava pulled her eyes from his to check on the swans, to make sure their attraction wasn't burning them. Then she sat on the bluff, her feet dangling off the edge of the world. A few moments passed before he lowered himself, too. They both noticed when he sat too close, then when he moved too far away, and finally when he settled somewhere in the middle.

Nixon spoke first, a welcomed break from their sizzling silence. "You did well," he said. "There are guards who have a difficult time keeping pace with me."

She brushed the compliment off her shoulders and cockily replied, "Haven't you heard that girls are better than boys?" She refused to look at him, it was too soon, but there was no mistaking that the *psh* sound he made was accompanied by a roll of his eyes.

"Anyway," he continued, a little too pointedly, "I—"

"I wanted you to kiss me," she interrupted in a rush, their I's overlapping. This time she did look at him, a slow turn of her head and a sheepish smile. "That morning, in my bedroom. I haven't stopped wanting you to kiss me. But I can't leave you with that guilt, either. I can't—I *won't*—betray Sebastian or Delilah like that."

"Delilah?" he asked, his brows scrunched under his confusion. "What does she have to do with anything?"

"I'm sure you've noticed she's pretty into you…"

"Well, yes," he said as he pulled the tie from his hair. His locks fell into place perfectly, a black onyx frame around the world's most cherished piece of art. "I'm not dense."

"She would hate me forever if she even *knew* I...how I feel for you. I can't risk that." She shook her head. "I will regret it more than anything."

He nodded his understanding. "Then what do we do?"

"I don't imagine there's a chance you'll just leave High House, is there?" Ava asked. "Just...pack up all your stuff and go somewhere else. I'm sure Cordellia would take you in in a heartbeat." She looked at him expectantly, so intensely he wasn't sure if she was joking; and as the ocean blue of her eyes rippled under a pool of hope, he started mentally packing his bags.

It was in this moment he realized he would do anything she asked of him.

When her veneer cracked, shattered like glass by her slow-grin laughter, he laughed too, his relief audible by the rush of breath from his lungs. "I hope you have a Plan B," he said, nudging her shoulder with his.

Then she turned serious again. "I can't handle you ignoring me. You, D and Sebastian are the only normal things in my life. And I don't have much time left for normalcy. I want to hold on to it as much as possible and I can't do that if I'm walking on eggshells around you. I get it. I understand what you were trying to do but..." She shook her head, letting the gesture fill in the rest. "So, since you're not going to be that easy to get rid of, we have to establish some rules."

"Rules I can do."

"Okay." She drummed her fingers against the side of her neck, thinking. "First and foremost, no kissing." Nixon snapped his fingers. The chuckle that escaped her was pure, like the air at the edge of existence and sweet like sugar on a bee's wing. It was his favorite sound in the world, aside from the way she said his name.

"And no physical contact," she added.

His face was stone, disapproval evident only in the lowering of his lids. "None?" The pieces of hair that had been plastered to her sweaty face were now dry, little baby curls that moved with her. His fingers ached to push them behind her ears.

"I don't trust you to not try and seduce me." She winked.

Nixon gawked, his eyes bigger than she'd ever seen them. "Me?!" he practically shouted, his head shaking in disbelief. Ava had never seen this side of him: fun, playfully flirtatious. What a twenty-four-year-old guy *should* be like.

"While we're on the subject," he said, "*you* are not allowed to give me lusty eyes."

A loud honk-like sound came out of her and broke the dome of silence around them. One of the swans trumpeted back. "I don't even know what that means," she defended.

"You think I haven't noticed how you look at me? Your eyes get all spacy and I can practically feel you undressing me with them."

She opened her mouth to argue but no words came. It just hung there, held open by the truth of his words. He pushed it closed with his fingertip and said sternly, "No lusty eyes."

Exasperated, she turned away from him. Up here, there was nowhere to hide so he wouldn't see the intense blush radiating across her cheeks. "Fine," she mumbled, "no lusty eyes."

Nixon leaned back on his hands, a satisfied look on his face. She wanted to wipe it away. No, she wanted to kiss it away—kiss *him* so hard it was the only thing he'd have to be satisfied about. But instead she asked, "Anything else?"

He shook his head before sitting back up and gathering his hair into a short ponytail. "Those rules should keep us out of trouble," he said as he pushed himself to his feet. Ava copied him and stretched her arms into the sky. Her spine cracked in the most satisfying way. Nixon didn't look away fast enough and she caught him drinking in her form, but she didn't say anything.

As they started back down the hill, side by side this time, Nixon said, "I think we should kiss." She raised her brows but kept her eyes on the path. They were going down faster than they'd gone up, and he wasn't ahead of her this time to warn her of all the dangers.

"It's been two minutes and you already want to break rule number one?" she teased.

She saw him shrug in her peripheral. "It might help. We won't have to be tempted, constantly wondering what we're missing. Maybe you'll be a horrible kisser and I won't want to kiss you again, but at least we'd know."

"I am not a bad kisser," she replied between breaths. "And I'm not going to kiss you."

They ran the next mile in silence, their feet pounding the ground in harmonious synchronicity. Even their inhales and exhales matched, as if they were sharing one pair of lungs.

"I'll make you a deal," Nixon said as they dashed through a pile of dead leaves. They crunched under their shoes, like a bag of chips being crushed.

"What?" she huffed, inhaling through her nose as quickly as possible. Her lungs were on fire again, but she welcomed the burn. Physical pain meant she was still alive. She could handle physical pain. It was the emotional stuff she tried to avoid. That's why setting rules with Nixon, and *following* them—despite how hard it would undoubtedly be—was so important. She knew the damage, the destruction of self that betrayal could cause someone. She'd experienced it more than once in her short twenty years of life. She would do everything in her power to avoid bringing such pain to Delilah and Sebastian.

Even if it meant never kissing Nixon.

"If we go a month. Without breaking any of the rules. Then we kiss. Just a quick one. To get it out of the way."

She rolled her eyes and chuckled. "You don't. Give up. D'you?" she said between labored breaths. He gifted her with a wicked smile that made her heart beat so fast it was like propellers, and she would have floated away if gravity didn't have her anchored so tightly.

"I'll agree…" She picked up her pace steadily, forcing her legs to move through the pain. "If you can beat me home." Ava put everything she had behind the sprint as she took off, swallowed every bit of determination into her lungs; not because she didn't want to kiss Nixon, but because she wanted the pleasure of beating him. As she neared the metal gates, she glanced back to gauge their distance apart.

"One month," he whispered as he passed her on the other side, his beautiful lips bemusedly contorted.

One month, she thought while watching his hand slapp the gates. *How hard can it be?*

XXV.

Every single part of her body ached. It was as though someone had injected liquid lead into her veins, and now it had hardened, keeping her hostage in her overly-comfortable bed.

As soon as she'd returned from her run, she'd gone through two circuits of yoga, hoping to loosen her muscles. After dinner she'd utilized the bathtub, submerged to her neck in water as hot as she could handle. She'd added bath salts designed specifically for muscle tension. All either of those had done were help her collapse into the deepest sleep she'd gotten since her arrival at High House. So when the knocking started on her bedroom door, she made no effort to move. She wasn't entirely sure she could, even if she *wanted* to get up. She groaned her protest, as did Delilah, who was face-first in a pillow.

They had dedicated the time after dinner to one another. During her soaking, Delilah had sat outside the bathroom door, her back against the wall as they had done hundreds of times growing up. As Delilah coated her fingernails in polish and Ava prayed that whatever magic existed in the salts Helen had given her would work, D tossed out as nonchalantly as if she were talking about the day of the week, "I saw my parents while you were on tour."

"You did? Did they come here?"

Delilah shook her head even though Ava couldn't see. "No, I went home for a day."

"And how was it?"

She was silent for a second, searching her brain for a word that would adequately sum up her trip back to Typhony. "It was weird," she settled upon.

"Did Ashton ask about me?" Ava teased, her words light.

"Of course he did," Delilah replied, blowing on her hand. "Well, he asked when he would be able to come and visit, but I'm sure he specifically wants to see you."

Ava laughed, "I'll make sure to send him a formal invite soon," as she sank lower into the water. It was cloudy and smelled of lavender. Whether it was the additives or the near scalding temperature of the water—perhaps a combination of the two—she was starting to feel like spaghetti. Her run with Nixon had left her mentally, emotionally, and physically drained. She couldn't wait to crawl into bed, burrow under the blankets and just sleep. As she was thinking about her bed, with its mattress that was too perfect to be true, Delilah's words snapped her back to reality.

"I saw Cordellia, too," she'd said, almost too quietly.

Ava sat up quickly, water splashing over the sides of the tub, and looked toward the bathroom door. "Out in public?" she asked, her voice shaking. She missed her mother, worried about her daily, but she was too proud to apologize yet. A bridge had been burned between them, and though repairable, Ava wasn't quite ready to put in the effort.

Looking over the threshold, the scrunch of Delilah's face told Ava everything she needed to know. "I went by your house," she explained, shaking another bottle of nail polish.

Ava settled back into the tub, but she wasn't as relaxed as she had been before. This was the first time since their fight that Cordellia had been a topic of conversation. Between the Welcome Dinner, prepping for and then going on the tour, she hadn't even had time to tell Delilah what had transpired between the two women. Though many weeks had passed, it still felt too raw, like it had happened only minutes ago. Ava had felt let down by her mother before, but never like this.

It had never hurt this bad.

Maybe I'm overreacting, she had considered on more than one occasion. But she couldn't seem to fully convince herself 100% of the possibility, which led her to believe that no, she *wasn't* overreacting. She had a reason, a right, to feel how she was feeling. It would pass—time could change one's outlook, she was learning; it could wear mountains down to hills, make the impossible possible, but one had to allow it, had to give time its space to work. That's what she was doing with the Cordellia situation. Instead of running backwards, trying to put broken pieces of history back together, she was allowing time to work its magic. Eventually, the sharp edges would be dull enough that she could handle them without fear of cutting herself, but for now they were still too jagged.

It didn't stop her from asking, "How is she?"

"She seemed okay. Cordellia okay, not normal people okay." Cordellia okay was good. It meant she was functioning. Eating and sleeping and working, not sitting in whatever dark corner she could find, hiding from the monsters on the other side of the mirror. It also meant she was still taking the pills, and that they were still doing their job.

"She told me what happened between you two."

Ava groaned. She turned the faucet on and off with her big toe. "It wasn't pretty."

"No," Delilah replied, her voice spacey as she concentrated on the pink polka-dots she was dabbing onto her toenails. The two friends were quiet for a few moments, Delilah lost in her artwork and Ava in her thoughts: thoughts of Cordellia, thoughts of Nixon; of Sebastian and where he was, what he was doing and with whom.

"She asked me to tell you something."

With a sigh, Ava pulled the stopper in the bathtub before standing. It gave a long, continuous gurgle of goodbye as it carried with it lavender scented salt and at least one, if not two, layers of stress. It hadn't been a bad day really, but as soon as she'd gotten back to High House Ava began to question the 3-Rule Truce she and Nixon had established. Knowing he felt for her what she felt for him was making her attraction to him even more intense. She could barely look at him without panting like a thirsty dog, and so she kept him out of her vision as best as possible. Not that it mattered though, because the air buzzed with a constant charge, the electricity dancing across her skin as if they were his hands, his fingers...

She shook her head, clearing the thoughts away, and wrapped a towel around herself. "I'm not sure I want to hear what she has to say," she said to Delilah as she swiped her hand over the mirror. Her face was pink from the heat, as well as the licentious images of Nixon plastered to the walls of her imagination.

"Well..." Delilah pushed herself off the floor and spread out belly-down on the bed. "I told her I would relay the message, and I refuse to be made a liar." Ava shot her a sharp glance of annoyance on the way to her dresser.

"Why do I keep thinking what I want matters?" she muttered to herself. Pajamas in hand, she stepped into the closet to dress.

Ignoring her, Delilah delivered Cordellia's message. "She saw your speech. She said they set up one of those screens in Cottonwood Park and she watched you with like…a thousand people."

Ava stuck her head out of the closet and looked at Delilah. The corners of her eyes were soft, turned down, and she blinked rapidly to quell the tears pooling in them. "She went out?"

"That's what she told me," Delilah replied with a casual shrug.

Ava rolled her eyes as she tugged her t-shirt over her hair, the bottom portion of her curls damp from the bathwater. Cordellia didn't venture outside very often, not unless she was meeting a miner to trade gems, and even then, she kept her eyes down and stayed on course. Orders were either picked up at the house or delivered by Ava. There were too many voices, too many eyes outside of their house. Too much risk.

Too many faces on which she could see Dante.

The world was inconsiderate. It took lives without half a thought and crushed people with its decision. There was no rhyme or reason why some people were allowed to keep breathing while others—like Dante—were stolen in the blink of an eye.

Cordellia hated the outside world, and so she hid from it.

The fact that she had gone someplace where there were people, a place not involving her work, should have filled Ava with pride; but all it did was further rip open the wound their fight had caused.

"You're not as excited as I thought you'd be…" Delilah said as she moved to the other side of the bed. Disappointment was evident in her tone.

Ava turned off the bedroom light then crawled into bed. "She made zero effort to come to the dinner to see my speech live, to see *me*…but she somehow found the strength to watch it on a projection screen in a sea of people?" Anger about the whole situation was mounting with each syllable. How her mother or Delilah thought this would bring Ava comfort was beyond any understanding. She punched the pillow a few times before settling under the blankets. Her eyes danced across the ceiling as she tried to make her own constellations in the sticky stars.

"You know," Delilah said as she flipped over to face her. "You'd be less disappointed by your mother if you lowered your expectations of her."

Ava rolled her eyes as her head lolled. "You think I ask too much of people?"

"People, no. But Cordellia…" Delilah gave a tiny shrug. "She's been the way she is your entire life, yet you keep thinking one day things will change. I'm just saying, if you accept that she's probably never going to be the type of mother you want, you'll appreciate the kind of mother she's capable of being. She's never going to be Zarah."

The friends looked at one another for a second longer before Ava redirected her attention to the ceiling. More seconds passed, then Delilah shifted to her other side. As stillness settled in both the bedroom and High House, as both women were drifting away, Delilah's voice crept over the crests and waves of the blankets. "At least your mother is happy for you…" she said sluggishly.

All Ava had ever wanted from her mother was guidance and support, the things parents are supposed to instinctively give to their children. She had never considered that maybe Cordellia couldn't give those things because she didn't know how. Sometimes Ava wondered if her mother had her because it was something Dante had wanted, this dream they had built together that was severed in a single second. At his death, she was left with this small representation of all the hopes and dreams that would never happen. Ava knew her mother loved her, but there were times when she questioned that, if Cordellia had known what was going to happen, would she still have tried to get pregnant?

Maybe I do hold her to too high a standard. Delilah had not been wrong. Ava was always, unintentionally, comparing Cordellia to Zarah. Cordellia had had parents who doted on her and cared about her, but had died when Ava was five. Cordellia had had two examples of good parents, two examples of what being a parent meant. Zarah on the other hand had been number six of eight children. She'd been looked over and given the bare minimum of love and attention, and maybe in Cordellia's lack of mothering abilities, Zarah had seen her past reflected. She took care of Ava as if she were her own, perhaps to keep the tyke from feeling the same neglect she'd once experienced.

Zarah wasn't here anymore, though; and Cordellia was. She wasn't going to win Mother of the Year anytime soon, but as Delilah had said, she *was* happy for her. She'd always wanted better for Ava, and wasn't that the purpose of a parent?

To support, to hope for greater.

To want their children to live the lives they never had…

These thoughts swirled in Ava's subconscious as she fell into a dark sleep. And it was that darkness that held onto her as a repetitive tapping tried to pull her away. It was not loud, but it was invasive, and it rapped against each layer of unconsciousness, tugging her from colorless black to greys and dark blues. Her body protested as she forced it into an upright position. After a thoughtless look at the clock, she shuffled across the room, grumbling.

"This better be important," she mumbled, her tongue heavy. Her feet weighed 50 pounds each and her legs a little less than that. She teetered and tottered to the door like a drunken toddler.

"What?" she snapped as she yanked it open. She squinted against the brightness of the hall, blinking rapidly.

"Oh, sorry." Sebastian touched something on the wall next to the door and the lights dimmed into a soft, buttery hue. Then he was back in her line-of-sight. "Hey," he said.

His silver hair was a wind-tossed shag hanging over his eyes. It stuck up a little in the back, as though he'd fallen asleep sitting up. There was a fine layer of brown scruff on his jaw and hollow circles under his vibrant green eyes. The wrinkled grey shirt he wore had a snag in the shoulder, but aside from that he looked no worse for wear. Just a little ransacked. He shifted the bag on his back, which was fuller than it had been before he'd left. It made a gentle clinking sound, like a round of 'cheers!' at a celebration.

"You're back," she said flatly. Her throat was dry, and she coughed, clearing it.

"I'm back," he echoed.

Behind her, Delilah groaned, "Shut up," and the bed shifted as she turned away from the light. Ava stepped into the hall and closed the door almost completely. "It's early," she said as she crossed her arms over her chest.

"Or late," Sebastian replied, his smirk a bit skewed, almost hesitant. "Depending on how you look at it." There was no mistaking what the draw of her eyebrows or the firm set of her lips meant. "Anyway, I just wanted to let you know I was home."

"Was it a successful trip?"

"It was," Sebastian replied as he jostled the backpack, making the clinking more evident. He looked at Ava as if it meant anything to her. She looked back, assuring him it didn't.

Running his hand through his hair, he pushed the strands away from his face. There was a sallowness to his complexion she hadn't noticed before. "I'm sorry I woke you. I wanted…" He sighed. "You were the first person I wanted to see, and I didn't want to wait until morning. It was selfish of me, though."

Ava wanted to stay mad at him, but the truth was she had missed him, too. She had gone from spending a lot of time with him to him being gone completely. Not just busy, but physically elsewhere. Sebastian was also a buffer to the things she felt for Nixon. When he was around, her mind didn't have time to focus on what she felt for Nixon. She could channel all her thinking hours on the man who would become her husband; on the man she *needed* to have feelings for.

Needed to, at some point, love.

"Well," she said as she dropped her arms, visibly removing a piece of the barrier between them. "I'm glad you made it back from the great unknown. You should really get some sleep. You look a little haggard."

Sebastian chuckled, though there was very little genuineness behind it. "That's the best advice I've heard in a while. I'll see you at breakfast, hopefully. If not, lunch for sure."

Nodding once, Ava pushed the bedroom door open with her heel. "Rest well," she said as she stepped out of the hallway. She was careful to not disturb Delilah, who was nothing short of a monster when her sleep was interrupted, as she resituated herself.

She couldn't help but think of Delilah's words again as she floated back into the abyss of slumber. Was she being unfair to Sebastian by expecting him to be a distraction? What she needed to do was quell her feelings for Nixon once and for all. The attraction was going to be there because he was an attractive guy. There was a genuine connection between them she could do nothing about. But she didn't want to be torn between two guys, didn't want to stand at the fork of two different paths—one that was barricaded off by thicket bushes and booby-traps.

There is no second option, she thought as colors swirled behind her eyes and her breathing settled into a shallow cadence. Somehow, she would have to kill the idea of Nixon and find solace in the actuality of Sebastian. *Even if you're never completely happy,* her conscience reminded sadly.

It was the last thought she had before sleep overtook her once again.

XXVI.

High House had its own heartbeat when fully awake. It was made up of a cacophony of voices that fought over one another, footsteps that made imprints into the carpets, the grumble of trucks as they delivered produce for the day's meals. A coaxing of awareness that was soft and noninvasive. Unless, that is, one sleeps through it all, then it shatters their dreams like a brick through a window, startling them into consciousness.

This, for the first time since she'd moved into the mansion, was exactly what happened to Ava the following morning. She hadn't even heard Delilah leave the room and would have, without question, slept through most of the day if not for her bladder.

She dressed quickly in an outfit equally as comfortable but less revealing than her pajamas, finger-combed her hair into a high ponytail and slid into the dining room a second before the kitchen doors swung open. The lateness earned her a condescending brow flick from the queen and a father-like scowl from the king, but luckily the bustling staff shielded her from any sort of lecture.

Sebastian was the only one noticeably absent from the meal. She asked Levi to check on him after they finished eating and was informed he was still dead to the world. She used his absence for another run up the hill with Nixon and another defeat to the gates at the end. She showered, washing away the sweat and dirt, and finished dressing with ten minutes to spare before lunch. Then, with two pieces of garlic bread stacked atop her bowl of pasta, all of which was balanced on her cup, she made her way to the gazebo. Why people were suddenly using it as their own lunch spot, she wasn't sure, but she once again took no issue with the current guest. She smiled without thought, approaching quietly.

He didn't see her right away, giving her a few seconds to absorb him. The sun bounced off the ends of his hair, turning the silver flecks nearly white. His face was again smooth, free of stubble, and though his gaze wasn't directed toward her, she could still see the brightness of his irises. They were a much paler green than normal, less emerald and more a bleached malachite. It was such a startling color that when he finally did look at her, her breath caught in her chest. Even his ivory skin seemed to glitter and glow as though it had been dusted with crushed diamonds. As soon as she blinked, however, it faded and his pupils were once again swimming in a lily pad. Her head, too, was swimming for a few seconds, the colors of the world blending together. Then, that was also gone. Both obscurities ended so quickly she couldn't help but wonder if she'd imagined everything.

"Hi," she said once the cobwebs cleared.

Sebastian stood as she approached the table, a bundle in his arms. "You look stunning," he said, acknowledging her marigold sundress. She set her food on the table then moved to him, returning the kiss he brushed onto her lips. He tasted like lemonade and she savored the lingering flavor as they parted.

"And you look much better than this morning," she replied, smiling sheepishly. It grew into a full, bashful grin as he presented her a beautiful bouquet of flowers. There was a mixture of purple tulips, deep magenta roses, white orchids with pink speckles like flicked paint, and sprigs of baby's breath. She was awed not only by the uniqueness of it, but by the gesture itself.

She looked at him with large, glassy eyes and whispered, "It's gorgeous."

He ran a finger down the side of her face. He was clearly happy with her response. "Only the best for my girl."

The sentiment clenched her heart in a vice grip of guilt. It should have made her ecstatic; should have brought a blush to her cheeks and sent the butterflies in her stomach into a tizzy. But she could feel nothing over the ghosting fingers of static that stroked the back of her legs and whispered wicked words into her ears. She gave the prince her most appreciative look before taking the seat he had pulled out for her. She rested the flowers in her lap.

"I'd heard rumors," he started to say as he took his place across from her, "that you tend to forego shoes during lunch time."

"They aren't rumors if they're true." She wiggled her toes under the table and cocked her head to the side just an inch. "Though I'm sure the truth of it was spoken with high fondness," she added with unhidden sarcasm. She was certain she knew exactly from who the words had come, and the slight corner-flick of Sebastian's mouth confirmed her suspicions.

Ava rolled her eyes. "I could become her shadow and she would still find something wrong with me."

"She's a very difficult woman to please." Sebastian's abhorrence matched hers evenly.

"She seems proud of you," Ava challenged.

"Only when I obey," he said. "I'm her eldest. Everything she is as a mother and as a matriarch is wrapped up in the sort of person, the kind of king, I become. How I could possibly dare to digress from any path she's envisioned for me is beyond her understanding. So, when I do…" He let the rest hang in the air between them as he took a sip of his drink. "What she doesn't see is that I don't want to become like her."

Ava offered him an encouraging look. She sometimes forgot his title of prince didn't necessarily mean he wasn't his own person. She had seen him challenge Bernadette, openly defy her orders. Those times made her feel less alone, because though Delilah was her best friend, she was not entirely in tune with Ava's feelings regarding this whole shebang. Delilah would have been the sort of princess to watch the queen's every step, every movement, with a desire to fit perfectly in the old queen's crown. She wouldn't have dared question tradition, let alone speak against the king and queen.

Ava, however, had every intention of growing into her own crown.

Maybe Sebastian and I are *a good match,* she thought, eyeing him over the brim of her glass. "Does she want me to stop doing it?"

As the prince cut into a meatball with the quickness of a surgeon, one shoulder gravitated toward his ear. The look on his face could only be interpreted as *who cares*? "We've asked a lot of you these last few months," he replied while gathering noodles and meat onto his fork. "I think allowing you to spend your lunchtime shoeless is something we can afford."

"Even if your mother disapproves?"

"Even then." She tipped her head to him in thanks then bit into her sauce-dipped bread. "I am curious," he continued while she chewed. "*Why* you do it?"

"I like the feel of the grass under my feet," she explained. "It keeps me connected to the earth. Reminds me I'm just a small fragment in a big world, and that I am being given the *opportunity* to exist. It makes the things that seem significant, the things that seem impossible less..." She struggled to find the right word. "Just less," she settled on.

Sebastian sat back in his chair and ran a finger across his bottom lip, regarding her. Then he nodded once and continued eating. They did so in silence for a few minutes, studying one another on occasion. When they were being two people doing typical, mundane things like playing board games or twirling pasta around their forks, this too felt natural. It felt nice, even, and Ava reveled in it. It was easy to forget the big house looming over them, or the thrones inside of it which would, in a short time, be theirs.

She could forget about how she got here and be content in Sebastian's presence.

It wasn't much beyond surface-level feelings, but it was also something she could handle. Even the light flirting and the thoughtless connecting of lips were easy to get lost in. It was the pet names and the almost bellicose way he looked at her sometimes—as if her soul were made up of millions of jumbled words he was trying to make sense of—she was having a difficult time getting used to.

She hated the fact she didn't want to—*couldn't*—fully open herself up to Sebastian.

Suddenly, her thoughts became too much, the silence too heavy, so she broke it. "Are you happy to be home?" she asked.

"Of course," Sebastian answered without missing a beat. "Not that I'm not good company—" His smile was dazzling. "But there is a renewal that happens when you are once again surrounded by the people you care about." He nudged her leg with the toe of his shoe.

She took the gesture a bit further and ran her bare foot against the back of his calf. Flirty mischief tugged on her lips. "I don't suppose you want to tell me where you went," she pried, her voice dripping with a sickly sweetness.

"One day," he said after a few seconds of consideration. She opened her mouth to argue but he continued to speak, his calm words halting her. "When you are my wife, I will tell you all of my secrets. I will tell you where I go and why and what it all means. But there is so much on your plate already, so many things you must still learn about yourself." He paused, then added, "About Havaan. Bombarding you with any more would be cruel." He reached across the table and rested his hand palm-up in the center. She looked at him from under lowered brows and then sighed, a slight growl of frustration escaping with it, as she linked her fingers with his. "You asked me to be patient with you, and I ask you to do the same with this."

"That isn't fair," she pouted, "but fine."

Sebastian brought her hand to his mouth and grazed her knuckles. When his lips met her skin, sparks exploded in her veins. Her heart raced with the extra charge and her eyes darted around too quickly in search of the source.

As always, she sensed Nixon before she saw him. When he rounded the corner and his heated gaze immediately locked on her, she knew he'd felt her, too. She wondered if he experienced what she did or if it was something else entirely. She made herself a note to ask him, though it was difficult to focus on anything other than his physical appearance right then. His grey shirt was made charcoal with sweat where it settled into the grooves of his stomach. When he lifted the hem of his tank-top to wipe his face, Ava was certain she whimpered. She shoved a large piece of bread into her mouth as both men glanced at her. Then they turned their attention to one another for the first time.

"I will never understand how you work up such a sweat," Sebastian joked as he and Nixon exchanged a complicated handshake.

"That's because you never put in enough effort to work one up yourself," Nixon replied. He patted the prince on his shoulder once before squeezing it. "Welcome home, by the way."

Sebastian nodded his appreciation. "As I was just telling Ava, it's good to be home."

As if Sebastian saying her name granted Nixon permission to acknowledge Ava, he tipped his head her way ever so slightly. "I'm sure she's equally as happy to have you back." Ava gave a noncommittal shrug but winked at Sebastian at the same time.

"I'll let you two to get back to your lunch," Nixon said. "I didn't realize how late it was. I'm hoping there's some left."

"Your men came through after I did, so I wouldn't hold your breath," Ava said, smiling.

"Maybe if you stopped working out through the meal you wouldn't have to worry so much," Sebastian added, his tone only slightly teasing. Ava had also noticed Nixon's habit of forgoing lunch to train longer. His breakfast helpings were large, full of protein, but there was no way that one meal gave him adequate energy to avoid lunch. She worried he would overwork himself to the point of exhaustion one day. She was glad Sebastian had voiced her concerns. He could say things like this to his best friend, chastise him for pushing himself too hard.

Ava didn't have that clearance yet.

"Yes, Dad," Nixon replied dryly. He clearly hated being told what to do, and when he looked at Ava, she simply replied, "You heard your father."

"You two are horrid," the guard said, shaking his head. His words rumbled with a hint of amusement, and though it wasn't laughter, it was similar. It washed over Ava like the summer sun. "I will see you both for dinner," he added before continuing to the house. Ava's eyes tracked him to the back door, where he was intercepted by Levi.

Whatever the second prince of Havaan said to his not-by-blood-brother brought a small smile to Nixon's face. The gentle curve of his lips, the way his hard features softened, caused the world to explode inside of Ava.

Some people in the old days believed existence had started from a big bang, a seismic boom that brought with it the beginning of everything. It was a concept Ava had never been able to wrap her mind around until that very moment.

She glanced at Sebastian and was surprised to find his jaw set, his brows pulled so low it was hard to see his eyes under the shadow. She squeezed his hand gently. There was a small flare to his nose before it was all erased, as if a filter had suddenly been slipped into place.

They stared at one another for a second, then Sebastian spoke as if their previous conversation had never been interrupted. "I know my leaving and all the secrecy surrounding it hurts you, which is something I never wanted to do. So, I'm going to make it up to you."

Resting her elbows on the table, Ava steepled her fingers and set her chin against them. "I'm interested in knowing how you plan to do such a thing."

Sebastian mimicked her. His eyes clouded over as he replied, "We're going to go away together. But to where, you'll find out when we arrive."

"I don't do well with surprises."

There was a slight, amused twitch to his lips. "No," he started as he leaned back in his chair. "You don't do well with things being outside of your control."

Her eyebrows curved and her lips puckered, sealing behind them barbwire-wrapped words. There was much throughout her life over which she'd had no control. Hell, *most* of her life had been one uncontrollable thing after another, yet she'd survived it. Every morning she put on her 'deal with it' pants and got through whatever the universe decided to throw her way. The reason she and Sebastian were even having this meal together was just one instance of when the authority over her life had been stripped away.

How dare you, she wanted to yell.

They had spent such a small amount of time together in the month she'd been at High House, that such an assumption was totally asinine. The fact he had the audacity to pass such a ridiculous judgment on her was equally daft. Foul rebuttals pressed against her clenched teeth, threatening to shatter them into a million tiny fragments.

"You wouldn't know that," she replied. The lowness of her voice was an indicator of her umbrage, and the drop of the prince's face showed his understanding.

"You're right," he said gently. "I'm sorry, Avaleigh. I shouldn't pretend I know anything more about you than what you've told me." He pushed his chair back and rounded the table to her. Squatting beside her chair, he rested a hand on her kneecap and looked up at her, his green eyes drooping at the corners. As his fingertips grazed the curve of her ear and down the side of her neck, he continued. "Come away with me this weekend and let me discover more of you."

She swallowed against his touch. Her heart was beating so loudly she wondered if he could hear it—if Nixon could hear it through the thick walls of their home.

"What happens if I say no?"

"Then we stay here," Sebastian said, the answer obvious. He had no intentions of forcing her into anything, at least not in the way his parents had. Ava hated that she still needed these reminders.

"But I assure you," Sebastian continued, "the scenery at our destination is far better."

Ava crossed one leg over her knee and swung it like a pendulum, a steady beat of contemplation. When he shifted on his haunches, a sign of his discomfort, she rolled her eyes. "It better be the most beautiful place ever," she said flatly.

Sebastian grinned at her, the corners of his eyes bunching a little, and reached for her face. "The most beautiful place for the most beautiful woman," he said before he kissed her. His lips were soft and his movements slow, deliberately drawn out. She couldn't help the sigh of contentment that escaped her lungs. He swallowed her approval and his mouth curled against hers. When they finally parted and their eyes met, longing swirled in them; a ravenous storm threatening to sweep the two of them out to sea. For the briefest of seconds, Ava wanted to let the waves crash over her ankles.

Sebastian cleared his throat, and in return, the haze that was settling over her mind. She felt flushed and pressed her hands to her neck to try and cool herself down.

"I'll make arrangements and we'll leave tomorrow afternoon," he said, his voice far away and distant, as he gathered their dishes.

Ava returned to the moment at hand. "Tomorrow?" she repeated, pushing her chair away from the table. "That doesn't leave much time to pack, Sebastian. Not that I have any idea *what* to pack, since you won't tell me where we're headed."

"The weather is no different there than it is here." Stack of plates, cups, and bowls in hand, he walked past her and out of the gazebo. She gathered the bouquet of flowers hastily and hurried after him, finally catching up half-way to the door.

"That doesn't really help," Ava complained. "Do I pack to impress, or are we going to laze around all weekend in our underwear?" She said the last part sarcastically, hoping to drive home the extent of his unhelpfulness, but after what had just transpired between them, perhaps it was too soon a comment.

Sebastian's lips twisted fiendishly. "I would have no objections to the latter."

As she held the door open for him, she reprimanded him with a look, though the flush of crimson blotting her cheeks gave away the truth. He made his way into the kitchen while she followed, mentally scolding herself. Less than an hour ago she had been certain she wasn't ready for more than a bare-bones relationship. Less than that she had been practically drooling over Sebastian's best friend. Now she was suggesting they spend a weekend together in nothing but their undergarments?

What is wrong with me? she wondered.

"Pack whatever sort of dress you feel the most comfortable in," Sebastian said, dragging her attention back to the present. "It's a private location, so the chance of anyone wandering around is improbable." He nudged the swinging doors to the kitchen open with his foot. "I wouldn't *not* suggest a bathing suit," he added before slipping through the prince-sized crack and vanishing entirely. She could have followed, and for a pause considered it, but instead she forced herself up the stairs and to her bedroom.

She made a pit-stop at Delilah's door first.

If she was expected to adequately prepare for a weekend alone with Sebastian, at an undisclosed, private location no less, she was going to need her best friend.

XXVII.

Delilah made an unnecessary amount of noise the following morning, tromping her way into Ava's bedroom with a tray of vibrant fruit, fresh squeezed orange juice, and buttery croissants.

"What in the world?" Ava grumbled as daylight chased away the darkness of her dreams. She pulled the blanket over her head and swore into her pillow while Delilah fluttered around the room, arranging plates and bowls and silverware. By the time Ava finally forced herself from the cloud-like confines of her bed and shuffled like a caveman to the plush rug, Delilah had set up the daintiest breakfast arrangement. There was even a thin vase with a single white lily on the tray.

As she sat, Ava teased, "I'm not sure how much Sebastian will appreciate you trying to romance me."

"He appreciates it because it's from him," Delilah replied. She took her seat across from her best friend. "There were a few things he needed to take care of before whisking you away, so he asked me to present you your breakfast."

"What's wrong with me eating in the dining room with everyone else?" Ava asked before dropping a chunk of pineapple into her mouth.

Delilah shrugged. "Why is it so hard for you to enjoy a nice gesture without asking fifty questions? Any other woman in Havaan would be flattered by breakfast in bed."

Lowering her eyebrows a fraction, Ava replied, "Even if it's with their best friend and not their significant other?"

"You act as though there's a better alternative," Delilah said confidently.

Despite her best efforts, Ava's mouth corkscrewed into a smirk and the two women enjoyed a simple but delicious breakfast together. It was so reminiscent of the mornings they'd had back home that Ava had nearly forgotten where they were until Delilah began shooing her into the bathroom to shower. Under the waterfall sprayer, Ava's worry about the prince's expectations for the weekend rose with the steam. Was he going to try and take their courtship to the next level? If he did, would she allow it? Was she ready for such a big step with a guy she hardly knew?

She had made Connor work for it. Not because she'd been a prude, but because despite her aloofness to all things fairytale driven, that part mattered. In the end, it hadn't been the romantic rose-petals on the bed scenario she'd envisioned and she had felt cheated ever since that night. Though Sebastian was to be her husband, he was still a stranger in most regards. Giving such an important piece of herself to someone she'd barely skimmed the surface with was scary. She overanalyzed the whole situation, and by the time she stepped out of the shower, her breakfast was threatening to rewind itself.

Once she gathered herself and dressed for the day, she made her way to the front porch with her rolling suitcase. She and Sebastian were scheduled to leave around eleven that morning, but her being outside early was two-fold.

"Where are you going?" Nixon asked as he acknowledged her luggage.

She looked at him sadly and exhaled a deep, slow breath. "Home," she lied.

"What?" he replied, his emotions pulling on his brow.

Ava shrugged a shoulder and did her best to commit to her prank. "Apparently I've failed to meet the prince's standards and so...I'm being dismissed." She looked away from him as a smile threatened to give the whole thing away. It was a little cruel, maybe, but if anyone would find amusement in the joke, it would be Nixon. His sense of humor was often dry and a bit sarcastic. At times it was nearly impossible to sort a joke and the truth from one another. Yet when she looked back at him, her resolve began to crumble. The glow of his eyes was dimmed, overlaid with confusion. His mouth formed single letters as he tried to find the right words.

"Do you know what this means?" he asked, his low bravado rumbling even more.

"You can start running alone again?"

A ghost of a whisper teased his lips. "We could be together now," he whispered, the conviction—the *desire*—too great to speak at its full volume. At the same time, as each unexpected syllable slammed into Ava, rocking her world at its very core, the front door opened.

"Sebastian is bringing the car around," Delilah said. Her tone was too chipper, too happy and too wrong amongst the tension. "He wanted me to let you know he'll be here in a sec," she added. Her excited smile matched the way her rose-gold hair caught the rays of the sun. "Are you two okay?" she asked, her eyes flickering between her best friend and her momentary crush.

Ava pulled her attention from Nixon, from the way his face warped with realization and the light of his irises was snuffed out completely. "We're fine." She hoped she sounded reassuring, but the doubtful look Delilah gave told her otherwise.

"Okay…" she replied, dragging the word out. Then her tone changed, and her words were heavy with enthusiasm Ava could not match. "Have fun this weekend. I can't wait to hear all about it."

"I'll make sure to fill you in when I return," she promised.

"Duh." Delilah winked. Then she looked at Nixon, who was still looking at Ava, before vanishing inside without another word. Nixon blinked with the gentle latching of the door.

"So where are you really going?" His voice was flat and emotionless.

"I don't know," Ava answered honestly this time. "Sebastian won't tell me." Nodding once, Nixon ran a hand over his jaw. She could hear the scratch of stubble against his palm. "About what you said," she started. Her throat was tight and his words repeated in rhythm with her racing heart, like a metronome keeping track of her longing.

He looked away, the forest of ferns and evergreens suddenly more interesting. When he returned his attention to her, he didn't look *at* her, but instead *through* her, as though she were a mirror he wanted to shatter. Then, with nothing more than a small shake of his head, he leaped over the stairs and strode toward the wrought iron fence.

"Stop!" she called after him.

And he did.

For a microsecond he went statuesque, as if maybe he was considering something, but then his fingers twitched and he began his stroll again. "Forget it," he said into the wind.

"But I don't…" He didn't even stop to speak to Sebastian as the prince came coasting up the cobblestone driveway in a bright red car with its top down. "Want to," she finished to herself. Sebastian came to a stop in front of the stairs.

He hurried out and spread his arms wide, a dramatic presentation of the vehicle. The sun bounced off the polished car and the clouds above reflected off the chrome. "Your chariot, m'lady," he said with a deep bow.

Most everyone in Havaan who owned a car drove moderately sized vehicles to keep from exhausting the solar-charged battery too quickly. The first generation had done away with fuel pilfering and instead turned to more economical solutions for electricity and gasoline. It was simple: not magic, but nature. To harness the power of the sun, they installed solar panels beneath the ground as well as amongst the shingles atop houses and in the batteries of cars. As long as the citizens were conscious and considerate with their usage during the spring and summer months, there was no shortage of reserves in the fall and winter.

Ava, despite the way Nixon's words pulled her anxiety taut like a piano string, let a coy smile round her full lips. "If I'm going to be whisked away to secret locations, at least I'll be riding in style." Sebastian winked as he opened her door. Her fingertips danced along the top of his hand as she slid into the cushy, upholstered seats. The interior surfaces were as buffed as the body, not a trace of dust in sight. The dash was classic, with rounded windows that framed the battery gauge and gear setting. Tall, narrow numbers indicated the speed. As far as cars went, it was beautiful and sophisticated and incredibly out of place as they merged with the slight traffic of Havaan.

"Where did you get this?" Ava asked as they slowed at a stop light.

Sebastian's head angled toward her, but his eyes remained hidden behind a dark pair of sunglasses. "It's mine," he answered proudly. He looked relaxed behind the wheel; young and carefree, as if he were just a citizen of their country and not the man who was expected to rule it by the start of the next year. Ava tried to mimic his lackadaisical demeanor. She let the wind carry her hair behind her and with it the unexpected confession of Nixon. *There's nothing I can do about it now.* The car floated effortlessly around the curves of the road, twisting and shaping the guilt in her stomach. *Even if I want to.*

Ava rolled her eyes behind her own pair of sunglasses at Sebastian's simple remark. "I assumed you hadn't stolen it," she replied, her voice light and playful. "After all, you are Sebastian Calder, first prince of Havaan. Thievery seems like a low hobby for such a noble title."

"Even if it's car theft?" He smiled.

She draped her arm across the back of the seat, the grey fabric warm from the sun, and ran her fingers through his silver locks. They were soft, like a feather, and fell back into place unharmed. "That seems a little risky. I'm not sure you're the dangerous type," she teased.

Sebastian looked at her over the brim of his glasses, his green eyes sparkling like emeralds, before he laughed. She couldn't help but echo him, their sounds of jollity carrying into the wind.

They made one pit-stop on their journey, and that was to Mr. Fillion's market. "We're going to need food," Sebastian had said to her when they'd started their trip, and Ava refused to stock up anywhere else. It was impossible Mr. F hadn't heard news of her life-promotion, but he treated her as though she were still the same old Ava who lived on Holland Avenue and had once taken care of his children on date-nights. He continued to refuse payment for the four bags of groceries she'd gotten, but as he was carrying the last one to Sebastian's car, she tucked $200 worth of Havannian bills under his Crossword puzzle.

Conversation flowed between Sebastian an Ava, but as houses faded into nothing more than nature at its purest, their conversation lulled into a comfortable quiet. Ava closed her eyes and leaned her head against the seat. As the car glided along the twists and turns of a mountain, she reveled in the momentary peace. Her hand was warm in Sebastian's where it rested gently on his knee. The sun peaked through whipped clouds and kissed the exposed parts of her body. Sandwiched between a wall of sandstone and granite, and a divider of trees nearly touching the sky, there were no words except for the ones which looped through her mind with every twitter of a bird.

She couldn't forget the way Nixon's eyes had blazed—an inferno fueled by gasoline-like desire—when he thought they finally had a chance. Her guilt flashed images of his disappointment when he realized they didn't. *Why can't you, though?* her subconscious toyed, teasing what a future with Nixon would be like.

It was in that question, in those daydreams, where Ava recognized the importance of this weekend.

The attraction between her and Sebastian was there. He was beautifully handsome with a kind heart and easy disposition. He was respectful and caring. He was her partner in this crazy journey they'd both been forced to endure; the only person who had any sort of idea what Ava was feeling. As far as arranged husbands went, she had been gifted an excellent one. Yet she still didn't feel for Sebastian anything close to what she felt for Nixon. She didn't seek the prince in a crowded room or crave his approval like an addict. His smile didn't halt her world or his voice her heart. There was no shift in the air when Sebastian was near, or a nervous excitement when she knew she'd get to see him. His laugh, while melodic, didn't sing in her veins.

Ava knew these conflicting feelings would never bode well for the future. If she couldn't feel for Sebastian what she felt for his best friend, their relationship and all the prospects it held would amount to nothing.

It wasn't that she was looking to fall in love with the prince during their mystery getaway, but if she could just reach the point where she could *see* herself loving him, she would allow it to be enough. She could hang her faith in their relationship on that.

What will I do, she asked herself, if it I can't get myself to see him as anything more than just an attractive friend?

"Hey." Sebastian's soft voice cut through the haze of thoughts. She opened her eyes and looked at him as his lips grazed her knuckles. "We're here."

Excitedly, she sat up in her seat and took in the scenery. She gasped. They were surrounded in every direction by ocean. The water was a canvas of blue—light at the horizon where the sky met the waves—and darker as it kissed the sugar-white sand. Ava emerged from the car slowly, afraid the slightest movement would shatter the illusion before her. She turned in a languid circle and grinned at the structure behind her.

"She's a beauty, isn't she?" Sebastian's voice was full of marvel, as if it were the first time he was seeing it, too.

Ava nodded as she took in the small house. The faded eggshell paint was chipped in some areas and the red thatched roof sloped slightly, but even those imperfections couldn't distract from its simple charm.

"Is she yours, too?" Ava asked as, hand in hand, Sebastian led her up a small flight of wooden stairs. He let his cheesy smile and the ring of keys he pulled from his pocket answer for him.

As he slipped an old, antique key into the lock, he said, "No one knows about this place. I'm trusting you to keep its existence a secret."

Zipping her lips, she returned his grin before stepping inside. The air was stale and salty. The heat that had been trapped in the walls hit them like the opening of an oven as it rushed to escape through the jarred door.

Dust particles danced in the few streaks of sunshine breaking through the drawn curtains.

Odd shapes under cloths of white dotted the open floor space like sleeping ghosts; and the mattress to the full-sized daybed was flush against the wall, stripped of its bedding.

An eerie sepia film coated the entire space like an old-timey dream, giving it a feeling of abandonment. Not the depressing kind, though, where there are still remnants of a life once lived but the inhabitants too quickly gone. It was quiet and still and small and nothing like High House—the complete opposite, actually—and Ava loved every single inch of it. More than she had the cottages during their tour.

After they unloaded the car and pulled the protective sheets from the furniture—homey, mismatched pieces Sebastian had thrifted—they made dinner together. Ava did most of the actual cooking, but Sebastian was surprisingly a genius with spices and flavors. Between the two of them, they created a delicious meal which they ate on a blanket next to the water.

"This is nice," Ava said happily as she reclined back on her elbows. She watched the painted water surge and retreat rhythmically. Little waves moved over her bare feet. The sky was a rainbow of unnaturally bright colors that reflected off Sebastian's chrome hair, dyeing it pastel orange, yellow and blue.

Sebastian pulled his knees to his chest and smiled down at her. "I love it here. There are no people, unlike back home. There, you wake up and the first thing you see is people. Whether you're inside, outside, upstairs or down, you're bound to run into someone. Hell," he sighed, "you come out of the bathroom and surprise!"

"Let me guess," Ava chimed. "People?"

With a wink, the prince replied, "You got it."

"I'm starting to think you don't like people."

Sebastian chuckled and twisted a piece of her hair around his finger. Every time he did this, he marveled at the strand as though he'd never seen anything like it. It was the same look Ava caught him giving *her* when she wasn't looking.

When he spoke again, his voice was soft, distant almost. "I like some." Her lips curved a little as he let the curl go. "I don't have to worry about anyone here, though. At least not for nine miles in any direction. It's just me and my thoughts. I can be alone, even if it's for a day or two."

"You're not alone this time," Ava reminded, sitting up.

As warm sand slipped through his slender fingers, Sebastian answered, "No, but you're going to be my wife—"

She looked at him wide-eyed with feigned shock. "I *am*?!"

"That's what they tell me."

Avaleigh couldn't help the foolish grin that stretched across her jaw with his words. They were the exact ones she had spoken to him at the market, when he'd stopped to chat with her despite the attention it brought them both. That day sometimes felt like mere seconds ago, as if she were still trying to grasp everything that had happened; while a minute later it was as though eons had passed. Years since her life had changed in the most unexpected, but at times, exciting of ways.

"Can I ask you something?" Sebastian's voice interrupted the quiet into which they'd fallen once more.

"Go for it," she replied as she signed her name into the sand.

He didn't speak immediately, not until she looked over at him. "Where are your parents?" He sighed, exasperated at how he'd worded the question and by the look on her face, then he tried again. "Why haven't I met them yet, I mean?"

It was the last thing she'd expected from him, but she also wasn't surprised by the question. They'd been a part of one another's lives for two months, with plenty of opportunities for introductions to take place.

Ava swallowed the lump forming in her throat while she watched the ocean wash away her name. When she looked back at him, he was an open window, ready and willing to give her as much time as she needed if it meant she would let him in.

Making herself vulnerable was hard. She never wanted to give people something they could use against her, something they could use to hurt her. But she had also made a vow to herself—and unbeknownst to Sebastian—to him as well, that she would be honest with him this weekend. She would fillet apart the skeletons hanging in her heart and expose all the gritty, dirty, ugly parts that made her Avaleigh Nicolette Toliver. Because there were many, and if he was going to love her, he needed to love her beyond her ocean eyes and pretty face.

"You don't have to tell me if you don't want," Sebastian said, misreading her hesitating breath.

She shook her head. "No. I want to, I just…" *Need to find the right words.* Finally, she began, "You and my mother have something in common." Her attention returned to the melting sky for a second.

"We both think you're amazing?" She could hear his smile in the words.

She rolled her eyes anyway, even as her lips stretched into a slow grin of her own. Then he kissed her. It wasn't anything special, just flesh upon flesh; soft and reassuring. When they separated she was thankful for the setting sun, the red projection providing a place for the blush across her cheeks to hide.

"Two things then," she answered, nudging his shoulder with hers. "Specifically, your need for isolation. She's…sad…a lot. Always. She is always sad." Ava chewed her bottom lip, searching for the best way to aptly explain her mother. "Some days she hides it well. But there are other days when she gets lost in her emotions and she can't fight her way out." She looked at Sebastian, her eyes homing in on his. "I asked her one time to explain it to me. I spent most of my life watching it, but I never understood it. Not really, because how could I? I mean, I get upset sometimes but never in the same way she does. So I asked her to try and make me understand how it feels when she gets——"

"Sad?" Sebastian finished, his voice kind; not that she would ever expect anything less from him.

Ava nodded. "She told me it's like walking through quicksand. Every step is harder than the one before, and by the end of the day she's so tired that doing it again tomorrow seems impossible. But she just keeps trekking, trying to keep from sinking, even though when she sees light, even when she sees anything that could be misconstrued as an end to the struggle, there is always a black cloud looming above her. She's constantly in the dark with no way to fully escape it." Ava sighed. "I think the outside world reminds her of all the things she's missing out on, of what her life was supposed to be. Instead of being reminded, she avoids it. It's easier that way. So you may unfortunately never meet her, because the likelihood of her making her way to High House is pretty improbable." Ava exhaled quickly, deeply, and flicked away the single tear on her cheek.

She could feel Sebastian staring at her but she refused to look at him. Refused to be confronted with the pity she didn't want.

Instead, they sat in silence. The only audible sounds were the crashing of waves as they came together in the midnight blue ocean and the rush of blood in her ears as her heart beat wildly. She had accepted long ago that she would never really understand why her mother's illness embarrassed her so much, why it was so difficult to tell someone about it. Delilah was the only other living person who had experienced Cordellia at her worst. Multiple times D had helped Ava lug her mother from room to room, dragging her catatonic body around as if it were nothing more than a breathing corpse. But it had also taken Ava a few years into their friendship to even hint that her mother wasn't necessarily normal, and even longer for Ava to accept her best friend's secrecy.

"We could always go to her," Sebastian said quietly, though it sounded ten times louder against the dome surrounding them.

Ava turned her head quickly to face him, ready to accept whatever judgment he was passing. Her heart contracted against her ribs, trying to break through them, at the look that contorted his features. There was no pity in his eyes, no pull of disappointment to his brow when he realized how weak his future mother-in-law was. There was just kindness and understanding and concern—maybe a little—though it came from a place of caring.

He rested a hand on the side of her neck and rubbed her earlobe, a gesture which would have melted her kneecaps if she'd been standing. "If she won't come to our home, we can go visit where she's the most comfortable."

Ava smiled at him, her thankfulness evident in the gesture. "I hadn't thought about that," she admitted, laughing at herself.

Sebastian returned her look before pulling her closer. She thought he was going to kiss her again—she anticipated it—but instead he butted his forehead against hers. "You don't have to carry these things on your own anymore," he whispered so softly they were nothing more than a breath.

Nodding, Ava looked into his eyes as best as possible. This close, she could almost count each eyelash, each freckle she had never noticed before. His breath smelled sweet, like the fruit salad that had been part of their dinner, and her mouth was drawn to his like a bee to nectar. Without overthinking it, without giving him a chance to make a move, she did it instead. She let her emotions control her for once, and in his arms she let go of Cordellia and the shackles her sadness had created, holding Ava hostage all these years. She kissed him with an intensity she didn't know she had inside of her, a desire to feel alive, to try and experience what her mother and Dante had once had. She wanted to know what it felt like to invest herself so deeply in another person's existence that if she were to lose him, she too would walk through quicksand while trying to outrun his memories.

It worked for a while, for however long they were at the ocean's edge, his body pressing hers into the warm soil of the beach. Then suddenly there was a crackle in the air, a static charge that tingled her toes and Nixon's face flashed behind her eyelids. Her eyes snapped open, like blinds being raised, and she inhaled deeply—this time tasting salt and wind and air. She glanced around her, and when a flash of lightening illuminated the shadows, she half expected Nixon to step out from them.

Sebastian looked down at her curiously; his swollen lips parted as he, too, remembered what it meant to breathe without her. His hair was a mess, pulled in all directions by her hands.

"Ava—"

A boom above them cut his words short and they both jumped. Without warning, the sky opened and a bucketful of cold rain dropped on them. They looked at one another before Ava started to chuckle, a deep rumbling sound that rivaled the thunder. She pushed Sebastian off her, and between non-stop laughter they gathered the remnants of their picnic and ran for the safety of the house. They fought against the wind, against the rain, against the ground that was becoming softer with each passing second. *Like quicksand,* she thought as she fought to keep up with the prince.

Noticing her struggle, Sebastian turned, and as if he'd done it a million times before, hoisted Ava over his shoulder. At first, she demanded he set her down and she writhed in his arms, but soon her shouts, which were occasionally drowned out by clashes of thunder, turned into squeals of delight as the prince spun them in circles and zigzagged through the mud, bits of wet sand splattering against their skin.

It wasn't until they were back on solid ground did he place her on her feet. Her hair was stuck to her face and mascara trailed down her flushed cheeks, but she didn't care—*couldn't* care—not with the way Sebastian was looking at her: as if she were the last remaining beautiful thing in Havaan.

He slid a hand along the side of her neck again and Ava was certain he could trace her pulse with his fingertips. "As long as you are with me," he started, "I will not let you sink."

Tears prickled her eyes with the safety of his words. She searched within herself to find something to say that would even slightly mirror his compassion, his care and concern for her well-being. When she found she had none, she pressed her lips to his instead. It was not frantic and desperate like on the beach, but it still spoke volumes, saying the things she couldn't.

There was no religion in Havaan, no deities or gods like in the old world. But Zarah had shared with her the history of faith, how people had believed in giants living amongst the clouds, controlling the lives of those below. Their belief had been so strong in these gods that asking things of them was common. Sometimes those wishes were granted, while other times their requests went unanswered. Ava had never understood the purpose of asking the cosmos for anything, but tonight, as the sky continued to split and the rain to fall, Ava prayed. In that prayer she asked the universe to let her love him, to open her heart to Sebastian so they could have a chance at the beautiful future everyone around them seemed to believe they deserved.

The prince had promised her that sinking was not an option.

But Ava wasn't worried about sinking; she was worried about falling.

XXVIII.

"What about your father?" Ava spun on her heels to face the question, toothbrush paused in her mouth. "You didn't mention anything about him earlier," Sebastian continued as he tucked the corners of the fitted sheet onto the mattress.

Ava swallowed hard before rinsing her mouth. She put her toothbrush next to Sebastian's in the holder then turned off the light to the small bathroom. It was the only room in the house that had a door. The rest of the space—living room, kitchen and bedroom—were all one open area, designated only by the change of flooring.

The curious gaze of the prince followed her as she wordlessly helped him finish assembling the bed. As she fluffed her pillows, punching them harder than necessary, she exhaled a shaky breath. If talking about Cordellia was difficult, telling someone about Dante was even harder. Even though she didn't feel his loss the same way her mother did, she felt his loss *because* Cordellia radiated it so greatly.

Finally, when Sebastian rested a hand on hers, saving the pillow from any further abuse, she said, "He's dead."

Sebastian's brown eyebrows furrowed and the corners of his eyes drooped. "I'm sorry," he said, his voice reverent.

Climbing into bed, Ava gave a nonchalant shrug of her shoulder. They laid beside one another, each facing the ceiling with its slabs of knotted wood. The rain continued to beat against the house, knocking on the roof and pelting the windows. A chilled breeze pressed through the old siding.

"It happened when I was really young," she continued after a few minutes of silence. "I don't have any memories of him." She turned her head, unexpectedly coming face-to-face with Sebastian. His green eyes glowed with each flash of lightning, as if they were charged by the storm. "But my mother does. Those are the dark clouds that follow her around. She loved him so much that facing the outside world without him became…pointless. Impossible."

Sebastian rolled onto his side and tucked an arm under his head. Ava mimicked him. Now that her eyes had adjusted to the pitch black of the house, she could faintly see his features, could barely make out the slight upturn to his lips. "It must have been difficult for you, being raised by someone who was so—"

"Sad?" she interrupted, replaying his words from earlier.

"Sad. Lost. Scared. Alone."

"It was," Ava agreed. "But we survived."

Something pulled at her vocal chords, Zarah's name on the very tip of her tongue, but she bit it back and swallowed it down. She had already put too much of herself on display tonight, opened wounds and bled on the cards of her life's story. The salt in the air stung the scars and even the compassionate words of her betrothed could not heal them enough to make her want to open a Zarah-sized vein right now. Maybe one day, when he held the entire deck in his hand and she was the only card left to play.

Instead, Ava focused on the feel of Sebastian's fingertips moving down the side of her face. "You more than survived," he started. "You defied odds, Avaleigh. You should be a mess—"

"You're assuming I'm not," she teased.

"You're anything *but*. Your mother did an exceptional job raising a brilliantly beautiful woman with a heart of gold. You should be proud of her. And she herself."

Ava bit the side of her cheek and blinked a few times to keep her eyes dry. "You can tell her that when you meet her," she whispered before Sebastian pulled her into his body. She snuggled against him, her head buried in his chest. His nails traced the length of her spine. She did not deserve a man like Sebastian, someone who saw her wholeness through the cracks; what she would be once all the pieces were tucked into one another.

She fell asleep in the comfort of his arms, to the steady cadence of his heart, and for the first time since she'd met the bronze-eyed guard, Nixon did not enter her dreams.

They spent the next morning around the tiny dining table eating a late breakfast of omelets and diced fruit. Laughter filled the house as they made small talk, sharing lighthearted stories of their childhoods. Ava playfully swatted at Sebastian's hand when he reached across the table to snag a strawberry from her plate, and Sebastian occasionally nudged her foot with his under the table.

Everything was simpler here.

The casual banter and tasteful flirting were the most normal things she had done since she'd moved. Being with Sebastian felt normal, as if they were just two people who'd sneaked away to paradise for the weekend. This is what was supposed to happen. She was expected to want to kiss him, and hold his hand, to catch his eye when no one else was looking.

Sebastian was easy.

Sebastian was allowed.

Why is it so difficult for me to fall for him, then…?

Unlike at High House, here there was no shouting of orders or foot traffic up and down the hallways. They'd slept past 8:00 a.m., nearly into noon. Ava had woken earlier, the first time, just as dawn was beginning to break the horizon. The rising sun cast everything in a golden hue, a soft yellow that drizzled over the entire landscape and permeated the dark corners of the house.

She had watched Sebastian sleep, matched her breathing with his. Over and over again, around each of his fingertips, she had traced the shape of his hand until she could draw it with her eyes closed.

She woke again later, when the sun was at its highest and morning had brought with it a thin layer of heat even the clouds could not lessen. Her back was pressed tightly against Sebastian's chest and each exhale from his parted lips blew fine pieces of hair away from her neck. Though his closeness was stifling and sweat gathered in the space behind her knees, she reveled in the normalcy of the whole thing: of waking up next to someone—of waking up in safety.

Only when the tide began to roll in full force and the seagulls squawked their mid-morning greetings did they strip off clinging blankets and pull themselves from bed. Brunch was uncomplicated but filling. They ignored the dirty dishes in the sink as they changed into bathing suits and headed out to meet the waves.

Ava did yoga by the water's edge, the sand smooth where the waves lapped over it, while Sebastian swam the half-mile to the buoy and back. The afternoon was spent in the water, with Sebastian attempting to teach Ava to surf. For the first time in her life, her otherworldly grace could not save her from the multitude of tumbles and slips she took into the ocean. Each failed effort earned her a kiss of praise though, so they kept at it until the salt tangled her hair and their skin tingled from the sun. They returned to the kitchen as the midnight blue of night was beginning to bleed into the pale blue of the day.

As Ava added spices to the simmering sauce on the stove, she said to Sebastian, who was carefully folding lobster and shrimp stuffed pasta into tortellini noodles, "Tell me about *your* parents." Her tone was teasing, a little playful, but also hopeful. She wanted to know the king and queen beyond what the rest of Havaan knew, beyond the masks they put on for everyone. She wanted to know who they were when they weren't being the first patriarch and matriarch of the new world, but instead simply Mom and Dad.

"You know my parents," Sebastian replied, his face twisted in concentration.

Ava gathered a handful of finished pasta and dropped it into boiling water. "I know that your father loves to play Checkers and that your mother hates me. There has to be more to them than that."

"No, that's about it," he said, a coy turn to his lips.

Ava did not return his look, but instead challenged him with one of her own. "I find it hard to believe your mother would dislike someone so much just because." Her voice was unsteady as anger mounted inside of her. She hated that everyone took the queen's disdain toward her so lightly. Maybe they couldn't see the malevolence that flashed in her eyes whenever she looked at Ava, but Ava could. Her insides knotted together every time the two women were in the same room, and even though Ava refused to let the queen know the effect she had, it was there, bubbling just below her skin.

"I can understand her not liking me from the impression she got the night of the gala," she continued, "but I was being told my life was about to change in a way I had never anticipated. I don't know what else to do to prove I'm not that same person. I'm here." She let out a lung full of exasperated air. "I'm trying."

Leaning back against the counter, Sebastian ran his finger along his bottom lip as he regarded her. Finally, when he realized she wasn't going to let him off the hook, he sighed. "My mother believes respect comes from fear, from the ability to manipulate people. If she can't control you somehow, then you're a bigger threat than you are an ally." As he spoke, he moved around the kitchen retrieving dishes and cutlery. "My father wanted to be king for the popularity, for the parties and idolization that comes with a crown. But he never wanted the power. Not really. He never wanted to make decisions or decrees that would anger citizens. Every law he *has* made, the one banning magic for example, he's made knowing he's going to have support. He once told me that he had wanted to issue a decree against the separation, but Mother convinced him it would be a poor move, that they—that *I*, as incoming king—could not afford to have members of the upper-class angry at our family. And so, as you're aware, no decree was made."

"I've seen him stand up to her, though," Ava reminded as she recalled the Welcome Dinner and the queen's insistence that Connor had been there as some sort of ploy.

"He will," Sebastian said. He waved away the cloud of steam rising from the pasta he'd dumped into the strainer. "Occasionally. He's not afraid of her, but he still picks his battles wisely. He knows what will upset her, so he doesn't venture there. He defies her just enough, as if to remind her who's actually in charge. Though they'd disagree about who that is."

As Ava spooned noodles into two bowls, she said, "That still doesn't explain why your mother has a vendetta against me."

Sebastian pressed a firm kiss to her temple. "Probably because she doesn't intimidate you."

"She does sometimes," she admitted, her voice quiet, as if speaking too loudly would alert the queen, all the way from here, that her scare tactics worked. Ava looked at Sebastian across the table with an almost sad, apologetic look.

A look which crumbled his heart.

He reached across the space between them and entwined their fingers. "You can't let her know that," he said, an edge to his voice that she had never heard before. "She will use it against you if you do. Even if you're terrified, you must project bravery, okay?"

The words, a reflection of the ones Nixon had said to her in the car once before, were said with the same intensity; an insistence which told her, without saying such, that remaining steadfast and true to herself was necessary.

Ava nodded, and said with more assurance than she felt, "I will." Sebastian smiled at her, his boyish grin flashing over the top of her hand before he kissed her knuckles.

"I'm not entirely convinced she didn't have something to do with the whole Brisbane situation," Sebastian said as he took a drink.

Ava glanced up from cutting a noodle in half with her fork and asked, "What do you mean?"

"Brisbane is cold and calculated now, with priorities that come before being a decent human, but she wasn't always." Sebastian took a small bite of his food and Ava did the same while waiting for him to continue. "When she and Nixon first started dating, she was kind. It just seems like too elaborate of a plan. To invest four years of your life in a relationship with someone you know you're going to screw over for his best friend—"

"When she could have gone after you from the start," Ava finished for him, following his train of thought.

He nodded. "Exactly."

"So where does your mother come into this?"

Sebastian sighed. "I think she got to Brisbane. I think she whispered promises in her ear, ones any young girl would willingly chase after. Having something like the crown dangled in front of you can change someone, and that's exactly what happened. But mother underestimated my loyalty to Nixon."

"Have you told Nixon of your suspicions?"

With a firm shake of his head, Sebastian replied, "And you can't either. We're his family and if he feels that someone who's supposed to care about him is so willing to hurt him—"

It would crush him, she thought, but instead assured, "I won't say anything. I promise."

She couldn't help but wonder if Sebastian would regret his decision, his allegiance, if he knew of the feelings developing between herself and Nixon. It became more imperative than ever for things with Sebastian and Ava to work out. Whatever barrier was keeping them separated needed to be knocked down and demolished.

Immediately.

They dropped the subject of his family and betrayal for the rest of the evening, instead focusing on hypothetical plans for the future, including the number of children they wanted with the most obscure names they could come up with. They laughed until their sides ached and brushed their teeth at the same time, making eyes at each other through the mirror.

"I have something for you," the prince said as he finished checking all the locks on the windows and doors. The king and queen had not been easily convinced to let the two of them come away together without guards, but the fact there were very few people who even knew of the house—let alone who owned it—eased their concerns enough. "It's either that," Sebastian had said, "or we slip the guards." He wanted an uninterrupted weekend with Ava, a chance to show her who he was as nothing more than Sebastian Calder. Not the prince, not the future king. Just himself.

Ava kneeled excitedly at the foot of the bed, her face split with excitement. "A gift?" she cooed.

"Delilah did say that gifts make things better," he replied, returning her grin.

"She wasn't wrong," Ava joked.

From behind a stack of books on the small shelf next to the bathroom, he produced a long rectangular box. Ava recognized it as the sort in which Cordellia put finished necklaces. There was nothing extraordinary about the case; it was unremarkable and black. What was inside, however, made Ava look at Sebastian with confused eyebrows.

She removed the keyring and held it in her palm. The three rings attached were different sizes and shapes, their teeth cut in different patterns, but at the top of each stem was a small, carved-out emblem.

"This," Sebastian said, fingering the one with a sun, "is the extra key to this house." He tapped the largest of the three next, a heavy chunk of metal with interwoven rope-knots twisted together for the bow. "This one will open all of the doors at High House."

"All of them?" she echoed, her surprise evident.

"From the kitchen to the library and all the doors in between," he answered lightly, though there was a bit of warning to his tone. There was power in this key, power that Sebastian was handing over to her, trusting her not to misuse. "And this one," he said lifting the last key, "goes to the greenhouse." Ava traced the grooves of the whittled iron rose. "I will give you a tour of it when we return, if you'd like."

Her gaze moved from the key to the prince. Her smile reached her eyes, crinkling the corners of them. "I would like that very much," she replied as she tossed her arms around his neck, pulling him onto the bed with her. She kissed his face, repeating "thank you" between each. His laughter was infectious, and in no time they were both lost in fits of it, tears tickling their lashes.

Then they laid together, their feet hanging over the side of the bed, just looking at the ceiling. Somewhere around midnight they maneuvered themselves into a comfortable sleeping position. The temperature had dropped to a chill by that time, and Ava took up her role as little spoon without complaint or hesitation.

This is what normalcy is, and it's great, she thought as dreams began to settle in place, the edges shimmering with black glitter.

XXIX.

They returned home shortly before dinner the following day. They didn't even have time to unpack their luggage; just a few minutes to freshen up before gathering in the dining room. Those in attendance—all members of the Calder clan as well as Delilah and Helen—were eager to hear about their trip. More eager, in fact, than they had been when they'd returned from their cross-country tour. While Delilah sat forward in her chair, her elbows impolitely resting on the edge of the table, Queen Bernadette lounged against the back of her chair, seemingly paying little attention to the recounting.

"There isn't much to tell," they insisted, but provided some of the boring details, anyway. They told of the storm that interrupted their dinner and of their many failed attempts at surfing, leaving out the intimate parts, of course. The look Delilah gave Ava from across the table assured her those details would be rehashed later, in the privacy of Ava's bedroom. Which they were, welcomed with many squeals of delight.

For the week following, things at High House were good.

Ava divided her time between Sebastian and Delilah. Even Madeline—when she wasn't busy in the kitchen—was becoming a quick friend. Ava also spent an hour a day playing Checkers with the king.

He had found her by the pool a couple days after her return as she was reading some etiquette book Bernadette had given her. He'd stood at the edge of her vision for a few moments, then stepped into the space, blotting out the sun. With him he had a large box, though its size was a bit diminished in his giant hands.

"Do you play?" he asked, shaking it.

She pushed her sunglasses into her hair and looked at him curiously. "Play...what?"

"Checkers."

"I do," she said, nodding. "I haven't for quite some time though."

"No one around here plays," King Orion said, a little downhearted.

Ava removed her empty glass and sunglass case from the table next to her chair. "I've got some time," she said, smiling.

"As do I," Orion replied. He pulled a folding chair up to the table and began to set out the pieces. The board was made of glass and could fold into thirds via hinges. It was like the Backgammon game Zarah and Cordellia had spent nights playing.

Instead of the traditional colors, the squares were white and gold. The red and black discs were also glass, notches hand-carved into each one. Meticulously painted onto the center of the pieces was the king's symbol, three stars between the points of two crossed blades. Ava had never played on anything more than a cheap, flimsy board, and she was in awe of the intricacy and personalization of the king's game.

They played the first half in moderate silence, each one focused on their off-the-cuff, constantly changing strategies. Orion was aggressive, going full-force down the board while surrounding as many of Ava's chips as he could. Ava, however, was more careful, imagining the most obvious outcome of each move before making it. And she never opened her back row until it was the only option.

"You remind me of someone," Orion said as Ava double-jumped him with her first king. He said it so casually, so out of the blue, she wondered if he'd been talking to himself. But then he glanced up at her with green eyes the same shade as his son's.

She slid a piece from one white square to the next. "Who?"

King Orion scratched his beard a few times then shrugged. "I don't remember. King me." A bashful smile nudged his lips at the irony of the words. "Someone I cared about though, I think."

Ava wondered, as they continued to trap and jump one another's game pieces, if perhaps the person was maybe an ex-lover, someone he had courted when he was just Orion Calder, a normal, everyday citizen of Havaan. *Just another reason for the queen to hate me.* She also wondered if he had always wanted to be king or if his appointment to such had been one of opportunity. Sebastian said he'd wanted the title for the notoriety, but there had to be more to it than just that.

There were risks involved with wearing the crown.

Havaan had been close to turmoil, mere weeks away from destroying itself because of the greed and selfishness the second generation exhibited. They'd wanted power, too. Established the division between classes out of necessity, they had claimed. A necessity they hadn't bothered to explain, because those chosen to be a part of the upper class had followed like blind sheep. As long as it meant they got bragging rights, got to be better than *someone*. Even if those somebodies were people with whom they had been friends.

Best friends, even.

Bridges are easy to burn when you're the one with the match.

Which class had Orion been a part of?

One day she would find out, but this was the first occasion in which she'd spent time with the king, and she wasn't about to push her luck by asking too many questions. So long as the king didn't try to pry too much into her personal life, she would respect his as well.

They played three games before lunch was announced, the king winning two.

"Tomorrow?" he asked as he carefully placed the pieces into the velvet-lined box.

Ava smiled. "I would like that."

So, they played tomorrow, and the next day, and the one following. Every day before lunch they would meet under the cabana for as many rounds as they could get in. Ava found herself anticipating the meeting as soon as she awoke. Plus, she had plenty of hours to waste between breakfast and lunch now that Nixon was back to ignoring her.

He acknowledged her presence only when others were around. He had even gone so far as to switch his daily run-time, fluctuating between early morning, midafternoon and pre-dawn. Annoyed by his childish behavior, Ava resigned to not chase him, because she deserved his silence this time. But she couldn't make things right again if he refused to look at—let alone speak—to her.

Instead of trying to track his whereabouts, she wrote him a letter and slipped it under his bedroom door. Four days later, when she and Sebastian had been home for almost two weeks, she woke to a folded piece of paper at the threshold of her bedroom. In thick lettering it said: **11 TODAY.**

It would mean missing out on her time with Orion, but amending the rift that her carelessness had caused between she and Nixon was more pressing. She scrawled to the king a quick apology and had Delilah deliver it, despite her best friend's objections.

"Where are you going that you can't do it yourself?" she'd asked, a sculpted brow higher than it should be, as she pushed the envelope back into Ava's hands.

"I have to take care of something," Ava said, shoving the letter at her. "Besides, your job as my assistant isn't to question my motives, D. It's to do as I request with the biggest, happiest smile on your face." She pinched her best friend's cheeks before closing her mouth, which hung open at Ava's authoritative voice.

"The crown has changed you," Delilah replied, her tone serious despite the wink she gave.

Ava grinned. "I just ask myself 'what would Delilah do?' and then tone it down by ten."

With a shrug and swish of her hair, Delilah had started out of the bedroom. "I can't help that I know what I want and how to get it."

Shaking her head, Ava's laughter had followed Delilah down the hall, leaving the future queen time to not only change into workout gear, but also rehearse what she wanted to say to Nixon.

Ava arrived at the porch early and spent the extra minutes limbering up. She hadn't gone running for two weeks and if Nixon was still angry at her, then today's trek was not going to be an easy one. She deserved whatever torture he decided to put her body through. She would take it with teeth clenched and burning muscles if it meant his forgiveness.

She hated when people were mad at her, especially those she cared about.

And there was certainly no shortage of care for Nixon—maybe a little too much at times. His presence in her life was needed, though. He had been instrumental in getting her ready for the move, in coaxing the lengthening of her backbone, in igniting the small fire that now burned in her stomach. Nothing was right when there was distance between them, when their friendship was frayed. Bernadette already did an excellent job of making Ava uncomfortable around her own home, but with Nixon it was like the walls were closing around her. When she couldn't speak to him, the words that longed to pass her lips gathered in her throat like marbles and made it difficult to breathe at times.

She wanted to be able to exhale again, even if it meant gasping for air until they reached the top of the trail.

His voice broke through her thoughts as he stepped out of the house. His tone when he asked "Ready?" and strolled past her was short, but the single, deep word slid over her flesh like melted chocolate. His voice was equally decadent and did things a voice shouldn't be able to do.

With a cleansing exhale of breath, she answered, "Ready," to his back and began a slow jog, matching his rhythm until they passed the gates. Then he took off, faster than he ever had. He made no effort to set a pace with which she would be comfortable. Nor did he look back to check on her as they wove through the dense forest. He took her partially up the path she was familiar with, but then he veered right. The trees here were closer together, making it almost impossible to maneuver if she didn't look both down and ahead. The tops of the trees blocked out the sun entirely, causing shadows appear deeper and more ominous. Sometimes Nixon faded into them and she would lose track of him, but he always reappeared, and she pushed herself harder to catch up.

By the time they came to a stop at the bank of a river deep into the woods, her legs felt like rubber and her lungs burned. Every breath scorched her from the inside out. She wouldn't have been surprised if she started coughing up ash. There wasn't a single part of her that didn't hurt. Even her eyes stung from the sweat dripping into them.

Nixon was no better off, in which she found a bit of joy. It had been taxing on him as well. There were two black upside-down triangles on the front and back of his grey tank-top, the fabric stretched so tightly over his muscles she could count each ab.

Before she could fall into her attraction, she squatted by the river and gathered a handful of cold water, dousing her face with it.

Think of Sebastian. Think of Sebastian. She repeated the mantra to her steadying heart until nothing, but his green eyes and boyish grin filled her thoughts.

Things between them were going so well. Great, even. Their time away had brought them to a place they would have unlikely reached otherwise. As far as she knew, he was not attracted to Delilah, and she owed him the same respect. She would stitch her relationship with Nixon back together, but then she would limit her exposure to him. His presence, while a vital part of her existence at High House, was too dangerous; too tempting.

A second-long look at him could send her into a place where there was just them, free to do whatever they wanted with one another.

That was not the reality in which she needed to live.

Her dreams would have to be enough.

She felt him next to her before she even opened her eyes. The charge of his closeness tingled against her skin, as if someone had run their nails against her sides. The two of them looked across the river at the thick mass of saplings and evergreens.

"I'm sorry," she finally said. She watched him from the corners of her eyes. It was the same view she'd had of him the first time they'd met, before he had turned his full face to her. Before she had gotten captured in the bonfire of his eyes or his conviction in her ability to rule.

Before he said the words that would alter the course of her life forever. Before any of this mattered.

Before *he* mattered.

Nixon nodded once and unclenched his jaw. "I know," he said. A whoosh escaped her, a breath she hadn't held on purpose. He turned his gaze to her, the gold of his eyes more bronze than normal. "You good?" he asked as he turned away from her, heading back toward the trail.

Without a thought she reached out and grabbed his wrist, her fingers not even making it fully around the bone. "Are *we* good?" Her voice trembled.

He looked at her with lowered brows, as if he were considering the question. Maybe he was. Maybe he, too, had reservations about their friendship and whether he could look at her as nothing more than his future queen and his best friend's significant other. And if he couldn't? What would that mean? What would the end result be?

A boiling of fear began in her stomach as the seconds passed, the gurgling of the stream behind them the only thing she heard. Even her heart had quieted.

Finally, after what felt like half of her life, the corners of his lips twitched. "We're good," he finally said.

Relief flooded through her, sending her emotions into overdrive. Watery relief clouded her vision, but she blinked it away before it could escape. Almost reluctantly, she let go of his wrist, the tips of her fingers grazing his palm as she pulled away.

Damn it, she scolded.

"Let's go," she said with more tenacity than she felt. Nixon held her gaze a few seconds longer then he took off from where they'd come, reversing their path.

This time, when they emerged, they didn't race to the gates, but arrived wordlessly together. They entered the house without saying anything, and each mounted a staircase by themselves. At the top landing, they gave one another a tight-lipped smile full of uncertainty and gravitas, and then headed to their separate bedrooms.

There was still a weirdness lingering like early morning fog, but as they washed the dirt and grime from their tightly wound bodies, they tugged on the tiny, invisible string binding them together and twisted it around their fingers. It was a reminder of what they had and what they could be, but also a ken of what they would never have.

Each other.

XXX.

As May's cool weather birthed June's heat, life at High House lazed along. Ava, Delilah and Madi were quickly becoming a trio. They spent evenings together gossiping in Ava's bedroom, with bowls of popcorn or plates of ice cream-topped brownies. Ava and Delilah had also begun spending more time in the training barn, acting as extra eyes for Levi. Sebastian and Nixon, as well as Levi and Josiah (Levi's fencing instructor, though Ava had started to suspect there was something more between the two young men) often joined the girls during their free time. The group would sit under a shaded oak tree or along the edge of the pool, their feet submerged in the cool water, joking with one another. Ava and Cordellia had even started communicating again—not face-to-face but through weekly letters.

To Ava's surprise, her mother had been the first to extend the olive branch. In her careful handwriting she'd apologized for letting her down, but also insisted she was trying to get better. *I go into town occasionally,* she had written, and though the information had initially ignited a spark of anger in Ava, she'd quelled it. She was trying to take Delilah's advice and lower her expectations of her mother; to not look at her too-late successes as anything less than small footsteps in the right direction. *There is still so much I need to tell you. I hope one day to visit you at High House, that the memory of your father will not follow me but guide me there instead. He is not here to see you get married, to watch you take your vows and accept the crown. I am, though, and it is my greatest desire to see it happen in person. For the both of us.* She had signed the first letter and each one thereafter the same way: *I will leave a light on for you if you ever decide to make your way home again.*

It had taken Ava a few days to perfect her reply. Each letter sent and received was a nail put into the rebuilding of their ramshackle relationship. It was a slow process. A lot of trust had been lost between them, but if all went well, Cordellia would be there at year's end, celebrating with Ava as she went from future queen of Havaan to Second Queen of Havaan.

June was in its final week, and July brought not only stifling heat but one of the first big events at High House since the Welcome Dinner: The Meeting of the Regions.

"I expect you and Sebastian to be present," the king had announced one night at dinner.

Ava glanced up from the piece of chicken she'd been cutting and asked, "And what is that exactly?"

"One of the most grueling things you'll experience," Sebastian mumbled as he shoved a piece of bread into his mouth. He smiled around his food in response to the scolding look his father shot his direction.

"It may not be thrilling," Orion began, "but it is necessary. The meeting is a yearly gathering in which the governors of each region bring us the death, birth and marriage statistics of their areas. The records are kept in individual census books at each of the governors' homes, but we also keep a mass one here. It lists the histories of such events for every citizen of Havaan."

Ava's eyes went wide at the thought of such books. Did they go back beyond the last 25 years? Did the roots of her family tree stretch deeper than the generations she had known: past her grandparents into *their* grandparents, and maybe even more? She couldn't imagine the sheer volume of such a thing, but she was eager and excited to see it. The same could not be said about having to sit around and listen to the men rattle off names of hundreds—if not thousands—of people. Orion *had* mentioned over one of their daily Checkers games that she and Sebastian would start getting introductions into their future responsibilities.

This was just one of them.

"The only positive thing about the meeting is the banquet at the end of the weekend," Sebastian said.

"Food is always a good reward," Ava replied, smiling at the king.

King Orion took a sip of his amber drink. "It won't be the most exciting thing you'll endure as queen, that's for sure."

"It can't be all fun and games around here," Bernadette added from her end of the table, her usual air of displeasure buzzing around her like flies to a carcass.

She looked slightly worse for wear than normal. Her skin had lost a bit of its glow and the bags under her eyes had deepened, multi-leveled creases that hung low. She was showing her age more than she had been just a week ago. No one mentioned the change, but they had to have noticed it.

Unfortunately, her appearance did nothing to lessen her criticism of Ava.

They were tangible at times, the jabs she directed at her successor. The flick of her thin eyebrow or flash of a sneer were not difficult to interpret. There had been numerous occasions in which she'd made some sort of snide comment about Ava's lax demeanor, from her time spent lounging around with a book in her hands to her "lollygagging" in the kitchen, "distracting" the staff from their duties. Yet the queen had seemingly given up on prepping Ava for the crown.

For a month or so, she had made it her mission to supply Ava the driest reading material possible, like which spoon to stir her tea with and the history of the waltz as it pertained to the old ruling system. Then she'd quiz Ava, firing random questions at her whenever the mood struck. But it had been weeks since a stack of books had waited by Ava's bedroom door or she'd been asked some obscure question.

Perhaps it was so Bernadette had another thing about which to berate Ava, but Ava had decided to ignore the things Bernadette said to or about her. After her weekend away with Sebastian, she'd been given a greater insight into the queen and why she behaved the way she did. She had also accepted she would never know why Bernadette's dislike toward her was so vehement, but there was nothing she could do about it. She wasn't here for the king and queen, though thankfully the former seemed pleasantly taken with her. She had been chosen to marry their son, who was without question smitten with their choice.

"Just do what they brought you here to do," Nixon had said to her one day while catching their breaths after a shorter trek through the woods. The encroaching heat was shortening their distance each day.

Ava considered his words, but she wasn't always sure what purpose she had in the grand scheme of things. To make matters worse, as the days grew hotter, her heart was being pulled more and more in two directions. That seemed to be a magic number for Havaan: two social classes that shouldn't exist; two rulers who could not seem to agree on Ava.

And two amazing men who, without knowing it, *did* agree on her.

Those two guys each held different parts of her being, made up varying pieces of her soul. She consciously tried to keep herself from Nixon's reach, but it seemed the harder she tried, the more her heart begged to be his. It made being around him, even when he was at the opposite end of the long dining table, difficult.

"Sounds like it should be a boring, though informative time," Ava said in reference to the Meeting of the Regions.

Next to her, Sebastian took her hand and squeezed. "At least we'll endure it together." He flashed his coy smile before bringing her knuckles to his lips.

From the end of the table came a sharp sound, like metal gears grinding against one another. Everyone's eyes shifted, searching for the source. Ava caught the flash of fire; a million bombs exploding behind an eclipsing sun.

"Sorry," Nixon said, his voice low. He pulled his gaze from hers and glanced around the table. "Got a tender spot."

Chuckling from deep in his gut, Orion raised his glass. "There can be no better compliment to the chefs," he boasted before taking a long swig.

What Orion failed to understand was Nixon hadn't been talking about the chicken.

Her dreams that night, like all nights it seemed, were flooded with Nixon. Three times his breath woke her and three times she fell back asleep, only to be thrust into the loop once more.

A frustrated growl erupted from her throat as she kicked the covers off. They were suffocating her, depriving her of air, much like Nixon's dream-kiss had. Her legs trembled as she crossed her bedroom and made her way silently down the hall. The thudding of her heart resonated so loudly in her ears she worried it would wake High House, but she made it to the kitchen without disturbing another soul.

She was warm—too warm to be comfortable—as though her body was cooking from the inside out. The dreams were becoming more realistic with each passing night. Sometimes, she was convinced that when she opened her eyes she would find him next to her. They were too much, too intense, and left her body uncomfortably warm. Normally she could extinguish the flames with a few glasses of water. "But tonight calls for something more," she said to herself as she pulled a tub of vanilla ice cream from the freezer. Even in the dark, she moved around the large space efficiently, locating the scooper, bowl, silverware, and sprinkles in the dark without issue.

Seated on the stainless-steel counter, her back propped against the humming refrigerator, Ava ate slowly, each spoonful cooling her core. She tried to think of anything besides the dreams and the man who invaded them without permission.

She focused on the upcoming meeting. She thought about Cordellia. She wondered if Sebastian would go for them getting a puppy once they were married. She thought about where Orion and Bernadette would go when they were booted from the throne. Would they continue to live in High House?

By all the stars, I hope not.

"The king can stay," she rationalized out loud, "but Bernadette has got to go."

As she scooped another mouthful of ice cream onto her spoon, a sound disrupted the stillness. Aside from the dull whirring of the industrial sized fridge at her back and the occasional scrape of her spoon against the bowl, High House was deathly quiet.

It wasn't a bang that alerted her to another life, or even footfall; but rather a breath. Holding her own, she wedged herself in the crevice between the refrigerator and cupboards above her. It was a shallow alcove and she had to fold herself into it, but she hid seamlessly amongst the shadows the depth created.

She wasn't sure why she was hiding. It's not like she was doing anything wrong. Perhaps it came knowing that if Bernadette happened to be wandering around, she would have *something* to say about Ava's midnight snack. Another transgression to add to her growing list.

Ava was not in the mood to deal with the queen tonight, so she stayed buried in the darkness, waiting.

The doors swung inward and the haze from the sconces on the dining room wall created a silhouette of the visitor. Then the air shifted. Molecules in the atmosphere rearranged themselves into a static charge. Inwardly, Ava groaned.

She watched him from her cave as he rounded the prep-island and made his way into the pantry. When he came back, tossing an object from hand to hand, he passed by her.

"Whatareyadoing?" she growled, the sound almost demonic as it vibrated in her chest.

"Shit!"

He gasped and spun in a half circle toward the noise. Whatever he'd been carrying dropped to the ground with an echoless thud and his fists came up in a fighter's stance.

A loud, full-belly guffaw exploded from her. Her sides pinched with each shallow breath she took, only to release another lungful of laughter. Tears welled in the corners of her eyes and she made no effort to wipe them away as she slid from the dark. Nixon stumbled to the light switch. He nearly tripped over the object on the ground in the process, his foot rolling over the now bruised and dirty apple in his haste to reach the wall. When he turned back toward her, his face was red with either embarrassment or anger—maybe both—and it made Ava laugh even harder. "It hurts, it hurts," she exclaimed, grabbing her sides.

"Good," he replied as he tossed his apple in the garbage. "I hope it hurts forever," he added, his voice tense.

"Oh man," she chuckled, using her fingers to brush away the humor dripping down her cheeks. "That was awesome."

Arms crossed over his broad chest, Nixon leaned his panther-like body against the island. He did not seem to find the same amusement, and he glared at her under thick eyebrows. Finally, after a few hiccups and stray giggles, she returned his stern look, though her lips twitched with the need to smile.

He ran his hands through his hair, pushing it away from his face. There was a thin layer of scruff on his jawline and as he raked his nails down his face, it sounded like sandpaper. "I could have killed you," he finally said.

"I doubt it," Ava replied, sliding closer to the edge of the counter.

"The king will be disappointed to hear all my training is for nothing, then."

Ava tapped the space above her heart, using their sign to let him know his secret was safe.

"What are you even doing in here?" he asked.

She held up her bowl, which was now a layer of thick soup with rainbow veins. "I couldn't sleep."

"Bad dreams?"

She shook her head and averted her eyes. "Not bad, no." When she added, "Just annoying," her gaze inadvertently flicked his direction.

"Was I in them?" he joked, smirking.

"No," she replied a little too quickly. He raised a skeptical brow as the Cheshire-like grin on his face widened. "I can understand hearing the word annoying and automatically finding it synonymous with yourself," she said, "but in this case you are not the reason for my inability to sleep."

If there wasn't a perilous attraction between them, she wouldn't feel the need to cover her tracks. She'd be able to laugh it off and even reply with a sarcastic, "Oh you know it!" But it was already hard enough for them to be in the same room throughout the day. She didn't want him knowing he haunted her sleeping moments, too.

"That's good to know," he said as he pushed off the island.

She looked at him, one brow curving higher than the other. "Is it now?"

"Of course," he replied, the word moving him a step. He invaded the space between her knees, hovering in the safe zone. When he continued to speak, his voice an octave lower than normal, his words—like fingers—wrapped around her calves and pulled her closer to the edge of the counter.

"I want to be there if I'm keeping you up at night."

Breathe! her brain screamed, but she'd forgotten how. All she could do was watch him step further into her bubble, his body overtaking the emptiness between them. He was so close…

As he waited for her to say something, to grant or refuse him permission, she studied the features of his face that she hadn't before. There was a tiny scar at the tail of his eyebrow, an almost microscopic disruption in the hairs. He also had a small freckle on the right side of his bottom lip, as if someone had tapped a taupe-inked pen there.

Nixon was noticing things about Ava, as well. Like the way her eyelashes curled even without makeup, and the smattering of almost white flecks in her ocean-blue eyes. He saw her lips, the tops of them more triangular than rounded, whisper his name.

Her hands were on his chest, rising and falling with each breath. "I'm pretty sure that would be a violation of the rules," she whispered in response to his comment.

It was getting harder for him to fight what he was feeling for her, to douse the desire she fueled. If the way her breathing had changed and the faraway look in her eyes meant anything, it wasn't so easy for her, either.

Reaching up, he cupped her neck gently in his hands. "Rules are meant to be broken," he answered, using his thumbs to tilt her face upward.

She leaned forward, reducing the distance between their mouths.

He followed suit, bringing her face another inch toward his.

Rules be damned, they both thought as their eyes closed, as they leaned closer and closer…

A loud, sudden crash shattered the world and echoed in the spaces between their ribs, expelling their hearts from their chests.

XXXI.

Ava screamed then instantly bit down on her lip to stifle it. At the same time, Nixon took a giant step back, his hip connecting with the island behind him. He swore, and she shook her head, trying to clear it. Cobwebs hung from her brain as though it were a rafter in an abandoned house.

Their gazes dropped to the floor, to the bowl that had put a stop to the nearly committed transgression. Pushing off the counter, her legs like cooked spaghetti, Ava stumbled to the sink. She returned a minute later, a wet rag in her hand. She refused to look at Nixon, who had moved closer to the door, his hands lodged in his hair.

"You should go," she said. She set the bowl back on the counter then began cleaning what remained of her ice cream.

Her name slipped from Nixon's lungs, drawing her attention upward.

His eyes were wild, a world on fire. Loss pulled his brows and his jaw worked as he chewed his words. It took everything in her to stay rooted to the ground, to not crash into him.

"Nixon, please," she begged, the second word lodging in her throat. "I…I need you to go, okay? I can't…*we* can't…" She let him fill in the blank. "You know that, right?"

He started to take a step forward, but before his heel could hit the ground, Ava held up her hand, warding him off. "I know we *shouldn't*," he said from his spot.

Ava wanted to tell him they never would, she wouldn't let it get to that point—but she couldn't find the truth to back up the words.

"You need to go before someone comes down here," she said almost robotically as she dropped the damp rag on the floor and used her foot to wipe up the rest of the mess. Mesmerized by the back and forth motion, she didn't notice him leave until the air was cold and empty.

In a fog, she washed the dishes she'd used and set them in the drying rack. When she turned the kitchen light off, smothering the stainless steel appliances in darkness, she wanted the last ten minutes to stay behind as well; for her indiscretions to hide under the counters. Better yet, to lodge themselves in the garbage disposal. But they followed her through the dining room, up the stairs and down the hall, weaving between her feet like a needy cat.

She didn't want to go to her room.

Nixon lived there.

After what had almost happened, facing even dream-Nixon was a torture she had no desire to endure. On a whim she tried Delilah's door handle. Surprisingly, it turned easily in her hand and she pushed the door open just enough to slip inside.

D's bedroom was barely smaller than Ava's, and though their closets were the same size, Delilah's seemed to be incapable of holding all her clothing. There were no books on the shelves, just cases full of makeup. The walls were covered in photographs. There was also the lingering vanilla and cherry scent of Delilah's lotion. Even though it was a different bedroom than the one the friends had spent hours growing up in, the chaos of it was familiar. As Ava climbed into Delilah's plush, overly-pillowed bed, she could pretend they were back in Typhony.

Before the gala. Before Sebastian. Before Nixon.

Before her heart knew it was possible to betray so many people at once.

"You'kay?" Delilah asked, sleep holding its gentle hand over her mouth.

Swallowing the lump in her throat, Ava nodded. "Bad dream," she whispered, rolling away from her best friend. Even in the dark she couldn't stand to lie to her face.

Though it wasn't *really* a lie.

It did feel like a bad dream.

Not one where she was being chased by monsters with glowing red eyes, but instead by a knight with fire in his soul.

She wasn't quite sure which was worse.

Morning came too soon.

Too soon to wake up, too soon to face what had almost happened.

It was also too soon to see anyone.

Thankfully, Delilah was in the shower when Ava tiptoed out of her bedroom. When she returned to her own sanctuary, she brushed the spoiled milk taste from her mouth then returned to bed. Delilah knocked on her door to summon her to breakfast, but Ava ignored it. The second round of knocking was insistent; each pound of fist louder than the one before until Ava had no choice but to get up.

She opened the door harder than necessary. "What?" she asked, the singular word clipped.

"Did you not hear me the first time?" Delilah took a step toward the bedroom but Ava blocked her, closing the door a little. "What's going on?" she asked, retreating.

"Nothing," Ava replied. "I just don't feel well."

Guilt had a way of doing that to a person, manifesting in physical ailments like dark circles and upset stomachs.

"You don't look sick."

Ava glowered. "Well, I am.

With cynical eyes, Delilah regarded her. Ava didn't get sick often. She'd only seen it happen a handful of times during their friendship and each time she'd looked close to death. This time, her skin hadn't lost any of its bronze nor had her voice taken on a raspy bravado. But Cordellia didn't physically look ill most of the time either, unless she was in a catatonic state.

"Are you depressed?" Delilah asked. "Because if you are, I need to know." Needed to be prepared to force Ava into the bath and to eat a meal if worse came to worse. The exaggerated roll of eyes and groan of fulmination which came from her best friend was all D needed. She held up her hands in surrender. "Okay, sorry." Then she tried again with a softer approach. "Do you need anything? Some oatmeal, maybe? Soup?"

"Thanks," Ava started, "but I think I'm just going to rest for a while and see if I can't drag myself downstairs for lunch. If I don't though, soup would be great."

"I'll deliver it myself," Delilah said. She touched Ava's arm softly. "Let me know if you want anything, even company."

Nodding, Ava gave her a tiny smile. "I will. Thank you." Then she closed the door without another word and made her way back to bed.

She tried to tune out the sounds around her, to focus on nothing but her breathing and the tap, tap, tap of her heart. Eventually, the movements of the house and people shuffling to-and-fro soothed her, became a rhythmic machine that lulled her into oblivion. Her body sank into the softness of her bed and her blankets enveloped her, tucked her safely away like a letter.

She stayed in the nothingness of her sleep until footsteps, loud and thunderous, walked through her empty subconscious. Then there were words, muffled and bubbly as though they were coming from under water. She didn't recognize them at first, but slowly they became clearer.

A name.

Her name.

She pried her lids apart. "Hey," she said, her voice thick with sleep she couldn't shake.

"Hi," Sebastian whispered. "How are you feeling?"

She yawned and rolled onto her side before stretching, her spine cracking. "Tired," she answered, smiling sleepily. "But okay, I guess."

His fingers wove between a chunk of her hair, and as it slid around them, his voice sounded spacey. "Good, good," he said.

"What's wrong?" Ava asked as she took his hand, forcing him to look at her. It wasn't until she sat up did she notice the bag by the door. Brown. Limp. Its strap hanging loosely over the top flap.

"Oh," she said, acknowledging his going-away satchel.

It was empty for now. But when he returned it would be full. Full of secrets. Something it seemed they both possessed. *Maybe I'll tell you mine when you're my husband,* the voice in her head said maliciously, using his words against him.

Tell you how I've wanted your best friend since the first moment I saw him.

How I've almost given myself to him more than once.

How we had to draw lines, make rules, because even our loyalty to other people doesn't seem to be enough.

How we were seconds away from kissing and the *only* thing that stopped us was a damn bowl.

How even after all this time I still can't love you…

"It's that time again," Sebastian said, glancing over his shoulder as he followed her line of sight.

"How long this time?" she asked. "Will you be back in time for the region meeting?"

Sebastian brushed his lips over her knuckles before kissing the top of her hand. "Absolutely. I won't let you have all the fun." He winked as his lips tilted into a lopsided smirk.

Letting go of his hand, she looked at him, squarely in his lush, forest-green eyes. "I know you won't tell me where you're off to," she began, "but can you at least promise me it's necessary? That you're not keeping this from me over something stupid. Because I hate not knowing where you're going. I hate…" She sighed. "I hate the scenarios that play in my head."

"It's necessary," he assured, his tone soft and kind. Nothing less than what she'd expect from the prince. He was always so placid with her and it hurt knowing she didn't deserve his gentleness.

He wanted to give her more than she wanted to return.

"Not just for our family," he continued, "but for Havaan as well. I wouldn't do it otherwise."

"Why does it have to be you though?" she asked.

He didn't answer immediately, just mushed his lips together as he tried to find the right words. "It's safer for me than it would be for my father. Or for Levi. Or anyone else."

Right words or not, they were not reassuring.

She couldn't think of a place in Havaan that would be dangerous, because such a place no longer existed. The only place that came close was Nopels, and Nopels wasn't real. Which meant, if what Sebastian was saying was true, there was an area of their country where bad things lingered; somewhere she, nor the citizens of Havaan, knew anything about.

Some place where Sebastian was sent.

She didn't like it.

Just because she didn't love him didn't mean she didn't care for him. She *did* care about him, harbored some sort of feelings for him. Though what those feelings meant, she was hesitant to explore.

Sebastian could read her eyes: the two black discs of her pupils overtook most of the blue.

"Avaleigh," he said, redirecting her attention. "I'll be fine. I always am. I'll be gone so few days you won't have time to miss me." There was no wobble to his words, no fear hanging on each serif.

Ava tried to let that be enough. "Well, be careful either way, please."

"Of course," Sebastian said as he stood and kissed her forehead. "I hope you continue to get better."

Better? she thought, her eyebrows drawing together with confusion.

Oh. Right.

"I'll try," she replied, giving him her own promise.

He kissed her tenderly, and she returned it automatically. How free she was to kiss Sebastian, to press their lips together without having to worry about being caught. Even if they were, who cares? She was *supposed* to be kissing him. So why wasn't it enough? Why weren't his sweet words and looks of admiration and gentle caresses and beautiful green eyes and unique silver hair able to keep her from wanting someone else?

As soon as he was out of the room, she fell back against her bed.

With a pillow over her face, she screamed her frustrations.

XXXII.

Avoiding Nixon the next couple of days was easy. She wasn't trying to keep her distance this time around, but a new set of guard trainees had rolled in; a fleet of over one hundred men ages eighteen through forty. They would spend the next three days training under Raymon, Ramiro and Nixon. With Madi busy in the kitchen, prepping for the upcoming Meeting of the Regions, Sebastian off on his top-secret mission and Delilah chasing guards like they were butterflies, Ava was thankful Orion continued to carve out an hour for Checkers. She enjoyed his quiet company, but also the conversations they had.

The end-of-July heat was unbearable, especially in the afternoon, when the sun was at its highest. Everyone avoided being outside unless otherwise necessary. Even those who often took their lunches in the lush grass had resigned to eating in the house, finding different rooms in which to spread out and gorge themselves. King Orion and Ava had changed their gaming location from the pool deck to the impressive library. With dark wood furniture and soft, apricot paint, it was a calming, tranquil room. Arranged neatly on the floor-to-ceiling shelves were thousands of books, some old and some newer, all assigned by a system Ava would never fully grasp. There were also two plush couches with deep red fabric arranged in front of the hearth, and a small drink cart in the corner of the room that was refreshed daily.

The library was on the second floor of the manor, right next door to the Throne Room. Large windows overlooked the yard, providing a bird's-eye view of the greenhouse, gazebo, and training barn. The table upon which the game had been set up gave her an uninterrupted view of the backyard.

As Orion set the pieces atop the game board, Ava watched the guards—all in black gear—file into the giant shed. "Why is this a thing?" she asked, waving her hand toward the window and motioning to the happenings below.

Orion glanced outside. "The training? Your move."

"The training," Ava replied as she slid a disc. "The guards."

The king looked at her, his eyebrows low and his mouth a straight line, as if no one had ever asked such a thing. Maybe they hadn't. Questions weren't often voiced in Havaan, *especially* not when it came to the actions and choices of the king and queen.

And never *to* the royal family.

Three moves took place before Orion spoke again.

"When the war was over, the regime was created out of necessity. There was no way to be sure another rebellion wouldn't take place. If it happened, and we weren't prepared, gathering forces would be nearly impossible. So, I made sure we were as equipped." Ava jumped one of his pieces and collected the cool-to-touch glass orb. He gave her a scolding look for the play then continued his explanation. "As the years went by, the need for precautions lessened, but the interest in becoming a guard didn't. It gives people a purpose, and I've never seen a reason to take that away. Some won't make it through training," he said as he moved into Ava's back row, eliciting a kinged chip. "And there will be those who do, but will leave a few years from now to start a family or pursue a different occupation. There will always be new recruits, though, which is good. Just in case."

Ava looked up from the board quickly, her brows hitched. "In case of what?"

"In case of another war," Orion replied nonchalantly, as if the idea of such a thing wouldn't spell disaster.

"That isn't possible, is it?" She tried to match his casual disposition.

"Possible, yes," Orion replied, jumping three of Ava's pieces. He gave her a kind smile, the lopsided one he shared with both of his sons. "Probable, however, no. Unless you and Sebastian do something to anger everyone, that is."

Ava glared at him as he kinged her disc. "Like get rid of the class divide?" she challenged.

"Combining the social classes isn't a bad move."

"So why didn't you ever do it?" Ava asked without missing a beat. It wasn't a question asked maliciously, or even meant to be a jab at his rule. She was genuinely curious. Although Sebastian had given his own take on his father's lax decision making, she wanted the reasoning straight from the source. There had to be more than just 'it would upset a bunch of people.' She was at least willing to give King Orion the benefit of the doubt.

King Orion leaned his large frame back in his chair and wove a glass piece between his fingers, moving it up and down his hand smoothly. "I wanted to," he started, "but establishing myself as king was more important. The division of social classes isn't what almost destroyed Havaan. It was magic, so eliminating *that* was my first order of business. It had to be, or we weren't going to survive. It wasn't easy, though. It took months to track down the magicians and drain their power. Then, we had to follow up with their kin, test each person to ensure there was no magic running through *their* veins. If there was, we had to strip them of it, as well. People were...not happy right then.

"We needed time to heal. I was a new king, something we'd never had before. I needed to earn their trust, just like you and Sebastian will have to do, and making another drastic change so soon would ruin everything. Eventually, issuing a decree about the class divide fell off my radar. Should I have done it? Maybe. But people are happy and to most the divide isn't an issue."

"How would you know that, though?" A bit of anger painted her words this time. "You've never immersed yourself in a crowd and asked for complaints. When Sebastian and I were out there, when we took time to talk to the citizens, we learned it isn't all rainbows and butterflies. There are citizens who are being denied opportunities because they happen to live on the wrong side of some invisible, nonexistent line. People *are* unsatisfied with the social division, with what it means for them. They may not be shouting it from the rooftops, but it's there, bubbling under the surface. I am not the only one who feels this way."

"I never implied you were," Orion replied, his voice calmer than hers. "You asked me a question and I answered. Perhaps I could have done more as king." He shrugged. "You will understand the necessity in picking your battles wisely and deciding what actions to take in order to leave your mark when you wear the crown. Freeing Havaan of magic was mine. If getting rid of the divide is yours, then so be it. It's a great mission to undertake, one which will speak highly of your ability as queen."

Orion sat still for a few seconds, the green of his eyes flashing as if tiny fireworks were going off in front of him, and then he slid a

Checker piece across the board. "Why is the divide such a big deal to you?" he asked.

"Because," Ava started as she mimicked him. "It's pointless."

"A lot of pointless things exist."

"And a lot of things that exist shouldn't," she replied. Instead of arguing, the king bowed his head slightly, so she continued. "If it was discovered that there are other people out there, and they asked us what makes Havaan so great, we would inevitably answer that it's our unity, our togetherness. But when a separation gives power to one group, allows them to hold dominion over another, to dictate what their lives can and cannot be, we're no more united than the old world was. If we continue to allow two social classes, those in the middle are always going to exist simply to serve those in the upper." Looking out the window, a small smile touched Ava's lips as Delilah made her way toward the barn. While her attention remained on Nixon, D was also having a field day with the influx of new recruits. Ava coveted the freedom Delilah had to bat her eyelashes and flash her marvelous, vixen-like grin at whomever she wished.

There were many things about her best friend Ava envied; almost as many that she didn't.

When Ava spoke again, her cadence was less powerful, less passionate. "The divide changes people," she said, the words caught in her throat.

Before she turned back to the king, she fixed her face, refused to let him see any part of her weaknesses. "It tells little girls they can only aspire to so much, whatever is within the wheelhouse of their social class. It gives the impression that only certain people can dream of being queen. I don't want..." She paused for a moment, the right words bouncing around in her head. "I don't want the next generation to feel worthless. I don't want them to be told what and who they're allowed to be. I want everyone on equal ground—*true* equality. If we're going to claim to be one nation, then we need to be. If for nothing more than fairness and respect for one another."

"If you had known you were eligible, would it have made my choice any less difficult for you to accept?" Orion asked.

Ava shrugged. "I have no way of knowing, because you were too busy hosting galas and keeping everyone on this side of the river happy." Ava swallowed the lump in her throat then pushed all her pieces into the center of the board. "I forfeit," she said as she stood.

"Avaleigh." King Orion sighed like a parent annoyed at the hissy-fit their child was throwing.

Without looking back, Ava exited the grand library, with its rows and rows of books and giant painting of King Orion. She used the door that connected to the Throne Room and hurried through it, the heels of her sandals slapping against the floor. She walked past the carved pillars with their tiny scenes of Havaan's rebuilding. Stopping in front of one, she ran her finger over the small figure, his arms raised above his head as the dead pulled themselves from their graves.

The war had happened only a few short years before she was born. She'd been delivered into a world where the ground was still pregnant with magic. Birthed into a society where people refused to give up the power the dead had allotted them. Raised under the rule of a king and queen who made no effort to change it.

Would it have made a difference in her accepting her fate?

Perhaps if she had grown up knowing nothing of an upper class, if she had been looked at as an equal, then her appointment to queen wouldn't have rocked her world as much. She could have prepared, would have written her name with 'queen of Havaan' attached like so many of her classmates had.

And if that version of herself hadn't gotten chosen?

Then she would have been disappointed, but she would have been free to continue with life as she saw fit; marrying who she wanted to marry. She wouldn't have to feel guilty about her heart being defiant, about her feelings going in every direction except for where they were supposed to go.

Maybe that's what it all boiled down to: control of her life had been taken away from the moment she was conceived. The two social classes meant she would never be good enough to dream of being more than the daughter of a dead fisherman and a crazed jewelry maker.

Well, look at me now, she thought sarcastically as she continued her way through the Throne Room, down the staircase, and out the back door.

She hadn't meant to blow up at the king.

There was just so much going on inside of her lately. Between her feelings for Nixon becoming more difficult to avoid, Sebastian's need to keep secrets, Bernadette's constant vendetta and Orion's lackadaisical approach to being king, she was a whirlwind of frustration.

I need a distraction, she thought as she crossed the backyard. *And I know exactly where to find one.*

XXXIII.

There was no difference in the heat between the outside world and inside the barn. Both were an inferno that made clothes stick to skin immediately. Two industrial sized fans had been brought in, though they helped little. All they did was create a loud, obnoxious sound, like that of a wind turbine. It stifled the commands from the training guards and kicked up cyclones of dirt.

As Ava made her way across the barn, she pulled off her t-shirt and wrapped it around her waist. Being in just her blush colored tank-top and shorts was hardly cooler. She gathered her thick hair into a bun atop her head and climbed half-way up the bleachers.

"How's it going over here?" she asked. She plopped down next to Delilah, who managed to look effortlessly beautiful in a simple sundress.

"Hot," she replied. Then she wiggled her eyebrows and added, "And I'm not just talking about the heat."

Ava laughed and leaned against the bleacher behind her. She did a quick scan of the hundred-plus men below them. They were all rugged, with dirt caked on their muscles and sweat coating their bodies. Even the ones who were a bit older were still in top-notch shape. They kept up with the sparring without stumbling or stuttering. Although they were all an exquisite display of the male physique, Ava couldn't keep her eyes from one specific person.

Where Raymon and Ramiro circled different groups of future-guards, barking orders at them and tossing in the occasional insult,

Nixon wasn't afraid to get physical. He would demonstrate a takedown move and then allow himself to be tossed to the ground—sometimes so incorrectly a chorus of sympathetic groans would sound—until the trainee mastered the proper technique. It was art the way his body curved and moved, how he could almost anticipate what was coming next. He swatted away grapples and dogged weak kicks as if it were second nature. Which, Ava supposed, it was. He'd started his own training at thirteen and had devoted his life to the king's sentinel ever since.

Considering this, the matchups were quite uneven. Ava almost felt bad for the trainees. She knew Nixon wasn't going easy on them just because they were new. They would be returning home with their governors by week's end, which meant there were only four days to get them into proper form.

"What's up with you?" Delilah asked, noticing the way Ava was staring into the nothingness. When those moments happened, when she forgot there were eyes on her, Ava's mask would slip. It didn't happen often, but it opened her up, showed her true feelings, displayed the vulnerability she worked so hard to keep hidden.

She hated it.

Blue eyes moved to brown ones as Ava returned to reality. "Nothing," Ava said, shaking her head. "I'm okay." She sighed. "I—"

"You miss Sebastian, don't you?" Delilah cut in, her voice fluttery. Delilah was a hopeless romantic and loved the idea of Ava and Sebastian being head over heels for one another. In her mind, Ava had it made. Not only was she going to be queen, but she was going to do so by way of Sebastian Calder, the dreamiest of dreamboats. It was the greatest fairytale ever told.

If Ava could transfer her crown to Delilah, she would do so in a heartbeat. Sebastian deserved a woman who would lap at his kindness like a cat to milk; someone who would admire him as much as he admired his wife.

Not someone who lusted after his best friend so intensely it would make the Devil blush.

"Oh yeah," Ava replied, not hiding her sarcasm. "That's exactly it."

"He'll be home soon, though, right? Don't the governors arrive tomorrow?"

Ava nodded. "He said he would be, but who knows."

"Water break!" came a loud command from below.

There was an outburst of cheers from the crowd. Like fragments of a bomb, they dispersed toward the water coolers. Some poured half of the contents from bottles over their heads before guzzling the rest in three gulps. Others simply collapsed onto the hard-packed dirt, as if their skeletons had vacated their bodies the first chance they got.

Delilah stood and dusted the back of her dress. "I should go see if any of them need anything," she said.

"Like mouth-to-mouth?" Ava joked, grinning up at her.

"Hey," she replied, shrugging. "If that's what is required, who am I to deny our brave guardsmen?" Then suddenly she sat back down. Ava looked at her curiously. "It can wait." She spoke the words out of the side of her mouth and cocked her head to the right.

Ava felt the static charge down her spine before she noted Nixon coming their way. His charcoal locks were a wavy mess and pieces stuck to the back of his neck. His tank top suctioned to the definition of his stomach with each deep breath he took.

It was unfair someone could be so attractive, even when dripping sweat and panting like an overheated animal. The look Delilah tossed over her shoulder told Ava both women shared the sentiment.

"Hey," Nixon said, approaching them.

"Hi." The word dripped from Delilah's lips like gooey honey and melted chocolate wrapped in cotton candy. "Thirsty?" She offered him a bottle of water. Where she'd been hiding it was a mystery, but Nixon accepted it without question and drained most of the contents in a couple of swigs.

"Thanks," he said as he poured some in his hands then splashed his face with it.

"You look good," Ava blurted out, her face reddening instantly. Nixon glanced over his fingertips, one thick eyebrow arched. "Out there. With the training. Things are coming along well." She stumbled over her words, trying to rectify her embarrassment.

He flashed Ava a quick smile. Not long enough for it to linger, but enough to send her heart into overdrive. "Glad you're enjoying the show."

"Show?" a familiar voice echoed, demanding the attention of not only the small group but the entire fleet of men. "This is the most uninteresting show I've ever seen," Sebastian said as he made his way up the bleachers. "Although, having all of my favorite people—" A kiss to Ava's temple. "In one general location—" A brotherly handshake and slap on the back to Nixon. "Is quite nice." Turning his eyes to Delilah, he playfully asked, "Did you manage to keep my girl out of trouble while I was gone?"

Delilah grinned at him as he took his place next to Ava. "As best as possible. You know how difficult she can be."

"That I do," he agreed.

"How was your trip?" Nixon asked.

"Uneventful, but successful," Sebastian replied nonchalantly. Refusing to say more on the topic, he gestured below. "I know it's only day one, but how do you feel the new recruits are shaping up?" He took Ava's hand in his and kissed across her knuckles before entwining their fingers. She smiled at him, but it felt forced. She was uncomfortable with Sebastian's affinity for public affection, but even more so while Nixon was hovering above them.

She avoided Nixon's eyes when he replied, "Okay, I suppose."

"But?" Delilah asked, filling in the blank space.

Nixon sighed, and this time Ava did look at him. "But they're not getting it as quickly as we need them to. It's a little frustrating, is all."

"Maybe they need a demonstration," Ava said. He cocked his head slightly but said nothing, waiting for her to continue. "I learn better when I'm shown how to do something versus being told. I know you're in there with them, trying to help them, but they can only see one side of it when it's you versus them." She shrugged, then added, "Just a thought."

"It's a great thought," Nixon replied before draining the rest of his water. "But the last time Ramiro and I sparred, he got a mild concussion. And Raymon is healing from three broken fingers. So unless you're volunteering…"

Ava was more than willing to roll around in the dirt with Nixon, but because she didn't think Sebastian or Delilah would appreciate her admitting such a thing, she just glared playfully at the wink he sent her way.

"She's definitely not volunteering," Sebastian said, a bit of bite to his words. "But I will."

Six eyes turned toward him at once. "Is that a good idea?" Ava asked him. "I mean…is it safe? Are you as good as Nixon?" Though she'd tried to stifle it, doubt still hung on the question.

"Maybe not *as* good," Sebastian replied, "but he did train me, so I can't be too bad. And if anything, it'll be amusing. Which is really our job, isn't it?" He winked at Delilah. "To keep our ladies amused."

Nixon combed his fingers through his dark locks, pulling them back into a low bun. "You haven't trained in a while. Are you sure you're not too rusty?"

Laughing, Sebastian stood. He punched his friend in the shoulder gently. "You're not scared, are you?"

Nixon glared, an ominous look that did nothing to soften his harsh, "Never."

Suddenly an idea, the spark of a light bulb, formed in Ava's brain.

She had slowly come to realize that the only way she was going to be able to resist Nixon was if he became unavailable. She had hoped Delilah having a crush on him would be enough to quell her own attraction toward him, but as her dreams proved night after night, it wasn't. What she needed was for him to be completely entwined with someone else, so head-over-heels for her that Ava wasn't even in his peripheral anymore. Maybe, just maybe, if she could force Nixon to spend time with D, he would realize how charming she was and his attention would shift from Ava. It was a sad thought, but it was necessary if she had any hope of moving forward with Sebastian.

Too much time had been spent trying to feel for the prince something that reached beyond friendship. Yes, she was attracted to him, but it wasn't enough. It had been almost four months since she'd moved to High House. Her obsession with Nixon had continued to grow, while her feelings for Sebastian remained stagnant.

"I'll sweeten the deal," Ava started, looking at both guys. "If you do this, for the sake of training and education, of course, then I'll cook dinner for the two of you tonight."

Nixon regarded her through fiery slits. "Is your cooking worth possibly breaking every bone in my best friend's body?"

"Yes," Delilah and Sebastian said simultaneously.

"The actual question is," Nixon replied, "why are you even encouraging this? Don't you want Sebastian's face to remain pretty?"

Sebastian turned to Nixon and smiled his lopsided grin. "You think I'm pretty?"

"Very," Nixon answered.

Ava laughed at their banter. It was the first time she'd seen such an exchange between them, the sort of back-and-forth more common with her and Delilah. It made her genuinely happy, something she hadn't felt in a few weeks if she really thought about it. Lately she'd been on autopilot, a human robot whose emotion setting had been cranked to low.

"I don't want you to rearrange his face," she said, "but it'll be a good opportunity for the new recruits to see what they're working so hard for. What their full potential can be if they put in the effort."

Ava raised her eyebrows at Sebastian and then flashed Nixon her best lusty eyes. It was the dumbest rule they'd set, but also the safest to break. *Rules are meant to be broken,* he had whispered to her that night in the kitchen. She shivered just thinking about his closeness, the heat which had radiated off his body...

Sebastian and Nixon looked at one another as if mentally agreeing on their own rules. Perhaps no one else noticed the flash of challenge in Nixon's eyes, like a match being lit in a dark room. "You *really* want to do this?" he asked, offering his friend an out. Just as he hadn't gone easy with the recruits, he was even less willing to do so for Sebastian— for his brother.

The prince turned his attention to Ava and in his gaze she found not what she thought she would find: fear, hesitation. Instead, his green eyes glistened with excitement, eagerness.

Life.

If Orion and Bernadette knew of the shenanigans transpiring between the future king and the man in charge of protecting him, they would refuse to hand over the throne so soon. Bernadette would, without question, blame Ava for perpetuating such foolishness, and she would admit to it, just to push the queen's buttons. This is what guys did—they displayed their core, their basic genetic need to fight for and impress their mate.

They were reminded every day how much their appearance mattered. Business casual dress even when they spent the whole day inside. Bruises and gashes were not acceptable on the prince or the king or the queen. Sebastian, especially, had been bred from birth to be this pristine trophy, like an untarnished representation of a god the citizens were meant to worship. But here, in the barn, he could leave that all behind.

This was the first time, even in those moments when it was just the two of them, that Sebastian looked ready for something. For anything

For everything.

Ava stood, and as he did so often to her, she took Sebastian's face in her hands. "Go get 'im, Tiger," she said, smiling. Then she smacked him on the rear.

"For my lady!" he shouted as he shoved Nixon's shoulder on his way down the bleachers.

As Nixon began to follow, Ava grabbed his hand. She turned their backs on Delilah and the crowd below. "Are you going to give me a good luck pat, too?" he joked.

She smiled slightly. "Be nice to him," she whispered.

Squeezing her hand, he whispered back, "For my lady." Then he trailed after Sebastian.

"What was that about?" Delilah asked as Ava sat back down.

"Just warning them to play nice."

Trails of dirt puffed around the feet of Nixon and Sebastian as they made their way across the barn floor to the senior guards. They exchanged hushed words, gestured a few things with their hands, and then Raymon, with his bald head and red Viking beard, whooped loudly, startling some of the new guards. He patted both men on the shoulder before stepping into the center of the floor.

"Gentlemen," he started. He waved a hand Ava and Delilah's direction as he added, "and ladies, we have a very special show for you today. Your future king and your favorite guardsman have offered to demonstrate the skills you lads are working so hard toward."

Cheers, whistles and applause broke out in the barn, drowning out the roar of the fans. Delilah nudged Ava excitedly as they leaned forward, their feet on the bleacher below them. Both men glanced up at them as they took their place across from one another.

Raymon stood between them, a hand on each shoulder. "Make sure it's clean, you two, or I'll pummel you both into the ground," he said, loud enough for everyone to hear. Chuckles followed. Then he dropped a hand in front of their faces, as if severing the barrier keeping them separated.

In that moment, Ava could understand Sebastian's eagerness to undertake this challenge, because she, too, felt very alive.

XXXIV.

Ava had been lusted over before. She'd been ogled and visually craved like the rarest piece of art. She'd experienced it from both Sebastian *and* Nixon in their time together. But neither of them, nor anyone else, had ever looked at her the way the two men were looking at the plates she'd just set in front of them. They drooled over the feta, spinach and herb stuffed mini Cornish hens, glazed baby carrots and oven-baked red potatoes. She and Delilah had barely tucked the hems of their dresses beneath them when the guys cut into their food. The sound of utensils on plates, the sighs of exhalation, and the whisper of, "Have they ever eaten before?" that came from Delilah stretched a satisfied smile across Ava's lips.

Sebastian and Nixon had certainly earned the meal.

They had put on one hell of a demonstration, tossing each other around and punching at one another as if the other were simply one of the bags hanging in the corner of the barn. Neither had gone easy on his friend, but every motion, every knee to the stomach and punch to the back was done with an efficient grace and careful necessity.

This was not to say either had gone unscathed. There was a small dark spot forming under Nixon's left eye and Sebastian had more than a couple of bruised ribs. The knuckles of both men were cracked; blood had dripped into the ground and congealed there like wax from a candle.

It had all been worth it for the awe and admiration that shone in the eyes of each guard. There was respect and with that came an eagerness to be even a fraction as good as their role models. *This is what King Orion meant,* Ava had thought to herself as she'd watch the crowd surround them once Raymon called the match. There wasn't an official winner, but they'd both come out victorious for one reason or another.

Now they were redeeming their bruises and spilled blood with a promised meal. Chef Audart had, with great reluctance, allowed Madi to assist in the more technical elements of the meal, mainly stuffing and preparing the bird. Mrs. Markum had happily passed off the filling of cupcake papers to one of her assistants to help Ava perfect a key lime pie. Ava had lucked out that most of High House's staff seemed to adore and care for her as much as she did them.

"Is it worth it?" she asked as she cut into her own food, though with more grace and control. Strings of cheese, like tendons, stretched across her plate as she brought her fork to her mouth.

Nixon grunted his reply while Sebastian nodded and smiled at her. The foursome ate in silence for a few minutes. It was Sebastian who spoke first, taking the time between bites for a long sip of his iced tea. "Father said the two of you got into a bit of an argument this afternoon." He looked at Ava over the brim of his glass before drinking again.

As she cut into a potato, the skins glistening with melted butter, she answered, "More a disagreement really."

"You stomped out of the room," Sebastian replied. There was a hint of admonishment in his words, a scolding undertone. There were many things Ava hated and being treated like a child was one of them.

She lowered her brows, a silent warning that he was treading on thin ice. "I forfeited the game. It's not like I knocked over the board because I was losing. And I didn't *stomp* out."

Sebastian shrugged a shoulder. "I wasn't there," he said, "I can only—"

"No," Ava interrupted. She broke a soft carrot in two with her fork, administering more force than necessary. "You weren't there." She looked up at him again and held his gaze for three beats of her angering heart.

A fork in one and a knife in the other, Sebastian held up his hands in surrender. "I didn't mean to upset you."

"Why did you bring it up, then?" she snapped.

Next to her, a hand brushed her knee. The simple gesture sent a spark through her veins and straight to her chest, calming her nerves almost immediately. She risked a quick look at Nixon. His fire met her water with an intensity that could set the world ablaze. She turned her attention back to her plate before they burned Havaan.

"I was just making conversation, my love," Sebastian replied, his voice collected. Ava wanted to fling a spoonful of food at him. Instead, she shoved it into her mouth. Otherwise she would keep arguing, and the last thing she wanted to do was ruin the evening. This night was for Delilah; a chance to show Nixon her true self and hopefully—for both women—convince him she was worth investing his time.

Ava hoped her best friend would take the opportunity to shift the uncomfortable tension elsewhere, maybe ask the guard a question about himself, but instead she directed her words at Ava.

"What in the world could you have possibly gotten into an argument with the king about?"

"Disagreement," Ava corrected, lifting her eyes to her friend. "And nothing important."

Delilah sighed, and when she asked, "It was about the divide, wasn't it?" her question was laced with the same disappointment as Sebastian's.

"I said it wasn't important." *Let it go,* was what she really meant, and she wanted Delilah to desperately take the hint.

"It is to you," Delilah argued. Ava dropped her silverware. It clattered against her plate as she folded her hands on the table and focused on Delilah, who was clearly not in the mood to take not-so-subtle hints. "Otherwise you wouldn't make such a big deal out of it every chance you get. We get that it's your legacy. But it isn't a point you have to keep drilling home. It isn't something worth burning bridges over." Each word she spoke was level, even. As if she were simply telling Ava about color theory or reciting the alphabet. But each word she spoke slashed at Ava, cut into her until they were grating against bone.

She didn't argue back, however. Simply asked, "Are you finished?"

"You don't need to get snippy with me, Avie. I was just saying."

Ava wasn't sure if she was more annoyed Delilah hadn't dropped the whole thing when asked, or that D was siding with Sebastian and the king. That she, too, believed Ava had been in the wrong.

"This is my fault," Sebastian chimed, his voice apologetic. He stood and extended a hand to Ava. Her gaze roved up his palm, along the inside of his arm where red fingerprint marks were stained into his pale flesh, and to his face. His eyes were kind and there was a small lift to the corner of his lips. "Come with me. I want to show you something."

"Pass," she said as she picked up her utensils again.

A thrilled rumble rolled from Sebastian. "You can't pass."

She looked up at him again, her face set. "Like hell I can't."

He smiled wider. "Stop being so stubborn for once."

"That's like asking me not to breathe," she retorted. Then with a deep, agitated sigh she tossed her napkin onto the table and placed her hand in his. She let him tug her to her feet and with his free hand he pushed in her chair. "Madi will bring dessert out soon. We'll be back in time," Ava said to Delilah.

Her best friend nodded once. It was then that Ava noticed how large Delilah's eyes had gotten. Was it possible that Delilah was…nervous? Witty, charming, Delilah, ruler of men and breaker of hearts? Ava's gaze danced between the two at the table. On the final pass, her eyes locked with Nixon's. His face was passive. A lock of hair lay over his brow. The tips of it brushed against lashes too long to be masculine and his nostrils flared just a little. Ava's lips quirked a voiceless apology before she followed Sebastian.

They rounded the back of the gazebo and walked slowly, hand in hand, toward the padlocked door of the greenhouse.

"I'm sorry I said anything," Sebastian said. His fingers wrapped around hers and he squeezed.

"It's fine," she assured. It wasn't. Not really. She was annoyed. She didn't want to fight, though. It left her drained, exhausted physically and mentally. The scuffle between Sebastian and Nixon had been a nice distraction, but as soon as it was over she'd felt the weight of her *disagreement* with the king. She didn't want to think about that, either, so she shook her head to clear the memory and focused on Sebastian.

"What was that?" She'd heard him say something, but no part of the question had registered.

"I asked if you had your keys." The look she gave him was followed by a loud, drawn out sigh. He gripped the brass padlock and tugged.

The thick chains looped through the weathered handles rattled against the door.

She patted the front of her dress then shrugged. "Nowhere to put them."

As Sebastian pulled a hand from his pocket, he said, "You should always have them on you. At least the skeleton key. You never know when you'll have to sneak into a bedroom." He winked. "Or a greenhouse."

The walls and ceiling of the structure was constructed of blue-green glass. A large part of the greenhouse's exterior was covered in ivy. It spread up the walls and over the ceiling like mold, reaching toward the tall spire at the top. The spire was ornate, with swirls and curlicues which echoed those carved into High House's staircase bannister.

The greenhouse was as alluring as it was eerie, like a Victorian ghost.

It didn't seem to fit in at a place like High House, which is why it had always demanded Ava's attention.

It was her in building form: a little damaged and a lot misplaced.

At some point Sebastian had let go of her hand, and in the space between their words came an audible *click*. It was not soft, like the tapping of nails on a mattress, but louder, like the echo of a gun cocking. Within the next second a slinking, slithering sound cut through the air, followed by the clatter of chains coiling in on themselves.

With the heel of his loafer he pushed against the center of the greenhouse doors. They creaked open, folding into the edifice as if they'd been unused for eons, their hinges rusted in place.

"Ready?" Sebastian asked, leading her inside.

The air was heavy, not at all what she had been expecting. It hung like high noon in the summertime, suffocating as though someone had taken a towel fresh from the dryer and covered her mouth. But there was also moisture swirled within. The humidity suctioned Ava's midnight blue sundress to her body and made her curls tighten around one another.

A gasp caught in her throat as she fully entered the conservatory. It was mostly dark, but small lights strategically placed throughout permeated the shadows. Some of the ivy had crept through fissures in the glass ceiling and hung like stalactites from the roof. There was a large path for walking, its cracked stone leading around the entire circumference of the indoor garden. Tuffs of grass reached through the broken pieces, creating a mossy trail.

The earthiness of all the foliage assaulted her nose as Ava meandered, one slow step in front of the next, along the green carpet. There were ledges and shelves full of potted plants, each labeled in a tilted font: oregano, garlic, thyme, basil, lavender and cilantro; as well as other spices she couldn't identify. She got a whiff of each plant as she passed.

Resting a hand on the small of her back, Sebastian ushered her forward. She lifted her head and looked around, taking in as much of their surroundings as she could, until she paused at a wall of flora. It took up a decent chunk of space and was almost like a curtain of ivy. The leaves were different, however. These were more heart-shaped, thousands of them as black as Nixon's hair.

"What is this?" she asked Sebastian.

He ran a hand through his hair, pushing it out of his eyes. His scholarly voice—the one he always used when discussing the backstory of Havaan—came out as he began to speak. "It is said that the magicians had countless portals hidden throughout Havaan. There's no way they could have done the amount of business they did without a way to go from place to place quickly. Not much is known about the Portalis Dievas, aside from that. Its translation literally means 'portal of the Gods' and it is believed to have been the markers for these portals. It was smart." He flicked one of the petals. "If you didn't know what you were looking at, you'd just assume it was——"

"A wall of leaves," Ava finished.

Nodding, Sebastian continued. "They weren't always black, of course, but as magic was syphoned from Havaan, they couldn't survive. They needed those powers to draw from, and when it dried up, so did they."

Ava asked, "Why is it here if it's so useless?"

"A curiosity of Mother's. She doesn't have many interests, but she has always been quite fascinated with the magicians."

Ava gave a small grunt but said nothing more. Bernadette seemed like the sort of woman who would take interest in magically-based plants and flowers, even if they were for nothing more than decoration. Bragging rights. Owning such a piece of their sordid history came at a price. In fact, it was a crime in Havaan to possess anything from those days, and for anyone else it would mean automatic banishment to Nopels.

They continued around a bend until Sebastian stopped her with a touch to the shoulder. In front of them, a rustic wooden table contained three plants in weathered clay pots. Soil the color of onyx surrounded their stems, and when Ava later touched it, it was soft like feathers or crushed pearls. The plants themselves glowed, pulsating with neon hues of violet purple, bright yellow and chartreuse green.

"What are *these*?" Ava asked in breathless wonder.

Gently, Sebastian replied, "They are the last three enchanted plants from before the war."

In the days of the magicians, fields of such flora stretched for miles across Havaan. They were harvested and used for incantations, potions and hermetics. Later, when the second generation took over, the plants were hoarded; sold and bartered for whatever would help keep the magicians in power. After the war, King Orion ordered the fields destroyed, burned to the soil from which they grew. All traces of their existence were carried away in the wind.

"How are they here?"

"Because Mother wants them," Sebastian answered simply.

Eyeing him skeptically, Ava asked, "But how are they growing? Thriving? Why haven't they died like the Portalis?"

Sebastian picked up a few grains of the black dirt and rubbed them between his thumb and middle finger. "Sand from the river banks," he explained. "It was collected hours after the war ended and they were planted just as fast, when the magic and blood of the magicians had just begun to taint it."

"So it's true that the battle was fought at the river's edge?"

Smirking, the prince shrugged. "Most of the history the citizens have been told is truth. It's just ugly. It's easier to believe it isn't as violent or dark as it really is."

The glow of the flowers played with the shadows and valleys of Sebastian's face. He looked older, almost as rugged as his best friend. His hair was tinted blue in this light and his eyes shone like small green orbs, illuminating his lashes. He was still beautiful, but in the halogen-like neon lights he also looked a bit dangerous.

It was the first time he reminded her of Bernadette.

Slowly, Ava pulled her gaze away and focused on the purple flower. It was unlike any she had ever seen. The petals, shaped like that of a tulip, were lavender and violet swirled. The stamen inside were spiky with small pink bulbs on the tips. It looked as though someone had stuck sewing pins in the center of the flower, which throbbed with a rhythm matching that of her heart.

"What is this one?" This time she was inquiring not about its origin but its power.

"This one," Sebastian began as he stroked a curling vine of the purple flower, "is called Everlove. It is said to be able to manipulate the feelings of the consumer, make them believe they felt something toward another when they hadn't previously. It was the active ingredient in love potions."

Moving to the next pot, the yellow bulbs, Ava asked, "And these?" She looked up at him with eager eyes, the blue of her irises bright with wonder. The plant looked like small ears of corn, except the kernels were petals and from the tops of them bloomed grey puffballs.

"Wayrinwood. Its sole purpose is to weaken someone, make them easy to control." Ava's hand hovered above the blue plant next. It was the most enchanting one, with its star-shaped, blue speckled petals. The center of it glowed brightly, illuminating the spots the same way a black light would distort colors. Ava didn't have to ask Sebastian to tell her what it was.

"Paraloxia. Also known as The Truth Seeker. It—"

"Makes a person unable to lie?" Ava guessed. Sebastian smiled. "They all seem so surreal," she said. Biting the inside of her lip she grinned at him, completely punch-drunk on the moment.

"Beautiful, aren't they?" Sebastian's voice was soft, barely more than a whisper. Ava could do nothing but nod. She was transfixed by the beating cores of the flowers. They reminded her of the lights at the nightclub she and Delilah had ventured to a handful of times. As much as Ava loved Meridian, there were still times when it suffocated her—suffocated both girls—and they needed an escape.

Brene was special because it was where the main house of the royal family resided.

Paranick, which was two regions west from Brene, was known for its nightlife; its bars and dance clubs where people could get lost in a sea of bodies jumping and writhing to lyric-less beats. They hadn't gone in quite a while—years really—and Ava hadn't realized how much she missed the sweaty crowds and nonstop dancing until just then.

Maybe I can convince Sebastian to take me, she thought, smiling to herself at the idea of the prince in such an environment.

"Imagine having them spread throughout Havaan."

Ava realized, after blinking a few times to clear the memories of her past away, that he hadn't been talking about nightclubs or gyrating citizens. "Having what spread amongst Havaan?" Waving a hand with the pizzazz of someone presenting a prize, Sebastian gestured to the three plants on the table. They seemed to shiver with his acknowledgment. Her brows furrowed. "I still don't understand…" she said slowly.

"The plants, Ava. Imagine having field after rolling field of Everlove or Wayrinwood or…or Madergal or Semboisia. Hemlock. Or any of the other ones that once existed." With each word he became more animated. Each syllable was punched with eagerness. Passion. He was suddenly filled with a jocund Ava could not understand.

And then, like a light bulb being flicked on, she understood what he wasn't saying. "You want to bring magic back to Havaan." She didn't voice it like a question, but Sebastian still nodded and breathed out a whispered, "Yes."

Ava took a tentative step from him, as if she could somehow contract his insanity. "Sebastian," she started. She tried to keep her voice level, even when she finished with, "That's ludicrous."

"What do you mean?" the prince asked.

"I mean it's a terrible idea," Ava replied. This time she could not keep her disapproval from creeping out.

Now it was Sebastian who looked as though *she* were spewing senselessness. "I don't…what do you mean?" he asked again. "Avaleigh." He begged her understanding. "Just imagine the things we can achieve as king and queen with magic running through Havaan again."

Ava swallowed the lump in her throat. "You've read the history books, you know the stories." Pushing away the curls fused to her forehead, Ava said, "Damn it, Sebastian—your own *father* fought in the war that defeated the magicians. What is the point of us trying to get rid of the social divide if you're going to reintroduce magic to the regions?"

"What does one have to do with the other? We can still make one social class. We can still—"

Ava held up a hand to stop him. "How would you even do it?" she asked. There was no explanation he could give that would convince her any of this was a good idea, nor was she asking him to try and do so. She just needed to know his plan, to see how far he'd thought out what he was suggesting.

Sebastian exhaled a deep breath. The warm air caressed her neck and moved across her bare shoulders. The greenhouse suddenly felt twenty degrees hotter but neither of them noticed. Even the plants had stilled as if they, too, were waiting with bated breath to hear the prince's proposal.

"Do you honestly believe there aren't *any* citizens, in *all* of Havaan, who don't still have traces of magic in their veins? We just have to find a way to trigger it."

The corner of Ava's eyes drooped. "What about those who *don't* have any magic in their veins?"

Sebastian opened and closed his mouth a couple of times, trying to force an answer to his lips, but nothing came. Sighing, she gave him a look that said more than her words could. She pushed past him, but he grabbed her arm and admitted, "I don't have everything worked out yet, okay? But I can't imagine there isn't a way to share it, to get it to those who want it."

Turning to face him, she asked "What if someone *doesn't* want it? What then? Do you really want to go against an army of people who have a weapon we can't defeat?"

"I don't know, Ava!" Sebastian shouted. His fists balled and his eyelids dropped to half-mast.

In that moment, when his voice raised to a level it never had before, two things happened. One, and perhaps the most concerning, was the flare in his eyes. It was purple—the same neon hue of the plant now behind him—but it wasn't a trick of the flower. The flash covered the green of his irises completely, like the moon overlapping the sun during an eclipse. It swirled with flecks of silver, like the shavings often dusting Cordellia's work smock.

The second thing took place from the corner of Ava's eye. Some of the leaves of the Portalis, black and long dead, shook as though someone had run their hand across them. It drew her attention, but when she looked at the wall, all was still. *That,* she rationalized later, could have been a trick of light and shadows. Even the wind.

Sebastian's words pulled her gaze back to him. When her eyes locked on his, they were green again. No glittery, scary sparks of amethyst. Everything was so normal she questioned if she'd actually seen anything.

It was gone as soon as he blinked, but she had seen it…*Right?*

She was angry, emotional, tired.

All of which could account for what she thought she saw, a point Delilah would make further down the line.

"Why is it so hard for you to support me, to support *my* legacy, when I've done nothing but support yours? I have happily done so. I have, without complaint, followed your every lead, done *everything* you have asked of me since day one. Why can you not extend even a bit of faith for *my* dreams?"

"Because my dreams will unite Havaan," she said. She realized how selfish the words sounded, but that didn't make them any less true. "Yours will divide us. Again. It will separate citizens into those who have powers and those who do not. You know what happened before—greed and selfishness took over and it almost destroyed everyone." Ava took a tentative step toward him. She wrapped her fingers around the angry fists he was making. "Do you really want to be the king who brings chaos and disorder amongst his people? The king who brings another war?"

"You're assuming people can't learn from the past."

"And you're assuming they can. Is that a risk you're honestly willing to take?" His name caught in her throat and when she finally pushed it out it was full of desperation. "War will be inevitable. People *will* rebel." She didn't know why she was so sure of this, but it felt as certain as her eyes were blue and her hair brown. "Families will be shattered and children will lose their parents."

Again.

He looked at her, and for a second she thought she'd gotten through to him, but when he said, "I have faith in my people," she knew she was wrong. He was as dead-set on this plan as she was against.

"It's blind faith, Sebastian. It's misguided and it's clouding your judgment. The divide of social classes is so small, so insignificant but it's caused such a drastic rift between citizens. It's oppressed people by giving control to a secondary group. How do you not see, how do you not *understand*, that bringing back magic is going to be so much worse? It's *magic*. People will no doubt do what they can to either get it or hold it over those who don't have it. And those who are against it will fight." Dropping his hands, she sighed sadly. "I will not support you in this," she finished, almost apologetically.

"Even if that means I no longer support you in *your* vision for Havaan?"

Ava knew she could not bridge the social gap by herself. Sure, she had gained support from a large number of citizens, but that would mean nothing if the prince—if the future king—was not rallying with them. She was a nobody. A stranger to them.

She was picked to be queen based on nothing more than her looks.

The strength she possessed was not enough. She could not fight alone. Yet knowing this, knowing in the deepest part of her heart that her dreams, her legacy was going to vanish within the next few seconds, she replied, "Even then."

They stared at one another. It could have been seconds. It could have been minutes. But the time ticked by, eroded away by the heavy truth of what had just been revealed, until finally Sebastian said, "Perhaps when I iron out some of the wrinkles, we can revisit. Perhaps then I can convince you of the brilliance behind this."

Tired of fighting and a little afraid of what would happen if she continued to disagree with him, continued to question the ideas of which he was so strongly sure, she smiled sadly. "We should head back out," she answered instead.

With a nod, Sebastian led her through the greenhouse to the large doors made of glass and iron. Before she stepped out, she glanced over her shoulder at the wall of dried leaves. They were still, continued to be as dead as they had been when they'd first arrived.

Everything in the greenhouse was normal. The same as it had always been.

Outside of the greenhouse, nothing would be the same again. Ava understood, as she cast her eyes toward Sebastian, that whatever alliance they'd had was now gone. Nothing between them would be the way it had been less than half an hour ago. It was a harder realization to swallow than she ever thought it would be, but that was her life: constantly being let down and disappointed by the ones she cared about; by those who were supposed to care about her.

She was beginning to wonder if it had something to do with her, if maybe Delilah had been right. Perhaps she really did expect too much from people, asked for more than they could ever give.

She didn't know, and realistically she probably never would.

The only thing of which she was certain was that she was tired of always feeling this way.

XXXV.

There was a firm knock on the bedroom door, as though someone were trying to break into the room.

Let them come, Ava thought as she groaned and pulled her pillow over her ears. There had been a continuous barrage of pounding from morning and into the afternoon. First it had been Sebastian coming to walk her to breakfast, which she'd ignored, and then Delilah, who had requested Ava make some sort of sound to let her know she was at least alive. Ava had felt a twisted bit of delight in the startled yelp that came from the other side of the door when the hardcover book made contact.

Even Nixon had tried to coax her from her room, but she wanted to see him even less.

After last night she didn't want to see anyone.

When she and Sebastian had come back to the table, Ava excused herself from the rest of the meal. "I think the greenhouse was a little too warm. I'm not feeling very well."

She really had felt awful. Partially from the way Delilah's hand had rested on Nixon's arm, removed quickly when she and Sebastian returned, but mostly from the confrontation with the prince. From the crushing reality that the one mission she'd had, the *only* thing she'd hoped to accomplish as queen, was not going to happen.

In fact, it was going to be the complete opposite of what she'd expected.

She had no doubt Sebastian's plan would only divide citizens once again, creating between classes a chasm where currently there existed a crack. From two would come...how many? The current divisions would reconfigure into those with and those without magic.

Where Ava had promised unity and equality, Sebastian's reintroduction of magic would not only make her a liar, but also usher in mutiny and mass separation. People would rebel, of this she was sure; just as certain as she was that their rejection to such a change would bring another war.

"Avaleigh Toliver," a voice said from outside the door. "You open up right now."

"No!" Ava shouted from under her pillow. She pulled the blanket up around her as an extra barrier.

A few seconds of silence passed, followed by, "It'd be a shame if I had to eat all these ooey, gooey cookies by myself."

Ava glared at the door, her eyes peeking over the top of her blanket, and then she was across the room in a matter of steps. Wordlessly, she allowed entrance to her chamber and stepped aside. Helen crossed in front of her with a tray, on which was a plate full of cookies, the chocolate chips still melting as they cooled. There were also two smaller plates, two upturned glasses and a pitcher of cold milk.

After locking the bedroom door once again, Ava shuffled back to her bed on bare feet. She pulled her hair, which was another disaster entirely, into a bun at the nape of her neck before settling against the pillows.

"This is a cheap trick," Ava said, though she gladly accepted the small plate of cookies and the glass of milk Helen handed her.

"I had to do something," Helen replied as she crawled in next to Ava. She struggled a bit with the lush softness of the mattress, but she got there, nearly tumbling into the center of the bed. "Since you apparently think holing up in your room for a full day is acceptable behavior for a queen."

Ava cracked open one of the cookies. Chocolate dripped from a slightly under-baked center. It was just the way she liked them: golden brown and slightly crunchy on the outside, a little mushy on the inside.

"Is it written somewhere in the handbook of the newly appointed that the queen isn't allowed to have a day to herself?" she asked before shoving a milk-soaked half into her mouth.

"You would know better than I about the rules of being queen," Helen responded. She took a small bite of her cookie then washed it down with a dainty sip.

Scoffing, Ava answered, making no effort to hide the disdain in her voice. "Aside from a handful of quizzes, I've had zero training on what it means to be queen. I know the rules about as well as I would if they were tattooed on my lower back." She exhaled a humorless laugh. "At this point, I'm convinced Bernadette is taking a hands-off approach to ensure I make a fool of myself."

The corner of Helen's lips turned up slightly, but she did not partake in Ava's rant against the queen. Bernadette and her assistant were not friends like Ava and Delilah, but she knew better than to feed into such talk. She needed to keep her position at High House, if not for her own wellbeing then for Ava's, even if she didn't yet know it.

Instead, Helen said, "Bernadette would say the only job of a queen is to support her husband in everything he does."

Ava made a skeptical face Helen couldn't see, but it transferred into her tone. "I highly doubt the queen agrees with everything the king has done."

"I said support, not agree."

Sighing deeply, Ava counted to five before pulling out the submerged piece of cookie. She let a few drops of milk fall back into the glass as she mumbled, "I wonder how she would feel if her husband wanted to reintroduce magic back to Havaan." She looked at Helen then, a tight smile stretching her lips before the chunk of baked dough vanished between them.

"Oh." Helen paused, finishing off the last bit of milk in her glass. "She'd be ecstatic," she finished nonchalantly.

Choked with surprise, Ava downed the rest of her milk, clearing her throat. When she could speak again, she hacked out a loud, "What?!"

Helen set the tray at the end of the bed, then leaned into the pillows. Her hands rested on the curve of her stomach and she linked her fingers together. "Bernadette comes from a long line of magicians, although the old world would have called them witches." Ava put her empty plate and glass on the side table before turning toward the older woman, her legs crossed underneath her. "She, of course, was one of the citizens who had her powers taken from her when Orion ascended the throne. She pushed for the reinstatement of magic a few years into their marriage, but he refused adamantly. I think after *many* years of trying to change his mind and being told no, she folded. Not happily of course, but he's allowed her to keep a few trinkets here and there, memories that bind her to her ancestry."

The flowers Ava knew of, but she couldn't help wondering onto what other mementoes the queen was holding.

Sebastian and his mother had never seemed close. Ava had seen them argue countless times, mostly over Ava herself. She had witnessed his coldness toward her and had seen the control the queen tried to hold over her eldest son. Was it possible, though, that Queen Bernadette was to blame for Sebastian's passionate stance on magic's reintroduction? She was manipulative, so it wasn't farfetched to believe she had somehow planted this idea in her son's mind.

Considering how vehement Sebastian had been about it last night, it now struck Ava as strange that he'd never hinted at it before. Was Bernadette the reason for his sudden vagary? Would she be willing to destroy their country to get what she wanted? Would she sink so low as to use her own flesh and blood to benefit herself?

"Sebastian wants to bring magic back," Ava said sadly.

"And you don't agree with him," Helen rebutted. It wasn't a question, but Ava shook her head, anyway. "Why not?"

"It'll end us." Her words were heavy with conviction.

Helen adjusted, sitting up higher. "You seem quite certain of this," she said. There was more to the tone of the statement, and she eyed Ava with piqued interest.

"Should I not be?"

Shrugging, Helen said, "I have lived long enough to know that history has a way of repeating itself. One way or another."

"So I'm right? Nothing good will come from letting magic back."

"Perhaps. But perhaps not. It is possible we have learned from the mistakes we made before."

"Anything is possible," Ava replied, looking around the room. "But I can't support it, Helen, knowing there's even a small chance it'll divide us more."

Taking one of Ava's hands in hers, Helen looked her squarely in her eyes. "You're forgetting one thing. By that point, the regions will be united."

Ava pulled her hands away and knotted them in her lap. "I'm not going forward with that," she said, her voice low, wobbly. Tears pressed against her sternum. She didn't want to cry, not again. She had done enough of that last night, allowing her anger and frustrations to drag her to sleep.

"Why not?" Helen asked for the second time that afternoon. This time, however, surprise hung on the cusp.

Ava looked up. Her brows pulled together and her eyes swam with confusion. She didn't understand the question. The reason seemed obvious, but she explained anyway. "There's no point putting in the work to get rid of the social divide if Sebastian is going to come in and completely undo it." Ava shoulders lifted to her ears. A sad gesture. "It isn't worth it."

"I never took you for someone who gave up so easily."

Wide blue eyes became thin slits. "I'm not giving up," Ava refuted, her words short. "I just…I can't do it on my own. People have bowed to Sebastian since he was in the womb. They know his face, they respect his name. They will look to him to make sure they're allowed to support me." With a flick of her finger, Ava brushed away the tears dripping down her cheeks. "I'm no one to them. Just a girl who was chosen to marry him. They won't support me the way they will him and if he's not there…" Ava shook her head. "It won't matter," she ground out.

Helen reached toward her, but Ava crawled off the bed, away from her touch, and rushed into the bathroom. She turned on the faucet and risked a glance at herself in the mirror. She looked like a woman driven mad. Her hair was a nest of curls, all of them twisted in different tightness. Her eyes shone like marbles in the bottom of a red-rimmed glass. Her cheeks were splotchy, and her nose looked as though it'd been dipped in rose powder.

She was a mess.

She tried to wash it away with handfuls of cold water, but it didn't do anything besides turn her into a drowning mess.

Which is sort of how she felt.

Like she was sinking in her emotions. In her disappointment. In her anger and pain. She had wanted so bad to make a difference, to feel justified in wearing the crown. She had wanted to give those who dreamt of being more than a service to someone else the chance to do so. To work not in factories or printing presses unless they wanted; to not settle for being a sous chef when they wanted to run their own restaurant.

She wanted them to know they were better than she'd ever been.

Than she'd ever had a *chance* to be.

This dream wasn't just for her, but for Havaan's growth and continued peace. And in the blink of an eye it had been ripped away from her. From them. She'd been let down before, but this one hurt worse, because in turn she was being made to let everyone else down, as well.

"Let me ask you a question," Helen said. Ava turned to face the voice and found the portly woman sitting on the edge of the claw foot bathtub. She hadn't even heard her enter the room. Pulling herself onto the counter next to the sink, Ava nodded her head once. "Are you against bringing magic back because you honestly, in your heart of hearts, believe it will be detrimental to us? Or is it because you fear it's going to ruin *your* plans for us?"

Ava had been ready to answer when the first half of the question was presented. But the second gave her pause. *Was* she against Sebastian's proposal for nothing more than her own selfishness? She didn't have much in her life of which she could be proud, that she could show off or use to prove her worth. Amalgamating Havaan would be her legacy. It would ultimately show people she was more than just a nobody from a middle class.

Was that honestly the core of it? Did she care so much about being somebody that she was willing to go against something that could be good for their country?

In her rush against the prince's plan, she hadn't stopped to consider if it was possible they would work together, side by side, achieving what they both wanted.

Was it doable?

"No," Ava breathed out finally. Helen raised an eyebrow. "Yes, I am upset my dream isn't going to be achieved. But it's not the reason I don't want to see magic brought back. I've been taught the history of Havaan since I was a child. I've heard the stories of the sacrifices people made to get their hands on just a little bit of magic. Parents selling their sons and daughters to magicians for a vile of youth. Individuals hired to drain magicians of their powers so those without could finally get a taste of it. I cannot—I will not—be the queen who watches from the balcony as the world below her kills itself."

Helen stood and made her way across the bathroom. She slid her short fingers over Ava's slender ones and uncurled them from the edge of the countertop. Ava hadn't even realized how tight her grip had become until feeling began flowing back into them, little pinpricks of pain that distracted her from what she was feeling in her chest, in her heart.

In her soul.

A hand was placed against her face and she snuggled into the caress. "Child," Helen said, her kind voice even softer than normal. "How do you not realize that your plans must happen for Sebastian's to work?"

"What are you talking about?" Ava asked.

"He's not going to introduce something as powerful as magic into a society currently divided. There is too much risk. He doesn't want it to fail any more than you do."

Pushing her hand away, Ava slid from the counter and stomped back into her room. "I am not going to fix Havaan so he can turn around and break it again." She turned on Helen. "What is the logic behind that?"

"Because, Avaleigh, there is a chance, although very small, that history will not repeat itself. But *only* if we are united before risking it. Sebastian's success hinges on your success. You could unite Havaan and then, if magic returns, everyone will be on equal footing—"

"They won't be, though!" Ava cut in. "Some people will have magic and others won't. That's what it all boils down to, Helen. It's as simple as that."

"There is a possibility magic won't create violence and death, that it won't call for sacrifice," Helen continued as though Ava hadn't spoken. "You have to admit that."

"There is also a chance that it will." How could Helen ask her to even risk it? "I thought you'd be on my side," she added. Her voice was getting thick, her emotions wrapping around her throat like a hungry snake. It squeezed and squeezed, trying to suffocate her into submission.

Helen moved to her with more speed than Ava would have thought possible. Suddenly, her arms were around her. Ava stood still, her own arms hanging rigid at her sides, nail digging into her palms. "I *am* on your side," Helen whispered. "Which is why I am begging you to stay steadfast. Try and bring everyone together. Create as solid a foundation as possible. If he attempts to do what he plans and it does fail, you will never forgive yourself for giving up so easily. Knowing you could have done something to at least try and change the outcome."

Every conceivable emotion rushed from Ava at the truth of Helen's words. They came out in a harsh breath that shook her body. She was right. Ava *would* hate herself if she did nothing to stop their inevitable end. Even if, in the long run it was pointless, she would curse herself as she watched the country burn in flames of purple and blue and green and yellow. The screams of those below would haunt her dreams until death came for her if she didn't at least try and change the ugly course Sebastian's legacy could potentially put them on.

Ava sank into Helen's plushness and finally returned the hug. "What if people rebel against the unity?" she whispered, too drained to raise her voice.

"Some will," Helen replied without conviction or hesitation. "It is the unfortunate nature of people." By her shoulders she pulled Ava back enough that she could look at her, puffy face and all. "But keep in mind that most of the opposition is going to come from those in the upper class. Not the middle, where the number of citizens is higher than the other." Helen gripped Ava's hands tightly. "You have connections on the ground. You are one of them, and they will rally behind you because you understand them. You speak their language. You have shared in their dreams. They want a better life, better chances, more opportunities and you can give it to them. Sebastian, for as much as he may try, will never get it because he's never been affected by the division. You don't need him to make a change, Avaleigh. You can do it just as well, just as easily, on your own. It won't be easy, but it's not impossible."

"What if the transition doesn't go as smoothly as I expect?" Ava replied. "What if *I'm* the one who brings a war?"

Helen's assured, "You won't be," did not comfort Ava, because there was no way she could guarantee such a thing. Her hope in Ava was too strong. It was clouding her judgment, leading her blindly by faith alone.

"Some people will complain," Helen continued, trying to smooth the worried crease from Ava's brow. "And some will do so loudly. But if you were a citizen in the upper class, would you want to stand in the way of those who care for your child, or prepare your food, or repair the breaks on your car?" She gave Ava a knowing look. "Besides, do you think they'll really go against the decree of the queen?"

Shaking her head, Ava smiled, but just a little. A true Nixon smirk if ever there had been one.

"You can do this. But you cannot do it by hiding in your room whenever things become a bit more difficult than you'd planned. You are better than that."

Ava let out a deep, slow breath. For the first time since last night, before the bubble she was settling into shattered around her, she felt okay. Part of her was still twisted, wound too tight, but for the most part her head was clear. When had she become so engrossed in the royal life that she expected things to come easy? Nothing in her life had ever been simple, and she was stupid to think living in High House would change that. Helen had put her back on track.

She would do everything possible to continue with her plan. And then maybe they could find a way to work magic back in, as well.

In a way that wouldn't beckon death.

Sebastian could get behind her if he wanted to, or he could watch from the sidelines. That was up to him. Ava would not force him to back her. She would not beg and plead for his support. Because Helen was right about something else, too: he was never going to truly grasp the importance of what she was doing. And shy of having some incantation that could make them switch places for the first twenty years of their lives, he never would.

It was up to her to fight the good fight.

Even if that meant fighting on her own.

Which was something she'd been doing all along.

XXXVI.

There was something nice about eating every meal in the comfort of her bed and changing from one pair of pajamas to another. Ava would have preferred spending the following day in her room as well, locked away from the world for another 24 hours, but with the arrival of the governors that morning, staying hidden was not an option.

"You are expected to be ready and waiting tomorrow morning," Bernadette had hissed from the other side of the door last night. Ava had felt the words like cold fingers down her spine.

That chill lingered even in the August sun, which beat down on their shoulders as if to remind everyone it was there.

How is it August already? Ava had thought to herself while bathing. So much, and not enough, had happened in four months. In another four months she would become queen. Sebastian would slip a ring on her finger while Bernadette stabbed a crown into her skull.

She wasn't sure which would be more painful.

It was only ten hours into the day and already sweat was gathering behind her knees. She was wearing a pale brown sleeveless top with a mint green polka-dotted skirt and brown belt. Her shoes were a caramel color peep-toe. Her hair was behaving for the most part, a thick mane of tight curls waterfalling over her shoulders. She at least *looked* put together, even if she didn't feel it.

Nixon and Delilah had assumed their ever-vigilant positions behind the rest of the family. Sporadically, a fit of giggles would erupt from them, filling Ava with jealousy so thick it was like sludge trying to move through her veins.

This is what you wanted, she had to remind herself. She had needed Nixon to be unavailable so that she could focus all her efforts on wanting Sebastian. But that was before things had changed.

Helen's pep-talk had helped, giving her both the courage and passion to move forward with her mission. But it could not mend the rip that had been torn between her and Sebastian. Before, when she had looked at him she'd felt…*something*. Attraction, definitely, but there *had* been something more. Feelings she wasn't sure would ever come had begun to slowly arrive. She had felt connected to him in a way she didn't with anyone else. They were two people forced into a union and they would get through it as best as they could together. Together, the transition from prince and citizen to king and queen would be easier.

They'd been a unit.

A team.

Now when she looked at him, she felt nothing.

It was like looking at a stranger, someone she had never met before. It was like the day in the market, when she'd recognized him as Sebastian Calder, first prince of Havaan, but nothing more. The man engaged in conversation with his mother—which Ava now considered suspicious—was not the person with whom she had spent a week traveling through Havaan, spreading their mission statement. He was not the same person who'd made her feel safe and wanted and appreciated with waves and sand and keys.

She wanted to go back before the greenhouse.

Before Sebastian had shattered whatever mirage in which she'd started to believe.

They had taken breakfast together that morning, apart from everyone else.

"Things are different between us," he'd said. He had seemed sad about it, almost as disappointed as she was. Their time together was full of uncomfortable silence and melancholic sighs. They hadn't said much but they *had* agreed to act like things hadn't changed, at least around other people. "Fake it until we hopefully make it," he'd added while walking her back to High House.

Little did he know, this had been Ava's motto for as long as she could remember.

Fake it she could do. Making it would be another story entirely.

As if he could feel her contemplation, Sebastian turned from the queen, his eyebrows raised in a silent question. Ava's gaze traveled lazily to Bernadette. She looked worse than she had a couple of days ago. Her complexion, which was normally smooth and alabaster white, was marred with thin lines etched into grey skin like unbaked clay. They were hard to see unless the sun hit her in a particular way. She looked tired, the green of her pupils a bit cloudy. Her silver hair was in a long braid and tossed over her shoulder, though the tresses seemed to have lost a bit of their luster.

Somehow, despite her harried imperfections, the queen still managed to look elegant. A simplified version of her crown balanced atop her head and her rod-straight spine displayed her willowy figure. The dress she wore was simple, but the diamonds encrusted into the collar were a constant reminder of who she was.

Sometimes the queen appeared too flawless, painted to perfection.

Right now, she looked human.

A conniving, devious and dangerous human.

Because despite everything, her lips were still twisted in a malevolent smirk, as though she knew Ava's deepest, darkest secret and was waiting for the most opportune time to take her down.

"Is your mother feeling okay?" Ava asked when Sebastian came closer to her.

"What do you mean?" he asked, as if he was oblivious to his mother's lackluster semblance.

Shrugging, Ava replied, "She just looks a little…off."

"Oh, that," he said, waving a hand in front of his face. "She's been a bit under the weather lately. There was a lot to be done for this weekend and I think she wore herself out."

Ava wasn't convinced but she nodded anyway. There had been one other time when Bernadette appeared a bit weathered, and that was after they'd returned home from the cross-Havaan tour. She'd shuffled through High House, at least when she'd found the energy to show herself, in a silky crimson robe that dragged behind her like the train of a wedding dress. Her hair had lost its sheen and she refused to face anyone. She just floated from room to room until she ghosted into her bedroom once more. No one saw her for a couple of days, but once she reemerged she was a new woman.

There was something niggling at the back of Ava's mind about the whole situation, something that didn't sit quite right about Sebastian's nonchalance over his mother's apparent un-wellness, but she didn't have time to dwell on it. The crunching of wheels over the cobblestone drive diverted her attention. She tugged on the hem of her dress, ensuring there were no wrinkles, and instinctively stood straighter.

Today was an important day.

The three days to follow were also important, at least that's what the king and queen kept reminding everyone. Ava would need support from the most powerful people in Havaan if she intended to move forward with uniting the country. She couldn't rely on it to come from Sebastian, no matter how certain Helen had seemed, and Orion and Bernadette were either going to stay neutral or side with their son.

Which left the second-best option and that was the governors. They had as much power over their regions as Orion deemed necessary, but it didn't mean they weren't influential or that their opinions weren't respected. They could prove to be a vital part in the success of her plan, but she had to gain their trust first. She had to make a good enough impression that they would see beyond Meridian. She needed to prove to them that she was worthy of their faith, which meant she needed to stand like she'd already earned it.

They had all met the night of the Welcome Dinner, though their interactions then had been brief. They had shaken her hands and told her they looked forward to getting to know her better. At that time, she had been a sourpuss with a vendetta against everyone and everything that had put her here. Now, she was a sourpuss with a mission, a goal worth being here for.

The governors arrived in the traditional black cars, from west coast to east. Since the royal family's headquarters was in Brene there was only a need for three governors. Three seemed like such a small number when Ava thought about how much aid she would need to rally the regions, and if she allowed herself to overthink it, she would feel defeated before they even emerged from the vehicles.

So, she didn't, and instead pulled herself up higher.

The first to exit the car was the governor from the west region of Zyprah. He oversaw Usealie (the upper) and Conley (the middle). Archibald Revenwood met Orion inch for inch, which put him a little over six feet tall. He was incredibly thin, as if his body had been made of taffy and stretched until his bones threatened to crack. The widow's peak of his black hair nearly met his bushy salt-and-pepper brows and made him look like a villain. But his smile was kind and his laugh infectious. When Ava had first met him, the king had introduced him as Archibald.

"Archie," he had insisted. And then added with a wink, "I'm only called Archibald when I'm in trouble." Ava could relate, since no one ever called her Avaleigh unless she was being scolded. Or exasperating.

The gentleman in charge of Paranick (Oxphyn and Ramenell respectively) was named Clive Kendal. Where Archie was tall, Clive was not. He clocked in at no more than 5'4", making him shorter than Ava, even. He had a round belly and small eyes so brown they almost looked black. What had once been thick red hair was now thinning, a few pieces hanging on for dear life. He combed them across the bald spot, though it was a weak camouflage.

"Governor Kendal," Ava greeted, her hand held out in front of her. He wrapped it between both of his like a sandwich. "It's so great to see you again."

"You are as lovely as ever, my dear," he replied. He kissed the top of her hand before freeing it from his grasp.

"I'm a lucky guy, that's for sure," Sebastian said as the portly man moved down the line. Once the men reached Levi, they were escorted to the library by Delilah and Nixon. This was where they would conduct most of their business this weekend.

As the first two cars drove away and the last car approached, Ava couldn't help the smile spreading across her lips. Kai Roberts was her favorite of all the governors. Perhaps it was because he was the closest to her age, although 32 still left quite a difference. It might have been because he was the only governor who came to the meet-and-greet during the tour. Or maybe it was the fact he was the only one who had asked her to dance the night of the Welcome Dinner. It could have been his charming disposition or genuinely pleasant personality, but whatever it was, she liked Kai the best.

He slinked from the car with the grace of a panther; all long legs and well-built body which belonged to a man who had been a guard before taking over as chief of Diatin. His skin was the color of cinnamon sticks and his eyes an intense green that, against his complexion, sometimes looked translucent. His brown hair was a layer of close-cropped curls and a pair of silver-rimmed glasses tied his distinguished look together.

"Your man is here," Nixon whispered from behind her.

Ava looked over her shoulder at him and smiled. "Jealous?" she whispered back. The look he gave her said *yeah right*, even if his lips never did. He had no reason to be jealous. Kai was a great guy wrapped in an attractive package, but he wasn't Nixon. He didn't weaken her knees and set her pulse on a race to outdo the galloping of her heart.

After greeting Orion, Kai moved to Ava. "If it isn't my favorite future queen," he said, his voice deep and rich, like expensive chocolate.

"Hi, Kai!" Ava said into his chest as she returned his hug. He was also the only governor brazen enough to skip the handshake and go straight for the embrace.

"You'll save me a dance Saturday, right?"

She grinned at him as she hooked her arm through his. Together, they brought up the rear, following the rest of the entourage into the house. "Of course. I wouldn't let you leave without gracing me with your dancing skills." Kai flashed her two rows of perfectly straight teeth.

At the door, Bernadette kissed her husband goodbye. Before following the men, Ava turned to her. "I hope you feel better," she said, much to the obvious surprise of the queen. She cocked a thin eyebrow, deepening the creases in her normally smooth forehead.

"Thank you," she replied slowly. Suspiciously. It hooked at the end like a question.

King Orion's words tugged at Ava as he called her name. She turned and found him waiting in the doorway, the large door being held open by his baseball-mitt of a hand. "Sorry," she said, ducking under his arm. She hurried up the stairs and into the library.

A large table had been brought in and around it was placed six chairs: four on each side and two at the heads. Orion took one and Sebastian the other. Kai and Ava sat across from Archie and Clive and the group made small talk while drinks were served and the census books retrieved from bags. It was the job of each governor to keep track of every birth, death and marriage in his region, as well as financial transactions on any businesses in which the royal family had investments; the biggest being the six small vineyards that supplied Havaan with its wine. Four were in Diatin's middle class—Tykon—and the other two in Oxphyn. Aside from the contributions of citizens, which allowed them to participate in the grand events of High House, most of the royal family's revenue came from these businesses.

There was also a smaller table a foot or so away from the large one. On it sat a thick ledger in which the last five years of Havaan's population was listed. The information presented by each governor was transcribed into the big book by a frail woman named Eleanor. Ava was surprised the woman could still see well enough to do her job, but when she looked at the book later, she would be even more amazed by how immaculately organized it was.

As Eleanor settled into her seat and flipped to the next available blank page—the one that would start the 2160 records, King Orion spoke. "First, I would like to thank you all for your dedication to not only Havaan, but your designated regions. I cannot be everywhere all the time, but I am forever appreciative knowing our great country is in the best hands possible. We would not be as strong, flourishing in the way we are, if not for your hard work." He acknowledged each of the men with a tip of his glass. "Second, I want to welcome my son Sebastian and his intended, Avaleigh, to their first Governor's Meeting as the future king and queen." Orion turned his attention to Ava for a moment. "As you know, the queen doesn't typically take part in such mundane matters of Havaan, but I thought it would be nice for you to get a glimpse behind the scenes."

Ava smiled and saluted him with her own glass. "It is an honor to be here with all of you fine gents. Thank you for this opportunity."

"Don't thank him too soon," Kai said as he brought his goblet to his lips. "Mundane is just another word for boring."

Orion cleared his throat, which elicited another toothy grin from Kai. The others, including Ava, chuckled.

"Shall we get on with the boring business, then?" the king asked. "Eleanor, are you ready to begin?" Eleanor simply nodded then cracked her knuckles before picking up her pen. "Kai," Orion addressed, "why don't you start?"

"It would be my pleasure," he replied with what sounded like genuine enthusiasm. "We had thirty-three marriages this last year…" he began.

Ava learned very quickly that mundane had been an understatement.

XXXVII.

Ava adored the cadence of Kai's voice. The deep, cavernous swell of it recalled warm springs and lazy summers. But after an hour and a half of listening to him drone on about the thirty-three marriages, forty-five deaths and sixty-four births of his region, Ava never wanted to hear him speak again. To make matters worse, he had to pause after each name so Eleanor could document it in the big ledger, which only prolonged the torture. There was also time allotted to discuss the positive things taking place in each region and to report any infractions that had happened within the year. As expected, Kai had much to say about the former and little to say about the latter.

By the time they finished with Diatin, there was only fifteen minutes before lunch.

"Does anyone have any questions for Kai?" Orion asked before finishing the last swig of his wine. He was on his third glass. Ava had one and then switched to water. While she would have *loved* to drink the minutes away, the last thing she needed was to fall asleep during the meeting. She was already finding it difficult to keep her eyes open.

"I do," Ava said when no one else spoke up.

Kai turned toward her and smiled. "Why does that not surprise me?" he joked.

She glared at him in jest. "What's the response been to the proposition of merging social classes?" she asked.

"Very little opposition from what I have heard," Kai replied. "There was great excitement during your tour and I think citizens are just waiting to see what will come of your promises."

She couldn't keep the worried wobble from her voice. "But there *has* been opposition?"

"Whispers of it." Kai shrugged. "Mostly from the older generation who have a hard time adjusting to change of any kind. But I can't believe you didn't expect some, no?"

Ava nodded. "Of course I did, but it's still scary."

"Change is scary," Kai said. He reached over and patted her hands. "But things that are worth it rarely come without risk. Most citizens seem very receptive to the merge. Excited, even, about the opportunities it will provide."

Ava looked across the table at Clive and Archie. "And what of your regions?"

"Much the same," Archie replied. "People aren't typically vocal about their complaints, so if there are any regarding your idea I haven't been made privy to them. You have my full support though, Ava."

That was what she wanted to hear. *Needed* to hear.

All concern for going at this alone dissipated with those six words.

Three was a small number, but it was doable. Success was a possibility.

Afraid that speaking would let them know how scared she had been and how relieved she now was, she smiled her thanks.

"And mine," Clive answered, though his dark eyes had a hard time meeting hers. Still, she gave him the same appreciated grin.

"I expect I can count on you, too?" Ava said, addressing Kai.

He shook his head as he stood. "Absolutely not." He winked.

"It brings me much happiness knowing my son and daughter-in-law will have the support of such great men at their backs," Orion chimed while he and the rest of those gathered pushed their chairs away from the table. "We will reconvene after lunch. Clive, I look forward to hearing of the wonderful things taking place in Paranick."

Orion helped Eleanor from her seat and with her hand hooked into his large arm, the two of them meandered to the door.

"I'm going to go and let the guards know lunch is being served," Sebastian said as he kissed Ava's temple. His lips were firm, not soft like they had once been. She swallowed uncomfortably and nodded, flashing her most convincing smile before he vanished through the door.

"How *are* the new guards shaping up?" Clive asked as the six-some made their way down the staircase.

"Quite well," Ava praised. "I think you'll be impressed by the progress they've made."

Archie, who was behind her, squeezed her shoulder. "We always are. We are lucky to have such a well-trained group of men willing to pass on their skills to the newcomers."

"Perhaps we can arrange a bit of a demonstration this weekend," Orion said. "I'm sure they would love to show off a bit."

"I'll set it up personally," Ava said as they filed into the lunch line. Bernadette, Helen, Levi and a handful of other staff were in front of them.

As she was putting the top of her bun over the pulled chicken, from behind her Clive asked, "Do you intend to keep the guards once you're queen, Ava?"

She looked at him, taken aback. "It's never crossed my mind to get rid of them," she admitted. "Do you feel differently?" she asked as they sat. Instinctively, she placed a napkin at the spot next to her, saving it for Sebastian. It was weird how small things had become habit, like waiting for him to walk to breakfast or ensuring he had the chair beside hers at meals. These practices had mattered less than two days ago, but now felt hollow and robotic.

Things had changed so quickly it felt a bit like she'd been sucked up in a whirlwind, spun around a thousand times, and then dropped into a foreign land where nothing was familiar.

It made her a bit sad.

She had wanted such great things from their union and now—

"...it's become a bit pointless," Clive said, bringing Ava back to the moment. The look she gave him must have shown her confusion because he sighed, "The guards?"

"Pointless?"

"The regime was established as a failsafe against another war that never came," Clive explained. His beady eyes held hers. "Now they've become, and I hate to say it, meaningless. They may be necessary for the royal family, but past that they have no use."

"Perhaps they have no use against a war that's never happened," Ava began, as Sebastian slowly lowered himself into his chair. His eyes flickered between Ava and Clive, but he remained silent. At least until he heard the word war. When he opened his mouth, no doubt to reprimand Ava for speaking of business which she had no reason to speak *of*, she held up her hand. "But they have a point," she continued. The warning look she offered Sebastian was enough to ease the tension in his shoulders.

Clive wiped his mouth with his napkin. "I'm interested in hearing what you believe that to be."

"You mean aside from a safety precaution in case another war does break out in the future?" Clive lowered his eyes a fraction, creating thin slits as black as an abyss, and nodded curtly. "It gives meaning to them. They may never see battle. They may spend their whole lives at the ready and die never having put their training to use. But it gives them a purpose outside of just being fathers, or teachers, carpenters and bankers. It is the one thing in Havaan that doesn't discriminate based on where you're from. There is a brotherhood established that only those within it will ever understand."

"She's right," Kai said before he bit into his sandwich. "There *is* an indescribable feeling knowing you have membership to an elite club."

"We may never need them. By all the stars I *hope* we never do. But I would never take such an important honor away from them." She downed the rest of her lemonade and as she crumpled her napkin said, "You are more than welcome to issue a decree banning men in your region from joining the guardsmen, however."

Clive shook his head with each, "No no no no no. I've never thought of their importance beyond means of protection. I see your point."

As a swarm of guards, sweaty and caked in dirt, spilled into the dining room, Kai mumbled, "Speak of the devils." Their voices and greetings to others in the room broke the tension that had settled on Ava's table like a layer of fog on a fall morning. The room filled with conversation, as well as the sickly-sweet smell of sweat mixed with the rich scent of meat and barbeque sauce.

Ava waited for the air to change, for there to be an increase in electricity, but nothing shifted, and it was then she noticed the emptiness surrounding her whenever Nixon's wasn't around. She excused herself from the conversation she wasn't paying attention to and dropped her plate—along with those of Sebastian and Archie—into the trash. Then she grabbed a clean one and loaded it with food. On her way out of the dining room, she was stopped by a voice that was as smooth as silk and as cold as ice.

"Did all the excitement of your meeting today increase your appetite?" Bernadette asked. She made her way toward Ava, her gaze taking inventory of the two sandwiches, pile of carrots, side of potato salad, and smaller plate with two pieces of cheesecake. The queen looked better than she had that morning. The sun pouring in from the windowed ceiling danced along shiny silk strands and her skin was as smooth and lustrous as marble. Even the dark circles had vanished.

"It's for Nixon," Ava replied flatly. "He's skipping lunch again."

With her beauty returned the queen's vindictiveness and it dripped like muck from her words. "And you've taken it upon yourself to feed him. How very considerate of you."

Ava wasn't in the mood for a confrontation, but she heard herself responding before she could capture the words behind her teeth. "It's his job to get the guards into shape and he can't do that if he doesn't keep up his energy. Forgive me if I decide to concern myself with the health of the staff."

"Nixon is a big boy. It isn't your job to mother him," Bernadette hissed. She took a step closer to Ava and maneuvered so she was blocking them from view of the dining room. Ava's eyes met those of the queen. "It is also not your job to dash the dreams of your husband for your own selfish gain."

Ava laughed once, dry and humorlessly. "I don't need to defend my actions to you, Bernadette," she said, lowering her voice as well. "I may not agree with what Sebastian wants to do, but I will not stand in his way of doing so. And when the country burns, which it will, I will not abandon him, because despite what you believe about me, nothing I've done up to this point has been selfish."

Bernadette's thin brows lowered, and before Ava could step out of her reach, her hand gripped her upper arm. Nails dug into her skin, not enough to break flesh but enough to sting. Ava swallowed the pain and refused to divert her gaze. "The only thing I believe about you," Bernadette whispered, "is that you were right when you said we made a mistake in choosing you."

Wrenching her arm loose, Ava returned the hostile look. It was a stare-down, one which Ava refused to lose. Bernadette may be a cold-hearted bitch naturally, but Ava had spent sixteen years being best friends with the queen of glares. "Why? Because you're finally realizing you can't manipulate me, that you can't use me the way you tried to do with Brisbane?"

Bernadette's face faltered for just a second, half a blink and her mask was back in place, but Ava had seen it. "I had nothing to do with that situation," she replied, but even she didn't fully believe her own lie.

"That's not what your son seems to think." Ava watched Bernadette swallow before she continued. "You're stuck with me," she said, her words coated in a slimy self-assurance that matched her slow, wicked grin. "So maybe you should spend less time worrying about what I am and am not doing, and worry about yourself. Because you're starting to look like shit, Bernadette."

Ava turned on her heels without another word and smiled to herself at the audible gasp from behind her. There was no question the queen would rant about her unruly behavior to the king, but right now she didn't care. She was tired of the royal family trying to bully her into things. She was not a mound of dirt they could use their wet hands to mold. She was not putty. She was granite, stone that life had slowly chipped away at and formed.

She was a…a Toliver.

Her last name had never brought her pride. Growing up it had been synonymous with never fitting in, with always feeling like a minnow in a sea of hungry sharks. It always meant sadness and loss.

Weakness.

It never meant strength; and no matter how many times people told Ava she was strong, she couldn't believe it, because she was a product of her mother, who could barely find the power to breathe some days.

She had spent her entire life wanting to *not* be a Toliver.

But her mother's constant state of mourning was for a reason. She had experienced more loss in a handful of years than most people experienced in their entire existence. First her partner, the love of her life, was stolen from her. Then her parents died, one right after the other. Then, as if the universe hadn't stripped her of enough, it stole her best friend, as well.

No wonder she was afraid to live.

Yet, she had.

She did.

She *was*.

She was alive; and Ava was alive, too. She, too, had experienced loss. Loss of her father, loss of her grandparents. Loss of her second mother and subsequently her first. She lost a part of her best friend and then, more recently, pieces of herself. The person who had existed a few months ago had been ripped away from a life she'd always known and dropped into one she was still trying to figure out. There had been times—the nights of listening to Cordellia cry into the morning and sitting by Zarah's bed as illness devoured her from the inside out—when she had wanted to give up. Hell, there had been a few occasions in her time at High House when she had wanted to let go and be made into the person everyone expected.

Even if it meant becoming someone she wasn't.

But there was a reason she was still standing. And that's because she was a Toliver. She owed it to her name to remain constant, to hold fast to herself—to her lineage.

To make something of her legacy.

She would take up the crown and she would unite Havaan, and then she would do everything in her power to hold off the war she was certain was going to come.

Life had taken enough away from her.

She refused to let it take anymore.

XXXVIII.

Thankful, not for the first time for her cat-like agility, Ava managed to keep the two plates balanced on one another as the heavy door to the barn opened. She took a quick step back to avoid splattering food on the person exiting. She expected Nixon to step out, but was surprised when it was instead Levi. Sweat had soaked through his t-shirt and a thin sheen glistened on his forehead.

"Ava!" he gasped, equally as startled.

She raised an inquisitive brow. "Were you training?" she asked. She had watched the guards enough to recognize the sort of sweat Levi had worked up.

"No," he said slowly, eyeing her. "I was—"

"You don't need to lie to me, Levi. I think you should know how to defend yourself."

He smiled sheepishly. "You won't tell my parents?"

"I never saw you here," Ava replied, winking. "But you're late for lunch and your mother's in a horrid mood. Don't let her see you like that."

"When isn't she in a bad mood?" the younger prince mumbled as he stepped around her.

With a smile on her face, Ava slipped inside the barn and used her toe to close the door fully. As always, it was as hot as a furnace in the training facility, the giant fans making little difference. The air was a wall of sweat and dirt that vibrated with ripples of heat.

She made her way around the wall that acted as a short barrier and stopped at the edge. Someone had moved the portable punching bag into the center of the room and Nixon circled it, his arms jutting out repeatedly. Each swish and stab glinted in the dim halogen lights. It took a minute for Ava to realize that in his hands were two long blades. After a couple of attacks, he would slip the daggers into the band of his pants, the hilts of them sticking out over his shirt, and he'd throw punches into the bag. Randomly, he would pull one knife, other times both, and use them against the bag again.

Most of his hair had come loose from the tie and it clung to his face. Even from this distance, Ava could see the intense glow of his eyes, like a raging bonfire at the end of a dark tunnel. He bounced on his toes a few times between reps then went back to the bag, the *whop-whop-whop* of his fists echoing while the stabbing was as silent as death itself.

Finally—it could have been hours just as easily as minutes—he tossed the weapons to the ground and put his hands behind his head. His shirt, drenched with sweat, clung to the muscles beneath. Ava gulped and took a deep, calming breath. She was about to announce her presence when Nixon's gravelly voice cut over the fans.

"You can come out, Ava."

On shaky legs she stepped from the shadows and made her way across the hard-packed dirt. "How did you know I was here?" she asked, genuinely curious.

The corner of Nixon's lips lifted slightly. The hint of a smile turned her entire body into Jell-O. She needed to set the plates down immediately or he was going to be eating a literal sand-wich.

"I can feel you," he said, suddenly behind her. His voice was low and slid over her.

She put his lunch on the bleachers as calmly as possible and questioned, her voice shaking, "What do I feel like to you?" She had wondered if he could sense her nearness the way she could his; and if so, was it the same?

"You feel," he started, his words a breath down her spine, "as if someone brushed their fingertips against the back of my neck." She shivered with first his words and then with his touch as he grazed her flesh, his finger nothing more than a feather. She teetered on her heels, her back falling into his chest. If he hadn't been there to catch her, she would have shattered on the ground. Her head was spinning. She was drunk on his nearness, on the smell of perspiration and mint and laundry.

"So, cold?" she joked.

"No," he answered. "Like danger. Like temptation."

It would have been so easy to give into that temptation, to let Nixon's touch move past her arms. She was angry with Sebastian, felt abandoned by him in a way she never considered possible. It hurt. *She* was hurt. Disappointed. But even so, she wasn't sure she was ready to make him feel the same. She was a bleeding heart. She wanted Nixon, more than she wanted to breathe, but she didn't want him this way.

Not out of vengeance.

Damn my conscience, she thought the same time she whimpered. "Stop." His hands paused at her wrists and it took everything in her to say, "You have to eat," and step out of his reach. She ran her fingers through her hair, needing something to keep her hands from reaching for him, and then she turned.

Nixon's eyes were on fire, as if someone had lit a match and dropped it into his soul. His breathing came in heavy pants and Ava knew it wasn't from working out. They looked at one another for a hundred thudding heartbeats, the air crackling around her. He exhaled, the air escaping in a whoosh, and that was all it took to break the trance. He forced his eyes away from her and looked at the plates.

"You...you weren't at lunch," Ava stuttered as she tried to find herself again. "You're going to need your strength for later."

As he straddled the bottom bleacher, a devious smile moved over his lips. "Is that so?" he teased.

Just like that, things were back to normal between them.

At least as normal as things between them could be.

Ava could feel the blush creeping up her neck and over her cheeks. "Not for me," she replied as she took a seat on the ledge above him. "For the governors."

Nixon made a face. "They're not really my type."

Her lips struggled to contain the amused smirk. "They want to see the progress the guards are making."

"And you volunteered us to put on a show?" he guessed before snapping a carrot with his teeth.

Shaking her head, Ava said, "Orion did."

"Mhm," he replied skeptically. "I know what watching Sebastian and I go at it did to you."

She gawked at him, her mouth a wide O. Then she shrugged a shoulder. "I have no idea what you're talking about."

"Your lusty eyes gave it all away."

"I think you overestimate my attraction to you."

Nixon gave her a look that said *really?* but he didn't argue. Instead, he brought one of the sandwiches to his mouth and asked, "How was your meeting?" before taking a massive bite.

"Super awesome." The lie dripped with exaggerated enthusiasm. She placed her hands on her cheeks and squished her face slightly. "It was so boring," she said through fish-lips.

"I'll trade you places for a day," Nixon said. He twisted the cap off a bottle of water and downed half in a few swallows.

"Are they still not doing well?"

"No," Nixon began. "They're actually doing great. I think the demonstration helped a lot."

Ava rested her forearms on the tops of her knees and leaned forward. "So, what you're saying is that I was right?" She batted her lashes. Nixon snorted then tapped the end of her nose with his fork. She scrunched her face. He groaned. "What's wrong?" she asked, confused by the sound.

"Nothing," he said, scowling a little. "You just look…adorable when you do that."

Adorable was not the sort of word she ever thought she'd hear Nixon say. In fact, she hated when people called her such. It was too cutesy, too frilly dresses, but she liked the way it sounded coming from him.

"Eat," Ava said, nudging his plate toward him more with the toe of her shoe. "I have a meeting to get back to."

"You don't have to sit here and watch me," he said as he forked most of the potato salad into his mouth.

"I know," she replied, "but the sooner you finish eating the quicker we get to dessert." Nixon wiggled his eyebrows and she laughed. It echoed off the rafters, swirled around the blades of the fans and came back to her. It was the sound of someone who was really, truly happy.

It sounded nice, like something she wanted to hold onto.

"I'll eat," Nixon said, "if you tell me what really happened the other night." He raised an expectant eyebrow at her as he washed his food down with another swig of water.

She pulled her hair over her shoulder. "I told you what happened," she replied as she scanned for split ends. "I got too warm in the greenhouse and didn't feel well." The lie could not have sounded more like a lie. It fell flat even to her. Nixon scoffed, and she looked up at him, met his sympathetic eyes. The ring of fire was just that: his pupils eclipsing most of the flame. But even in the darkest pools she found serenity. She found understanding.

Nixon was the one person from the beginning of this crazy journey who had wanted nothing more than for her to remain resolute. His faith in her had been unwavering, even when they hadn't been on speaking terms. It was what drove her forward, pushed her when all she wanted to do was stop running. Whispered her battle cry when all she wanted to do was stop fighting. There was something between them—something past the obvious and palpable attraction—that made her want to trust him; to burden him with all her fears and lay her dreams in his hands. Because she knew they would be safe.

That *she* would be safe.

Which was why she found herself asking, "What do you think about reintroducing magic to Havaan?"

She caught him off-guard with the question and it showed in the way he choked on the last bit of sandwich. When he recovered he said, "I think a lot of lives were lost getting magic *out* of Havaan."

"Do you think we could handle it this time around?"

Nixon exhaled from his nose as he gathered his hair at the base of his neck. "I don't know," he answered honestly. "It's nothing I've ever thought about. What do you think?"

Ava took the clean fork he was offering and stabbed at her piece of cheesecake. "I think you guys would see a lot more action than you've ever expected."

"Is this something Sebastian plans on doing?" She tapped the end of her nose but said nothing as she chewed another bite. "Interesting," Nixon stretched the word. "I take it you're not a fan of this plan?"

She exhaled a lungful of irritated air. "I'm scared," she started, her emotions tugging on each word, "that what happened once will happen again. Bernadette and Sebastian think I'm crazy for believing nothing good will come from something in which nothing good came from before. I don't want to be a cynic, but I can't shake this feeling that if he moves forward with this, then I am either going to wind up standing across from him on a battlefield or beside him as we watch Havaan destroy itself.

"I just…" She worried the inside of her cheek and wrapped her arms around her waist protectively. Nixon moved to sit beside her, still straddling the bench so he could face her. His hand came to rest on her calf, his thumb stroking the bare flesh with the gentlest of touches. It set her skin alight and calmed her heart at the same time.

"I have spent my whole life afraid of failing. Of failing my mother, of looking away for four seconds and losing her forever. I'm scared of losing my *own* sanity and ending up like her." She mushed her lips together as tears wobbled on her waterline. "I'm worried about failing Zarah and never living up to the greatness she saw in me. And now I'm *petrified* of failing as queen, of being unable to change Sebastian's mind and having to watch as everything falls apart.

"Maybe I *am* selfish, but I don't want to have to shoulder that blame. I don't want to be affiliated with the consequences of Havaan getting caught up in the madness of magic again. I know it's possible it will work out, that we will handle it better the second time around. That we, as a world, will have learned from the generations before and won't repeat their mistakes. But as much as I would love to believe it wholeheartedly, I can't."

She turned to him and his hand cupped her face. He ran a rough thumb along her cheek, swiping away the tear that had dared escape. "You're definitely a cynic," he said. She laughed a shaky sound. "But I don't think your fears are unfounded. Magic changed everyone. It turned good people bad and made bad people into monsters. It took a lot of blood and sacrifice, a lot of death, to get us where we are now. Being asked to play a part in doing that again is unfair. And grounds for being terrified."

"I told him I wouldn't support him in this," Ava said. Her voice was stronger now. For some reason, confessing her fears to Nixon had unburdened from her a load she hadn't known she was carrying. It didn't take away those fears; they still settled in her stomach like snakes, slithering over one another to keep warm, but she no longer felt like they were slipping through her ribs and wrapping around her throat. "I will stand by his side when the cities burn, not because I want to, but because it will be my responsibility as his wife. But I will not hold one of his hands while the other strikes the match." Flicking away another tear she added, "I don't know what to do, Nixon. Tell me what the right choice is."

Nixon half-smiled at her. "There is, like you said, a chance it could work. Maybe if it is moderated, controlled by two people who are kind-hearted and willing to put in the work to see it succeed, then it will. But—" He put a finger to her lips when she went to argue. "I think in this situation you have to follow your heart. Your instincts. If it leads you to his side then go with sure, confident feet. If it doesn't, if it tells you to distance yourself as much as possible and to deal with the consequences later, then listen. And go *that* way with sure, confident feet. Whatever you decide, though, you will not be alone."

There it was.

The constant support and endless faith she had come to rely on before she'd even understood its importance.

"I don't deserve you," she whispered as his hand came to rest on the side of her neck. He could feel her pulse against his palm, and when she nipped his thumb the world began to collapse in on itself. They were treading dangerous territory, walking too close to the edge. Even if they had wanted to step away, there was a force keeping them tethered to the inevitable.

There was no longer any doubt that at some point they would give in. One day, they would stop fighting the pull between them and they would fall. But that day was not today.

A familiar voice cut through the tension brewing between them like a summer storm. "Avie?"

Ava groaned her frustration as Nixon's hand dropped away. Her skin was still warm from where he'd touched her, an invisible flame lingering just below the surface.

She cleared her throat and yelled, "I'm here."

A second later, Delilah came around the corner. Her brown eyes flicked between her best friend and the guard a few times. "Hey," she finally said, her attention settling on Ava.

"Hey," Ava said back as she stood.

"Sebastian sent me to find you. Your uh…your meeting is starting."

Ava nodded. "Thanks," she said while gathering the now empty plates and used silverware. As Delilah began to retreat Ava called after her. "Hold on. I'll walk with you."

Delilah paused by the wall, her hands shoved into the pockets of her tangerine-colored skirt. She was pulled in on herself in a way Ava had never seen before. She couldn't help but wonder if part of it was her doing. They hadn't had a sit-down, girl time vent fest in a while. Thinking back on the last couple of weeks, Ava couldn't remember half of what had happened. Everything before the greenhouse was a blur.

She vowed right then to carve out a chunk of time for her best friend.

"Thank you for lunch," Nixon said as he, with his arm on Ava's elbow, helped her down the bleacher.

"Thank you for listening to me whine and complain," she replied, smiling up at him.

The corner of his lips twitched and he lowered his voice so only the two of them could hear. "What I said, about you not being alone. I meant it. Regardless of what choices you make, whatever direction those choices take you, I will be by your side. I will follow you anywhere."

There was so much she wanted to say and no adequate way to say it. She really didn't deserve him. He would put himself through hell for her. He was going to have to stand behind her as she said her vows to

Sebastian. And he would take up position next to her if the time came to fight against his brother.

She wasn't sure of much in life, but she had no doubt Nixon would die for her.

Would I be willing to do those things for him?

"I appreciate you," she said, smiling. "I better see you at dinner," she added, her words half threatening.

"I get food brought to me when I don't make an appearance," he replied as he wrapped his arms around the punching bag. His muscles flexed. Something tightened in her core. "It's almost as good as breakfast in bed," he added, winking so only she could see it.

Ava couldn't help the laugh that escaped her. "Closest thing to breakfast in bed you'll get from me."

He smiled, the fullness of it making a brief and rare appearance. "Go before they decide to come in here and hold court."

"I would never do that to you. I don't think you can afford to have any of your brain cells killed by the boredom."

Nixon pushed the bag and let it swing. "I could probably use a little more room," he said as he nudged it with his fist. "Especially since you take up so much space."

She swallowed his words and turned her back to him. Dropping the pile of trash in the bin by the door, she linked her arm with Delilah's and smiled at her. The steady *whop-whop-whop* followed them out, but this time she couldn't be sure it wasn't her heart.

XXXIX.

Ava used her foot to close the door to the library and then stood there, simply reveling in the silence of the room. She would never tire of the ink and paper smell or that of the polish slicked over the wooden furniture. The sun cut across the floor in warm beams and etched leafy shadows around the room. In here, High House faded into a hum. Sometimes it felt separate from that world, allowing her to be, as well.

Day two of the Meeting of the Regions had been just as boring as day one. Yesterday, Clive had taken close to three hours regaling them with the last year in Paranick. This morning, Archie had used a little under two hours to do the same for his region. Ava hadn't known it was possible for boredom to hurt so much, but the tightness in her shoulders and the crick in her spine proved otherwise.

Fortunately, Orion was the only man left to give his report.

Unfortunately, the population of Brene was the highest of all the regions. There was something enchanting about living close to High House, apparently. Ava had lived in Brene her entire life and had never once understood the appeal.

To each their own, Ava thought as she ran her finger along the spines of the thick census books. She pulled the first one from the row and had to cradle it in both arms. There wasn't much documentation from the time before Orion, but from his first year on the throne he'd been insistent on keeping the census.

The book dropped onto the table with an echoing thud. Ava flinched, waiting for someone to come investigate, but when the door remained closed, she sighed. "Who knew five years could weigh so much?" she wondered aloud as she fell into her chair. It was still warm from earlier. She was half expecting there to be a permanent indent of her butt by the end of the weekend.

"Alright Eleanor, let's see how good you are." Ava turned the first couple of pages carefully, the paper stiff with time. The ink had begun to bleed in some places, but for the most part it was all legible. She didn't know where to begin, wasn't entirely sure she knew what she was looking for either, so she started at the most logical place: Dante.

Year three of Orion's reign began more than halfway through the massive ledger. Ava didn't know much about her father, but she did know he had died sometime within that span. If she could find a starting point, maybe she could work her way backward, finally get some answers.

"Newsome….Nichols….Nieman…Norbert…" It took some time to scan through the small, elegant font but her finger finally stumbled over the name. "Noriega." Below his last name were a few details, including his birthday, the names of his parents, and his death date. May. She had missed the anniversary of his passing and couldn't help but wonder how Cordellia had celebrated it.

As she tried to connect with her father, Ava's eyes lingered uncertainly on a word she hadn't expected. It hurt in a way she couldn't quite understand. On the line that said CHILDREN, scrawled across it in a script too beautiful to have been done by hand, it said *none*.

She rubbed at the spot above her heart.

She'd been born the second year of Orion's rule, yet had somehow gone unreported. It didn't make sense. There'd been plenty of time between her birth and his death for their names to be connected.

With more haste than the old book could handle, Ava flipped toward the end of year three. She found the T's then turned the pages until she found her last name. She paused at her grandparents and was shocked to learn they'd had not one child but two: her mother and a little boy named Samuel who had died at age four.

Yet another death that shackled Cordellia to the cemetery.

Under Ava's grandparents was her mother.

Toliver, Cordellia. BORN *13 September 2115.* DEATH   .
CHILD(REN) *Toliver, Avaleigh.*

Ava dropped to the next citizen.

Toliver, Avaleigh. BORN *19 April 2140.* DEATH   . MOTHER
Toliver, Cordellia. FATHER *unknown.*

Unknown?

The room tilted.

Cordellia had loved Dante with every fiber of her being. His death had made it nearly impossible for her to look at Ava sometimes. Too much of Dante's spirit existed in Ava's eyes and hair.

What if…

What if Dante *wasn't* her father?

Ava sat back in her chair and dug her nails into her legs. The pain kept the tears at bay. Then she stood and paced the room. Her eyes came back to the book more than once, as if she expected the words to rearrange themselves into something that made sense.

There had to be an explanation aside from the most obvious one.

Children none. Father unknown.

The words were a never-ending loop, a riddle without a solution.

At some point she made it to the couch and stared into the unused fireplace. The portrait of Orion loomed over her and she wanted nothing more than to stab his arrogant face with a fire poker. As she considered it, wondered how she could get up that high, the clock in the library chimed. It was the only clock in the house that was ten minutes fast, so she knew she had time.

Dazed, she dragged her feet across the hardwood floor and retrieved Volume One. She nestled it back in its spot on the shelf and began to make her way across the large room. The last leg of the meeting would begin soon, and she planned on using the extra time to eat her feelings. There had been the makings for ice cream sundaes in the dining room and she needed one.

Immediately.

As she reached for the handle, a singular word slithered through the keyhole. "Sir," a familiar voice said.

"What is it, Raymon?" the king's voice chimed.

"There's been a…*situation*…in Usealie." The way the guard said situation grabbed Ava's attention. She forgot about her own predicament and pressed her ear to the door.

"What sort of situation?" Orion asked, his voice low.

"The kind that would be better discussed in private."

Orion sighed and the doorknob wiggled. "Come into the library then," he said, clearly not pleased.

Ava ran across the room on as light of feet as possible and launched herself over the back of the loveseat. She settled as deeply into the cushions as she could and closed her eyes. If they moved this way and saw her, they would think she was sleeping. *Hopefully*. She heard the soft click of the latch as the door closed, then the heavy reverberations of two pairs of feet as they moved into the room. She held her breath, afraid even that would give her away.

"Tell me what has happened," Orion ordered.

Raymon exhaled. "A woman was found wandering the streets yesterday afternoon," he said.

"That hardly seems grounds for concern," the king replied. Ava had never heard him sound so grouchy, as if he'd rather be doing *anything* but dealing with the affairs of Havaan.

"It is once you find out she was beaten."

Ava bit her gasp and strained to hear the conversation better. Both men had dropped their voices to an almost inaudible level.

"Explain."

Raymon cleared his throat and then said, "She was stumbling through the market, blood dripping down her face. Her dress was torn. A couple of citizens pulled her aside until a guard could get there. When questioned, she claimed her husband was at fault. By her statement, it was not the first time he'd put his hands on her, but that this was the worst."

"What did the husband have to say?"

"When two guards entered their home, they found him sitting there, his knuckles bloody. There was also a hole in the wall where he'd slammed her head repeatedly. When asked what happened he said he was tired of being married."

There was a sudden explosion, like a wrecking ball meeting stone. Ava flinched and clenched her teeth to keep from yelping. "Damn it!" King Orion shouted as his fist met the table again. "Where is he now?"

Ava swore she could hear Raymon swallow. "He's being kept at the governor's home. There are guards stationed with him at all times."

Both men were silent for three thundering beats of a heart before Orion asked, "Why are we just hearing about it now?"

"The message carrier got here as soon as he could. I asked him to wait around to relay a message back."

The king's, "Good, good," sounded spacey, as if he were distracted. Ava tracked his pacing, holding her breath and squeezing her eyes shut each time he sounded too close. They would never believe she was sleeping now, not with the way she was trembling.

Vibrating not from fear, but anger.

"Sir?" Raymon said. He sounded unsure and maybe a little scared. Ava couldn't begin to imagine how Orion looked.

"What happened to his wife?" Orion asked finally, his tone rough. Though he hadn't raised his voice, the question bounced around in the near perfect silence.

The senior guard released a shuddering exhalation that spoke volumes. It wasn't necessary for him to say, "She died," and the confirmation did nothing to settle Ava. Tears had already begun to gather at the corner of her eyes. Things like this were not supposed to happen in Havaan. Darkness was not supposed to permeate the seams holding their country together. It happened, of course, but acknowledging it was hard to swallow. Probably more so for the king, who slumped into the closest chair. The legs of it screeched across the floor and the table creaked when he rested his elbows on it.

Finally, after what felt like a year of silence, Orion said, "Inform Archie of what has happened in his region. Tell Ava, Eleanor, and the other governors that the meeting is postponed for an hour. Then I need you to send Sebastian to me and ask the carrier to wait a few more minutes."

Raymon didn't reply, but the quiet closing assured his leaving. Ava needed the room to clear fully so she, too, could leave. Petulance and sadness warred in her veins, flowing through them like adrenaline. She wanted to hit something, preferably the man who had dug his wife's grave with his fist. Her thoughts could not help but drift to those of Juliet. Ava had sent her three letters suggesting they meet up for lunch or dinner. She'd kept them as casual as possible, in case Connor got his hands on them, but her ultimate goal was to get Juliet and her son away from him. Away from the violence and the bruises. Juliet had replied once, saying she appreciated Ava's willingness to let the past go and move forward, and that she would be in contact to set up a time to get together. That was two months ago and Ava's last letter had gone unanswered.

If she didn't know for a fact that Juliet and Connor lived in Lyyard, she would have worried it was Juliet who had been found. Still, knowing it wasn't did nothing to quell the intense hatred she felt for a man she'd never met; and the extreme grief for a woman who had suffered, and died, at his hands.

The door to the library creaked open and then closed again, the click of the lock covered by Sebastian's, "You wanted to see me?"

"We've had an incident," Orion began. He explained what had occurred, but the words felt robotic, as if it were happening to some other country, under the rule of some other king. Sebastian listened in what Ava could only assume was stunned silence.

When his father finished speaking, the prince asked, "What do you want me to do?" It wasn't sarcastic, but rather a question of acceptance, as if Orion had asked this of him more than once.

"Go to Usealie, get the man, and escort him to Nopels."

Nopels?

That couldn't be right.

Nopels was nothing more than a scare tactic. It wasn't a real place and yet…that's what Orion had said. She was sure of it. This last hour had been one surprise after another. Her stomach roiled as if she'd been on a rollercoaster all this time, the rickety cart pulling her up each crest and shoving her over each hill, only to send her into a series of continuous loops.

Nothing about this afternoon was making sense.

She pinched her arm to make sure she wasn't dreaming.

"I understand," Sebastian said flatly. No arguing. No questions.

Which meant this was not a place unfamiliar to him.

"There's a mail carrier waiting downstairs. You and Archie are to return with him."

"Okay."

"This is not good news for us, my son," Orion said as he stood. The chair sighed its appreciation.

"It never is, Father," Sebastian replied as the two men made their way across the room.

"Mention this to no one," the king warned as the door opened.

The door closed on his response, leaving her once again alone, with nothing more than the thoughts colliding with one another.

She counted to ten to make sure the coast was clear, then jumped up and hurried across the room. As carefully as possible, she pried the door open and glanced up and down the hallway. Relieved to find the area empty, she took off down the hallway as if someone were chasing her. It felt good to move, quickly at that, even for just a few seconds.

If history repeated itself, Sebastian would come down to her room before leaving. She made oblong circles in the soft carpet and tried to sort through everything she'd learned in such a short period. She pushed the information about her father—or not her father?—to the back of her mind for now. In the extra space, she shuffled the questions to which she needed answers, ranking them from most important to least.

She would demand them if it came down to it.

She had not a shred of doubt that if she hadn't been hiding in the library, she would know nothing of what had taken place in Usealie. Whether it was because the queen remained constantly uninformed of such happenings, or they didn't think she could handle it, or they wanted to protect her from the true horrors of Havaan…or the hundred other excuses Orion and Sebastian would come up with.

She was tired of being kept in the dark.

She would no longer stand there and allow them to turn off the light.

If necessary, she would bring her own matches, build her own fire, and force them to answer her questions. Or she would burn trying.

Her heart leapt to her throat when the expected knocking filled the room like a bell. She was ready for it and flung the door open before his knuckles could rap a second time. Ava said nothing, just stepped aside as Sebastian entered, the strap of his messenger bag crossed over his torso. It swelled slightly with a softness that could only be clothing.

"Going somewhere?" she asked as she closed the door then stood in front of it.

Sebastian ran a hand through his already messy locks. It was the same look he had whenever he was sent away on his secret mission. It was the look of someone who wasn't happy about it, but would do what was asked without complaint because that's what was expected of him.

"There's a situation in Usealie I need to deal with. I won't be gone longer than a day. Two at the most, but that's unlikely."

"What sort of situation?" Ava asked.

Shaking his head Sebastian answered, "It doesn't matter."

Without missing a beat Ava replied, "It never does." She made no effort to hide the sarcasm.

Sebastian sighed again, this time the one with which she was most familiar. It told her she was pushing his buttons without him having to say it. "I don't have time for this right now." He took a step toward the door and reached for the handle. With a slight shift of hips, Ava positioned herself in his way. "Get out of my way, Avaleigh," he said, leveling his gaze. He'd meant it to be threatening, but she stood up straighter and met his eyes.

"Or what?" she started. The tail of her brow rose. "Are you going to hit me?"

Shocked by the question, by the implication he would do such a thing, Sebastian took a giant step back. His eyes widened, forcing his brows to his hairline. Nothing in the look indicated he'd connected what she had said to the situation he was off to police. No part of him would ever suspect she could know about the violence that had taken place a day ago. She wasn't *supposed* to know.

It was just dumb luck that she'd been in the right place at the wrong time. How much of her time as queen would be spent that way? How many secrets would build between them until there was a wall too big to scale?

"I'll move," she offered, "if you answer a question. And you do it truthfully."

Sebastian threw his hands up. "It doesn't seem like I have much of a choice."

Welcome to my life, pal, Ava thought but did not say.

Crossing her arms over her chest and leaning against the door, she asked, "What is Nopels?"

It was not the question he had been expecting.

Where are you going? *Why* are you going? What's happened?

Those he'd been ready for, was already crafting lies on his tongue; but this...

"What do you mean?" His throat was tight, the question pushed suspiciously through the space.

"All my life, I was told it was a made-up place. A dangerous, scary place meant to terrify children into behaving. But it's real, isn't it?"

His mouth opened and closed a few times as he struggled with what to say. Finally, he nodded his head once. "The legend was partially right. It is a dangerous and very scary place, but it exists."

She was surprised Sebastian had admitted it. "What is it?" she asked eagerly.

"You said one question."

"That was my original question."

"It's a highly guarded prison of sorts," he answered finally. Short. Simple. But informative. "Can I go now?"

No matter how hard she tried, she could not keep the worry out of her voice. "Why do you have to be the one to go?"

Sebastian gave her a weak smile. "Father has sent a lot of people there. It's unsafe for him to go. If something happens to him, the consequences will be dire."

"The consequences will be dire if something happens to you, too."
As angry as she was at the prince, she didn't want to see anything bad
happen to him. He wasn't the right person for her, she knew this, but
they could be friends. Their friendship could benefit Havaan if they
found a way to look past their differences and get on the same page
with the whole magic thing.

Her page, preferably.

Just because she didn't agree with him, just because she didn't love
him like she had hoped, didn't mean she wanted unscrupulous things to
befall him. If that happened, there would be a void in her life that no
one would ever be able to fill. She had seen firsthand what that could
do to a person.

Sebastian looked at her sadly. "At least you would be free of me," he
said dully, with no conviction behind his words.

Gnawing on the inside of her bottom lip, she let it slip through her
teeth before replying. "My freedom is not worth your life."

He pushed the rebellious pieces of hair out of his eyes and adjusted
the hem of his shirt. "I appreciate the sentiment," he said. "I really have
to go."

With an exhausted sigh, Ava stepped aside. She motioned to the
handle with a flourish of her hand, as if she were presenting him the
greatest gift in history. By the way he grabbed for it, perhaps it was.
Before he could fully leave, she gripped his arm. "Please be careful,"
she whispered.

Without looking at her, he nodded. "I always am." Then, she let go
of his arm and watched him walk down the hall. He disappeared
around the corner before she closed the door again. Pressing her back

against the cold wood, she slid to the floor, just as she'd done her first day at High House.

While she waited to be summoned for the last part of their meeting, she thought back to day one.

So much had happened since then.

So much had changed.

More vicissitudes were coming. She could feel it, just as sure as she could feel each pressing beat of her heart against her ribs.

She knew without question that one of those changes—perhaps the biggest one yet—would take place by the end of the night.

XL.

Despite the moon hovering in the sky like a spotlight, the heat of the morning still hung heavy and low like a circus canopy. The air was uncomfortably thick and acidic, each inhale burning the throat a little more. The warmth caused clothes to stick to the body, yet Ava chose to sit outside, her back pressed to the railing of her balcony. The things that had been revealed earlier in the day had piled ontop of one another until they filled the rooms of High House, making it impossible to breathe. The tension in the library had been equally as suffocating after Orion told them of the incident in Zyprah.

"Sebastian and Archie have gone to sort it out," he'd said, offering no further explanation. "I assure you there is no reason to worry." When he'd delivered the last lines, his eyes had darted to Ava.

Did he suspect she knew the truth? Was he worried she would spew it like a fountain?

She'd expected Orion to confront her, but his own thoughts and worries had kept him distant. For this, Ava was grateful.

She twisted, cracking her spine. Her bones were tight, as though swollen with the secrets of the day. She was having a difficult time processing everything, no matter how many mental boxes she sorted it all into.

First there was the possibility that Dante—the man she'd been made to believe was her father—may not be. And if he *was*, why weren't they connected in the census book? What was being protected by keeping their relationship a secret?

Then there was Nopels, kept hidden for a reason Ava couldn't even begin to fathom.

About this she would ask Sebastian when he returned. Why the hush-hush? Why all the lies, the half-truths? Then, she would demand he take her there; show her what the big deal was. If it was nothing more than a prison like he said, he wouldn't put up a fight. There shouldn't be any resistance. Ava couldn't help but chuckle at the thought.

"Everything comes with resistance here," she wrote in her journal by the dying light of the day. *"Resistance and lies."* The disclosure of Nopels' existence opened a Pandora's Box of questions. How much of the story was true? Legend said the magicians who'd refused to give up their abilities had been banished there, de-tongued and their hands shackled. Was *that* part real? And if not, where had Orion sent them?

If he'd sent them anywhere at all…

There were too many unknowns. Too many missing pieces to even start seeing the big picture. When she tried to organize all her thoughts into something cohesive, the impossibility of it all began to gather, closing in around her. She needed to be outside of High House, but she also had a plan, one that required her to stick close.

She'd taken up residence on the balcony, where she had a perfect view of the backyard, from the lush green lawns and floral gardens to the greenhouse, with its broken windows and clingy vines, all the way to the training barn.

The shouts and whoops and grunts that seeped from the slightly ajar door provided an aggressive, almost primal soundtrack to her writing. In a way, it matched how she was feeling.

Outside, with the nickel-taste of heat on her tongue, she responded to Cordellia's latest letter. It seemed her mother was doing quite well, both on her own and mentally. Whatever medication Sebastian had gotten for her was doing its job. Ava would forever be thankful to him for procuring the pills, and it made her feel guilty how quick she'd been to turn on him. Perhaps one day things would be okay between them again. Never how they had been, but better than now.

At last, the guards trickled from the barn. Some were on their way home to wives and children, or comfy couches and oven-nuked frozen dinners. Others would merely disperse to their bedrooms at High House, shower off the stench and dirt of the day then collapse into bed. Even Raymon and Ramiro left as soon as training for the day was finished. Some days it was right before dinner, while other nights not until the moon had taken its place in the sky.

They all left, except for one.

Ava waited a few minutes, in case he decided to call it an early evening for once, before crossing the yard and pushing open the door. If ever a place needed to be aired out, the training barn was it. Yet there was something humbling when you entered the space. Hard work, sweat, and sometimes blood held up the walls. Years' worth of dedication and determination had packed the earth, sculpted bodies. Changed lives. It was as holy a place as Havaan had and Ava felt a sort of reverence whenever the hot air trapped inside whooshed past her like a prayer.

"Do you know where Sebastian went?" she asked as she rounded the wall. She didn't say it as if he was missing and she was inquiring his whereabouts. Instead, it was laced with conspiratorial intent, his location a secret she was about to disclose.

Nixon shook his head as he continued to loop a thick cord around his hand and elbow. "I have no clue."

"He went to Zyprah," Ava said. She made her way to him with slow, deliberate steps, dragging the toe of each shoe across the dirt. "Do you know why?"

"Again, no clue. I have a feeling you're going to tell me, though."

"A woman was beaten to death by her husband." Nixon's thick brows rose toward the wavy pieces of hair resting on his forehead. "Sebastian had to go and take the man to prison. To Nopels."

Ava watched Nixon's face for any signs of change, a twitch of surprise or acknowledgement. She wanted to know if he knew the truth about Nopels as well, or if they—his family—had left him in the dark all these years. The way his lids dropped to half-mast told her he didn't believe what she had just said.

Which meant he didn't know, either.

"Nopels isn't a real place," he dragged out as if questioning her sanity.

Nodding once, Ava replied, "That's what I thought, too. But Sebastian confirmed today that it's real. What it is, beyond a maximum-security prison, I don't know. But it exists in some form."

Nixon let out a stunned breath. "Well shit," he finally said. He ran his hands through his hair and rested them on the top of his damp locks. The bottom of his shirt lifted, flashing a thin line of golden skin. Ava swallowed and raised her eyes to his. She knew, from the flare of his nose and bob of his Adam's apple, that she was giving him lusty eyes.

"Like something you see?" His voice dropped an octave, making it even deeper. Enticement dripped from the tail of each letter and flowed toward her in dark, smoky curls.

"Of course," she replied.

Nixon's lips twitched, a small smile crossing them as he gripped the bottom of his shirt. "I can take it off so you can be sure."

Her throat went dry. There was a ball of "yes" and "please do" and "take it off!" lodged there, but she swallowed the lump then clicked her tongue in disappointment. "Unfortunately, I didn't come here to ogle you. It's a shame, really. It's definitely a body worth idolizing." Nixon grinned and it nearly stopped her heart. "I need something from you," she said, all joking erased from her tone. "I want you to train me."

His head cocked and an eyebrow curved. "What?"

"Not like you train the guards," she began, "but like you trained Levi. Basic self-defense techniques."

Nixon looked at her curiously, and then his face shifted. It wasn't a look she understood until he asked, "Is there a reason you feel you need to be trained?" His voice was rough, scratchy, as if the idea of her needing to defend herself caused him physical pain.

Taking a step forward, her hands out in front of her, she shook her head repeatedly. "No, no, no. It's nothing like that," she assured. He visibly relaxed and she dropped her arms. "It's just…" She laughed her frustration. She'd practiced what she was going to say to him, but Nixon made her forget her fears and sadness and filled those missing spaces with peace. Calm. A rightness she'd never experienced before.

Instead of looking at him, she looked over his shoulder at the wooden walls that had started to warp from the heat. She thought about all the things she didn't find attractive—battered wives and bruised vows, death of true love and the heartbreak that followed—and then she returned her eyes to his and tried again.

"That woman in Zyprah probably thought she didn't have a reason, either. But maybe if she'd been able to defend herself, just a little, she wouldn't be where she is now. I don't want to end up like her, dead because I was told I didn't *need* to learn to fight for myself. We're made to believe it isn't true, but there *are* monsters in Havaan, Nixon. They live in the shadows and they walk the streets and they can strike at any time."

"You will never end up in a situation where you have to defend yourself," Nixon replied. "You will always have more than one of us with you."

"I know that, but...I don't want to risk it. I want to be able to take care of myself if, for whatever reason, someone else can't." Ava shrugged. "If you don't want to, if you don't feel comfortable doing it, it's fine. I can ask Raymon or Ramiro or...anyone else, I suppose." She looked up at him through her lashes, her lips twisted coquettishly. "I just thought I would offer you the chance to break rule number two."

Nixon growled from low in his throat. It was a carnal sound and sent a shiver up her spine. "I can think of a million better reasons to put my hands on you than attacking you."

"That's because you're a heathen," she joked, winking. Then she gave him her best puppy eyes and took a step closer. She toyed with his fingers and whispered, "Please." She saw the very moment his resolve crumbled and she beamed up at him before he verbally agreed.

"When do we start?" she asked excitedly.

"Right now," Nixon replied. This time it was her turn to be surprised.

"Right *now?*"

Nixon raised a brow. "Unless you have something more important to do?"

She shook her head. "No, it's just…you've been training all day. I figured you'd be exhausted."

"I had a good lunch," he said. "And dinner."

Ava hadn't. She'd skipped lunch for information that had only led her to more questions. They'd smothered her appetite and made her unable to do anything but nibble on her dinner. She wasn't hungry though, at least not for food. A nervous excitement rushed through her blood and quelled her need to eat.

"Is that why you asked me late at night?" Nixon teased. "Because you figured I'd be so tired I wouldn't be able to turn you down?"

"Of course not. I had no doubt you would—"

Ava jumped back as Nixon rushed her. Before she could blink, he was behind her, one arm wrapped tightly around her waist. She had no time to release a startled yelp before his hand covered her mouth.

"Get free," he said casually, though there was a bit of command to his voice.

"Oy cat," she mumbled into his hand.

He chuckled, the sound vibrating against her back. "What?" he laughed.

She tapped at his hand and he pulled it back enough for her to speak. "I said I can't. That's what you're supposed to be training me to do, remember?"

"Your instincts are telling you to fight, right?" She nodded. "To kick and claw and do whatever you can to break my hold. But—" He slid his hand back up, covering her mouth once again. With his lips brushing the outer shell of her ear, he whispered, "If I want you bad enough, I will have you." Ava inhaled deeply, her body pressing back against his instinctively. Part of her was certain he wasn't speaking just as her assailant. "Your kicking and squirming will be annoying, sure, but by this point I've accounted for your weight and how to use your movements against you. You're going to tire yourself out long before you exhaust me. However, one of the hardest forces to work against is dead weight. I know you're going to want to fight, but fight smart. If you can—"

Midsentence, Ava went limp, using the weight of her body against him. He grunted at the unexpected change and shifted his feet to accommodate. "Very good," he praised. "I'm going to have to adjust my grip and when I do, that's the best time for you to go on the defensive. When a person is caught off guard, they're vulnerable, and that is when you should attack. If you can, use your elbow and aim for the face as hard as possible. The nose is one of the most sensitive parts of the body and if you can break it, you're going to break the grip your assailant has on you. Their instinct will be to protect their nose from further harm. If you can't get to the nose," he continued, "then aim for the throat. And then get out of there. Scream. Run, but never in a straight line. Keep your attacker as off balance as you can. Got it?"

Ava nodded and said into his hand, "Gaht dit."

"Good," he replied as he released her. "Now turn around and walk toward me, as if you're out and about enjoying a Sunday stroll."

Laughing, Ava did as she was told. She sashayed her hips for added effect. "I don't know how many strolls you thin—"

He was on her again before she could finish her sentence. Even though she knew it was coming, it still surprised her, and her fight or flight instincts kicked in. But she pushed them down and instead let Nixon drag her a foot or so before she sagged into a bag of bones. Nixon was ready for it this time, but he still adjusted as if he hadn't been. Ava followed his instruction, and while she refused to *actually* drive her elbow into his throat, she pressed against it enough that she could feel his words when he said, "Excellent. You're a quick learner."

"I have a good teacher," she retorted as she reluctantly stepped from his grip. "Again," she demanded.

Nixon nodded firmly as she began her prowl to him again.

An hour later, she'd learned three variations of the maneuver. Whether or not she'd be able to successfully execute them in the real world was yet—and hopefully never—to be seen.

She'd even managed to throw Nixon off his game, slipping out from his arms as if she'd been practicing for months. It happened only once, but it was enough to make her proud. She would have never thought, in her wildest dreams, she would be learning self-defense skills from one of the king's guards. She was also aware of the risks she was taking in doing so. Each time he grabbed her, each time his hand slid over her stomach and she was pulled against his body, it became more difficult to focus on the task and not the way they fit together.

"I think that's enough for tonight," Nixon said when he released her the final time. They were both covered in sweat, a sheen coating on their skin, and their breaths came in quick pants.

Who knew making yourself dead weight could be so exhausting?

Dramatically, Ava slumped onto the hard ground and landed on her back, her arms and legs out as if she were going to make a dirt angel.

"You alive down there?" Nixon chuckled as he grabbed the last two bottles of water from the cooler. The ice had long ago melted, leaving the bottles submerged in a shallow pool. He flicked the lukewarm droplets from his hands and onto Ava.

"Can't move. Might need CPR." She opened one eye and smiled up at him before closing it again. The hard-packed earth felt nice. She lifted her hips, trying to ease the tension in her lower back. As she lowered them, the insides of her eyelids darkened even more and when they snapped up, Nixon's face was mere inches away. Her lungs froze at the intensity of his eyes. Strands of hair fell over his face like a black curtain, making him look even more dangerous. His lips were parted slightly and she could see the very edge of his teeth. It was too similar to the way she and Sebastian had been on the beach. The reminder made her heart hurt.

As Nixon leaned closer, his mouth a fraction from hers, she put her hands on his chest and pushed. "We can't," she whispered, desperation clinging to each word. She wanted to let go, to free-fall into Nixon so bad it was a physical ache. But she couldn't—not here, not like this. It wasn't even guilt stopping her—she felt none of that—but something she couldn't identify right then.

Very soon, she would recognize it as fear.

She shifted her gaze from Nixon's face, unable to stand the look of defeat marring it.

He exhaled his frustration, the warm breath caressing her neck. "Why do you keep fighting what's between us?" he asked through clenched teeth. The pain was evident even in his voice. *There* was the remorse she'd been missing a few minutes ago. "Can't you tell it's killing me having you so close but never close enough?"

"I'm sorry," she forced out. "I don't want to hurt you. I don't want—"

Nixon sat up and kneeled between her knees. His hair was a wavy mess that brushed against his working jaw. Ava pushed herself upright, using her arms to support herself.

"You're so good at knowing what you don't want, Ava, but what *do* you want?"

Ava didn't know how to answer him. There were too many things to list, and none that would comfort him. Instead, she shrugged and said, "I don't know."

They regarded one another. The rings of his irises glistened like honey from a hive then dulled like a hand covering the beam of a flashlight. Pushing his hair away from his face, he stood in one fluid motion. "You were right," he said flatly. "I've been at this all day. I'm going to go to bed." From her spot on the ground, she just nodded. He said nothing more as he walked past her.

"I'm sorry," she called out. She'd said the words so many times at High House, apologized for so many things, at this point they were becoming meaningless.

"Turn out the lights when you leave," Nixon replied as his feet continued to carry him away. She heard the door slide open on its tracks and then slam shut, the sound reverberating through the empty barn. Taking slow, deliberate sips of her water, Ava remained seated until her body began to ache and her legs to tingle from loss of feeling. Finally, with a heavy heart and strained muscles, she pushed herself up and dusted dirt from the back of her pants. All the adrenaline had dripped out of her body through each bead of sweat now soaked into her shirt or splattered on the ground.

She wanted—*needed*—to marinate in the bathtub and thirty minutes of pure silence.

Hell, she would take fifteen minutes if it gave her enough time to shut off the thoughts in her head. If it allowed her to put her doubts in time-out and quell all the questions, the unknowns, the what-ifs.

As she turned off the lights, closing the gym down for the next twelve hours, two particular what-ifs followed her back to the house.

What if I did stop fighting?

What if I finally got what I wanted?

XLI.

Ava was undressed by the time she crossed the threshold into her bathroom, dirt-covered workout clothes shed like a second skin in a trail across her bedroom floor. As the tub filled with water, the steam fogged the mirror. Wiping a face-sized space clean, Ava scrutinized her reflection. She tried to see what everyone else saw, the parts of her they considered beautiful.

The pieces that would make someone as honorable as Nixon willing to betray his best friend.

She'd never considered herself something worth looking at. Nothing stood out, except for the blue of her eyes. She'd always been told she had her father's eyes, but were they the eyes of Dante Noriega or someone else? Some man who was an even bigger stranger than the one her mother mourned.

The vapor continued to mist around the room and filled the clean spot on the mirror again, distorting her features. Features of which she still didn't understand the appeal. She shrugged and stepped into the bath. Her body broke the surface as she sank into the almost too hot water. She skimmed her palms along the top, making tiny waves that tickled her palms. If she closed her eyes, she could almost bring back the feeling of Nixon's body against hers.

"No," she said to herself, shaking her head as if to magically erase the thoughts. This is exactly what she *didn't* want—*Yeesh, Nixon was right.* She wanted peace, silence. A brain void of who her father was, of

Nopels, of violence and secrets and lies. And especially of Nixon. Of all the things she had on her mind, he was the hardest to avoid.

On a deep breath, she submerged herself fully underwater. One reason she loved the clawfoot tub was its length. It was long enough to encompass her full height, as if it had been built with her specific measurements in mind. Maybe it was. Maybe, while she'd been preparing for High House, the royal family had been preparing for her.

She couldn't help but wonder at what point would she disappoint them all?

The water settled around her like a liquescent coffin, the echoing rush of stillness filling her ears. For the next thirty seconds, all she heard was the swishing of the water as it tried to settle and the steady barroom of her heart. Sound, or lack thereof, was intensified as if being played over a microphone at a grand pavilion.

It was exactly what she needed.

Her hair moved around her like octopus tentacles and when she breathed out she could hear each *pop-pop-pop* of the bubbles. She stayed submerged until her lungs burned, begging for oxygen. Even then, she remained hidden until her eyes hurt from the pressure and her body felt as light as the air it was being refused.

Coughing, she came up finally.

Water splashed over the sides of the tub and splattered onto the tiled floor. She leaned her head against the porcelain, now warm to the touch, and counted to three hundred. She focused on nothing more than the numbers, filled her head with a steady rhythm as they danced across her closed eyes like little sheep. When she reached the end, she finally forced herself up and out, her hands gripping the edge of the bathtub.

She tugged on a pair of faded shorts—the hem of the leg holes frayed from too many washings—and an oversized t-shirt before stepping into her bedroom. The steam billowed around her feet, holding her in place.

No, that wasn't what locked her legs. It was the white dress hanging over the French veranda door like a curtain.

Had it been there when she'd first walked in?

She forced her feet to move, willed them to take one heavy step and then another. There was a barrier keeping her from reaching the gown, but she fought against it until she was close enough to comb her fingers through the frills and lace. Pinned to the corset-like bodice was a note, the words scrawled in a flourishing calligraphy she knew all too well.

Avaleigh,

With the days toward your wedding nearing closer, perhaps seeing my dress will inspire you to begin thinking about yours. -Bernadette.

Ava ripped the note from the safety pin and let it flutter to the ground. Bolts of panic shot through her and she bit her lip to keep from crying out. She sank to the edge of the bed and ran her palms up and down the top of her legs. Her eyes, which she could not pry from the dress, filled with tears, no matter how many times she blinked them away. The twill unraveled and made its way across the room, tying itself into a noose around her neck.

But then her brain, which had moments ago been obsessed with ones and fives and hundreds, began playing the reel of all the times Nixon's hands had been on her skin, his fingertips grazing her neck. It reminded her of each time his lips had hovered within kissing distance of her own and the way those same lips smiled her name. The hangman's knot loosened until she could breathe again.

This is my future, she thought.

Suddenly, she could think of nothing but Nixon.

Replayed the dreams she'd had of him until they felt like memories.

She paced the room, laid in bed, brushed her teeth, and paced some more, all the time keeping watch of the dress, as though it would crawl off the hanger and wrap itself around her. It was gaudy, with too many layers of fluff. Ava hated it. Wanted to burn it and draw warrior marks on her face with the ashes.

"Damn it," she whispered as her nails dug into her sides.

Before she knew it, she was hurrying down the hallway, the teeth of the key biting into her palm. The discomfort kept her focused, drove her forward. Even if she'd wanted to turn back, it was too late as she shoved the skeleton key into the lock. The bolt slid easily and she pushed the door open, stepping inside the room before anyone spotted her.

Ava had never been inside any of the bedrooms down this hall, not even Sebastian's. The one in which she now found herself was a mass of dark oak, hunter green and heather grey. It was clean and organized, the large space overtly masculine. The only light was from an array of white candles staggered across the windowsill, the wax dripping and hardening on the ledge before it reached the bare floor. There was a faint hint of cotton and mint in the air, which did nothing to eliminate the desire clawing at her stomach as though she were famished.

In a way she was.

Starved for Nixon in a way she'd never yearned for another.

The bed was large and, unlike hers, made. The corners were tucked neatly in place and the pillows arranged along the head. Four wooden beams holding up the bed frame touched the ceiling. She was running fingers along the t-shirts hanging in the closet, most with the king's crest sewn into the sleeves, when a sound she hadn't noticed—the running of water—stopped abruptly. In the few seconds between the shower turning off and the bathroom door opening, she debated leaving. She could slip out, go back to her own bedroom, and he would never know she'd been here…But licentious hunger held her in place.

The door to the bathroom swung open, a wave of steam escaping at the same time. The light turned off and then Nixon stepped out.

Everything around her faded away, all her attention zeroed in on the man before her.

Astonishment left her in one breath. The sound drew his eyes to her. Immediately, they blazed like gasoline fed to an inferno. His nostrils flared. His jet-black locks were combed away from his face and lay against the back of his neck. The ends curled upward like baby hair. He was all muscle, formed and shaped by hard work. When she finally made it to his face again, he looked startled, his features lifted in surprise. Then they sank, pulled by confusion.

"Ava?" He said her name as though it were impossible that *she,* of all people, would be standing in his bedroom. She smiled sheepishly and waved. *Slick.* "What are you doing here? How did you *get* in here?"

She swallowed her nerves and held up her key ring. "Skeleton key," she answered, as if that would explain everything. He turned his head slightly and regarded her from the side of his eye. He didn't speak, and Ava realized he was waiting for her to explain herself.

Her fingers twisted around one another and her gaze dropped to the floor. *Speak,* the voice in her head commanded the same time she said, "You." She raised her eyes back to his and stumbled over her words. "You asked me what I want, and the answer is you. It has been since the night of the gala. But I am terrified of the consequences, because I want you beyond just your body." She couldn't help but trace the perfectly defined parts of him with her eyes. Her lusty eyes. "By all the stars, it's a great body," she whispered, more to herself than anyone else. The corner of Nixon's mouth twitched in amusement.

Smiling a little, she continued. "I've tried to resist the pull between us because I know that if we collide, it'll be catastrophic. We will not be the only ones affected and I just...I don't want to hurt anyone." Her voice was sad. It trembled with the underlying anxiety of what her choice would ultimately mean. "But I can't fight it anymore. I want you, and I think if I don't have you I might die."

Nixon took slow strides, but he still crossed the room in less than four. Ava, her back against the door, inhaled sharply as his hands rested on the sides of her head, his arms caging her in. She gave him a look that left no room for misinterpretation.

"If we do this," Nixon said, his voice raspy, "there is no going back." Cupping her face, he traced her bottom lip with his thumb. "I will not be able to let you go, and you will have to kill me to get rid of me."

With hands that shook as though she were holding a quaking Earth, she let her fingers trace the ridges of his stomach. Ava raised her eyes to meet his, and in his returned stare she saw the same pining she felt.

"Are you going to stand there and try to talk me out of this," she whispered, "or are you finally going to kiss me?" Her teeth nipped his thumb. Anticipation brewed in the room, swirled like the layers of a wedding dress, but this time it didn't create shackles. Instead, it chased away all the doubt and fear she'd been harboring the last couple of months.

The last couple of hours.

Nixon ran a finger down the side of her face to her chin. With two fingers, he tilted her face up toward him. His lips, like they'd done so many times before, hovered over hers with barely enough room for a breath. "I'm not trying to talk you out of anything," he said. "I just want—"

"Shut up, Nixon." As the words left her mouth, she fisted his hair with both hands and pulled him down. His mouth sealed hers and he swallowed the satisfied sound that escaped. Her arms encircled his neck, deepening their kiss.

This was what they had been waiting for.

She had not been lying when she'd said the consequences of their surrender would be dire. If their indiscretion was discovered it would cause a rift in their lives too grand to repair. Which is why, as Nixon carried her to his perfectly made bed, their lips never parting, they both knew tonight would have to remain a secret. No shouting about it from the bleachers of the training barn or gossiping about it with her girlfriends. No bragging to his best friend about his conquest or memorializing it in the pages of her journal.

There could be no mention of it, which, if he kept kissing her the way he was, wouldn't be a problem. Ava wouldn't have the ability to speak ever again. Yet she would willingly give him her last breath, just as surely and easily as she was about to give up herself.

Delilah's words filled her mind: *"Don't you think you should tell him? What if he's expecting a virginal wife? He's going to be a little disappointed when he goes to—"* She'd been talking about Sebastian at that time but they still rang true.

A bit of apprehension leaked out when Ava whispered, "Nixon," breaking the connection of their lips. When he focused on her, his eyes were wild, like a raging forest fire hell-bent on destroying everything in its path. He looked like a man possessed. His hair stood up and was twisted in places where her fingers had plunged. The tresses were as soft as she'd always imagined.

"I'm not a virgin," she blurted. Her face heated with shame; not that she had given herself to someone before, but that she couldn't give that part of herself to Nixon first.

He smiled down at her. "That's okay," he reassured. His teeth grazed the edge of her bottom lip and he mumbled, "Neither am I."

Ava laughed, and any reservation she'd been holding onto left as his mouth came down again. This time there was less haste. Now that the initial first kiss was out of the way, they took their time memorizing one another. Her fingers got lost in his hair and her mind in what was finally happening.

Emotions ricocheted through her as though she were a pinball machine at an old arcade.

Except this was no game.

There was not a single thing in Havaan that could compare to this moment. She had known from their first encounter that he would be the end of everything she thought she knew.

She had not been wrong.

XLII.

Night still blanketed the room the first time she woke. Hung-over with sleep, her surroundings were hazy and unfamiliar. Shadows that shouldn't be there now existed and the bed on which she laid was too firm. She tried to sit up, but something anchored her around the waist. When she looked down at the tanned arm, the previous hours rushed back.

She rolled as much as his arm would allow and studied Nixon's features by the glow of the nearly full moon shining through the window. He had never been this vulnerable before, and for the first time since she'd met him he looked…peaceful. Like the morning after a tornado, when memories have been reduced to nothing more than rubble, but the tumultuous grey sky becomes the purest blue.

Nixon was not only the eye of her storm, but also the calm which followed.

The shadow of his lashes raked across his cheek and meshed with the grains of his stubble. His hair lay across his face like ink spilled from a well. She had never found him so beautiful in all his delicate manliness.

Something stirred inside of her and the intensity of it was almost painful. The realization of her feelings for him was too enormous to grasp, to even think about in her state of mind. Instead, she settled back into his arms, her slender fingers lacing with his.

His arm tightened around her waist. "Mine," he whispered, as he kissed her shoulder.

Smiling to herself, she brought their joined fists to her mouth. "Yours," she replied just as softly, her lips brushing one of his knuckles before she was pulled back into a dream that, for once in her life, couldn't compare to reality.

When she woke again, it was in her own bed. The cloudlike mattress curved around her body like a warm, fluffy hug. Before dawn, when color was just beginning to bleed into the horizon, she'd reluctantly untangled herself from a still-sleeping Nixon and sneaked back to her room before the rest of High House yawned awake.

Stretching, she took inventory of all the aches and pains. Some were from being dragged around the gym like a bag of bricks, but the others—the ones reaching beyond bone and muscles—were from the greatest mistake she'd ever made. The emptiness she felt when Nixon wasn't around became a steady, dull throb in her soul.

Breakfast would be starting in a little less than an hour, which meant she had just enough time to shower and make herself semi-presentable before Sebastian came to walk her down.

"No," she reminded herself. "Sebastian is still gone." *Sebastian is always gone,* she thought bitterly as she tossed the blankets aside. She glanced down at the beautiful silk robe wrapped around her body. It was black with white and pink cherry blossoms printed throughout. When she stood, it hit just below her knees and the neckline plunged to a degree that would cause even Delilah to blush. Then she remembered she had snagged it from the back of Nixon's closet, her clothing discarded somewhere in the darkness of his room. At that time, it was the least inconspicuous thing she could think to grab; no one would suspect anything if she was discovered tiptoeing through the halls in a woman's robe. But now that she was conscious, she was a little confused.

Mainly as to why Nixon was in possession of such a thing.

Shrugging off the garment, she stepped into the shower and washed the transgressions of her night down the drain. As she conditioned her hair, she realized something was missing…something which should exist but didn't.

"Do you feel guilty?" Nixon would ask her later.

"I feel guilty that I don't feel guilty," she would reply, and he would agree.

In the present, she dressed in a pair of high-waisted khaki shorts, a black and white Aztec printed tank-top that was an inch longer than a crop-top, and a thin red cardigan that flared out behind her like a cape. She slipped her feet into a pair of strappy sandals, folded the silk robe over her arm, and headed out of her room.

Delilah stepped into the hall at the same time and smiled at her, the pull of her lips slow and lazy, laced with lingering lassitude. It would take D a couple of hours to fully wake up, even if she were dressed to the nines with a full face of makeup. Which, she was.

"'Morning," she yawned. She ran her fingers through her hair, adding some volume to the crown while the rest fell flawlessly into place.

"Good morning," Ava replied.

"Where were you last night?" D asked as her best friend approached.

Ava's eyes widened a fraction. "Why? What?" she asked a little too quickly.

"Last night?" Delilah's brown eyes were full of suspicion, even though her tone was nonchalant. "I went to your room to check on you and you weren't there."

The two women began walking down the hall, their steps dragging. "Oh," Ava started. "I um...I couldn't sleep," she continued, which was true. "So, I went down to the library to do a little research and I crashed. I woke up there this morning and crept back to my room a few hours ago."

Ava hated the way the untruth flowed so easily from her lips. She was not the kind of person who lied, and *never* to her best friend. Delilah was the *one* person Ava had always been honest with, even when it stung. That was the sort of relationship they'd had from day one, when six-year-old Delilah had asked if she could stay the night at Ava's house.

"Probably not," little Ava had replied.

"Why not?" D had asked. Then, she hadn't been tainted by the pretty lights of Typhony, and the question was asked with innocent curiosity.

"My mom is sick." Even at that age Ava was aware of her mother's disorder, was conscious of how it would make their family look. She'd known she needed to keep it a secret from as many people as possible.

"Maybe when she's better," Delilah, with her waterfall of pink hair, had said. She'd been such an adorable child, one of those kids who were destined to skip the awkward phase and rocket straight into her inevitable beauty. Which is exactly what she had done.

Little Ava had shrugged. "She's been sick for a while. I don't know if she'll ever get better."

"Is it contagious?"

Unruly curls bouncing, Ava shook her head. "No. She's just been really sad since my dad died."

There was an understanding no child should possess when Delilah said, "My mom was sad when my dad left, too. He just packed up in the middle of the night and never came back. That bastard."

Ava had never heard that word, but any time she thought back on the exchange, it always made her giggle. It was probably something Celeste had said multiple times around her impressionable daughter. He really had been a bastard, though.

"That's okay. I'll just ask my mom if you can stay with me," Delilah had said, her purple pencil case swinging in her small hand.

"No," Ava had refuted. "I'll ask mine." Two things happened that afternoon. One, it was the moment Ava realized she wanted a life outside of her mother's illness; and two, she made her first and only best friend.

And now she was lying to her. A lie Delilah seemed to accept.

That was until she glanced at Ava's arm. "How did you get Nixon's robe?"

Ava couldn't help the way her eyes lowered. "How do you know it's Nixon's?"

Shrugging, Delilah said, "I saw it in his closet when I was in his room one day."

Her head was spinning. "When were you in Nixon's room?" Ava asked. She tried to keep the jealousy from her tone, but this was something Delilah had never mentioned. This was the sort of thing you told your best friend, like you told your best friend about your mother's incurable sadness.

Like you told your best friend when you were falling for someone…

Perhaps Ava wasn't the only one with a secret.

Delilah shrugged again, the motion full of indifference. "When you and Seb were off on your tour, I sort of invited myself to hang out, thought maybe I could convince him there could be something between us. As you can see though, it didn't work. How did *you* get it?"

This time, it was Ava's turn to make a noncommittal movement. "I woke up covered with it. I was going to take it to breakfast to see if I could find its rightful owner, but I'll check with Nixon first. As long as you're sure it belongs to him."

"I mean, I don't think it *belongs* to him, unless he has a habit of dressing in women's clothing. But I'm pretty sure it's the same one I saw."

Ava smiled at her best friend as they reached the top landing of the staircase. "Good enough for me. I'm going to go and drop it off. I'll see you at breakfast."

"Are you sure?" Delilah asked. Ava halted at the coating of sadness on the words.

"Am I sure of what?"

"That you'll make it to breakfast. There have been multiple times when you've *said* you'll see me there and well...you don't."

There was a deafening sound of Ava's heart breaking. She *had* been unintentionally neglecting Delilah. While it wasn't on purpose, Ava still felt bad. Yes, Delilah had wanted this more than Ava, but that didn't mean she wasn't being affected by all the changes, as well. She, too, had been pulled from her family and dropped into a completely different life. Ava was Delilah's anchor to her old one, and lately Ava had done a shitty job of keeping her best friend close.

"I will be there unless something comes up," Ava promised. Because it was possible that between point A and point B she would be intercepted two or three times and ultimately never make it to the dining room. At least this way, if she *didn't* make it, it wouldn't be another lie. "But I'm starving so I'm going to do my best."

Delilah nodded. "I'll make you a plate just in case. And if I don't see you down there, it'll be waiting in your room."

"Thanks, D," Ava replied, smiling although it wasn't totally convincing.

A few steps down, Delilah turned back to her. "What are you wearing tonight?"

Ava raised a confused brow. "Tonight? What's tonight?"

Incensed, Delilah sighed. "The Governor's dinner? The dance?"

"Shit," Ava groaned. "That's tonight?" Delilah gave her a look that could mean nothing less than *duh*. Ava chewed her lip anxiously. "It's been a crazy couple of days. A lot has happened." Delilah looked around, her eyes darting from wall to wall and then she nodded once. Her lips were drawn together, two rose-colored lines that kept her from saying whatever was knocking behind them. But Ava understood the look: *how nice of you to keep your best friend in the loop.*

"I want to tell you about it," Ava said, hoping to convey as much honesty as she could. She really did want to fill D in, at least on her maybe-not-father.

And maybe Nopels.

Not so much the whole Nixon thing. That she would take to her grave.

"Well, you know where to find me," Delilah replied. She gave a weak smile at the end.

Ava watched as her best friend made her way down the stairs, catching up with Tavion, a very handsome guard from Oxphyn, at the bottom. She giggled at something he said. By the way his eyes scanned her from head to toe, one would have to be blind to not see how drawn Tavion was to Delilah. Ava was envious of the way Delilah could just flip between masks. She wanted to be able to stop caring about something in the blink of an eye; or at least *appear* like she didn't care. But she had been blessed—all sarcasm intended—with a face that made it impossible to betray her feelings. Sometimes it was nice, but more often than not, it just got her into trouble.

Ava made her way down the guy's hall. Music played from behind a couple of doors, the different notes and melodies tripping over one another. Thumps and bangs echoed through the empty hallway as the men began to rise for the day. She knocked on Nixon's door a few times. While she waited for him to answer, she traced her fingers along the pale flowers on the robe, the sheeny fabric soft beneath her fingers. It reminded her of the way Nixon's hair had felt as she'd combed her fingers through it, trying to get to every part of him. She had wanted to absorb every molecule of his being so that she would always have a piece of him.

She exhaled through her nose. "Get a grip, you feen," she scolded under her breath a second before the door swung open.

Nixon's eyes were on fire. His hair fell in waves around his handsome yet fraught face.

"Hi," she said, then cleared her throat when the word got stuck. "Hi," she said again, clearer this time.

He replied, the word deep and gargled, "Hey." Then he stepped aside, a silent invitation that Ava accepted. "You weren't here when I woke," he said as he closed them in. Now that the night had been chased away, so too had the shadows and she could pick out the features of his room more clearly. She hadn't noticed the wooden chair in the corner last night, her discarded clothing folded neatly in a pile. His bed was made again, the corners crisp and the pillows arranged.

"I wasn't sure if Sebastian would be home this morning," she offered as explanation to his statement. Nixon nodded and raked his nails down his face. The sound against his stubble was like sandpaper. Her skin tingled in memory of the scruff against her skin.

"I brought this back." She held the robe out in front of her, hoping to distract herself from the memories reeling through her mind. "Whoever it belongs to will probably want it at some point." She tried for light, casual jest but even she could hear the sharp edges of her words. She had no right to be angry about another woman warming his bed. Hell, she was practically engaged to someone else. But there was never a time when she *wasn't* jealous about the women he'd already met and those he would meet in the future. She already hated his wife.

Almost as if in slow motion, Nixon took the garment, and once it was in his hands he looked down at it as though he'd never seen it before. "No," he started, his voice thick. He walked over to the bed and sat on the edge of it, his fingers dancing over the flowers as hers had done moments ago. Finally, his eyes moved to Ava's and her breath caught in her chest. He looked so...*sad*. She wanted to cry for him, though she had no idea why.

"It was my mother's," Nixon added.

"Oh," Ava said. She felt like an idiot. After a few silent seconds, she moved across the room and climbed onto the hard mattress. Her back rested against one of the pillows as she faced him, her legs tucked under. She asked, "Do you want to tell me about her?"

Considering her question, it looked as though he was going to close himself off, but then he said, "Would you like to hear about her?"

"Of course," she breathed out in one overly excited breath. Her soft smile at the end was returned and it melted her heart.

Nixon stood and walked over to the closet. Ava watched as he hung up the robe, hiding it in the back of his clothes, and then returned to the bed. He sat across from her, using one of the sturdy posts to rest upon. When he began speaking, his voice was reverent, dreamlike but also somewhat disconnected. Ava knew the tone all too well.

He was still mourning.

"My mother was an amazing woman. Both of my parents, from what I can recall of my father, were great people. When Orion declared war on the magicians, my father was one of the first to volunteer. They were best friends even before secret meetings and battle preparations were ever a part of their life. My mother always spoke of him as a brave warrior, a loyal man, which of course meant my father would be a part of the war whether he agreed with it or not. For two days he fought, dragged fallen brothers and sisters to safety in between assaults." Nixon's chest expanded as he inhaled deeply. Ava used the break in his words to move closer. She offered him her hand, and after tracing her palm a couple of times, he locked their fingers together and squeezed.

"Even though Orion's side ultimately won, there were lives lost on both fronts. My father's included. My mother was distraught. I was only two and a half when he died, but I remember her scooping me up and squeezing me so tight I thought I was going to suffocate. I remember the way her tears fell onto my face and how she just screamed his name repeatedly until there was nothing left of either of our voices."

"It sounds like loss has touched both of us," she said quietly.

Nixon gave her a sympathetic smile then leaned forward and kissed her. She sighed as their lips connected. Kissing Nixon would forever and always be her favorite thing. She would gladly give up every morsel of sweet treats if it meant his lips would never be too far away.

When they separated, he continued, though more breathlessly than before. "My mother pulled herself together after his death. She was strong like that. She had other lives to worry about." He paused. "I had a sister. Did you know that?" Ava shook her head. "She was two years older than me. Her name was Arabella and she was very kind. I always wanted to be like her and she encouraged it. When she got her first bike, I wanted my first bike. When she learned to fly off the swings, I was right behind her. And when I skinned my knees doing both, she had a band-aid ready."

"She sounds great," Ava said. Her throat was tight, as if she'd taken a lung-full of his sorrow.

Nixon blinked a few times. "She was. I think if she had gotten the chance to grow up, the two of you would have gotten along. You share the same feisty, no-holds-barred spirit. The strength I see in you is the strength I always admired in both her and my mother. But she didn't get to grow up. When she was twelve, she saw this little boy getting bullied and she stood up to the kids doing it. They spared her nothing, even though she was a girl."

Ava brought her free hand to her mouth and bit her knuckle in preparation for what she knew he was going to say. She didn't want him to have to relive the moment his big sister died. She didn't want him to think he was obligated to tell her about the way her limp body had lain in the grass at the park under the spiral slide for hours until her mother ran around frantically looking for her daughter. When he told her about the way she'd screamed, wailing over her as she carried her home, the memory had gotten trapped in his throat. His anger over the fact that the boys involved were never punished was obvious in the way he nearly crushed her hand.

He kissed it better afterwards, though.

"After Arabella's funeral, my mother was convinced the magicians had put a hex on the families of those who'd battled against them and that they were finally making good on it. Of course, it was lunacy. We weren't cursed, we were just…unlucky. Death isn't choosy. It takes who it wants, when it wants. But to save me, she took her own life before death could do it for her." He shrugged a shoulder, not as if it didn't matter but because he still, after all these years, couldn't comprehend the reasoning behind her actions. Couldn't understand how she thought leaving Nixon alone was a good solution to anything.

Cordellia may have her demons, but she had never tried to end her life.

There had been times when Ava wondered if her mother even loved her, but she now knew she did. She wouldn't have stuck around, being tormented by this life thing, if she didn't. If Ava wasn't so heartbroken for both little Nixon and grownup Nixon, she would have felt guilty for the way she'd always looked at her mother.

The way she had always considered her behavior weak.

Now she understood that it took more courage to live than it did to die.

"I didn't have anywhere to go," Nixon continued after Ava had settled against his side. He'd pulled her to him with one swift motion and she snuggled into his chest, her arms wrapped tightly around his middle. His fingers combed through her hair and if she were a cat she would have purred. "The only place I knew other people was here. Orion came by a couple of times a month to check on us, a promise he'd apparently made to my father. He'd bring Sebastian, or sometimes I'd spend the weekend here. I didn't have anyone else. I remember sending a message to Orion, telling him my mother was dead, but the time between that letter getting sent and the king showing up is a blur. I do remember the way he and Martin, a guard who retired a few years ago, were almost repelled by the smell of decay. I remember him covering my eyes, as if I hadn't been living with my mother's corpse for almost two days. Orion took me to my room and helped me pack a bag. Then we were leaving. Leaving my life and my home with my dead mother inside. Leaving it all behind.

"I took up training with the guards as soon as I turned twelve. I wanted to start earlier but Orion was insistent I have at least a couple of years to still be a kid. I'm lucky I ended up here. Who knows what would have happened to me if my father hadn't mattered to the king."

Ava nipped his chin and then said, "I'm glad you ended up here. You turned out pretty alright."

He laughed, a low rumble in his chest that made her heart swell. "I'm glad *you* ended up here," he said as he coiled a piece of her hair around his finger.

"Me, too, sometimes."

"Just sometimes?" he asked looking down at her.

She nodded. "Times like these, when I'm with you. I feel like I'm exactly where I'm supposed to be when you're around. Any other time, I still feel like a misfit, like I'm that girl again who's trying desperately to fit in but will always be an outcast."

"I'm sorry your life was altered the way it was." He kissed the top of her head. "I know it was never something you intended. You've been quite clear."

She feigned offense and chuckled. "You didn't have much to do with it aside from fetching me for the king, but I'll forgive you anyway."

"I'm afraid I had more of a role than that," he replied, almost sheepishly.

She sat straight up and looked him directly in his eyes. Perplexity distorted her features. "What do you mean?"

Nixon licked his lips, his bottom one slipping through his teeth slowly before he spoke. He was uncomfortable, worry tugging on his brows. "I was wandering the crowd the night of the gala. I saw you come in and I…I had never seen someone so beautiful. The way you looked around with this intense awe. I was so lost in everything you did." She blushed. "Sebastian was gone and I had unofficially been tasked with the job of finding him a match. I didn't know I had been assigned this role, but Orion just assumed that as his best friend I would know what he liked. But I couldn't keep my eyes off you. If I was in the crowd, I was following you. If I was up in the library watching the party, I was seeking you out. Orion must have caught me looking because the next thing I know he congratulated me, told me Sebastian would be thrilled with our choice. So, in a way, I'm at fault for you being chosen."

Ava pursed her lips to the side as she considered his confession. He wanted so desperately to kiss her, but he was a good interpreter of body language and the glare she was giving him did not read as *come hither*.

"You could have told me this before," she finally said.

"I tried, but it never seemed to be the right time. Something would always interrupt me. After a while, I worried you would hate me."

"I probably would have," she admitted, "if you'd told me early on. But I guess I can't be too mad at you now. I mean, it's a little annoying since you're always scolding me about *my* lusty eyes, but it's too late to hold grudges."

"Grudges would mean you wouldn't get to kiss me anymore," Nixon joked.

"Definitely not worth holding a grudge then," she teased back before his lips found hers again. She threaded her hands in his hair, drawing him closer.

Neither of them made it down to breakfast.

XLIII.

Summer was in full swing. It was pushing 90 degrees at 10:30 in the morning. Waves of heat sizzled on the blacktop of the roads. Even the plants felt the effect as they curled in on themselves, wilting at the edges even though they'd been watered just hours ago. Holed away in the library, listening to the droll of finances was the last place Ava wanted to be; and thanks to Orion, she wasn't.

"There isn't much need for you to be present," he'd said before she'd even stepped into the room. "Spend the time doing something enjoyable."

"Well, if you insist," she'd said, giving him a chance to change his mind though she was already backing away.

The king chuckled and waved her off, and with an appreciative smile she'd hurried back down the hall to her bedroom. She had no reservations about how she was going to spend her free time. She switched her modest maxi dress for a red-and-white striped bikini top and black bottoms. Sunglasses in hand and flip-flops on her feet, she'd made a beeline for the pool.

She intended to stay planted in a lounge chair until lunch.

Maybe even through it.

Chef Audart had given both she and Nixon a scolding look when they'd slipped into the otherwise empty dining room at the tail-end of breakfast. The kitchen staff was already clearing the serving pans and removing the remaining muffins and bagels. Ava returned the look with her best apologetic grimace, then they loaded up their plates.

Ava had tried to find Delilah afterwards to apologize—again—but she was unsuccessful. She'd knocked on her bedroom door before going to the pool, but that had gone unanswered as well.

Now her skin was warm to the touch, the sun kissing all the exposed parts. She let the rays burn away every concern she'd brought down with her. She soaked up the heat, reveled in the comfort it brought. That was until the sunshine was eclipsed, sending an automatic shiver down her spine.

She sighed. "Can I help you?"

"Just admiring the view," Nixon replied. Ava could hear the smile in his voice.

She rolled her eyes behind her sunglasses to keep her own grin at bay. "Shouldn't you be admiring the inside of the barn?"

When he said, "Probably," the word came from far away. Ava lowered her sunglasses and looked around from under the brim of her floppy hat. "But I took the day off," he added over the sound of a lounge chair being dragged across the smooth stone of the deck.

"You can just do that?"

He shrugged and settled into the edge of the chair, his back to her. He pulled off his shirt, then balled it up. Before he leaned back, using his shirt as a pillow, Ava caught her first glance of his back tattoo. It was a battle scene, the bright, full moon in the background silhouetting the people fighting one another. The soldiers were a mass of black, with small circles for their heads, but one person stood out amongst them all. He was leading them, his shadowed body running while he sliced through a blast of purple with a large sword.

"Tell me about your tattoo," Ava said.

"It's how I imagine my father looked in the war," he said simply.

Blue eyes locked on golden ones and she smiled softly. "You must admire him."

"I admire his memory. I admire the version of him I've worked up in my head from all the stories I've been told."

She wanted to reach over and take his hand, to feel his fingers linked with hers. Instead, she forced assurance into her words. "He would be very proud of the man you've become."

"I hope so," Nixon replied. Then he cleared his throat of the emotions creeping up and changed the subject to his favorite topic. "What are you doing out here and not—" He motioned with his head the general direction of *up there*.

"Orion felt my time would be better spent lounging by the pool, and who was I to argue with his logic?" Nixon laughed, and it was the purest sound in the world. It was her second favorite sound, falling only slightly behind her mother's singing voice. "Are you going to get into trouble for taking time away from training? Especially with this being the last day the new guards will be here?" That evening they would celebrate the hard work of Havaan, from its trainees to its governors. The immediate members of the governor's families would be arriving later in the afternoon, and following dinner there would be a party with music and dancing, wine and snacks.

Oddly enough, Ava was looking forward to all of it, specifically the last bit.

Tomorrow morning, all the guests would load into their cars and depart for their regions until next year. Ava would miss the new guards most of all. They'd added a fun, jovial excitement to the otherwise mundane existence of High House. She'd enjoyed watching them go from sloppy, bumbling citizens to able and ready guards. They'd done an extraordinary amount of work in the last week, their level of commitment impressive.

"They're as trained as they're going to get," Nixon said. "Raymon and Ramiro will put them through drills this afternoon and then they'll get to bum around the rest of the day. Really isn't much of a reason for me to be there. Besides…" He paused and settled into the chair more, closing his eyes against the blaring brightness above them. "I didn't get much sleep last night." His head lolled and he opened one eye, grinning at her.

Cinching her laughter behind pursed lips, Ava answered, "I hope it was worth it."

"Oh," he said, sighing dramatically, "she was."

They eased into the comfortable silence of which only they were capable. It was permeated by the occasional sounds custom to High House: the shouts of voices, the clanging of dishes, the startup of a lawnmower, the whir of a vacuum cleaner. Even the pool added to the cacophony with the gentle gurgle of its cleaning pump.

The peace comforted Ava like a pillow, its quiet a gentle lullaby. She was teetering on the brink of sleep when Nixon's voice pulled her back from the edge. "Aren't you worried you're going to burn?"

She shook her head. "Noriega skin doesn't burn, it just tans. It's one of the few things my father blessed me with. Now, if I had my *mother's* skin tone I'd be a lobster the minute I stepped into the sun."

Nixon turned toward her so suddenly that she jumped a little. "What's your father's last name?"

"Noriega," she answered slowly. "Why?"

He stared at her for a few seconds, his eyebrows furrowed, and then he sighed. "It sounds familiar."

"I've probably said it before," she offered, shrugging.

"Maybe," he replied as he sat back. He didn't sound entirely convinced.

Wordless quiet overtook them again until Nixon yawned theatrically then sighed just as loud. "I'm bored," he said.

Ava laughed as she adjusted the lounger, making it completely flat. Then she flipped onto her stomach and replied, "You aren't very good at relaxing, are you?" When she turned to look at him, if the sun hadn't been warming her, his gaze would have.

He blinked a few times when Ava whistled. "What?"

Shaking her head, Ava rested her cheek on the top of her folded hands. "You. Relaxing. Not good at it."

"Oh," he said, clearing his throat as if she *hadn't* caught him checking her out. "I don't think I do it enough to be good at it. I prefer to be doing things. Not always guard related things, but in-motion things."

"Okay," she started, "what kind of in-motion thing would you like to do?"

Nixon glanced around as if looking for the answer in the otherwise empty cabana. Then his eyes came to rest on the neatly folded net at the other end of the pool. "How good are you at volleyball?"

"I'm okay," Ava replied, shrugging. If okay meant playing for five years in school and being team captain her second year of high school. She would have played until graduation, but Zarah got sick when she was sixteen and she gave it up to care for both her mothers. She hadn't played, let alone touched a ball in four years, but she imagined it was like riding a bike.

"We should play," Nixon said excitedly. "Sebastian and I used to play all summer when we were younger. There hasn't been much time in the recent years, with training and him being gone so often."

Ava raised a brow. "His leaving on these secret missions isn't new?" "No," Nixon confirmed. "Sometimes Orion would take him on 'king business,' but once a month, maybe every other, he'd vanish for a couple of days by himself." Nixon shrugged as if it didn't faze him any, but his following words revealed the truth he wouldn't admit. "I wasn't a fan of it initially," he said. "He was the only person I hung out with around here, but when his trips became more frequent, I shifted my focus to training diligently."

It was weird to think that only a couple of months ago this exchange would not be happening. He'd been closed off, revealing dribbles of himself here and there. Now his feelings seemed to flow freely, as though their night together had shaken something loose. Ava liked that he trusted her with his memories as much as she trusted him with her own.

There was one downfall to the change, though.

Every time he opened up, her feelings intensified.

"Do you really want to play volleyball?" A chunk of hair had slipped from her loose braid. The ends brushed against her bare shoulder.

"I do," Nixon replied.

Ava sat on the edge of the lounger and pushed her feet into her sandals. "Well, okay then," she said as she pulled the knee-length cover-up over her swimsuit. No need to go prancing around High House in her bikini. "We're going to need to recruit more players."

"Are you afraid to go against me?" Nixon teased.

"Terrified." Ava winked. "But aside from that it'll—"

A loud screeching ripped through their playful banter. It was as though someone was dragging a sledgehammer across concrete. They looked at one another, faces contorted under their flinching. Then, it stopped just as suddenly as it had started. A couple of seconds later, Sebastian came from the back of the greenhouse. His hair was a tousled mess, as though he'd just crawled out of bed, and his messenger bag swelled against his hip, this time filled with more than just clothes. His tan shorts were wrinkled and the hem of his shirt had come partially un-tucked.

"Hey!" Ava called after him.

His head snapped up and he looked around, his eyelids fluttering as though he had no idea where he was. She held a finger up to Sebastian, a wordless wait, and then turned back to Nixon.

"Let the guards out of their drills and see how many you can get to come join us. I'll see if I can steal Madi from the kitchen and find Delilah." Nixon nodded at her then jogged away, patting Sebastian on the shoulder as he passed. His best friend stood in place, his eyes unfocused on Ava as she approached him. "Are you okay?" she asked.

Sebastian took a deep breath and exhaled, "I'm fine." Ava didn't believe him, and he could tell by the way her eyebrow cocked. "Just tired."

For once, Ava decided to let it go. If he wasn't in the mood to defend his temperament, she wasn't going to force him to talk. He took her weary silence as the end of their conversation. As he began to turn from her, something clicked in her mind. "Did you just come from the greenhouse?" she asked, stopping him mid-motion.

"I didn't *come* from there. I was in there, though."

Ava couldn't help the way her confusion painted itself on her face. She was used to Sebastian giving circular answers, but she had no idea how to make heads or tails of this one. She was also growing tired of it. So much of their relationship had been built on secrets, on lies, on truths he would tell her "when the time was right" or "when she was officially queen."

"What's the difference?" she asked. Annoyance tiptoed across her words.

Sebastian pushed his hands through his hair then ran them down his face. "I don't know, Avaleigh. I told you I was tired."

"When did you get home?"

"Just a bit ago."

"Did you take the train?" she asked. That could account for his exhaustion. It hadn't been built for sleeping, but for convenience and speed. If he hadn't been to bed yet, that could explain his rumpled appearance. She knew she should want to welcome him home with loving arms, not an onslaught of questions, but she couldn't. There was a barrier between the two of them now, one they'd both had a hand in building. Of course, she'd built onto it last night, looping barbed wire along the top.

The worst part was that she still didn't feel bad about what had happened with Nixon.

Being with him was right, even if it was wrong.

Life at High House had changed her, sometimes for the good and sometimes for the bad. She just wasn't sure which changes she was okay with and which she could do without.

"Um…no," Sebastian started in response to the latest question in her inquisition. "I came back with Archie."

"That was nice of him," Ava replied and Sebastian nodded. "Listen, I know you're probably exhausted and you just want to get some sleep, but Nixon and I are trying to get a couple of teams together for some water volleyball if you're interested."

A sad, lopsided smile pulled at his lips, though it looked as if it were having difficulty forming. "Thanks," he said, "but I'm going to check in with my parents and catch a few hours of sleep before tonight. Have fun for me though, yeah?"

"Sure," Ava answered.

As if he were on autopilot, Sebastian closed the distance between them and pressed his lips against hers. She turned, offering him the edge of her mouth. When they pulled away, she dropped her eyes to the ground behind him.

"I'm glad you're home," she said, glancing up at him quickly.

The low hang of his brow bone cast a shadow over his eyes, and in them was a coil of light purple. It looked almost white in the summer sun. It twisted and swirled with the green like watercolor paint. It tugged at her mind, beckoned her forth like a smoky finger, but a second later it was gone and she was left staring at the emerald green she knew.

"Me, too," Sebastian said. As he adjusted the strap of his bag, shifting it off his hip, a clattering like wind chimes came from the canvas.

Ava was about to question him—again—when he cut her off. "Enjoy your time in the pool. You've earned a little R&R. I will see you tonight for dinner, if not before." Before she could say anything else, he turned and vanished into the house through the back door. She stood in a stupor, trying to figure out what had just happened, until a ruckus of manly voices broke through her muddled conscience.

As he hurried away from the group of guys trailing into High House, Levi and Josiah bringing up the end, Nixon's excited smile faltered when he saw her. "What's wrong?"

She blinked to clear the last bit of cobwebs and then Ava replied, "Sebastian's being super weird."

"Do you think he knows?" he asked, leaning closer. She shook her head in disagreement. "Is he joining us?"

"No. He said he was tired."

Nixon nodded a couple of times as if he understood. "I got six guys. Did you have any luck?"

"I haven't started yet," Ava answered honestly. "But if I can find Delilah I'm sure she'll join."

"Well get moving," he joked, winking. "We don't have much time before the lunch bell tolls. I'll set up the net while you're gone." "You're so useful." Ava grinned at him then scrunched her nose as he pushed her over-sized hat over her eyes.

She made her way into High House, and as she entered the foyer, the front door swung open and deposited Delilah.

"There you are," Ava said as she met her friend at the bottom of the stairs.

"Here I am," Delilah replied dryly. From both arms hung bags of different sizes and colors.

"Where were you? I came to find you earlier to see if you wanted to sunbathe with me."

"I went to the market," D said as they started up the stairs.

"For…?"

"Something to wear tonight. I would have invited you if you'd made it to breakfast. But big surprise, you didn't." There was no misinterpreting the pained sarcasm dripping from each word. If they were poison they'd have burned holes in the carpet.

"I'm sorry. Nixon and I started talking and I lost track of time. Turns out the robe belonged to his dead mother."

Delilah raised two perfectly sculpted brows. "He opened up to you about his family?"

"A little."

"Huh," Delilah scoffed. "You penetrated Fort Nixon."

"I guess," Ava replied.

"Good for you. I hope your bonding time was enjoyable." Delilah turned her back on Ava as she reached for the handle on her bedroom door.

"Are you upset with me?" Ava asked before her best friend could retreat.

"Yes," Delilah answered honestly.

Sighing, Ava rested a hand on Delilah's shoulder, halting her. "Listen, D. I know I've been kind of a shitty friend lately. There's been a lot going on and I just…I haven't been very good at finding time for us. I feel like I'm being pulled in all these directions, trying to make everyone happy, but I can't. Someone is always going to get the short end of the stick, but I'm sorry that recently it's been you."

After setting her bags inside her room, Delilah faced Ava again. Her eyes were red-rimmed but her cheeks were dry. "I thought us being here together would mean we'd see each other every day and talk every night, but I feel like I have less time with you now."

"I know," Ava said as she reached for Delilah's hands. "I know I keep disappointing you and there is so much I want, I *need* to tell you. It's not like I don't want to hang out with you, I do, but I've got an entire staff I have to get to know, I had the tour. I had the meeting with the governors. I've had to try and fall in love with Sebastian." She let out an exasperated breath, her lips vibrating at the same time. "Things are a lot different than I thought they would be."

"For me as well," Delilah agreed.

"Can you forgive me long enough to join my team for water volleyball?"

"Who are you playing against?"

"Levi. Nixon. Some of the guards. I'm going to see if Ms. Markham will let me borrow Madi for an hour."

Delilah's brown eyes sparkled. "It's unfair you're using shirtless guards to win my forgiveness, but it's working."

Ava laughed. For the time they were splashing around in the pool, their friendship would be as it should. "I'm not sure how I feel about your compassion being based on abs, but I'll take it." Before she knew it, she'd tossed her arms around Delilah in the tightest hug she could muster.

Chuckling, Delilah's small hand patted Ava's back. "If you keep squeezing me like that I'm not going to have enough oxygen to help you kick ass."

When the two friends parted, there were wide grins plastered on both faces. "Go get ready while I snag Madi. I'll see you downstairs in a bit."

"Are you actually going to show up this time, or are you and Nixon going to have another heart-to-heart?" Delilah half-teased as she stepped into her bedroom. She flashed Ava one of her flawless smiles before the door closed.

Swirling her goblet around, the sparkling red liquid sloshing against the sides like a bloody tidal wave, she could feel the lines in her face pulling back together. She didn't need to look in the mirror to know her skin-tone was returning to its natural paleness or that the bags under her eyes were being erased. Even her bones felt better and she pulled herself into her authoritative stance. Though the outside was righting itself, restoring her to the beauty and poise everyone expected, no amount of the drink could remedy the anger seething inside her as she watched the atrocity taking place below her window.

Not once, in the twenty-four years she'd been queen, had any of the staff so flippantly taken time off. Especially not as a group. *Especially* not to frolic in the pool as though they were on vacation; as if they didn't have an important dinner to prepare for. Some even had the audacity to just sit at the pool's edge, watching the shenanigans— *supporting* the mayhem!

Ever since *that girl* had arrived, the atmosphere around High House had become lackadaisical. She took no shame in greeting most of the help by name, asking how their families were. Ava had turned them all into smiling idiots, gave them the impression they could now treat Bernadette with the same welcoming disposition. As queen, she had never taken the time to memorize their names or learn anything personal about them. She didn't even know that much about Helen, and they spent nearly every day together. Bernadette had worked hard to exert her dominance, to make everyone in her service quiver in her presence.

Power and fear went hand-in-hand; fear and respect could not exist without the other.

It was a lesson she had learned long ago, but her husband was oblivious to such things. He believed respect came from comradery, that if you gave it you would be given it back. He didn't see how his relaxed approach to everything made him just as foolish as the help was becoming.

She did, though.

Bernadette understood the damage that could happen if one's authority looked questionable.

She'd known Ava was going to be trouble the moment she'd blatantly refused the nomination for queen, as if she were too good for the job. If things with Brisbane had worked out, none of them would be in this predicament, but she had been careless and effete with her.

Bernadette had no one to blame but herself for the predicament in which they now found themselves. It was blame she sorely shouldered.

If her dislike for Ava weren't so strong, Bernadette could almost admire her brazenness. As it was, she didn't admire her any more than she trusted her intentions. She had brought her concerns to her husband one night after she'd witnessed yet another chummy exchange between Ava and the chefs.

"What exactly are you angry about, my love? Is it that she's friendly with the staff?" he'd asked.

"Yes! They are her employees. There isn't a reason for her to try and make friends with them," she had replied, "unless she's out to turn them against us."

Orion had acknowledged the comment with a sideways glance, and for a moment she was convinced she'd gotten to him. They were words which had worked before. Her *fragile,* always nice, carefree husband's one fear was another war. Even the mere threat of such had always sent him into a panic, turned him into the strong king she wanted him to be, and in those anxiety-ridden moments she'd been able to work her magic.

But when Orion said, "I think she's just trying to establish a relationship with them before she takes over," her hopes were dashed. Yet again. By *that girl.* First, she'd turned her own son against her: he was always at the ready to defend his betrothed. And now her husband was jaded by her, too? Bernadette had wanted to scream that night.

Instead, she'd kept her composure and tried again. "She's going to ruin everything *we've* worked hard to establish. How are you not worried about this?"

Flipping to the next page in the *Havaan Weekly,* Orion had sighed. "I'm not worried because in a few short months we won't be here for them to turn against. Any issues that arise because of her will be hers to deal with. I can't imagine she has intentions of creating a mess too big to clean up." Then, as he'd folded his paper and turned his back to her, he'd added, "I don't want to hear another word of this paranoid melodrama, Bernadette. I just want to spend my last days as king as blissfully as possible."

She'd promised to let it go, had lied her assurance that he was right—it was more than likely just fear of having to hand over the reign to another—but Bernadette had not stopped plotting against Ava. She knew the girl wasn't as perfect as she seemed; that her valor and bravery toward Bernadette were more than likely a mask for *something.*

Bernadette just needed to find the weakest spot in Ava's falsified strength.

Then, one day, she figured out what it was.

"Of course," she had whispered to herself as she'd watched the two of them giggle with one another. "It's always the best friend."

As her plans so often did, it dug its nails into her brain and whispered ideas in her ear until it was foolproof. By now the wheels were set in motion. She just had to hope she'd greased them enough that by the time they built up speed, there would be no stopping. If all went according to plan, by the time they reached the end, Ava and everything she stood for would crash and burn.

It was hard to see the coming chaos and heartbreak through the bonhomie taking place below, but it was coming. She could feel it in her veins, as sure as she could feel the red fluid doing its job.

Unable to stand the show any longer, the queen swished away from the window, the train of her robe billowing behind her. The movement disturbed the long curtain that had hidden her from view, drawing Ava's attention. Looking up, she swore she saw Bernadette, a wicked grin stamped across her jaw, but she was gone in the blink of an eye.

"Another game?" Nixon asked from the other side of the net. He juggled the wet volleyball between his hands.

She pulled her eyes from the third floor and erased the confusion etched on her face with a smile. "Only if your team is ready to lose again," she replied, laughing as a wave of water hit her in the face. "OH!" she sputtered. "You are so going down!"

"Kick his ass, Ava!" Raymon cheered from his lounger.

"I intend to," she said, winking. Then she took her spot next to Delilah, high-fived her best friend, and readied herself.

"Serving!" Nixon shouted a second before his hand whapped against the ball.

XLIV.

The smell of chlorine followed her around. Molecules of it stuck to the ends of her hair and soaked into her pores. Her skin felt tight, and no amount of lotion she slathered on could help. What she needed was a long, hot stay in the shower—for which there would be plenty of time before the party—but more importantly, she needed food.

She felt like she was floating as she made her way down the stairs. Today had been just what she needed. Hanging out with people she genuinely enjoyed being around while doing something she genuinely enjoyed doing. For the 45 minutes they'd volleyed a ball back and forth, she'd been able to pretend she was a normal girl. When she'd returned to her room, though, and saw her red dress hanging beside the veranda door, she was reminded that life was not as simple as splashing around in the pool with her crazy group of friends. She wasn't sure what it was about dresses and the disappointment they seemed to be made of, but this one was not enough to clip the wings of joy which carried her off the last step.

"You look happy," Archie said as he closed the front door.

"You know what, Archie," Ava said, grinning, "I am. Today has been a pretty good day."

"We only get a select number of those in our life. It's wise to acknowledge them when they arise."

"You are a wise man, Archibald."

"I appreciate your kind words, Avaleigh," he replied.

"Did you get everything squared away with the *incident* back home?" Ava asked, her tone suddenly serious.

"It has been addressed and taken care of." Ava hated that he was being careful not to give too much away. She desperately wanted him to confide in her, but she had to remind herself he was under the assumption she was as clueless as they liked to keep her.

"Good," she replied, playing along. "Can I ask you something else?"

"Always," Archie said as he took a step toward her and leaned down, giving her his full attention.

She looked around to make sure they were alone. "Did Sebastian seem…strange to you this morning?"

Archie's brows lowered. "I don't know what you mean?" he answered.

"Was he different? Quieter than normal, or did he seem okay with you?"

Holding up one of his hands, the governor shook his head. "I meant I don't know what you mean about me seeing the prince today. I haven't seen him since yesterday."

This time it was Ava's face that pinched in befuddlement. "But he told me you and he rode back together this morning."

"I've just returned, Ava." He raised the small travel bag he was holding. It was the first time she'd noticed it.

Ava blinked a few times, trying to clear the cloud of questions away, and pursed her lips to the side. "Maybe I misunderstood him?" she wondered, more to herself than the man standing before her. Then she looked up into his kind eyes. "Did he say where he was going when you last saw him?"

Ava did not miss the way his eyes dropped for a second, or the way he swallowed his lie. "No."

She opened her mouth to ask a follow-up question, but Delilah's voice cut her off.

"Are you actually dining with us peasants today?" D joked as she came down the stairs. "Oh. Hi…"

"Archie," the tall man replied. He bowed slightly to Delilah. "Please, go enjoy your lunch. I didn't mean to hold you up," he apologized, even though it was Ava who had stopped him.

"My fault entirely," Ava countered. "Enjoy the rest of your afternoon, Archie. I will see you and Mrs. Revenwood for dinner tonight."

"We are looking forward to it," he replied. Then he dipped his head, as if tipping an imaginary hat, to both women before heading up the staircase.

Delilah turned to her best friend, her eyebrows knitted in a question mark. "Everything okay?"

Nodding, Ava hooked her arm with D's and pulled them toward the dining room. "Everything is fine," she lied, hoping her soft smile would be convincing enough.

Why had Sebastian lied to her about something as simple as how he'd gotten home? Where had he gone once he'd left Archie? While Ava had been in the arms of another, had Sebastian been, as well?

Question after question assaulted her, distracting her from the conversations taking place around her. Sebastian wasn't at lunch, so she couldn't purge herself of her endless list of queries, but she vowed to do so the next time she saw him. She would force answers from him, even if she had to corner him to do so.

Little did she know, however, that the time would never come.

After lunch, with full bellies and muscles sore from exertion, the best friends took an hour-long power nap in the frosting pink silk sheets of Delilah's bed. Later, as they sorted through the hoard of her closet, trying to make an executive decision about what the future assistant would wear that evening, Ava filled her in on what she'd uncovered in Volume I of Havaan's history.

"Who knew Cordellia had it in her to be so scandalous?" Delilah said as she held two dresses up to herself, alternating between them in the mirror.

"The silver one," Ava said when D turned to her for her opinion. "And it's a potential scandal. Maybe there's a logical reason I went unreported on Dante's side. Maybe all the information she's kept from me about him goes back to this. Or vice versa."

"I like the idea of a torrid love affair better."

Rolling her eyes, Ava replied, "I know." She swung her legs over the edge of the bed and stood. Her calves and thighs were sore from treading water that afternoon. She moved diligently across the room. "I'm going to go figure out what *I'm* wearing tonight before Helen arrives."

"I pulled the red dress out for you," Delilah reminded.

"I know," Ava replied, "I'm just not sure the red dress is appropriate for tonight."

Delilah rolled her eyes away from Ava. "Just make sure you pick something other than the blue dress," she suggested as she stepped back into her closet.

"I'll see what I can do to not let you down."

Ava was in her bedroom only a few minutes, standing in front of the red dress in nothing more than a tank-top and underwear, when a frantic knock at the door shattered her contemplative thoughts.

Helen's way early, she thought as she grabbed for her shorts and called out, "Hold—"

The door swung open in a static charged flurry of black hair and golden eyes.

"What in the world!" she exclaimed as Nixon strode toward her. Her fingers gripped the fabric of her bottoms, as if simply holding them made her more dressed. He had seen her in less—*far* less—but the last thing he needed was Helen, or Delilah, or worse of all *Sebastian* to come barging in, as well.

"I said hold on," she scolded without much gusto.

"I have something to show you," Nixon said as he pulled his hand from his back pocket.

Snapping the elastic band of her shorts into place, Ava asked, "And you couldn't wait four seconds?"

"I didn't think you would want me to."

Ava raised a curious brow. "Show me."

A smirk tugged his lips as he took his place beside her. In his hand was an old, faded photograph, the last third of it folded. "This," he started, pointing at a dark-haired man, "is my father."

"Obviously," Ava replied, smiling up at him. Even if he hadn't pointed him out, she would have known. The similarities were uncanny, from their luscious onyx locks and square jaw, to the way their smiles softened their hard features.

Nixon's father had his arm around the man in the middle. "That—"

"Is King Orion," Ava finished. He was younger, not much older than Sebastian's current age. His face was still kind, though baby soft and without the grooves of the years.

Nodding once, Nixon unfolded the last part of the photo. Ava's breath caught in her throat. Genuine smiles stretched across all three men. Orion's arm was slung over the new man's shoulders, too, tugging him close. A mop-top of curls blew in an invisible wind, pulling them away from his handsome face.

A face with which Ava shared parts.

Taking the picture from Nixon, her hands shaking as she held it like a fragile egg, she traced the third man with her thumb. "Dante," she whispered.

"I knew I'd heard his last name before," Nixon said softly, as though speaking too loudly would startle her. He turned the photo over in her hands. Scrawled across the back in handwriting she recognized from birthday cards and letters sitting in a pile in her dresser were their names: Dante Noriega. Orion Calder. Felix Haldonai.

"Your last name is Haldonai?" Ava asked, casting her gaze at Nixon.

"It is."

"I don't think I knew that." Smiling softly, she added, "It's nice." Nixon kissed her forehead before she turned her attention back to the object in her hand. "How did you get this?"

"It was in a box of things I took from home. Photos, mostly. Some letters, documents. There's something else I need to show you."

Ava tucked the photo in the pocket of her shorts then trailed him out of her bedroom, down the halls—the long one then the short—and into the library. The wooden floors were cold against her bare feet. Nixon's boots echoed through the large room, each step a determined thud that matched the increasing rhythm of her heart. He was on a mission, so she sat on the arm of the couch and watched him. He made a beeline to a bookshelf at the far right. He didn't even stop to scan the bindings of the countless books, just stretched to his full height and retrieved one from the top shelf.

Sudden nerves crawled through her like spiders, their spindly legs weaving a ball of uncertainty. She wasn't sure why she was uneasy, but she knew, without him having to say anything, that what he was about to show her would change things.

"What is this?" Ava asked as Nixon settled onto the couch. She slid from her perch to the cushions, and across their laps he settled the massive tome.

"It's the written history of Havaan," Nixon said as he thumbed through the pages. "The *actual* history. Not stories or myths, but the truth. Orion treats it almost like a journal. I'm not entirely sure why it's even down here."

A little over halfway through, Nixon found the spot. "This will not be easy for you to read," he said, looking pointedly into Ava's eyes.

"Should I not?" she asked, premature tears gathering. The tone of his voice, the seriousness of his words, shook her already raw emotions. If she hadn't been worried before, she was now.

Nixon pushed the book onto her lap more, and with a sigh replied, "You, of all people, deserve to know the truth." Then he cupped her cheek with one hand and brushed his lips against hers. "I am sorry in advance," he whispered before kissing her. His lips lingered like he was trying to prolong her pain.

If it was meant to bring her any sort of comfort, it failed.

After swallowing the nervous lump in her throat, Ava filled her lungs, exhaled the warm breath slowly, and then began reading the thick, all-caps script of the king.

What she read, as assumed, changed *everything*.

XLV.

I have decided to declare war against the magicians. They have already instigated miniature wars throughout our country, and we will continue to destroy one another if someone doesn't put a stop to it. It is clear no one else has the guts to do so, so I will be the one. I may die at the battle lines, but at least I will die for a cause.

The next page and a half were ramblings of the King's plans and how he would gather a big enough force to defeat the other side: **I have asked only my most trusted companions to spread the word. We will keep our war efforts a secret for now, but when we have a strong enough army we will make the official announcement. Only a coward would attack without giving the opposition time to prepare. Besides, I want citizens to have a chance to choose their side. It will take time, time we don't have, but we need to plan. We need to acquire. We need to be as strong as possible to win.**

"None of this is important to me," Ava said, looking up at Nixon.

He smiled at her. It was quick and tight-lipped and sad. She sighed, rolled her eyes and skimmed some more. It took a while to get to the part she thought he wanted her to see, and once she did, she understood his earlier apology.

We won. It was, as expected, a violent battle but we came out victorious. We lost many citizens on both sides of the battle lines,

my friend and closest ally Felix included. His death has not gone unnoticed; not only in our regiment but also my life...I have declared myself the new king of Havaan. There has been little opposition to my rule, and Felix's bravery and insight would be useful as I ascend the throne. Luckily, the warfare did not take Dante from me as well. Though he is hesitant to join my side, I am hopeful I can change his mind. His skillset was essential in our winning, just as his logic and knowledge will be useful in my rule....

...It has taken quite some time, but we have rid Havaan of nearly all magic. Many gave it up without a fight, but then again who wouldn't when faced with the consequences? Those who didn't were sentenced to a life in Nopels. It is more humane than the alternative. There are a few still in possession of their powers, as agreed to before the war, but they will be monitored closely. If there is even the smallest indication they are using their abilities they, too, will be stripped and sent to reside with their traitorous brothers and sisters.

While all of this was interesting, it wasn't anything more than confirmation of the stories they'd been told. But when she turned the page, it wasn't necessarily the words that caught her attention but the style in which they were written. Orion's handwriting was blocky, thick—masculine—but it had never seemed angry. At least up until now. Ava could feel the rage behind each letter he'd slashed into the page. They were placed down without thought, rather a purging of emotion.

There were also sections that looked as though the words had been erased, or at least an attempt had been made to remove them. Smudged remnants remained, like fading ghosts. Under the word "sources" there was an R, maybe two T's, and an E. It was hard to say, but *something* had been scrawled there before; words that no one was meant to read.

Truths no one was meant to know.

Sources have revealed to me whisperings of a new rebellion. One formed by those who I have held closest to my heart. Those I have trusted with my life. What they are angry about I haven't a clue, but the threats, if true, would be detrimental to myself as well as my country. While I am hesitant to act without confirmation, I am more hesitant to tip them off that I know. I gave the opposition a chance to plan once before, and while it ultimately worked in my favor, the number of deaths was beyond prediction. As much as I care for the conspirators, I cannot give them a chance to attack, especially if their threats are real. But at the same time, am I willing to sacrifice the few remaining friends I have on nothing more than a hunch?

…It has been done. I have watched and observed them, and I believe their rebellion to be true. How can this be? How can those I have called friend—nay, brother, turn on me so quickly? Without reason, without coming to me first and giving me a chance to fix whatever issues have arisen? Whatever their reasons, they have left me no choice. I have done what I always promised myself I would never do: I have relied on magic to do my bidding. I made a deal with evil incarnate, sold a part of my soul

to protect my country, my people. I needed to make five deaths look natural as to divert suspicion from myself. I needed to use their passing as a warning to those in the rebellion that I have not flushed out. This is what happens when you turn against the king.

As I stood on the shoreline and watched the boat capsize, taking with it people I had once considered the most loyal of my friends, the wind and the rain could do nothing to mask my misery and loss. I felt, with each death, a part of myself die, as well. I will miss them: Henry Harvey, Barren Carper, Sarah Nedeski, Georgio Lembardi, and most of all, Dante Noriega.

I will mourn their deaths until the day of my own, but Havaan needs a ruler to keep them in line. We have watched, with our own eyes, the failure that comes when left to our own devices. As painful is the loss of a few, it is better than the loss of our entire country.

With shaking hands, Ava closed the book gently. She stared at nothing for a full minute while her mind tried to organize all the pieces of information floating around.

"Are you—" Nixon started but she held up her hand, cutting him off.

She worried her bottom lip until blood trickled onto her tongue. She swallowed the truth repeatedly until it gathered like stones in her throat, pushing their way to the top. "He killed them," she finally whispered. The realization of it tugged on her tear ducts, but she refused to let them fall. "Orion *murdered* my father." Springing to her feet, she paced in front of the fireplace, the oversized portrait of the king looking down. She stopped and turned on Nixon. "Did you know?" she asked, anger at his possible betrayal already bubbling to the surface.

"No," he replied quickly, standing at the same time. He held up his hands as though he were surrendering. She took a step from him, her head shaking repeatedly. "Ava, I promise you I had no idea until a bit ago. I'd read the story before, but I didn't make the connection until I realized what your father's name was." Taking a tentative step, he reached for her, but she curled in on herself. "I would never keep this from you intentionally. You believe that, right?"

She nodded while taking quick, panicked breaths. The revelation of Dante's death—of the treachery behind it—felt like a bolder sitting on her chest. His loved ones had always been made to believe his death was some tragic misfortune of his job, which was hard enough to handle. But murdered...? By his best friend? By the *king?!* How was anyone supposed to stomach that?

She had always wanted answers, but maybe she'd been better off without them.

Because this...this was too much.

Her eyes snapped to Nixon's. The golden irises blazed with heated concern. "How could you stay?" Her emotions bled through each word. "How could you keep serving him after you learned what he did? How could you live in a house with him and stand by his side and do his bidding? How could you stay here and protect him?"

When Nixon spoke, his voice was almost as strained as hers, his throat raw as though he'd been screaming into the abyss. "Where was I supposed to go, Ava? My family is dead. The Calders are all I have left in this world. This is my home. *They*...they are my family."

"Your family is dead because he killed them, just as much as he killed my father. Is being on your own, not having anywhere to go and not knowing anyone *really* worse than facing him day after day after day? Was it so easy for you to ignore the truth for comfort? For familiarity? How did you not, every day, plan your revenge?"

Nixon ran his hands through his hair and gripped the locks. Ava's insinuations were getting to him. He had struggled, from the first time he'd accidentally stumbled across the book. It had been lodged at the very top of the bookshelf, shoved flat behind other novels and ledgers tall enough to hide it. The relationship between he and Orion was never the same after he learned, letter by painful letter, the evil side of the only father-figure he could remember. He had a difficult time balancing the man who had raised him with the man who had taken upon the role of Death all those years ago; and even after all this time he still found it impossible to do. He knew Ava would never understand anything through her anger, but he was going to try to explain himself anyway. He *needed* her to understand that it had not been as easy for him as she was assuming. But before he could speak, Ava's words silenced him.

"He doesn't deserve to live," she said, her voice spacey, as though she were speaking to herself more than him. Then her deep blue eyes met his and she repeated herself, louder this time.

He whispered her name and she focused on him once again. "I know what you're thinking. I know how bad you want your pound of flesh—because I have been there, too, despite what you may believe—but you will not get it. Orion is protected. He is guarded all of the time and they will not hesitate *to* protect him. Even against you. No matter the cost. Your life does not mean as much to them as his does, regardless of how much they like you. You *will* end up in jail, in Nopels, or dead, long before he does."

Through clenched teeth, Ava replied, "It isn't fair that he gets to walk around pretending to be this good king when he took my father from me." Her bottom lip trembled as she tried to keep her feelings at bay.

"I know." Nixon took another step toward her. He wanted to hold her, to give her the strength she'd need to fall apart, because he knew she wouldn't do so on her own. She would bottle it up, as dangerous as it was, and strap it to her chest. She would wear her pain like armor until it suffocated her.

When she was within arm's reach, he felt a sense of relief, because he was certain she was going to step into him. But when she asked, "Would you protect him from me?" he faltered in his stride.

Nixon rolled the words around in his mouth, boulders he was afraid to let into the world. Finally, he said, "If it meant protecting you from yourself, then yes. I will not allow you to put yourself in the position for the consequences that would follow. Do you honestly want his head on a spike so bad you would be willing to leave behind Delilah, or your mother? Or *me?*"

"Would you kill me?" Ava asked as flatly as before, ignoring everything Nixon had said.

"I'm hoping we never have to find out," he replied. The tremor of his voice betrayed his emotions. "Please, Ava, I know...I can see in your eyes how badly you want to avenge your father, but now is not the time to do so."

"If not now, then when?" she nearly shouted. "How much longer does he get to keep walking around without repercussions for the blood on his hands?"

Nixon shrugged. "I don't know," he said solemnly. "Maybe forever. But is his life worth your own? Would you be in such haste to lose it, all in the name of a man you don't know? A man who maybe…possibly…*was* actually working against—"

"Stop," Ava hissed. "Don't you dare—"

"Your mother kept things from you for a reason. Maybe this is why. Maybe she didn't want to taint your opinion of your father. You don't know for sure whether he was or wasn't conspiring, Ava. There *is* a chance that—"

"*Orion* didn't know for sure! Even if Dante *was* planning a rebellion, that does not give Orion the right to take my father from me! He stripped me of not only one parent, but both. He stole my childhood. I had to take care of myself, and my mom, all because Orion couldn't handle some whispers? He *murdered* people, Nixon. He took their lives in his own hands and ended them without considering how it would affect anyone else." Ava laughed once, from disbelief instead of humor. "The fact that you can stand here and defend him—"

"I'm not defending him," Nixon snapped. "I don't condone what he did. But Ava, he is my family. Whether or not I agree with the choices he made, I cannot stand by while someone plots his murder. Would you turn around and exact the very thing you are angry about on someone else?"

"How can you not want the same thing as me?" she asked. Her hands gripped the fabric of her shirt so tightly her knuckles turned white—a stark contrast against the black top she wore. "This man who you share dinners with, who you look up to and respect, took your family from you, too. How can you not see that?"

"It isn't about seeing it. It's about knowing when to pick your battles, knowing when to draw your swords. And right now is not that time." Nixon rested a hand on her clenched ones. His eyes bore into hers, as though his gaze could change her mind. Even if he couldn't, he would try. He could not stomach what would happen if he failed to talk her off this ledge. "Please, Ava. I've already betrayed my best friend for you. Do not make me betray my king."

Ava dropped her arms, shaking off Nixon's touch at the same time. "I have to go," she said robotically as she turned from him. When he called her name, she stopped and looked over her shoulder. "Don't worry, Nixon. I'm not going to do something stupid like murder Orion." She smiled at him, a look that was full of sadness. There was no better word for it, and it crushed every resolve he had.

It was in that moment he knew he would hand her the knife to take her revenge if she asked.

"I wouldn't want to put you in the position to have to choose between the two of us. I don't think I would like what decision you'd make." Then she hurried out of the library, leaving Nixon under the watchful, painted eye of the executioner king.

She'd meant part of what she had said to the guard. She wasn't going to kill Orion, not yet at least. But some people might argue that stealing one of the cars of the royal family constituted being stupid.

Ava didn't care.

She didn't care about the consequences of grand theft auto or of missing the governor's dinner or the pandemonium her sudden disappearance would cause. Helen would find the room empty when she arrived to get Ava ready, and it would remain so for longer than it should. By the time High House would erupt into frenzy, she would be far away.

Not far enough that no one could find her, though.

There was no plan to vanish. She had business to deal with at High House, but she needed answers first. Now, more than ever, they were imperative. And there was only one place—from one person—where she could get them.

Holland Avenue was as she had left it. The shorter school days in the summer lent to later dinners. It left the streets littered with children. Three houses down, a group of girls practicing their jump-roping recited sing-song chants. A bike gang, with playing cards shoved into the spokes of their tires, raced up and down the sidewalks. The same young couple that had been there when Ava had left for High House was still on the porch, her head on the shoulder of her beau. Book spines were being cracked in the lounged-upon grass or by splashed-in pools.

Even the light of house number six was still a welcoming beacon in the blazing mid-day sun.

The normalcy, the nostalgia, clenched at Ava's heart in a way she hadn't expected. It hammered at her soul with a force so painful she had to sit in the car until the sobs ceased. Then, with red-rimmed eyes and a slight pressure building in the front of her skull, she stepped out of the car, mounted the two steps to the front door, and turned the knob.

XLVI.

Home will always have a certain smell. It soaks into fabrics and permeates the counter tops. It settles into the grout of a bathtub and seeps into the paint on the walls. For some, it is fresh laundry and homecooked meals. For others, it is baby powder and spices. For Ava, it was always earth, like fresh tilled soil; the staleness of a house where the windows were hardly opened and dust particles settled on the unused surfaces. It was metal shavings and herbal tea and lavender.

If she'd had to imagine what mourning smelled like, that would be it.

For years, she had found it unbecoming, a constant reminder of the disarray of her life, of the unlived-in-ness of it. But stepping into it now was the most welcoming homecoming. The stuffy warmth of the house enveloped her like first love and the steady bass coming from the basement tied it all together.

Holland Avenue Number Six had never felt so right.

Instead of immediately letting Cordellia know she was there, she took a few minutes to walk the floors. The kitchen was as it had always been: pictures stuck to the fridge with an assortment of magnets, a few dishes from the day drying in the rack. The tea kettle sat on a back burner and a washrag hung over the center divider of the sink. The living room furniture, which had never been moved in all her years here, was in different spots, however. The couch was pushed under the wide window, the curtains partially open. Two chairs had been placed in front of the couch, as though they were expecting company, and a small wooden coffee table had been added. Ava traced her finger around the imprint left behind by a glass that had sat there without a coaster. The pictures on the fireplace mantel were the same, aside from the one she had stolen. In its place was one clipped from a newspaper: Sebastian held her close and her head was tipped back in laughter. It took a moment to recognize the image that had been snapped during their tour. She'd been so unsuspecting, so unaware of everything that would follow their crazy week together, that she'd allowed herself to believe in happiness.

In the possibility of love in the arms of a stranger.

Looking at it, she expected some sort of reaction; one of regret maybe? Loss? But she felt nothing, and it was in this lack of turmoil where she realized she would never love him. Despite his goodness and kindness, he just wasn't the one with whom she was meant to endure life.

Which reassured, above everything, that she couldn't marry him.

Ava had always hoped one day she would have the kind of love to rival that of Cordellia and Dante. She wanted that can't eat, can't sleep, can't exist without him sort of love. She wanted to know that, without fear, in his hands she could break into a million pieces and he wouldn't hesitate to put her back together. She wanted someone who would make her a better person. Someone who would not try to change her, but instead admire her flaws and find beauty in them.

Sebastian wasn't that guy.

Which meant she needed to find a way to get out of marrying him.

Maybe I can blackmail Orion, she thought as she flicked the light switch at the top of the basement stairs. Cordellia's work music cut out almost immediately and Ava settled onto the couch. While she waited for her mother, she considered this option. If she presented Orion with what she knew, threatened to take it to the papers, would he believe her?

Would he be scared enough to just let her leave? What were the chances he wouldn't have some sinister backup plan, like having her murdered the moment she passed through the gates?

It *was* his go-to method, after all.

There are risks, but is the possibility of being free of High House, of the lies it is built upon, worth them? Or is ending his life the better option, ensuring he doesn't have a chance to kill me first?

Nixon was right, of course. She wouldn't make it out alive if she took that route. Unfortunately, there were too many ways it could all end, and she didn't have the mental capacity to work them out right now. She needed to stay focused on the reason she was here and the questions gathering in her mouth.

"Avaleigh?" The frantic voice of her mother shattered her thoughts as Cordellia rounded the corner and stepped into the living room. Her grey apron looked like a nebula, with specks of greens, purples, reds, silvers and gold from gemstones and metals. Her hair was a disaster and she had smudges all over her face, but she looked good. Healthier than Ava had ever seen. She'd put on some weight, which meant she was eating, and her hair, despite its disorder, had a shine to it.

Tears sprang to Ava's eyes as she took in the woman in front of her. It was a projection of the person she had always wanted her mother to become, but never believed possible.

"Hi, Mom," she said as she brushed at her wet cheek.

Cordellia stared at her only child. Her eyes were wild, as if she couldn't believe what she was seeing. Then, before Ava could register she was even moving, she crossed the room and stepped into her mother's arms. She sank into the embrace and inhaled the familiar metallic scent. It was laced with hints of mango and vanilla. The two women held one another until their arms ached from the grip, both afraid that if they let go, the mirage would disintegrate like wet sand.

It was the older of the two who finally pulled away, although only enough to cup Ava's face. "I forgot how beautiful you are," she whispered before kissing Ava on the forehead. Ava couldn't help but smile at the gesture. She'd been kissed on the forehead by both Sebastian and Nixon, but neither had come as close to comforting as that of her mother. It was a simple thing, and it was just what she needed to steel herself again.

"Are you good?" she asked. She didn't need to explain what she meant.

Cordellia nodded and smiled. "I am," she said, and Ava believed her. "The medication is working wonders and my head is clearer than it's been in years. Some days are still hard, I still miss you and your father, but I get through them. I *want* to get through them. So yes, I'm good."

"That's great," Ava replied, hugging her again.

"Are *you* good?"

Laughing once, Ava detangled herself from her mother and took a seat on the couch again. Patting the spot next to her, she waited while Cordellia settled beside her. "I need something from you," she said as she took her mother's hands in hers.

"Of course."

"Before I ask for it, you have to promise me you'll be honest. No matter how hard it is, you have to give me the truth. Don't worry about protecting me, okay? Because that isn't what matters right now. If you can't do that, if you can't promise me transparency, then I'll go."

A handful of seconds passed while Cordellia considered this small but terrifying request. She had a feeling she knew why Ava had come, the words that would follow once she agreed, and the mere idea of pulling off that band-aid terrified her. But the look of desperation straining the face of her child—her pride and absolute joy—chased away any apprehension. She was ready to let the wound breathe, to finally start the healing process.

She nodded once. "Honesty and transparency I can give you."

Ava smiled her thanks, though it was tight lipped and quick, and then she swallowed. "Is Dante my father?" she blurted. It was the hardest question, with the most important answer, which is why it tumbled out first. If she could get the worst stuff out of the way, then everything that followed would, theoretically, be easy-peasy.

This was certainly not the question Cordellia had been expecting, and the weight of it forced her back a step. "Of course he is your father," she replied, a hint of incredulity on the cusp of her answer. "Why would you ever doubt that?"

Pressing her palms against her eyes, Ava sighed. "The king has this book," she began, lowering her hands, "and in it are the marriages, births, and deaths of all of Havaan. Under my name you're listed as my mother, but the father part says father unknown—"

"And your first instinct was I had lied to you all these years?"

"You haven't told me much about Dante," Ava reminded. "It was a natural assumption. It didn't make me feel great, if that helps." Looking at her mother again Ava asked, "Why wasn't he recorded as my father? Was he ashamed of—"

"No, Avaleigh, he wasn't ashamed of you. Your father loved you more than words." Cordellia exhaled deeply and used her fingers to push away the grey wisps tickling her forehead. "Because he loved you, he wanted to protect you."

"Protect me from what? From *who?*"

Cordellia shook her head. It was a signal Ava recognized all too well. It meant she was about to shut down, vanish into the place she went when facing the world became too scary. But when she said, "It's complicated," her voice was at least clear. Not frantic like it normally became.

"It doesn't get to be complicated, Mom. Transparency, remember? I'm not a little girl anymore. I don't need you to protect me from the monsters. I promise you, I have already faced them."

The look that passed behind her mother's eyes could be interpreted as nothing more than failure. Shame. All her life, Cordellia had tried to guard Ava against the ugliness of the world. She had not been successful behind closed doors, but her daughter had survived life just fine, grew from the ashes with a strength and self-awareness Cordellia both envied and admired. Sometime in the night, Ava had become an adult. In the blink of an eye she'd gone from learning words to having a powerful gamut of her own, ones with a voice strong enough to back them up. Cordellia did not know where this woman had come from— this tough, independent lioness—but she was proud it was her daughter.

"Your dad was magic," she began. Her fingers worked the wrinkled, metallic-dusted fabric of her apron. "I don't know what his abilities were, but they were rare. And those powers were one of the biggest reasons Orion won the war. When it was over, Dante wanted a simple life again. He wanted nothing more to do with battles or ridding Havaan of magic. For a while, he had it. We had it. It was as though the war had been nothing more than a dream, one of those that feel so real you get déjà vu.

"But Orion grew paranoid, and though your father tried to keep that part of his life separate from the one he had with us, it was impossible. The king would summon him at all hours of the day, pull him from the boat early. At one point, it got so extreme that a messenger would knock on the door almost daily. Sometimes it would be in the evening during dinner, while other times Dante left in nothing more than pajamas and slippers. As these summonses became more frequent, your father became more…cautious. I asked him if the king was dangerous, if *we* were in danger. When he said there wasn't a cause for concern, I could tell he was lying. I don't know what he thought Orion was up to and I don't know if part of his fear came from someone discovering your bloodline, but when you were born he asked we not link the two of you together." A single tear rolled down Cordellia's cheek and she dabbed it away with the hem of her apron. The action deposited microscopic shards of metal that highlighted her face whenever the light kissed her. It was like she was glowing from the inside out, and not for the first time, Ava wondered how different their life would be if Dante hadn't died.

If he hadn't been murdered.

"Do you come from magic, as well?" she asked.

Cordellia smiled sadly. "I don't have a thread of it anywhere in my bloodline. But your father's family…" She shook her head slowly, as though the magnitude of what she needed to say was too big. "Both of his parents were full magician, which meant your father was, as well. Which means, yes, sweet girl, you would have been, too. Not fully, of course, but there *is* magic in you. Somewhere, lying dormant in your veins, is untapped power."

Sebastian's words echoed through her mind: "Do you honestly believe there aren't any citizens, in all of Havaan, who don't still have traces of magic in their veins? We just have to find a way to trigger it."

Swallowing the lump in her throat, Ava slumped back against the couch. Power. *Magic.* The thing which had driven a wedge between she and Sebastian was the thing she possessed. Passed to her by, if what both Cordellia and Orion claimed was true, an incredibly strong thaumaturge.

Never once had she been made to believe she was special. Quite the contrary. Her entire existence, her importance and aspirations, had been overshadowed by the happenstance of which side of the social divide she lived.

What is going on in my life? she asked herself as she tried to digest it all. First, she was chosen as queen based on nothing more than the fact that Nixon couldn't keep his eyes off her, and now this. She sat up quickly, as if pulled by invisible strings, when another question struck. This one she couldn't help voice aloud.

"Did you ever meet Orion?"

Cordellia nodded. "Once. Many years ago, before the thought of a war was on anyone's mind. But Dante never called me Cordellia. He called me Daisy, because of the flower crown I wore the night we met."

Tiny pieces of things were beginning to come together. She was starting to see the larger picture in the fragments. "Is that why you didn't go to the Welcome Dinner?"

"I don't know if Orion would recognize me, but I didn't want to risk it. If he did, he would connect your father and his abilities to you and they would take advantage of you, if not worse. Dante wanted to keep you safe, so I did what I had to in order to honor that. Even if I didn't understand it fully. Even if I knew it would hurt you."

Each answer gave way to two, even three more. They filed through Ava's mind so quickly she barely had time to process the first before the next was out of her mouth. Instead of asking the one begging to be set free—why her mother had been so insistent on Ava accepting the crown—unexpected panic filled her and pushed forth a different one.

"Is it possible Orion found out who my father is? Could he have somehow pieced it together and that's why I was chosen?" Orion had always been nice to her, though, had never seemed vindictive or worried that she somehow knew the truth of what had happened all those years ago. If anyone had been less than kind it had been the queen, but the king had also, on many occasions, told Ava she reminded him of someone. Had he been testing her, trying to gauge whether she was privy to his secrets?

Was it possible he'd meant to bring her to High House so he could keep her under a microscope in case she…what…? Picked up where Dante had left off?

Cordellia's hand, as it gently squeezed her knee, brought Ava back to the living room, with its rearranged furniture and sunlight slicing across the center of the couch. "There's no reason for him to suspect anything, I promise you. Your father was diligent in keeping you safe. I'm not sure what your father was trying to protect you from, but I can't imagine he didn't cover every possible trail leading back to you." Resting her other hand on the side of Ava's face, she tucked a loose piece of hair behind her ear. "Why the necessity for answers now? Has something happened?"

Ava wanted nothing more than to unload the past couple of days into her mother's lap, to purge the secrets tucked behind her ribcage. But Cordellia was just starting to get better. Her mind seemed calm. She wasn't a mess of misery buried six feet under a mound of blankets and mourning shrouds. She was present—more so than she had been in all twenty years of Ava's life. Now was not the time to put her back by the grave when she was just beginning to live again.

Instead, Ava pulled the photo Nixon had given her from the pocket of her shorts and handed it to her mother. "I found this, tucked away in a book in the library. I recognized your handwriting. Between this and the census book, I just...I felt now was the time."

A slow smile spread across Cordellia's lips and when she glanced up at her daughter, her grey eyes glistened. Then she looked back down at the picture and traced Dante's face with her finger, exactly as Ava had done. "Nixon looks so much like his dad, doesn't he? The first time I saw him, I could have sworn I was looking at a ghost."

"Did you know Felix?"

"I did. He was your dad's best friend, long before talks of war. He was the magnet which pulled Dante and Orion together. When he died, I think the two of them anchored themselves together through his memory, through this commonality they shared. If it hadn't been for Felix, I don't think your dad and Orion would have had any reason to associate."

How ironic it was that Ava and Nixon had found their way to one another. Was it purely coincidence their paths had crossed, then looped, then merged into one? Or had there been a bigger force at work all these years?

"Do you blame Felix for Dante's death?" Ava asked.

"Not anymore," Cordellia replied honestly. "Dante never wanted to be a soldier, had promised me he was only helping to plan, but he was loyal to a fault and that drew him to the field." *Just like Felix*, Ava thought. As if looking at Dante for too long hurt too much, Cordellia flipped the photo over and handed it back to Ava.

"The war did something to your father," she continued. Her voice was steady, though it swirled with both anger and sadness. "It took a part of him and left scars no one could see. As they healed…" She cleared her throat. "The war took one man, gave me back another, and I was never sure if the one he was before was ever going to come back."

"But he did, right?" There was a sense of eagerness to the question which Ava didn't understand at first. She knew so little of Dante as it was, but what stories her mother *had* told her——from what Zarah had shared——Dante wasn't weak. He wasn't like Cordellia was now. A part of the mirage she'd formed of her father had already begun to crack under the possibility of him being a traitor.

She wasn't sure it would survive finding out he'd been lost to his grief, as well.

"He did," Cordellia answered, pushing away the lingering bits of Ava's worry. Pressing a hand to her stomach, Cordellia continued. "When I found out I was pregnant, the mere idea of you filled in all the pieces that had gone missing. Your life renewed the sense of his own." This time when she smiled, it was radiant. Honest. Pure in only the way a mother's love can be. "I always thought I would be jealous if he ever loved someone more than he loved me. But he loved *you* in a way I never knew possible. He loved you with a ferocity I don't think another man will ever be able to match. All he wanted was for you to be safe and happy. For you to grow strong, not only in strength, but mentally as well. For you to follow your own path. He would be so proud to know that, despite his absence, you've become more than he could have dreamed. That despite *my* absence and all the darkness I have filtered into your life, you have always shown bright."

Cordellia locked her gaze with Ava's, this time holding it. "I'm sorry I kept him from you for so long. It just seemed unfair to tell you about the amazing man who helped create you when you would never get to meet him. But I guess hiding behind his death, hoarding my memories of him, was unfair too, wasn't it?"

Wiping her nose on the back of her hand, Ava sniffled, then used her fingers to push away the rest of her tears. It was hard to find the positive in everything she'd uncovered lately, and it had taken a lot of awful days to get here, but she was abundantly thankful she and her mother had finally reached this point.

When Cordellia said, "Why don't you dig out the makings for S'mores and meet me in the backyard? I think it's time I introduced you to your father," that thankfulness increased tenfold.

By the light of the summer moon and the roaring flames of a bonfire, Cordellia produced picture after picture and story after story of Dante Noriega. Ava read and re-read letters written in his masculine script. The two women laughed at his shenanigans and cried over the memories they would never make.

At the very bottom of the box, which Cordellia had kept under her bed all these years, was a vibrant red piece of paper folded into thirds. The two halves met at the middle, and at one point had been sealed by a waxed crest of the king.

"What's this?" Ava asked when she reached it.

"That's the letter they delivered when your father died. They send it to the family of the deceased when they pass away in service for the royal family." Cordellia snarled at the letter. Ava scanned the page, disgusted by how generic the words were. "For as close as Orion and your father were," Cordellia said when she mentioned it, "you'd think he'd have taken time to write a personalized message. I never thought too highly of him, but that sealed the deal for me." Taking the piece of paper from Ava, she flipped it over and over. "I've thought about burning it countless times."

"Why don't you?" Ava asked.

Cordellia shook her head. "I don't know." Then without another word, she flung the note into the fire. They sat in silence as the words that had sent Cordellia on her downward spiral ignited, the edges of the paper curling then burning until they were nothing but ash.

They were not the kind of memories that belonged buried under so many good ones.

After a while, Ava brought her hand to her mouth to cover a long yawn. She wasn't sure what time it was, just that night had arrived with its midnight cloak. They had watched the sky change from baby blue to navy while they sorted through the two shoeboxes Cordellia had brought outside. As they'd toasted marshmallows and squeezed the gooey center out between graham crackers and chocolate bars, the sun had set; the black of night erasing the stripes of violet-red and orange-yellow painted above Havaan.

Now the events of the faded day were catching up with Ava, the smoke of the fire syphoning her energy with each pop of a log.

"I don't want to go back to High House," Ava mumbled while pulling her knees to her chest. Just the thought of returning to the mansion, with its bricks of lies and foundation of bones, was suffocating. The last thing she wanted to do was look any of them in the eye or share the same air with them. Even Nixon, who had done nothing but try and help. She had never felt such an overwhelming sense of loneliness and isolation. This included the three days in fifth grade when Delilah had been out with the flu and Ava had eaten lunch in one of the bathroom stalls, too uncomfortable under the judgmental glares of her classmates to sit at the table she had since the start of the school year.

D had always been her buffer in times like this. When the weight of the world was too much to bear, she was right there, taking her half of the heft. But Ava didn't want even her best friend right now. Who she wanted was the woman sitting next to her, the one who couldn't take her eyes off the flickering flames. She was no doubt thinking about Dante and how they had first met; how she had glimpsed him through the fire when she was eighteen years old, with a crown of daisies on her head and a life of opportunities at her feet.

"Then don't go back," Cordellia said as though it were the simplest answer in all of Havaan.

Ava sighed. "I have to."

"But you don't have to go back *tonight*," her mother replied. When she turned toward her, Ava saw the woman her father must have seen: intense grey eyes the color of burned charcoal, full lips, small button nose, cheekbones that could only be described as regal. Cordellia had said many times she couldn't understand why Dante had been attracted to her, but Ava could. Her mother was beautiful, even with the reminder of time lightly drawn into her skin. She had no doubt Dante would find her just as beautiful *now* as he had the night they met.

"Whatever brought you here tonight will still be at High House tomorrow. There's no need to hurry back to them if you're not ready. Even a future queen needs time to herself." Ava nodded. As Cordellia stood, crumbs from the graham crackers falling to the ground, she added, "I'll make up your bedroom."

"Don't," Ava insisted. "I'll sleep in the guest room."

Looking down, the fire playing with the angles and depths of her face, Cordellia asked, "Are you sure?"

Ava had spent many days and nights in the guest room when it had been Zarah's: first when she was healthy and later when she wasn't. They played card games when she could sit up, and in the hours when she couldn't, they would lay side by side while Ava read poetry—some allotted but much forbidden—out loud. Pieces by Walt Whitman, Langston Hughes, Maya Angelou and John Milton.

When Zarah had passed away, so too did Ava's need to waste hours in the room.

It wasn't until the nights when Nixon stayed with them had she even gone into the bedroom, afraid she might find Zarah's ghost sitting on the edge of the bed, leafing through the disorganized manuscript she'd passed on to Ava.

Even now, as she let the door fall open on squeaky hinges, part of her worried at what she would find. Yet when the light turned on and the darkness vacated, it was as it had always been: just a room with a neatly made bed and the smell of lavender captured in the bedding. Before crawling under the blankets, Ava had showered in the small bathroom with its tub/shower combo and rose-printed curtain. She had missed the sound of the water hitting the plastic. The muted *plop*s were so different than the *plinks* they made against the glass wall of the one at High House. Here, it was comforting, and if she didn't think about it, she could act—like her father had done—as if the last couple of months had been nothing but a never-ending dream. She couldn't say nightmare, because there had been some good moments.

There had even been great moments.

Now, dressed in a pair of old pajama bottoms and a faded t-shirt too short to wear in public, Ava settled between the sheets that had, not so long ago, encased Nixon. Turning into the pillow, she inhaled deeply. Though Zarah's scent still lingered, there was also an underlying hint of mint and cotton, a cleanliness that didn't come from the detergent Cordellia used.

"I miss you," she whispered into the darkness as she let the heaviness of her eyes drag them closed.

It was a message sent to the three out of four people she cared about the most in this world: two who had shaped her in more ways than she'd ever thought possible; and one she didn't know but who had done just the same.

XLVII.

The next morning, after a breakfast of eggs, bacon and toast, and dressed in clothes the queen would frown upon, Ava followed the winding road away from Holland Avenue and back to High House. As she drove, the wind drying her curls and a soft jazz rhythm trickling from the radio, she was at peace. At least as much as she could be with everything looming ahead. Oddly enough, she left home with more questions than with which she'd arrived. Different questions, particularly about Dante's abilities and what that meant for her.

If anything.

Though many of the answers she had gotten from her mother had only verified Orion's words, more importantly they had broken through a barrier. One that had been there for twenty years, keeping mother and daughter apart even when they were sitting side-by-side. Ava would never know her father outside memories Cordellia could provide, but she had learned more about him in twelve hours than she had her entire life. All things considered, that was a win. It was a victory she would gladly accept.

Part of her wished she could speak to Orion about Dante, gain a different kind of insight than the mushy, love-struck one her mother offered, but she knew she couldn't do such a thing without raising suspicions.

She also knew what she had to do about her future…and that was leave High House.

At one point, not so long ago, she had entertained the idea of being queen, of sitting next to Sebastian and ruling by his side, harvesting good in their country. Giving all of that up would mean giving up full unity in Havaan. Sebastian would move forward with his dreams of bringing magic back to their country, and as a result, a division greater than the current one would take its place. This was a certainty Ava could not shake. It pained her and was almost enough to convince her to tough it out, but she could not stay in a place where so much evil existed. It was only a matter of time before it consumed all the good residing there. She had already felt it beginning to seep its way into her bones. It wove ideas of murder into her mind and formed the whisperings into tangible shapes. The promise of the crown was already changing her, and it was not a change she liked.

It was not hard to believe it would ultimately do the same to Sebastian.

He was the byproduct of two people who had wicked souls. From day one, from the moment he took his first breath, hands that dripped with violence and malevolence had molded him and readied him for the day he would take his place as king.

As good and as kind as he was now, there was no way he could escape his genetics.

So, Ava needed to escape, instead.

Until then, she needed to be on high alert. She could not trust the shadows at her back.

Because if she could connect the dots, put pieces of information together, that meant someone else would be able to, as well. She could not be around when and if that happened; if and when someone figured out the connection between her and Dante.

Between she and the king.

She would have to temporarily ignore her instinct to fight. She would become complacent, overlook everything she knew and pretend to be unaware of Orion's unsavory actions. He alone could grant her the exit she needed, but to get to that point she had to appeal to his better nature. It was not a plan with which she was happy, but one that must be done.

If she had known that in a matter of weeks things would change in the most unexpected of ways, she might have considered another course of action all together. As it was, whatever abilities her father may or may not have passed onto her, seeing into the future was not one of them.

If she had known magic swam in her body, would she have been more eager to listen to Sebastian's harebrained idea?

Perhaps he's come further along, she thought, then immediately scolded herself at how quickly she had changed her tune. If she could be so easily teased by the prospect of magic, the rest of Havaan would not fare well.

When the iron gates of High House yawned open, activated by a switch in the vehicle, Ava drove the car around the right side of the house and back into the garage. She returned the keys to the lockbox. Being the future queen had allowed her the combination. It hadn't needed to be used until last night, and after the stunt she'd pulled, she wouldn't be surprised if they took the privilege away.

Ava made her way to the front of the house and halted mid-step when Delilah's head snapped up. Her brown eyes tossed daggers at her best friend from her place on the porch.

"Where in the hell were you?" she shouted as Ava approached. D's small body shook with not only anger, but also relief. A million scenarios had plagued her waking hours, as well as her sleeping ones, and only one of them had ended with Ava returning in one piece. None had planned for the casualness with which she strolled up: as if she'd just been out for a leisurely, every day walk around the gardens and not missing for seventeen hours.

"Home," Ava replied coolly, though she made a conscious effort to keep her distance from Delilah. She had only ever seen D get violent once, and when it had happened she'd been wearing the exact same expression. "Some stuff came up and I just needed to get away from everything. From all of this." Without thought her eyes flickered to the house.

"And you didn't think to tell anyone? I have been so worried about you. I didn't know if you were coming back, if you were dead. No one had *any* clue where you had gone. You can't just do shit like that anymore, Ava. You're important now!"

Ava blinked away the words. It was not the first time Delilah had tossed them at her feet. Before, Ava had tripped over them, the implication skinning her knees. Now, she hopscotched her way around them. she opened her mouth to apologize, then closed it again. She didn't have anything to apologize *for*. She felt bad Delilah had been made to worry, but aside from being kidnapped, there were only a few places Ava would intentionally venture.

Besides, she was done apologizing for looking out for her best interests.

"I'm back now," she said as she stepped around Delilah.

Slender fingers wrapped around her wrist, holding her in place. "I'm supposed to be the one you go to when things hit the fan. You're not supposed to run away. Not from me."

Ava looked at Delilah. A part of her resolve crumbled at the look on her face. It was obvious she hadn't gotten much sleep, whereas Ava had slept like a rock.

"You're right," Ava said by way of apology. "It was wrong of me to go without letting anyone know. It won't happen again."

Dropping her hand, Delilah firmly replied, "Don't let it."

"How mad is everyone else?" Ava asked as the two women planted themselves on the porch.

"Sebastian was a mess, scared you weren't going to come back. He sent Nixon out to try and find you, but when he came back empty handed, it only made things worse." Ava couldn't help the small twitch of a smile that teased her lips. Nixon, of all people, would have thought to look at Cordellia's. She hadn't heard the roar of his motorcycle, but that didn't mean he hadn't done a pass. She'd have to thank him for covering for her later. "Orion tried to ignore everything and keep the festivities going, but it's hard to be in a partying mood when the future queen is missing. And Bernadette…" Delilah shrugged. "She was pissed."

Ava scoffed. "Bernadette gets pissed if I breathe wrong. I'm not concerned about her wrath." The two women sat in silence, or as much as High House would allow. Ava had never noticed how loud it really was. There was always something going on, some sort of sound taking place, and it surprised her how quickly she had gotten used to the ruckus. Being back home had reminded her of what comfortable, peaceful silence sounded like. There were still noises, but they lingered in the background; a white hum that added to the ambience, like the rush of waves or cricket songs. Here, everything was so invasive, a twelve-piece marching band that made it hard to think sometimes.

Suddenly, Delilah sighed. "Why won't you talk to me?" she asked. "Whatever is going on, you can tell me. I'm your assistant. That's what I'm here for."

When Ava looked at her, she was startled by the look of genuine dolefulness with which she was met. It was a look of vulnerability, and it took Ava back to the days when she and D both lived in Meridian: when they were young and innocent and had no qualms about sharing their emotions. There was no need to fear the susceptibility, no understanding that the more you opened yourself up to it, the more it allowed people to hurt you. It was a face Delilah had not worn in a very long time and it filled Ava with so much guilt she almost vomited everything right there on the cobblestone. By all the stars over Havaan—by all the secrets of the king—she wanted to tell Delilah *everything.*

But at the last minute, she swallowed it back down and instead said, "The queen doesn't tell her assistant all her secrets, Delilah."

"Then as your best friend, tell me."

Ava shook her head and begged, with her eyes, for Delilah to let it go. "I can tell you even less as my best friend."

Rolling her eyes, Delilah complained, "That makes no sense."

"I have learned things lately that are dangerous," Ava explained as simply as she could. "If I gave them to you it would be like handing you a bomb. Knowing what I know could destroy a lot. A lot of people, including myself, and I don't want you to be caught up in the wreckage. I wish I could tell you, I do, but I need you to let me protect you from this, okay? Please." Tears tickled her bottom lashes, but she blinked them away. She had never cried as much as she had since the night of the gala, and frankly she was getting a bit bored of it.

If her moment of weakness had any effect on Delilah, she wasn't going to let on. "I don't need you to protect me, Avie."

Ava tried a different approach, one she wasn't happy with. "I'm not going to put you at risk, Delilah. Do not ask me about this again," she said, her voice firm.

Delilah hooked an eyebrow at her. "Are you *demanding* this as the future queen or my best friend?"

Standing, because sitting was making her anxious, Ava replied, "Whoever you respect more. I need to talk to Sebastian." Then she moved to the door and left Delilah sitting on the stoop, simmering in her confusion and anger.

Ava had been weird lately—distant. Delilah could feel her pulling away more and more each day. She had tried to pinpoint exactly when things had changed and *why,* but she couldn't. The days were all mushed together into one discombobulated mess and within the mobocracy it was impossible to distinguish one turn of events from another. But if she didn't figure it out soon, and then find a way to fix it, she was going to lose her best friend completely. There would be a void they would be unable to traverse no matter how close they stood to one another.

As Delilah watched Ava retreat, she felt that gap increasing just a little more.

At the door, with her hand on the knob, Ava said, "I love you." Then she tacked on two words she had refused to say again. "I'm sorry." Before the words could reach Delilah, Ava pushed her way into the foyer.

She half expected the Calder family to bum-rush her upon her arrival. To corner her by the coatrack and demand an explanation for a vanishing act that would impress Houdini himself. But the foyer was empty. The natural melodies of the day-to-day flooded the space from all sides, like a living surround sound system. The kitchen reverberated with pots and pans clanking against one another and the shouts of recipes from chef to assistant. The far-off hum of a vacuum came from the right. The growl of a lawnmower seeped in from the back yard. Footsteps thudded back and forth across the hallway upstairs. Doors opened and closed as ghosts entered and exited the numerous rooms. Pipes groaned as water was transported throughout the mansion. It grated on her, each sound filtering into her brain and pushing aside all other thoughts. She wanted to cover her ears with her hands and scream for it to stop, but that would not bode well for her plan of acting calm and collected, as though nothing were wrong.

She needed to fake her way through the next couple of days—weeks, at the most—until she had a solid plan to get out of here. Away from the voices and the noise, the anger and the lies. Away from all the things she didn't want and back to the things she did.

Some moments it felt as if High House would become her mausoleum, that she would die in this place, destined to forever pass through its walls. But as quickly as those thoughts arrived, she shooed them away. If she let them linger, she would lose her sanity. She would not give up hope, not until she had to. Not until she was lying in a cell in Nopels or taking her last ragged breath.

Whichever came first.

Instead of acting like a spoiled child and demanding silence, Ava went up the left staircase and down the boy's hall. She'd told Delilah she needed to talk to Sebastian, and she did, but she stopped at another door first.

She knocked on the door of the bedroom with which she was more familiar—it was not lost on her that she *still* hadn't seen the bedroom of the man she was supposed to marry—and waited.

When she'd made her great escape, she had been angry at Nixon, not because of what he had shown her—for that she was grateful—but because he had stood by the king's side after learning what he had done. In the heat of her ire, she couldn't grasp why he had done so, but after her night away she was less upset. She didn't agree with it—still couldn't fully wrap her mind around why he had stayed—but she wanted to better understand it from his perspective. More than that, she wanted him to know she was still on his side and that she wasn't going to put him in a position to choose between herself and the king.

Despite the bond the two of them had formed, she didn't want to know what choice he would ultimately make. She was not naïve enough to believe that whatever feelings he had for her would be stronger than the relationship between he and Orion.

She cared about Nixon too much to ask him to choose.

For now, at least.

If in the long run things did not go as planned, if something forced her to take Orion's life, she would. What Nixon did then would be up to him, and she would accept whatever decision he made.

All she wanted to do right now was apologize and thank him for covering for her, but after knocking a couple more times and getting no response, she put it on the back burner. *He's probably training,* she rationalized as she went downstairs and out the back door. However, instead of taking the path toward the aggressive grunts of the guards, she went to the greenhouse and unlocked the heavy padlock.

If Dante had indeed passed something onto her, there was only one way to find out.

The greenhouse was as hot as it had been the first time and the heat stole her breath. Sweat beaded on her upper lip, rolled down the center of her chest, and gathered along the back of her neck. The spotlight glows of the potted plants danced across the ceiling. Ava wondered why their vibrancy was never visible from the outside. Maybe it was impossible to penetrate the layer of ivy blanketing the glass. Or maybe the glass itself was the clue. Or maybe it was just because they were magic and enchanted things operated with their own set of rules.

Ava let out an exasperated sigh and pulled her attention from the lights. She planted herself in front of the wall of dead leaves. If what Sebastian had said was true, if magic did indeed need magic to operate, then it was possible she had enough juice in her to make the Portalis do *something*.

"Right?" she asked no one. Shaking her hands out, she realized she had absolutely no idea where or how to start. Why did she think just standing in front of a bunch of dead plants would trigger her magic? Or that her magic would have the power to revitalize something as big as a portal?

"Because you're an idiot," she mumbled to herself, then she rolled her shoulders. She tried to block out the words in her head and the sounds filtering around her. She concentrated everything she had on making something—anything—happen.

And she refused to leave until it did.

But when ten minutes slipped into twenty, and twenty dragged into thirty, and there was change in nothing more than her patience and confidence, she was beginning to realize how futile it all was. The time was drawing closer when she would have to admit Dante had passed along nothing more than his curly hair and big blue eyes.

It would make sense she hadn't gotten the magical part of his bloodline.

She was an ordinary person with an ordinary life and being able to activate some hidden genetic ability in less than an hour didn't fit in with that.

"Shut up," she scolded.

"I didn't say anything," a voice replied. She yelped and turned around. "What are you doing?" Levi asked, offering his lopsided smile.

"Nothing," Ava lied. She hoped he couldn't hear the thundering in her chest.

Taking slow, tentative steps toward her he said, "It looks like you were staring at a wall of dead leaves." He brushed a finger down one of them and it fluttered to the ground like paper confetti.

"Well then, that's exactly what I was doing. You act as though it's weird or something."

Levi chuckled. "Totally natural," he said, his voice light and playful. "Welcome back, by the way."

"Thanks." She pursed her lips to the side. "Are you mad at me, too?"

"Nah. I knew you were safe."

Ava raised a questioning brow. "How?"

"Nixon and I found the car at your mother's house. It was like, the first place we looked. Once we saw you were there we figured you'd be okay. Then we drove around and got shaved ice from the market before returning. Don't tell anyone, though."

Miming a zipper across the lips, Ava tossed Levi the invisible key. He played along and caught it, then swallowed it. She didn't spend much time with Levi, which was kind of a bummer, because the little bits of it that she got here and there, she enjoyed greatly.

Once the key was safe in his stomach, Ava said, "Well, thank you for covering for me. I'll have to thank Nixon later, too. And apologize. To everyone."

"You'll have to wait a couple of days for the last part. Mom, Nixon and Sebastian aren't here right now."

Ava's eyebrows lowered. "Oh. Where are they?"

Dropping himself to the ground, his back pressed against the conservatory wall, Levi said, "They went to visit my aunt."

The glass, as Ava sank down next to Levi, was cool against her back despite the heat. She wanted to press her entire body against it, but she didn't think she could brush that off as easily as she had the leaf-wall weirdness.

"The future queen goes missing and they just flounce away for a family vacation?"

"You left all of your stuff here. It was safe to say you were coming back."

"Hm," Ava huffed. If they had suspected she would return, why did Delilah act as though all of Havaan had been put on high alert? Was it just another ploy, a way for the king and queen to say they checked all the boxes in case something happened to Ava? She was annoyed with herself that she was annoyed by this, so she changed the subject.

"I didn't know you had an aunt," she said. It occurred to her then how little she knew about any of the Calders, even after all this time. Was that why things kept surprising her? Maybe Nixon had always known how devious and dangerous the king was, and so his betrayal hadn't come as a great shock. Helen wasn't taken aback when Ava had revealed Sebastian's hopeful magic reintroduction because it had been a topic of conversation before.

Ava was, and would always be, years behind.

A ghost at their dinner table which memories and stories passed through.

Which was another reason she couldn't stick around.

She couldn't marry into a family that would always have layers of secrets too thick for her to ever permeate.

Eventually it would crush her.

"I do," Levi said. "Just one. She's older than my mother. I guess she isn't doing too well health-wise."

"I'm sorry to hear that," Ava said, offering her sympathies. "Why didn't you go with them?"

Levi shrugged. "We're not really that close. And she's always liked Sebastian better."

"I doubt that."

"It's true," he countered. "She told me." A look of pure shock dropped Ava's jaw and widened her eyes. It seemed that Bernadette and her sister shared their bluntness. Ava disliked her almost immediately. "I don't take it personally," Levi continued, his voice even with truth. "She's had more time with Sebastian. And he's the heir. Stuff like that matters to her."

"Even so. That's still really shitty."

Levi laughed and nodded once. "It can be. But not everyone in life is going to like everyone else. I have enough people who *do* like me."

Nudging his shoulder with hers, Ava said, "I think you're pretty great."

"I think you're pretty great, too, Ava."

Her heart contracted with a painful kind of happiness, and she smiled at him, doing her best to keep the sadness from leaking through. Ava adored Levi in a way she didn't anyone else in his family. She had never gotten a glimpse of anything but goodness and kindness from him. He was a great person, with a purity she hoped he would always hold onto—and she would miss him if—*when*—she left this awful place behind.

He was almost enough to make her want to stay.

"Did you get the answers you were looking for?" Levi asked.

"How did you know I went home looking for answers?" Ava cocked her head to the side slightly. Her eyes squinted half a centimeter under her curiosity.

"Nixon told me you'd uncovered some stuff and that you went home to question your mother about it. He didn't tell me what sort of stuff, though, and I didn't ask. It isn't my business."

"I got answers, but also more questions. Seems like a never-ending thing recently."

"We would stop learning if we stopped having questions to ask."

Ava regarded the guy sitting next to her. He was so unlike his brother it was as though the four-year difference had made them into two entirely different people, spun from completely opposite threads, with no semblance of sameness in their personalities. The physical similarities they shared were the only thing linking them as siblings.

His brown hair was longer than when she'd first met him, and while he kept the sides closely shaved, the top was growing in like a Chia pet. In his gentler features was a sincerity that seemed to have skipped the rest of the Calder family. Ava wondered, if he had been born first, what sort of king he would have been. Sebastian was kind, but he was also secretive and hard to read at times. He had dark parts that showed themselves at random junctures, and when they did it was as though she didn't know him.

In those moments, he changed into more of a stranger than he'd been when they began this journey together.

Levi was always open. He said what he was thinking without filter. He was honest and sincere, intelligent and logical. In the days to come, Ava would find herself relying heavily on those characteristics.

In the greenhouse, she nodded at his statement. "You are a wise one, young prince." He offered her a full grin, the dimples in his cheeks making a rare appearance. Before she could stop the words, they were out of her mouth. "Can I tell you something? Something you can't tell anyone else right now?"

Mimicking her from before, he zipped his lips and handed her the key. A small part of her felt guilty that she was going to tell Levi this information before she told Delilah. When had it become easier to talk to others than her best friend?

I will *tell Delilah*, she rationalized, if for nothing more than to alleviate the penitence.

There, on the broken ground of the greenhouse, with its surreal flowers and wall of ex-magical foliage, she told him what she had learned. Not about how *his* father had killed *her* father, but the part about Dante's powers, how he'd been strong with abilities that rivaled the most common ones. He listened to her without interruption, although his eyebrows remained raised the entire time. Ava didn't have the unique features of someone who had been created by a strong magician. A part of her still doubted what her mother had told her—what Orion had written—about Dante.

"I don't even know if he passed anything onto me," she explained, "but that's why I'm out here." She laughed once, humorously. "It's stupid."

"It's not stupid," Levi replied. "You have spent your whole life in the dark about this dude and now you have something to go on. You're looking for a connection to him, something you and he share. That isn't dumb. It's rational. And normal."

"Thanks." Ava gave him a tight smile and then leaned her head on his shoulder. Levi rested his cheek atop her curls.

"I could do some research if you want. See if there's some way to stimulate whatever powers you might have."

Ava sat up and looked at him. "You would do that?"

He shrugged a single shoulder. "Sure. I don't do much with my days, aside from fencing and helping in the barn. It'll be nice to have something to occupy my time."

Squeezing his hand, Ava said, "That would be great," around her wide grin. "How are things with Josiah, by the way?"

Levi looked startled. He blinked quickly and then stammered, "Wha...what? What do you mean?" The question tumbled from clumsy lips. He scratched at the back of his neck before running his fingers through the waves at the top of his head.

"With your...fencing?" Ava drew her response out slowly. She narrowed her eyes at him, her curiosity piqued.

"Oh." He exhaled an uneven breath and visibly relaxed. "They're going fine."

The corner of Ava's lips twitched as she tried to contain an understanding smirk. "Good to know."

They sat on the ground for a while longer, making small talk while pulling the weeds growing through the cracks in the walkway. When the bell for lunch sounded, a loud buzz that came from the barn, and the excited voices from the choir of guards filtered by the greenhouse, Ava and Levi pushed themselves up and joined the crowd.

They agreed to start their research after lunch, but even that felt too far away to Ava. She was suddenly desperate to feel Dante's magic pouring through her. Hell—she would even settle for a tickle, a pop; any indication that she was more. Ava was no longer content with being just a citizen of Havaan.

Delilah had said Ava was important now and she wanted that to be true. For the first time in her life, she had a purpose. Not one that centered around the crown, but because of the blood swirling inside of her. If Sebastian found out about her eagerness to trip the live wire in her veins, he could use it against her. Call her a hypocrite. *This* was a title she would gladly accept.

Ava's need to understand her powers—Dante's powers—went beyond just connecting with him. She still wasn't sold on the idea of magic running rampant in Havaan, but she also had a gut-wrenching feeling Sebastian would find a way to make it happen. If he did, and if the war she imagined followed, she wanted to be able to defend herself and those she loved with more than just steel.

The only way to beat magic was with magic.

Before, she had been willing to stand by Sebastian's side, to fight beside him even if she was shouting, "I told you so!" over the flames. But things had changed. If war ensued, she and the prince would be on opposite sides of the battle lines. And if she was forced to fight, she would make sure she did everything in her power to win.

XLVIII.

Ava became futilely obsessed with figuring out if Dante had passed along any of his magic, and if so, how to activate it. With Bernadette and her traveling entourage still absent, she was left with plenty of time to feed the beast. When she wasn't in the library—sometimes with Levi and sometimes without— scouring through page after page of text, she was in the greenhouse testing the theories that came from said research. Each time she failed, every time there was no change—she still wasn't sure what that change would be—her need only increased. She lost sleep, and any she did get was atop opened books. The ink would tattoo itself onto her skin and even in the mirror the words still made little sense.

Soon her mission stopped being about Dante's magic and more about him in general. Her attention shifted to collecting ammunition she could use against Orion.

When she got tired of rifling through the rows of unorganized books, with permission she borrowed one of the king's cars and spent the day at home with Cordellia's box of memories. The rubber-banded love letters were sappy but eloquently written, with beautiful prose that on occasion brought tears to her eyes. They spoke of Cordellia's beauty and of the ugliness of the upcoming war. They spoke of King Orion's excitement and then his paranoia. They laid out the plans Dante wanted with his leading ladies when all was said and done.

Every letter was signed with the mantra Ava had grown up hearing, like some sort of lullaby she could not understand: *mikor orada es tidak svar, enged dashuri fi itu clave.*

But the notes never mentioned Dante's abilities, never gave any indication he even had any. Each refolded and re-enveloped correspondence left Ava as uninformed as before.

Her quest for information and subsequently her failed attempts at triggering her abilities—of which she was really starting to doubt—had one bright spot: it allowed her to avoid the king. Where once he would have sought her out for a game of Checkers, he now kept his distance. Perhaps he could sense Ava's sudden distrust of him. Maybe the hate she felt was visible to him like ugly, festering sores.

Whatever the reason for his sudden disinterest in her, she was thankful.

The only time she was forced to be in the same room with him was during dinner. While Bernadette, Sebastian, and Nixon were gone, they could get away with eating at different times, blame it on scheduling conflicts or unintended naps. But when the trio returned three days later, the routines of High House resumed. At their first dinner together, Ava apologized to both Orion and Bernadette for her actions the night of the Governor's Dinner.

Bernadette's patented sneer assured Ava she didn't agree with her husband's response of, "We're just glad you're back safe and sound." Ava had little doubt the queen would have shed few tears if something horrific had happened to her. But Ava didn't care. She had no illusions that Bernadette would ever like her. The feeling was mutual.

Perhaps that's what made it easier to stomach.

Sometimes, Ava would stare at the king, astonished he could sit there so casually, so cavalier, after all the pain he had inflicted on his citizens. Because it wasn't just Ava's life that had been turned upside down by his actions. Others had suffered, too. Others had had their loved ones ripped away. The only difference was that they didn't know the truth. They had the joy of living in the dark, believing it had been a freak accident. A temper tantrum of Mother Nature and not of the man to whom they shouted their praises.

During these times, Nixon watched her like a hawk.

Ava could read the expectation on his face, as though he were waiting for her to jump up and bleed Orion's life onto his beef wellington. Like he was waiting for the king to face plant into his scallops, his throat closed via some poison she'd slipped into his glass.

"I'm not going to kill him," Ava confessed to Nixon one night as she was redressing. Sometimes her research became so grueling that she needed a temporary distraction.

Nixon was her favorite one.

He had been reluctant the first time she had come to him. The words they'd shouted at one another still coated their skin like sawdust. The tension between them was obvious, though it wasn't their typical kind. It didn't hum with need but crackled uncomfortably. Their attraction was still a live wire, but now it was unsecured, each spark a warning.

When she'd dropped her bathrobe on his bedroom floor and stood in front of him in nothing but her bare apology, any caution he'd been feeling vanished in the crash of lips and collision of skin.

Now, though, she didn't stay. As soon as she came down from the high he injected into her bloodstream, she untangled from him, avoided his eyes as she rewrapped herself. Nixon watched her from the bed, his head propped up in his hand.

"That's good to know," he'd replied, the relief evident in his tone. "I can't imagine you're just going to let this go, though."

Ava's lips curled into a small smile as her blue eyes settled on him. The bags under her oceans were dark, like the edge of the water where the moon never touches. "I have another plan," she replied as she buttoned her jeans. "I'm going to get out of here."

A black eyebrow rose, lifting the strand of hair that had fallen across his forehead. "Just like that, you think?"

"I hope," she answered. She gathered her hair in a messy bun on the top of her head. "Or I'll die trying."

"I would prefer you just leave if that's the only other option."

"Me, too," she agreed. She pushed her feet into her sandals. She hadn't been back to her room all day, even though it was ticking past midnight. It was imperative she wait until the entire house was asleep before she crept into Nixon's room. Not that she did it often.

Ava had become an apparition of High House's library, floating in and out of the room, appearing elsewhere only when summoned. She went to bed disappointed every night, but woke the next morning with renewed vigor. Failure drove her, unanswered questions fueled her need for more answers. Every morsel of information loosened her connection to High House, pushed her further from the crown and closer to the door. It was slow-going, and countless time she'd considered giving up, but then a vision of her father disappearing into the darkness of a raging ocean would flood her mind.

She would bring justice to Dante's name.

If nothing else came from all of this, that would be enough.

Before Ava left Nixon's room the last time, she looked over her shoulder at him and said, "You could come with me." They were an echo of the words Delilah had said to her all those months ago, when they'd been nothing more than two friends in their fancy dresses heading to a soiree that would, unknowingly, alter both of their lives in the craziest of ways. She would give so much to go back to that day. But Ava was a big believer in fate, and even if she'd done everything differently—if she'd hidden in the shadows more, kept out of Nixon's line of sight—anything besides simply staying home, she would be in the exact same situation she was now.

Nixon had just stared at her, his eyebrows pulled so low his forehead cast a shadow over his alluring eyes. His lips parted, as if he was going to say something, agree to come with her or out-right refuse, but she spoke first. She was afraid to hear the latter. Even though things were tense between them right now, she still cared for him in a way she never had anyone else before.

The feelings she had for him would not allow her to handle his rejection.

Not now. Not when she was already broken.

Instead, she had added, "Just...the offer is on the table." Then she'd slipped out of his room, making sure to close the door as quietly as possible. She kept her eyes diverted, refused to glance at the one a couple away. She didn't want to risk catching Sebastian's gaze through the wood.

As the days crept into weeks, life at High House seemed back to normal, though there was a lingering tension; smoke that pushed its way through the cracks and filled the rooms in a thin haze. Everyone smiled and joked as if they were trying to fan it away with laughter. Even Ava pretended to ignore the discomfort.

She needed everyone at ease and as unsuspecting of her as possible.

It was an illusion of calm before the storm.

A storm that would come, not a couple of days later, but weeks, when the end of the month was nearing and the heat was at its highest.

It would come at the worst time, conjured by the last person she'd ever expect.

Ava entered her bedroom with an armful of books dug from the very bottom shelves of the library. The spines were cracked and the pages hung on to the binding like the last baby tooth. They were the oldest books she'd been able to find. Thick layers of dust, which peeled away when she swiped her finger through it, obscured the titles. They were her last resort. If there was any text regarding magic and potentially how it all came to be, it would be in these pages. While magic was a genetic thing, the second generation had also shared it with others. Some who hadn't come from a charmed lineage had died as part of one. Which meant, theoretically, there had to be a way to jumpstart it.

If nothing came from this batch, that was it. There were no more chances after today.

As she stepped in to her bedroom and nudged the door closed, she stopped short when she turned, nearly dropping the stack of books.

"You scared me," she said to Delilah. Her best friend's brown eyes met hers. Ava recognized the look in them immediately. As she set the books down quickly, but carefully, on top of her bookshelf she asked, "What's wrong?" then moved to Delilah. She sat on the edge of the bed, one leg tucked under her, and waited for her friend to respond.

"Do you love him?" Delilah asked. There was no emotion behind the question. It was collected, as though she were simply asking what day it was.

"Which him?" Ava replied a little too quickly. Then she flinched. It was all she could do to pray Delilah hadn't caught her slip-up. But her friend was observant. When Ava looked at her and the sad half-smile tugging at her lips, Ava knew she had.

"The him you're supposed to marry," D answered regardless. Wringing her hands, Ava opened her mouth, but Delilah added, "And don't lie to me, Avie. Don't tell me what you think I want to hear. For once, in a really long time, just be honest. That is, if you even know how to anymore."

Ava swallowed the barb of the words. "No," she said, "I don't love Sebastian."

"But at one point you wanted to, right?" Ava nodded. "So, what changed?"

"I don't know," she half-lied. She worried her bottom lip, the sting a distraction from the pained look on her best friend's face.

"I hadn't even realized something was awry, but Sebastian noticed the change," Delilah started. Her voice was flat, emotionless, as though she were reciting words she'd been rehearsing for weeks. When she turned and faced Ava fully, the corners of her eyes drooped. "He came to me one day and asked if I knew why things were suddenly different. Why you were so distant, so withdrawn from him. And I *didn't* know why because I didn't see it. Maybe because I didn't want to. Maybe my expectations for you and Sebastian were so high I couldn't believe anything could come between you two.

"But once he mentioned it, I started to pay attention. It didn't take me long to realize what it was, why you were distracted." The beat of Ava's heart was so loud she wondered if Delilah could hear it, too. The hairs on the back of her neck stood straight up as though they, too, were listening to her confession, waiting for the rest of it.

The painful rest that was most certainly coming.

Delilah's voice took on a new tone, a level of franticness, like she couldn't believe what she was saying. "The way you looked at each other, the little jokes and how you're the only one who can make him smile. It was so glaringly obvious." It took Ava a moment to understand that the *he* wasn't Sebastian, but instead Nixon. "I wasn't going to say anything at first. I figured whatever was going on between the two of you was your business. But then I felt bad for Sebastian, because each time he came to talk to me, to vent about how it was becoming almost impossible for him to connect with you, I could sense his pain. When I saw how he was hurting I just…I couldn't sit there and watch him fall apart." Using a dainty finger, Delilah flicked a fallen tear from her smooth cheek. She wasn't wearing any makeup and her hair was in a nondescript ponytail, but she still looked tragically beautiful.

Delilah took a second to gather herself. "I did something," she croaked out. Her throat was suddenly tight.

"Okay…?" Ava said slowly. It was all she could manage. She didn't trust herself to speak.

Locking her almond shaped brown eyes on Ava's blue doe-like ones, Delilah reached across the small space and took her best friend's hands. "You're going to hate me." The fear that her words held buckets of truth was evident in the way she clung to Ava.

"I've never hated you," Ava reassured. "Tell me what you did."

Taking a deep breath did nothing to calm Delilah. Her hands shook and Ava gripped them tighter to try and stop the tremors. "I…um…" Tears welled instantly. "I told Sebastian."

"Told him what…?"

"My suspicions about you and Nixon."

Ava had never felt the world freeze. She had never had her lungs stop working entirely, as well as her heart. Her brain kicked into overdrive trying to process Delilah's words. Even when she'd learned the truth about her father's death it hadn't felt like this; like everything was on pause except for her.

"Delilah," she whispered. Speaking any louder would shatter the world, and it was already leaning unsteadily, like a block tower balanced on a single brick.

Delilah stood and paced in front of the bed. "You didn't see the look on his face, Avie. The sheer and utter defeat when he talked about how much he cares for you and how badly he wants things to work. I couldn't handle seeing him that way and it just…it came out. I told him I thought maybe there was something going on between you and Nixon. He didn't believe me at first, but the more we talked about it…" She fell to her knees in front of Ava. "I'm sorry. I know I messed up, but…but I protected you. And all you have to do is play along, okay? And then things will be fine, and…and you and Sebastian can work through this and…and you can be happy. Please understand. I did this for you. I did it so that you—"

"You did it for me?" Ava repeated. Her voice was steady, though her body buzzed with ten thousand angry bees. "You did it for *me*?!" she said again, this time louder. She pushed herself off the bed and stepped away from Delilah. "I hope you have a good reason as to why you'd betray me like this, because I'm having a really difficult time believing it was all over Sebastian's melancholy. And even if it was, you're supposed to have *my* back. You're not supposed to stab me in it. So please, help me understand. What was the real motive behind this? Was it jealousy?"

Delilah stood and positioned herself in front of Ava. Both women were shaking, but for two entirely different reasons. Anger and frustration bubbled under Ava's skin. It was flames beneath her flesh, burning from the inside out. Delilah's emotions were roaring waves crashing upon her ribcage. It left salt streaks down her cheeks. Each woman was a disaster, a windstorm of words and feelings, and their friendship was the only thing in its path.

"I can see why you would think that," Delilah said. "I spent years wanting the crown. Years wanting Sebastian. I spent months wanting Nixon. And somehow you got all three. So yes, I was jealous of you, but that wasn't why I did it."

She took a step toward Ava, one hand reaching out, but Ava pulled away. Delilah's hand hovered in the air for a second then dropped. "You have the chance to make the changes you've always wanted to see in Havaan. But you were willing to toss it all aside for an affair that could not continue. You've never been one of those girls with their heads in the clouds, which is why I can't believe you would be so naïve as to think otherwise. Once you are married, once you are queen, whatever you and Nixon have could not continue. One way or another it *had* to end. I saved you from the pain you would feel. And if it wasn't for Bernadette I—"

"Bernadette?" Ava asked, confused as to what the queen had to do with anything. Suddenly, a memory clicked, like progressing to the next image in a slide projector.

She had just come back from a run with Nixon, long before anything romantic had sprouted between them, and as she was rounding the hallway to her bedroom, Delilah's door opened.

"It was such a pleasure spending this time with you," a familiar voice—like nails on a chalkboard—sounded before two figures stepped from the room. Delilah had been looking up at the queen with a smile so big it was a wonder it still fit on her small face. Neither had noticed Ava, and she never mentioned overhearing the exchange. "I know what I am asking of you is a lot, but I have no doubt you will do what is best for our family. And for Havaan. Always remember that the greatest risks have the greatest rewards."

"What reward was she talking about?" Then another thought crossed Ava's mind, and she narrowed her eyes at Delilah. "Did she promise you the crown? That if you were willing to rat me out and things between Sebastian and I ended, you could take my place?"

Shaking her head repeatedly, Delilah held out her hands. "No. It was nothing like that. She just wanted to remind me of my duties as your assistant, that they're different than the ones I hold as your best friend. It's my job to keep you focused. To ensure your path to the throne is without temptation and distraction. And if, for whatever reason you were to divert from it, it's my job to right you."

Ava looked at Delilah, her eyes wide. Nothing D was saying was making sense. Or maybe it was, but there was a much bigger issue at the forefront of Ava's thoughts. If Sebastian knew about she and

Nixon, if he even suspected something was going on, he would no doubt confront his best friend.

Shaking her head, Ava said, "I don't even know who you are anymore. The Delilah I consider my friend would never betray me like this."

"How dare you talk about betrayal as though you're innocent in all of this." Delilah's tone was suddenly sharp. The words cut Ava, but she was right. With that, Ava could not argue. "I was just trying to help!" Delilah shouted. "I saved you from inevitable heartbreak. I saved you from having to go home. I saved you from ending up like your mother."

"Don't you dare."

"One of your biggest fears in life is becoming like her. And whatever feelings you have for Nixon cannot continue. You would have been willing to give it all up for him. For lust or worse—love. The wrong kind of love. Maybe you'll never love Sebastian fully, and perhaps that's for the best. Love destroys. Your mother is a prime example of that."

"My mother was destroyed by loss."

"Lost love," Delilah retorted without missing a beat. "Avie—" She took a step toward Ava again, but the recoil from her best friend stopped her. "Think about it. The longer Nixon remained a part of your life, the deeper your feelings were going to get. I've seen you leaving his room at all hours of the night. You turn to *him* when you have a problem. Over Sebastian. Over *me*. Tell me I'm wrong. Tell me I have read the signs incorrectly and I will make amends." Before Ava could deny or confirm her suspicions, she continued. "I'm sorry you are hurting right now, but after a while you will see that I was not wrong. The crown belongs on your head. You *are* the best choice. And now it can happen."

The most heartbreaking thing was that Delilah honestly believed what she was saying, that what she had done really was for the best. But even her naivety could not staunch Ava's anger.

"Do you really believe that after what you told Sebastian, things are going to continue on as planned? That he's going to want to marry me? That I'm still going to be queen?"

"Yes, because I protected you," Delilah said again. Ava still didn't know what it meant but she didn't care. She didn't feel very protected. In fact, she felt the opposite. "If you would just listen to me!"

Ava held up a hand. "I'm tired of listening to you. I don't even recognize you." She shook her head and laughed without merit. It took every bit of energy she had, which wasn't much, to speak the following words. But she pulled herself to her full height, her spine straight, and looked down at Delilah. "I asked my best friend to come here with me, to stand by my side, to support me in my decisions, both the good and the bad. It is not your job to fix whatever I have broken or right the injustices *you* believe are happening. It is not your job to play judge and jury against my transgressions. It is your job to council me, to bring to my attention when I am making a mistake and then be there while I try to figure it out." Ava took a deep breath. "At least, it *was* your job."

"What does that mean?" Delilah asked. The question shook with uncertainty.

"Delilah Witicker," Ava started. Each word caught in her throat and she had to push around the tightness, had to look through the blur of tears. "I denounce you as my assistant."

"No. Ava no, please…" Delilah reached for her again, but Ava twisted away from the grab.

Ignoring the pleading, she continued. "You have thirty minutes to gather your belongings and leave High House." Then Ava spoke, not as the future queen but as Avaleigh Toliver. "I have been let down my entire life by people I love and care about, but none of it has hurt as much as it does right now. I may have betrayed Sebastian, but he is a stranger to me. You betrayed your best friend in a way that can never be undone. You have done far more damage than I think you realize."

"Avie, I'm sorry," Delilah cried, tears cascading down her face. "Please don't do this. *Please*. I'll do anything, but don't send me away. I can't go back home. Back to that tomb, with my judgmental mother and her always happy husband and their perfect little son. I will die there."

Ignoring her as best as possible, Ava went to the bedroom door and opened it. She didn't have time to stand there and wait for Delilah to leave. But she did pause. She refused to look at Delilah, afraid that if she did, she would lose her resolve. She also knew she couldn't. Some would consider her actions hypocritical, but she owed Sebastian nothing. All those years ago when they were knobby kneed kids on the playground, she had given Delilah something she'd never given to anyone else: her trust. And now that was gone.

"You were right about one thing," Ava said over her shoulder. "Love does destroy."

And then, leaving no time for Delilah to reply, Ava took off down the hall, the beseeching wails of the woman she left behind following her. She needed to find Sebastian. She needed to find Nixon. It was Ava's actions that had brought them to this point, her inability to stay away from Nixon, but she could not control who her heart wanted. Eventually, fighting had become impossible. What Delilah—nor anyone else—would ever understand was how complete she felt because of Nixon. In his arms she had become worth more than her social class had designated. With him she was worth more than even the crown, more than the title of queen.

With him, because of him, she was excited about the future.

Long before she'd discovered what Orion had done, she was already working on plans to get out of High House. Before the truth of her father was revealed, she had known Sebastian wasn't the man with whom she was meant to be. The man she was destined to spend forever with—the one who would rival the love story of Dante and Cordellia—had hair the color of pure midnight and eyes that blazed with the fire he lit inside of her.

She didn't know what Sebastian would do, but she knew he was capable of far more than anyone was aware. There was a gnawing pain in the pit of her stomach letting her know she was wasting precious time. Taking off down the hall, she left behind the one person who she had always been certain she would grow old with.

She wasn't sure which hurt worse.

The fact Delilah would never be by her side again or the possibility that neither would Nixon.

XLIV.

The side of her fist ached as she pounded on two doors, first Nixon's and then Sebastian's, back and forth between them.

"What's going on out here?" a loud voice boomed a second before Raymon's head appeared from a couple of doors down. His fingers massaged his temples and he squinted at the faint light from the sconces, as if it burned his eyes.

"I'm sorry. I'm…I'm looking for Sebastian. And Nixon." Ava tried to control the tremor of her voice. "Have you seen either of them?"

Stepping out of the room, Raymon said, "Nixon was in the training barn when I was there a bit ago." He moved a step closer. "Is everything alright? You don't look so well."

"I just…I have to find them," she rushed out. She made to turn on her heels then stopped. "I've released Delilah as my assistant." Holding up a hand, she halted him when he opened his mouth to speak. "She's been given half an hour to get off the premises. I can tell you're not feeling well, but please see that she does so." Then, leaving no room for questions, Ava sprinted back through the hall, down the staircase and across the yard. Her feet weren't carrying her fast enough and even though she pushed, ran through the burn in her calves and the stitch in her side, the barn seemed to get further and further away.

She was out of breath and her body burned with exertion when she reached it. It took every bit of strength to slide open the door. The assault of heat made her stumble a little, nausea from lack of both sleep and food setting in at the worst time. But she pushed through that, as well. She wasn't sure why, but she had a sickly feeling Sebastian was not going to be as forgiving as Delilah had believed.

She needed to warn Nixon, then find Sebastian and explain everything, apologize for hurting him. Then, if lucky, she needed to get the hell out of this place. They could come after her, chase her from one edge of their world to the other, but hopefully Nixon would be by her side. If he was, it didn't matter how long or far they had to run. They would do it together, and she would be happy.

It had become such a foreign concept lately she wondered if she would recognize it when and if it ever returned.

The grunts of fighting and the echo of fists on punching bags carried her forward. She looked at each face, all familiar but not the one she wanted. The feeling of dread expanded in her stomach, like a black hole sucking all her hope away.

"Ava?" a voice called from across the barn. Most of the guards stopped what they were doing and looked at her, their eyes large as though she had grown a second head. She could only imagine the crazed look on her face.

"Where's Nixon?" she asked Ramiro as he started across the dirt floor.

When he got too close, she took a step back and he froze. "Is everything okay?"

"No," she said curtly. "Where is Nixon?"

Ramiro's dark eyes darted toward the barn door then back to her. "Sebastian came and pulled him aside. Said he needed to talk to him about something."

"When?" she asked, unable to keep the panic from her voice.

"I don't know. An hour ago?"

Ava swore under her breath then turned and retreated. Her feet kicked up dirt as she took off. Chased by a barrage of questions from the men, she ignored them and headed back toward High House. Midway between the triangular paths that connected the barn, the house, and the greenhouse, she stopped. With hands on her hips and head tilted back, the high noon sun warming her face, she screamed. The sound ripped through her and echoed around the vast space of the backyard. The few grounds keepers present froze, as though someone had hit a giant pause button, and stared at her. Hoses continued to spray water, drenching one patch of flowers, and gardening sheers hovered over perfectly pruned bushes. Ava ignored them all and counted to ten. As the sun continued to blow its warm breath on her skin, she focused not on the events that had already happened, but tried to figure out where Sebastian and Nixon could be. High House was full of rooms she'd yet to explore, and many that she had. They could be in any of them.

There was a pressure building in both her head and her chest. Her heart was breaking. She could feel it falling apart, as though little pieces were being torn off by a creature with huge talons. That creature's name was Deceit and it had been out to get her the first time her feet touched the grounds. This place did something to people, something that made even the kindest, gentlest, purest souls into vindictive and evil beings. Ava was not innocent, had not gone untouched in all of this. She, too, had been caressed by Deceit's tender touch. She had listened to the whispers of temptation and given in. She, too, had lost herself in the labyrinth to the throne. And now she was paying for it.

She forced her feet forward, pointed toward the front of the house, hoping that maybe the guys had just gone for a "let's talk this out" walk. A loud screeching to her right stopped her mid-step and she slowly pivoted the direction of the sound. Sebastian, his silver hair standing up at all angles, came staggering from the greenhouse. The hem of his shirt was ripped, as though he'd snagged it on something, and through the slash she could see the paleness of his skin. When she croaked out his name, he looked at her, his green eyes rimmed in red. She had never seen him look so downtrodden before.

Running to him, Ava caught him under the arm as he crumbled. "Are you okay?" she whispered as she offered him what little strength she had. They stood there, the plush grass under their feet, for a few minutes in silence. Sebastian's breathing was shallow and quick, but with time it slowed to a less frantic rhythm. "What happened?" she asked. "Where's Nixon?"

With the last question, his eyes darted to her, and the pull of his brow seemed too angry for the anguish on his face. He looked murderous, and it took everything in her to not push him away.

"So, it's true?" he hissed as he pulled himself free from her grasp.

"Let me explain," she started, her voice nothing but a choked murmur. "I—"

"You don't have to explain anything," Sebastian replied. "That treacherous bastard confessed to everything."

Ava squinted at him in confusion. "What are you talking about? Confessed to *what*?"

She was prepared for anything. If Sebastian knew about her and Nixon, believed anything beyond just speculation, she was ready for that. She was not, however, ready for his response of, "For poisoning you."

Dumfounded, Ava stumbled backwards, the weight of the words hitting her like a physical force. Nothing came from her mouth, though it opened and closed like a puppet. She shook her head, trying to clear her shock, then said, "He hasn't been poisoning me."

"Ava, he admitted it to me. How he even knew about Everlove is beyond me but—"

"Everlove?"

Delilah's words filtered back to her: *"I protected you. You just have to play along…"* Is this what she had meant? But Delilah didn't know about the flower, either, unless…Unless Bernadette had told her. Had they worked this plan out together? Had they conspired with one another—her best friend and her undeclared enemy—to make this happen? To get rid of Nixon so that things between Ava and Sebastian wouldn't be ruined? It would make sense. A scandal like the future queen bedding a guard—the best friend of the future king—would cast doubt on the royal family. It would rock Havaan at its core. Ava had no doubt Bernadette would sink this low to save face. And Delilah, in her dire need to remain at High House, would go along with whatever crazy plan the queen concocted.

For a brief second, Ava felt bad she had been so hasty in her releasing of Delilah, but D had made her choice on her own accord. Despite how manipulative Bernadette could be, Delilah had made the conscious decision to side with her, to forego all their friendship had meant for a room in a big house.

For *that* she could not be forgiven. For that, trust could not be restored.

"I don't understand what you're saying right now," Ava finally said.

"Do you love him?" Sebastian asked. The pain, the fear of her answer, was evident in his tone. The way she bit her bottom lip, so hard that blood trickled down her chin, was as good as a confession. "It's not your fault," he assured. He was so calm, *too* calm, and it scared her a little. Irrational she could handle. Had expected. But calm, almost understanding, was worse than him breaking things and screaming accusations at her.

"He couldn't handle the fact that you were starting to feel something for me, so he manipulated those feelings."

"No," Ava whispered, shaking her head repeatedly. Tears dripped down her cheeks, but she paid them no mind. Everything inside of her was cracking, like the top layer of a frozen pond. Every word Sebastian said was a nail to the ice, creating little spider webs in her already fractured soul.

Sebastian reached for her, his hand ghostlike on her arm. She could feel nothing, sense nothing but the shock and pain radiating within. "I know this is hard for you to hear right now, but you need to listen to me. He told me how he observed you at the gala, how he wanted to have you to himself, but Father choosing you made that impossible. He was obsessed with you, Ava, desperate to be with you, and so he used Everlove to get you."

"But...but I never drank anything from him. He never gave me anything...How..."

"He could have had it on his body somewhere. You just had to ingest it somehow. Avaleigh, my love, I am sorry I didn't see what was happening. I'm sorry I didn't protect you from this." His hands moved from her arms to her shoulders, and then her neck. He held it loosely, intimately, and this time she did pull away.

"I don't believe you," she said, more strength in the words than she felt. "What I feel for him wasn't because of some stupid magical flower. It's because he's the one for me. It's because—"

Sebastian interrupted her. "How do you know that, though? How can you be so sure your feelings for him are your own doing and not his?" Ava frowned, her brows furrowed. She blinked a few times as the weight of his question wrapped around the truth. As much as she hated to admit it, she *couldn't* be sure. She was *pretty* sure Nixon hadn't drugged her, hadn't used one of the queen's forbidden plants to grow forbidden feelings, but part of what he had told Sebastian had been true: he had noticed her at the gala. He had been drawn to her. Was it so insane to believe the rest of what he'd admitted was true, as well? Ava was having a difficult time believing so, but then again, if she had been poisoned...

Swallowing the lump in her throat, Ava asked, "What did you do to him?"

The look Sebastian gave her could only be described as sympathetic. "You're only concerned with his wellbeing because of the plant. The good thing about Everlove is it only stays in your system for forty-eight hours."

"Please, Sebastian," she begged, the lump of emotions returning. "Just tell me where he is..."

The prince released an exasperated sigh. He was trying to hold it together, trying to keep his anger reigned in and undirected at her. It wasn't her fault she'd been made to believe she felt something for another. It wasn't her fault the feelings she'd had for Sebastian had changed. Where she'd once looked at him with admiration, she now looked at him with hate, with an uncaring that—though he wouldn't admit it—hurt. Almost as much as learning his best friend, his most trusted and relied upon confidant, had turned against him all for the sake of a pretty face. Sebastian was determined to win her back though, to prove he was the better man, the *right* man for her. She didn't need the likes of Nixon Haldonai to feel loved and cared for.

To be happy.

"If in two days, when the flower is out of your system, you still want to know what I did to Nixon, I'll tell you."

"D…do you p…ro…promise?" she asked through the struggled breaths she took between deep sobs.

"I promise." Sebastian offered her a soft smile, and while it didn't reach his eyes, it was still comforting. Sort of. Nothing could comfort her right now. First, she'd lost the only friend she really had and now she lost the man she was pretty sure was her soulmate.

As much as she hated it, the rational side of Ava knew there was only one way to find out how true her feelings for Nixon were, and that was to wait it out. Two days of not knowing if he was okay, if he was even alive, seemed like torture, but Sebastian wasn't going to give her the answers she sought until then. So, she did the only thing she knew was right, and nodded.

Sebastian slid his arm around her waist and pulled her to his side. "Let's go inside. It's been a long day and we need to rest." Nodding again, because she could do nothing more, she curled against him. As her shaking arms came around his torso, bile rose in her throat. She didn't want to be touching him. She didn't want to be this close to him. Not because he repulsed her, because despite all that had taken place between them, he was a good man. Sure, he had a darker side, one that flashed in his eyes like the strike of a match, but who among them didn't?

He was not the worst person she could have ended up with, but he wasn't the best. He wasn't the right one. Which is why his touch was painful and his nearness like acid in her stomach. But she swallowed it down and let him guide her into the house. She wasn't entirely sure she'd have been able to make it there on her own, anyway.

As they entered the foyer, Ava's head lifted when a familiar voice called her name.

"Avie! Avie please. Please, just listen to me," Delilah begged—shouted—as Raymon, with his large hand wrapped around her arm, steered her down the stairs.

Sebastian looked between the spectacle and Ava before asking, "What is the meaning of this?"

"I want her out," Ava whispered as she barely raised her head. Her eyes, however, locked on Sebastian's. "Regardless of what you believe Nixon was doing, she still betrayed me. She told you what she did out of her own selfishness, and that is not a person I want around. Especially as my assistant." She gripped his shirt tightly in her hands, and when his thumb traced her cheek, brushing away the freshly fallen tears, she nuzzled into his palm. "We cannot move forward with traitors by our sides," she said quietly.

The corner of Sebastian's lips hooked and with his eyes still on hers he nodded. Then he turned to Delilah. "I appreciate you bringing this situation to my attention, but I will not go against Ava's wishes." Glancing at the large guard he added, "Please see that Ms. Witicker gets to where she's going safely."

"No!" Delilah screamed as she fell to the ground. There was sheer agony in her voice, a pain Ava felt in her core but couldn't acknowledge. Refusing to look at her, Ava buried her head in Sebastian's chest. He carried the two of them up the opposite staircase, Delilah's shouts of refusal and her cries for mercy following them up every step. Each letter crashed into Ava's back, tore through her spine and clawed at her heart. By the time they reached the door, she was nothing more than a beating bloody pulp. Sebastian had to practically drag her down the hallway. Her toes left trails in the carpet.

Slipping his key into the lock, Sebastian said, "I think it's best if you stay here for the next couple of days." Ava looked into the room, confusion blanketing her, and then she glanced down the hall. She had expected him to take her to her bedroom, or his, but instead they were at a door at the farthest end of the men's hall.

"What...what are you doing? Why here?" she asked, panic seizing her.

"It's for your protection," he assured as he stepped them over the threshold. Ava used her body against his as she tried to remain outside. She didn't want to go into this unfamiliar room. It felt like punishment. It was dark and cold—not a comfortable cool but frigid. "You need a neutral space, Ava. We can't have you running off to find Nixon." Sebastian tried to wrestle her in. "It's just...for a couple..." Grunting, he gripped her arm and shoved her into the room. The force was surprising and left her with no time to brace against the momentum. She fell to the ground and let out a stunned cry. "Of days," he finished as he tugged on his shirt, making the tear in it bigger. "Everything you need is in here, and meals will be brought to you. Please, Ava, I am doing this for you." His words echoed Delilah's. "It's not a good idea for you to be roaming around High House in such a state. Take the next couple of days to rest. Get your strength back, and when the Everlove is out of your system we will move forward with our lives. I am not the bad guy here, regardless of what you think." As he began to close the door, with a softer voice—the one she had almost come to love—he added, "I am sorry to have to do this."

Then he was gone.

The click of the lock sliding into place made her shudder.

She was alone. Not just in this room, with its single window placed close the ceiling, but in the world as well. The two people she had cared for most, who had kept her sane, were gone. And her mother, the only other person she could rely on, was out there. After this, there was no way the king was going to let her go, no matter how much information she had as blackmail.

Then, another thought crossed her mind as she stood and turned on the light to the room. What if after all of this, after her two days of quarantine, she no longer wanted to leave? It hurt, the thought that Nixon would do something like use magic to alter her feelings for him. She didn't even want to entertain the idea of it, but it was necessary. Because there was a possibility, although small, that he had done what he'd said.

Nixon wasn't a liar.

He had never lied to her, at least from what she knew. Quite the contrary. He had been open with her. Honest. He had let her see parts of himself she didn't think a lot of other people got to see. He had shared the tragedy of his family with her, and later he had told her about his childhood before and after High House. He had provided her with information about her father and the king that he knew would not only help her but also possibly affect the way she looked at him.

He could have left her in the dark.

He'd had no reason to make himself a vulnerable target for the anger that would then follow the big reveal.

Yet he had.

Which was what made it difficult for her to believe that the man who had put himself at such a risk would sink so low as to use magic against her. That he would risk her finding this out, as well, and hating him.

Ava took a moment to look around the room. The bed was small, built for one person, and uninviting. In both the closet and the dresser were some of her favorite clothing items. *How much time had passed since Delilah told Sebastian her suspicions and the time I found him?* Ava wondered. He'd had time to stock the room with a couple of books, as well as the bathroom with her necessities.

Sitting on the edge of the bed first, then seconds later curling into a ball on the mattress, Ava wasn't sure what she was more afraid of: coming to learn that all she felt for Nixon was a lie, or that it wasn't.

L.

Two full days passed.

Ava spent those days sorting out her feelings, most of it done in the bathtub. Though it wasn't as nice as the one in her bedroom, it sufficed for soaking. When the water eked toward anything less than near scalding, she would drain half then refill the tub. Sometimes she would test how long she could hold her breath, but for the most part she just sat there, wilting away while the time crept by.

When she wasn't becoming a human prune, she paced the mustard colored carpet. Or she read. Or she slept. A lot. As promised, she received three meals a day, which she ate by herself. Most were delivered by staff she recognized but had yet to form any sort of relationship. They entered, set the tray inside the door, then left. No one showed any hesitation, no fear that at any moment she might attack them. They gave her knives and forks and never once worried she would use them to make her great escape. They didn't even flinch when they opened the door and she was just standing there, wordlessly watching them with a curious, albeit creepy, tilt to her head.

They knew, just as she did, that she wasn't going to attack them. What they didn't know was that she had considered it the first couple of hours, when the reality of her confinement had set in. The lonely silence was too much and she was pretty sure by the end of it she would be clawing at the walls. But she did her best to stay somewhat amused, and in the hours when she couldn't stand reading another line or her legs felt like jelly from the circles she was making in the floor, she slept. Her dreams were peppered with flashes of her life, of her existence before High House as well as during, and all the things she had taken for granted with both.

Each time she woke, she stared at the knotted print of the ceiling. Sometimes she missed Delilah and wondered where she'd ended up. Was she back home, holed away in her bedroom, avoiding the veracity of her decisions? Or had she left Typhony as she had discussed in the carriage? There were brief pings of regret at dismissing her, and Ava had to scold herself when she entertained them. Delilah had done what she had done, and Ava had done what she had done as a result. There was no going back. Only forward. Though it saddened her that forward would be without her best friend.

She also thought of Nixon, though she tried to avoid him, as well.

After what seemed like years, the forty-eight hours were up. She was released early in the morning, when dawn was just beginning to peek over the horizon. It tinted the leaves with soft yellow and vibrant orange, giving the impression of fall in the summer. *Oh, how I would give anything to return to the fall,* Ava thought as she made her way to her bedroom. She faltered involuntarily as she passed the door that had once belonged to Delilah. The nameplate was gone and the door itself was open a crack. When she peeked in, she saw how it had been stripped of the life it once held.

It was the perfect metaphor for how she felt.

She showered in her own bathroom and dressed in clothing she picked out. She did her hair and applied a bit of makeup. Then she waited, poised perfectly on the edge of the bed.

As expected, the knock came at 8:00 a.m. exactly.

"Good morning," she said, smiling at Sebastian.

"Wow," he exhaled as his green eyes rove her body. The sundress she'd chosen was white and blue striped. The lowcut neckline flashed a comfortable amount of skin. The yellow belt that cinched her middle only emphasized her better assets. It was short, hitting above the knee, and the light brown ankle boots she'd paired with it lengthened her legs. Perhaps it was a little too promiscuous, but it was also tempting—which was exactly what she wanted: to impress Sebastian, to remind him of what he was getting when she became his wife. The way his eyes hooded when he looked at her assured her success.

Blushing, she tucked a loose piece of hair behind her ear and grinned. "Well, thank you," she said. "You look quite dashing, as well."

Sebastian offered her his arm and she took it happily. They made their way into the dining room, each step flawlessly synchronized. Ava was surprised to find the rest of the Calder family seated around the table. Breakfast typically involved everyone serving themselves from the buffet-style chafing pans the kitchen set out.

She greeted each member of the family before taking her seat. As they waited for the kitchen staff to bring out their plates, Ava made eye contact with everyone in attendance, starting with Orion. Having not forgotten the horrible things he had done, meeting his gaze was difficult, but she managed. The corners of them crinkled with his age as he smiled kindly at her. Bernadette eyed her suspiciously, her brows lowered a fraction. Levi, however, refused to break contact. His eyes bore into her, a silent question swimming around the irises.

As plates of croque madame were slid in front of each person, Ava asked the queen, "How is your sister feeling, Bernadette?"

Tentative seafoam eyes met hers. "Pardon?" Suspicion teetered on the cusp of her voice.

"Your sister. I heard she was unwell. I was wondering how she's feeling now."

Bernadette looked at her husband, then both of her sons, as though she didn't understand what was happening, before she settled her attention back on Ava. "She's...better. Thank you for asking..."

"I would like to send her flowers. Unless you think that would be inappropriate?"

The queen stared at her. She looked like someone attempting to decipher Havaan's most difficult riddle. Ava cut into her egg. The yolk ran over the layer of béchamel sauce and down the edges of the toasted bread beneath. When she looked back up at Bernadette, she smiled sweetly before shoving a forkful of food into her mouth.

"Um..." Bernadette started, still unable to grasp the kindness of the gesture. Ava could see the gears turning as she tried to figure out the hidden agenda behind the request. "I think that would be fine," she finally said. "I'll have Helen get her address for you."

"Thank you," Ava replied before taking another bite of her meal.

Clearing his throat before speaking, Orion asked, "So Ava, are *you* feeling better?" The question was careful, a bit uncertain.

Swallowing both the nervous lump in her throat as well as her food, Ava nodded. She hadn't even thought to ask Sebastian what he had told his parents, or the rest of High House, about why she was missing for the last two days. Had he also made an excuse for Nixon's sudden disappearance? If so, what had it been?

"That's a ray of good news in all the bad we've had lately," the king praised. "I am also sorry to hear about your falling out with Delilah."

"Trust is a difficult thing to come by these days," Bernadette added. Her voice was flat, non-threatening, but laced with the perniciousness

Ava had come to expect in everything she said. The queen couldn't speak without having to remind everyone what a total and complete bitch she was. Ava had come to accept this long before the current meal.

Though the comment stirred her on the inside, outwardly Ava remained calm and unnerved. "It is," she agreed, "which is why she had to go. As unfortunate as it is, and though her actions were not entirely her own, that trust was lost. It was not something I wanted to take time to mend." Ava reached across the table and took Sebastian's hand in hers. "I would rather spend the time repairing something worth fixing."

Sebastian squeezed her fingers before she pulled her hand away.

"Have you thought about who you'd like to replace Ms. Witicker as your assistant? I would not wait too long to think it through, if not," Bernadette said.

Before replying, Ava took a leisurely sip from her flute of orange juice. "I was thinking Helen's niece, Madeline. We're friends, but not close. Maybe that was my first mistake in selecting Delilah."

Both the king and queen nodded, whether in agreement over her new choice or her second statement, she wasn't sure, but the answers seemed to satisfy them well enough.

"It has been a very tumultuous couple of weeks," Orion said. "We have all experienced loss in it, but I think it's best if we focus on the future and move on from all that has taken place."

"I agree," Ava said, giving him a quick smile and a slight tip of her glass.

After breakfast, after Sebastian had kissed her lips tenderly and stated how happy he was that she was back to her normal self, Ava was in the kitchen giving her compliments to the chef when Levi stuck in his head.

"Ava?" he said softly, afraid to disturb the exuberant ruckus taking place.

Turning from Madi, Ava smiled kindly at her future brother-in-law. "Hey there," she said.

Levi stuffed his hands in the deep pockets of his olive-green shorts. "Can I um…can we talk?" His eyes briefly met hers before he glanced around the kitchen uncomfortably.

"Of course." After bidding Madi farewell and meeting Levi at the door, she said, "Shall we walk the garden?"

He offered her his arm, just as his brother had done that morning, and together they entered the large space of the backyard. In silence, they walked along the wrought-iron fence encasing the property. Near the back, where the yard ended and changed into forested area, Levi stopped. "Are you okay?" he asked, his voice pregnant with concern.

"Yes?" she replied, confused by his question.

After looking around to ensure they were alone, Levi took a small step toward her and lowered his voice. "Sebastian told me what Nixon had done to you, what he *claimed* he had done." The youngest Calder's eyes dropped at the corner and fear swam in the green pools like tiny minnows. "Is it true?" he whispered, his throat tight.

Ava rested her hand on his arm and giving him a small, barely noticeable smile, shook her head. "No," she replied, "it's not true."

She'd spent the hours in confinement thinking about Nixon, analyzing every look and touch and word that she could remember. She tried to pinpoint the exact second things had shifted, but she couldn't. It felt like he had always been a part of her, there in the spaces between each heartbeat. Her need for him was like flames simmering just below her skin, and it was his touch that both ignited and abolished them. From their first moment of contact, from the first spark of electricity down her spine, she had been his.

The possibility that all of it had been the work of some flower had terrified her.

As she'd fallen asleep the final night, she worried that when the sun came up she would find her feelings for him gone.

But in the morning, before she was released from her cage, she'd sat on the edge of the bed and felt her heart swell.

Then she'd wept with a relief she had never known before.

She didn't think she could handle it if he'd betrayed her, and now she knew he hadn't. Now she knew he had lied to protect her, and all she had to do was play along.

The look that passed over Levi's face was of the same respite. She squeezed his arm in comfort and gave him time to gather himself. "You were very convincing," he said when he could finally speak without his voice cracking.

"I had to be. I *have* to be."

"Where is he?" There was desperation in his question, one she understood. Nixon was just as much Levi's brother as Sebastian, if not more.

"Sebastian told me he'd taken care of him," Levi continued, "but he won't tell me what that means. I was hoping you knew. I've been out of my mind these last few days."

Ava shook her head again. "I don't know either," she replied, and when his face fell she quickly added, "But I am going to find out. And then I'm going to find him."

"I'm going with you."

"Levi. That's not a safe option."

"You don't know that. And even if it isn't, who's to say you won't need backup? How about, until we know for sure where he is and what it's gonna take to rescue him, you just agree I can come?"

Bringing her hand to his face, she touched his cheek softly with the palm. "Your dedication to him is admirable." Then she nodded once. "For now, we'll agree you can come. But if it turns out it's going to be too dangerous, *you* agree to stay here, okay?"

Though reluctantly, Levi nodded, then pushed his faux glasses higher onto his nose. "So, what now? What do we do?"

"*We* don't do anything." Ava's eyes traveled to High House as she sighed. "*I* get the information from your brother."

Levi blinked at her a few times. "How do you plan on doing that?"

"A girl has her ways," she replied, laughing at the coral blush that kissed his cheeks. "It's going to be a few more days, though." Ava hooked her arm through Levi's again and they continued their stroll, taking slow, leisurely steps. "I need him to trust me, to continue believing Nixon manipulated me. I need to convince him I am his now, and if I try to pry Nixon's location from him too soon he'll get suspicious. That can't happen. I have one chance."

Levi said, "Then I'll wait impatiently. And continue on as if nothing's wrong."

"Good," Ava replied.

She had a plan, but it would take time.

Time she wasn't willing to sacrifice, but if it meant getting the truth and then getting Nixon back, there was, unfortunately, no other option.

LI.

For five days, Ava put on a show fit for the stage.

For five days, Ava played her heart to Sebastian's name.

They kissed and cuddled. They laughed and held hands. She wore clothing that revealed extra skin and his fingertips grazed the flesh it exposed. On day three, they ventured to the market so Ava could find a birthday gift for Cordellia. They made no announcement ahead of time and wandered the congested streets as though they were newlyweds. To anyone looking, they were the epitome of marital bliss.

Outwardly Ava was calm, happy. Inwardly, she was humming with pent-up rage.

Outwardly she giggled; inwardly she plotted.

In the mornings, she took to the hill she and Nixon had so many times ascended. At the top, where they had laid down rules they'd later broken, she apologized to the wind. Could Nixon feel each light touch and brush of lips? Did it stab him a little each time, just as it did her?

"Tell him I'm sorry," she whispered to the birds, hoping they would deliver her message to him, wherever he was.

Because he *was* somewhere.

She would know if he was dead.

Cordellia had always said that she knew the exact moment Dante died, felt it like a punch to her stomach. She still carried that ache around with her, her organs swollen and hemorrhaging his memories every day. Ava hoped her mother had passed along that sixth sense. As long as she could feel the tension of their tether, she could believe

Nixon was alive. If she later discovered he wasn't, that Sebastian and his father shared more than their green eyes, she would kill them both. Without a second thought she would murder father and son in cold blood, then follow Nixon into the afterlife.

Until then, Ava blushed at Sebastian's flirtatious remarks and shied away from the glances he sent her way. For five days she walked around High House as though Nixon had been nothing more than a figment of her imagination. She avoided the barn, as well as the eyes of the other guards, though she couldn't help but wonder how much they knew. Had Sebastian told them what Nixon had supposedly done? Did they, too, believe him to be so perfidious he would sink to such levels? Or did they know him better than that?

She could have asked them and Sebastian what they had been told, but any mention of Nixon would be a bleep on Sebastian's doubt-o-meter, and that wasn't a risk she was willing to take.

So, for five days she wasted time luring Sebastian back to her.

For five days, she planned.

And midmorning of the sixth, almost a full week since Nixon had gone missing, Ava put that plan into motion.

She stood nervously in front of the prince's bedroom door. She wasn't nervous about what she was going to do, at least not entirely. She was worried it wouldn't work, that he would see through her façade; and in that truth, he would refuse her the answers she so desperately needed.

"For Nixon," she whispered as she reluctantly shook her limbs free of the nerves. She exhaled a deep breath and then knocked.

Once upon a time she had stood outside the door a few down, anxiety the same bubbling volcano that now erupted in her stomach.

Then, she had waited on this side with restless excitement. Now there was only fear and dread and a desire to get through it as quickly as possible.

The door opened, and in the doorway loomed Sebastian. He was dressed as he had been an hour ago when they'd enjoyed lunch in the pavilion. She'd only assumed he would be in his bedroom, working on a more cohesive plan for magic's reintroduction, and a thankful breath left her when she realized she'd been right.

For the last five days, while Ava had been preparing, so had the prince.

"Ava?" The uncertain tone of his voice matched the confusion on his face. "What's wrong?"

"Nothing," she replied sheepishly. "I just missed you." Looking up at him through thick lashes she asked, "Can I come in?"

"Of course," he said as he stepped aside. Ava entered the bedroom of her would-be husband for the first time and looked around. Where Nixon's room had been dark wood and earthy neutrals, Sebastian's was light textures and bright colors. It wasn't messy, but it wasn't obsessively clean, either. It was a lived-in, comfortable room. It was only slightly bigger than hers with large windows that let in a massive amount of light. The walls were a light pumpkin color and the carpet a soft beige. The bedding was a grey so pale it was almost white, and the pillows—of which there were only two—had blue, orange and green striped cases. There was a small table in the middle of the room and scattered atop it were opened books and loose papers with doodles and notes in quick, scratchy handwriting.

"How's all of this going?" Ava asked as she picked up a piece of paper.

Coming up behind her, Sebastian took the notes from her hand and said, "Slow." He tucked the rest of his research into one of the books and closed it with a loud *whap*.

"You've been at it a while. I figured," she started as she leaned against the table and ran her fingers over the tie on her robe, "that you could use a break." On the final word, the silk fabric gathered like a puddle at her feet.

Sebastian gulped as he took in the image before him. She stood there in a too revealing matching underwear set. Delilah had forced her to buy it one day while they were out and about. She had never tried it on, and while it fit, it was just barely. It did the job though, as Sebastian's eyes flared.

"I could use a break," he choked out. Smiling, she motioned him forward, and as if in a trance he floated to her. Once he was within distance, she wrapped her arms around his neck.

"I wanted to thank you for being so patient and kind through all of this," she began, dropping her voice. "I also wanted to apologize for what happened. I know it wasn't really my fault, but I should have been more aware. I should have come to you when I realized my feelings were changing and maybe we could have put a stop to it sooner." Resting a hand on the side of Sebastian's face, his cheek smooth against her palm, she continued. "You've been so great to me from day one and I think…I think it's time I show you my gratitude." She assured her words could not be misconstrued. There could be no doubt in Sebastian's mind what she was implying, and she could tell by the sharp inhale that there wasn't. She made no sound of protest as they moved to the bed. They could have easily used the table, but in retrospect the bed was a safer place for what was about to happen.

As they collapsed onto the mattress, his mouth sealed over hers. She gave him control, became pliable in his hands. She took him back to the beach, to a frozen moment when he'd trusted her. She used that, wrapped his belief of their relationship around him like a blanket. It wasn't long before his lips moved from hers and over her skin. She egged him on, whispered praises.

Outwardly, she craved him. Inwardly, she was counting.

Slipping her hands under the prince's shirt and dragging her nails down his spine lightly, she bit his earlobe. Her voice was so sugary sweet she had to force it out when she cooed, "Sebastian?"

"Hmm?" he mumbled against her neck.

In the same sing-songy voice she asked, "Where's Nixon?"

Rearing back, the prince looked down at her. A flash of anger sparked in his eyes but the question mark on his face was more prominent. "Why are you asking me about him?"

She slid her hands up and down his arms calmly. "You promised me that once the flower was out of my system, if I still wanted to know, you would tell me." Tracing his parted lips with her finger she continued before he could interrupt. "What I do and don't feel for him has nothing to do with my curiosity." In the second it took for Sebastian to blink, Ava flipped their positions. His eyes wandered her curves from under drooping lids. "He used me. He used me against you. I just want to know that the punishment fits the crime. Tell me…" Leaning down, she brushed her lips against his. Sharing one breath, she whispered, "And we can celebrate his demise."

Looking up at her, Sebastian's eyes hazed over, a milky blue that glowed too bright, like that pop of brilliance right before a light bulb burns out. Then his pupils dilated, as though he was overly focused, and the swelling of black pushed the blue away. Just as quickly as the Paraloxia kicked in—aka the Truth Seeker—so too did the sleeping pill she'd crushed into her lotion. His eyelids were a curtain being lifted and lowered by heavy ropes.

"Sebastian." She shook him and his eyes opened wide. "Where is he? Where is Nixon?"

"I sent…him…away…" he replied. Each word was forced through lips which were beginning to slope at the corners. His head lolled and each time he got too close to sleep, it snapped back up, his eyes springing open once again.

"*Where* did you send him?" Ava asked, her voice rising with desperation. He was fading faster than she'd thought, and if she didn't get Nixon's location now she wasn't going to get it ever. Without thinking, she raised her hand and swiped it across Sebastian's cheek. The echo of the slap was loud and she grimaced.

"Ow!" Sebastian complained, rubbing the spot. Her hand stung and she balled it into a fist around the fabric of his shirt, gripping it tightly in her fingers.

"Tell me where he is! Please," she begged. "Please Sebastian."

As if his tongue were too heavy for his mouth, Sebastian lapped it against the roof. "He's in…" He exhaled deeply as his eyes closed again.

"Where?!" Ava shouted, shaking the prince. His body was limp. "Damn it!" she said through clinched teeth.

Suddenly, Sebastian's eyelids lifted just slightly. She could see the unfocused sliver of green. "The beast."

"The beast? What does that mean?" Panic was starting to set in. She only had a couple of seconds before he was down for the count. The precious ticks of a clock had never mattered so much to her as they did now.

As she was starting to accept the fact he was too far gone to answer her anymore, a word slipped from his lips. "Nope…" The word came out sluggish and she wondered if he was already dreaming, mumbling incoherently in his sleep. Then she sat up on him and shook him once more.

"Nope? As in Nopels?"

Ava scrambled off him as he started to roll to his side. He gathered his pillow into a lump and nodded repeatedly, a movement outside of his control. "Nopels," he mumbled.

Exhaling a lungful of relieved air, Ava crawled off the bed as quickly as possible and snagged her robe on the way to the door. Tying the sash back around her waist, she smiled to herself. She had a location. And although it didn't give her much to go on, it was better than nothing.

He was in Nopels.

Now all she had to do was figure out what it meant and how to get there, which would soon prove easier said than done.

LII.

The door opened before she had a chance to knock, and she slipped inside unnoticed. She could only imagine the rumors that would start if she'd been caught. It didn't matter, though, if something was spread. She had no intentions of remaining at High House after today.

"Did you get what you needed?" Levi asked as he handed her the pile of clothes she'd stashed in his bedroom earlier that morning.

"Sort of," Ava replied to his back. He gave her privacy while she changed into a pair of jeans and a long, flowing t-shirt. "Not much, but it's better than nothing. I'm finished."

Turning back around, concern creased his forehead. Green eyes darted toward the wall as he asked, "Is he okay?"

"He's sleeping. Hopefully the pill will last the full eight hours, but I don't want to rely on that. We need to figure out how to get to Nixon as soon as possible."

Levi nodded, though the movement was clunky, spacey almost. The last five days had not been easy for him, either. His concern for Nixon was evident, even though he did a decent job of hiding it. Watching Ava interact with his brother had been difficult. She'd done such a convincing job he sometimes wondered if she really was in love with him, if maybe the magic flower had taken longer to wear off than expected. But when she'd come to his door that morning with a stack of clothing and a plan, he'd never been more relieved. Sebastian was his brother by blood, but Nixon had always treated him as though it were the two of them who were related. He was willing to do what he had to do to save Nixon and right their lives again.   "So, where is he?" he asked while Ava laced up her boots.

Glancing at him she answered, "He gave me two locations. First, he said he was in 'the beast' and then he said 'Nopels'. I don't know if the beast is a nickname for Nopels or if they're two different locations, but it's more than we had twenty minutes ago." As she wrapped her thick hair around her hand and secured it with a tie she asked, "Are you ready to get started?" Her voice was authoritative and surprisingly controlled.

Without hesitation, Levi nodded.

They walked as casually as possible to the library and locked the door behind them. There wasn't typically a steady flow of traffic in and out of the room, but it was better to be safe than sorry.

Once they were settled around the large coffee table between the fireplace and the couch, under the watchful eyes of the king's portrait, they spread open multiple books. Ava had searched through the library while trying to find answers about her father, but she didn't remember coming across the words 'beast' or 'Nopels'. They could exclude the census books, and she was almost certain a handful of others wouldn't yield the answers they needed, so they set those aside. It was a risk, but she didn't want to spend time researching something only to come up empty handed.

As one hour crept into two, they had zilch to show for their wasted time. Ava and Levi didn't so much read each page as they did skim them, looking specifically for those two key words. Each time one of them closed a volume and set it aside, that little bit of hope they had depleted. Dinner would be served within the next couple of hours, and only a few after that Sebastian would wake. He would return as her ever vigilant shadow and there'd be no hope for rescuing Nixon.

This was D-Day.

Ava reluctantly gave her eyes a break and took in the large quantity of books still left to look through. She felt defeated. They hadn't even gone through half of the tomes and their deadline was inching closer with each useless word. It was safe to say that whatever power Dante may or may not have passed on to his daughter, it was not the ability to pinpoint necessary information by magical sonar.

"Of course," she whispered as she closed the book in front of her.

Looking over the rim of his rounded costume glasses, Levi asked, "What?"

Ava smiled and spoke with calm excitement. "Legend has it that Nopels is the place where all the magicians were sent once their magic was syphoned. Though small, there is always a chance your father missed a morsel of it and that in some vein there is still a spark. A microscopic drop that at any time could reactivate itself. It's the same principal Sebastian is banking on."

"Okay…?" Levi drew the word out.

"If you were your father, would you want to put more than two thousand powerful magicians in a place that is man-made? That could easily be destroyed if their abilities woke again?"

It was easy to track the exact moment the pieces fell into place for Levi. His eyes widened and his lips stretched into a slow, crooked grin. "Of course not," he said.

"It would have to be magic based." Then suddenly, upon hearing the words, the realization of what that meant sunk in and she folded in on herself. "Which means," she began, the disappointment laced through her words, "we're not going to find it in any of these books." Sighing, she fell onto her back and covered her eyes with her arms. "We're screwed." Her lungs felt like lead, as though the letdown was a tangible boulder growing from her chest.

She wanted to scream. She was tired of taking one step forward only to be catapulted one hundred back. All she wanted was to figure out how to get to Nixon, then *get* to Nixon, then leave everything behind with him by her side. But it seemed the universe did not agree with her plans.

Not that she should be surprised.

It rarely had.

Swimming in her pool of pity, resigned to accept the fact she was never going to see the fiery eyes that so often stole her breath, she barely heard Levi's, "Not necessarily," over her internal pouting.

But she *had* heard it and it yanked her up quickly. The boulder shifted a little and settled in her stomach instead. "What do you mean, not necessarily?"

This time it was Levi's turn to grin at her. She wasn't ready to accept the possibility of good news, but she was eager to hear some. "When I was younger, I was in my parent's bedroom and I came across this book. It was hidden in a closet under a bunch of other stuff, like it was never meant to be found. It was massive, and I didn't get to look through the whole thing, but it was full of spells and potions and all things magic. *If* Nopels is indeed what we're thinking it is and it's documented anywhere, it's going to be in that book."

"This is great! All we have to do is get the book and—"

Levi sighed and in that exhale of breath shrunk the optimism-balloon once again. Ava didn't even try to grasp the string; she just let it go. "My parents lock their bedroom from the outside. There're only two keys and I'm not in possession of either one. So, we really are screwed."

Laughing, Ava covered her face with her hands. This day had been such an emotional rollercoaster, she wasn't sure she could handle much more. Hesitantly, she dared to believe something good might come their way. When she lowered her hands, Levi was staring as though she'd lost her mind.

It was possible that she had.

"If I could get you into their bedroom, could you find the book?" she asked once her chuckles had ceased.

Eyeing her suspiciously, Levi nodded once, slowly. "Assuming she hasn't moved it."

"We'll just have to hope she hasn't." Ava pushed to her feet so sudden it startled the younger prince. "I need to go get something. I'll meet you in the Throne Room."

Following her to the door, Levi stuttered, "Wait…What? What do you have to get?"

"Something," she replied, refusing to slow. At the door, she paused and faced him. "Leave a few minutes after me." Then before he could say anything else, she checked the staircase landing and slipped out. Except instead of turning left toward the female hallway, she turned right.

What they were about to do, where they were potentially about to go, would be a risk. One that she might not be able to come back from. If that were the case, she needed to check all the necessary boxes before embarking. She knew that it was foolish to believe Nixon had somehow found his way back from Nopels on his own or that

Sebastian had lied through the Paraloxia and had just discarded him a few miles away. But she had to be sure.

When she turned the handle to Nixon's bedroom and the door swung open freely, she was.

She stepped into the darkness, permeated by nothing more than the small streaks that managed to push through the curtains. The veil of mint and cotton washed over her. She inhaled it, wanting to absorb the remnants into her pores. The familiar smell tingled over each of her senses and brought to her eyes a wave of tears. There was no way to adequately describe how much she missed him, how big of a hole his absence left in her heart. No one had ever completed her in the way Nixon did, and without him she was left without the biggest and best pieces of who she had become.

If he was lost to her forever, she would lose herself, as well.

As she turned to leave, because if she didn't now she never would, the sunlight glinted off something across the room. There were only a few things organized along the top of his dresser: a single photograph of Delilah, Nixon, Levi and Sebastian at the Welcome Dinner, their eyes glued to her, cheesy smiles on their faces, as she told them some animated story. It was so candid and natural it looked as though they had been a part of one another's lives for years instead of just days at that point.

It was hard to believe the five people in the shot would ever turn against one another.

Diverting her eyes from the image, she ran her fingers over the only other thing on the dresser: Nixon's daggers. He had been so unsuspecting of what was to become his fate that he hadn't even worn his blades. Ava had seen them only a handful of times, but she was always awed by their beautiful design. They were long, 8" or so, with black and gold handles. The leather had been molded over time by his fingers, but the luster it'd been dusted with still glinted and shimmered in the light. There was a slight curve to the razor-thin, razor-sharp blades and engraved into the metal were different sized flames.

The weapons were dangerous but sexy; cold like steel, but elegant.

Just like Nixon.

Without thinking, Ava belted the two-pocket holder around her waist and sheathed the weapons. She was surprised by how light they were but how safe they made her feel. As if planned, the shirt she wore covered the belt entirely. The pocketed blades slipped into her pants and rested against her hips comfortably. Armed and ready for whatever Nopels was, she exited the room. Yet again, she did not head toward her own bedroom, but instead found herself entering Sebastian's.

There was a possibility he was awake, that the pill had worn off quicker than expected. Would he remember she had drugged him and that in his unconscious state had told her the location of their supposed mutual nemesis? Would he be angry? Hurt? Upset?

Would he understand?

Unlikely.

With a hand on the top of the blade handle, she rounded the table. When she saw him, the air left her lungs in a whoosh. Not only was he still asleep, but he was halfway off the bed. For a fleeting second, she thought about leaving him that way and letting him wake upside down and with a sore back. But even *she* wasn't that mean, and with some struggle she wrestled him back into his bed. As she tucked the blankets around his chest, she couldn't help the sad smile that twitched her lips.

"I hope you make the best king possible," she whispered. She leaned down and pressed a soft kiss to his forehead. As she went to turn, his hand grabbed her arm. Before she could blink, one of the knives was out of its pocket and in her hand. She waited, watched his face. If his eyes opened, if he questioned what she was doing, if anything aside from a snore escaped him, she was ready. She didn't even question why she was ready to plunge the blade hilt-deep into his flesh.

It was the house.

It did something to people.

Awoke the evil inside them.

Thankfully, Sebastian's fingers uncurled from her wrist and he sank down into his pillows, rolling away from her entirely. She sent a word of thanks to the stars and then tiptoed out of the room.

Finally, she made it to her own.

Standing in the middle of it, Ava was reminded of a time, less than half a year ago, when she had been here for the very first time, wondering what her life had become. Now she did the same thing. Things had not turned out anything like she had expected. All she'd needed to do was fall in love with a handsome prince and rule by his side.

It had seemed so easy then.

Long before she knew about the murders Orion had committed. Nights before she'd learned the truth about her father. Days before she'd found herself gearing up to rescue a man who wasn't supposed to matter, but did, more than anything else she held precious in her life.

There was no time to reflect on the olden days or to feel embittered with nostalgia.

But this was the last time she would step foot into this room. She would be forced to leave behind family photos and memories from her life before High House. Walking away from it all meant never again wearing her favorite pair of pajama bottoms or sitting by the window, flipping through the pages Zarah had passed on to her. It meant never passing those stories to her own child. Getting to Nixon came with a cost, and while it was a heart-wrenching one, it was one she was willing to pay.

She shoved her anthology of old-world words and tales into the cushion of the loveseat. She'd sliced a hole in it on one of the first weeks here, creating a makeshift safe for the book. She hoped it would become a fossil when High House crumbled from its weak foundation.

Next, she went into the closet, and using one of Nixon's blades, cut the bottom hem off the blue dress. She tied the two ends together into a giant loop then wrapped it around her hair. It wasn't much, but it was something. A piece of home, a reminder of where she came from and the goodness others saw in her.

Then she freed one of her favorite photos from its frame—one of her and her mother and Zarah at Ava's fifteenth birthday—and tucked it into her pocket.

Lastly, she snagged the ring of keys from her dresser drawer. Without another glance, Ava left her bedroom one final time and ran to meet Levi in the Throne Room.

"What took you so long?" Levi loud-whispered when the door closed behind her. He was standing at the far end of the room, beyond the thrones, next to a door so well camouflaged into the paneling of the wall it was impossible to find if you didn't know it was there. The first time Ava had noticed it, she'd thought her eyes were deceiving her, the shadows playing some sort of trick. When she asked Sebastian about it, she learned that behind the panel was a staircase, which led to the bedroom of the king and queen.

"It'll be ours one day," he'd said, and at that time she had been excited about the notion of sleeping her life away next to him, in a room that was undoubtably beautiful and regal. Now, the thought made her shudder.

"You okay?" Levi asked.

As she made her way toward him, past the pillars with their tiny, intricate carvings, her eyes darted to the one of the legendary necromancer. Of all the scenes in the room, that one was her favorite. She wished she could saw out the image and take it with her. Instead of dreaming of impossibilities, she hurried to the younger prince. He was pacing back and forth, his worry obvious in each lap.

"Here," she said, placing the ring of keys in his hand. Pointing to the skeleton key, she informed him, "This one should open all the doors in High House. Whether or not it opens the one to your parent's bedroom I don't know, but it's our last hope."

Ava expected him to question where she'd gotten such a tool, but he simply nodded once and wrapped his long fingers around the ring. "I'll be back." Then, without another word, he pushed the panel. A soft click disengaged the mechanism and the piece of wall slid away like a whisper. *Just another secret here,* Ava thought as she watched him ascend the stairs. He vanished around a curve in the slight spiral of the steps, leaving her to wait alone in her impatience.

They hadn't considered the possibility that Orion would be up there, hanging out, doing whatever it was he did when he was by himself. Bernadette had gone to visit her sister again, so she wouldn't be a problem. Neither would Raymon or Benji, a lower ranking guard, who had both accompanied the queen. Their absences—more so Bernadette than the others—was the reason Ava had decided to execute her plan today. Ever since the afternoon when everything had fallen apart, Bernadette seemed to always be there. It was as though she suspected Ava's fakery, silently doubting each interaction between she and Sebastian.

Accompanied by the quiet of the room, Ava was suddenly exhausted.

The day had been taxing and the closer it got to dinner time, the more anxious she'd become. They had little less than an hour until the meal would be served and they would be expected to be there. There was no way they'd be around when that happened. There was no way they could spare any extra time. Having to look through yet another book was already going to steal precious moments.

Ava sank to the floor and rested her head on the wall. She had no intentions of falling asleep, but the next thing she knew, footsteps were shuffling around her. The sound startled her, and she was on her feet quicker than she'd thought possible, considering her fatigue. Levi came down the last step and looked at her, his eyes wide at the sight of

Nixon's dagger halfway from its sheath. When she'd become such a weapon-wielding lunatic she wasn't sure, but if she wasn't careful she was going to end a life she didn't intend to take.

Nodding at the large book cradled against Levi's chest, she said, "You found it."

When he dropped the grimoire on the platform of the thrones, Ava was pretty sure the thud would alert someone of their presence. Luckily, as they sank onto the dais, no one came barging in. Ava all but crumpled next to Levi. As he hoisted the book onto his lap, he gave her a sympathetic glance.

"You look tired."

"I *am* tired." As if on cue, a long yawn escaped.

"You should rest. I'll wake you if I find anything." She didn't know what face she was making, but Levi's dropped. "Do you not trust me?" The hurt in the question stung her, like the jolt of skinning one's knee.

She had never once, since this whole debacle took place, questioned Levi. But as soon as the words crossed his lips, a hint of doubt tickled the back of her neck. The young prince was related to the older by blood, but the bond he and Nixon had was stronger. There was mutual respect between the two men. She supposed it was possible he was leading her down a dangerous path—an insidious one even. If that proved to be the case, she wouldn't be surprised. Her life had been riddled with betrayal recently, but she couldn't bring herself to believe Levi would add another name to the list.

It could have been because he was her last and only hope in finding Nixon. Or maybe she just needed there to be one decent, good person left.

"I'm sorry." Ava rubbed her palms against her eyes—grateful she hadn't put on any eye makeup that morning, save for clear mascara. She hoped her voice didn't betray her sincerity when she added, "I trust you."

"Then rest. You aren't going to be any good to Nixon if you can't keep your eyes open." Levi set the massive book aside then removed the short-sleeved button up he was wearing. He smiled shyly at her as he now sat there in just a light green tank top. He wasn't super muscular like Nixon, but his time fencing had defined his arms somewhat.

"Thanks," she said as she took the shirt. It was warmed from his body and it instantly drained more of her energy. "Wake me as soon as you find something." Balling the fabric, she spread across the cold stone of the platform. As soon as her head hit the makeshift pillow, her eyes began to close. "We don't…" She yawned again. "…have much time…"

She wasn't sure how long she was down for. It was somewhere between being partially conscious, where sounds came as though from underwater, and the few moments where blackness threatened to swallow her so fully she wouldn't remember a single fragment of her dream. It was Levi's insistent calling of her name that eventually pulled her from the depths of her slumber.

When she realized what was happening, and simultaneously *remembered* what was happening, she sat up quickly. It took a few blinks for her to reorient herself and focus on the person sitting next to her, but once she did, he said, "I think I found it."

And just like that, the small spark of hope she'd been trying to keep lit, flared. It, like she, waited impatiently for him to continue.

"What does it say?" She scooted closer to him. There were thousands of words on the page and they all blurred together. Still, she pretended to follow along with his finger as he read.

"It says that *Los Nopellos*, or Nopels, roughly translates into 'the beast'. It was built as a warded place to keep the second-generation magicians, as well as those before and after who displayed any signs of magical abilities…Blah blah blah. As such, it is not accessible via any part of Havaan, since it is separate and not part of this realm. Only those who walk amongst the Gods have the right to enter."

When Levi looked up from the page and his eyes met hers, he let out a sad exhale. "Havaan doesn't believe in Gods, so how are we expected to walk amongst them? And why are you smiling like that?" Again, she had no idea what her face looked like, but she could feel the corners of her mouth threatening to rip her jaw in two. By the size of Levi's eyes, she must have looked insane.

"Because I know what it means." She was unable to keep the elation from her tone.

"How?" Levi asked.

Ava shook her head. "It's too much to explain. I'll show you though." As she made to stand, something caught her eye. The book had been typed, each letter lined up in neat little rows, but in the margin, coming off the word Nopels with a drawn arrow, was a handwritten word.

…*Tidak*…

Ava's finger grazed it. She swallowed the lump in her throat.

"I thought it was weird, too," Levi said, picking up on only half of Ava's sudden shift. "I've never seen it before."

"I have," Ava said, barely more than a whisper. She looked at Levi. His eyes were round, shadowed under the low-hanging awning of his brows.

"How?" he asked. "What does it mean?"

"I…I don't know," Ava stumbled. "It's part of something my mom says. Something my dad said to her, I guess." There were a hundred apologies graffitied across her face. "It's always been said as a mantra of love and support. Like a rally cry."

"Okay…" Levi said, stretching the word like taffy. Uncertainty danced in the green of his eyes.

"I'm not keeping it from you," Ava promised. "I've spent my entire life having answers withheld from me, answers that could have changed a lot if people had just been honest. If I knew what this meant" –She stabbed the word with her finger— "I would tell you."

"Okay," Levi said again after a brief pause. "I believe you." They smiled at each other. "So how did something your dad said wind up in a book about a thing that shouldn't exist? And more importantly, why is it linked with Nopels?"

Ava shrugged. "I have no idea."

Levi sighed and closed the book. The echo bounced around the rafters, wrapping itself around them like cobwebs. "Well then, let's worry about the things we do know." He pushed to his feet and held out his hand to Ava. "Show me how to walk amongst the Gods."

They hurried out of the Throne Room, down the stairs, out the backdoor and to the greenhouse. Using the correct key, she clicked open the padlock and unraveled the thick chain from the handles.

When they stepped inside, the sauna-like heat didn't faze her. She had a goal in mind and no time to focus on anything else. She was another step closer to Nixon and nothing was going to stop her now.

When they came to a halt in front of the black curtain of leaves, Levi asked, "What is this?"

"Portalis Dievas," Ava replied as though the words should mean something to Levi. He just blinked at her. "More commonly known as the portal of the Gods." She gave him the condensed version of what Sebastian had told her, how the magicians had been so egotistical that they considered themselves deities; Gods among men. "They used the portals to travel from place to place." As she took a tentative step forward and then another, she continued, "Your brother told me it was dead because it needed magic to thrive. But I would bet my life he was lying and just didn't want me to know the truth."

She had spent weeks trying to bring them back to life, convinced that if magic flowed in her blood, something would happen. But it never had, and maybe this was why. Maybe they weren't dead, but instead their color simply a mirage to keep people from trying to use the gateway.

"You might win that bet," Levi muttered. Then he shouted, "What are you doing?!" as Ava pushed her hand through. The leaves parted around her wrist, the rustling like turned pages in an old book. She wasn't sure what she'd expected—someone to pull her through? But that didn't happen. The other side was just…cool. As if someone had left the air conditioner on.

Levi watched her, worry seizing his breath. He let it out when she revealed her safe, undamaged appendage: much like a performer in a circus presenting the intact woman, who only minutes ago he had sawed in half.

"Did the book happen to say how to use the Portalis?"

Her partner-in-crime shook his head. "Not the section on Nopels, at least. You didn't give me a chance to read further." The last line sounded a bit bitter, but Ava let it slide. He was undeniably scared. She was, too. Neither of them knew what lay on the other side, what sort of misadventures would befall them in a realm not their own. Would Nixon be right there, waiting alone in the void? Or was there another layer to all of this, more twists and turns than a labyrinth? Was Nopels even real, or was the book nothing more than a fairytale?

There was only one way to find out.

Ava turned to Levi, whose eyes had gone wide once again. "Listen to me," she started as she gripped his shoulders. "I don't know any more than you do about what is waiting for us behind that. But you have to promise me that if things get hinky and it looks like it's going to be dangerous, you'll turn back. And if that's not possible, then you'll do your best to hide."

"I'm not leaving you alone," he argued. At the same time, he straightened his spine and tried to match Ava's height. He didn't, but it was a valiant effort.

"Nixon would want you safe."

"He would want *you* safe."

Ava gave Levi a kind smile. "He has known you for far longer than he has known me. You will forever matter more than I do. He would never forgive me, or himself, if something happened to you. So please, Levi, promise me you'll do whatever you must to stay safe. To stay alive."

Though he was clearly unhappy doing so, he agreed with a slight nod of his head. It was something *like* a nod, at least, but it sufficed. She didn't want to waste any more time.

"Are you ready to do this then?"

She didn't miss the flash of eagerness in his eyes. "Let's go get your man," he said as he offered Ava his hand. She wrapped her fingers around his and gave them an encouraging squeeze.

Then, without another word and without a moment's hesitation, they stepped through the leaves.

LIV.

It was dark.

Although dark didn't accurately describe the pure lack of light. This was a void, stripped of everything besides true black. Ava couldn't even see her hand as she waved it in front of her face. The emptiness did something to her physically, as well: disconnected her from her own body. Even with Levi's hand in hers, she felt entirely and utterly alone.

There were no sounds other than the blood rushing to her beating heart and the quick hiss of breath as it escaped through her teeth. She was afraid to speak, as though a single letter would splinter the darkness into nothingness and take her with it.

Levi's whispered, "Ava?" was too loud, too invasive.

The coldness she'd felt when she stuck her hand through swirled around her ankles. She couldn't shake the image of snakes slithering around the ground.

Squeezing Levi's hand, she replied, "I'm here."

He swallowed, and she could hear it loud and clear. "What do we do now?" he asked quietly.

"You didn't happen to bring a flashlight, did you?"

Levi laughed once. "Must have slipped my mind." Ava smiled, but when she realized he couldn't see it, she echoed his humorless chuckle. "Do we go back?"

"Nixon isn't back," Ava replied.

After a beat of silence Levi said, "So we go forward."

"We go forward," she repeated.

So, they did. One slow, nervous step in front of the other through the vastness of shadows and whatever else was lurking there. They stayed connected at the fingers and with their other hand tried to feel in front and beside them. Ava wanted to be able to get to the dagger in case something grabbed them, but with one hand keeping her linked to Levi, she was out of options. Sure, she could have let go of him, but it was like they needed to be joined; as if the other person was their one lifeline to sanity, to safety.

Besides, neither of them could fight their way out of a paper bag at this point. Still, no relief came when all their hands ghosted through was empty space and more black.

Many years ago, before Havaan was formed, when presidential elections relied on panic and threats, and chaos and violence bled into contaminated water, scientists had developed a color called vantablack. It was believed to be the purest, blackest shade known to man.

What surrounded Ava and Levi would put vantablack to shame.

That was, until the space began to lighten. At first Ava thought she was just adjusting to it, but when she began to see the outlined shape of the young prince, she realized the truth. Someone, or something, was slowly turning on the lights. It was like the chandelier in the dining room at High House, with its small lever one could raise, allowing them to control the amount of light the fixture gave off. That's what was happening in the void. The light didn't overpower the shadows, nor was it harsh or blinding. It was soft, warm, an almost tarnished gold, as though it were coming from inside a pumpkin.

Now that they could see, Ava and Levi let go of each other and looked around. If they reached out their hands, their fingertips touched smooth, unblemished walls. Walls that had not been there mere seconds ago.

"Well okay then," Levi said as he took in his surroundings. He looked up, trying to find the source of the light, almost certain it was coming from the ceiling, but that too was smooth. It was coming from everywhere, and nowhere, at the same time.

Ava gave him a second to marvel at it all and then said, "Let's keep going."

One less tentative step in front of another, they continued down the long, seemingly endless corridor. They could have walked inches or it could have been miles. The walls continued to look the same. Maybe grey, maybe brown. The ground was firm and went no other direction besides straight. The nippiness continued to keep them comfortable.

"Do you love him?" Levi asked after a long bout of silence. Even their footsteps gave off no sound.

"Which him?" she asked automatically, then shook her head. She really needed to stop doing that. She knew exactly which *him* Levi was asking about and he knew she knew.

Still, he replied, "The one you're risking your life for."

Ava hesitated only a second and then nodded. "I do," she said. Then she continued, a need to explain coming over her. "I tried to love your brother." She glanced at Levi. "But I couldn't."

Levi bobbed his head a little. "You can't help who your heart wants." His voice was distant, almost a little sad, especially when he finished with, "Even if it's the person the rest of the world considers wrong."

There was one thing Ava had suspected about Levi, but never knew how to bring up. Now that he'd given her an in, she took it. She treaded lightly when she asked, "Like you and Josiah?"

Green eyes snapped to her blue ones. Ava had observed the way Levi and his fencing partner behaved around one another, especially when they thought no one was watching. The looks, the casual but unnecessary touches, the cheesy smiles. She knew what love looked like.

Being gay wasn't a crime in Havaan. In fact, a large portion of their population was in same-sex relationships. It wasn't chastised or victimized like it had been in the old world. They had the same respect and rights as anyone else. Ava didn't imagine those same beliefs went for the person who was second in line for the throne, though. The Calder legacy was contingent on offspring, and if anything happened to Sebastian before he could produce an heir, Levi would take the crown. He couldn't keep the family name going with a husband.

After swallowing the lump in his throat, Levi diverted his eyes from her and nodded once.

"I'm sorry you can't be together in the way you want. I had hoped to make that possible for you as queen, but…" She paused. How was she supposed to finish that sentence? *But my feelings for Nixon trump your love and happiness?* Loving and rescuing Nixon suddenly felt very selfish. It felt unfair to put her relationship—which they didn't even officially have—above that of Levi's.

But then he gave her his cute, lopsided smile. "Don't," was all he said, because he knew what she had been thinking. It had been all over her face. "We get Nixon. And then we get as far away from High House as possible. Let them sort out the mess themselves. The throne was never meant for me. I don't want it anyway. I would make a piss-poor king."

"No," Ava said softly, "you would make an excellent king."

In the second it took for them to blink, suddenly appeared doors on either side of them. They were staggered along the walls of the antechamber, with signs anchored above each one as though they led to individual businesses. None of them made much sense to Ava or Levi. They were carved or printed with words they didn't recognize, in a language they didn't speak. Beside one door was a long, misshapen hieroglyphic. The sign above the door read *braykier*. Some of the doors were surrounded by a humming white light, the space behind it bright and luminescent. Others had a red hue. It reminded Ava of the photo developing room in the photography class she'd taken while in school.

"What will you do when you find him?" Levi asked, drawing Ava's eyes from the foreign signs. She'd been watching them like a cat to a mouse, making sure the one for Nopels didn't slip through their claws.

Ava paused before answering. "We'll leave, I guess."

"Without me?"

"I suppose," she finally sighed. The shadow of abandonment that crossed Levi's face shattered her into a million pieces. "I never considered you'd want to leave," she explained.

"Why not?"

"You're the prince."

Levi scoffed. "I am no more made for that throne than you are, Ava. No offense."

"None taken," she said, chuckling. A few minutes of contemplative silence stretched between them before she spoke again. "Okay." Levi looked at her, brows knitted in confusion. "When we come back, you can leave with us."

"Just like that?" His words were wavy hills of skepticism.

"Yeah. I'm not going to force you to exist in a future that you don't want, Le. We know better where we belong than anyone else does, and if you believe that place is with Nixon and I, carving out your own path, then who am I to argue?"

Levi chewed her explanation for a moment then nodded once. "Okay then."

They shared a comfortable smile before going back to the hanging placards. They continued walking, all the while scanning the hanging placards for something they would recognize. Finally, after what seemed like forever—when Ava was beginning to question the rationale behind what they were doing—Levi shouted, "There!"

Above a door exactly like all the others, was a sign exactly like the others.

Except this one had words she could read.

Los Nopellos.

Thankful reprieve sighed out of her in one deep breath. They had made it. Despite every obstacle that had been tossed their direction, they were here. Standing at the entrance of a place she had been told her entire life didn't exist. The thing of fables. And on the other side of it, somewhere behind this door that had not a white or red halo, but a translucent mustard one, was the love of her life.

Love.

It had been such a foreign concept to her for the last twenty years. Growing up, she had thought love made you sad. That it made you weep and wail until your throat was hoarse and it was impossible to believe there were any more tears left. She had believed that love tore families apart and cast shadows on even the brightest of mornings. She had never seen the beauty and purity of love, even when she was with Connor. Even when she'd thought she was in love with him. She'd given herself away and had gotten herself back in worse shape.

It had reaffirmed everything she'd been taught about love.

It was something she protected herself from so that she would never become her mother.

But here she was, traveling through enchanted leaves and wandering aimlessly in the dark, all so she could save the person who had saved her.

All because of love.

Ava touched the door. She wanted some sort of sign he was behind it. Wanted to feel his presence. Wanted her body to hum with his electricity. But it was just warm, like room temperature water, and nothing more. Still, this was where Sebastian had taken him. All signs pointed to this door.

And that was good enough for her.

With one hand on the hilt of the dagger, part of the blade freed from its pocket, and the other hand on the brass knob, Ava glanced over at Levi. The youngest Calder dipped his head and squared his shoulders. On a quick exhale, Ava turned the handle, pulled open the door, and stepped over the threshold.

LV.

"What. The. Hell."

Sand.

It was everywhere.

No matter which direction they looked, there was nothing but soft, golden silt as far as the eye could see. It didn't make sense. They were supposed to open the door and Nixon would be standing right there. Ava had *counted* on him being here. Sebastian had said this was where he was, and he hadn't been capable of lying, not with the Paraloxia in his system.

Unless...unless Nixon *was* here...It wasn't impossible that Sebastian had killed his best friend and to hide the body had buried him. Here. Under the sand.

Which was everywhere.

If that were the case, she would never find him.

Ava screamed. Tears threatened to choke her but she pushed through them and yelled instead. Her legs buckled and she collapsed onto the ground. She clawed at the silken dirt, tossed it aside, and her curses echoed back in their particles.

"Where is he?" she shouted at Levi, who stood a few feet away watching her breakdown. "What is this place? Why isn't he here?!"

"I don't know," Levi replied softly. "To all of those things."

"Damn it!" Ava cried. She swiped at her cheeks, brushing away tears she didn't realize had fallen. After a few quiet minutes, she whispered,

"I'm sorry. I'm just…I'm so tired. I want this to be over. I want to know he's okay."

Levi looked around. "Maybe…maybe there's something else we have to find. But we're not going to do it by just standing here, so let's get moving." His voice had taken on the authoritative tone she needed. Ava was in no position to be the brave leader right now. She was utterly defeated. Memories of the last week were piling on her, threatening to push her so far into the ground she would never be able to dig herself back out.

It would be a lie to say it wasn't a tempting thought.

"Go where?" she asked, the question coming out barely more than a breath. Her throat was raw from her emotional tantrum. "Are you not seeing the same thing I'm seeing?" She raised a brow at Levi's back. "What are you doing?"

Levi stood up and brushed his hands on his shorts. "Marking an X where we came in. We'll walk for a little in one direction and if we don't find anything, we'll go another. If we don't find him, we go home and try again tomorrow.

"There is no tomorrow, Levi! I drugged your brother. I used magic to get him to tell me where Nixon is. Do you really think there's a tomorrow that is going to allow me to continue to search for him? You can't be that stupid."

She had never seen him scowl before, but if looks could kill, the one he was giving her would have ended her life right there. He looked twice his age and so much like his brother, it startled her. "If this is all the time we have, then you need to get your ass up and we need to get moving. Because we aren't any closer to finding Nixon with you sitting there pouting."

Ava looked at him incredulously, her mouth hanging open. She exhaled through her nose, like an angry bull, then pushed herself off the ground and fell into step behind Levi. Wordlessly, they marched across the flat land. It wasn't a struggle, like it was at the beach. The earth was firm beneath their shoes with very little give. Occasionally, Ava glanced back, checking to ensure some invisible force hadn't come by and swept their footprints away, but they were there, two sets that vanished into the horizon.

It wasn't hot like she'd read a desert was. There were no deserts in Havaan, and the only thing similar was the thin strips that bordered the coasts. Even that was different though, rougher because of the mixed-in pebbles. This type of terrain was of the old world and she only knew of it from the history books. The air wasn't thick either, so it wasn't difficult to breathe, but every step was excruciating.

She was drained.

Even the thought of seeing Nixon's handsome face, of feeling his arms around her again, did little to propel her forward. At this point, she was on auto-pilot, moving onward because there was nothing else to do. As much as she hated *how* Levi had said what he had, he was right. They had to keep going if they had any hope of finding Nixon.

It was all she was hanging on to right now, but with time even that wasn't enough.

"This is stupid," Ava complained, kicking at the sand. They'd been walking for a while and her calves were starting to cramp. Bits of sand had crept into her shoes and were rubbing her heels raw. It clung to her eyelashes and sneaked into her mouth, grinding like salt in her teeth. "It can't be this difficult. We're missing something." She put her hands on her hips and surveyed the land, keeping her pouting face turned from Levi.

"Tidvak," Levi said.

"Gesundheit?" Ava replied.

"No. Tidvak," Levi repeated. "The word in the book. The piece of what your dad used to say."

"*Tidak*," Ava corrected, then she turned back to the younger prince. His face was sculpted from innocent faith, molded in the belief that the one word held all the answers. Ava didn't want to be the hammer that broke it. "I don't know, Le," she said uncomfortably. "It doesn't make sense…"

Levi waved his hands around him, as if to say *what about any of this does?* "Maybe not," he replied, "but you can't deny that it's weird. There has to be some sort of correlation between this mantra that's *only* a part of your family, and the fact that it's ended up in a book about a place that isn't supposed to exist. That's too many stars aligning for it to not mean something." The corner of his mouth dropped, pulling his entire face into a frown. "What's the worst that'll happen? Nothing? Then we'll be no worse off than we are now. But at least we'll know. And we can come up with another plan."

Ava was silent for a few seconds, trying to find a way to refute what he had said. There *were* too many pieces coming together for them not to belong to the same puzzle. But Ava was afraid to hang all her hope on this one possibility. It seemed *too* perfect, too plausible, and if it failed, she wasn't sure she'd be able to risk failing again.

When she could find nothing of Levi's statement with which to argue, she sucked a breath through her teeth and nodded. "Okay.

Yeah." Ava scanned the land again. "But stay here. I'm going to walk out and try it, I guess."

"Why do I have to stay here?"

"I don't know what this working might look like. I don't know if it's going to rip the world in two and I'm going to fall into an abyss or…" Ava shrugged. "I know it's not what you want to do but—"

"I'll stay here," Levi agreed, almost too easily.

Ava raised a brow. "You will?"

Levi nodded and flashed her his crooked grin. "I can be amiable sometimes."

A loud laugh pushed from Ava, and with it went some of the tension from her chest. "I could learn a few things from you," she said, smiling.

They stood there in the silence for a few seconds, savoring the mutual respect that had unexpectedly brewed between the two of them. Then Levi lifted his chin toward the horizon.

"Go on," he said, dropping his gaze.

Nodding a couple of times, mainly to psych herself up, Ava said. "Yeah, okay." Then she kissed Levi on the top of his head before ruffling his loose curls. "Just in case," she said. The words came out choked and she turned away before he could see his reflection in her eyes.

"Wish me luck," she called from ten steps away.

"Good luck!"

Ava had a feeling that this beast, and whatever all the sand had to do with it, was going to take more than just luck to figure out, but she was tired of wasting time being scared. She had not come this far, risked treason against the crown and trekked endless miles through a sea of marigold silk, to not at least *try*.

She walked a quarter of a mile or so from Levi, putting enough distance between them that if a fissure opened up or some other natural disaster decided to claim her, he'd have a chance of escape. When she felt far enough away, she turned and looked over her shoulder, waved at the small figure of the prince, then put her back to him again. He gave her two enthusiastic thumbs up.

"Alright dad," Ava said to the nothingness. "I followed all the breadcrumbs. Please don't let them lead to nowhere." She licked her lips, took a calming breath, and said, "*Tidak*."

She waited. Listened to the silence. Let it whisper to her that she was doing something wrong. Then she remembered not only that the word had been written, but *how*. With the ellipses, which meant there was more before it and more after it.

Another voice filled her head. "…the way he said them," her mother's words rang back. "The authority of his voice when they passed his lips, there was no way to doubt they were significant. Important."

Ava closed her eyes and tried to harness the queen—not Bernadette, but the one she'd almost become. The queen who'd wanted to lead her people to peace; who had wanted to rule with a firm but fair hand. She channeled the authority she'd used when dismissing Delilah, and in the space that it left, she filled with the sadness of losing her. The pain of missing Nixon and the fear she would never see him again coated it all. Like a balloon, she shaped her words with it. Then she popped it, let it out into the universe as she said, "*Mikor orada es tidak svar, enged dashuri fi itu clave.*"

At first there remained nothing. Just the final syllable echoing back. But then, from far off, came a gentle rumble, like the engine of Nixon's bike revving to life. In the next second, it was closer, became thunder over her head. It shook the ground so hard she had to lower herself, press her hands against the sand as it jostled and tumbled under her fingers. She looked back at Levi. He, too, was closer to the ground, kneeling on the trembling earth.

All around her, tiny S's began to form, like a hundred thousand snakes wiggling beneath the ground. Ava wanted to run to Levi, to throw them both back into the safety of the dark tunnel, but something kept her rooted in place—something more than the quaking Sahara. There was something under the sand and it began to circle her repeatedly. It kicked up a small tornado of dirt and she covered her face with her hands. It was loud inside the funnel, like the industrial fans that failed to cool the training barn.

Then, just as suddenly as it started, it ended. The sand settled, the wind vanished, and Ava dropped her hands. She searched for Levi, wanted to make sure he was okay. His mouth was unhinged, hanging low like a damaged puppet and his head was tilted back at an uncomfortable angle. For a second, she was worried something had happened to him, but then he raised his hand and pointed at her.

No, not *at* her…

Behind her.

Ava stood and turned slowly, a dancer inside a broken music box, its gears sticky.

And then, she screamed.

Standing in front of her was something, even in her wildest of dreams, she would have never been able to concoct. There was no other way to describe it besides a sand cobra with human parts. The creature was massive, easily four times taller than Ava, with a snakelike body as wide as two bumper-to-bumper semi-trucks. It had strong, defined arms that hung at its sides with long, slender fingers. When her eyes moved upwards, she expected a cobra head, but instead there was a weird hybrid. The face was the skeleton of a human. The space where its eyes should have been were hollow crevices, as were the cheekbones. Nothing but sunken in wells. But its nose and mouth were formed completely, as if a sculptor had just begun working on this strange monster. Around the skeletal head was the hood of a king cobra, made entirely of sand. It flared out, making the creature seem even grander than it already was.

The creature seemed to stare down at her, even though it didn't have the eyeballs to do so. It shouldn't have been able to move with the grace that it did given its size. It should have collapsed in on itself when it lowered, the back of its vertebrae-less body hunched as it brought itself face-to-face with Ava.

"What. Do you want?" it asked. It barely opened its mouth to speak. The voice that came from it was slithery and crisp, and almost like a whisper. She heard it more in her head than anything.

Ava opened and closed her mouth repeatedly, trying to figure out what to say. Finally, she settled for, "What are you?"

The creature smiled at her. Its wide mouth stretched and revealed two long rows of sharp, overlapping teeth. "You called. Upon me and yet. You don't know what. I am?" It emphasized the T on the end of every word. It made them sound much harsher than they should have.

Squaring her shoulders, Ava nodded once. "I'm looking for Nopels," she said, this time aiming to answer its original question.

Moving its head back and forth, much like a snake would, the creature replied, "I am Nopelsssss...." It hissed out the last word.

"The beast," Ava whispered.

"Issss that. What they call me?" She nodded.

Suddenly, the skull came closer and the nose inhaled deeply. She tried to step back but something shot up and blocked her exit. Running her hands against the form at her back, she shuddered when she realized it was the creature's reptilian tail. It was solid, despite being made of sand. "You smell. Familiar."

"Is…is that good?" she stuttered.

Again, the beast—Nopels, she supposed—grinned. This close she could almost count the teeth, not that she planned on doing so. "Dependss."

"On what?

"On what. You want."

Ava swallowed. "I'm looking for someone," she started. "I was told he would be here. That he was in Nopels."

"There are a lot. Of people. In Noplesss." Ava didn't like the sound of that. "Who. Are you?"

"Ava," she replied.

"But who. Do you belong to?"

"I don't understand," she answered honestly. "And what do you mean there are a lot of people inside of you?" Her mother had always said her curiosity would be her downfall one day. She hoped today wasn't it.

Nopels wove around her, its large serpent body coiling closer. Its face was right next to her ear. "I am. The guardian. Of Navah."

Turning her head just slightly she asked, "Of what?"

"Not what. Where." As if being rewound, Nopels unwrapped itself and settled in front of her again. Each time he moved the sand swished. "What. Does Havaan. Pride itsssself. On?"

Ava was getting tired of getting nowhere. While she was standing here having weird conversations with a skeleton-snake creature, Nixon was getting further and further away. She wanted to demand answers, demand Nopels tell her what she wanted to know, but something told her to stay calm. To play along. That if she let her frustrations rule her she would blow her chance to find Nixon.

So, she answered. "Unity."

"More."

"Peace. Goodness."

"Navah. Is none of. Those thingssss. Navah. Is the. Opposite. Navah runsss. On chaosss." Suddenly, a long black tongue jutted from Nopels' mouth and flicked against her skin. It was wet and smooth, like stripped rubber. Ava shuddered and couldn't help the way her body retracted in on itself, away from the forked appendage. "You. Have Noriega blood in you."

Pulling itself up to a height that forced Ava to crane her neck, she asked, "You know my father?"

"You. And I. Are created from the ssssame magic."

Ava took a step back, as though the words that had just been hissed held weight. She shook her head in disbelief as she questioned, "Dante made you?" What kind of powers did her father have that would allow him to create, not only an animated creature made of nothing but sand, but also an entire other world inside of it? Cordellia had said Dante was powerful, but Ava was starting to think just *how* powerful had been understated.

"Sssmart and pretty. Doesn't. Happen very often."

Blinking a few times, her head still refusing to believe what she'd just heard, Ava pushed down the million questions building in her brain. Except for one. It escaped before she could stop it. "If that's true, how do you still exist?" As if it didn't understand, the skull tilted sideways slightly. She was pretty sure the bridge above its would-be eye sockets furrowed. She didn't understand much about the rules of magic, but she knew one thing. "If my father's power created you, you would have died when he did, no?"

That slow, creepy smile spread across its skeleton jaw again. "Oh, little one. What. Liessss. Have they. Been telling you?"

"What do you—" She didn't need to finish her question before the truth hit her like a punch to the gut. Her lungs froze. When they decided to work again, the depth of her exhale brought with it warm tears. They stung her eyes and she pinched them shut, forced the salt water away. When she opened them again, she yelped. Nopels had brought its face to hers again. The skull itself was the size of a large boulder and the hood that flared around it was at least a yard wide on either side. It was terrifying, but for some reason Ava wasn't scared anymore. Creeped out, sure, but not scared.

She didn't have the mental capacity to be scared right now.

There was one single thought floating around up there, but it took up all the space.

"He's alive," she said. She hadn't worded it like a question, but Nopels nodded anyway. "Is he...is he in you? In Navah?" Again, the creature nodded. "The person I'm looking for, he would have come here with Seba—with the pri—with a silver-haired guy."

"The prince."

"Yeah."

The end of Nopels tail brushed against the back of her leg, but she ignored it.

"He. Is in Navah. Alsssso."

Relief flooded through her. She wanted to fall into the giant sand-snake and sob, but she shoved those feelings down. She was so close. "How do I get to him? How do I get him out?" Ava didn't specify which *him* she was talking about.

She should have been expecting it. This whole journey had been a prime example of give a little, take a lot back. But she still felt the crushing weight of defeat when Nopels murmured, "You. Can't."

"Why not?"

"It issss. Law. It isss. The ruless. Only those. Who enter of their own. Accord. Can leave."

"Shit."

The hood around the skull flared, shaking slightly like the last fall leaf. "Are you. So easily. Defeated?" With the tip of his large tail, Nopels tilted her head back up. "Father. Would be dissssappointed." The beast paused, considered something, and then said, "There. Is a way. To get him. Out." Nopels made no effort to distinguish which *him* it was speaking of either, but she didn't ask. Nor did she ask if it was possible for her to free both men.

"Tell me."

"It isss. By Noriega magic that I. Exist. And only by. Noriega magic can I. Be set. Free."

"Free?"

"No longer. Desssstined to guard. Navah. It isss. Not a good feeling. All this evilnesssss. Inside of me."

Ava raised a brow. "What does you being free look like? You're not going to go into Havaan and cause havoc, are you?"

"I will. Sssimply cease. To exist."

"But if you no longer exist," Ava worked out slowly, "then Navah won't either." Nopels nodded. "And the people inside of you?"

"Gone." Ava swallowed. "Do they. Matter ssso much to you. That you would. Be willing to ssacrifice. The one. With fire in. His eyessss?" It had her there. Before…before the gala and High House and Nixon, she would have hesitated. She would have never contemplated ending thousands of lives for one, but there wasn't anything she wouldn't give for the one with fire in his eyes.

Ava stood as straight as possible when she asked, "How do I set you free?"

"It'ssss. Easy. All you do. Is make a blood. Oath. Promisssing my freedom. And I. Will allow you entrance. To Navah. As well. As passage back to Havaan. For you. And your. Beau."

Ava considered this deal. The beast was the only way to get to Navah, and if that's where Nixon was, then that's where she wanted to go.

"How long do I have?" she asked, because she knew, without Nopels having to say anything, that she would not be granted infinite time. It wouldn't be that easy. Especially when the prospect of its freedom was hanging in the balance.

"Three. Daysss."

"Seven."

"Five. And you. Can bring back. Assss many people. As you desire." Nopels dropped to her level again and whispered, "Our father. Included."

Hesitating for fifteen seconds, less to think it over and more for dramatic effect, she finally nodded. "Deal."

As soon as the word was out of her mouth, a burning pain tore across her wrist. "What the hell?" She glanced down and frowned at the raised red tally marks that were quickly fading into pale white scars.

She hated when the beast smiled, especially when it was so close to her face, but she did everything in her power to hold her stance. "Sssso that. You don't lose. Track of. Time."

"Gee, thanks," she said flippantly. "Now tell me what to do."

"Cast the spell. And sssseal it. With your. Blood."

"Why blood?" Genuine curiosity won out this time over the time constraint.

"Magic. Requiressss. Sacrifice. Wordssss. Can be broken. Liesss. Can be told. Blood. Is life."

Ava flipped her hands over and looked at them. Her eyes settled on the faint blue rivers beneath her skin. "What if it doesn't work? You said magic is needed to undo all of this. What if I don't have any in me?"

"You do."

They were the words she'd hoped Nopels would say. She'd questioned it, even doubted the possibility, because things like that didn't happen in her life. Not to her. She had never been special. Just plain, simple, Avaleigh Toliver with the sad mother and the dead father. But now she was learning none of that was true. Even Cordellia wasn't as sad as she'd once been. And if Ava could rescue Dante, then she wouldn't be sad ever again. The promise of a life with both her mother *and* father, as well as Nixon, would have convinced her to do anything.

Even if it meant destroying a place and all its inhabitants.

And maybe even herself if she couldn't get out in time.

"Okay," she said. It was more for herself than Nopels, but the snake reared back and wiggled with what she could only guess was excitement. "I just…make something up?" she asked as she slipped one of Nixon's blades from the belt.

"That'sss. It. Make it. Eloquent, though. I have missed. People putting effort. Into their wordsss."

"Luckily for you, I got B's in all of my poetry classes." Ava took a deep breath and cleared her mind of everything but a spell. A chant? An incantation? Were there particular words she needed to use? Ones that would make it more official? Or could she just toss out any old thing and it have the same effect?

You'll never know if you don't try.

Nodding to herself, she opened her eyes, as well as her mouth and said:

"I give my word for what it is;

your freedom for my passage.

In five days' time it shall be done,

whether I return as three, or two, or none.

With my blood I vow it to thee…"

Ava raised the blade and rested the tip of it against her palm. Holding her breath, she sliced her skin. Blood pooled instantly. As if she'd done this a million times before, she dumped the puddle of crimson onto the ground and delivered the last line: "…my promise is binding so let it be."

Her eyes settled on the hollowed ones of Nopels as she closed her fingers around the gash, trying to stop the bleeding. "How was that?"

she asked, almost shyly. Why did it matter so much what some sand-man thought of her on-the-spot writing skills?

The beast shrugged one of his massive shoulders. Particles of sand shifted, trickling down his body. "I've. Heard worsssse." Ava glared. "But. It will. Work." She was pretty sure the creature was teasing her, but she didn't want to think of it being any more human than its arms and nose allowed.

Suddenly, a voice called out and two heads turned toward the sound. "Levi," she said as he made his way to them. She had all but forgotten he was there.

"Friend. Of yoursss?" Nopels asked. It slithered over to Levi like an eel, coiling its frame around his feet. The monster regarded the young prince with its eyeless sockets. Its head moved back and forth, as if hypnotized.

"A…Ava?" Levi stuttered. Nothing but his eyes moved her direction.

"He isn't going to hurt you," she said with more certainty than she felt. She didn't know if it was true, but she was banking on it being so.

"*He?*"

"It. Meet Nopels." Ava made the introduction casually, as if she and the beast had been best friends for years.

"Hello…" Levi said hesitantly. His voice had crept at least two octaves higher.

Nopels' top half snapped toward her. "He. Stays here," he droned.

"Agreed," Ava said without missing a beat.

"Stays here?" Levi stepped over the large body of Nopels and came to her. "Where are you going?"

"To get Nixon," she replied. Then she looked at the beast as it glided back and forth with impatience. "It's a guardian of some place called Navah. And that's where Nixon is."

Levi moved his face in her direct line of sight. "Let me go with you," he begged with both his words and his eyes.

Ava shook her head. "We agreed that if it was going to be dangerous you had to stay behind."

"I know, but—"

"Navah is the opposite of Havaan. I can't, in good conscience, allow you to come." She took his hand in hers. "Regardless of how bad I want you by my side."

Nopels slinked up next to them. "Time. Isss. Wasting."

"I have to go," Ava said. Tugging Levi to her, she crushed his body into hers. Their arms wrapped around each other and they squeezed. If Ava could absorb him and carry the young doyen into Navah with her, she would. As it was, she reluctantly let him go. With hands on each side of his face she whispered, "I will find him." Then she kissed his forehead.

Finally, and as ready as she was going to be, she turned back to Nopels. "Let's get this over with."

As much as she wanted to cower, she stood her ground as the large hand reached for her. It grabbed the back of her shirt and hoisted her into the air. Her heart dropped to her stomach and a wave of nausea passed.

"Whoa whoa whoa whoa whoa!" she screamed, all calm demeanor and faked confidence lost. If there was one thing she feared more than becoming her mother, it was heights. And this...this was high.

Nopels brought his face to hers and fixed her with his empty sockets. Even without eyes she could feel the intensity of his gaze. "Do. You love him?"

Why does everyone keep asking me that? "Does it matter one way or another?"

"Most of the people. In Navah are. Not kind. They will. Manipulate you and. Usssse you. For their own sself. Gain. If you do not. Love him. Then what you are about. To endure isss. Not. Worth it. Love must. Guide you. Otherwisssse. You *will* fail."

"Well that's reassuring," Ava said sarcastically. "But I do love him. Whether he knows it or not, I am his. Nothing will keep me from finding him." Her eyes watered, distorting the figure in front of her, but she blinked them away. Now was not the time to become a sobbing, emotional mess. She'd done enough of that the last couple of weeks.

"Trussst. No one," Noples warned. "Get in. Get out. Do not. Fall victim to their liesss."

Afraid that if she spoke she might vomit her nerves, Ava simply nodded.

Nopels grinned, his razor-sharp teeth in two neat lines. Then he opened his wide mouth. A cacophony of sound blared from the dark pit like a speaker. She could see nothing, but she could hear the ruckus.

Somewhere, at the bottom of the nothingness, was Nixon.

I'm coming, she thought, hoping the promise would somehow reach him. *Just hang on.*

In the next second, she was falling.

Ava didn't even scream as Nopels swallowed her whole.

ACKNOWLEDGEMENTS.

This book became something way bigger than I ever thought it would be. Especially when it started out as a literal dream, with a bunch of missing plot holes and underdeveloped themes. I knew I needed to write it though, and I wouldn't have done so without my sounding boards: Tiffany and Nicole, you guys were there from the first day, when I came into work and exclaimed that I had this idea for a book but didn't know how to get from point A to Z.

To my beta readers, Lexi, Nicole and Janelle. Thank you for telling me how much you loved this book. But more importantly, for telling me when and where I needed to make changes. More than that, I appreciate you talking me through all my temporary panics!

Without my fierce and honest editor Cindy, who spent hours upon hours going through each line and polishing my mistakes into bright, shining diamonds, thank you! This book would not be what it is without you.

Of course, to my parents, simply for being themselves. They truly are amazingly wonderful people.

Raymon and Ramiro, you guys finally got your cameo! I hope I did your names justice.

I owe a bigger thank you than they realize to my writing group. Being surrounded by brilliant and creative minds has done more than I think anyone will ever understand. You inspire me daily.

And finally, to you, the reader. If you made it this far, I hope you loved the story and characters as much as I do. I poured myself into Havaan and I cannot wait to explore Navah and all that awaits our friends in the next book…books?

Made in the USA
Monee, IL
06 December 2021

83202429R10385